PALACE WALK

Naguib Mahfouz

PALACE WALK

Translated by

William Maynard Hutchins

and Olive E. Kenny

The American University in Cairo Press

113 Sharia Kasr el Aini, Cairo, Egypt
www.aucpress.com

This edition 2001
Third printing 2004

First published in Arabic in 1956 as *Bayn al-qasrayn*

Dar el Kutub No. 8944/01
ISBN 977 424 681 0

Printed in Egypt

With appreciation to David Morse
—The Editor

PALACE WALK

1

She woke at midnight. She always woke up then without having to rely on an alarm clock. A wish that had taken root in her awoke her with great accuracy. For a few moments she was not sure she was awake. Images from her dreams and perceptions mixed together in her mind. She was troubled by anxiety before opening her eyes, afraid sleep had deceived her. Shaking her head gently, she gazed at the total darkness of the room. There was no clue by which to judge the time. The street noise outside her room would continue until dawn. She could hear the babble of voices from the coffeehouses and bars, whether it was early evening, midnight, or just before daybreak. She had no evidence to rely on except her intuition, like a conscious clock hand, and the silence encompassing the house, which revealed that her husband had not yet rapped at the door and that the tip of his stick had not yet struck against the steps of the staircase.

Habit woke her at this hour. It was an old habit she had developed when young and it had stayed with her as she matured. She had learned it along with the other rules of married life. She woke up at midnight to await her husband's return from his evening's entertainment. Then she would serve him until he went to sleep. She sat up in bed resolutely to overcome the temptation posed by sleep. After invoking the name of God, she slipped out from under the covers and onto the floor. Groping her way to the door, she guided herself by the bedpost and a panel of the window. As she opened the door, faint rays of light filtered in from a lamp set on a bracketed shelf in the sitting room. She went to fetch it, and the glass projected onto the ceiling a trembling circle of pale light hemmed in by darkness. She placed the lamp on the table by the sofa. The light shone throughout the room, revealing the large, square floor, high walls, and ceiling with parallel beams. The quality of the furnishings was evident: the Shiraz carpet, large brass bed, massive armoire, and long sofa draped with a small rug in a patchwork design of different motifs and colors.

The woman headed for the mirror to look at herself. She noted that her brown scarf was wrinkled and pushed back. Strands of chestnut hair had crept down over her forehead. Grasping the knot with her fingers, she untied it. She smoothed the scarf around her hair and retied the two ends slowly and carefully. She wiped the sides of her face with her hands as though trying to erase any last vestiges of sleep. In her forties and of medium build, she looked slender, although her body's soft skin was filled out to its narrow limits in a charmingly harmonious and symmetrical way. Her face was oblong, with a high forehead and delicate features. She had beautiful, small eyes with a sweet dreamy look. Her nose was petite and thin, flaring out a little at the nostrils. Beneath her tender lips, a tapered chin descended. The pure, fair skin of her cheek revealed a beauty spot of intensely pure black. She seemed to be in a hurry as she wrapped her veil about her and headed for the door to the balcony. Opening it, she entered the closed cage formed by the wooden latticework and stood there, turning her face right and left while she peeked out through the tiny, round openings of the latticework panels that protected her from being seen from the street.

The balcony overlooked the ancient building housing a cistern downstairs and a school upstairs which was situated in the middle of Palace Walk, or Bayn al-Qasrayn. Two roads met there: al-Nahhasin, or Coppersmiths Street, going south and Palace Walk, which went north. To her left, the street appeared narrow and twisting. It was enveloped in a gloom that was thicker overhead where the windows of the sleeping houses looked down, and less noticeable at street level, because of the light coming from the handcarts and from the vapor lamps of the coffeehouses and the shops that stayed open until dawn. To her right, the street was engulfed in darkness. There were no coffeehouses in that direction, only large stores, which closed early. There was nothing to attract the eye except the minarets of the ancient seminaries of Qala'un and Barquq, which loomed up like ghostly giants enjoying a night out by the light of the gleaming stars. It was a view that had grown on her over a quarter of a century. She never tired of it. Perhaps boredom was an irrelevant concept for a life as monotonous as hers. The view had been a companion for her in her solitude and a friend in her loneliness during a long period when she was deprived of friends and companions before her children were born, when for most of the day and night she had been the sole occupant of this large house with its two stories of spacious rooms with high ceilings, its dusty courtyard and deep well.

She had married before she turned fourteen and had soon found herself the mistress of the big house, following the deaths of her husband's parents. An elderly woman had assisted her in looking after it but deserted her at dusk to sleep in the oven room in the courtyard, leaving her alone in a nocturnal world teeming with spirits and ghosts. She would doze for an hour and lie awake the next, until her redoubtable husband returned from a long night out.

To set her mind at rest she had gotten into the habit of going from room to room, accompanied by her maid, who held the lamp for her, while she cast searching, frightened glances through the rooms, one after the other. She began with the first floor and continued with the upper story, reciting the Qur'an suras she knew in order to ward off demons. She would conclude with her room, lock the door, and get into bed, but her recitations would continue until she fell asleep.

She had been terrified of the night when she first lived in this house. She knew far more about the world of the jinn than that of mankind and remained convinced that she was not alone in the big house. There were demons who could not be lured away from these spacious, empty old rooms for long. Perhaps they had sought refuge there before she herself had been brought to the house, even before she saw the light of day. She frequently heard their whispers. Time and again she was awakened by their warm breath. When she was left alone, her only defense was reciting the opening prayer of the Qur'an and sura one hundred and twelve from it, about the absolute supremacy of God, or rushing to the latticework screen at the window to peer anxiously through it at the lights of the carts and the coffeehouses, listening carefully for a laugh or cough to help her regain her composure.

Then the children arrived, one after the other. In their early days in the world, though, they were tender sprouts unable to dispel her fears or reassure her. On the contrary, her fears were multiplied by her troubled soul's concern for them and her anxiety that they might be harmed. She would hold them tight, lavish affection on them, and surround them, whether awake or asleep, with a protective shield of Qur'an suras, amulets, charms, and incantations. True peace of mind she would not achieve until her husband returned from his evening's entertainment.

It was not uncommon for her, while she was alone with an infant, rocking him to sleep and cuddling him, to clasp him to her breast suddenly. She would listen intently with dread and alarm and then call out in a loud voice, as though addressing someone in the room, "Leave us alone. This isn't where you belong. We are Muslims and believe in the one God." Then she would quickly and fervently recite the one hundred and twelfth sura of the Qur'an about the uniqueness of God. Over the course of time as she gained more experience living with the spirits, her fears diminished a good deal. She was calm enough to jest with them without being frightened. If she happened to sense one of them prowling about, she would say in an almost intimate tone, "Have you no respect for those who worship God the Merciful? He will protect us from you, so do us the favor of going away." But her mind was never completely at rest until her husband returned. Indeed, the mere fact of his presence in the house, whether awake or asleep, was enough to make her feel secure. Then it did not matter whether the doors were open or locked, the lamp burning brightly or extinguished.

It had occurred to her once, during the first year she lived with him, to venture a polite objection to his repeated nights out. His response had been to seize her by the ears and tell her peremptorily in a loud voice, "I'm a man. I'm the one who commands and forbids. I will not accept any criticism of my behavior. All I ask of you is to obey me. Don't force me to discipline you."

She learned from this, and from the other lessons that followed, to adapt to everything, even living with the jinn, in order to escape the glare of his wrathful eye. It was her duty to obey him without reservation or condition. She yielded so wholeheartedly that she even disliked blaming him privately for his nights out. She became convinced that true manliness, tyranny, and staying out till after midnight were common characteristics of a single entity. With the passage of time she grew proud of whatever he meted out, whether it pleased or saddened her. No matter what happened, she remained a loving, obedient, and docile wife. She had no regrets at all about reconciling herself to a type of security based on surrender.

Whenever she thought back over her life, only goodness and happiness came to mind. Fears and sorrows seemed meaningless ghosts to her, worth nothing more than a smile of pity. Had she not lived with this husband and his shortcomings for a quarter century and been rewarded by children who were the apples of her eye, a home amply provided with comforts and blessings, and a happy, adult life? Of course she had. Being surrounded by the jinn had been bearable, just as each evening was bearable. None of them had attempted to hurt her or the children. They had only played some harmless pranks to tease her. Praise God, the merit was all God's. He calmed her heart and with His mercy brought order to her life.

She even profoundly loved this hour of waiting up, though it interrupted a pleasant sleep and forced her to do chores that should have ceased with the end of the day. Not only had it become an integral part of her life, tied to many of her memories, but it continued to be the living symbol of her affection for her spouse, of her wholehearted dedication to making him happy, which she revealed to him night after night. For this reason, she was filled with contentment as she stood in the balcony peering through the openings toward Palace Walk and al-Khurunfush streets and then towards Hammam al Sultan or the various minarets.

She let her eyes wander over the houses bunched together untidily on both sides of the road like a row of soldiers standing at ease, relaxing from harsh discipline. She smiled at the beloved view of this road, which stayed awake until the break of dawn, while the other streets, lanes, and alleys slept. It distracted her from her sleeplessness and kept her company when she was lonely, dispelling her fears. Night changed nothing save to envelop the surrounding areas with a profound silence that provided a setting in which the street's sounds could ring out clearly, like the shadows at the edges of a painting that give the work depth and clarity. A laugh would resound as though bursting out in her room, and a remark made in a normal tone of voice could be heard distinctly. She could listen to a cough rattle on until it ended in a kind of moan. A waiter's voice would ring out like the call of a muezzin: "Another ball of tobacco for the pipe," and she would merrily ask herself, "By God, are these people ordering a refill at this hour?"

They reminded her of her absent husband. She would wonder, "Where do you suppose he is now? What is he doing? . . . May he be safe and sound whatever he does."

It was suggested to her once that a man like Mr. Ahmad Abd al-Jawad, so wealthy, strong, and handsome, who stayed out night after night, must have other women in his life. At that time, her life was poisoned by jealousy, and intense sorrow overcame her. Her courage was not up to speaking to him about it, but she confided her grief to her mother, who sought as best she could to soothe her mind with fine words, telling her, "He married you after divorcing his first wife. He could have kept her too, if he'd wanted, or taken second, third, and fourth wives. His father had many wives. Thank our Lord that you remain his only wife."

Although her mother's words did not help much then, she eventually accepted their truth and validity. Even if the rumor was accurate, perhaps that was another characteristic of manliness, like late nights and tyranny. At any rate, a single evil was better than many. It would be a mistake to allow suspicion to wreck her good life filled with happiness and comfort. Moreover, in spite of everything, perhaps the rumor was idle speculation or a lie. She discovered that jealousy was no different from the other difficulties troubling her life. To accept them was an inevitable and binding decree. Her only means of combating them was, she found, to call on patience and rely on her inner strength, the one resource in the struggle against disagreeable things. Jealousy and its motivation became something she put up with like her husband's other troubling characteristics or living with the jinn.

She continued to watch the road and listen to the people chat until she heard a horse's hoofbeats. She turned her head toward al-Nahhasin Street and saw a carriage slowly approaching, its lamps shining in the darkness. She sighed with relief and murmured, "Finally . . ." It was the carriage of one of his friends, bringing him to the door of his house after their evening out before continuing on as usual to al-Khurunfush with the owner and some other friends who lived there. The carriage stopped in front of the house, and her husband's voice rang out cheerfully: "May God keep you."

She would listen lovingly and with amazement to her husband's voice when he said good night to his friends. If she had not heard him every night at about this hour, she would not have believed it. She and the children were accustomed to nothing but prudence, dignity, and gravity from him. How did he come by these joyful, jesting sounds, which flowed out so merrily and graciously?

The owner of the carriage teased her husband, asking, "Did you hear what the horse said to himself when you got out? He commented it's a pity I bring a man like you home every night when all you deserve is an ass."

The men in the vehicle exploded with laughter. Her husband waited for them to quiet down. Then he replied, "Didn't you hear the answer? He said in that case I'd be riding you."

The men burst out laughing once more. The vehicle's owner said, "We'll save the rest for tomorrow night."

The carriage proceeded along Palace Walk, and her husband headed for their door. She left the balcony for the bedroom. Picking up the lamp, she went to the sitting room and then to the hall to stand at the top of the stairs. She could hear the outside door being slammed shut and the bolt sliding into place. She imag-

slap. For this reason, he consumed his food cautiously and nervously, stealing a glance from time to time at what was left. The food's quick disappearance added to his anxiety. He waited apprehensively for a sign that his father was finished eating. Then he would have a chance to fill his belly. Kamal knew that although his father devoured his food quickly, taking huge helpings selected from many different dishes, the ultimate threat to the food, and therefore to him, came from his two brothers. His father ate quickly and got full quickly. His two brothers only began the battle in earnest once their father left the table. They did not give up until the plates were empty of anything edible.

Therefore, no sooner had his father risen and departed than Kamal rolled up his sleeves and attacked the food like a madman. He employed both his hands, one for the large dish and the other for the small ones. All the same, his endeavor seemed futile, given his brothers' energetic efforts. So Kamal fell back on a trick he resorted to when his welfare was threatened in circumstances like these. He deliberately sneezed on the food. His two brothers recoiled, looking at him furiously, but left the table, convulsed with laughter. Kamal's dream for the morning was realized. He found himself alone at the table.

The father returned to his room after washing his hands. Amina followed him there, bringing a cup containing three raw eggs mixed with a little milk, which she handed to him. After swallowing the concoction, he sat down to sip his morning coffee. The rich egg drink was the finale of his breakfast. It was one of a number of tonics he used regularly after meals or between them—like cod-liver oil and sugared walnuts, almonds, and hazelnuts—to safeguard the health of his huge body. They helped compensate for the wear and tear occasioned by his passions. He also limited his diet to meat and varieties of foods known for their richness. Indeed, he scorned light and even normal meals as a waste of time not befitting a man of his stature.

Hashish had been prescribed for him to stimulate his appetite, in addition to its other benefits. Although he had tried it, he had never been comfortable with it and had abandoned it without regret. He disliked it because it induced in him a stupor, both somber and still, and a predisposition toward silence as well as a feeling of isolation even when he was with his best friends. He disliked these symptoms that were in rude contrast to his normal disposition aflame with youthful outbursts of mirth, elated excitement, intimate delights, and bouts of jesting and laughter. For fear of losing the qualities required of an exceptionally virile lover, he dosed himself with an expensive narcotic for which Muhammad Ajami, the couscous vendor by the façade of the seminary of al-Salih Ayyub in the vicinity of the Goldsmiths Bazaar, was renowned. The vendor prepared it as a special favor for his most honored clients among the merchants and local notables. Al-Sayyid Ahmad was not addicted to the drug, but he would take some from time to time whenever he encountered a new love, particularly if the object of his passion was a woman experienced with men and their ways.

He finished sipping his coffee. He got up to look in the mirror and began putting on the garments Amina handed to him one at a time. He cast a searching look at his attire. He combed his hair, which hung down on both sides of his head. Then he smoothed and twisted his mustache. He scrutinized the appearance of his face and turned slowly to the right to inspect the left side and then to the left to study the right. When at last he was satisfied with what he saw, he stretched out his hand to his wife for the bottle of cologne Uncle Hasanayn, the barber, prepared for him. He cleansed his hands and face and moistened the chest of his caftan and his handkerchief with it. Then he put on his fez, took his walking stick, and left the room, spreading a pleasant fragrance before and after him. The whole family knew the scent, distilled from assorted flowers. Whenever they inhaled it, the image of the head of the house with his resolute, solemn face would come to mind. It would inspire in the heart, along with love, both awe and fear. At this hour of the morning, however, the fragrance was an announcement of their father's departure. Everyone greeted it with a relief that was innocent rather than reprehensible, like a prisoner's satisfaction on hearing the clatter of chains being unfastened from his hands and feet. Each knew he would shortly regain his liberty to talk, laugh, sing, and do many other things free from danger.

Yasin and Fahmy had finished putting on their clothes. Kamal rushed to the father's room, immediately after he left, to satisfy a desire to imitate his father's gestures that he had stealthily observed from the edge of the door, which was ajar. He stood in front of the mirror looking at himself with care and pleasure. Then he barked in a commanding tone of voice to his mother, "The cologne, Amina." He knew she would not honor this demand but proceeded to wipe his hands on his face, jacket, and short pants, as if moistening them with cologne. Although his mother was struggling not to laugh, he zealously kept up the pretense of being in deadly earnest. He proceeded to review his face in the mirror from the right side to the left. He went on to smooth his imaginary mustache and twist its ends. After that he turned away from the mirror and belched. He looked at his mother and, when he got no response from her except laughter, remonstrated with her: "You're supposed to wish me health and strength."

The woman laughingly mumbled, "Health and strength, sir." Then he left the room mimicking his father's gait and holding his hand as though leaning on a stick.

The mother and her two girls went at once to the balcony. They stood at the window overlooking al-Nahhasin Street to observe through the holes of its wooden grille the men of the family on the street. The father could be seen moving in a slow and dignified fashion. He projected an aura of grandeur and good looks, raising his hands in greeting from time to time. Uncle Hasanayn, the barber, Hajj Darwish, who sold beans, al-Fuli, the milkman, and al-Bayumi, the drinks vendor, all rose to greet him. The women watched him with eyes filled with love and pride. Fahmy followed behind him with hasty steps and then Yasin with the body of a bull and the elegance of a peacock. Finally Kamal made his appearance. He had scarcely taken two steps when he turned around and looked up at the window where he knew his mother and sisters were concealed. He smiled and then went on his way, clutching his book bag under his arm and searching the ground for a pebble to kick.

This moment was one of the happiest of the mother's day. All the same, her anxiety that her men might be harmed by the evil eye knew no limits. She continued reciting the Qur'anic verse "And from the mischief of the envious person in his envy" (113:5) until they were out of sight.

5

The mother left the balcony followed by Khadija, but Aisha tarried there till she was alone. Then she went to the side of the balcony overlooking Palace Walk. She peered out through the holes of the grille with interest and longing. The gleam in her eyes and the way she bit her lip showed she was expecting something to happen. She did not have long to wait, for a young police officer appeared from the corner of al-Khurunfush Street. He came closer, slowly making his way toward the Gamaliya police station. At that, the girl quickly left the balcony for the sitting room and headed for the side window. She turned the knob and opened the two panels a crack. She stood there, her heart pounding with a violence provoked by both fear and affection. When the officer neared the house, he raised his eyes cautiously but not his head, for in Egypt in those days it was not considered proper to raise your head in such circumstances. His face shone with the light of a hidden smile that was reflected on the girl's face as a shy radiance.

She sighed and closed the window, fastening it nervously as though hiding evidence of a bloody crime. She retreated, her eyes closed from the intensity of the emotion. She let herself sink into a chair and leaned her head on her hand. She roamed through the space of her infinite sensations, experiencing neither sheer happiness or total fear. Her heart was divided between the two emotions, each mercilessly trying to attract it. If she succumbed to the intoxication and enchantment of happiness, fear's hammer struck her heart, warning and threatening her. She did not know whether it would be better for her to abandon her adventure or to continue obeying her heart. Her love and fear were both intense. She lingered in her drowsy conflict for some time. Then the voices of fear and censure subsided, and during this truce she enjoyed an intoxicating dream.

She recalled with her usual delight how she had been shaking dust from the window curtain one day when she chanced to look at the street through the window, which was halfway open to let the dust fly out. Her glance had fallen on him as he looked up at her face with astonished admiration. She had drawn back in apparent alarm, but before he disappeared from sight he had made an unforgettable impression on her imagination with his gold star and red stripe. A vision to enchant the mind and ravish the imagination, it hovered before her eyes for a long time.

At the same hour the next day and for days after, she had gone to stand by the slit, where he could not see her. She would observe with triumphant happiness how he looked up at the closed window with concern and longing and then how his features were illumined by the light of joy as he began to discern her figure at the crack. Her heart, on fire and reaching out, awake for the first time, looked forward impatiently to this moment, savoring it happily and then dreamily bidding it adieu as it ended.

A month had passed and once more it had been time to dust the curtains. She had set about shaking them, deliberately leaving the window halfway open so she could be seen. In this manner, days and months had passed until her thirst for even more romance conquered her oppressive fear and she had taken an insane step. She had opened the two panels of the window and stood there, her heart beating violently from affection and fear. She might as well have proclaimed her love to him. She seemed to be a person throwing herself down from a vast height to escape a searing fire all around her.

The sentiments of fear and censure having subsided enough for a truce to be proclaimed, she enjoyed the intoxication of her dream. She awoke determined to shut out the fear troubling her serenity. In order to soothe her consicence she started to tell herself, "The earth didn't shake. Everything went off peacefully. No one saw me, and no one will. Moreover, I didn't do anything wrong!" She stood up and, to make herself think she had a clear conscience, sang in a sweet voice, "You there with the red stripe, you who have taken me prisoner, have pity on my humiliation." She sang it repeatedly, until her sister Khadija's voice reached her from the dining room.

Khadija shouted sarcastically, "Diva Munira al-Mahdiya, you renowned prima donna, please do us the favor of eating. Your servant has set the table for you."

This voice brought her back to her senses as though Khadija had shaken her. She fell from the Platonic world of ideal forms to reality, feeling somewhat frightened for no clear reason, since everything had passed peacefully, as she told herself. All the same, her sister's voice, objecting to her singing and to her images in particular, alarmed her, possibly because Khadija was so critical toward her. Nevertheless, she set aside this momentary anxiety and responded with a brief laugh. She ran to the dining room and found that the cloth had indeed been spread and that her mother was bringing in the tray of food.

Khadija said to her sharply the moment she entered, "You loll about, off by yourself, while I prepare everything. We've had enough singing."

Although Aisha usually spoke tenderly to Khadija to protect herself from Khadija's sharp tongue, the latter's insistence on reprimanding her whenever an opportunity arose occasionally made Aisha wish to rile her. Pretending to be in earnest, she said, "Didn't we agree to divide the work in the house between us? So you do the chores and I'll do the singing."

Khadija looked at her mother and said mockingly of her sister, "Perhaps she intends to become a professional."

Aisha did not get angry. To the contrary, she said, again with affected seriousness, "Why not! My voice is like a bird's, like a curlew's."

Although Aisha's previous words had not stirred Khadija's rage, since they were in jest, this last statement did, both because it was obviously true and because Khadija envied her the beauty of her voice along with her other attractions. So she attacked her: "Listen, madam, this is the home of an honorable man. There would be nothing wrong with his daughters having voices like donkeys, but it's a disgrace for them to be nothing but pretty pictures of no use or value."

"If your voice were beautiful like mine you wouldn't say that."

"Of course! We'd sing duets together. You'd say, 'You there with the red stripe, you who'—and I'd continue—'have taken me prisoner, have pity on my humiliation.' We'll let the lady"—pointing toward her mother—"do the sweeping, scrubbing, and cooking."

The mother, who was accustomed to this bickering, had taken her place and implored them, "Trust in God. Sit down. Let's eat our breakfast in peace."

They came over and sat down. Khadija observed, "Mother, you're not fit to raise anyone."

Her mother muttered calmly, "God forgive you. I'll leave the child rearing to you, so long as you don't forget your own manners." She stretched her hand out to the tray of food, reciting, "In the name of God the Merciful, the Compassionate."

Khadija was twenty and the eldest, except for Yasin, her half brother, who was about twenty-one. She was strong and plump, thanks to Umm Hanafi, although a trifle short. Her face had acquired its features from her parents but in a combination lacking in harmony or charm. She had inherited her mother's small, beautiful eyes and her father's huge nose, or a smaller version of it, although not small enough to be excused. While this nose on her father's face, where it fit, lent his face a noticeable majesty, it added nothing to the girl's looks.

Aisha was in her prime at sixteen. She was the very picture of beauty. She was of slender build and figure, but in her family circle this was considered a defect to be remedied by the ministrations of Umm Hanafi. Her face was as beautiful as the moon. She had a white complexion suffused with rosy highlights and her father's blue eyes, which went well with her mother's small nose. Unlike all the others, she had golden hair, inherited from her paternal grandmother, thanks to the laws of genetics.

It was natural that Khadija should grasp the differences between her and her sister. Neither her extraordinary proficiency in running the house and doing embroidery or her indefatigable vigor, which never dimmed or dulled, gained her anything. On the whole, Khadija felt a jealousy toward Aisha she did not bother to hide, thereby causing the beautiful girl to be upset with her frequently. Fortunately, this natural jealousy did not leave any negative residue deep in her soul. She was content to vent it through the sarcastic sauciness of her tongue. Moreover, she was a girl who, despite the handicaps nature had given her, had a heart full of affection for her family, even though she did not spare them her bitter mockery. Regardless of how long her jealousy lasted, it did not warp her disposition or become hatred or loathing.

Although her sarcasm was humorous when aimed at a member of her family, she was a scold of the first degree with regard to their neighbors and acquaintances. Her eyes, like the needle of a compass always attracted to the magnetic pole, lit first on people's imperfections. If their shortcomings were cloaked, she contrived to uncover and enlarge them. Then she applied epithets to her victims to match their defects. They were usually known by these in the family circle.

She called the widow of the late Mr. Shawkat, the oldest friend of her parents, "the machine gun," because of the way her spittle flew when she talked. Umm Maryam, their next-door neighbor, she named "Could you spare?" because she borrowed household utensils from them now and then. The teacher at the Qur'an school of Palace Walk was the "evilest of creation" because when he taught he frequently recited this verse from the Qur'an (113:2) along with the rest of the sura and because of his ugly face. The cooked-beans vendor was "baldy" because he had no hair, the milkman "one-eye" because his vision was impaired. The nicknames she gave the members of her family were less virulent. Her mother was "the muezzin" because she rose so early, Fahmy "the bedpost" because he was slender, and Aisha "the reed" for the same reason. Yasin she called "Bamba Kashar" after a notorious chanteuse of the day, since he was both plump and fastidious.

Her outspokenness was not merely satirical. There was truly no limit to her harshness if someone got in her family's way. Then her criticism of people was violent and devoid of tolerance and forgiveness. She showed a pronounced lack of interest in the sorrows that trouble people from day to day. This harshness was displayed domestically in her unparalleled treatment of Umm Hanafi and even in her handling of the domestic animals, such as the cats, which were pampered by Aisha in ways beyond description. Her rudeness to Umm Hanafi was a subject of controversy between her and her mother. The mother treated her servants exactly like part of her family. She thought everyone was an angel and did not know how to think ill of anyone. Khadija, on the other hand, was disposed to suspect the woman, since it was her nature to be suspicious of everyone. She did not hide her fear that the servant slept too close to the storeroom. She asked her mother, "How did she get so fat? From the remedies she concocts? We all consume those and we haven't gotten fat like her. It's the butter and honey she skims off without measure when we're asleep."

The mother defended Umm Hanafi as best she could. When her daughter's insistence got on her nerves, she said, "Let her eat what she wants. We have lots, and her belly has limits that cannot be exceeded. We'll not go hungry in any case."

Khadija was not pleased by this remark. She began to examine the tins of butter and jars of honey every morning. Umm Hanafi observed this behavior with a smile. She loved the whole family for the sake of her excellent mistress.

Khadija did not behave like this with members of her family. If one of them was indisposed, she was filled with tenderness and knew no rest. When Kamal came down with measles, she insisted on sharing his bed. She could not stand for even Aisha to be afflicted by the slightest misfortune. Her heart had no equal both in coldness and in compassion.

When she sat down to eat she abandoned her quarrel with Aisha. She attacked the beans and eggs with an appetite that was proverbial in the family. For all of them, food, in addition to its nutritional value, ultimately served an aesthetic goal, because it was the natural foundation for becoming well rounded. They ate deliberately and painstakingly. They did their very best to chew their food thoroughly. They did not even slow down when they were full. They kept on eating until they were stuffed, each according to her capacity. The mother was the first to finish, followed by Aisha. Khadija was left alone with the remaining food. She did not quit until all the dishes were wiped clean.

Aisha's slenderness did not correspond to the diligence with which she ate. The magic of the fattening potions failed on her. Khadija was moved to make fun of her, suggesting that evil machinations had caused her to be soil unfit for the good seed sowed in her. She also liked to ascribe Aisha's slenderness to the weakness of her faith. She would tell her, "We all fast during Ramadan except you. You pretend to fast and then slip into the storeroom like a mouse to fill your tummy with walnuts, almonds, and hazelnuts. Then you break your fast with us so ravenously that those who have been fasting envy your appetite. But God won't bless you."

The breakfast hour was one of the rare times when the three women were alone. Thus it was the most appropriate occasion for them to disclose and air secrets, especially about matters they would be embarrassed to discuss when the men of the family were present. Khadija had something she wanted to say, even though she was busy eating. She remarked in a calm voice, totally different from the yell she had recently employed, "Mother, I had a strange dream."

In deference to her intimidating daughter, the mother replied, even before she swallowed the morsel in her mouth, "A good dream, daughter, God willing."

Khadija said with increased concern, "I seemed to be walking on the wall of a roof terrace. Perhaps it was the roof of our house, or another. Then an unknown person pushed me off and I fell screaming."

Aisha's interest was serious enough to cause her to stop eating, but her sister was silent for a short time to create the greatest possible impression. Their mother murmured, "God grant it's for the best."

Trying not to smile, Aisha asked, "Wasn't I the unknown person who pushed you? Isn't that so?"

Khadija was afraid the mood would be ruined by this joke. She shouted at her, "It's a dream, not a game. Stop your foolishness." Then, addressing her mother, she said, "I fell screaming, but I didn't hit the ground as I expected. Instead I landed on a horse that carried me off and flew away."

Amina sighed with relief as though she had grasped the meaning of the dream and was reassured by it. She smiled and resumed eating. Then she said, "Who knows, Khadija? . . . Perhaps it's your bridegroom!"

Talk about bridegrooms was permitted only on an occasion like this and then only in the form of a terse allusion. The girl's heart throbbed. She was apprehensive about marriage in a way she was about nothing else. She believed in her dream and the interpretation. Therefore she was overjoyed by her mother's words. All the same, she wanted to disguise her embarrassment with irony as usual, even if it was at her own expense, and said, "You think the horse is a bridegroom? My bridegroom will have to be an ass."

Aisha laughed till bits of food flew from her mouth. Fearing Khadija would misinterpret her laughter, she said, "You put yourself down too much, Khadija. You're just fine."

Khadija cast her a glance full of suspicion and doubt. Then their mother started to speak: "You're an extraordinary girl. Who can match your skill or energy? Or your quick wit and pretty face? What more can you ask for?"

The girl touched the tip of her nose with her finger and asked with a laugh, "Doesn't this stand in the way of marriage?"

Smiling, her mother replied, "Nonsense . . . you're still young, daughter."

Khadija was distressed to have youth mentioned, since she did not consider herself young compared with the age most girls were when they married. She said to her mother, "You married, Mother, before you turned fourteen."

The mother, who was actually no less apprehensive than her daughter, replied, "Nothing comes early or late except as God grants."

Aisha sincerely wished: "May our Lord soon allow us to celebrate your wedding."

Khadija looked at her skeptically, remembering how one of the neighbor women had asked to marry Aisha to her son. Their father had refused to let the younger sister marry before the elder. She asked, "Do you really want me to marry, or do you hope it will leave the way clear for you to marry?"

Aisha answered with a laugh, "Both."

6

When they had finished breakfast, the mother said, "Aisha, you do the laundry today and Khadija will clean the house. Afterward meet me in the oven room."

Amina divided the work between them right after breakfast. They were content to be ruled by her, and Aisha would not question her assignment. Khadija would take the trouble to make a few comments, either to show her worth or to start a quarrel. Thus she said, "I'll let you clean the house if you think washing the clothes is too much. But if you make a fuss over the washing so you can stay in the bathroom till all the work in the kitchen is finished, that's an excuse that can be rejected in advance."

Aisha ignored her remark and went off to the bath humming. Khadija commented sarcastically, "Lucky for you that sound reverberates in the bathroom like a phonograph speaker. So sing and let the neighbors hear it."

Their mother left the room and went through the hall to the stairs. She climbed to the roof to make her morning rounds there before descending to the oven room. The bickering between her daughters was nothing new to her. Over the course of time it had turned into a customary way of life when the father was not at home and no one could think of anything pleasant to say. She had tried to stop it by using entreaty, humor, and tenderness. That was the only type of discipline she employed with her children. It fit her nature, which could not stand anything stronger. She lacked the firmness that rearing children occasionally requires. Perhaps she would have liked to be firm but was not able to. Perhaps she had attempted to be firm but had been overcome by her emotions and weakness. It seemed she could not bear for the ties between her and her children to be anything but love and affection. She let the father or his shadow, which dominated the children from afar, straighten them out and lay down the law. Thus their silly quarrel did not weaken her admiration for her two girls or her satisfaction with them. Even Aisha, who was insanely fond of singing and standing in front of the mirror, her laziness notwithstanding, was no less skillful and organized than Khadija.

Amina would have been justified in allowing herself long periods of relaxation, but she was prevented by a natural tendency that was almost a disease. She insisted on supervising everything in the house, no matter how small. When the girls finished their work, she would go around energetically inspecting the rooms, living areas, and halls, with a broom in one hand and a feather duster in the other. She searched the corners, walls, curtains, and all the furnishings to eliminate an overlooked speck of dust, finding as much pleasure and satisfaction in that as in removing a speck from her eye. She was by nature such a perfectionist that she examined the clothes about to be laundered. If she discovered a piece of clothing that was unusually dirty, she would not spare the owner a gentle reminder of his duty, whether it was Kamal, who was going on ten, or Yasin, who had two clear and contradictory approaches to caring for himself. He was excessively fastidious about his external appearance—his suit, fez, shirt, necktie, and shoes—but shockingly neglectful of his underwear.

Naturally this comprehensive concern of hers did not exclude the roof and the pigeons and chickens that inhabited it. In fact, the time she spent on the roof was filled with love and delight from the opportunities it presented for work, not to mention the joys of play and merriment she found there. No wonder, for the roof was a new world she had discovered. The big house had known nothing of it until she joined the family. She had created it afresh through the force of her spirit, back when the house retained the appearance it had always had since being built ages before. It was her idea to have these cages with the cooing pigeons put on some of the high walls. She had arranged these wooden chicken coops where the hens clucked as they foraged for food. How much joy she got from scattering grain for them or putting the water container on the ground as the hens raced for it, preceded by their rooster. Their beaks fell on the grain quickly and regularly, like sewing-machine needles, leaving little indentations in the dust like the pockmarks from a drizzle. How good she felt when she saw them gazing at her with clear little eyes, inquisitive and questioning, while they cackled and clucked with a shared affection that filled her heart with tenderness.

She loved the chickens and pigeons as she loved all of God's creatures. She made little noises to them, thinking they understood and responded. Her imagination had bestowed conscious, intelligent life on all animals and occasionally even on inanimate objects. She was quite certain that these beings praised her Lord and were in contact, by various means, with the spirit world. Her world with its earth and sky, animals and plants, was a living, intelligent one. Its merits were not confined to the blessing of life. It found its completion in worship. It was not strange, then, that, relying on one excuse or another, she prolonged the lives of the roosters and hens. One hen was full of life, another a good layer. This rooster woke her in the morning with his crowing. Perhaps if it had been left entirely to her, she would never have consented to put her knife to their throats. If circumstances did force her to slaughter one, she selected a chicken or pigeon with a feeling close to anguish. She would give it a drink, seek God's mercy for it, invoke God's name, ask forgiveness, and then slaughter it. Her consolation was that she was exercising a right that God the Benefactor had granted to all those who serve Him.

The most amazing aspect of the roof was the southern half overlooking al-Nahhasin Street. There in years past she had planted a special garden. There was not another one like it in the whole neighborhood on any of the other roofs, which were usually covered with chicken droppings. She had first begun with a small number of pots of carnations and roses. They had increased year by year and were arranged in rows parallel to the sides of the walls. They grew splendidly, and she had the idea of putting a trellis over the top. She got a carpenter to install it. Then she planted both jasmine and hyacinth bean vines. She attached them to the trellis and around the posts. They grew tall and spread out until the area was transformed into an arbor garden with a green sky from which jasmine flowed down. An enchanting, sweet fragrance was diffused throughout.

This roof, with its inhabitants of chickens and pigeons and its arbor garden, was her beautiful, beloved world and her favorite place for relaxation out of the whole universe, about which she knew nothing. As usual at this hour, she set about caring for it. She swept it, watered the plants, fed the chickens and pigeons. Then for a long time, with smiling lips and dreamy eyes, she enjoyed the scene surrounding her. She went to the end of the garden and stood behind the interwoven, coiling vines, to gaze out through the openings at the limitless space around her.

She was awed by the minarets which shot up, making a profound impression on her. Some were near enough for her to see their lamps and crescent distinctly, like those of Qala'un and Barquq. Others appeared to her as complete wholes, lacking details, like the minarets of the mosques of al-Husayn, al-Ghuri, and al-Azhar. Still other minarets were at the far horizon and seemed phantoms, like those of the Citadel and Rifa'i mosques. She turned her face toward them with devotion, fascination, thanksgiving, and hope. Her spirit soared over their tops, as close as possible to the heavens. Then her eyes would fix on the minaret of the mosque of al-Husayn, the dearest one to her because of her love for its namesake. She looked at it affectionately, and her yearnings mingled with the sorrow that pervaded her every time she remembered she was not allowed to visit the son of the Prophet of God's daughter, even though she lived only minutes away from his shrine.

She sighed audibly and that broke the spell. She began to amuse herself by looking at the roofs and streets. The yearnings would not leave her. She turned her back on the wall. Looking at the unknown had overwhelmed her: both what is unknown to most people, the invisible spirit world, and the unknown with respect to her in particular, Cairo, even the adjacent neighborhood, from which voices reached her. What could this world of which she saw nothing but the minarets and roofs be like? A quarter of a century had passed while she was confined to this house, leaving it only on infrequent occasions to visit her mother in al-Khurunfush. Her husband escorted her on each visit in a carriage, because he could not bear for anyone to see his wife, either alone or accompanied by him.

She was neither resentful nor discontented, quite the opposite. All the same, when she peeked through the openings between the jasmine and the hyacinth bean vines, off into space, at the minarets and rooftops, her delicate lips would rise in a tender, dreamy smile. Where might the law school be where Fahmy was sitting at this moment? Where was the Khalil Agha School, which Kamal assured her was only a minute's trip from the mosque of al-Husayn? Before leaving the roof, she spread her hands out in prayer and called on her Lord: "God, I ask you to watch over my husband and children, my mother and Yasin, and all the people: Muslims and Christians, even the English, my Lord, but drive them from our land as a favor to Fahmy, who does not like them."

7

When al-Sayyid Ahmad Abd al-Jawad reached his store, situated in front of the mosque of Barquq on al-Nahhasin Street, his assistant, Jamil al-Hamzawi, had already opened and readied it for their customers. The proprietor greeted him courteously and, smiling sweetly, headed for his desk. Al-Hamzawi was fifty. He had spent thirty of these years in this shop as an assistant to the founder, al-Hajj Abd al-Jawad, and then to al-Sayyid Ahmad after the father's death. He remained loyal to his master both for the sake of his job and out of devotion. He revered and loved him the way everyone did who had any dealings with him, whether of business or friendship.

The truth was that he was dreaded and feared only in his own family. With everyone else—friends, acquaintances, and customers—he was a different person. He received his share of respect and esteem but above all else was loved. He was loved for the charm of his personality more than for any of his many other fine characteristics. His acquaintances did not know what he was like at home. The members of his family did not know him as others did.

His store was of medium size. Containers of coffee beans, rice, nuts, dried fruit, and soap were crammed on the shelves and piled by the walls. The owner's desk with its ledgers, papers, and telephone stood on the left opposite the entrance. To the right of where he sat there was a green safe mounted in the wall. It looked reassuringly solid, and its color was reminiscent of bank notes. In the center of the wall over the desk hung an ebony frame containing an Arabic inscription illuminated in gold that read: "In the name of God."

Business was light early in the morning. The proprietor began to review the accounts of the previous day with a zeal inherited from his father but preserved with his own abundant vitality. Meanwhile al-Hamzawi stood by the entrance, his arms folded against his chest. He was reciting to himself the Qur'an verses he knew best. His voice could not be heard, but the continual motion of his lips gave him away. From time to time a faint whisper slipped out from a sibilant *s* sound. He continued his recitation until the arrival of the blind shaykh who had been retained to recite the Qur'an every morning.

Al-Sayyid Ahmad would raise his head from his ledger every so often to listen to the recitation or look out at the street and the endless flow of passersby, hand and horse carts, and the Suarès omnibus, which was so big and heavy it could scarcely wobble along. There were singing vendors who chanted jingles about their tomatoes, mallow greens, and okra, each in his own style. The commotion did not interfere with the proprietor's concentration. He had grown accustomed to it over a period of more than thirty years. He was so lulled by the noise that he was disturbed if it ceased.

A customer came in and al-Hamzawi waited on him. Some friends and neighbors who were merchants stopped by. They liked to visit with al-Sayyid Ahmad, even if only for a short time. They would exchange greetings and enjoy one of his pleasantries or witty sayings. They made him feel proud of his skill as a gifted storyteller. His conversation had brilliant touches relating to the popular culture that he had absorbed not from schooling, since he had never finished primary school, but from reading newspapers and befriending an elite group of gentry, government officials, and attorneys. His native wit, graciousness, charm, and status as a prosperous merchant qualified him to associate with them on an equal footing. He had molded a mentality for himself different from the limited mercantile one. The love, respect, and honor these fine people bestowed on him doubled his pride. When one of them sincerely and truthfully told him, "If you had had the opportunity to study law, you would have been an exceptionally eloquent attorney," this statement inflated his ego. All the same, he was good at hiding his pride with his charm, modesty, and affability. None of these visitors stayed long. They went off one after the other, and the pace of work increased in the shop.

All at once a man rushed in as though propelled by a powerful hand. He stood in the middle of the store, squinting his narrow eyes to see better. He aimed them at the owner's desk. Although he was no more than three meters away, his efforts to make him out were to no avail. So he called out, "Is al-Sayyid Ahmad Abd al-Jawad here?"

The proprietor replied with a smile, "Welcome, Shaykh Mutawalli Abd al-Samad. Have a seat. You bless us with your presence."

The man bent his head. It so happened that as al-Hamzawi approached to greet him, the visitor, who did not notice his outstretched hand, sneezed unexpectedly. Al-Hamzawi drew back and took out his handkerchief. A smile and a frown collided on his face. The shaykh plunged toward the desk, muttering, "Praise God, Lord of the universe." He raised the edge of his cloak and wiped his face with it. He sat down on the chair his host offered him.

The shaykh appeared to be in enviable health for his age, which was over seventy-five. If it had not been for his weak eyes, his eyelids that were inflamed at the edges, and his sunken mouth, he would have had nothing to complain of. He was wrapped in a faded, threadbare cloak. Although he could have exchanged it for a better one through the donations of benefactors, he clung to it. He said that al-Husayn had blessed him in a dream and thus had given the cloak he wore an excellence that would not fade away. The shaykh had performed miracles by penetrating the barriers of normal human knowledge to the invisible realm. He was known equally for his healing prayers, amulets, candor, and wit. He was at home with humor and mirth and that especially endeared him to al-Sayyid Ahmad. Although a resident of the quarter, he did not burden any of his disciples with his visits. Months might pass without anyone knowing where he was. When he dropped by after an absence, he received a warm welcome and presents.

The owner gestured to his assistant to prepare the usual present of rice, coffee, and soap for the shaykh. Then he said to welcome him, "We've missed you, Shaykh Mutawalli. We haven't had the pleasure of seeing you since the holiday of Ashura."

The man replied bluntly, "I'm absent when I think fit and present when I choose. You should not ask why."

The proprietor, who was used to his style, stammered, "Even when you are absent, your blessing is present."

The shaykh did not seem touched by this praise. On the contrary, he shook his head in a way that showed his patience was exhausted. He said gruffly, "Haven't I warned you more than once not to speak to me until I address you? You should be silent."

Feeling an urge to vex him, the proprietor said, "Sorry, Shaykh Abd al-Samad. I forgot your warning. My excuse is that I forgot it because you have been absent so long."

The shaykh struck his hands together and shouted, "An excuse is worse than a sin." Pointing his index finger in a threatening way, he continued: "If you persist in disobeying me, I'll be unable to accept your gift."

The proprietor sealed his lips and spread out his hands in submission, constraining himself to be quiet this time. Shaykh Mutawalli waited to be sure of his obedience. After clearing his throat he said,

"I commence with a prayer in honor of Muhammad, the beloved master of creation."

The proprietor responded from his depths, "God's blessing and peace on him."

"I praise your father as he deserves; may God have plentiful compassion for him and grant him a spacious abode in His paradise. I can almost see him sitting where you are. The difference between the two of you being that your late father retained the turban and you have traded it in for this fez."

The proprietor murmured with a smile, "May God forgive us."

The shaykh yawned till tears came to his eyes. Then he spoke again: "I pray to God that He may grant your children prosperity and piety: Yasin, Khadija, Fahmy, Aisha, and Kamal and their mother. Amen."

Hearing the shaykh pronounce the names Khadija and Aisha sounded odd to al-Sayyid Ahmad, even though he was the one who had told him their names a long time ago, so he could write amulet inscriptions for them. It was not the first time the shaykh had pronounced their names, nor would it be the last, but never would the name of any of his women be mentioned outside their chambers, even on the tongue of Shaykh Mutawalli, without its having a strange and unpleasant impact on him, even if only for a short time. All the same, he muttered, "Amen, O Lord of the universe."

The shaykh said with a sigh, "Then I ask God the Benefactor to return to us our leader Abbas, backed by one of the caliph's armies, which are without beginning or end."

"We so ask Him and it would not be difficult for Him."

The shaykh's voice rose as he said angrily, "And that He afflict the English and their allies with a shocking defeat, leaving them without a leg to stand on."

"May our Lord carry them all off."

The shaykh shook his head sorrowfully. He said with anguish, "Yesterday I was walking in the Muski when two Australian soldiers blocked my way. They told me to hand over everything I had. So I emptied my pockets for them and brought out the one thing I had, an ear of corn. One of them took it and kicked it like a ball. The other snatched my turban. He unwound the cloth from it, ripped it, and flung it in my face."

The proprietor listened closely, fighting off the temptation to smile. He quickly disguised it by an exaggerated display of disapproval. He shouted in condemnation, "May God destroy and annihilate them."

The other man concluded his account: "I raised my hand to the sky and called out, 'Almighty God, rip their nation to shreds the way they ripped my turban cloth.' "

"Your prayer will be answered, God willing."

The shaykh leaned back and closed his eyes to rest a little. Meanwhile the proprietor scrutinized his face and smiled. Then the religious guide opened his eyes and addressed him in a calm voice and a new tone, giving warning of a new subject. He said, "What an astute and gallant man you are, Ahmad, you son of Abd al-Jawad."

The proprietor smiled with pleasure. He responded in a low voice, "I ask God's forgiveness, Shaykh Abd al-Samad . . ."

The shaykh interrupted him, saying, "Not so fast. I'm the sort of person who praises only to clear the way to speak the truth, for the sake of encouragement, son of Abd al-Jawad."

A wary circumspection was evident in the eyes of the proprietor. He muttered, "May our Lord be gracious to us."

The shaykh gestured at him with his gnarled forefinger and asked him threateningly, "What do you have to say as a devout Muslim concerning your lust for women?"

The proprietor was accustomed to his candor. Thus he was not troubled by his assault. After a brief laugh he replied, "How can you fault me for that? Didn't the Messenger of God (the blessing and peace of God upon him) speak of his love for perfume and women?"

The shaykh frowned and looked even grimmer in protest against the proprietor's logic, which he did not like. He countered, "Licit acts are not the same as forbidden ones, you son of Abd al-Jawad. Marriage is not the same as chasing after hussies."

The proprietor stared at nothing in particular and said in a serious tone, "I have never allowed myself to offend against honor or dignity at all. Praise God for that."

The shaykh struck his hands on his knees and exclaimed with astonishment and disgust, "A weak excuse fit only for a weak person. Immorality is damnable even if it is with a debauched woman. Your father, may God have mercy on him, was crazy about women. He married twenty times. Why don't you follow his path and shun the sinner's?"

The proprietor laughed out loud. He asked, "Are you one of God's saints or a nuptial official? My father was almost sterile; so he married many times. Even though I was his only child, his property was split up between me and his last four wives, not to mention what he lost during his lifetime in divorce settlements. Now I'm the father of three males and two females. It wouldn't be proper for me to slip into more marriages and have to divide the wealth that God has bestowed on us. Don't forget, Shaykh Mutawalli, that the professional women entertainers of today are the slave girls of yesterday, whose purchase and sale God made legal. More than anything else, God is forgiving and merciful."

The shaykh moaned. Shaking his torso right and left, he said, "How adept you are, you sons of Adam, in embellishing evil. By God, you son of Abd al-Jawad, were it not for my love of you, I would not suffer you to speak to me, you fornicator."

The proprietor spread out his hands and said with a smile, "God grant . . ."

The shaykh snorted in annoyance and yelled, "If it weren't for your jokes, you'd be the most perfect of men."

"Perfection is God's alone."

The shaykh turned toward him and motioned with his hand as if to say, "Let's put this aside." Then he asked in the tone of an interrogator tightening his grip around his victim's throat, "And wine? What do you say about that?"

Suddenly the proprietor's spirits flagged. His discomfort was apparent in his eyes. He remained silent for some time. The shaykh sensed submission in his silence. He shouted in triumph, "Isn't it forbidden? No one would succumb to it who strives to obey and love God."

The proprietor interrupted with the zeal of a man fending off a veritable disaster: "I certainly strive to obey and love Him."

"By word or deed?"

Although he had an answer ready, he took some time to think about it before replying. He was not accustomed to busying himself with introspection or self-analysis. In this way he was like most people who are rarely alone. His mind did not swing into action until some external force required it: a man or woman or some element of his material life. He had surrendered himself to the busy current of his life, submerging himself totally in it. All he saw of himself was his reflection on the surface of the stream. Moreover, his zest for life had not diminished as he grew older. He was forty-five and still enjoyed an ardent and exuberant vigor like that of an adolescent youth. His life was composed of a diversity of mutually contradictory elements, wavering between piety and depravity. Contradictory though they were, they all met with his satisfaction, without needing to be propped up by any pillar of personal philosophy or hypocritical rationalization. His conduct issued directly from his special nature. Having a clear conscience, he was good-hearted and sincere in everything he did. His breast was not shaken by storms of doubt, and he passed his nights peacefully. His faith was deep. It was true that he had inherited it and that there was no room for innovation in it. All the same, his sensitivity, discernment, and sincerity had added an elevated, refined feeling to it, which prevented it from being a blind traditionalism or a ritualism inspired by nothing but desire or fear. The most striking characteristic of his faith as a whole was its pure, fertile love. Using it, he set about performing all his duties to God, like prayer, fasting, or almsgiving, with love, ease, and happiness; not to mention a clear conscience, a heart abounding in love for people, and a soul that was generous in its gallantry and help for others. These qualities made him a dear friend. People vied to enjoy the pleasures of his friendship.

With the same ardent, overflowing vitality, he opened his breast to the joys and pleasures of life. He delighted in fancy food. He was enchanted by vintage wine. He was crazy about a pretty face. He pursued each of these pleasures with gaiety, joy, and passion. His conscience was not weighed down by guilty feelings or anxious scruples. He was exercising a right granted him by life, as though there was no conflict between the duty life gave his heart and the duty God entrusted to his conscience. At no time in his life had he felt estranged from God or a target for His vengeance. He communed peacefully with Him. Was he two separate people combined into one personality? Was his faith in the divine magnanimity so strong that he could not believe these pleasures really had been forbidden? Even if they were forbidden, should they not be excused so long as no one was harmed? Most probably what happened was that he embraced life with his heart and emotions without resorting to thought or reflection. He found within himself strong instincts, some directed toward God and tamed through worship and others set for pleasure and quenched in play. The integration of all these within him was secure and carefree. His soul was not disturbed by any need to reconcile them. He was not forced to justify them in his thoughts, except under the pressure of criticism like that with which Shaykh Mutawalli Abd al-Samad confronted him. Under such circumstances, he found himself more distressed by thinking than by the accusation itself, not because he shrugged off being accused before God, but because he could not believe that he was actually being accused or that God would truly be angry at him for having a little fun that harmed no one. Thought, however, was a burden and revealed how trivial his knowledge of his religion was. For this reason, he frowned when the other man challengingly asked him whether his obedience was "by word or deed."

He responded in a tone that did not hide his distress, "By word and deed both. By prayer, fasting, and almsgiving. By remembering God whether I am standing or sitting. Why is it wrong for me, after that, to refresh myself with a little fun, harming no one, or for me to overlook one rule? Is nothing forbidden save these two things?"

The shaykh raised his eyebrows and closed his eyes to indicate that he did not agree. Then he muttered, "What a perverse defense!"

The proprietor suddenly went from anxiety to gaiety, as was his wont, and said expansively, "God is clement and merciful, Shaykh Abd al-Samad. I don't picture Him, may He be high and exalted, being in any way spiteful or sullen. Even His vengeance is mercy in disguise. I offer Him love, obedience, reverence, and a good deed is worth ten . . ."

"In the calculus of good deeds, you have the most to gain."

The proprietor motioned to Jamil al-Hamzawi to bring the shaykh's present. He said happily, "God's all we need, along with the favors of His deputy."

The proprietor's assistant brought him the parcel, which he took and presented to the shaykh. "To your health," he said with a laugh.

The shaykh accepted it and said, "May God provide for you generously and forgive you."

The proprietor mumbled, "Amen." Then, smiling, he asked him, "Weren't you well off once, master?"

The shaykh laughed and replied, "May God go easy on you. You're a generous man with a good heart. I take this occasion to caution you against excessive generosity, for it is not compatible with making a living as a merchant."

The proprietor asked in astonishment, "Are you tempting me to withdraw the gift?"

The man rose and replied, "The gift to me is not excessive. Begin somewhere else, you son of Abd al-Jawad. Peace to you and God's mercy."

The shaykh left the store in a hurry and disappeared from sight. The proprietor kept on thinking. He was mulling over the dispute that had flared up between him and the shaykh. Then he spread his hands out in entreaty. He mumbled, "God, forgive me both my bygone and recent sins. God, You are clement and merciful."

8

Kamal left the Khalil Agha School in the afternoon, bobbing along in the swelling current of pupils who blocked off the road with their flow. They began to scatter, some along al-Darrasa, some on New Street, others on al-Husayn. Meanwhile bands of them encircled the roving vendors stationed to catch them at the ends of the streets that branched out from the school. Their baskets contained melon seeds, peanuts, doum palm fruit, and sweets. At this hour, the street also witnessed fights, which broke out here and there between pupils forced to keep their disagreements quiet during the day to avoid school punishment.

Kamal had only rarely been embroiled in a fight, perhaps not more than twice during the two years he had been at the school. He had avoided fights, not from a lack of disputes, which actually were plentiful, nor because he disliked fighting. Being forced to renounce fighting caused him profound regret, but the overwhelming majority of the other pupils were much older, making him and a few of his companions aliens in the school. They stumbled along in their short pants surrounded by pupils over fifteen, many close to twenty. They plowed through the younger boys pompously and haughtily, sporting their mustaches. One of them would stop him in the school courtyard for no reason and snatch the book from his hand to toss far away like a ball. Another would take a piece of candy from him and pop it in his own mouth, without so much as asking, while carrying on a conversation with someone else.

Kamal's desire to fight did not desert him, but he suppressed it out of fear of the consequences. He responded only when one of his young companions provoked him. He found that attacking them vented his stifled rebellious feelings. It was a way to regain confidence in himself and his strength. Neither fighting nor being forced to refrain was the worst insult the aggressors could inflict. There were the curses and bad language that reached his ears, whether or not intended for him. He understood the meaning of some of the expressions and was cautious with them. Others he did not know and repeated innocently at home, thus stirring up a storm of outrage and indignation. This led to a complaint to the school disciplinarian, who was a friend of his father's.

It was nothing but bad luck which decreed that his adversary in one of his two fights was from a family of known toughs living in al-Darrasa. On the afternoon following the battle, Kamal found waiting for him at the door of the school a gang of youths armed with sticks, forming a ring of terrifying evil. When his adversary gestured to point him out, Kamal grasped the danger lying in wait for him. He fled back to the school and appealed to the disciplinary officer for help. The man tried in vain to dissuade the gang from its objective. They spoke so rudely to him that he was forced to summon a policeman to escort the boy home. The disciplinarian paid a call on Kamal's father at his shop and told him of the danger menacing his son. He advised him to attempt to resolve the matter prudently and diplomatically. The father had recourse to some merchants he knew in al-Darrasa. They went to the home of the toughs to intercede for him. Thus the father made use of his well-known forbearance and sensitivity to soothe their tempers. They not only forgave the boy but swore to protect him like one of their sons. The day was not over before al-Sayyid Ahmad sent someone to them with several presents. Kamal escaped from the sticks of the toughs, but it was like jumping out of the pan into the fire. His father's stick did more to his feet than tens of others would have.

Kamal started home from school. Although the sound of the bell signaling the end of the school day brought a joy to his soul unmatched by any other in those days, still the breeze of freedom he inhaled lightheartedly outside the school gates did not obliterate from his mind the echoes of the last class, which was also his favorite: religion. That day the shaykh had recited to them the Qur'an sura containing: "Say it is revealed unto me that a group of the jinn listened" (72:1). He had explained the passage to them. Kamal had concentrated his attention on it and raised his hand more than once to ask about points he did not understand. Since the teacher was favorably disposed toward him on account of the extraordinary interest he displayed in the lesson as well as his excellent memorization of Qur'an suras, he was much more open to the boy's questions than he usually was with his pupils. The shaykh had undertaken to tell him about the jinn and their different groups, including the Muslim jinn, and in particular the jinn who will gain entry to paradise in the end as an example for their brothers, the human beings. The boy learned by heart every word he said. He kept on turning the lesson around in his mind until he crossed the street to get to the pastry shop.

In addition to his enthusiasm for religious studies, he knew he was not just learning it for himself alone. He would have to repeat what he had grasped to his mother at home, as he had been doing since he was in Qur'anic kindergarten. He would tell her about the lesson and she would review, in the light of this new information, what she had previously learned from her father, a religious scholar trained at al-Azhar mosque university. They would discuss what they knew for a long time. Then he would teach her the new Qur'an suras she had not previously memorized.

He reached the pastry shop and stretched out his hand with the small change he had hung on to since morning. He took a piece of pastry with the total delight he experienced only on such a sweet occasion. It made him frequently dream of owning a candy store one day, not to sell the candy but to eat it. He continued on his way down al-Husayn Street, munching on the pastry with pleasure. He hummed and forgot he had been a prisoner all day long, not allowed to move, not to mention play or have fun. He was a sitting duck to be struck at any moment by the teacher's stick raised threateningly over the pupils' heads. In spite of all this, he did not hate school totally, since his accomplishments within its walls brought him praise and encouragement. His brother Fahmy was impressed because he did so well, but Kamal did not even receive one percent of his brother's appreciation from his father.

On his way, he passed by the tobacco store of Matoussian. He stopped under its sign, as he did every day at this hour, and raised his small eyes to the colored poster of a woman reclining on a divan with a cigarette between her crimson lips, from which rose a curling plume of smoke. She was leaning her arm on the windowsill. The curtain was drawn back to reveal a scene combining a grove of date palms and a branch of the Nile. He privately called the woman Aisha after his sister, since they both had golden hair and blue eyes. Although he was just going on ten, his admiration for the mistress of the poster was limitless. How often he thought of her enjoying life in its most splendid manifestations. How often he imagined himself sharing her carefree days in that luxurious room with its pristine view that offered her, in fact both of them, its earth, palms, water, and sky. He would swim in the green river valley or cross the water in the skiff that appeared ghostlike far off in the picture. He would shake the palm trees till the dates fell around him or sit near the beautiful woman with his eyes gazing at her dreamy ones.

He was not good-looking like his brothers. He was perhaps the one in the family who most resembled his sister Khadija. Like hers, his face combined his mother's small eyes and his father's huge nose, but without the refinements of Khadija's. He had a large head with a forehead that protruded noticeably, making his eyes seem even more sunken than they actually were. Unfortunately, he had first realized how strange he looked when a schoolmate teased him and called him a two-headed boy. Kamal had been enraged, and his anger had gotten him into one of his two fights. Even after he taught the boy a lesson, he was still upset and complained of his unhappiness to his mother. She was upset because he was. She tried to console him, telling him that people with large heads had large brains and that the Prophet (peace upon him) had a large head. To resemble the Prophet was the ultimate that anyone could aspire to.

He tore himself away from the picture of the smoking lady, and gazed this time at the mosque of al-Husayn. He had been taught to revere al-Husayn, and not surprisingly the holy martyr's shrine provided his imagination with countless sensations. Although his high regard for al-Husayn—matching the high status his mother in particular and the family in general accorded him—derived from al-Husayn's relationship to his grandfather, the Prophet, Kamal's knowledge of the Prophet had not provided him with what he knew about al-Husayn and the events of his life, nor did it explain the way his soul always hungered to have the saga of al-Husayn repeated, so he could draw from it the finest stories and the deepest faith. This centuries-old saga had found in Kamal an attentive, passionate, loving, believing, grieving, weeping listener. His suffering response was eased only by the fact that the martyr's head, after being severed from his immaculate body, chose Egypt from all the world for its resting place. Immaculate, it came to Cairo, glorifying God, and settled to the ground where al-Husayn's shrine now stands.

Kamal frequently stood in front of the shrine, dreaming and thinking. He wished his vision could penetrate it, to see the beautiful face. His mother assured him it had withstood the vicissitudes of time, because of its divine secret being. It had preserved its bloom and beauty, so that it lit up the darkness of its abode. Although unable to fulfill his wish, he stood there for long periods, communing with himself. He expressed his love and told his problems to the Prophet's grandson. These arose from his vivid daydreams about the jinn and his father's threats. He would implore al-Husayn's assistance for his exams, which he had to take every three months. He would usually conclude his private audience with a plea for a visit in his dreams. His custom of passing by the mosque both morning and evening had somewhat lessened its impact on him, but the moment his eyes fell on the shrine he would repeat the opening prayer of the Qur'an, even if he passed by repeatedly in a single day. Indeed, the shrine's familiarity could not rob his breast of his splendid dreams. The sight of the towering walls still evoked a response from his heart and the lofty minaret still called out to his soul, which quickly answered.

Reciting the Qur'anic prayer, he cut across al-Husayn Street and then turned into Khan Ja'far. From there he headed for Bayt al-Qadi Square. Instead of going home by way of al-Nahhasin, he crossed the square to Qirmiz Alley, despite its desolation and the fears it aroused in him, in order to avoid passing by his father's store. His father made him tremble with terror. He could not imagine that a jinni popping out at him would frighten him any more than his father screaming at him in anger. His distress was doubled, because he was never convinced of the appropriateness of the stern commands with which his father pursued him in his attempt to keep the boy from the fun and games he craved. Even if he had seriously wished to yield to his father's wishes and had tried to spend all his free time sitting quietly with his hands folded together, he would not have been able to obey that haughty, tyrannical will. He furtively took his fun behind his father's back whenever he felt like it, at home or in the street. His father knew nothing of this, unless a member of the household, exasperated when Kamal got out of hand and carried things too far, informed on him.

Kamal had gotten a ladder one day and climbed onto the arbor of hyacinth beans and jasmine, high above the roofs. His mother, seeing him there poised between earth and sky, had shrieked in terror until she had forced him to come down. Her concern over the consequences of such dangerous sport had won out over her fear of exposing him to his father's severity. She had told her husband what Kamal had been up to. He had immediately summoned him and ordered him to stretch out his feet. He had beaten them with his stick, paying no attention to Kamal's screams, which filled the house. Then the boy had limped out of the room to join his brothers and sisters in the sitting room. They had been trying not to laugh, except for Khadija. She had taken him in her arms and whispered to him, "You deserved it. . . . What were you doing, climbing the hyacinth beans and bumping your head against the sky? Did you think you were a zeppelin?" Except for such dangerous games, his mother shielded him and allowed him as much innocent play as he wanted.

He was often amazed to remember that this same father had been sweet and kind to him not so long ago, when he was a small child. Al-Sayyid Ahmad had enjoyed playing with him and from time to time had treated him to various kinds of sweets. He had done his best to lighten Kamal's circumcision day, hideous though it was, by filling his lap with chocolates and candy and smothering him with care and affection. Then how quickly everything had changed. Affection had turned to severity, tender conversation to shouts, and fondling to blows. He had even made circumcision itself a means for terrifying the boy. For a long time Kamal had been confused and had thought it possible they might inflict the same fate on what he had left.

It was not just fear which he felt toward his father. His respect for him was as great as his fear. He admired his strong, imposing appearance, his dignity that swept everyone along with it, the elegance of his clothing, and the ability he believed him to have to do anything. Perhaps it was the way his mother spoke about her husband that put him in such awe of him. He could not imagine that any other man in the world could equal al-Sayyid Ahmad's power, dignity, or wealth. As for love, everyone in the household loved the man to the point of worship. Kamal's small heart absorbed its love for him from this environment, but that love remained a hidden jewel, locked up inside him by fear and terror.

He approached Qirmiz Alley with its vaulted roof, which the jinn used as a theater for their nightly games. Although it frightened him, he preferred going that way to passing by his father's store. When he entered the cavelike space he started reciting, "Say He is the one God" (Qur'an, 112:1), in a loud voice that resounded in the gloom beneath the curves of the roof. His eyes looked eagerly ahead at the distant mouth of the tunnel where light shone from the street. He quickened his steps, still repeating the Qur'an sura to keep from thinking about the jinn, for jinn have no power over anyone who arms himself with God's verses. His father's anger, once it flared up, could not be averted, even if he recited all of God's Book. He left the vaulted section of the alley for the other half. At the end he could see Palace Walk and the entrance of Hammam al-Sultan. Then his eyes fell on his home's dark green wooden grilles and the large door with its bronze knocker. His mouth opened in a happy smile at the wide variety of amusements this place harbored for him. Soon the boys from all the neighboring houses would run to join him in his wide courtyard, with its several chambers, surrounding the oven room. There would be fun and games and sweet potatoes.

At that moment he saw the Suarès omnibus slowly crossing the street heading for Palace Walk. His heart leapt. Pleasure at his own cleverness filled him. At once he tucked his book bag under his left arm and raced to catch it. He jumped on the back steps, but the conductor did not let him enjoy his pleasure for very long. He came and asked the boy for his fare, giving him a suspicious, challenging look. Kamal told him ingratiatingly that he would get off as soon as it stopped but could not while it was moving. The conductor turned from him and yelled to the driver to stop the vehicle. He was angrily scolding Kamal, but when he looked away the boy seized the opportunity to tread on the instep of his foot, take a swing at him, and hop to the ground. He shot off in flight. The conductor's curses that followed him were filthier than balls of mud with stones inside. It had not been a deliberate plan or an original one. He had simply been delighted to see a boy do it that morning. When he got the chance to try it himself, he did.

9

Except for the father, the family gathered shortly before sunset for what they called the coffee hour. The chosen site was the first-floor sitting room surrounded by the children's bedrooms, the parlor, and a fourth small room set aside for studying. Its floor was spread with colored mats. Divans with pillows and cushions stood in the corners. Hanging from the ceiling was a large lantern illuminated by an equally large kerosene lamp. The mother sat on a sofa in the center. In front of her was a large brazier where the coffeepot was half buried in the embers topped by ashes. To her right was a table holding a brass tray with cups lined up on it. The children were seated opposite her, including those permitted to drink coffee with her, like Yasin and Fahmy, and those barred from it by custom and etiquette, like the two sisters and Kamal, who contented themselves with the conversation.

This hour was well loved by them. It was a time to enjoy being together as a family and to have a pleasant chat. They would cluster under their mother's wing with love and all-embracing affection. The very way they sat leaning back with their legs folded under them showed how free and relaxed they felt.

While Khadija and Aisha urged the coffee drinkers to finish so they could read their fortunes in the grounds, Yasin talked for a time and then read a story about two orphan girls from an anthology called *Evening Tales for the People.* He was in the habit of devoting some of his free time to reading stories and poems. It was not because he felt a need for more education, since at that time the primary certificate was no mean achievement. Rather, he loved to be entertained and was infatuated with poetry and good style. He looked, with his massive body in a loose house shirt, like an enormous water skin. Yet, by the standards of the time, his girth did not detract from the good looks of his full brown face with its seductive black eyes, joined eyebrows, and sensuous lips. Despite his youth—he was only twenty-one—his overall appearance revealed a full-fledged manliness.

Kamal clung to Yasin to garner whatever rare stories he would toss him now and again. He kept asking for more, oblivious to the distress his insistence caused his brother. Kamal wanted to satisfy the yearnings that set his imagination on fire at this time every day. How quickly Yasin would be distracted from him by the conversation or get caught up in the reading. From time to time Yasin would favor him, when his urging became intense, with some brief words which, even if they answered one of his questions, were very likely to arouse new questions he could not answer. Kamal kept looking, sadly and jealously, at his brother when he was busy reading. This skill furnished Yasin with the key to a magical world. Kamal's inability to read the story by himself vexed him. How sad it made him to have the book in his hands, to be able to turn the pages to his heart's content, and not be able to decipher the symbols and thus enter the world of visions and dreams. Kamal found in this facet of Yasin a stimulus for his imagination, supplying him with a variety of pleasures but also arousing painful cravings. He would often raise his eyes to his brother and ask him apprehensively, "What happened after that?"

The young man would snort in response: "Don't give me a hard time with your questions. Don't push your luck. If I don't tell you today, then tomorrow." Nothing made Kamal more unhappy than having to wait until the next day. The word "tomorrow" came to be linked in his mind with sadness. It was not unusual for him to turn to his mother after the gathering broke up in hopes that she would tell him what "happened after that," but she did not know the story of the two orphan girls or the others Yasin read. Since it grieved her to turn him away disappointed, she would tell him what stories she remembered about brigands and the jinn. Slowly his imagination would be diverted to these, and he would be partially consoled.

In that coffee hour Kamal frequently felt lost and neglected by his family. Hardly anyone paid attention to him. Their endless conversations made them forget him. He was not above fabricating something to excite their interest, if only briefly. Thus he threw himself into the course of the conversation, daringly interrupting its flow. Like a torpedo going off, he said suddenly in a high-pitched voice, as though he had all at once remembered a momentous event, "What an unforgettable sight I saw on my way home. I saw a boy jump on the steps of the Suarès omnibus. He slapped the conductor and then rushed off at top speed. But the man raced after him till he caught him. He kicked him in the stomach as hard as he could."

Kamal glanced at their faces to judge the impact of his story, but found no interest there. He noticed, rather, a rejection of his news and a determination to continue their conversation. He saw Aisha's hand stretching out to his mother's chin to turn her away from him, after she had begun to listen to him. He even glimpsed a mocking smile spread across Yasin's lips. He had not lifted his head from the book. Obstinately Kamal said in a loud voice, "The boy fell down writhing with pain and people crowded around him. Then what do you know, he had departed from this life."

His mother moved the cup from her lips and asked, "Son, are you saying he died?"

Kamal was gratified by her interest and concentrated his forces on her, like a desperate assailant throwing all his reserves against the weakest section of a forbidding wall. He said, "Yes, he died. With my own eyes I saw his blood pouring out."

Fahmy glanced at him scornfully as if to say, "I know it isn't the first story like this you've told." He asked sarcastically, "Didn't you say the conductor kicked him in the stomach? So where did this blood come from?"

The flame of victory that had been shining in his eyes since he caught his mother's attention went out. Flashes of confusion and exasperation took its place. Then his imagination came to his rescue, and his eyes recovered their lively look. He said, "When the man kicked him in the stomach, he fell on his face and split his head open."

At this, Yasin, without raising his eyes from the two orphan girls, commented, "Or the blood flowed from his mouth. Blood might come from his mouth without any need for an external injury. There is more than one explanation for your fake news, as usual. So have no fear."

Kamal protested against his brother's suggestion that he had made it up. He proceeded to swear the most awesome oaths that it was true, but his protests were lost in the clamorous laughter uniting harmoniously both the deep voices of the men and the high-pitched ones of the women.

Khadija's sarcastic nature was aroused. She remarked, "You certainly have a lot of victims. If the reports you give were true, you'd leave none of the inhabitants of al-Nahhasin alive. What will you tell our Lord if He takes you to account for these reports?"

Kamal found in Khadija a worthy adversary. As usual when he collided with her sarcasm, he began to allude to her nose. He said, "I'll tell Him it's the fault of my sister's snout."

She replied with a laugh, "It's just like yours! Don't we share this affliction?"

At this, Yasin spoke again: "You're telling the truth, sister." She turned toward him, ready to pounce on him, but he forestalled her by saying, "Have I made you angry? Why? All I did was to express openly my agreement with you."

She told him furiously, "Remember your own shortcomings before you allude to the defects of other people."

He raised his eyebrows, pretending to be perplexed. Then he murmured, "By God, the greatest defect is nothing compared to this nose."

Fahmy made a show of being displeased but asked in tones that indicated he was joining the fray, "What are you talking about, brother? A nose or a criminal offense?"

Since Fahmy rarely joined in a quarrel like this, Yasin welcomed his words enthusiastically. He said, "It's both at the same time. Think of the criminal responsibility assumed by the person who presents this bride to her ill-fated bridegroom."

Kamal crowed with laughter like a recurrent whistle. The mother was not happy to have her daughter fall victim to so many assailants. Wanting to bring the conversation back to its original subject, she said quietly, "Your idle chatter has drawn you away from the topic of the conversation, which was whether Mr. Kamal's story was true or not. All the same, I see no reason for doubting him since he has sworn to it. Yes, Kamal would never swear falsely about something."

The boy's pleasure at his revenge faded at once. Although his brothers and sisters continued the joke for a while, he withdrew into a world of his own. He exchanged an earnest glance with his mother and then isolated himself to reflect anxiously and uneasily. He had grasped the seriousness of a lying oath. It could stir the wrath of God and His saints. It distressed him deeply to swear falsely by al-Husayn, in particular, because of his love for him, but he frequently found himself in a serious dilemma, as he had today, from which in his opinion the only escape was a false oath. Drawn unwittingly into making one, he would still be worried and anxious, especially when he remembered his offense. He wished he could pull up his sinful past by the roots or begin with a clean, new page. He thought of al-Husayn and of standing at the base of his minaret that seemed to touch the sky. He entreated the Prophet's grandson to forgive his error. He felt the shame of having committed an unpardonable offense against a loved one. He was plunged in his supplications for some time. Then he began to pay attention to what was going on around him.

He opened his ears to the conversation that was continuing with a combination of old themes and new ones. Little of it interested him. It naturally consisted of a repetition of memories drawn from the family's past, whether recent or distant, of news about what was happening to the neighbors, their joys and sorrows, and of a discussion about the awkward relationship that his two brothers had with their tyrannical father. Khadija would embark on an exposition of this last subject and analyze it in a humorous or malicious fashion. Thus the boy acquired knowledge that developed in his imagination into a strange portrait, deeply indebted to the conflict between the aggressive, mocking spirit of Khadija and the indulgently forgiving spirit of his mother.

Kamal tuned in when Fahmy was telling Yasin, "Hindenburg's last offensive was extremely important. It's quite possible it will be the turning point of the war."

Yasin was sympathetic to his brother's hopes, but in a calm way tinged with indifference. Like his brother, he wished the Germans would win and consequently the Turks too. He wanted the caliphate claimed by the Ottoman sultans to regain its previous might and for Khedive Abbas II and Muhammad Farid to return to Egypt. None of these hopes, however, preoccupied his heart, except when he was talking about them. Shaking his head, he observed, "Four years have passed and we keep saying this same thing. . . ."

Fahmy replied with anxious longing, "Every war has an end. This war has got to end. I don't think the Germans will lose."

"This is what we pray to God will happen, but what will you say if we discover the Germans are just the way the English describe them?"

As the debate caught fire and grew more intense Fahmy raised his voice and said, "The important thing is to rid ourselves of the nightmare of the English and for the caliphate to return to its previous grandeur. Then we will find the way prepared for us."

Khadija interrupted in their conversation to ask, "Why do you love the Germans when they're the ones who sent a zeppelin to drop bombs on us?"

Fahmy proceeded to affirm, as he always did, that the Germans had intended their bombs for the English, not the Egyptians. Then the conversation turned to zeppelin airships and what was reported of their huge size, speed, and danger, until Yasin rose and went to his room to change, prior to leaving the house for his usual night on the town. He returned after a brief absence, ready and outfitted. His clothes looked elegant, and he made a handsome appearance. With his large body, sprouting mustache, and mature masculinity he seemed much older than he was. He said goodbye to them and went off.

Kamal gazed after him with a look revealing how much he envied him the enjoyment of his liberty with its enchanting freedom from restrictions. It was no secret to Kamal that his brother, since his appointment as a secretary at al-Nahhasin School, no longer had to account for his comings or goings. He could stay out as late as he wished and return whenever he wanted. How beautiful it was and how blissful. How happy a person would be to be able to come and go as he pleased and stay out nights as long as he desired. He could limit his reading, once he mastered the skills, to novels and poetry.

He suddenly asked his mother, "When I get a job, will I be able to go out nights like Yasin?"

His mother smiled and replied, "Going out nights is not a goal you should be dreaming about now."

He shouted in protest, "But my father goes out at night and so does Yasin." His mother raised her eyebrows in confusion and stammered, "Be patient till you become a man. Then you can get a job. When the time is right, God will grant you opportunities."

Kamal did not seem prepared to wait. He asked, "Why can't I get a job in three years when I have my primary certificate?"

Khadija yelled sarcastically, "You want to get a job before you're fourteen! What will you do if you wet your pants at work?"

Before Kamal could proclaim his outrage at his sister, Fahmy told him derisively, "What a donkey you are. . . . Why don't you think about going into law like me? If it weren't for circumstances beyond his control, Yasin would have gotten his primary certificate before he was twenty. Then he would have completed his education. Lazybones, you don't even know what to wish for."

10

When Fahmy and Kamal climbed to the roof of the house, the sun was about to disappear. It seemed a tranquil, white disk—its vitality faded, heat turned cold, and glow gone out. The garden with its ceiling of hyacinth beans and jasmine was already growing dark. The young man and the boy went to the far side of the roof where nothing barred the sun's last rays.

They headed for the wall adjoining their neighbors' roof. Fahmy brought Kamal to this spot every evening at sunset on the pretext of reviewing his lessons in the fresh air, even though it was chilly by this time of day in November. Fahmy stationed the boy with his back to the wall and stood facing him, in order to observe the neighbors' adjoining roof without having to turn. There, among the clotheslines, a girl appeared, a young woman of about twenty. She was busy gathering the dry clothes and piling them in a large basket. Although Kamal spoke in his usual loud voice, she kept on with her work as though she had not noticed the arrival of the two interlopers.

The hope that brought Fahmy at this hour was of catching a glimpse of her if some errand called her to the roof. Whenever his hope was fulfilled, his face, blushing with surprised delight, revealed how excited it made him. He began to listen to his younger brother absentmindedly while his eyes roamed about furtively.

She was visible one moment and concealed the next, or part of her could be seen while the rest was out of sight, depending on where she was in relation to the clothes and sheets. The girl was of medium build with a clear complexion verging on white. She had black eyes that radiated life, vivacity, and warmth, but her beauty and his surging emotions and feeling of victory at seeing her could not erase the anxiety pervading him, feebly when she was present and strongly when he was by himself, at her being so daring that she showed herself to him. Was he not man enough for a girl to hide from or was she a girl who did not mind showing herself to men? He kept asking himself why she did not turn and flee in alarm as Khadija or Aisha would have if either had found herself in the same situation. What strange spirit caused her to be an exception to commonly observed traditions and revered customs? Would he not have felt calmer if she had shown that customary modesty, even at the expense of his indescribable pleasure at seeing her? All the same, he invented excuses for her, based on the length of time they had been neighbors, her growing up alone, and perhaps affection too. He continued to argue and debate with his soul to encourage and satisfy it.

Since he was not as daring as she, he started to watch the nearby roofs stealthily to make sure that they were free of witnesses. For a young man of eighteen to violate the honor of the neighbors, especially such a good neighbor as al-Sayyid Muhammad Ridwan, was not a matter to be tolerated. For this reason he was always distressed by the gravity of his action. He was afraid news of it would reach his father, with calamitous results. The way love can disregard fears, however, is an age-old wonder. No fear is able to spoil love's development or keep it from dreaming of its appointed hour.

Fahmy watched her appear and disappear until no clothes were left to separate them. She faced him, her small hands rising and falling, her fingers slowly and deliberately grasping and releasing what she held, as though she was dragging out her work on purpose. His heart guessed it was on purpose, although he was torn between doubt and hope. He did not fight his feeling of being liberated to the farthest horizons by his happiness. He was conscious of nothing but dancing melodies. Although she did not glance up at him, her demeanor, the blush on her cheeks, and her avoidance of looking at him all betrayed how intensely conscious she was of his presence, or the impact he had made on her feelings.

Composed and still, she appeared to be very reserved, as though she was not the same girl who spread joy and delight throughout his house when she visited his sister and her voice carried through the house accompanied by her sonorous laughter. He would crouch behind the door of his room with a book in his hand, ready to pretend he was memorizing his lesson if anyone knocked on the door. He would intercept the melodious sounds of her words and laughter by concentrating on separating them from the other voices that blended with hers. His mind was like a magnet attracting to itself only the bits of steel from a mixture of various materials. He might catch a glimpse of her as he crossed the sitting room. Their eyes might meet in a glance which, though fleeting, would be enough to intoxicate him and stun him as though he had received a message with it so momentous it made his head spin.

He nourished his eyes and spirit with glimpses of her face. Even though the looks were furtive and fleeting, they took control of his spirit and senses. They were strong and penetrating. A single one conveyed more than a lengthy gaze or a deep investigation. They were like a burst of lightning glowing for a brief moment, its flash illuminating vast expanses and dazzling the eyes. His heart was drunk with a mysterious and intoxicating joy, even though it was never free of a sorrow which trailed it, like the troublesome Khamsin winds from the sandy desert trailing the advent of spring. He could not stop thinking about the four years it would take to complete his education. During that time, countless hands might stretch out to pluck this ripe fruit. If the atmosphere of the house had not been so suffocating, with his father's iron grip tight around his neck, he would have been able to seek a more direct route to reassure his heart. He was afraid to breathe a word about his hopes and expose them to the harsh rebuke of his father, which would scatter them and send them flying off.

He asked himself what she was thinking as he looked out over his brother's head. Was it really nothing more than taking in the laundry? Had she not yet felt what motivated him to stand here evening after evening? What was her heart's response to these daring steps of his? He imagined himself hopping over the wall that separated the roofs to join her where she stood in the dusk. He imagined her reaction in different ways. She would be waiting for him by appointment or would be surprised at his advance and start to flee. Then he thought about what would come next—the confession, complaint, and censure. In either case, hugging and kissing might follow, but these were mere speculations and flights of the imagination. Fahmy was well grounded in religion and manners and knew how unrealistic and absurd they were.

It was a silent scene, but the silence was electric and could almost speak without a tongue. Even Kamal had an anxious look in his small eyes, as though asking about the meaning of this strange seriousness that excited his curiosity pointlessly. Then, his patience exhausted, he raised his voice to say, "I've memorized the words. Aren't you going to listen to me?"

Fahmy was roused by his voice and took the notebook from

him. He proceeded to ask him the meanings of the words while Kamal answered, until Fahmy's eyes fell on a beloved one. He discovered an extraordinary link between it and his present situation. He raised his voice intentionally when he asked what it meant: "Heart?"

The boy answered him and spelled the word, while Fahmy tried to discern her reaction. He raised his voice once more and asked, "Love?"

Kamal was a little disconcerted. Then he said in a voice that showed he was objecting, "This word isn't in the notebook."

Smiling, Fahmy said, "But I've mentioned it to you repeatedly. You ought to know it by heart."

The boy frowned, as though by contracting the arch of his eyebrows he could fish out the fugitive word. His brother, though, did not wait for the results of this attempt. He continued his examination in the same loud voice, saying, "Marriage . . ."

He thought he noticed the semblance of a smile on her lips at that. His heart beat rapidly and feverishly. He was filled with a sense of victory, because he had at last been able to transmit to her a charge of the electricity blazing in his heart. He wondered why it was this word which elicited a reaction from her. Was it because she disapproved of what preceded, or was it the first she heard?

Before he knew it, he heard Kamal protesting, after being unable to remember the answer, "These words are very hard."

His heart affirmed his brother's innocent statement. He reflected on his situation in light of it. His joy at once subsided, or almost. He wanted to speak, but he saw she had bent over the basket. She picked it up and approached the wall adjoining the roof of his house. She placed the basket on top of the wall and began to press the laundry down with the palms of her hands. She was close to him, separated by little more than a meter. Had she wanted to, she could have chosen another place on the wall, but she had deliberately confronted him. She had acted so aggressively that she seemed daring to a degree that frightened and perplexed him. His heartbeats were fast and feverish once more. He felt life was disclosing to him a new variety of treasure he had never experienced before. It was charming, delightful, vital, and enjoyable. She did not stand close to him long, for at once she lifted the basket and turned to go to the door leading down from the roof. She darted away from him and disappeared from sight. He stared at the door for some time, oblivious to his brother, who repeated his complaint about the difficulty of the word.

Fahmy felt a desire to be alone to enjoy this new experience of love. He looked out into space and pretended to be astonished, as though he had just noticed for the first time the darkness marching across the horizon. He muttered, "It's time for us to go in. . . ."

11

Kamal was memorizing his lessons in the sitting room. He had left Fahmy alone in the study in order to be closer to his mother and sisters, who were enjoying a continuation of the coffee party limited to women. Their talk, however trifling, provided them with incomparable delight, and as usual they sat so close to each other they seemed a single body with three heads.

Kamal sat cross-legged on the sofa facing them. He had his book open in his lap. He would read for a while and then close his eyes to try to learn some by heart. At intervals he would amuse himself by looking at them and listening to their conversation. Fahmy only grudgingly agreed to let him study his lessons away from his supervision, but the boy's excellent performance in school provided him with an excuse to choose any place he wanted for studying. In fact, his diligence was his only virtue worth praising and, had it not been for his naughtiness, it would have won encouragement even from his father.

Despite his diligence and superior performance, he got bored at times and felt so disgusted with work and discipline that he envied his mother and sisters their ignorance and the rest and peace they enjoyed. Privately he even wished the destiny of men in this world was like that of women, but these were fleeting moments. He never forgot the advantages he possessed, which inspired him frequently to lord it over them and brag, even for no reason at all. It was not unusual for him to ask them, his voice resounding with challenge, "Who knows the capital of the Cape?" or "How do you say 'boy' in French?"

He would encounter a polite silence from Aisha. Khadija would acknowledge her ignorance, but retort, "Only a person with a head like yours can handle such riddles."

Her mother would comment with innocent self-confidence: "If you'd teach me these things the way you do religious studies, I'd know them as well as you." In spite of her gentleness and humility, she was intensely proud of her general knowledge, which had come down to her from antiquity through successive generations. She did not feel in need of further education or suspect there was any new knowledge worth adding to the religious, historical, and medical information she already possessed. Her faith her learning was doubled by the fact that she had gotten it straight from her father, or by growing up in his house, and that her father was a shaykh and one of the religious scholars God favored over all creation, because they knew the Qur'an by heart. It was inconceivable that any knowledge could equal his, although, in the interest of keeping the peace, she did not mention this to the others.

She frequently disapproved of things the boys were told in school. She was upset either because of the explanations provided or because young minds were allowed to learn such things. Fortunately, she did not detect a difference worth mentioning between what the boy was told in school about religion and her own knowledge of it. Since the school lesson consisted of little more than recitation of Qur'an suras along with commentaries on them and the first principles of religion, she had found it allowed her scope to narrate the legends she knew and believed to be an inseparable part of the reality and essence of religion. She may even have seen in them an eternal element of religion. Most recounted miracles of the Prophet and prodigies of the Prophet's companions and the saints, along with various spells for defense against the jinn, reptiles, and diseases.

The boy did not doubt these tales and believed in them, because they came from his mother and they did not conflict with what he learned about religion at school. Moreover, the mentality of his religion teacher, as revealed by his casual remarks, did not differ at all from the mother's. Kamal was enthralled by the legends in a way that none of his dry lessons could match. Filled with enjoyment and flights of the imagination, his mother's lesson was one of the happiest hours of his day.

On subjects outside religion, their disputes were not infrequent. For example, they differed once about whether the earth rotates on its own axis in space or stands on the head of an ox. When she found the boy insistent, she backed down and pretended to give in. All the same, she slipped off to Fahmy's room to ask him about the truth of the ox supporting the earth, and whether it still did. The young man thought he should be gentle with her and answer in language she would like. He told her that the earth is held up by the power and wisdom of God. His mother left content with this answer, which pleased her, and the large ox was not erased from her imagination.

Kamal, however, did not choose this gathering for his studies to boast about his learning or because he liked intellectual disputes. The truth was that he loved the women's company with all his heart and did not want to be separated from them even when he was working. Seeing them gave him a pleasure nothing else could equal. He loved his mother more than anything in the world. He could not imagine existing without her even for a moment. Khadija played the role of a second mother in his life, despite the impudence of her tongue and the bite of her temper. Aisha, although she never went out of her way to help anyone, loved him deeply, and he reciprocated her love totally. He would not take a drink of water from the jug without asking her to drink first. Then he would put his lips on the place she had drunk from.

As it did every evening, this gathering lasted until about eight, when the two girls rose, said good night to their mother, and went to their bedroom. At that, the boy hurried to finish reading his lesson. Then he took his religion textbook and moved next to his mother on her sofa. He told her temptingly, "Today we heard a commentary on a fantastic sura you'll really like."

The woman sat up and replied reverently and devoutly, "All the words of our Lord are fantastic."

He was pleased by her interest. A feeling of bliss and power he experienced only during this final lesson of the day coursed through him. Indeed he found in this religion lesson more than one reason to be happy. For at least half of it he had the role of teacher. So far as he was able, he would attempt to recall whatever he could about his teacher's bearing and gestures and the feeling of power and superiority he projected. In the other half of the lesson he would find enjoyment in the memories and legends she related to him. Throughout it all he would have his mother completely to himself.

Kamal looked in the book almost conceitedly. Then he recited, "In the name of God, the Compassionate, the Merciful. Say: It has been revealed to me that a group of the jinn listened in. They said, 'We have heard a wondrous Qur'an. It provides guidance to correct decisions. We declare our belief in it and shall worship our Lord exclusively." (72:1–2.) He recited "The Jinn" through the twenty-eighth verse.

His mother's eyes had an apprehensive and anxious look. She had warned him against uttering the words "jinn" and "afreet" as a precaution against dangers, some of which she mentioned in order to frighten him and others she withheld out of concern and circumspection. She did not know what to do when he recited one of these dangerous names in a holy sura. Indeed, she did not even know what to do to prevent him from memorizing this sura or what she would do if, as usual, he invited her to memorize it with him. The boy detected this anxiety in her face. He was overcome by a crafty pleasure. He recited the passage several times, emphatically pronouncing the dangerous word while he observed her anxiety. He expected she would ultimately express her concern apologetically, but her anxiety was so intense that she took refuge in silence.

He began to repeat the commentary to her the way he had heard it until he suggested, "So you see that some of the jinn listened to the Qur'an and believed in it; perhaps the ones living in our house are some of these Muslim jinn. Otherwise, why have they spared us all this time?"

The woman replied rather uneasily, "Perhaps they are, but it's possible some others are mixed in with them. So it would be best for us not to repeat their names."

"There's nothing to fear in repeating the word. That's what our teacher said."

His mother stared at him critically and said, "The teacher doesn't know everything."

"Even if the name is in a sacred verse?"

Confronted by his question she felt upset but found herself forced to respond, "The word of our Lord is a blessing in its entirety."

Kamal was satisfied and continued with his account of the commentary: "Our shaykh also says their bodies are made of fire!"

Her anxiety became extreme. She implored God's protection and invoked His name a number of times.

Kamal continued talking: "I asked the shaykh if the Muslims among them would enter paradise. He said, 'Yes.' I also asked him how they could, if their bodies are made of fire. He replied sharply that God can do anything."

"May His might be exalted."

He gazed at her with concern and then asked, "If we meet them in paradise, won't their fire burn us?"

The woman smiled and said confidently and devoutly, "There is no harm or fear there."

The boy's eyes wandered dreamily. Then he changed the course of the conversation suddenly by asking, "Will we see God in the next world with our eyes?"

His mother answered with the same confidence and devotion, "This is true. There can be no doubt of it."

Yearnings showed in his dreamy glance like rays of light shining through the darkness. He asked himself when he would see God. In what form would He appear? Abruptly shifting topics once more, he asked his mother, "Is my father afraid of God?"

She was astonished and said incredulously, "What a strange question! Son, your father is a pious man, a believer who fears his Lord."

Perplexed, he shook his head and said in a subdued voice, "I can't imagine my father being afraid of anything."

His mother shouted in censure: "May god forgive you. . . . God forgive you."

He apologized for what he had said with a tender smile. Then he invited her to memorize the new sura. They proceeded to recite it together, verse by verse, and repeat it. When they thought they had accomplished as much as they could, the boy rose to go to his bedroom.

She stayed with him until he had slipped under the covers of his little bed. Placing her hand on his forehead, she recited the Throne Verse from the Qur'an about God's all-encompassing, watchful care (2:255). She leaned over and kissed his cheek. He put his arms around her neck and gave her a long kiss that came from the depths of his small heart.

She always had trouble getting away from him when she said good night. He would use every trick he knew to keep her beside him for the longest time possible, even if he did not get her to stay till he fell asleep in her arms. He had found that the best way to attain his goal was to ask her to recite, when she finished the Throne Verse, a second and a third verse with her hand on his head. If he perceived she was excusing herself with a smile, he would implore her to continue, citing his fear of being alone in the room or the bad dreams he would have unless there was a lengthy recitation of sacred verses. He might go so far in trying to retain her as to pretend to be sick. He found nothing wrong in these stratagems. He was certain that they did not even compensate for a sacred right which had been violated in the most atrocious way the day he was unjustly and forcibly separated from his mother and brought to this solitary bed in his brother's room.

How often he remembered with sorrow the time not so far distant when he and his mother shared a bed. He would fall asleep, his head resting on her arm, while she filled his ear with the sound of her gentle voice recounting stories of the prophets and saints. He would be asleep before his father returned from his night out and wake only after the man had risen to bathe. He would not seen anyone else with his mother. The world belonged to him and he had no rival. Then a blind decree that made no sense had separated them. He had looked to her to see what impact his banishment had made on her.

How startled he had been by her encouragement, which, implied that she agreed with the decision. She had congratulated him, saying, "Now you've become a man. You have a right to a bed of your own." Who said it would make him happy to become a man or that he craved a bed of his own? Although he had soaked his first private pillow with his tears and warned his mother he would never forgive her so long as he lived, he had never dared slip back into his former bed. He knew that behind that treacherous, tyrannical action crouched his father's unalterable will. How sad he had been. The dregs of sorrow embittered his dreams. How furious he had been with his mother, not just because it was impossible for him to be furious at his father but because she was the last person he thought would disappoint his hopes. She knew, though, how to appease him and gradually cheer him up.

At first she took care not to leave him until sleep made off with him. She would tell him, "We haven't been separated the way you claim. Don't you see that we're together? We'll stay together always. Nothing but sleep will separate us. It did that even when we were in one bed."

Now the sorrow had sunk below the surface of his emotions. He had accepted his new life, although he would not allow her to leave until he had used up all his tricks to make her stay the longest possible time. He held her hand as avidly as a child grasping his toy when other children are trying to snatch it away. She kept on reciting verses from the Qur'an with a hand on his head until sleep took him by surprise.

She bade him good night with a tender smile and went to the next room. She opened the door gently and looked toward the blurred shape of the bed on the right. She asked softly, "Are you both asleep?"

She could hear Khadija's voice reply, "How can I fall asleep when Miss Aisha's snoring fills the room?"

Then Aisha's voice was heard, protesting sleepily, "No one has ever heard me snore. She keeps me awake with her constant chatter."

Their mother said critically, "Have you forgotten my advice to cease your banter when it's time to go to sleep?"

She closed the door again and went to the study. She knocked on the door gently. Then she opened it and poked her head in to ask with a smile, "Do you need anything, sir?"

Fahmy raised his head from the book and thanked her, his face aglow with a charming smile. She closed the door and crossed the sitting room to the outer hall, before climbing the stairs to the top floor, where her husband's bedroom was. The Qur'an verses she was reciting preceded her.

12

When Yasin left the house he naturally knew where he was going, since he went there every evening. He appeared, however, to have no idea where he was heading. He was always like this when walking in the street. He went along slowly in a friendly, complaisant manner. He strutted vainly and proudly, as though never forgetting for a moment his enormous body, his face radiating vitality and manliness, his elegant garments that received more than their fair share of attention, the fly whisk with its ivory handle that never left his hand winter or summer, and his tall fez tilted to the right so it almost touched his eyebrows.

As he walked, he was also in the habit of lifting his eyes but not his head to spy out what might just possibly be hiding behind the windows. By the time he got to the end of a street he would feel dizzy from moving his eyes around so much. His passion for the women he encountered was an incurable malady. He scrutinized them as they approached and gazed after their bodies as they drew away. He would get as agitated as a raging bull and then forget himself. He could no longer conceal his intentions discreetly. In time Uncle Hasanayn, the barber, Hajj Darwish, who sold beans, al-Fuli, the milkman, al-Bayumi, the drinks vendor, Abu Sari', who roasted seeds for snacks, and others like them noticed what was happening. Some of them joked about it, and others criticized him. The fact that Ahmad Abd al-Jawad was a neighbor and highly regarded by them gave them a reason to close their eyes and pardon Yasin.

The young man's vital forces were so powerful that they dominated him if he was otherwise at liberty. At no time did they grant him any relief from their proddings. He continually felt their tongues burning against his senses and consciousness. They were like a jinni on his back, guiding him wherever it wished. All the same it was not a jinni that frightened or upset him. He did not wish to be freed from it. In fact, he might even have desired more like it.

His jinni quickly disappeared and changed into a gentle angel when he approached his father's store. There he kept his eyes to himself and walked normally. He was polite and modest. He walked faster and did not let himself be distracted by anything. When he passed the door of the shop, he looked inside. There were many people present, but his eyes met those of his father, who sat behind his desk. He bowed respectfully and saluted his father politely. The man answered his greeting with a smile. Then Yasin continued on his way as delighted with this smile as though he had received an unparalleled boon.

The fact was that his father's accustomed violence, even though it had undergone a noticeable change since the youth joined the corps of government employees, still remained in Yasin's opinion a form of violence moderated by civility. The bureaucrat had not freed himself from his former fear, which had filled his heart when he was a schoolboy. He had never outgrown his feeling that he was the son and the other man the father. Huge as he was, he could not help feeling tiny in his father's presence, like a sparrow that would tremble if a pebble fell. As soon as he got past his father's store and safely out of sight, Yasin's airs returned. His eyes began to flutter about again, not discriminating between fine ladies and women who sold doum palm fruit and oranges on the street. The jinni controlling him was wild about women in general. It was unassuming and equally fond of refined and humble women. Although they resembled the ground on which they sat in their color and filth, even the women who sold doum palm fruit and oranges occasionally possessed some beautiful feature. They might have rounded breasts or eyes decorated with kohl. What more could his jinni wish for than that?

He headed toward the Goldsmiths Bazaar and then to al-Ghuriya. He turned into al-Sayyid Ali's coffee shop on the corner of al-Sanadiqiya. It resembled a store of medium size and had a door on al-Sanadiqiya and a window with bars overlooking al-Ghuriya. There were some padded benches arranged in the corners. Yasin took his place on the bench under the window. It had been his favorite for weeks. He ordered tea. He sat where he could look out the window easily without arousing suspicion. He could glance up whenever he wished at a small window of a house on the other side of the street. It was quite possibly the only shuttered window that had not been carefully closed. This oversight was not surprising since the window belonged to the residence of Zubayda the chanteuse. Yasin was not ready for the chanteuse herself. He would need to pass patiently and persistently through many more stages of wantonness before he could aspire to her. He was watching for Zanuba to appear. She was

Zubayda's foster daughter. She played the lute and was a gleaming star in the troupe.

The period of his employment with the government was a time full of memories and came to him after the long, obligatory asceticism he had endured out of respect for his father and the frightening shadow he cast on his life. Thereafter, he had plunged into the Ezbekiya entertainment district like water down the falls, in spite of the harassment of the soldiers brought to Cairo by the winds of war. Then the Australians appeared on the field, and Yasin had been obliged to forsake his places of amusement to escape their brutality. He had been at his wits' end and had begun to roam the alleys of his neighborhood like a madman. The greatest pleasure he could hope for was a woman selling oranges or a gypsy fortune-teller.

Then one day he had seen Zanuba and, dumbfounded, had followed her home. He had confronted her time after time but had almost nothing to show for it. She was a woman, and to him every woman was desirable. Moreover, she was beautiful and so he was wild about her. Even when his eyes were wide open, love for him was nothing but blind desire. It was the most elevated form of love he knew.

He looked out between the bars at the empty window with such apprehension and anxiety that he forgot what he was doing and drank hot tea without waiting for it to cool. He swallowed some and burned himself. He started to breathe out and put the glass back on the brass tray. He glanced about at the other patrons as though implying that their loud voices had disturbed him so much they were responsible for his accident and the reason that Zanuba had not appeared at the window.

"Where could that cursed woman be?" he wondered. "Is she hiding on purpose? She must certainly know I'm here. She may even have seen me arrive. If she continues to play the coquette right to the very end she'll make today one more day of torture."

He resumed his stealthy looks at the other men sitting there to see whether any of them had noticed. He found they were all immersed in their endless conversations. He was relieved and looked back at his targeted site, but the train of his thoughts was interrupted by memories of the troubles he had encountered during the day at school. The headmaster had questioned the honesty of a meat distributor and had undertaken an investigation in which Yasin, as school secretary, had participated. Then he had appeared a little slack in his work, and the headmaster had scolded him. That had spoiled the remainder of the day for him and made him think of complaining about the man to his father, for the two men were old friends. The only problem was he feared his father might be rougher on him than his boss.

"Get rid of these stupid ideas," he advised himself. "We're done with the school and the headmaster, curses on them. What I'm being put through by that smart-ass bitch, who's too stingy to let me see her, is enough for now."

Dreams of naked women began to swarm through his mind. Such visions frequently played on the stage of his imagination when he was looking at a woman or trying to remember her. They were created by a rash emotion that stripped bodies of their coverings and revealed them naked the way God created them. This emotion did not make an exception for his body either. His visions would progress through all types of fun and games with nothing held back.

He had just sunk into these dreams when the voice of a driver crying "whoa" to his donkey roused him. He looked in that direction and saw a donkey cart standing in front of the singer's house. He asked himself if the wagon might have come to carry the members of the troupe to some wedding. He summoned the waiter and paid him to be ready to leave at a moment's notice. Time passed while he waited and watched.

Then the door of the house opened and one of the women from the troupe emerged, leading a blind man. He was wearing a long shirt, an overcoat, and dark glasses and carried a zitherlike qanun under his arm. The woman climbed into the cart and took the qanun. She grasped the blind man's hand while the driver helped him from the other side till he reached the woman. They sat next to each other at the front of the wagon. They were followed immediately by a second woman carrying a tambourine and a third with a parcel under her arm. The women were concealed in their wraps but their faces were visible. In place of long veils they were wearing short ones embellished with brilliant colors that made them look like the candy bride dolls sold at festivals. And then what? . . . With yearning eyes and throbbing heart he saw the lute emerging from the door in its red case.

Finally Zanuba appeared. The edge of her wrap was placed far back on her head to reveal a crimson kerchief with little tassels. Beneath it there gleamed laughing black eyes with glances full of merriment and deviltry. She approached the wagon and held out the lute to a woman who took it. Zanuba raised a foot over the wheel. Yasin craned his neck and gulped. He caught a glimpse of her stocking, where it was fastened above her knee, and of a stretch of her bare leg. The pleasantly clear skin showed through the fringes of an orange dress.

"If only this bench would sink into the ground with me about a meter. My Lord, her face is brown, but where it doesn't show, her skin is white, really white. So what do her thighs look like? And her belly? Oh my goodness . . ."

Zanuba placed her hands on the top of the wagon and braced herself so she could get her knees on the edge. Then she began crawling onto the wagon on all fours.

"Good God, good gracious . . . Oh, if only I were at the door of her house or even in the shop of Muhammad the fez maker. Look at that son of a bitch staring at her ass with both eyes. After today he ought to call himself Muhammad the Conqueror. O God . . . O Deliverer."

Her back started to straighten and she stood up on the wagon. She opened her wrap and, taking the two ends in her hands, shook it repeatedly as though she were a bird flapping its wings. She draped the black cloth around her skillfully to reveal the details of her body's features and articulations. It especially highlighted her full, gleaming rump. Then she sat down at the rear of the wagon. Under the pressure of her weight, her buttocks were compressed and ballooned out to the right and left, making a fine cushion.

Yasin rose and left the coffee shop. He found that the wagon had moved off. He followed after it slowly, gasping and clenching his teeth in his excitement. The wagon proceeded on its way haltingly, dragging and swaying. The women on board were rocking back and forth. The young man trained his eyes on the lute player's cushion. He followed her motions so closely that after a while he imagined she was dancing. Darkness was engulfing the narrow street. Many of the shops had begun to close their doors. Most of the people in the street were workers returning to their homes, drained of strength. Between the weary crowds and the darkness Yasin found ample opportunity to devote himself to looking and dreaming in peace and quiet.

"O God, may this street never end. May this dancing movement never cease. What a royal rump combining both arrogance and graciousness. A wretch like me can almost feel its softness and its firmness both, merely by looking. This wonderful crack separating the two halves—you can almost hear the cloth covering it talk about it.

And what can't be seen is even better. . . . Now I understand why some men pray four prostrations before bedding a bride. Isn't this a dome? Why, yes, and under the dome lies the shaykh in his tomb. I'm certainly a devotee of this shaykh. Hear me, Shaykh Adawi!"

Yasin cleared his throat as the wagon approached Mutawalli Gate, known as Bab al-Zuwayla. Zanuba turned around. He saw her, and she saw him. It seemed to him he could detect the hint of a smile on her lips when she turned her head away. His heart beat violently, and an intoxicating, fiery pleasure penetrated his consciousness. The wagon went through Mutawalli Gate and then turned left. At that point the young man was forced to stop, since nearby he saw telltale decorations, lights, and a cheering crowd. He drew back a little, his eyes never leaving the lute player. He watched her avidly as she descended to the ground. She tossed a playful look his way and headed for the wedding party. She disappeared through the door in a clamor of joyous ululation. He sighed passionately and was overcome by a furious perplexity. He seemed anxious, as though he did not know which way to turn.

"God curse the Australians! Where are you, Ezbekiya, for me to disperse my care and sorrow in you and draw a little patience from you?"

He turned on his heels, muttering, "To the only consolation left . . . to Costaki." No sooner had he mentioned the name of the Greek grocer than his head began to perspire, longing for the intoxication of drink. Wine and women in his life were inseparable and complementary. It was in the company of a woman that he had first gotten a taste for wine. By force of habit it had become one of the valued ingredients and sources of pleasure for him. All the same, it was not always granted that the two, wine and women, came together. Many nights were devoid of women, and he had no choice but to relieve his anguish with drink. Over the course of time as the habit became established he seemed almost to have fallen in love with wine for its own sake.

He returned by the route he had come and made his way to the grocery store of Costaki at the head of New Street. It was a large saloon. The front was a grocery store and the inner room a bar; a small door connected the two. He stopped at the entrance, mixing with the customers, while examining the street to see if his father was in the vicinity. Then he headed for the small interior door, but he had scarcely taken a step when he noticed in front of him a man standing by the scales while Mr. Costaki himself weighed a large parcel for him. Involuntarily he turned his head toward the man. Yasin's face immediately became gloomy. A rude tremor shot through his body, making his heart contract with fear and disgust. There was nothing in the man's appearance to inspire these hostile emotions. He was in his sixth decade and was wearing a loose gown and a turban. His mustache was white and gave him a noble, gentle look. Yasin, however, proceeded on in consternation, as though fleeing before the man's eyes could fall on him. He pushed open the door of the bar rather forcefully and went in, as the earth seemed to sway beneath his feet.

13

Yasin threw himself down on the first chair he found. His strength seemed to have given out and he looked somber. He called the waiter and ordered a carafe of cognac in a tone that showed his patience was exhausted. The bar was just a room with a large lantern hanging from the ceiling. Wooden tables with rattan chairs were lined up along the sides. The patrons sitting there included rustic types, workers, and gentlemen. In the center of the room directly under the lantern, pots of carnations were grouped together.

It was strange that he had not forgotten the man and had recognized him at first glance. When was the last time he had seen him? He could not be sure, but most probably he had set eyes on him only twice during the past twelve years, the second time being the encounter that had just shaken him. The man had changed. There was no doubt about it. He had turned into a dignified, sedate old man. If God had only forbidden the blind coincidence that had brought them together . . . His lips curled in disgust and resentment. He felt he was swallowing a bitter humiliation. How degrading and demeaning! He would hardly recover, with pain and perseverance, from his anguish before it was resurrected by some repressed memory or cursed chance encounter like today's. Once again he would be abased, broken . . . lost. In spite of himself, he thought back over the odious past, with all the force of the strife lying behind it.

The darkness drew back to reveal the ugly apparitions that frequently grasped at him like emblems of torment and loathing. Among them he could make out the fruit store at the head of the cul-de-sac called the Palace of Desire, or Qasr al-Shawq. An image with blurred features came to him. It was himself as a boy. He saw the boy hurrying to the shop where that same man greeted him and brought him a bag filled with oranges and apples. Joyfully he took it back to the woman who had sent him and was waiting for him . . . to his mother, not someone else, alas. The memory made him frown with rage and anguish. Then he recalled the image of the man. He asked himself apprehensively whether that man could possibly recognize him if he saw him. Would he recognize in him the small boy he had once known as that woman's son? A tremor of alarm passed through him. His towering, bulky body seemed to fade and dwindle until he sensed it had become nothing at all.

At that point the carafe and glass were brought. He poured out some cognac and drank greedily and nervously. He was in a hurry to reap the drinker's share of refreshment and forgetfulness, but suddenly his mother's face appeared to him from the depths of the past. He could not keep himself from spitting. Which should he curse: fate, which made her his mother, or her beauty, which caused so many men to fall in love with her and enveloped him in disasters? It was beyond his power to change anything destined to befall him. All he could do was submit to the divine decree that mauled his self-esteem. After everything he had endured, it was surely unjust to expect him to make amends for what fate had decreed, as though he were the sinful offender. He did not know why he deserved that curse.

There were many children like him raised by divorced mothers. Unlike many of them, he had found with his mother pure affection, boundless love, and abundant fondling unrestrained by a father's control. He had enjoyed a happy childhood based on love, tenderness, and gentleness. He could still remember many things about the old house in Qasr al-Shawq, like its roof, which overlooked countless other ones. Minarets and domes were visible from it in all directions. Its enclosed balcony looked down on al-Gamaliya Street, where night after night wedding processions passed, lit by candles and flanked by toughs. Most would lead to brawls in which cudgels were wielded and blood flowed.

In that house he had loved his mother in a way that could not be surpassed. In it an obscure doubt had crept into his heart. There the first seeds of a strange aversion had been cast into his breast, the aversion of a son for his mother. These seeds were destined to grow and mature until they changed in time into a hatred like a chronic disease. He had often told himself that if a person had a strong enough will he might be able to carve out more than one future, but no matter how strong his will he could never have more than one inescapable and unavoidable past.

Now he asked himself, as he had frequently before, when he had realized that he and his mother were not alone. It was unlikely that he had known with any certainty. All he could remember was that at one point in his childhood his senses had noted with disdain a new person who intruded on the household from time to time. Perhaps he, Yasin, had looked at him skeptically and somewhat fearfully. The man had probably done everything in his power to amuse and please him.

He gazed back into the past with intense hatred and revulsion but found he could not fight it off. His past was like a boil he wished he could ignore, while his hand could not keep from touching it every now and then. Moreover, there were matters he could not possibly forget. In a certain place, at a time between daylight and darkness, from beneath the upper window or through a dining-room door with red and blue triangles of glass—in that place he remembered he had suddenly beheld, in circumstances corroded by forgetfulness, the intruder assaulting his mother. He had not been able to keep himself from screaming from the depths of his heart. He had howled and wept until the woman came to him, clearly disturbed. She had attempted to put his mind at rest and calm him down.

At that point the train of his thoughts was cut short by his intense resentment. He looked around him despondently. Then he filled his glass from the carafe and drank. When he set the glass back down he noticed a drop of liquid on the edge of his jacket. He thought it was wine and took out his handkerchief. He started patting the spot. Checking on a hunch, he examined the outside of the glass and saw drops of water clinging to it near the bottom. He surmised it was water and not wine that had fallen on his coat and thus regained his composure. But what a deceptive composure it was! His mind's eye had returned to the odious past.

He did not remember when the incident in question had taken place or how old he had been at the time. He did remember quite certainly that the seducer kept on coming to the old house and had frequently tried to ingratiate himself with Yasin by giving him sweet and tasty fruit. After that, he had seen the man in his fruit store at the head of the alley when his mother brought him along with her to run an errand. With childish innocence he had pointed the man out to her. She had dragged him forcefully away and forbidden him to point at the man. Thus Yasin learned to pretend not to know him when his mother was with him on the street. This incident had made the man seem even more mysterious and incomprehensible to him. She had also cautioned him against mentioning the man in the presence of an elderly uncle who was still alive at that time and who visited them occasionally. He had heeded her warning and become even more apprehensive.

Fate had not been satisfied with that. If the man had not visited the house for several days, his mother would send the boy to invite him to come "tonight." The man would receive him graciously and fill a bag with apples and bananas. He would give the boy his acceptance or apologies, as the case might be. It got to the point that when Yasin wanted some tasty fruit he would ask his mother's permission to go to the man to invite him for "tonight." When he remembered this, his forehead broke out in a sweat from shame, and he exhaled in annoyance. Then he poured some cognac and swallowed it.

Slowly the fiery intoxication spread through his system and began to play its magical role in helping him bear his troubles. "I've said a thousand times I've got to leave the past buried in its grave. It's no use. I don't have a mother. My stepmother, who is tender and good, is all the mother I need. Everything's fine except for an old memory I can get rid of. I wonder why I allow it to persist with me and exhume it time after time. Why? It was just bad luck which plunked that man in front of me today. He's destined to die one day. I wish a lot of men would die. He's not the only one."

Although his intellect forbade it, his rebellious imagination continued the journey through his gloomy past. Now he felt more relaxed about it. Indeed, there was not much more to the story itself. The rest of it differed from the beginning, perhaps, and seemed relatively bright after the dark period he had endured as a young child. This improvement came in the few years preceding his transfer to his father's custody. Then his mother had summoned up the courage to tell him openly that the fruit merchant had been visiting her in hopes of marrying her. She had hesitated to accept him and probably would refuse him for Yasin's sake. How much truth was there to what he had been told? It would be absurd to put too much faith in the details of his memories, but he had certainly attempted to understand and comprehend. He had been afflicted with an obscure doubt, revealing itself to the heart rather than the intellect. He had suffered enough distress to scare away the dove of peace and prepare the earth of his soul to receive the seed of the revulsion, which in time had grown to maturity.

When he was nine, he had been transferred to his father's custody. Before that, his father had only seen him a limited number of times, to avoid friction with Yasin's mother. When he came to his father's house as a boy he was ignorant even of the most elementary forms of knowledge and had to make up for the ill effects of his mother's excessive pampering. He hated learning and had little willpower to help him. Had it not been for the ferocity of his father and the pleasant atmosphere of his new home he would not have succeeded in obtaining the primary certificate even when he was over nineteen.

As he grew older and grasped the facts of life, he paraded in review his life in his mother's house and examined it from different perspectives, using his new expertise to cast a glaring light on it. Then the bitter and repugnant realities were revealed to him. Whenever he took a step forward in life, he found the past was like a poisoned weapon attacking him and his dignity from within.

At first his father had tried to ask him about life in his mother's home. Even though he was young, he had abstained from digging up the sad memories. His wounded pride defeated both a desire to arouse his father's interest and the love of chattering characteristic of small boys. He kept silent until he received strange news about his mother's marriage to a coal merchant in the Mubayyada region of al-Gamaliya. Then the boy wept for a long time. His anger was more than he could bear, and he burst out and told his father about the fruit merchant whose offer of marriage his mother had claimed, one day, she had refused for Yasin's sake.

His link to her had been severed at that time, eleven years ago. He knew nothing about her except what his father related from time to time, like her divorce from the coal merchant after two years of marriage to him. Then she had married a master sergeant the year later. After about two years she was divorced again, and so forth and so on.

During the lengthy separation, the woman had frequently endeavored to see him. She would send someone to his father to ask his permission for their son to visit her, but Yasin rejected her invitations with intense distaste and revulsion, even though his father advised him to be conciliatory and forgiving. The truth was that he held a fierce grudge against her that rose from the very core of his wounded heart. He closed the door of forgiveness and pardon on her and barricaded it with anger and hatred. He believed he was not being unjust to her. He had simply set her down at the level to which her activity had lowered her.

"A woman. Yes, she's nothing but a woman. Every woman is a filthy curse. A woman doesn't know what virtue is, unless she's denied all opportunities for adultery. Even my stepmother, who's a fine woman—God only knows what she would be like if it weren't for my father."

His thoughts were interrupted by a man's voice which rang out: "Wine has nothing but benefits. I'll cut off the head of anyone who disagrees. Hashish, dope, and opium are very harmful, but wine is full of benefits."

"What are its benefits?" his companion asked.

"Its benefits! What a strange question!" the man replied incredulously. "Everything about it is beneficial, as I told you. You know this. You believe it. . . ."

The companion said, "But hashish, opium, and other narcotics are also beneficial. You ought to know this and believe it. Everyone says so. Are you going to oppose this popular consensus?"

The first man hesitated a little. Then he observed, "Everything's beneficial, then. Everything. Wine, hashish, opium, narcotics, and whatever comes along."

His companion retorted in a victorious tone, "But wine is forbidden by Islam."

The man said angrily, "Is that all you can come up with? You should give alms righteously, go on pilgrimage, feed the poor. The opportunities for atonement are plentiful, and a good deed is worth ten others."

Yasin smiled with relief. Yes, at last he was able to smile. "Let her go to hell and take the past with her. I'm not responsible for any of it. Every man gets some dirt on him in this life. Anyone who could pull back the curtain would get an eyeful. The only thing that interests me is her real estate: the store on al-Hamzawi, the residence in al-Ghuriya, and the old house in the Palace of Desire. I swear to God that if I inherit all of it one day, I'll have no qualms about praying God to be compassionate to her. . . . Oh . . . Zanuba, I almost forgot about you, and only the devil could make me forget you. It was a woman who tormented me, and it's with a woman that I seek consolation. Oh, Zanuba, I didn't know until today that under your clothes you have such a fair complexion. . . . Ugh, I need to erase this thought from my head. The truth is that my mother's an aching molar that won't stop hurting till it's pulled."

14

Al-Sayyid Ahmad Abd al-Jawad sat behind the desk in his store. The fingers of his left hand were playing with his elegant mustache as they commonly did when he was carried off by the flow of his thoughts. He was staring into space, and the expression on his face suggested that he felt relaxed and contented. He was obviously pleased to feel the love and affection people harbored for him. If he could have discerned some sign of their love every day, that would have made each day happy and splendid in a way no amount of repetition could blunt. Today he had received yet another proof of their love.

The night before, he had been unable to attend a party to which one of his friends had invited him. Immediately after he had taken his seat in the store this morning, the man who had invited him and some comrades who were guests at the party had come to see him. They had reprimanded him for missing it and held him responsible for diminishing their delight and enjoyment. They had said, among other things, that they had not really laughed from the bottom of their hearts the way they did when he was present. They had not found the same pleasure in drinking that they did with him. Their party, as they put it, had lacked its soul.

Now he was joyfully and proudly reviewing their remarks. He was deeply touched by the intensity of their reproaches and the warmth of his own apologies. All the same, he did not escape the reprimands of his conscience, which by its very nature was bent on pleasing his dear friends and thirsty for a fond and sincere drink from the springs of friendship and affection. It might almost have spoiled his good humor, except for the contentment and pride he felt because of the love his friends' revolt against him revealed. Yes, how often the love that attracted him to others and them to him had cheered his heart with unlimited delight and satisfaction. He seemed to have been created for friendship more than for anything else.

He had encountered another manifestation of this love, or of a different type of love, later that morning. Umm Ali the matchmaker had called on him. She had told him, after beating around the bush for some time, "You surely know that Madam Nafusa, the widow of al-Hajj Ali al-Dasuqi, owns seven stores in al Mugharbilin?"

Al-Sayyid Ahmad had smiled. He had grasped intuitively what the woman was hinting at, and his heart had told him she was not simply playing the matchmaker this time but was a messenger sworn to secrecy. He had imagined on more than one occasion that Madam Nafusa had come close to announcing her affection for him during her frequent trips to his store to buy groceries. All the same, he had wanted to sound her out, if only to amuse himself. He had replied with apparent interest, "It's your job to find a suitable husband for her. And they're hard to come by!"

Umm Ali had thought she had achieved her objective. She had said, "I've chosen you out of all men. What do you say?"

The proprietor had laughed loudly and merrily, revealing his good humor and self-satisfaction, but had replied decisively, "I've been married twice. I failed the first time. God made me successful with the second. I will not be reckless with the blessing God has granted me."

The truth was that he had often overcome, by the force of his inalterable will, the temptations of another marriage, in spite of the suitable opportunities that came his way. It seemed he had not forgotten the example of his father, who had slipped inadvertently into a succession of marriages that squandered his fortune and caused him many problems. He, his father's only child, had been left with only a negligible amount of money. Now, through his own profits and income, he enjoyed an ample living that furnished his family happiness and comfort and provided him with as much as he wished to spend on his amusments and entertainments. How could he do something that would spoil this excellent and convenient situation that secured for him both honor and freedom? Indeed, he had not amassed a fortune, not from a lack of means of accumulating one, but because of the generosity that was part of his nature. Spending his wealth and enjoying what it brought him were the only reasons he could see for having it. Moreover, a deep faith in God and His benefactions filled his soul with a sense of trust and confidence that protected him from the fear afflicting many people with regard to their possessions and their future.

His rejection of the lures of further matrimony did not prevent him from being pleased and proud whenever a good opportunity came his way. Consequently, he could not overlook the fact that a beautiful woman like Madam Nafusa wanted him to be her husband. This thought dominated his mind now. He began to look at his assistant and the customers with vacant eyes and a dreamy, smiling face. He remembered, again with a smile, how one of his friends had teased him that morning about his elegance and his use of perfume: "Enough of that. Enough for you, old man."

Old man? He actually was forty-five, but what could this critic say about his enormous vitality, robust health, and stream of gleaming black hair? His feeling of youthfulness had not weakened or diminished. His boyish vigor seemed to increase with time, and he had lost none of his charms. Indeed, despite his modesty and complaisance, he was intensely conscious of his looks and secretly both proud and vain. He was enormously fond of praise. His humility and graciousness seemed designed to increase praise and to spur his companions gently on to say more nice things about him. He was so self-confident that he believed himself superior to other men in looks, grace, and elegance, but he was not a bore about it. His modesty also came to him naturally. It was an innate characteristic that arose from a disposition overflowing with good humor, sincerity, and love.

In fact, he made use of this native disposition, without any reservations, to scout for more love. Inspired by this thirst for love, his nature was inclined toward sincerity, faithfulness, serenity, humility: the attributes that attract love and approval the way flowers attract butterflies. Although his modesty seemed to be a skill, it was a natural characteristic. His skill came instinctively and not from any act of will, revealing itself naturally and simply, without any affectation or effort. He preferred to be silent about his good qualities and conceal his pleasing qualities, while joking about his faults and defects, in order to seek love and affection. To make his virtues known and brag about them could easily have incited an envious reaction. His effective and skillful use of modesty drove his admirers to praise what his wisdom and reserve passed over. Without his resorting to any unseemly boasting, his merits were made public in a way he could never have achieved by himself, thus increasing his charm and the affection lavished on him.

He sought guidance from this same intuitive inspiration even when he was clowning around, socializing, and enjoying music. On those occasions, no matter what effect drinking had on his mind, he never lost his skill and adroitness. If he had wanted to, he could easily have overwhelmed his companions with his quick wit, ability to improvise, excellent sense of humor, and scathing sarcasm, but he conducted parties in an expert and generous way, giving everyone present a chance to participate. When someone told a joke, even if it fell flat, he would favor him with his resounding laughter. He had an intense desire to prevent his own jokes from wounding anyone. If a jest required him to attack a companion, he would make up for his attack by encouraging the other man and flattering him, even if he had to make fun of himself. The party would not end until everyone present had stored up delightful and captivating memories.

The benefits of his natural delicacy, or delicate nature, were not limited to the comic side of his life. They also extended to important aspects of his social life and made themselves felt in the most magnificent way in his well-known generosity, whether manifested in the banquets he hosted in the big house from time to time or in the donations he made to needy people linked to him by some business or personal relationship. He was generous and gallant in his assistance to friends and acquaintances, acting as a guardian for them, but in a way imbued with love and trust. They relied on him when they needed advice, mediation, or a service, whether their problems related to work, money, or personal and domestic questions like an engagement, marriage, or divorce. He was happy to undertake these duties for no wage other than love, serving as an agent, marriage official, and referee. No matter how hard these tasks were, he always found that carrying them out filled his life with delight and joy.

A man like this, excelling in so many social graces and then concealing it, as though fearful of substantial harm if people knew, may allow his modesty to dissolve when alone with his thoughts. Such a man is then apt to savor his fine qualities for a long time and succumb to pride and vanity. Thus al-Sayyid Ahmad began to recall both the censure of his devoted friends and the offer of Umm Ali the matchmaker with pleasure, delight, and glee, which mixed together in his heart in an intoxicating but harmless fashion. Yet the sting of sorrow intruded on his reverie, and he started to tell himself, "Madam Nafusa is a lady with many estimable qualities. Many have desired her, but she wants me. All the same, I won't take another wife. That matter is settled. And she's not the kind of woman who would agree to live with a man without getting married. This is the way I am and that's the way she is. So how can we get together? . . . If she had come my way at any time but now when the Australians have us blocked in, it would have been easy. What a pity the roads are barricaded when we need to use them."

A carriage stopped at the entrance to the store then and interrupted his thoughts. He looked out to see what was happening. He saw the vehicle tip toward the store under the weight of a prodigious woman who began to alight from it very slowly, hampered by her folds of flesh and fat. A black maid had gotten down first and held a hand out for her to lean on while she descended. The woman paused for a moment, sighing as though seeking some relief from the arduous descent. Then, like the ceremonial camel litter that each year was a traditional highlight of the procession of pilgrims setting off for Mecca, she made her way into the store, swaying and trembling.

Meanwhile the maid's voice rang out almost oratorically to announce her mistress: "Make way, fellows, you and the other one, for Madam Zubayda, queen of the singers."

A muffled laugh escaped from Madam Zubayda. Addressing the maid in a counterfeit tone of reprimand, she said, "May God forgive you, Jaljal . . . Queen of the singers! That's enough. Haven't you learned the virtue of humility?"

Jamil al-Hamzawi rushed toward her, his mouth hanging open in a wide smile. He said, "Welcome! We should have spread the earth with sand for you."

Al-Sayyid Ahmad rose. He was examining her with a look both astonished and thoughtful. Then, to complete his employee's greeting, he said, "No, with henna and roses, but what can we do when good fortune arrives unannounced?"

The proprietor saw his assistant going to get a chair. He beat him to it with a broad step almost like a jump. The other man moved aside, concealing his smile. The proprietor presented the chair to the visitor himself. He gestured with his hand to invite her to have a seat, but as he did so his hand stretched out to its full extent, perhaps without his being conscious of it. The openings between his fingers spread apart till the hand resembled a fan. This manual expansion was influenced possibly by the effect on his imagination of her prodigious bottom, which would shortly fill the seat of the chair and certainly spill over the sides.

The woman thanked him with a smile. The beauty of her face shone, with no veil to conceal it. She sat down, gleaming in her finery and jewels. Then she turned toward her maid and addressed her, although what she said was not intended solely for her: "Didn't I tell you, Jaljal, there's no reason for us to wander hither and yon to do our shopping when we have this fine store?"

The maid agreed: "You were right as usual, Sultana. Why should we go far away when here we have the noble Mr. Ahmad Abd al-Jawad?"

The lady drew back her head as though shocked by what Jaljal had said. She cast her a disapproving look and then glanced back and forth between the proprietor and the maid so he could see her disapproval. Concealing a smile, she said, "How embarrassing! I was talking to you about the shop, Jaljal, not about al-Sayyid Ahmad."

The proprietor's experienced heart felt the affectionate atmosphere created by the woman's remarks. Guided by his quick instincts, he got into the spirit and murmured with a smile, "The shop and al-Sayyid Ahmad are one and the same, Sultana."

She raised her eyebrows coquettishly and replied with gentle obstinacy, "But we are interested in the store, not al-Sayyid Ahmad."

It seemed that al-Sayyid Ahmad was not the only person to feel the fine atmosphere created by the sultana, for here was Jamil al-Hamzawi, who alternated between haggling with the customers and stealing looks at any part of the singer's body he could get his eyes on, and there were the customers letting their eyes wander from the merchandise to pass over the lady. Indeed it seemed that this propitious visit had even caught the attention of passersby in the street. The proprietor decided to move closer to the sultana and turn his broad back on the door and the people to protect her from the disturbance of intruders. All the same, this did not make him forget where he was in the conversation. He continued with his little joke: "God, may His wisdom be exalted, decreed that inanimate things have better luck at times than man."

She answered suggestively, "I think you're exaggerating. Inanimate goods are no luckier than a man, but frequently they are more useful."

Al-Sayyid Ahmad gave her a piercing look with his blue eyes. Pretending to be astonished, he exclaimed, "More useful!" and then, pointing at the floor, "This store!"

She granted him a short, sweet laugh but said in a tone not without a deliberate harshness, "I want sugar, coffee, rice; the man needs his store for these things." Then she continued with an inflection free of any flirtatiousness: "Moreover, men are much harder on the heart."

The doors of desire had opened for the proprietor. He sensed he was faced with something far more significant than a simple purchase. He objected, "Not all men are the same, Sultana. Who told you that a man's no substitute for rice, sugar, and coffee? It's with a man that you truly find nourishment, sweetness, and satisfaction."

She laughed and asked him, "Are you talking about a man or a kitchen?"

He answered victoriously, "If you look closely, you'll discover an amazing similarity between a man and a kitchen. Each of them fills the belly with life."

The woman lowered her eyes for a time. The proprietor expected her to look up at him with a bright smile, but the glance she directed at him was serious. He sensed at once that she had changed strategy or perhaps was not really comfortable about slipping into a relationship so quickly. She turned away and then he heard her say quietly, "May God help you . . . but all we need today are rice, coffee, and sugar."

The proprietor stepped away from her and tried to look serious. He summoned his assistant and in a loud voice entrusted the lady's orders to him. He gave the impression that he too had decided to refrain from being too affectionate and to get back to business, but it was just a maneuver. Immediately afterward he went on the attack again with his smile and murmured to the sultana, "The store and its proprietor are yours to command."

The maneuver had its effect, for the woman said jokingly, "I want the store, and you insist on giving yourself."

"I'm no doubt better than my store, or the best thing in it."

She beamed with a mischievous smile and said, "This contradicts what we've heard about the excellence of your merchandise."

The proprietor laughed boisterously and said, "Why do you need sugar when there's all this sweetness on your tongue?"

This verbal battle was followed by a period of silence during which each of them appeared content with himself. Then the performer opened her purse and took out a small mirror with a silver handle. She began to look at herself. The proprietor went back to his desk. He stood, leaning on the edge of it, while he studied her face with interest.

The truth was that when his eyes had first noticed her, his heart had told him that she had not made her visit merely to buy something. Then her warm and responsive conversation had confirmed his suspicions. Now all that remained was for him to decide whether to respond or to bid her a final adieu. It was not the first time he had seen her, for he had frequently run into her at weddings hosted by his friends. He knew from secondhand reports that al-Sayyid Khalil al-Banan had been her lover for a long time but that they had recently separated. Perhaps it was for this reason that she was looking for goods at a new store. She was very beautiful, even though her status as a singer was only second-rate. All the same, he was more interested in her as a woman than as a singer. She certainly was desirable. Her folds of flesh and fat would warm a chilly man during the bitter cold of winter, which was at hand.

His reflections were cut short by al-Hamzawi, who brought the three parcels. The maid took them, and the lady thrust her hand into her purse, apparently to take out some money. Al-Sayyid Ahmad gestured to her not to try to pay: "That would be quite wrong."

The woman pretended to be astonished. "Wrong, Mr. al-Sayyid? How can doing what's right be wrong?"

"This is an auspicious visit. It's our duty to greet it with the honor it deserves. It would be impossible for me to do justice to it."

While he was talking, she stood up. She did not offer any serious resistance to his generosity but warned, "Your generosity will make me hesitate more than once before I come back to you again."

The proprietor laughed boisterously and replied, "Have no fear! I'm generous to a customer the first time, but I make up for my loss later, even if I have to cheat. This is the way merchants operate."

The lady smiled and held out her hand to him. She commented, "When a generous man like you cheats, it isn't really cheating. Thank you, Sayyid Ahmad."

He responded from the depths of his heart, "Don't mention it, Sultana."

He stood watching her strut toward the door and then climb into the carriage. She took her place, and Jaljal sat on the small seat opposite her. The carriage rolled off with its precious cargo and disappeared from sight.

Then here was al-Hamzawi, asking as he turned a page of the ledger, "How can this sum be accounted for?"

The proprietor looked at his assistant with a smile and replied, "Write beside it: 'Goods destroyed by an act of God.' " He murmured to himself as he returned to his desk, "God is beautiful and loves beauty."

15

That evening al-Sayyid Ahmad closed his store and set off surrounded by respectful glances and diffusing a pleasant fragrance. He proceeded to the Goldsmiths Bazaar and from there to al-Ghuriya till he reached al-Sayyid Ali's coffee shop. As he passed it, he looked at the singer's house and the adjoining buildings. He observed that the string of shops on both sides of it were still open and that the flow of pedestrian traffic was at its height. He continued on to a friend's house, where he passed an hour. Then he excused himself and returned to al-Ghuriya, which was engulfed in darkness and almost deserted.

Confident and relaxed, he approached the house. He knocked on the door and waited, looking carefully at everything around him. The only light came from the window of al-Sayyid Ali's coffee shop and from a kerosene lamp on a handcart at the corner of New Street. The door opened and the form of a young servant girl could be seen. Without any hesitation, in order to inspire in the girl trust and confidence, he asked her in a forceful voice, "Is Madam Zubayda at home?"

The girl looked up at him and asked with the reserve her job required, "Who are you, sir?"

He responded determinedly, "A person who wishes to reach an agreement with her for an evening's entertainment."

The girl was gone for some minutes before returning to invite him in. She stepped aside to allow him to enter. He followed her up the narrow steps of the staircase to a hallway. She opened the door facing him, and he passed through it into a darkened room. He stood there near the entrance, listening to her footsteps as she ran to fetch a lamp. He watched her place it on a table. She moved a chair to the center of the room to stand on while she lit the large lamp hanging from the ceiling. Then she put the chair back where it belonged. She took the small lamp and left the room, saying politely, "Please have a seat, sir."

He went over to a sofa at the front of the room and sat there confidently and calmly, demonstrating that he was accustomed to situations like this and certain the results would be to his liking. He removed his fez and placed it on a cushion at the center of the sofa. He stretched his legs out and made himself comfortable. He saw a room of medium size with sofas and chairs arranged around the sides. The floor was covered with a Persian carpet. In front of each of the three large sofas stood a serving table inlaid with mother-of-pearl. The windows and door were hung with curtains that prevented the aroma of incense he enjoyed from escaping. He amused himself by watching a moth flutter nervously and eagerly around the lamp. While he waited, the servant brought him coffee. It was some time before he heard the rhythmic thump of slippers striking the floor.

He became fully alert and stared at the opening of the door, which was immediately filled by the prodigious body, its pronounced curves sensuously draped in a blue dress. The moment the woman's eyes fell on him she stopped in astonishment and shouted, "In the name of God, the Compassionate, the Merciful! . . . You!"

His eyes ran over her body as quickly and greedily as a mouse on a sack of rice looking for a place to get in. He said admiringly, "In the name of God. God's will be done."

After her pause, she continued to advance, smiling. She said with pretended fear, "Your eye! God protect me from it."

Al-Sayyid Ahmad rose to take her outstretched hand. Sniffing the fragrant incense with his enormous nose, he asked, "Are you afraid of an envious eye even when protected by this incense?"

She freed her hand from his and stepped back to sit on one of the side couches. She replied, "My incense is a boon and a blessing. It's a mixture of various kinds, some Arab and some Indian that I blend myself. It's capable of ridding the body of a thousand and one jinn."

He sat down again and said, waving his hands in despair, "But not my body. My body has a jinni of a different sort. Incense doesn't do any good with him. The matter is more severe and dangerous."

The woman struck her chest like a heaving water skin and shouted, "But I perform at weddings, not exorcisms."

He said hopefully, "We'll see if you have a remedy for what ails me."

They were silent for a time. The sultana started to look at him somewhat reflectively, as though trying to discern the secret of his visit and whether he really had come to ask her to perform at a party, as he had told the servant. Her curiosity got the better of her and she asked, "A wedding or a circumcision?"

Smiling he replied, "Whichever you wish."

"Do you have an uncircumcised boy or a bridegroom?"

"I've got everything."

She gave him a warning look as if to say, "How tiresome you are!" Then she muttered sarcastically, "We'll be happy to serve you, whatever it happens to be."

Al-Sayyid Ahmad raised his hands to the top of his head in a gesture of thanks. He said with a gravity that belied his intentions, "God bless you! All the same, I'm still determined to leave the choice to you."

She sighed with a rage that was half humorous and replied, "I prefer weddings, of course."

"But I'm a married man. I don't need any more wedding processions."

She yelled at him, "What a joker you are ... Then let it be a circumcision."

"So be it."

She asked cautiously, "Your son?"

Twisting his mustache, he answered simply, "Me."

The sultana let out a flowing laugh. She decided to stop thinking about the question of an evening performance. She guessed what kind of performance it would be. She shouted at him, "What a crafty man you are. If my arm were long enough I'd break your back."

He rose and approached, saying, "I won't deprive you of anything you want." He sat down beside her. She started to hit him but hesitated and then stopped. He asked her anxiously, "Why don't you honor me with a beating?"

She shook her head and replied scornfully, "I'm afraid I would have to repeat my ritual ablutions."

He asked longingly, "May I hope we can pray together?" He privately asked God's forgiveness as soon as he had made this joke. Although there were no limits to his impudence when he was intoxicated by his sense of humor, his heart was always troubled and uneasy until he secretly and sincerely asked God's forgiveness for the humorous excesses of his tongue.

The woman asked with ironic coquetry, "Do you mean, reverend sir, the kind of prayer the muezzin says is better than sleep?"

"No, prayer which is a form of sleep."

She could not keep herself from saying with a laugh, "What a man you are! On the outside you are dignified and pious, but inside you're licentious and debauched. Now I really believe what I was told about you."

Al-Sayyid Ahmad sat up with interest and asked, "What were you told? . . . May God spare us the evil of what people say."

"They told me you're a womanizer and a heavy drinker."

He sighed audibly in relief and commented, "I thought it would be criticism of some fault, thank God."

"Didn't I tell you you're a crafty sinner?"

"Here's the evidence, then, that I've won your acceptance, God willing."

The woman raised her head haughtily and replied, "Keep your distance. . . . I'm not like the women you've had. Zubayda is known, if I do say so myself, for her self-respect and good taste."

The man raised his hands to his chest and looked at her in a way both challenging and gentle. He remarked calmly, "It's when a man is tested that he's honored or despised."

"How come you're so cocky when, according to you, you haven't even been circumcised yet?"

Al-Sayyid Ahmad laughed loudly for a long time. Then he said, "You don't believe me, you circumciser. Well, if you're in doubt . . ."

She punched him in the shoulder before he could finish his sentence. He stopped talking, and then they burst out laughing together. He was happy she laughed along with him. He surmised that, given both the veiled and open remarks that had passed between them, her laughter constituted an announcement of her consent. The flirtatious smile, visible in her eyes with their shadow of kohl, served to confirm this idea in his mind. He thought he would greet this flirtation in kind, but she cautioned him, "Don't make me think even worse of you."

Her statement reminded him of her reference to things she had heard. He asked her with interest, "Who's been talking to you about me?"

She replied tersely, giving him an accusing look, "Jalila."

This name took him by surprise. It was like a critic interrupting their tête-à-tête. He smiled in a way that showed he was uncomfortable. Jalila was the famous performer he had loved for such a long time, until they separated after the fire had died in their romance. They continued to like each other but had gone their separate ways. Relying on his experience with women, he thought he had better say, as though he really meant it, "God curse her face and voice!" Then, trying to avoid this topic, he continued: "Let's skip all this and talk seriously."

She asked sarcastically, "Doesn't Jalila deserve a gentler and more gracious comment? Or are you always like this when you talk about a woman you've dumped?"

Al-Sayyid Ahmad felt a little uneasy, but he was awash with the sexual conceit aroused in him when a new lover discussed one of his former girlfriends. He enjoyed the sweet intoxication of triumph for some time. Then he remarked with his customary suavity, "In the presence of beauty like yours, I'm unable to put it aside for memories that are buried and forgotten."

Although the sultana retained her ironic look, she responded to the praise by raising her eyebrows and concealing a faint smile that had stolen across her lips. All the same, she addressed him scornfully: "A merchant is generous with his sweet talk until he gets what he wants."

"We merchants deserve to go to paradise because people are so unfair to us."

She shrugged her shoulders with disdain and then asked him with unconcealed interest, "When were you seeing each other?"

He waved his arm as if to say, "What a long time ago!" Then he muttered, "Ages and ages ago."

She laughed mockingly and said in a tone of revenge, "In the days of your youth, which have passed."

He looked at her reproachfully and said, "I wish I could suck the venom from your tongue."

She continued with what she was saying in the same tone: "She took you in when your flesh was firm and left you nothing but bones."

He gestured with his forefinger to caution her, saying, "I'm one of those hardy men who get married in their sixties."

"Motivated by passion or senility?"

He roared with laughter and said, "Lady, fear God. Let's have a serious talk."

"Serious? . . . You mean about the evening's entertainment you came to arrange?"

"I seek entertainment for a whole lifetime."

"A whole lifetime or just half?"

"May our Lord grant us what is good for us. . . ."

"May our Lord grant us what is pleasant."

He secretly requested God's forgiveness in advance before he asked, "Shall we recite the opening prayer of the Qur'an?"

She jumped up suddenly, ignoring his invitation, and cried out in alarm, "My Lord . . . it's later than I thought. I have an important engagement tonight."

Al-Sayyid Ahmad rose too. He stretched out his hand to take hers. He spread open her palm tinted with henna and looked at it with desire and fascination. He kept on holding it even after she tried repeatedly to withdraw it. Finally she pinched his finger and raised her hand to his mustache. She shouted menacingly to him, "Let go of me or you'll leave my house with only half a mustache."

He saw that her forearm was near his mouth. He abandoned the dispute and slowly brought his lips to her arm until they sank into its soft flesh. A delicious fragrance of carnations wafted from her. He sighed and murmured, "Till tomorrow?"

She escaped from his hand without any resistance this time. She gave him a lengthy look. Then she smiled and recited softly:

My sparrow, Mother, my little bird,
I'll play and show him what I have learned.

She repeated these lines several times as she saw him out. Al-Sayyid Ahmad left the room singing the opening of this song in a low voice both dignified and sedate. He seemed to be examining the words for their hidden meaning.

16

In the home of the singer Zubayda there was a room like a hall in the middle of her residence that was dubbed the recital chamber. Actually it was a hall for which new uses had been found. Perhaps the most important of these for her and her troupe was rehearsing their songs and learning new material. It had been chosen because it was far from the public street and separated from it by bedrooms and reception chambers. Its size also made it a suitable location for her private parties, which usually were either exorcisms or recitals to which she would invite her special friends and close acquaintances. The motive for hosting these parties was not simply generosity, for any generosity manifested was almost always that of the guests themselves. The aim was to increase the number of fine friends able to invite her to perform at their parties or to help promote her by praising her in the circles where they were received. It was also from these men that she selected lover after lover.

Now it was al-Sayyid Ahmad Abd al-Jawad's turn to honor the festive hall, accompanied by some of his most distinguished acquaintances. He had displayed boundless energy following the daring meeting that had taken place between them at her house. His messengers had immediately taken her a generous gift of candied nuts and dried fruit, sweets and other presents, in addition to a stove he commissioned which was decorated with silver plate. These gifts were all a token of the affection to follow. Leaving the guest list entirely up to him, the sultana had invited him to a get-acquainted party in honor of their newfound love.

The chamber was remarkable for its attractive, Egyptian look. A row of comfortable sofas with brocade upholstery, suggesting both luxury and dissipation, stretched out on either side of the sultana's divan, which was flanked by mattresses and cushions for her troupe. The long expanse of floor was covered with carpets of many different colors and types. On a table suspended from the right wall, halfway along it, candles were arranged in candelabra where they looked as lovely and intense as a beauty mark on a cheek. There was a huge lamp hanging from the peak of a skylight in the center of the ceiling.

The skylight's windows looked out on the roof terrace and were left open on warm evenings, but closed when it was cold.

Zubayda sat cross-legged on the divan. At her right was Zanuba, the lute player, her foster daughter. On her left was Abduh, the blind performer on the zitherlike qanun. The women of the troupe sat on both sides, some clasping tambourines, others stroking their conical drums or playing with finger cymbals. The sultana had selected for al-Sayyid Ahmad the first seat on the right. The other men, his friends, found places for themselves without any hesitation, as though they lived there. This was not odd since there was nothing novel about the situation for them and it was not the first time they had seen the sultana. Al Sayyid Ahmad presented his friends to the performer, beginning with al-Sayyid Ali, the flour merchant.

Zubayda laughed and said, "Al-Sayyid Ali is no stranger to me. I performed at his daughter's wedding last year."

Then he turned to the copper merchant. One of the men accused him of being a fan of the vocalist Bamba Kashar, and the merchant quickly remarked, "Lady, I've come to repent."

The introductions continued until everyone was presented. Then Jaljal, the maid, brought in glasses of wine and served the guests. The men started to feel a vitality mixed with liberality and mirth. Al-Sayyid Ahmad was undeniably the bridegroom of the party. His friends called him that and he felt it too, deep inside. At first he had been a little uncomfortable in a way rare for him but had concealed his discomfort with an extra amount of laughter and mirth. Once he began drinking, the embarrassment left him spontaneously and his composure returned. He threw himself wholeheartedly into the excitement.

Whenever he felt a surge of desire—and desires are aroused at musical entertainments—he would gaze greedily at the sultana of the soiree. His eyes would linger on the folds of her massive body. He felt good about the blessing fortune had bestowed on him. He congratulated himself on the sweet delights he could look forward to that night and following ones.

" 'It's when a man is tested that he's honored or despised.' I challenged her with this declaration. I've got to live up to my word. I wonder what she's like as a woman and how far she'll go? I'll discover the truth at a suitable time. In any case, I'll play by her rules. To ensure a victory over an opponent, you must assume she's vigilant and strong. I won't deviate from my long-standing practice of making my own pleasure a secondary objective after hers, which is the real goal and climax. In that way my pleasure will be achieved in the most perfect fashion."

Despite his great number of amorous adventures, out of all the different varieties of love, al-Sayyid Ahmad had experienced only lust. All the same, he had progressed in his pursuit of it to its purest and most delicate form. He was not simply an animal. In addition to his sensuality, he was endowed with a delicacy of feeling, a sensitivity of emotion, and an ingrained love for song and music. He had elevated lust to its most exalted type. It was for the sake of this lust alone that he had married the first time and then for the second. Over the course of time, his conjugal love was affected by calm new elements of affection and familiarity, but in essence it continued to be based on bodily desire. When an emotion is of this type, especially when it has acquired a renewed power and exuberant vitality, it cannot be content with only one form of expression. Thus he had shot off in pursuit of all the varieties of love and passion, like a wild bull. Whenever desire called, he answered, deliriously and enthusiastically. No woman was anything more than a body to him. All the same, he would not bow his head before that body unless he found it truly worthy of being seen, touched, smelled, tasted, and heard. It was lust, yes, but not bestial or blind. It had been refined by a craft that was at least partially an art, setting his lust in a framework of delight, humor, and good cheer. Nothing was so like his lust as his body, since both were huge and powerful, qualities that bring to mind roughness and savagery. Yet both concealed within them grace, delicacy, and affection, even though he might intentionally cloak those characteristics at times with sternness and severity. While he was devouring the sultana with his glances he did not limit his active imagination to having sex with her. It also wandered through various dreams of amusing pastimes and tuneful celebrations.

Zubayda felt the warmth of his gaze. Glancing around at the faces of the guests vainly and coquettishly, she told him, "Bridegroom, control yourself. Aren't you embarrassed in front of your associates?"

"There's no point trying to be chaste in the presence of such a prodigious and voluptuous body."

The songstress released a resounding laugh. Then with great delight she asked the men, "What do you think of your friend?"

They all replied in one breath, "He's excused!"

At this the blind qanun player shook his head to the right and left, his lower lip hanging open. He muttered, "He's excused who gives a warning."

Although the man's proverb was well received, the lady turned on him in mock anger and punched him in the chest, yelling, "You hush and shut your big mouth."

The blind man accepted the blow laughingly. He opened his mouth as though to speak but closed it again to be safe. The woman turned her head toward al-Sayyid Ahmad and told him threateningly, "This is what happens to people who get out of line."

Pretending to be alarmed, he replied, "But I came to learn how to get out of line."

The woman struck her chest with her hand and shouted, "What cheek! . . . Did you all hear what he said?"

More than one of them said at the same time, "It's the best thing we've heard so far."

One of the group added, "You ought to hit him if he doesn't get out of line."

Someone else suggested, "You ought to obey him so long as he stays out of line."

The woman raised her eyebrows to show an astonishment she did not feel and asked, "Do you love being naughty this much?"

Al-Sayyid Ahmad sighed and said, "May our Lord perpetuate our naughtiness."

At that the performer picked up a tambourine and said, "Here's something better for you to listen to."

She struck the tambourine in a rather nonchalant way, but the sound rose above the babbling commotion like an alarm and silenced it. The noise of her tambourine teased their ears. Everyone gradually dropped what he was doing. The members of the troupe got ready to play while the gentlemen drained their glasses. Then they gazed at the sultana. The room was so silent it almost declared their eagerness to enjoy the music.

The maestra gestured to her troupe and they burst out playing an overture by the composer Muhammad Uthman. Heads started to sway with the music. Al-Sayyid Ahmad surrendered himself to the resonant sound of the qanun, which set his heart on fire. Echoes of many different melodies from a long era filled with nights of musical ecstasy burst into flame within him, as though small drops of gasoline had fallen on a hidden ember. The qanun certainly was his favorite instrument, not only because of the virtuosity of a performer like al-Aqqad, but because of something about the very nature of the strings. Although he knew he was not going to hear a famous virtuoso like al-Aqqad or al-Sayyid Abduh, his enthusiastic heart made up for the defects of the performance with its passion.

The moment the troupe finished the five-part overture, the singer began "The sweetness of your lips intoxicates me." The troupe joined her enthusiastically. The most movingly beautiful part of this song was the harmony between two voices: the blind musician's gruff, expansive one and Zanuba the lutanist's delicate, childlike one. Al-Sayyid Ahmad was deeply touched. He quickly drained his glass to join in the chorus. In his haste to start singing he forgot to clear his throat and at first sounded choked. Others in the group soon plucked up their courage and followed his example. Soon everyone in the room was part of the troupe singing as though with one voice.

When that piece was finished, al-Sayyid Ahmad expected to hear some instrumental solos and vocal improvisation as usual, but Zubayda capped the ending with one of her resounding laughs to demonstrate her pleasure and amazement. She began to congratulate the new members of the troupe jokingly and asked them what they would like to hear. Al-Sayyid Ahmad was secretly distressed and momentarily depressed, since his passion for singing was intense. Few of those around him noticed anything. Then he realized that Zubayda, like most others of her profession, including the famous Bamba Kashar herself, was not capable of doing solo improvisations. He hoped she would pick a light ditty of the kind sung to the ladies at a wedding party. He would prefer that to having her attempt a virtuoso piece and fail to get it right. He tried to spare his ears the suffering he anticipated by suggesting an easy song suitable for the lady's voice. He asked, "What would you all think of 'My sparrow, Mother'?"

He looked at her suggestively, trying to arouse in her an interest in this ditty with which she had crowned their conversation a few days before in the reception room. A voice from the far end of the hall cried out sarcastically, "It would be better to ask your mother for that one."

The suggestion was quickly lost in the outburst of guffaws that spoiled his plan for him. Before he could try again, one group requested "O Muslims, O People of God" and another wanted "Get well, my heart."

Zubayda was wary about favoring one bunch over the other and announced she would sing for them "I'm an accomplice against myself." Her announcement was warmly received. Al-Sayyid Ahmad saw no alternative to resigning himself and seeking his pleasure in wine and dreams about his promising chances for the evening. His lips gleamed with a sincere smile that the gang of inebriates cheerfully perceived. He was touched by the woman's desire to imitate the virtuosi in order to please her knowledgeable listeners, even though her actions were not totally free of the vanity common among singers.

As the troupe was getting ready to sing, one of the men rose and called out enthusiastically, "Give the tambourine to al Sayyid Ahmad. He's an expert."

Zubayda shook her head in amazement and asked, "Really?"

Al-Sayyid Ahmad moved his fingers quickly and nimbly as if giving her a demonstration of his skill. Zubayda smiled and remarked, "No wonder! You were Jalila's pupil."

The gentlemen laughed uproariously. The laughter continued until Mr. al-Far's voice rose to ask the sultana, "What are you planning to teach him?"

She replied teasingly, "I'll teach him to play the qanun. Wouldn't you like that?"

Al-Sayyid Ahmad implored her, "Teach me internal repetitions, if you will."

Many of them encouraged him to join the musicians and he took the tambourine. Then he rose and removed his outer cloak. In his chestnut caftan he looked so tall and broad that he could have been a charger prancing on its hind legs. He pushed back his sleeves and went to the divan to take his place beside the lady. To make room for him she rose halfway and scooted to the left. Her red dress slipped back to reveal a strong, fleshy leg which was white brushed with pink where she had plucked the hair. The bottom of her leg was adorned with a gold anklet that could barely encompass it.

One of the men who glimpsed that sight shouted in a voice like thunder, "The Ottoman caliphate forever!"

Al-Sayyid Ahmad, who was ogling the woman's breasts, yelled after him, "Say: the Ottoman grand brassiere forever!"

The performer shouted to caution them: "Lower your voices or the English will throw us in jail for the night."

Al-Sayyid Ahmad, whose head was feeling the effects of the wine, yelled, "If you're with me, I'll go for life at hard labor."

More than one voice called out, "Death to anyone who lets you two go there alone."

The woman wanted to end the debate begun by the sight of her leg and handed the tambourine to al-Sayyid Ahmad. She told him, "Show me what you can do."

He took the tambourine and smiled as he rubbed it with the palm of his hand. His fingers began to strike it skillfully and then the other instruments started playing. Zubayda glanced at the eyes fixed on her and sang:

I'm an accomplice against myself
When my lover steals my heart.

Al-Sayyid Ahmad found himself in a wonderfully intoxicating situation. The sultana's breath fluttered toward him each time she turned his way, meeting the vapors which rose to the top of his head with every sip. He quickly forgot the refrains of the famous musicians al-Hamuli, Muhammad Uthman, and al-Manilawi, and lived in the present, happy and content. The inflections of her voice made the strings of his heart vibrate. His energy flared up and he beat the tambourine in a way no professional could match. His intoxication became a burning, titillating, inspiring, raging drunkenness the moment the woman sang:

You who are going to see him
Take a kiss from me as a pledge for my
Sweetheart's mouth.

His companions kept pace with him or surpassed him as the wine made its ultimate impact on them. They were so agitated by desire they seemed trees dancing in the frenzy of a hurricane.

Slowly, gradually the time came for the song to close. Zubayda ended by repeating the same phrase that began it: "I'm an accomplice against myself," but with a spirit that was calm, reflective, and valedictory, and then final. The melodies vanished like an airplane carrying a lover over the horizon. Although the conclusion was greeted by a storm of applause and clapping, silence soon reigned over the hall, for their souls were worn out by all the exertion and emotion. A period passed when nothing was heard except the sound of someone coughing, clearing his throat, striking a match, or uttering a word that required no reply. The guests realized it was time to say good night. Some could be seen looking for articles of clothing they had stripped off in the heat of their musical ecstasy and placed behind them on the cushions. Others were having too good a time to leave until they had sipped every possible drop of this sweet wine.

One of these cried out, "We won't go until we have a wedding procession to present the sultana to al-Sayyid Ahmad."

The suggestion was warmly received and widely supported. Incredulous, the gentleman and the entertainer collapsed with laughter. Before they knew what was happening, several men had surrounded them and dragged them to their feet, gesturing to the troupe to commence the joyous anthem. The couple stood side by side, she like the ceremonial camel litter bound for Mecca and he like the camel. They were giants made less threatening by their good looks. Coquettishly she placed her arm under his and gestured to those surrounding them to clear the way. The woman with the tambourine started playing it, and the troupe along with many of the guests began to sing the wedding song: "Look this way, you handsome fellow." The bridal couple proceeded with deliberate steps, strutting forward, animated by both the music and the wine.

When she saw this sight, Zanuba stopped playing her lute and could not keep from emitting a long, ringing trill or shriek of joy. If it could have taken bodily form, it would have been a twisting tongue of flame splitting the heavens like a shooting star.

Their friends tried to outdo each other in offering their congratulations: "A happy marriage and many sons."

"Healthy children who are good dancers and singers."

One of the men shouted to caution them, "Don't put off until tomorrow what you can do today."

The troupe kept playing and the friends kept waving their hands until al-Sayyid Ahmad and the woman disappeared through the door leading to the interior of the house.

17

Al-Sayyid Ahmad was sitting at his desk in the store when Yasin walked in unexpectedly. The visit was not merely unexpected but extraordinary, since it was unusual for the young man to visit his father at the store. Even at home he avoided him to the best of his ability. Moreover, Yasin looked absentminded and serious. He approached his father, giving him nothing more than a mechanical salute. Seeming to forget himself, he neglected to show the pronounced respect and deference customary when in his father's presence. Then he said in a voice that showed how upset he was, "Greetings, Father. I've come to talk to you about something important."

His father looked up at him quizzically. Although he felt anxious he relied on his willpower to conceal it and asked calmly, "Good news, God willing."

Jamil al-Hamzawi brought Yasin a chair as he welcomed him, and his father ordered him to have a seat. The young man brought the chair closer to the desk and sat down. He seemed to hesitate for a few moments. Then he sighed in exasperation at his own hesitation and said in a quavering voice with touching brevity, "The thing is, my mother's going to get married."

Although al-Sayyid Ahmad was expecting bad news, his forebodings had not wandered in the direction of this outgrown corner of his past. Therefore the announcement caught him off guard. He frowned as he always did when he remembered anything about his first wife. It upset him and he was alarmed because of the direct threat to his son's honor. "Who told you so?" he inquired, asking not to seek information but to escape from an unpleasant reality or provide himself time to deliberate and calm his nerves.

"Her relative Shaykh Hamdi. He visited me at al-Nahhasin School and told me the news. He confirmed it would take place within a month."

The news, then, was a fact beyond doubt, and it was nothing novel for her. If the past was any guide, it would not be her last marriage either. But what sin had this youth committed to be subjected to this harsh punishment, which hurt him again and again? The man felt pity and affection for his son. It was hard on him that he, to whom people turned in times of trouble, could do nothing to relieve Yasin's pain. He asked himself what he would have done if he had been afflicted with such a mother. He was distressed, and his pity and affection for his son became more intense. Then he wanted to ask about her fiancé but resisted the temptation, because he was worried about making his son's wound worse and could not bring himself to ask. Given the current disaster, curiosity about the woman who had been his wife would not be appropriate.

Yasin, as though reading his mind, volunteered emotionally, "And who's she marrying! A person called Ya'qub Zaynhum who has a bakery in al-Darrasa. He's in his thirties!"

He became even more agitated, and his voice trembled as he spat out the final phrase like a fish bone. His feeling of disgust and aversion passed over to his father, who began repeating to himself: "In his thirties. . . . What a disgrace! It's adultery disguised as marriage." The man was angry because his son was and for his own sake too. He always got angry when news of her private affairs reached him. It appeared to reawaken his sense of responsibility for what she did, since she had once been his wife. He also seemed, even after such a long time, to be hurt by the fact that she had escaped from his discipline and had disobeyed his will. He remembered the days he had lived with her, however few, with the exceptional clarity of a man recalling an illness he has had. It was hardly surprising that a man as sure of himself as he was should see in the mere wish to disobey him an inexcusable crime and crushing defeat.

Moreover, she had been and perhaps still was beautiful and full of feminine attractions. He had enjoyed living with her for a few months until she displayed some resistance to his will, which he imposed on close family members. She saw no harm in enjoying some freedom, even if it was limited to visiting her father from time to time. Al-Sayyid Ahmad had grown angry and had attempted to restrain her, at first by scolding her and then by violent beatings. The spoiled woman had fled to her parents, and anger had blinded the haughty man. He thought the best way to discipline her and bring her back to her senses was to divorce her for a time—naturally just for a time, since he was very attached to her. He did divorce her and pretended to forget about her for a period of days and then weeks, while he waited for a representative of her family to bring him good news. When no one knocked on his door, he swallowed his pride and sent someone to sound out the situation to prepare for a reconciliation.

The messenger returned saying they would welcome him on the condition that he would not forbid her to leave the house and would not beat her. He had expected that they would agree without any stipulation or condition. He became violently angry and swore never to marry her again. Thus they had gone their separate ways, and Yasin's fate was to be born away from his father and to suffer humiliation and pain in his mother's house.

Although the woman had married more than once and although, in her son's eyes, marriage was the most honorable of her offenses, this anticipated marriage seemed more outrageous than the previous ones and more calculated to cause pain. The woman was at least forty, and Yasin was now fully grown and aware of his ability to defend his honor from harm and humiliation. He was no longer in his previous situation when, because of his youth, he could only react to the disturbing rumors about his mother with astonishment, alarm, and tears. He now considered himself a responsible adult who should not sit on his hands when humiliated. These thoughts passed through the father's head. He was painfully aware of how serious they were, but he resolved to downplay their significance as best he could in order to spare his eldest son the vexation.

He shook his broad shoulders as though it did not matter very much and said, "Didn't we vow to consider her a person who never existed?"

Yasin replied sadly and despondently, "But she does exist, Father. No matter what we vow, she continues to be my mother so long as God spares her, both in my eyes and in everyone else's."

The young man breathed out heavily. With the handsome, black eyes he had inherited from his mother he gazed at his father in a penetrating plea for help. He seemed to be telling him, "You're my powerful, mighty father. Give me your hand."

Al-Sayyid Ahmad was even more profoundly moved but continued to pretend to be calm and unconcerned. He remarked, "I don't blame you for feeling hurt, but don't exaggerate. I can understand your anger, but if you'll just be reasonable, you'll get over it without too much trouble. Ask yourself calmly how her marriage harms you. . . . A woman gets married? Women get married every day and every hour. In view of her past conduct, she cannot be held responsible for a marriage like this. Perhaps she even ought to be thanked for it. As I've told you repeatedly, your mind won't be at rest till you stop thinking about her and pretend she never existed. Trust in God and don't take it so hard. No matter what people say, you should find consolation in the fact that marriage is a legal relationship sanctioned by religion."

He said these things without meaning them, since they totally contradicted his extreme, innate sensitivity over anything relating to family etiquette. He said it all with such warmth that he seemed to be telling the truth, thanks to the diplomatic skills he had acquired while learning to become a wise arbitrator and beneficent intermediary capable of settling disputes between people. Although his words were not lost on Yasin, since it was inconceivable that any of his children would ignore what he said, the young man's anger was too profound to evaporate all at once. The words affected him like a cup of cold water poured into a boiling pot.

He immediately replied to his father, "It's a legal relationship of course, Father, but at times it seems as far removed as possible from piety or legality. I ask myself: What could motivate this man to marry her?"

Despite the gravity of the situation the father said to himself a bit sarcastically, "You ought to ask what's motivating her!"

Before al-Sayyid Ahmad could answer, Yasin continued: "It's greed and nothing else."

"Or maybe a sincere desire to marry her."

The youth flew into a rage and shouted in a hurt and furious way, "No, it's nothing but greed!"

Although it was a serious situation, al-Sayyid Ahmad could not help noticing the sharpness of the tone with which his son had addressed him. Given his son's condition and grief, he felt uncomfortable simply reaffirming what he had said before. Hearing no further objection, Yasin continued with relative composure: "What makes him marry a woman ten years older is greed for her money and property."

The father shrewdly saw the benefit in shifting the conversation to this topic. It would divert the young man from dwelling on more sensitive and painful matters. Thinking about that man might keep him from examining his mother's motives for getting married. In addition, he realized how well founded his son's opinion probably was regarding this fiancé. He was quickly convinced and embraced his son's fears. Yes, Haniya, Yasin's mother, was well-to-do. Her fortune in real estate had remained intact in spite of her experiments with marriage and love. Although in the past she had been a beautiful young woman with both magic and majesty, to be feared and not feared for, now it was unlikely that she had as much control over herself as she once did, not to mention control over others. Her fortune might well be squandered on the battlefield of love, where she was no longer so competitive. It would be outrageous in the extreme if Yasin emerged from the inferno of this tragedy with both wounded honor and empty hands.

Al-Sayyid Ahmad remarked to his son as though thinking it over by himself, "I see you're right, son, in what you say. A woman her age is an easy mark and could well be a temptation to greedy men. What can we do? Should we seek to contact that man and force him to abandon his adventure? To try to intimidate him, threatening and menacing him, runs contrary to our ethics and what people know we stand for. To attempt to entreat and persuade him would be a humiliation our honor could not bear. That leaves us only the woman herself. I'm not overlooking your break with her that she richly deserved and still does. The truth is, I'd not be comfortable about your reestablishing a link with her, if the new circumstances did not require it. Necessity has its own rules. No matter how difficult it is for you to visit her, it's your own mother you're returning to, after all. Who knows? Perhaps your surprise appearance on her horizon will bring her back to her right mind."

Yasin looked like a hypnotist's subject in the moments preceding the hypnotic suggestion. He was silent and dazed. His state revealed the profound impact his father had on him or indicated that this suggestion had not taken him by surprise. All the same, he stammered, "Isn't there any better solution?"

His father replied forcefully and plainly, "I think it is the best solution."

As though addressing himself, Yasin asked, "How can I go back to her? How can I force myself back into a past I fled and want more than anything to erase from my life? I have no mother . . . no mother at all."

Despite what Yasin appeared to be saying, his father felt he had succeeded in converting him to his opinion. He told him diplomatically, "True, but I think if you appear in front of her, after this long absence, it will have an effect. Perhaps if she sees you before her, a full-grown man, her maternal instincts will be awakened. Then she'll mend her ways and shy away from anything that might damage your honor. Who knows?"

Plunged in thought, Yasin calmed his mind, heedless of his despairing, anguished appearance. He was shuddering from fear of the scandal awaiting him. That was possibly the most heinous thing troubling him, but his fear of losing the fortune he expected to inherit one day was no less appalling. What could he do? No matter how he approached the issue he could find no better solution than the one his father had suggested. Indeed, no matter how shaky he felt, the fact that the idea came from his father lent it, in his opinion, validity and spared him a lot of worry. "So be it," he said to himself. Then, addressing his father, he said, "Just as you wish, Father."

18

When his feet brought him to al-Gamaliya Street, he was so choked up he felt he would die. He had not been there for eleven years, eleven years that had passed without his heart yearning for it once. Any memory of the area that had flashed into his mind had been surrounded by a depressing black halo and ornamented with the stuff from which nightmares are woven. The truth was that he had not simply left home but, when the opportunity arose, had fled. Angry and dejected, he had turned his back on it and avoided it completely. It was not a place he sought out or even cut across on the way to some other district.

Yet it remained exactly the way it had been when he was growing up. Nothing had changed. The street was still so narrow a handcart would almost block it when passing by. The protruding balconies of the houses almost touched each other overhead. The small shops resembled the cells of a beehive, they were so close together and crowded with patrons, so noisy and humming. The street was unpaved, with gaping holes full of mud. The boys who swarmed along the sides of the street made footprints in the dirt with their bare feet. There was the same never-ending stream of pedestrian traffic. Uncle Hasan's snack shop and Uncle Sulayman's restaurant too remained just as he had known them. If it had not been for the bitterness of the past and his present suffering, a tender smile, which the child in him wished to display, might well have traced itself on his lips.

The cul-de-sac known as the Palace of Desire or Qasr al-Shawq came into sight. His heart pounded so strongly it almost deafened his ears. At the corner on the right could be seen baskets of oranges and apples arranged on the ground in front of the fruit store. He bit his lip and lowered his eyes in shame. The past was stained with dishonor and buried in the muck of disgrace, constantly emitting a lament of shame and pain. Even so, the past as a whole was not nearly so heavy a burden as this one store, which was a living symbol, enduring through time. Its owner, baskets, fruit, location, and memories seemed a combination of shameless boasting and painful defeat.

Since the past was composed of events and memories, by its very nature it was apt to fade away and be forgotten. This store provided physical evidence to restore what had faded and fill in what he had forgotten. With each step he took toward the cul-de-sac he moved several steps away from the present, traveling back through time, in spite of himself.

He could almost see a boy in the store looking up at the proprietor and saying, "Mama invites you to come tonight." He saw him returning home with a bag of fruit, grinning happily. There he was, pointing the man out to his mother as they walked along the street. She was pulling him away by the arm, so he would not attract attention. He was sobbing with tears at the man's savage assault on his mother, which he re-created afresh with his current level of sophistication each time he thought about it, thus turning it into an ultimate manifestation of horror. These searing visions began to pursue him. He strove to flee from them, but no sooner would he escape from the clutches of one than he would be grabbed violently by another, stirring deep inside him a volcano of hatred and anger.

He kept on walking toward his destination but in a miserable state. "How can I enter this dead-end street when that store's at the corner? . . . And the man . . . will he be in his usual spot? I won't look that way. What devilish force is tempting me to look? Will he recognize me if our eyes meet? If he seems to recognize me, I'll kill him. But how could he know me? Not him, not anyone in this neighborhood . . . eleven years. I left here a boy and return a bull . . . with two horns! Don't we have the power to exterminate the poisonous vermin that keep on stinging us?"

He headed into the cul-de-sac, hurrying a little. He imagined people would be looking inquisitively at him and asking, "Where and when have we seen that face?" He went along the alley, which rose unevenly uphill, forcing himself to shake the suffocating dust from his face and head, if only temporarily. To make it easier to carry through with his resolve, he distanced himself from his surroundings, which he began to study. He told himself, "Don't be impatient with this tiresome street. When you were young you really enjoyed sliding down it on a board." All the same, when he could see the wall of the house, he started wondering again, "Where am I going? To my mother! . . . How amazing! I don't believe it. What will I say to her? How will she receive me? . . . I wish. . . ."

He turned right, into a subsidiary cul-de-sac, and approached the first door on the left. Without the slightest doubt it was the old house.

He crossed the street to it the way he did when he was young, without any hesitation or reflection, as though he had only left it the day before, but this time he stormed through the door with unaccustomed anguish. He climbed the stairs with slow, heavy steps. Despite his anxiety, he caught himself examining things carefully to compare them with what he remembered. He found the stairway a little narrower. It was worn in some places and small chips had fallen from the edges of the treads where they protruded over the risers. His memories quickly obscured the present entirely. In this state he passed the two floors that were rented out and reached the top one. He stopped for a few moments to regain his strength, his chest heaving. Then he shook his shoulders disdainfully and knocked on the door. After a minute or so, it was opened, revealing a middle-aged servant. The moment she saw that he was a stranger, she hid behind the door and asked him politely what he wanted.

Although it was unreasonable to expect the servant to recognize him, he became agitated and resolutely made his way inside, heading for the parlor. He said in a commanding voice, "Tell your mistress Yasin's here."

"What do you suppose the servant thinks of me?" He turned around and saw her hastening away inside, either because his imperious tone had cowed her or . . . He bit his lip and walked into the room. In his haste and fury he assumed unconsciously that it was the parlor, although in different circumstances his memory would have known every corner of the house without a guide. Then, dredging up memories, he would have made a tour from the bath, to which he was carried in tears, on to the enclosed balcony, where evening after evening he had watched wedding processions, through the spaces between the wooden spindles. Was the current furniture in the room the same as in the distant past?

All he remembered of the old furnishings was a long mirror set on a gilded basin with openings in the cover, from which sprouted artificial roses of various colors. There were candelabra attached to the edges of the mirror. Dangling from their necks were crystal crescents, which he had frequently enjoyed playing with while he looked through them at the room, which would shimmer in strange disguises. He could remember their fascination even when he could not see them. There was no reason to wonder, for today's furnishings were different and not merely because they were newer. The decor of a frequently married woman was subject to change and renovation, in the same way that his mother had traded in his father, the coal dealer, and the master sergeant. Yasin felt tense and anxious. He perceived that he had not only knocked on the door of his former home but had scraped the scab off an inflamed sore and plunged into its pus.

He did not have long to wait, perhaps even less time than he imagined. He soon heard quick footsteps approaching and a person talking to herself. The voice was loud, but Yasin could not make out the words. Then he sensed she was there, although his back was turned to the doorway. Her shoulder jarred against the second door, which was still closed. He heard her call out breathlessly, "Yasin! My son! . . . How can I believe my eyes? . . . My Lord. . . . You've become a man. . . ."

Blood rushed to his beefy face. He turned toward her anxiously, not knowing how to address her or how their meeting would turn out, but the woman spared him from having to form any plan. She rushed to him and put her arms around him. She embraced him nervously and intensely. She began kissing his chest, the highest part of his tall body her lips could reach. Then she was sobbing and her eyes were bathed in tears. She buried her face against his breast, forgetting herself for a while until she could catch her breath. All that time he had not moved or spoken a word. He felt deeply and painfully the unbearable awkwardness of his rigidity, yet no indication of life, of any life at all, was revealed by him. He remained motionless and dumb. He was profoundly touched, although at first it was not clear to him what kind of emotion it was. Despite the warmth of his reception he experienced no desire to throw himself into her arms or kiss her. He was unable to pluck out the sad memories lodged inside him like a chronic disease afflicting him since childhood.

Although he was resolved and determined to clear the past from the stage of the present and retain control of his mind and his wits, the discarded past threw dark shadows on the surface of his heart, like a fly brushed away from the mouth which has left behind infectious germs. He perceived at that terrifying moment, more than he had throughout his past life, the sad truth that had clouded his heart for a long time: he no longer felt anything for his mother. The woman raised her head, as though beseeching him to bring his face close to hers. He was not able to refuse and leaned over. She kissed him on the cheeks and forehead. As they embraced, their eyes met, and he kissed her forehead, moved by his frustration at being so ill at ease and embarrassed, not by any other sentiment.

Then he heard her murmur, "She told me Yasin was here. I said,

'Yasin! Who could that be? But who else could he be? I only have one Yasin, the person who deprived himself of my house and deprived me of him. So what has happened? How come he's accepted my invitation after such a long time?' I ran here like a madwoman, not believing my ears. Here you are. You, not someone else, praise to God. You left me a boy and have returned a man. I have been dying to see you and you didn't even know I was alive."

She took him by the arm and led him to the sofa. He accompanied her, asking himself when this tumultuous wave of affectionate welcome would roll by so he could see the way clear to achieve his objective. He began to look at her stealthily, with a curiosity mixed with astonishment and anxiety. She seemed not to have changed except that her body had filled out. She still retained her beautiful figure. Her fair, round face and black eyes accentuated with kohl were just as beautiful as ever. He was not comfortable with the makeup he observed on her face and neck. He seemed to have been expecting that the years would have changed her dedication to taking care of herself and her passion for personal adornment even when she was all alone.

They sat side by side while she gazed affectionately at his face for a time and then measured his height and girth with admiring eyes. In a trembling voice she said, "Oh, my Lord. I can hardly believe my eyes. I'm in a dream. This is Yasin! A whole lifetime has gone up in smoke. How often I invited you and begged you. I sent you messenger after messenger. What can I say? . . . Let me ask you why you were so hardhearted to me. How could you turn away from my loving pleas? How could you turn a deaf ear to the cry of my grieving heart? How? . . . How? How could you forget you had a mother secluded here?"

Her final sentence caught his attention. He found it so strange that it invited both his sarcasm and his lamentation. It might well have slipped out because of her bewildered emotional state. Yes, there had been something, things, to remind him morning and evening that he had a mother, but what kind of thing or things?

He looked up anxiously without speaking, and their eyes met for a moment. The woman jumped in, longingly, to ask: "Why don't you speak?"

Yasin overcame his uncertainty with an audible sigh. Then he replied, as though finding no alternative, "I thought about you a lot, but my pain was unbearable."

Before he could complete what he was going to say, the light sparkling in her eyes faded, and a cloud of disappointment and listlessness, driven by a wind from the depths of the sad past, settled over her pupils. She could not stand to look him in the eye any longer. She glanced down and said in a mournful voice, "I thought you were over the sorrows of the past. God knows they weren't worth the anger you displayed, keeping you away from me for eleven years."

He was amazed and infuriated by her criticism. He found it so reprehensible that it felt like salt poured on his angry wound. He was upset and would have exploded had it not been for the goal of his visit. Did the woman really mean what she said? Did her deeds really seem so insignificant to her? Or did she think he did not know what had happened? Although he controlled his nerves by exerting his will, he replied, "Are you saying my anger was unmerited? What took place merited the utmost anger and even more."

She let her back collapse against the sofa cushion. She cast him a look combining censure with an appeal for affection. She asked, "What's wrong with a woman remarrying after she gets divorced?"

He felt the fires of anger flaming through his veins, but the only apparent effect was the closing and tightening of his lips. She still made it seem so simple when she talked, as though she was convinced of the certainty of her innocence. She asked what was wrong with a woman getting married after she had been divorced. Fine, there was nothing wrong with some woman remarrying after her divorce, but if that woman was his mother, then it was a different story, a very different story. And to which marriage was she referring? There had been a marriage and a divorce, a marriage and a divorce, and then a marriage and a divorce. And there was something even more bitter and calamitous: that fruitmonger. . . . Did she remember him? Should he slap her in the face with those memories? Should he tell her frankly that he was no longer as ignorant as she thought? The intensity of his memories forced him to abandon his moderation this time. With great resentment he said, "Marriage and divorce, marriage and divorce, these are disgraceful affairs that should not have seemed right to you. How often they have shredded my heart, mercilessly."

She folded her arms across her chest in despondent surrender and remarked with mournful tenderness, "It's bad luck and nothing else. I've been unlucky, that's all there is to it."

He cut her off short, contracting his facial muscles and making his neck swell out, saying, as though the words he uttered were repulsive and revolted him, "Don't try to justify your actions. That only hurts me more. It's best if we pull down the curtain on our pains and hide them, since we're unable to wipe them out of existence."

She reluctantly took refuge in silence. Her heart was apprehensive that stormy memories would spoil the happy reunion and the hopes it had inspired in her. She began to observe him anxiously, as though trying to guess what he was concealing in his chest. When she could not stand his silence any longer she said plaintively, "Don't keep on tormenting me. You're my only child."

These words had a strange effect on him as though revealing to him for the first time that he truly was her son and that she was the only mother he had. All the same, it served him as a new incentive for outrage and anxiety. How many men! He turned his face away to conceal from her the traces of revulsion and anger sketched on its surface. He closed his eyes to flee from memories of vile sights.

At that moment he heard her say gently and imploringly, "Let me believe that my present happiness is a reality and not an illusion and that you came to me having rid your heart forever of all the sorrows of the past."

He gave her a long, hard look that revealed the serious nature of his thoughts, but there was nothing then that could have deterred him from trying to achieve his objective or even postponed it for a while. In a voice indicating that the words he spoke were far less important than what they implied, he remarked, "This depends on you. If you wish, you will have everything you want."

An anxious look could be seen in the woman's eyes, revealing the reawakened fear she was suffering. She replied, "I desire your love from the depths of my heart. How often have I yearned and striven for it, only to have you reject me mercilessly."

He was distracted from her affectionate words by the thought disturbing his mind. He continued: "What you crave is within your grasp. It is in your hands alone, if you take wisdom for your guide."

The woman asked with alarm, "What do you mean?"

Her feigned ignorance infuriated him and he said, "The import of my words is plain. You should refrain from doing something which, if the information reaching me is correct, would be a fatal blow for me."

She opened her eyes wide and then frowned with unconcealed despair. She muttered unwittingly, "What do you mean?"

Assuming that she was playing dumb on purpose he responded with rage, "I mean that you should annul the plan to remarry. Don't even consider doing something like this again. I'm not a child anymore. My patience won't stand for any further insults."

She bowed her head with unmistakable sorrow. She kept it down for some time, as though asleep. Then she raised her head slowly. The grief visible in her expression was too profound to measure. In a feeble voice, as though addressing herself, she said, "So you came because of that!"

Without considering what he was saying, he replied, "Yes!"

His answer could just as well have been a burst of gunfire, for everything around him changed and was transformed suddenly. The atmosphere became gloomy. Later, when he was alone, he went back over that conversation. He was comfortable with everything he had said until this final answer. He pondered over it, not knowing whether he had made a mistake or said the right thing.

His mother murmured as she looked around her, "How I wish my ears were deceiving me."

He realized only too late that he had gone too fast. He was angry with himself, furious, and poured his wrath on everything but himself. In an attempt to conceal his error at the expense of an even greater one, without stopping to think, he burst out: "You do just what you want without thinking about the consequences. I've always been the victim who has been hurt for no fault of his own. I would have thought that life would have taught you some lessons. So imagine my surprise when someone tells me you're planning to get married again. What a scandal, and it keeps recurring every few years, without any end in sight."

Her despair was so intense that she listened to him with apparent disinterest. Then she said sorrowfully, "You're a victim and I'm a victim. Each of us becomes a victim when your father and that woman who has taken you under her wing start whispering to you."

He was amazed by this shift in the course of the conversation. It appeared ludicrous to him, but he did not laugh. If anything, he was even angrier and said, "What bearing do my father and his wife have on this matter? Don't try to evade responsibility for your actions by throwing accusations in the faces of innocent people."

She protested in a voice like a groan, "I've never seen a son crueler than you. . . . Is this what you have to tell me after a separation of eleven years?"

He waved his hand in angry rejection and said sharply and furiously, "A sinful mother is likely to give birth to a cruel son."

"I'm no sinner. . . . I'm not a sinner. But you are as cruel and hard-hearted as your father."

He snorted with vexation and shouted, "We're back to my father! We have enough to discuss without him. Fear God and retreat from this new scandal . . . I wish to prevent this scandal at any price."

Her despair and sorrow were so intense that her voice sounded cold when she said, "How does it concern you?"

Astonished, he yelled back, "My mother's scandal shouldn't concern me?"

She replied with a sorrow blended with a slight amount of sarcasm, "You have the right to stop thinking of me as your mother."

"What do you mean?"

Ignoring his question, she muttered, "Since you have no feelings for me anymore, the best thing is for you to leave me and my concerns alone."

He shouted angrily, "What's already happened is all I can bear. I will not permit you to soil my reputation again."

Swallowing bitterly, she replied, "With God as my witness, there's nothing about it that will soil anyone's reputation."

He asked her disapprovingly, "Are you determined to go through with this marriage?"

She was silent for a time. Her head was bowed sadly and she was sunk in despair. A deep sigh escaped her. Then she said in a scarcely audible voice, "The matter's settled. The marriage contract has been drawn up. I'm no longer in a position to stop it."

Yasin jumped to his feet. His corpulent body was rigid and his face pale. Boiling with anger, he stared at her bowed head. Then he roared at her. "What a woman you are. . . . You criminal!"

She mumbled in choked voice revealing her total surrender, "May God forgive you."

At that moment it occurred to him to blast her with what he knew about her past conduct, things she assumed he did not know, like the sinister story of the fruit seller. It would be a bomb he could drop on her head suddenly and blow her to bits, exacting the most hideous revenge. There was a terrifying flash from his eyes, flying out from beneath a frowning, gloomy brow with furrows that seemed threatening suggestions of forthcoming evil. He opened his mouth to drop his bombshell, but his tongue would not move. It stuck to the roof of his mouth as though forced there by his brain, which had not been blinded by his suffering to the calamity that would result. The dreadful instant passed with the speed of a fleeting earthquake during which a person feels death breathing on his face repeatedly for a few moments before everything returns to normal. He groaned but suppressed his anger. He backed down, without regrets. His forehead was dripping with cold sweat. Later, when he remembered various moments of this strange meeting, he recalled how he had acted then and felt relieved that he had held back, even though he was totally amazed by his restraint. What most surprised him was his feeling that he held back out of compassion for himself, not for her. Although he already knew what he would have revealed, he seemed to have been shielding his own honor rather than hers.

He blew off steam by striking his hands together and saying, "Criminal! . . . Scandal incarnate! . . . How I'll laugh at my foolishness every time I remember that I hoped something good might come from this visit. . . ." Then he continued sarcastically: "I'm amazed you can desire my affection after this."

She was distraught and sad. He heard her say, "My soul made me hope we could live together with love, in spite of everything. Your surprise visit inspired warm hopes in my heart that made me imagine I could give you the most exalted form of love my heart possesses . . . unblemished."

He backed away from her, as though fleeing from the tenderness of her words. Nothing could have excited his anger more than that. Filled with anger and despair, he sensed there was no longer anything to be gained from staying on in this hateful atmosphere. Turning around to make his way out, he said, "I wish I could kill you."

She lowered her eyes and said with unconcealed sorrow, "If you do, you'll relieve me of the sufferings of my life."

His anguish reached its peak. He threw her a final look filled with loathing. As he left the place, the floor of the room shook with his footsteps. When he reached the street and began to come to his senses, he remembered for the first time that he had forgotten to discuss the real estate and property. He had not mentioned so much as a word about it. How had he forgotten when it was the main reason for his visit?

19

Mrs. Amina opened the door and stuck her head in, saying with her customary tenderness, "Is there anything I can do for you, sir?"

She heard Fahmy's voice reply, "Come here, Mother. It will only take five minutes."

The woman entered, happy to comply with his request. She found him standing in front of his desk with a serious and concerned expression on his face. He took her hand and led her to a sofa near the door. He seated her and then sat down beside her, asking, "Is everyone asleep?"

The woman realized that she had not been invited to perform some trivial favor; otherwise what need was there for such care or this interest in privacy? His concern was quickly transmitted to her sensitive soul. She answered, "Khadija and Aisha went to their room at their usual time and I just left Kamal in his bed now."

Fahmy had been waiting for this moment since he retired to the study early in the evening. He had not been able to concentrate his attention on the book before him as usual. Off and on he had been following the conversation between his mother and his sisters, worried that they would never stop talking. Then he had listened to his mother and Kamal memorize a section of the seventy-eighth sura of the Qur'an, beginning: "Concerning what are they disputing?" Finally the house had become quiet and his mother had come to say good night. He had invited her to come in, and the tension of waiting had ended for him.

Although his mother was gentle as a dove and he felt no reserve or fear with her, he found it difficult to express what he wanted to say. He was overcome by a shy embarrassment. A long period of silence passed before, twitching his eyelids, he said, "Mother, I've invited you to advise me on a topic of great concern to me."

The woman's anxiety became so intense that her tender heart almost transformed it into fear. She replied, "I'm listening, son."

He breathed deeply to relieve his nerves and said, "What would you think if . . . I mean, isn't possible that . . ." He came to a hesitant stop. Then he changed his tone and said delicately but anxiously, "I have no one to confide my innermost feelings to except for you. . . ."

"Of course, my son, that's only natural."

Taking courage from this, he said, "What would you think about trying to arrange an engagement between me and Maryam, the daughter of our neighbor al-Sayyid Muhammad Ridwan?"

At first Amina was astonished by his suggestion. Her initial response was a smile revealing more anxiety than joy. Then the fear that had gripped her while she was waiting for him to declare what he had in mind dispersed. Her smile broadened and shone, announcing her unqualified delight. She hesitated for some moments, not knowing what to say, then she burst out: "Is this really what you want? . . . I'll give you my frank opinion. . . . The day I go to arrange an engagement for you with a decent girl will be the happiest day of my life."

The youth blushed and said gratefully, "Thank you, Mother."

His mother gazed at him with a tender smile and remarked wistfully, "What a happy day! I've had to work hard and be patient many times. It's not too much to ask that God reward me for my exertion and patience with a day like this I've been hoping for; indeed with many more like it when I rejoice for you and your sisters Khadija and Aisha."

Her mind wandered off in happy dreams until something occurred to her that suddenly roused her. She drew her head back anxiously like a cat that sees a dog approaching. She muttered sympathetically, "But . . . your father?"

Fahmy smiled angrily and replied, "That's why I'm asking for your advice. . . ."

The woman thought a little. Then she said, as though to herself, "I don't know how he'll react to this request. Your father's a strange man, different from anyone else. What others take for granted, he considers a crime."

Fahmy frowned and said, "There's nothing in the affair to warrant anger or opposition."

"That's what I think."

"It goes without saying that the marriage won't take place until I have completed my studies and found myself a job."

"Of course, of course."

"So what could anyone object to, then?"

She gave him a look that seemed to say, "Who's going to remonstrate with your father if he doesn't care to listen to reason?" After all, her known stance toward him was blind obedience, whether he was right or wrong, just or tyrannical. What she said, however, was: "I hope your request will be blessed by acceptance."

The young man responded enthusastically, "My father married when he was my age, and I don't even intend to do that. I'm planning to wait till my marriage seems so normal there will be no objection to it from any quarter. . . ."

"May our Lord grant our request."

They were still for a time, looking at each other, united by a single thought, knowing instinctively that they understood each other perfectly. It was not hard for them to read each other's thoughts. Then Fahmy expressed what was preoccupying both of them: "Now we need to think about who ought to raise the topic with him. . . ."

The woman smiled, but anxiety had robbed her smile of its spirit. She realized that her resourceful son was reminding her of a duty only she could perform. She did not object to doing it, since there was no alternative, but she accepted the task reluctantly, as she did many others. She asked God that it would end well. She remarked tenderly and affectionately, "Who should bring it up but me? . . . May our Lord be with us."

"I'm sorry. . . . If I could, I'd do it myself."

"I'll talk to him, and it will be successful, God willing. Maryam's a pretty girl, polite and from a fine family."

She was silent for a moment. Then, as though it had only just occurred to her, she asked, to clarify something, "But isn't she your age or even older?"

The youth replied uneasily, "That doesn't matter to me at all!"

Smiling, she replied, "With God's blessing; may our Lord be with us." Then, as she stood up, she added, "I leave you now in the Master's care. Until tomorrow." She leaned toward him and kissed him, then she left the room, closing the door behind her. She was astonished to find Kamal sitting on a sofa, bent over a notebook. She shouted at him, "What are you doing here?"

Smiling in embarrassment, he rose and replied, "I remembered that I'd left my English notebook. So I came to get it. Then I thought I'd review the words one more time."

Once again she went with him to the bedroom. She did not leave him until he was stretched out under the cover, but he did not fall asleep. The lively thoughts racing through his mind defeated sleep. As soon as he heard his mother's footsteps going upstairs to the top floor, he leapt out of bed. Then he opened the door and ran to his sisters' room. He shoved the door open and went in without shutting it, so the lamp in the hall could illumine some of the darkness blanketing the room. He rushed to the bed and whispered, "Khadija!"

Astonished, the young woman sat up in bed. He jumped up beside her, so excited he was breathless. As though not satisfied with entrusting the secret that had kept him from falling asleep to only one listener, he put his hand on Aisha and shook her. The girl had already noticed his arrival. She threw back the cover and raised her head, half out of curiosity and half in protest. She asked, "What brings you now?"

He paid no attention to her tone of protest, because he was certain that a single word hinting at his secret would be enough to turn them head over heels. His heart jumped with delight and joy at this thought. Then he whispered, as though he was afraid someone else would hear him, "I've got an amazing secret."

Khadija asked him, "What secret? . . . Tell us what you've got and show us how clever you are."

He could not conceal it any longer. He replied, "My brother Fahmy wants to get engaged to Maryam."

At that, Aisha sat up in bed too, with a quick, mechanical motion, as though the revelation was cold water splashed on her face and teeth. The three shadows moved close together in a mound resembling a pyramid in the faint light penetrating the room, which was reflected on the floor near the open door as a trapezoidal panel. Its edges fluctuated with the oscillations of the lamp's wick, which had been exposed to a draft when the door was left open. The breeze reached the hall in gentle whispers, flowing surreptitiously from the small openings of the girls' window.

Khadija asked with great interest, "How do you know that?"

"I got out of bed to fetch my English notebook. When I reached the door of the study I heard my brother's voice. So I stayed there on the sofa." Then he repeated what he had overheard. They listened to him, spellbound, until he finished. At that point Aisha asked, as though she needed further convincing, "Do you believe this, Khadija?"

In a voice that sounded as though she was speaking by telephone from a distant city, her sister replied, "Do you imagine he's invented a long, complicated story like this?"

"You're right." Aisha laughed to relieve her tension and continued: "There's a big difference between the death of the boy in the street and this story."

Paying no attention to Kamal's objection to the insinuation directed at him, Khadija asked, "How do you suppose this came about?"

Aisha laughed and observed, "Didn't I tell you once I doubted it was the hyacinth beans that enticed Fahmy to the roof every day?"

"It's another kind of fragrant vine that's wound itself around his leg."

Aisha sang softly: "You're not to be blamed, my eyes, for loving him."

Khadija chided her: "Hush . . . this isn't the time for singing. . . . Maryam's in her twenties and Fahmy's eighteen. How can Mother agree to that?"

"Mother? . . . Mother's a gentle dove and wouldn't know how to say no. But wait a minute; it's only fair to say that Maryam's beautiful and a fine girl. . . . Moreover, our house is the only one in the neighborhood that hasn't had a wedding yet. . . ."

Both Khadija and Aisha loved Maryam, but love had never been able to hide a loved one's defects from Khadija's eyes, regardless of the circumstances, and when provoked she would not limit herself to criticizing defects. Since the marriage saga stirred her latent fears and jealousy, she turned on her friend without any qualms. Her heart refused to accept her as a wife for her brother. She proceeded to say, "Are you crazy? . . . Maryam's pretty, but she's not nearly good enough for Fahmy. You donkey, Fahmy's getting an advanced degree. He'll be a judge someday. Can you imagine Maryam as the wife of a high-ranking judge? She's like us in most respects. Indeed, in more than one respect she's not as good as we are, and neither of us is ever going to marry a judge. "

Aisha asked herself, "Who says a judge is better than an officer?" Then she said to her sister argumentatively, "Why not?"

Without paying attention to her sister's protest, Khadija continued: "Fahmy will be able to marry a girl a hundred times more beautiful than Maryam and at the same time one who's educated, rich, and the daughter of a bey or even a pasha. So why should he be in a hurry to get engaged to Maryam? She's nothing but an illiterate with a sharp tongue. You don't know her as well as I do."

Aisha perceived that in Khadija's eyes Maryam had been transformed into a bundle of faults and defects. All the same, she could not keep from smiling secretly in the dark at the description of Maryam as sharp-tongued, since the epithet was much more suitable for Khadija. She abandoned her protest and said submissively, "Let's leave the matter to God. . . ."

Khadija replied with conviction, "The matter is in God's hands in heaven and in Daddy's here on earth. We'll find out what he thinks about it tomorrow." Then she told Kamal, "It's time for you to go quietly to your bed."

Kamal returned to his room, telling himself, "That only leaves Yasin, and I'll tell him tomorrow."

20

Khadija and Aisha were sitting beside the closed door of their parents' room on the top floor. They were facing each other with their legs crossed beneath them, warily trying not to breathe too loud as they strained with great interest to hear what was being said inside. It was shortly before the afternoon prayer, and their father had risen from his siesta and performed his ablutions. As usual, he was sitting drinking his coffee while he waited for the call to prayer. He would pray and then return to the store. The sisters expected their mother to broach the subject Kamal had told them about, since there would be no more suitable time for this purpose. Their father's loud voice carried to them from inside, discussing ordinary household matters. They listened apprehensively and attentively, exchanging questioning glances, until finally they heard their mother say in an exceptionally polite and submissive way, "Sir, if you will allow me, I'll tell you something Fahmy requested me to bring to your attention."

At that, Aisha gestured with her chin toward the room as though saying, "Here it comes." Meanwhile Khadija was imagining her mother's condition as she prepared to utter the dangerous words. Her heart went out to her and she bit her lip in her intense sympathy.

Then they heard their father's voice asking, "What does he want?"

Silence reigned for a short time, although it seemed long to the eavesdroppers. Then the woman said gently, "Fahmy, sir, is a fine young man. He has gained favor with you through his seriousness, success in school, and good manners, may God protect him from the evil eye. Perhaps he has entrusted his request to me hoping that his status with his father will be an argument on his behalf."

Their father responded in a tone the girls thought showed his pleasure with their mother's proposal so far: "What does he want? . . . Speak."

They leaned their heads against the door. Each of them was staring at the other, but hardly seeing her. They made out the feeble voice saying, "Sir, you know our excellent neighbor Muhammad Ridwan?"

"Naturally."

"He is a fine man like you, sir. It's a good family and they're exceptional neighbors."

"Yes."

She continued after some hesitation: "Fahmy asks, sir, whether his father will allow him . . . to become engaged to Maryam, the daughter of our excellent neighbor, so that she will be under his supervision until he is ready to get married."

The father's voice grew louder and his tone was harsh with anger and disapproval: "Get engaged? . . . What are you saying, woman? . . . He's only a boy! . . . God's will be done. . . . Repeat what you just said."

Khadija imagined that their mother had recoiled in alarm. The trembling voice said, "All he did was ask. It was just a question, sir, with the decision left entirely to you. . . ."

He replied in an explosion of anger: "What is this spineless pampering? I'm not accustomed to it and he shouldn't be either. I don't know what could corrupt a schoolboy to the extent that he would make such an outrageous request. . . . But a mother like you could well ruin her children. If you were the kind of mother you ought to be, he would never have dared discuss such insolent nonsense with you."

The two girls were seized by fear and anxiety, but for Khadija these were mixed with relief. Then they heard their mother say in a trembling, subservient voice, "Don't burden yourself, sir, with the trouble of getting angry. Nothing matters except your anger. I certainly did not intend any offense, nor did my son when he innocently conveyed his request to me. He came to me with the best of intentions; so I thought I would present the matter to you. Since this is what you think, I'll tell him. He will submit to it totally, just as he obeys all your commands."

"He'll obey me whether he wishes to or not. But I want to tell you that you're a weak mother and nothing good can be hoped from you."

"I'm careful to see they do as you command."

"Tell me: What led him to think of making this request?"

The girls listened intently and anxiously. They were surprised by this unexpected question. They did not hear any answer from their mother but imagined she was blinking her eyes in confusion and fear. They felt great sympathy for her.

"What's struck you dumb? . . . Tell me: Has he seen her?"

"Of course not, sir. My son doesn't lift his eyes to look at a neighbor girl or anyone else."

"How can he want to get engaged to her if he hasn't seen her? I didn't know I had sons who were sneaking looks at the respectable women of our neighbors."

"God shelter us, sir. God shelter us.... When my son walks in the street he turns neither to the right nor to the left. When he's at home he scarcely leaves his room unless he has to."

"So what made him ask for her, then?"

"Perhaps, sir, he heard his sisters talking about her..."

A tremor passed through the bodies of the two girls. Their mouths were gaping open in alarm as they listened.

"Since when are his sisters matchmakers? Glory to God, am I going to have to leave my store and job to squat at home in order to patrol it and rid it of corruption?"

The mother cried out in a sobbing voice, "Your house is the most respectable one of all. By God, sir, if you hadn't got angry so quickly, the matter would be over and done with."

The man yelled in a threatening voice, "Tell him to mind his manners, have some shame, and know his place. The best thing for him would be to concentrate on his studies."

The girls heard some movement inside the room. They rose cautiously and tiptoed away.

Mrs. Amina thought it best to leave the room, according to the policy she followed whenever she accidentally let something slip out that stirred his anger. She would not return unless he summoned her. She had learned from experience that for her to remain when he was angry and try to calm him down with gentle words only made him more furious.

Al-Sayyid Ahmad found himself alone. The observable effects of his anger, like the rage apparent in his eyes, complexion, words, and the gestures of his hands, subsided, but the anger deep within his chest lingered on like dregs at the bottom of a pot.

It was an established fact that he got angry at home for the most trivial reasons and not merely because of his plan for the management of his home. He was also affected by his sharp temper, which was not held in check at home by the brakes of civility that he employed to perfection outside his household. His domestic rage presumably granted him some relief from the effort he exerted with other people, when he suffered in the interest of self-control, tolerance, graciousness, and concern for other people's feelings and affection. Not infrequently he realized he had gotten angry for no reason at all, but even then he did not regret it. He believed that getting angry over a trivial matter would prevent serious offenses, which would truly merit his anger.

All the same, he did not consider what he had heard concerning Fahmy that afternoon to be a minor error. He discerned in it an unseemly turbulence that should not be agitating the soul of a schoolboy from his family. He could not imagine that the world of the emotions had infiltrated the atmosphere of his home, which he vigilantly strove to keep one of stern purity and immaculate innocence. Then it was time for the afternoon prayer, a good opportunity for spiritual exercise. He emerged from his prayers with a calmer heart and a more relaxed mind. He sat on the prayer rug, spread out his hands, and asked God to bless him with both offspring and money. He prayed especially that he have reason for pride in his children's good sense, integrity, and success.

By the time he left the house his frown was merely a device intended to frighten his family. At the store he told some of his friends about the event as though it was a silly prank, not a calamity, because he did not like to bore people with calamities. They made some humorous comments about it of the kind they enjoyed, and before long he was joining in their jokes. When they left, he was roaring with laughter. At his store, the event did not seem as serious to him as it had in his room at home. He was able to laugh about it and even sympathize with the request. He ended up telling himself happily, with a smile, "There's nothing wrong with a kid who takes after his old man."

21

When Kamal darted out of the door of his house, evening was beginning to darken the streets, alleys, minarets, and domes. His happiness at this unexpected excursion at a time he was rarely allowed out was matched only by his pride in the message Fahmy had entrusted to him. It was not lost on him that Fahmy had chosen him instead of anyone else. That the atmosphere had been one of circumspect secrecy lent the message and therefore Kamal a special importance. His young heart felt it and danced with excitement and pride. He wondered with amazement what had shaken Fahmy enough to plunge him into a sad and anxious state, making him seem a different person, one Kamal had never seen or heard before.

Fahmy was known for his self-control. Their father would explode like a volcano for the most trifling reason. Yasin spoke sweetly but was prone to sudden outbursts. Even Khadija and Aisha had their moments of irrational behavior. Only Fahmy was exemplary in his self-control. His laughter was a smile and his anger a frown. Yet his profoundly calm character did not diminish the sincerity of his emotions or the steadfastness of his zeal.

Kamal could not remember seeing his brother in such a state. He would never forget Fahmy's condition when they talked privately in the study: eyes wandering, soul troubled, and voice trembling. For the first time in his life Fahmy had spoken to him in a tone of warm entreaty, totally shocking Kamal, who had memorized the message and repeated it over and over again to Fahmy.

From the tenor of the message itself he realized that the affair was closely linked to the strange conversation he had overheard and conveyed to his sisters, stirring up an argument between them. It all related to Maryam, that girl with whom he frequently exchanged taunts. There were times when he liked her and others when she annoyed him, but he did not understand why there should be an important connection between her and his brother's peace of mind and welfare. Maryam! Why was she, rather than any other person, able to do all this to his dear and wonderful brother? He felt there was a mystery to the situation like that surrounding the existence of spirits and ghosts, which had often aroused both curiosity and fear in him. Thus his heart resolved eagerly but anxiously to get to the bottom of this secret.

His anxiety did not prevent him from repeating the message to himself the way he had gone over it with his brother, so he could be sure not to forget a single syllable of it. He was reciting it when he passed the home of the Ridwan family. Then at its corner he turned into the alley where the door was located.

He knew the house well, for he had often slipped into its small courtyard, where a handcart, missing its wheels, was pushed into a corner. He would climb in, relying on his imagination to supply the wheels and make it go wherever he wished. He had often wandered through the rooms uninvited to be greeted and petted by the lady of the house and her daughter. Despite his youth, he thought of them as old friends. He knew the house—its three rooms arranged around a small sitting room that had a sewing machine below a window overlooking Hammam al-Sultan—as well as he knew his own house with its big rooms surrounding the large sitting room where their coffee hour was held evening after evening.

Some aspects of Maryam's house had made a lasting impression on him, like the dove's nest on the roof of the enclosed balcony of her room. Its edge could be seen above the wooden grille at the corner adjoining the wall of the house, looking like a semicircle to which a mat of straw and feathers had been attached. Sometimes the mother dove's tail stuck out, sometimes her beak, depending on how she happened to be sitting. As he looked at it, he would be torn between two desires. One, based on instinct, urged him to destroy it and snatch the babies, and the other, acquired from his mother, would have him sympathetically investigate the life of the dove and her family.

There was also the picture of the Ambassadress Aziza, a flamboyant character from popular literature, which hung in Maryam's room. The colors of the print were brilliant. The heroine's complexion was radiant and her features pretty. She was even more beautiful than the belle whose picture gazed down at him every afternoon at Matoussian's store. He would look for a long time at the picture, wondering about her. Then Maryam would tell him as much of her story as she knew. Even things she did not know would slip easily from her tongue, enchanting and fascinating him.

Thus there was nothing strange about the house for him. He made his way to the sitting room without anyone noticing him. He cast a fleeting glance into the first room and found Mr. Muhammad Ridwan lying in bed as usual. He knew the old man had been sick for years. He had heard him described as "paralyzed" so often that he had asked his mother what the word meant. She had been alarmed and had begun to seek refuge with God from the evil suggested by this term. He had shrunk back in retreat. From that day on, Mr. Muhammad Ridwan had aroused his pity and a curiosity mixed with fear.

He passed by the next room and saw Maryam's mother standing in front of the mirror. There was a doughlike substance in her hand which she was stretching over her cheek and neck. She pulled it off in rapid, successive motions. Then she felt where it had been with her fingers to assure herself that the hair had been pulled out and her skin was smooth. Although she was over forty, she was as extraordinarily beautiful as her daughter. She loved to laugh and joke. Whenever she saw him she would greet him merrily, kiss him, and ask him, as though her patience was exhausted, "When are you going to grow up so I can marry you?" He would be overcome by embarrassment and confusion, but he enjoyed her jesting and would have liked even more.

He was curious about this procedure she carried out in front of the mirror from time to time. He had asked his mother about it once, but she had scolded him, reprimanding him for asking about something that did not concern him. That was the most extreme form of discipline she employed. Maryam's mother had been more indulgent and gracious. Once when she noticed he was watching her with astonishment, she had him stand on a chair in front of her. She stuck on his fingers what he at first thought was dough. She held her face out to him and said laughingly, "Go to work and show me how clever you are."

He had begun to imitate what she had been doing and established his cleverness to her satisfaction and his delight. He had not been content with the pleasure of doing it but had asked her, "Why do you do this?"

She had laughed loudly and suggested, "Why don't you wait ten more years to find out for yourself? But there's no need to wait. Isn't smooth skin better than rough skin? That's all there is to it."

He went by her door softly so she would not know he was there. His message was too important for him to meet anyone except Maryam. She was in the last room, sitting on her bed, her legs crossed beneath her, eating melon seeds. There was a saucer in front of her filled with shells. When she saw him she exclaimed in astonishment,

"Kamal!" She was about to ask him why he had come at such an hour, but she did not, for fear that that would frighten or annoy him. "You honor our house," she continued. "Come sit beside me."

He shook hands with her. Then he unfastened the buttons of his high boots. He removed them and jumped onto the bed. He was wearing a striped shirt that went to his ankles and a blue skullcap decorated with red lines. Maryam laughed tenderly and put some seeds in his hand. She told him, "Crack these open, sparrow, and move your pearl-like teeth. . . . Do you remember the day you bit my wrist when I was tickling you . . . like this. . . ?" She stretched her hand toward his armpit, but he moved in the opposite direction and crossed his arms over his chest to protect himself.

A nervous laugh escaped him, as though her fingers actually were tickling him. He yelled at her, "Have mercy, Miss Maryam."

She let him alone but expressed her amazement at his fear: "Why does your body shrink from being tickled? Look: I don't mind it at all." She began to tickle herself nonchalantly while giving him a scornful look.

He could not refrain from challenging her: "Let me tickle you and then we'll see."

She raised her hands over her head. His fingers attacked under her arms and proceeded to tickle her as gently and quickly as possible. He fixed his eyes on her beautiful black ones so he could catch the first sign of any weakening on her part. Finally he was forced to give up, sighing with despair and embarrassment.

She greeted his defeat with a gently sarcastic laugh and said, "So you see, you weak little man. . . . Don't claim you're a man anymore." Then she continued as though she had suddenly remembered something important: "What a calamity! You forgot to kiss me. . . . Haven't I repeatedly told you that the greeting when we meet is a kiss?" She moved her face toward him. He put out his lips and kissed her cheek. Then he saw that scraps of melon seeds had escaped from the corner of his mouth and stuck to her cheek. He brushed them away with embarrassment. Maryam grasped his chin with her right hand and kissed his lips time and again. Then she asked him with amazement, "How were you able to get away from them at this time of the day? Maybe your mother's looking for you right now in every room of the house."

"Oḥ . . ." He had been having such fun talking and playing that he had almost forgotten the message he had come to deliver. Her question reminded him of his mission. He looked at her with a different eye, an eye that wished to delve deep inside her to learn the secret power that was rocking his fine, sober brother. When he realized that he was the bearer of unhappy news, his inquisitive look disintegrated. He said despondently, "Fahmy sent me."

A new, serious look came into her eyes. She searched his face attentively for a clue to his mission. He felt that the atmosphere had changed, as though he had gone from one class to another. Then he heard her ask in a soft voice, "Why?"

He answered her with a frankness that indicated he did not understand the seriousness of the news he brought, even though he felt it instinctively: "He told me, 'Give her my greetings and tell her that Fahmy asked his father's permission to become engaged to her. He did not consent for the engagement to be announced while Fahmy was still a student. He asked him to wait till he completed his studies.' "

She was staring at his face with intense interest. When he fell silent, she lowered her eyes without uttering a word. Their tête-à-tête degenerated into a despondent silence which his young heart found hard to bear. He longed to scare it away no matter what. Kamal continued: "He assures you that the refusal came in spite of him and that he'll hurry to finish his studies so that what he desires may come to pass."

When he found that his words did not help free her from the clutches of silence, his wish to restore her former happiness and good humor increased. He asked her enticingly, "Should I tell you what Fahmy and Mother said when they talked about you?"

She responded in a neutral tone, halfway between interest and disinterest, "So what did they have to say?"

He felt good about this partial victory and recounted to her what he had overheard from beginning to end. It seemed to him that she sighed. Then she commented crossly, "Your father's a harsh, frightening man. Everyone knows he's that way."

Without thinking he agreed: "Yes . . . Daddy's like that."

Fearfully and cautiously he raised his head to look at her, but he found her lost in thought. Remembering his brother's instructions, he asked, "What shall I tell him?"

She laughed through her nose and shook her shoulders. She started to speak but paused to think for a moment. Then she replied with a naughty gleam in her eyes: "Tell him that she won't know what to do if a suitor asks to marry her during this long period of waiting."

Kamal was more concerned about memorizing the new message than he was about understanding it. He sensed at once that his mission had ended. He put the remainder of the melon seeds in his shirt pocket. Then he shook hands with her, slipped to the floor, and departed.

22

Whenever Aisha looked at herself in the mirror, she was immensely pleased with what she saw. Who else from her illustrious family, indeed from the whole neighborhood, was adorned by golden tresses and blue eyes like hers? Yasin flirted openly with her, and Fahmy, when he spoke to her about one thing or another, did not neglect to give her admiring glances. Even little Kamal did not want to drink from the water jug unless her mouth had moistened the lip. Her mother spoiled her and said she was as beautiful as the moon, although she did not conceal her anxiety that Aisha was too thin and delicate. For this reason she had encouraged Umm Hanafi to concoct a remedy to fatten her up. Aisha herself was perhaps more conscious of her extraordinary beauty than any of the others. Her intense solicitude for every detail of her appearance made this clear.

Khadija did not let her sister's excessive concern for her beauty pass without comment, rebuke, and criticism. It was not that Khadija would have been pleased if Aisha had neglected herself. She took after her mother more than any of the others when it came to cleanliness and neatness. But it annoyed her to observe her sister greet the day by combing her hair and fixing her attire before doing the household chores, as though Aisha could not bear for her beauty to be left untended for even one hour out of her whole life.

It was not simply interest in her own beauty that caused Aisha to want to fix herself up first thing in the morning. When the men went off to work, she wanted to be ready to repair to the parlor and open the shutters of the window overlooking Palace Walk just the least bit. Then she would stand searching the street, while she waited anxiously and fearfully.

She stood there this morning with her eyes wandering from Hammam al-Sultan to the ancient building that housed the public cistern. Her young heart pounded while she waited for "him." Then he appeared in the distance. He turned the corner, coming from al-Khurunfush, and strutted along in his uniform with the two stars gleaming on the shoulder. As he approached the house, he cautiously began to raise his eyes but not his head. When he was close, the faintest of smiles flickered across his face, one more clearly perceived by the heart than the eyes, like the crescent moon the first night. Then he disappeared beneath the balcony.

She whirled around to continue watching him from the other window overlooking al-Nahhasin but was shocked to see Khadija, standing on the sofa between the two windows, looking over her head at the street. A moan escaped Aisha. Her eyes grew big with unmistakable alarm. She stood rooted to the spot. When and how had her sister come? How had she gotten up on the sofa without Aisha being aware of it? What had she seen? . . . When and how and what?

Meanwhile Khadija fixed her eyes on her sister, slowly and silently narrowing them. She extended the silence as though to prolong Aisha's suffering.

Aisha gained partial control of herself. She lowered her eyes with great effort and turned toward the couch, futilely pretending to have steadied her nerves. She stammered, "Lady, you frightened me!"

Khadija did not show any interest. She remained where she was on the sofa. Her gaze was directed at the street through the crack. Then she muttered sarcastically, "Did I frighten you? . . . May the name of God protect you. . . . I must be the bogeyman."

After retreating a little to escape from Khadija's eyes, Aisha gritted her teeth in rage. In a calm voice she said, "I suddenly saw you, over my head, without knowing you'd come in. Why did you sneak up?"

Khadija jumped down. She sat on the sofa, completely and scornfully at ease. "I'm sorry, sister," she said. "Next time I'll hang a bell around my neck like a fire truck so you'll know I'm here and won't be frightened."

Still terrified, Aisha answered, "There's no need to wear a bell. It would be enough if you'd just walk the way God intended us to. . . ."

Casting her a knowing look, Khadija continued in the same sarcastic tone: "Our Lord knows I walk the way He intended. What's clear is that you, when you stand behind the window, I mean behind this crack, are so caught up in what's in front of you that you're no longer conscious of what is happening around you and don't act the way our Lord intended."

Aisha snorted and mumbled, "You'll never change."

Khadija was silent again for a moment. She turned her eyes away from her victim and raised her eyebrows as if thinking about a difficult puzzle. Then she pretended to be pleased, as though she had found the right answer. Speaking to herself this time, without looking at her sister she said, "Then this is the reason she frequently sings: 'You there with the red stripe, you who have taken me prisoner, have pity on my humiliation.' Not being suspicious, darling, I just thought it was an innocent song, merely for your amusement."

Aisha's heart beat wildly. What she feared most had happened. It was no use anymore to cling to the phantoms of false hopes. She was afflicted by a disturbance that rocked the very pillars of her being, and she almost choked on her tears. All the same, her despair forced her to risk everything to defend herself. In a voice that shook so much the words were hard to understand, she yelled, "What's this nonsense you're saying?"

Khadija appeared not to have heard her. She continued to herself: "This is also the reason she fixes herself up so early in the morning. I've often asked myself if it made sense for a girl to get all dolled up before she does the sweeping and dusting. But what sweeping and what dusting? Oh, Khadija, you poor dear, you'll live a fool and die a fool. You're the one who'll do the sweeping and dusting, and you won't have time to worry about your appearance either before or after work. You miserable creature, why should you deck yourself out? You could look through the crack of the window day after day, and if even one officer out on patrol took an interest in you, I'd be so surprised I'd chop my arm off."

Upset and nervous, Aisha shouted at her, "Shame on you. Shame."

"She's right, Khadija. You with your muddled mind aren't able to understand these arts. Blue eyes, hair of spun gold, a red stripe, and a gleaming star, these all fit together nicely in a rational way."

"Khadija, you're mistaken. I was looking at the street. That's all. I wasn't trying to see someone or be seen by him."

Khadija turned toward her as though hearing her protest for the first time. She asked apologetically, "Were you talking to me, sweetheart, Shushu? Excuse me, I'm thinking about some important matters. So don't say anything just now." She shook her head thoughtfully again and said to herself, "Yes, it all makes perfect sense, but is this your fault, Mr. Ahmad Abd al-Jawad? I feel sorry for you, sir, you noble and generous man. Come see your women, sir, you whom I honor most of all."

Aisha's hair stood up on end at the mention of her father. Her head whirled. She remembered what he had said to her mother when he was attacking Fahmy's request to get engaged to Maryam: "Tell me:

Has he seen her? . . . I didn't know I had sons who were sneaking looks at the respectable women of our neighbors." That was what he thought about his son; so what would he think about his daughter? She nearly choked as she cried out, "Khadija . . . this isn't right. . . . You're mistaken. . . . You're wrong."

Khadija kept on talking to herself without paying any attention to her sister: "Do you suppose this is love? Perhaps! Don't they say, 'Love has penetrated my heart. . . . It won't be long till I'm taken to Tokar Prison'? I wonder where this notorious Tokar Prison is? Perhaps it's in al-Nahhasin; indeed perhaps it's in the home of Mr. Ahmad Abd al-Jawad."

"I can't bear what you're saying. Have mercy on me and spare me your tongue. Oh Lord . . . why won't you believe me?"

"Think carefully about what you're going to do, Khadija. It's not a game. You're the older sister. A duty is a duty, no matter how bitter it may seem. The authorities must be informed. Should you confide the secret to your father? The truth is that I wouldn't know how to tell him such an important secret. Yasin? He might as well not exist for all the help he can provide. The most that can be hoped from him is for him to chant some incomprehensible words. Fahmy? But he's also sweet on the golden-haired wonder who is the source of the whole problem. I suspect the best thing is for me to tell Mother. I'll let her do what she thinks is right."

Khadija moved as though she intended to get up. Aisha rushed at her like a chicken without a head. She grabbed her shoulders and shouted, as her chest heaved, "What do you want?"

Khadija asked, "Are you threatening me?"

Aisha started to speak but all at once choked on her tears. She murmured some words that were mangled by her sobs. Khadija stared at her silently and thoughtfully. Then the mischievous sarcasm of her expression changed to a frown as she listened uncomfortably to the girl's sobs. Speaking in a serious tone for the first time, she remarked, "What you did was wrong, Aisha."

Then she stopped. The frown on her face became more pronounced. Her nose seemed to stick out even farther. She was clearly moved. She started speaking again: "You've got to confess you made a mistake. Tell me how you talked yourself into this mischief, you crazy girl."

Drying her eyes, Aisha mumbled, "You misjudge me."

Khadija snorted and scowled as though she could not stand any more of this lamentable obstinacy. All the same, she abandoned the notion of acting hostilely toward Aisha or of mistreating her. She always knew when and where to stop. She would not let things get out of hand. Her sarcasm had satisfied her rough and hostile tendencies. As usual, she was content to draw the line there. Her other inclinations, as far removed as possible from hostility and harshness, still had not been satisfied. They were impulses arising from the affections of an older sister. Indeed her feelings were almost maternal and embraced every member of the family, no matter how fierce her attack against one of them might be, or his against her.

Impelled by these affectionate urges, Khadija said, "Don't be obstinate. I saw it all with my own eyes. I'm not joking now. I want to tell you frankly that you made a big mistake. Our family has not known this kind of mischief in the past and we don't want to experience it again, now or in the future. It's nothing but recklessness that has landed you here. Listen to me and pay attention to my advice. Don't ever do this again. Nothing remains a secret forever, no matter how long it may be concealed. Imagine the situation for all of us if someone on the street or one of our neighbors noticed you. You know very well how people talk. Imagine what would happen if the news reached Daddy. God help us!"

Aisha bowed her head and allowed her silence to serve as a confession. Her face was stained red with shame in a physical manifestation of remorse that conscience releases inside us when injured by one of our offenses.

Khadija sighed and said, "Beware, beware. Understand?" Then a wave of sarcasm swept across her and her tone changed somewhat: "Hasn't he seen you? What's keeping him from asking for your hand like an honorable man? When that happens, we'll gladly say farewell to you, lady, or even good riddance."

Aisha got her breath back. Her smile resembled the first glimmer of consciousness after a long swoon. The sight of this smile seemed to make Khadija disinclined to let her sister escape from her grasp so soon, after she had enjoyed dominating her for a long time. She shouted at her, "Don't think you're off the hook. My tongue won't be still unless you do a good job of entertaining it."

Aisha asked her cheerfully, "What do you mean?"

"Don't neglect it. Otherwise it might yield to a malicious urge. Divert it with some candy so it'll be occupied with that and not you, a box of bonbons from Shangarly, for example."

"You can have all you want and more."

Silence reigned while each of them was busy with her own thoughts. Khadija's heart, as it had been from the beginning of the encounter, was a breeding ground for all sorts of different emotions . . . jealousy, anger, sympathy, and affection.

23

Mrs. Amina was busy getting ready for the traditional family coffee hour when Umm Hanafi rushed up to her. The gleam in her eyes suggested that she was bringing good news. She announced importantly, "Three ladies I've never seen before wish to call on you."

The mother set everything down and straightened up quickly in a way that showed the impact of the news on her. She stared at the servant with a look of intense interest, as though it was likely the visitors were from the royal family or even from heaven. Then, seeking confirmation, she stammered, "Strangers?"

Umm Hanafi replied in a tone that had a happy, triumphant ring to it, "Yes, my lady. They knocked on the door and I opened it. They asked me, 'Isn't this the home of al-Sayyid Ahmad Abd al-Jawad?' I said, 'Yes, indeed.' They said, 'Are the ladies in?' I replied, 'Yes.' They said, 'We would like to have the honor of calling on them.' I asked them, 'Shall I say who the visitors are?' One of them told me with a laugh, 'Leave that to us. All the messenger needs to do is carry the message.' So I flew to you, my lady. I've been saying to myself, 'May our Lord make our dreams come true.' "

Her interest still showing in her eyes, the mother said quickly, "Invite them to the parlor . . . hurry."

For a few seconds Amina did not move. She was sunk in these new thoughts, in a happy dream world that suddenly revealed its riches to her, after she had worked for nothing else all these past years. Then she snapped out of her reverie and called Khadija in a voice that made it clear she would not tolerate any delay. The girl came at once. The moment their eyes met she smiled and, unable to restrain her joy, told her daughter, "Three ladies we've never seen before are in the parlor. . . . Put on your best clothes and get yourself ready."

When Khadija blushed, Amina blushed too, as though she had caught this contagious embarrassment from her daughter. Then she left the sitting room to retire to her room on the top floor to prepare herself as well to receive the visitors. Khadija was looking vacantly at the door through which her mother had vanished. Her heart was pounding so much it almost hurt. She asked herself, "What's behind this visit?" Then she pulled herself together. Her mind immediately resumed functioning. She summoned Kamal from Fahmy's room and told him, "Go to Miss Maryam and give her my greetings. Tell her that Khadija asks her to send some powder, kohl, and rouge."

The boy jumped at the chance to obey this order and rushed out of the house. Khadija hastened to her room and proceeded to remove her housedress. Aisha looked at her with inquiring eyes. Khadija told her, "Pick out the best dress for me . . . absolutely the best one."

Aisha asked her, "Why are you in such a state? . . . Is there a visitor? Who?"

Khadija replied in a faint voice, "Three ladies. . . ." With special emphasis, she added, "Strangers. . . ."

Aisha drew back her head in astonishment. Then her beautiful eyes grew wide with delight. She cried out, "Oh! . . . Should we understand from this that . . . Oh, what news!"

"Don't get your hopes up . . . for who knows what it really means."

Aisha headed for the armoire to select an appropriate dress. She was laughing and saying, "There's something in the air. . . . A wedding smells like pure perfume."

Khadija laughed to hide her uneasiness. She went to the mirror and looked carefully at herself. She covered her nose with her hand and said ironically, "There's nothing wrong with my face now." Removing her hand from her face, she commented, "Now, like this, only God can save me."

While helping her sister put on a white dress embroidered with lavender flowers, Aisha laughingly remarked, "Don't be so hard on yourself. Can't your tongue spare anything? There's more to a bride than her nose. What about your eyes, long hair, and quick wit?"

Khadija wrinkled her nose as she answered, "All people see are the defects."

"That's true for people with your temperament, but not everyone is like you, thank God."

"I'll answer you when I can find the time."

As Aisha smoothed her sister's dress, she patted her waist and said,

"And don't forget your soft, plump body.... What a great body you've got."

Khadija laughed happily and said, "If the bridegroom was blind I wouldn't worry about anything.... I wouldn't mind a blind one, even if he was a religious scholar from al-Azhar Mosque."

"What's wrong with the religious scholars from al-Azhar? Don't some of them have treasures as boundless as the ocean?"

When they were done with the dress, a murmur of displeasure escaped from Aisha. Khadija asked her, "What's the matter?"

She grumbled, "There isn't a bit of powder, kohl, or rouge in our house, as though there weren't any women living here."

"The best thing would be to take this complaint to Father."

"Isn't Mother a lady? Doesn't she have a right to use cosmetics?"

"She's beautiful just the way she is, without any need for them."

"What about you? Are you going to meet the visitors like this?"

Khadija laughed and replied, "I sent Kamal to Maryam to get the powder, kohl, and rouge. Is my face one to leave bare when I meet matchmakers?"

Since there was not enough time to waste even a minute, Khadija removed her scarf and began to take down her two long, thick braids. Aisha started combing the flowing hair. She remarked, "What long, straight hair you have. What do you think? I'll plait it into a single braid. Wouldn't that be the more beautiful?"

"No, two braids.... But tell me: Should I leave on my stockings or have bare legs when I meet them?"

"It's winter and people would normally wear wool stockings, but I'm afraid if you leave them on they'll think there's something wrong with your foot or leg that you're deliberately trying to hide."

"You're right. A court of law is more merciful than the room of women waiting for me now."

"Be brave. Our Lord has promised us..."

At that moment Kamal hurried into the room. He was panting. He gave his sister the containers of cosmetics and told her, "I ran all the way and even up the stairs."

Khadija smiled and said, "Bravo! Bravo! What did Maryam say?"

"She asked me if we had company... and who they were. I told her I didn't know."

Concern was visible in Khadija's eyes when she asked him, "Was she satisfied with that answer?"

"She asked me to swear by al-Husayn to tell her everything I knew. I swore I'd told her everything."

Aisha laughed. Her hands kept on with their work as she observed, "She'll guess what's happening."

Khadija was spreading powder on her face and said, "She wasn't born yesterday. It's not likely that anything will escape her. I bet you she'll come visit us tomorrow at the latest to conduct a thorough investigation."

Kamal should have left the room then, but he did not want to, and perhaps could not, he was so interested in the scene unfolding before his eyes. For the first time in his life he witnessed his sister's face undergo this transformation into a new face altogether, boasting white skin, pink cheeks, and eyelids with delicate black lines along their edges that enhanced her eyes and made them look splendidly clear. His heart rejoiced at this new face. He shouted with excitement, "Sister, now you're just like those beautiful candy bride dolls Papa buys for the festival of the Prophet's Birthday."

The two girls laughed. Khadija asked him, "Do you like the way I look now?"

He rushed up to her and put his hand out to the tip of her nose, saying, "If only this would go away."

She evaded his hand and told her sister, "Throw out this slanderer."

Although he resisted, Aisha seized his hand, dragged him outside, and bolted the door. Then she went back to her beautifying task. The sisters proceeded with their endeavors seriously and silently. Although it was understood in the family that matchmakers would be allowed to meet only Khadija, she told Aisha mischievously, "You need to prepare yourself to meet the visitors too."

Aisha replied as slyly as her sister, "That won't be until you've been escorted to your bridegroom." Then she corrected herself before Khadija could speak: "Now that the moon is rising how can little stars be seen?"

Her sister cast her a skeptical look and asked, "Which of us is the moon?"

Laughing, Aisha replied, "Me of course."

Khadija gave her a poke with her elbow and sighed: "I wish you could lend me your nose the way Maryam lent me her powder."

"Forget your nose, even if only for this one evening. A nose is like a sore that grows larger every time you think about it."

By then they had practically finished their work as beauticians.

Khadija's interest in her appearance waned. Her thoughts shifted fearfully to her pending examination. She was afraid in a new way, not simply because it was a novel situation but because of its serious consequences.

She soon complained, "What's this meeting that's being inflicted on me? Picture yourself in my place, surrounded by strangers. You don't know the least thing about them or their background. Have they come with good intentions or am I just an amusing spectacle for them? What will become of me if they are abusive faultfinders, like me . . . huh?" She laughed briefly. "What can I do but sit beside them politely and submissively while they stare at me from left and right, front and back? I'll have to obey their orders without the slightest hesitation. If they ask me to stand, I stand. 'Walk'—I walk. 'Sit'—I sit. Nothing will slip by them: the way I sit or stand, if I'm silent or speak, my limbs and features. In addition to putting up with all this abuse, we must be nice to them and lavishly praise their kindness and generosity. Afterward we still won't know whether we've won their approval or displeasure. My, oh my . . . I could curse the man who sent them."

Aisha quickly replied in a tone that revealed her personal interest in the subject: "May no evil harm him."

"Don't pray for him till we're sure he's ours. . . . Oh, how my heart is pounding. . . ."

Aisha stepped back to be out of range of her sister's elbow before she replied, "Be patient. . . . You'll find many opportunities in the future to get your revenge for today's frightful meeting. How often they'll be roasted by the fire of your tongue once you're the mistress of the house. Perhaps they'll recall today's inspection and say to themselves, 'I wish that had never happened.' "

Khadija confined her response to a smile. There was no time for a counterattack. In any case, she would not have gotten the salutary delight from it she usually derived, or any pleasure at all, because she was dominated by her terror and anxiously wavering between hope and fear.

When they had finished their work, Khadija paused to give her reflection in the mirror a thorough examination. Aisha, who was two steps behind her, looked back and forth from the reflection to the original.

Khadija began to murmur, "Bless your hands. I look good, don't I? This is the true Khadija. Never mind my nose now. O Lord, may Your wisdom be exalted. It took a little effort, but everything turned out all right. So why . . ." Then she realized she had said too much and quickly added, "I ask God's forgiveness. May Your wisdom prevail in everything."

She moved a few steps farther away from the mirror, still examining her image carefully. She recited the opening prayer of the Qur'an to herself. She turned toward Aisha and said, "Pray for me, girl." Then she left the room.

24

With the advent of winter, the coffee hour acquired a new aspect represented by the large stove placed in the center of the room. The family clustered around it, the men in their overcoats and the women wrapped up in their shawls. The coffee hour offered them, in addition to the appetizing refreshments and pleasant conversation, a chance to get warm.

Although Fahmy had been sad and silent for the past few days, he seemed ready to spring some important news on the family. His hesitation and reflection only served to show how momentous and important the news was. After giving the matter a little more thought he decided to reveal it and transfer the burden to his parents and the fates. He said, "I've got some important news for you. Listen."

All eyes were fixed on him attentively. He was known to be such a sensible young man that everyone expected his news would be as important as he claimed. He continued: "Mr. Hasan Ibrahim, an officer in the Gamaliya police station, who is one of my acquaintances, as you all know, came to see me and asked me to tell my father of his wish to become engaged to Aisha."

Just as Fahmy had expected, the news affected people in extremely different ways. That was the reason he had hesitated and thought for so long before revealing it. His mother looked at him with intense interest. Yasin whistled, gazed at Aisha flirtatiously, and shook his head. The young girl bowed her head out of embarrassment and to hide her face from prying eyes that might detect the turmoil of her throbbing heart. Khadija's first reaction was surprise, which soon turned to fear and foreboding. There was no clear reason for either, but she felt like a pupil waiting impatiently for examination results who hears privately of a comrade's success.

The mother asked with an anxiety inappropriate for the topic of a joyous wedding, "Is that all he said?"

Taking care to avoid looking at Khadija, Fahmy replied, "He began by stating he wished to have the honor of asking for the hand of my younger sister."

"What did you tell him?"

"I naturally thanked him for his good intentions."

His mother was not questioning him to find out something. She was attempting to conceal her uneasiness and wished time to mull things over. She began to wonder if there might be a connection between this request and the ladies who had called on them a few days before. She remembered then that one had observed before Khadija had appeared, in the context of a general conversation about the family of al-Sayyid Ahmad, that they had heard the gentleman had two daughters. She had understood then that they had come to see both daughters but had turned a deaf ear to the suggestion. Those ladies had been related to the family of a merchant in al-Darb al-Ahmar. Fahmy had said once that the father of the officer, on the other hand, was an employee in the Ministry of Works. This fact did not decisively rule out the possibility of some link between the two families. It was customary for a family to send marriage scouts selected from one of its branches, not from the bridegroom's immediate family, as a precaution. She dearly wished to ask Fahmy about this point but seemed afraid his answer would confirm her fears, thereby putting an end to the hopes of her elder daughter and bringing her a new disappointment.

It so happened that Khadija posed the question for her mother. She veiled her frustration with a listless laugh as the issue troubling her breast emerged in these words: "Perhaps he's the one who sent those ladies to visit us a few days ago?"

Fahmy replied at once, "Of course not. He told me he'd send his mother to us if his request is approved."

Although he spoke in a way that inspired trust, he was not telling the truth. He had gathered from his conversation with the officer that the ladies were his relatives. Although he loved Aisha and was convinced that his friend the officer was worthy of her, he was unwilling to cause pain to his older sister. He felt a brotherly affection for her and was very upset at her bad luck. Perhaps the disappointment he had suffered played a powerful role in strengthening this affection.

Yasin guffawed and remarked with childish glee, "It seems we'll soon have two weddings."

The mother cried out with heartfelt joy, "May our Lord answer you. . . ."

"Will you speak to Daddy for me?" When the question escaped from Fahmy, he was preoccupied with this engagement, but afterward his words sounded odd to him, as though they came not from his tongue but from his memories. These words plunged into his inner depths, before floating to consciousness again with memories clinging to them. He remembered the comparable question he had addressed to his mother in similar circumstances. His heart became dispirited, and his pains were inflamed. He felt once more the tyranny that had buried his hopes. He began to tell himself, as he had done repeatedly during the preceding days, how happy he would have felt about the present, how hopeful he would have been about the future, how content he would have been with life as a whole, had it not been for his father's stern will. This memory made it impossible for him to be concerned about anything but himself. He surrendered himself to the sorrow gnawing at his heart.

The mother thought for a time and then asked, "Wouldn't it be a good idea for us to think about what I can say to your father if he asks me why the officer requested Aisha specifically and didn't ask for Khadija's hand? Since he hasn't seen either one . . ."

The two girls both focused their attention on their mother's remark. They both remembered their scene at the window. The annoyance Khadija felt at that memory doubled her unhappiness about the current situation. Her heart protested against blind fate, which refused to reward reckless frivolity with anything but good. Aisha felt her flow of delight obstructed by her mother's observation, as if a throat happily swallowing a tasty and delicious morsel had been obstructed by a sharp thorn stuck in the food. Fear quickly sucked the heart out of the happiness that had been making her spirit quiver.

Only Fahmy rebelled against his mother's words. He was not defending Aisha, as it might have seemed, since on such a delicate issue he could not defend Aisha in Khadija's presence. He was angry because of his suppressed sorrow, about which he could not speak openly with his father. Unconsciously addressing his father in the person of his mother, he remarked angrily, "This would be unjust and arbitrary. Reason and intellect provide no support for such an objection. Don't men learn a lot of things about decent women kept secluded from the street by talking to female relatives, whose only goal is the formation of a legal union between a man and a woman?"

Their mother had meant nothing by her remark. She was merely trying to hide behind her husband until she could discover some way out of the bind she found herself in with Aisha and Khadija. When Fahmy voiced his objections to her so frankly, she found herself forced to answer with similar frankness: "Don't you think it would be best for us to wait till we hear something from those women who visited us?"

Khadija could not bear to remain silent. Driven by her pride, which forced her to declare that she cared nothing about the matter at all, despite the anxiety and forebodings struggling inside her, she said, "This is one thing and that's quite another. So there's no reason to postpone one because of the other."

Their mother remarked in a calm but forceful way, "We're all agreed that Aisha's wedding will be delayed until after Khadija's."

Aisha could only say, gently and submissively, "The matter's not open to discussion."

Khadija's breast filled with resentment when she heard the gentle tone of Aisha's voice. Perhaps it was this gentleness that angered her most of all. It may have suggested to her that she deserved to be pitied, which she absolutely rejected. It may also have been that she would have liked for Aisha to declare her opposition openly so she could attack her sister and find some outlet for her anger. Aisha had armed herself with that hateful fake sympathy to defend herself from harm, thus doubling Khadija's resentment, which was lying in ambush, waiting for a chance to pop out. Finally she found herself obliged to say, if a bit sharply, "I don't agree that this matter's not open to debate. It's not fair that someone's bad luck should cause you to destroy another person's good luck."

Fahmy noticed the angry sorrow concealed behind the altruism of Khadija's words. He wrenched himself free from his personal grief. He regretted what he had said in a moment of anger, fearful that Khadija would interpret it to mean he sided openly with her sister. Addressing Khadija, he said, "Telling Papa about Hasan Effendi's request doesn't mean we agree Aisha should marry before you. There would be no harm in our making acceptance of the engagement conditional on postponement of its announcement to an appropriate time."

Yasin was not convinced it was right to require one marriage to precede the other, but he could not muster enough courage to express his opinion. He found some comfort in making a general statement that could be understood in different ways. He said, "Marriage is the fate of every living creature. Anyone not getting married today will marry tomorrow."

Kamal had been following the conversation with interest and at this point his shrill voice rang out, asking unexpectedly, "Mother, why is marriage the fate of every creature?"

His mother ignored his question. The only response he received was a loud laugh from Yasin, who made no other comment. Then the mother observed, "I know every girl will marry today or tomorrow, but there are considerations not to be overlooked. . . ."

Kamal tried asking his mother another question: "And will you be getting married too, Mother?"

They all roared with laughter, and this relieved the tension. Yasin seized the favorable opportunity and found the courage to say, "Present the matter to Father. Whatever he says will be final in any case."

With a curious insistence, Khadija said, "That's the only way. That's the way it has to be."

She meant what she said, because she knew how impossible it was to conceal a matter like this from her father and firmly believed her father would not allow Aisha to marry first. In addition to these reasons, she also wished to continue pretending indifference to the issue. Although she did not know of the connection between the officer and the visitors, her anxious forebodings had not left her for a moment.

25

Although Mrs. Amina had encountered more than one cause for unhappiness during her life, she had had no experience with this unforeseen problem and its unique character, since it seemed to pertain to one of the essential foundations of happiness in this world. Even so, in her household and in her heart in particular, it had turned into a cause for anxiety and distress. How right she was when she asked herself, "Who would have suspected that the arrival of a bridegroom, something we have been avidly awaiting, would cause us all this trouble?" Yet that was what had happened.

Several views struggled for control of her mind without her being comfortable about any of them. For a time she thought that agreeing to let Aisha marry before Khadija would destroy her elder daughter's future. On other occasions she thought that stubborn opposition to destiny would create an extremely dangerous situation, with sinister repercussions for both girls. It also troubled her a great deal to close the door in the face of a bridegroom as splendid as the young officer. It was asking a lot to expect that luck would provide another one as good. But what would Khadija's position be and what kind of luck and future would she have if the agreement was concluded? Mrs. Amina could not make up her mind. It was especially difficult since all the prospects seemed so bleak, leaving her unable to find any solution. She was ready to cast the whole burden on the shoulders of her husband and felt relieved, despite the apprehension that swept through her every time she was about to bring up a topic she feared might upset him.

She waited until he finished his coffee. Then she said in her soft voice clearly intended to be polite and submissive, "Sir . . . Fahmy told me one of his friends asked him to present his request to become engaged to Aisha."

From his place on the sofa he looked down at her on her pallet not far from his feet. His blue eyes were filled with interest and astonishment. He seemed to be asking her, "How can you be talking to me about Aisha when I've been waiting for news about Khadija since hearing about the three women visitors?" He asked, to make sure he had heard correctly, "Aisha?"

"Yes, sir."

Al-Sayyid Ahmad looked straight ahead of him with annoyance. Then, as though addressing himself, he said, "I decided a long time ago which order to follow."

The woman quickly said, so he would not think she was opposing his opinion, "I know how you feel about it, sir, but I have to inform you of everything that goes on here."

He scrutinized her keenly, as though probing to discover how much of her statement was true and sincere, but his scrutiny was interrupted by a new thought that shone in his eyes. He asked her with concern and anxiety, "Do you suppose there's a connection between this and the ladies who visited you?"

Once they were alone, Fahmy had told her, that there was a connection. The young man had suggested keeping it from his father when she broke the news to him. She had promised to think about it carefully and had hesitated between accepting and rejecting the idea. Finally she had been inclined to keep it a secret, as Fahmy had suggested, but when her husband's question put her on the spot and she felt his eyes looking at her like blazing sunlight, her resolve crumbled and her conviction melted. She replied without hesitation, "Yes, sir. Fahmy learned they were relatives of his friend."

Al-Sayyid Ahmad frowned in anger. As usual when he was angry, his white complexion became flushed and sparks flew from his eyes. It seemed that anyone who belittled Khadija was belittling him. Whoever questioned her honor attacked his, head-on. Yet the only way he knew to show his anger was through his voice, which grew loud and coarse. He asked angrily and scornfully, "Who is this friend?"

She did not know why, but she was uneasy about mentioning the name. "Hasan Ibrahim, an officer at the Gamaliya police station," she said.

He asked her excitedly, "Didn't you tell me you showed only Khadija to the ladies?"

"Yes, sir."

"Did they visit you again?"

"Certainly not, sir. Otherwise I would have told you."

He scolded her as though she were responsible for this peculiar behavior: "He sent his relatives. They saw Khadija. Then he asks for Aisha! . . . What's the meaning of this?"

The mother swallowed and cleared her throat, which was dry from the give-and-take of their conversation. She murmured, "In a case like this, the matchmakers don't go to the house in question until they have visited many of the neighboring households to make inquiries about matters of concern to them. In fact, they did hint in their conversation with me that they had heard you had two daughters. Perhaps presenting only one instead of both . . ."

She had meant to say, "Perhaps presenting only one instead of both served to confirm for them the rumor they had heard about the beauty of the younger girl." She stopped herself partly from fear of increasing his anger and partly from apprehension at openly stating this fact that was linked in her mind to gloomy anxieties and worries. She caught herself and concluded her statement with a mere gesture of her hand, as if to say, "And so on and so forth."

Al-Sayyid Ahmad glared at her until she lowered her eyes submissively. He became resentful and sad, compressing the anger within his heart. He began to pound his chest, trying to get some relief or company for his sorrow. Then he shouted in a stormy voice, "Now we know everything. Here's a suitor asking for your daughter's hand. So let me hear your opinion."

She felt that his question was dragging her into a bottomless pit. Holding her hands out subserviently, she replied without any hesitation, "My opinion is the same as yours, sir. I have no opinion of my own."

He roared back, "If that was so, you wouldn't have mentioned the matter to me at all."

She said apprehensively and devotedly, "Sir, I mentioned it to you only to keep you informed about the new development, since it's my duty to let you know everything that affects your home, coming from near or far."

He shook his head peevishly and said, "Who knows . . . yes, by God, who knows? You're just a woman, and no woman has a fully developed mind. And the topic of marriage in particular is enough to make you women lose your senses. So perhaps you . . ."

She interrupted him in a trembling voice: "Sir, I seek refuge with God from what you suspect. Khadija is my daughter and my flesh and blood just as much as yours. . . . What's happening to her is breaking my heart. Aisha's still in the first bloom of youth. It won't hurt her to wait till God brings help for her sister."

Her husband was nervously smoothing his thick mustache with the palm of his hand. Then he stopped suddenly as though he had remembered something. He asked, "Does Khadija know?"

"Yes, sir."

He waved his hand angrily and shouted, "How can this officer ask for the hand of Aisha despite the fact that no one has seen her?"

Although her heart was throbbing, she replied heatedly, "I told you, sir, perhaps they heard something about her."

"But he works in the Gamaliya police station—in other words, in our area. It's as though he lived here."

His wife replied very emotionally, "No man has ever seen either of my daughters since they stopped going to school when they were little girls."

He struck his hands together and shouted at her, "Not so fast.... Slow down. Do you think I have any doubts about that, woman? If I did, not even murder would satisfy me. I'm just talking about what will go through the minds of some people who don't know us. 'No man has ever seen either of my daughters...' God's will be done. Would you have wanted a man to see them? What a crazy prattler you are. I'm repeating what might be rumored by fools. Yes ... he's an officer in the area. He walks along our streets morning and evening. So it's not out of the question that people, if they learned he was marrying one of the girls, would suspect that he might have seen one of them. I would despise giving my daughter to someone if that meant stirring up doubts about my honor. No daughter of mine will marry a man until I am satisfied that his primary motive for marrying her is a sincere desire to be related to me ... me ... me ... me. 'No man has ever seen either of my daughters ... ' Congratulations, Mrs. Amina, congratulations."

The mother listened with her head bowed, not uttering a word. The room was still. Then the man rose, signaling that he was going to put on his street clothes and return to his shop. She quickly got up. Her husband took his arms out of the sleeves of his house shirt and raised it to take it off but stopped before the neck of the shirt had gone past his chin. With the garment folded around his shoulders like the mane of a lion, he asked, "Didn't Mr. Fahmy understand the seriousness of the request his friend was making?" Nodding his head sadly, he continued: "People envy me my three sons. The truth is that all I've got are daughters ... five daughters."

26

Once al-Sayyid Ahmad left the house, they soon learned what he thought about Aisha's engagement. Although his opinion was accepted without opposition by people obliged to agree with him, it reverberated inside each of them in different ways. Fahmy was sorry to hear the news. He was unhappy Aisha was going to lose a fine husband like his friend Hasan Ibrahim. Before his father's decision, Fahmy had wavered between enthusiasm for the prospective bridegroom and sympathy for Khadija's delicate position. When the matter was settled, the part of him pitying Khadija found relief, while the other part wishing for Aisha's happiness was sad. This sorrow gave him the courage to state his opinion openly: "Without any doubt, Khadija's future is of concern to all of us, but I don't agree with the insistence on forbidding Aisha to take advantage of her opportunities. A person's fortune is part of the invisible world known only to God. Perhaps God has stored up an even better fortune for the person forced to wait."

Khadija was possibly the one who felt most uncomfortable, since this was the second time she had stood in the way of her sister's getting married. She brooded about her anguish, not while her future was on the line, but after her father's categorical decision, when the danger threatening her had retreated. Then her anger and pain faded away, to be replaced by a distressing feeling of embarrassment and anguish. Fahmy's words did not please her, because deep inside she wanted everyone to support her father's decision and leave her the only one opposing it. All the same, she commented, "Fahmy was right in what he said. That's what I've thought all along."

Yasin reaffirmed his idea: "Marriage is the destiny of every living creature. . . . Have no fear. . . . Don't panic."

He contented himself with this general observation, even though he was very fond of Aisha and indignant over the injustice that had befallen her. He was afraid that if he stated his opinion frankly, Khadija might misunderstand and suspect some link between this and the innocent squabbles that frequently broke out between them. His sensitivity about being a half brother also prevented him from volunteering an opinion that might offend a family member whenever they confronted a serious matter of delicate family business.

Aisha had not uttered a word but finally forced herself to speak, so her silence would not betray her pain, which she was determined to conceal. She would pretend to have no feelings about the engagement, no matter how much that distressed her, and announce her relief about the outcome, to conform with the atmosphere of the household that did not allow human emotions their rightful place and where the affections of the heart were hidden behind veils of self-denial and hypocrisy. So she said, "It wouldn't be right for me to marry before Khadija. The best thing by far is what my father has decided." She continued with a smile: "Why should you all be in such a hurry to get married? How do you know that we'll enjoy as happy a life in our spouse's home as we do here in our father's house?"

When, as usual, they picked up their conversation around the stove that evening, Aisha did not hesitate to participate in it as much as she was able, given her wandering thoughts and the disintegration of her ego. In truth, she resembled nothing so much as a chicken with its head cut off, darting about with outspread wings, bursting with vitality and energy at the very moment blood flowed from its neck, draining away the last drops of life.

Aisha had anticipated what would happen even before the matter was presented to her father. All the same, she had nourished a glimmer of hope in her dreams, like one of us tempted by the hope of winning first prize in a major lottery. At first, influenced by the generosity that comes with victory or happiness and by affection for her unlucky sister, she had been willing to object to getting married. Now her generosity had faded away and her affection had dwindled. Nothing remained but resentment, anger, and despair. There was not a thing she could do about it. This was her father's will and she could not criticize it. All she could do was submit and obey. In fact, she had to be happy and content. To be despondent would be an unforgivable offense. To protest would be a sin her conscience and sense of etiquette could not allow. From the intoxication of bounteous happiness that had elated her night and day she awoke to despair. How gloomy the darkness seemed coming immediately after dazzling light. Thus the pain was not limited to the current darkness but was doubled many times over by regret for the light that had vanished. She asked herself why, since light had been able to shine for a while, it could not keep on shining. Why should it die out? Why had it died out? It was a new regret to add to the others—drawn from memories, the present, and dreams of the future—that sorrow was weaving around her heart. Although she was sunk in thought about this and it dominated her feelings, she wondered again, as though for the first time, whether the light had really gone out. The bitter truth seemed to be bombarding her emotions for the very first time.

Had the ties been severed between her and the young man who had filled her heart and imagination? Here was a new question, no matter how often it was repeated, and a new shock even though it had already penetrated her very bones. Her searing regret kept getting buffeted by the despair consuming her and the hopes fluttering in the air. Whenever a hope took flight, regret returned and settled deep inside her, to float back to the surface time and again, until it was firmly established. When her soul had bade farewell to the last of her hopes, regret became an inseparable part of her.

It was over, as though he had never existed. There was no way to get him now. How easy it was for them. They treated it like an everyday affair, as though remarking, "What are we going to eat tomorrow?" or "I had a strange dream last night" or even "You can smell the jasmine all over the roof terrace." A word here and a word there . . . a suggestion to announce and an opinion to explain. They were strangely calm and reserved, offering her smiling condolences and jesting encouragement. Then the topic of conversation would change and branch out.

Everything had ended. It would be incorporated into the family history and forgotten. How did her heart fit in with all this? She did not have a heart. No one imagined she had one. So in reality it did not exist. How alienated she felt. She was lost and abandoned. They were not part of her. She was not part of them. She was alone, banished, disowned. How could she forget that a single word bestowed by her father's tongue would suffice to change the face of the world and turn her into a new person? Just one word, the expression "yes," would be enough to produce a miracle. It would not have cost him a tenth of the effort that went into the long discussion leading to his refusal. Yet he had willed otherwise and had been pleased to let her suffer all this torment.

Although she was hurt, angry, and resentful, these emotions could not touch her father. They fell back impotently like a wild animal stopped by its trainer, whom it loves and fears. Aisha was not able to attack her father, not even in the depths of her heart. She continued in her love and devotion for him. She felt sincerely dutiful to him, as though he were a god whose decree could only be received with submission, love, and loyalty.

That evening the young girl tightened the rope of despair around her delicate neck. Her sensitive heart believed it had dried up and become barren forever. The role of happy indifference she had resolved to assume with her family doubled her nervous tension, as did participation in their conversation, which she imposed on herself. Finally her golden head bowed under the strain and their voices became a dull clamor in her ears. As soon as it was time to withdraw to the bedroom she collapsed there in exhaustion like an invalid. In the security provided by the darkness of the room, her face frowned for the first time, presenting an accurate reflection of the state of her heart.

Someone was still watching her, Khadija, but Aisha had been sure from the start that dissimulation would be useless with her. When they were at the coffee hour, she had avoided her eyes. Now that she was sitting beside her, there was no escape and no place to flee. Aisha expected her sister to pounce on the subject with her customary resolve. She waited from one moment to the next for the sound of her voice. Her heart welcomed the conversation, but not because it would give birth to any new hope. She wished to find some consolation in the excuses and anguish her sister would certainly express truthfully.

She did not have long to wait before Khadija's voice did make its way to her through the darkness: "Aisha, I'm really sorry, but God knows there's nothing I can do. I wish I had enough courage to ask Father to change his mind."

Aisha wondered whether these words were sincere or hypocritical. She reacted immediately to her sister's sad tones with a feeling of annoyance. Even so, she was forced to resume the false voice of happy indifference she had used throughout the coffee hour with her mother. She replied, "What's there to be sad or despondent about? My father wasn't in error. He wasn't unjust. There's no need to be in a hurry."

"This is the second time your marriage has been delayed because of me."

"I'm not sorry at all."

Khadija observed pointedly, "But this time's not like the first."

As quick as lightning Aisha realized what her sister meant. Her heart pounded painfully with love and regret, weeping from passion and love. It was a hidden love, which could be awakened by any hint reaching it from outside, whether intentional or accidental, like a sore or a boil that hurts when touched or pierced. She started to talk, but was forced to stop because she was out of breath. She was afraid her voice would give her away.

Then Khadija sighed and remarked, "That's why you find me so sad and melancholy. But our Lord is generous. There's no distress that's not followed by relief. Perhaps he'll wait and be patient, so he becomes your destiny no matter how unlikely that seems now."

Every part of Aisha's body cried out, "If only that were so!" But her tongue said, "It's all the same to me. The matter's simpler than you think."

"I hope that's the case. I'm very sad and upset, Aisha."

The door opened suddenly, and the form of Kamal could be made out in the faint light slipping in from the crack of the door. Khadija shouted at him crossly, "Why have you come? What do you want?"

The boy answered in a tone that revealed his indignation at her rude reception, "Don't drive me away. . . . Make room for me."

He jumped onto the bed and knelt between them. He put out a hand to each of them and began to tickle them. He wished to create a better atmosphere for his discussion than that suggested by Khadija's rebuff. They grabbed his hands, however, and said one after the other, "It's time for you to go to bed. Go and sleep."

He shouted angrily, "I won't go until I learn what I've come to ask you about."

"What do you want to ask about at this hour of the night?"

Changing his tone in hopes they would pay attention to him, he asked, "I want to know whether you'll both leave the house when you get married."

Khadija yelled at him, "Wait till the marriage takes place!"

He asked obstinately, "But what is marriage?"

"How can I answer you when I haven't been married? . . . Go and sleep. May God protect you from evil."

"I won't go until I find out."

"My dear, trust in God and leave us."

In a sad voice he said, "I want to know if you'll both leave the house when you get married."

She replied angrily, "Yes, sir. . . . What else do you want?"

He said anxiously, "Then don't get married. That's what I want."

"We hear and obey."

Then he went on, protesting excitedly, "I can't bear for you to go far away from us. I'll pray to God that you never get married."

Khadija shouted, "Straight from your mouth to the portals of heaven. . . . Great . . . wonderful. May our Lord be generous to you. Be kind enough to leave us in peace."

27

A feeling spread through the household that they would have a day's reprieve from their oppressively prim life. Safe from their guardian's eye, they would be able, if they so desired, to get an innocent breath of fresh air. Kamal was of the opinion that he could do as he wished and spend the whole day playing, inside the house and out. Khadija and Aisha wondered if they might slip over to Maryam's house in the evening to spend an hour there having fun and amusing themselves.

This break did not come as a result of the passing of the gloomy winter months and the arrival of the first signs of spring with intimations of warmth and good cheer. It was not occasioned by spring granting this family liberty they had been deprived of by winter. This respite came as a natural consequence of a business trip, lasting a day or more, that al-Sayyid Ahmad made to Port Said every few years. It so happened that he set out on a Friday morning when the weekly holiday brought the family together. They all responded eagerly to the freedom and the peaceful, relaxed atmosphere the father's departure from Cairo had unexpectedly created.

The mother hesitantly dashed the girls' hopes and the young boy's high spirits. She wanted to make sure the family persisted with its customary schedule and adhered, even when the father was absent, to the same rules it observed when he was present. She was more concerned to keep from vexing him than she was convinced that he was right to be so severe and stern.

Before she knew what was happening, though, here was Yasin saying, "Don't oppose God's plan. . . . Nobody else lives like us. In fact, I want to say something novel. . . . Why don't you have some fun too? What do you all think about this suggestion?"

Their eyes looked at him in astonishment, but no one said a word. Perhaps, like their mother, who gave him a critical look, they did not take what he was saying seriously. All the same, he continued: "Why are you looking at me like this? I haven't contravened any of the directives of the Prophet recorded in the revered collection of al-Bukhari. Praise God, no crime has been committed. All it would amount to is a brief excursion to have a look at a little of the district you've lived in for forty years but never seen."

The woman sighed and murmured, "May God be merciful to you."

The young man laughed out loud. He said, "Why should you ask God to be merciful to me? Have I committed some unforgivable sin? By God, if I were you, I'd go as far as the mosque of our master al-Husayn. . . . Our master al-Husayn, don't you hear? . . . Your beloved saint whom you adore from afar when he's so near. Go to him. He's calling you."

Her heart pounded and the effect could be seen in her blush. She lowered her head to hide how deeply she was affected. Her heart responded to the call with a force that exploded suddenly in her soul. She was taken by surprise. No one around her could have anticipated this, not even Yasin himself. It was as though an earthquake had shaken a land that had never experienced one before. She did not understand how her heart could answer this appeal, how her eyes could look beyond the limits of what was allowed, or how she could consider the adventure possible and even tempting, no—irresistible. Of course, since it was such a sacred pilgrimage, a visit to the shrine of al-Husayn appeared a powerful excuse for the radical leap her will was making, but that was not the only factor influencing her soul. Deep inside her, imprisoned currents yearning for release responded to this call in the same way that eager, aggressive instincts answer the call for a war proclaimed to be in defense of freedom and peace.

She did not know how to announce her fateful surrender. She looked at Yasin and said in a trembling voice, "A visit to the shrine of al-Husayn is something my heart has wished for all my life . . . but . . . your father?"

Yasin laughed and answered, "My father's on his way to Port Said. He won't be back until tomorrow morning. As an extra precaution you can borrow Umm Hanafi's wrap, so anyone who sees you leaving the house or returning will think you're a visitor."

She looked back and forth between her children with embarrassment and dread, as though seeking more encouragement. Khadija and Aisha were enthusiastic about the suggestion. In their enthusiasm they seemed to be expressing both their own imprisoned desire to break free and their joy at the visit to Maryam, which had become, after this revolution, a certainty.

Expressing his heartfelt approval, Kamal shouted, "I'll go with you, Mother, and show you the way."

Fahmy gazed at her affectionately when he saw the expression of anxious pleasure on her face, like that of a child hoping to get a new toy. To encourage her and play down the importance of the adventure, he said, "Have a look at the world. There's nothing wrong with that. I'm afraid you'll forget how to walk after staying home so much."

In an outburst of enthusiasm Khadija ran to Umm Hanafi to get the black cloth she wrapped around herself when she went out. Everyone was laughing and offering their comments. The day turned into a more joyous festival than any they had experienced. They all participated, unwittingly, in the revolution against their absent father's will. Mrs. Amina wrapped the cloth around her and pulled the black veil down over her face. She looked in the mirror and laughed until her torso shook. Kamal put on his suit and fez and got to the courtyard before her, but she did not follow him. She was afflicted by the kind of fear people feel at crucial turning points. She raised her eyes to Fahmy and asked, "What do you think? Should I really go?"

Yasin yelled at her, "Trust God."

Khadija went up to her. Placing her hands on her shoulders, she gave her a gentle push, saying, "Reciting the opening prayer of the Qur'an will protect you." Khadija propelled her all the way to the stairs. Then she withdrew her hands. The woman descended, with everyone following her. She found Umm Hanafi waiting for her. The servant cast a searching look at her mistress, or rather at the cloth encompassing her. She shook her head disapprovingly, went to her, and wrapped the cloth around her again. She taught her how to hold the edge in the right place. Her mistress, who was wearing this wrap for the first time, followed the servant's directions. Then the angles and curves of her figure, ordinarily concealed by her flowing housedresses, were visible in all their details. Smiling, Khadija gave her an admiring look and winked at Aisha. They burst into laughter.

As she crossed the threshold of the outer door and entered the street, she experienced a moment of panic. Her mouth felt dry and her pleasure was dispelled by a fit of anxiety. She had an oppressive feeling of doing something wrong. She moved slowly and grasped Kamal's hand nervously. Her gait seemed disturbed and unsteady, as though she had not mastered the first principles of walking. She was gripped by intense embarrassment as she showed herself to the eyes of people she had known for ages but only through the peephole of the enclosed balcony. Uncle Hasanayn, the barber, Darwish, who sold beans, al-Fuli, the milkman, Bayumi, the drinks vendor, and Abu Sari', who sold snacks—she imagined that they all recognized her just as she did them. She had difficulty convincing herself of the obvious fact that none of them had ever seen her before in their lives.

They crossed the street to Qirmiz Alley. It was not the shortest route to the mosque of al-Husayn, but unlike al-Nahhasin Street, it did not pass by al-Sayyid Ahmad's store or any other shops and was little frequented. She stopped for a moment before plunging into the alley. She turned to look at her latticed balcony. She could make out the shadows of her two daughters behind one panel. Another panel was raised to reveal the smiling faces of Fahmy and Yasin. The sight of them gave her some courage for her project.

Then she hurried along with her son down the desolate alley, feeling almost calm. Her anxiety and sense of doing something wrong did not leave her, but they retreated to the edges of her conscious emotions. Center stage was occupied by an eager interest in exploring the world as it revealed one of its alleys, a square, novel buildings, and lots of people. She found an innocent pleasure in sharing the motion and freedom of other living creatures. It was the pleasure of someone who had spent a quarter of a century imprisoned by the walls of her home, except for a limited number of visits to her mother in al-Khurunfush, where she would go a few times a year but in a carriage and chaperoned by her husband. Then she would not even have the courage to steal a look at the street.

She began to ask Kamal about the sights, buildings, and places they encountered on their way. The boy was proud to serve as her guide and volunteered lengthy explanations. Here was the famous vaulted ceiling of Qirmiz Alley. Before walking beneath it one needed to recite the opening prayer of the Qur'an as a defense against the jinn living there. This was Bayt al-Qadi Square with its tall trees. She might have heard him refer to the square as Pasha's Beard Square, from the popular name for its flowering lebbek trees, or at times also as Shangarly Square, giving it the name of the Turkish owner of a chocolate shop. This large building was the Gamaliya police station. Although the boy found little there to merit his attention, except the sword dangling from the sentry's waist, the mother looked at it with curiosity, since it was the place of employment of a man who had sought Aisha's hand. They went on until they reached Khan Ja'far Primary School, where Kamal had spent a year before enrolling at Khalil Agha Elementary School. He pointed to its historic balcony and remarked, "On this balcony Shaykh Mahdi made us put our faces to the wall for the least offense. Then he would kick us five, six, or ten times. Whatever he felt like."

Gesturing toward a store situated directly under the balcony, he stopped walking and said in a tone she could not mistake, "This is Uncle Sadiq, who sells sweets." He refused to budge until he had extracted a coin from her and bought himself a gummy red candy.

After that they turned into Khan Ja'far Alley. Then in the distance they could see part of the exterior of the mosque of al-Husayn. In the center was an expansive window decorated with arabesques. The façade was topped by a parapet with merlons like spear points bunched tightly together.

With joy singing in her breast, she asked, "Our master al-Husayn?" He confirmed her guess. Her pace quickened for the first time since she left the house. She began to compare what she saw with the picture created by her imagination and based on what she had seen from her home of mosques like Qala'un and Barquq. She found the reality to be less grand than she had imagined. In her imagination she had made its size correspond to the veneration in which she held its holy occupant. This difference between imagination and reality, however, in no way affected the pervasive intoxication of her joy at being there.

They walked around the outside of the mosque until they reached the green door. They entered, surrounded by a crowd of women visitors. When the woman's feet touched the floor of the shrine, she felt that her body was dissolving into tenderness, affection, and love and that she was being transformed into a spirit fluttering in the sky, radiant with the glow of prophetic inspiration. Her eyes swam with tears that helped relieve the agitation of her breast, the warmth of her love and belief, and the flood of her benevolent joy. She proceeded to devour the place with greedy, curious eyes: the walls, ceiling, pillars, carpets, chandeliers, pulpit, and the mihrab niches indicating the direction of Mecca.

Kamal, by her side, looked at these things from his own special point of view, assuming that the mosque served as a shrine for people during the day and the early evening but afterward was the home for his martyred master al-Husayn. The Prophet's grandson would come and go there, making use of the furnishings in much the same way any owner uses his possessions. Al-Husayn would walk around inside and pray facing a prayer niche. He would climb into the pulpit and ascend to the windows to look out at his district surrounding the mosque. How dearly Kamal wished, in a dreamy kind of way, that they would forget him in the mosque when they locked the doors so he would be able to meet al-Husayn face to face and pass a whole night in his presence until morning. He imagined the manifestations of love and submission appropriate for him to present to al-Husayn when they met and the hopes and requests suitable for him to lay at his feet. In addition to all that, he looked forward to the affection and blessing he would find with al-Husayn. He pictured himself with his head bowed, approaching the martyr, who would ask him gently, "Who are you?"

He would answer, before kissing his hand, "Kamal Ahmad Abd al-Jawad." Al-Husayn would ask what his profession was. He would reply, "A pupil in Khalil Agha School," and not forget to hint that he was doing well. Al-Husayn would ask what brought him at that hour of the night. Kamal would reply that it was love for all the Prophet's family and especially for him.

Al-Husayn would smile affectionately and invite him to accompany him on his nightly rounds. At that, Kamal would reveal all his requests at once: "Please grant me these things. I want to play as much as I like, inside the house and out. I want Aisha and Khadija to stay in our house always. Please change my father's temper and prolong my mother's life forever. I would like to have as much spending money as I can use and for us all to enter paradise without having to be judged."

The slowly moving flow of women carried them along until they found themselves near the tomb itself. How often she had longed to visit this site, as though yearning for a dream that could never be achieved on this earth. Here she was standing within the shrine. Indeed, here she was touching the walls of the tomb itself, looking at it through her tears. She wished she could linger to savor this taste of happiness, but the pressure of the crowd was too great. She stretched out her hands to the wooden walls and Kamal imitated her. Then they recited the opening prayer of the Qur'an. She stroked the walls and kissed them, never tiring of her prayers and entreaties. She would have liked to stand there a long time or sit in a corner to gaze at it and then circle around again, but the mosque attendant was watching everyone closely. He would not allow any of the women to tarry. He urged on women who slowed down and waved his long stick at them threateningly. He entreated them all to finish their visit before the Friday prayer service.

She had sipped from the sweet spiritual waters of the shrine but had not drunk her fill. There was no way to quench her thirst. Visiting the shrine had so stirred up her yearnings that they gushed forth from their springs, flowed out, and burst over their banks. She would never stop wanting more of this intimacy and delight. When she found herself obliged to leave the mosque, she had to tear herself away, her heart bidding it farewell. She left very regretfully, tormented by the feeling that she was saying farewell to it forever, but her characteristic temperance and resignation intervened to chide her for giving in to her sorrow. Thus she was able to enjoy the happiness she had gained and use it to banish the anxieties aroused by leaving the shrine.

Kamal invited her to look at his school and they went to see it at the end of al-Husayn Street. They paused there for a long time. When she wanted to return the way they had come, the mention of returning signaled the conclusion of this happy excursion with his mother, which he had never before dreamed would be possible. He refused to abandon it so quickly and fought desperately to prolong it. He proposed a walk along New Street to al-Ghuriya. In order to put an end to the opposition suggested by the smiling frown visible through her veil, he made her swear by al-Husayn. She sighed and surrendered herself to his young hand.

They made their way through the thick crowd and in and out of the clashing currents of pedestrians flowing in every direction. She would not have encountered even a hundredth of this traffic on the quiet route by which she had come. She began to be uneasy and almost beside herself with anxiety. She soon complained of discomfort and fatigue, but his desperation to complete this happy excursion made him turn a deaf ear to her complaints. He encouraged her to continue the journey. He tried to distract her by directing her attention to the shops, vehicles, and passersby. They were very slowly approaching the corner of al-Ghuriya. When they reached it, his eyes fell on a pastry shop, and his mouth watered. His eyes were fixed intently on the shop. He began to think of a way to persuade his mother to enter the store and purchase a pastry. He was still thinking about it when they reached the shop, but before he knew what was happening his mother had slipped from his hand. He turned toward her questioningly and saw her fall flat on her face, after a deep moan escaped her.

His eyes grew wide with astonishment and terror. He was unable to move. At approximately the same time, despite his dismay and alarm, he saw an automobile out of the corner of his eye. The driver was applying the brakes with a screeching sound, while the vehicle spewed a trail of dust and smoke. It came within a few inches of running over the prostrate woman, swerving just in time.

Everyone started shouting and a great clamor arose. People dashed to the spot from every direction like children following a magician's whistle. They formed a deep ring around her that seemed to consist of eyes peering, heads craning, and mouths shouting words, as questions got mixed up with answers.

Kamal recovered a little from the shock. He looked back and forth from his prostrate mother at his feet to the people around them, expressing his fear and need for help. Then he threw himself down on his knees beside her. He put his hand on her shoulder and called to her in a voice that was heartrending, but she did not respond. He raised his head and stared at the surrounding faces. Then he screamed out a fervent, sobbing lament that rose above the din around him and almost silenced it. Some people volunteered meaningless words of consolation. Others bent over his mother, examining her curiously, moved by two contrary impulses. Although they hoped the victim was all right, in case there was no hope for recovery they were grateful to see that death, that final conclusion which can only be delayed, had knocked on someone else's door and spirited away someone else's soul. They seemed to want a rehearsal free of any risks of that most perilous role each of them was destined to end his life playing.

One of them shouted, "The left door of the vehicle hit her in the back."

The driver had gotten out of the car and stood there half blinded by the glare of the accusations leveled at him. He protested, "She suddenly swerved off the sidewalk. I couldn't keep from hitting her. I quickly put on my brakes, so I just grazed her. But for the grace of God I would have run her down."

One of the men staring at her said, "She's still breathing. . . . She's just unconscious."

Seeing a policeman approaching, with the sword he carried on his left side swinging back and forth, the driver began speaking again: "It was only a little bump. . . . It couldn't have done anything to her. . . . She's fine . . . fine, everybody, by God."

The first man to examine her stood up straight and as though delivering a sermon said, "Get back. Let her have air. . . . She's opened her eyes. She's all right . . . fine, praise God." He spoke with a joy not devoid of pride, as though he was the one who had brought her back to life. Then he turned to Kamal, who was weeping so hysterically that the consolation of the bystanders had been without effect. He patted Kamal on the cheek sympathetically and told him, "That's enough, son. . . . Your mother's fine. . . . Look. . . . Come help me get her to her feet."

Even so, Kamal did not stop crying until he saw his mother move. He bent toward her and put her left hand on his shoulder. He helped the man lift her up. With great difficulty she was able to stand between them, exhausted and faint. Her wrap had fallen off her and some people helped put it back in place as best they could, wrapping it around her shoulders. Then the pastry merchant, in front of whose store the accident had taken place, brought her a chair. They helped her sit down, and he brought a glass of water. She swallowed some, but half of it spilled down her neck and chest. She wiped off her chest with a reflex motion and groaned. She was breathing with difficulty and looked in bewilderment at the faces staring at her. She asked, "What happened? . . . What happened? . . . Oh Lord, why are you crying, Kamal?"

At that point the policeman came forward. He asked her, "Are you injured, lady? Can you walk to the police station?"

The words "police station" came as a blow to her and shook her to the core. She shouted in alarm, "Why should I go to the police station? I'll never go there."

The policeman replied, "The car hit you and knocked you down. If you're injured, you and the driver must go to the police station to fill out a report."

Gasping for breath, she protested, "No . . . certainly not. I won't go. . . . I'm fine."

The policeman told her, "Prove it to me. Get up and walk so we can see if you're injured."

Driven by the alarm that the mention of the police station aroused in her, she got up at once. Surrounded by inquisitive eyes, she adjusted her wrap and began to walk. Kamal was by her side, brushing away the dust that clung to her. Hoping this painful situation would come to an end, no matter what it cost her, she told the policeman, "I'm fine." Then she gestured toward the driver and continued: "Let him go. . . . There's nothing the matter with me." She was so afraid that she no longer felt faint. The sight of the men staring at her horrified her, especially the policeman, who was in front of the others. She trembled from the impact of these looks directed at her from everywhere. They were a clear challenge and affront to a long life spent in seclusion and concealment from strangers. She imagined she saw the image of al-Sayyid Ahmad rising above all the other men. He seemed to be studying her face with cold, stony eyes, threatening her with more evil than she could bear to imagine.

She lost no time in grabbing the boy's hand and heading off with him toward the Goldsmiths Bazaar. No one tried to stop her. No sooner had they turned the corner and escaped from sight than she moaned. Speaking to Kamal as though addressing herself, she said, "My Lord, how did this happen? What have I seen, Kamal? It was like a terrifying dream. I imagined I was falling into a dark pit from high up. The earth was revolving under my feet. Then I didn't know anything at all until I opened my eyes on that frightening scene. My Lord . . . did he really want to take me to the police station? O Gracious One, O Lord . . . my Savior, my Lord. How soon will we reach home? You cried a lot, Kamal. May you never lose your eyes. Dry your eyes with this handkerchief. You can wash your face at home. . . . Oh."

She stopped when they were almost at the end of the Goldsmiths Bazaar. She rested her hand on the boy's shoulder. Her face was contorted.

Kamal looked up with alarm and asked her, "What's the matter?"

She closed her eyes and said in a weak voice, "I'm tired, very tired. My feet can barely support me. Get the first vehicle you can find, Kamal."

Kamal looked around. All he could see was a donkey cart standing by the doorway of the ancient hospital of Qala'un. He summoned the driver, who quickly brought the cart to them. Leaning on Kamal's shoulder, the mother made her way to it. She clambered on board with his help, supporting herself on the driver's shoulder. He held steady until she was seated cross-legged in the cart. She sighed from her extreme exhaustion and Kamal sat down beside her. Then the driver leaped onto the front of the cart and prodded the donkey with the handle of his whip. The donkey walked off slowly, with the cart swaying and clattering behind him.

The woman moaned. She complained, "My pain's severe. The bones of my shoulder must be smashed." Meanwhile Kamal watched her with alarm and anxiety.

The vehicle passed by al-Sayyid Ahmad's store without either of them paying any attention. Kamal watched the road ahead until he saw the latticed balconies of their house. All he could remember of the happy expedition was its miserable conclusion.

28

When Umm Hanafi opened the door she was startled to see her mistress sitting cross-legged on a donkey cart. Her first thought was that Mrs. Amina had decided to conclude her excursion with a cart ride just for the fun of it. So she smiled but only briefly, for she saw that Kamal's eyes were red from crying. She looked back at her mistress with alarm. This time she was able to fathom the exhaustion and pain the lady was suffering. She moaned and rushed to the cart, crying out, "My lady, what's the matter? May evil stay far away from you."

The driver replied, "God willing, it's nothing serious. Help me get her down."

Umm Hanafi grasped the woman in her arms and carried her inside. Kamal followed them, sad and dejected. Khadija and Aisha had left the kitchen to wait for them in the courtyard, thinking about some joke they could make when the two returned from their excursion. They were terribly surprised when Umm Hanafi appeared, struggling to carry their mother in from the outer hall. They both screamed and ran to her. Terrified, they were shouting, "Mother . . . Mother . . . what's wrong?"

They all helped carry her. At the same time Khadija kept asking Kamal what had happened. Finally the boy was forced to mutter with profound fear, "A car!"

"A car!"

The two girls shouted it together, repeating the word, which sounded incredibly alarming to them. Khadija wailed and screamed, "What terrible news! . . . May evil stay far away from you, Mother."

Aisha could not speak. She burst into tears. Their mother was not unconscious but extremely weak. Despite her fatigue she whispered to calm them, "I'm all right. No harm's done. I'm just tired."

The clamor reached Yasin and Fahmy. They came to the head of the stairs and looked down over the railing. Alarmed, they immediately hurried down, asking what had happened. From fear of repeating the dreadful word, Khadija gestured to Kamal to answer for himself. The two young men went over to the boy, who once again muttered sadly and anxiously, "A car!"

Then he started sobbing. The young men turned away from him, postponing for a time the questions that were troubling them. Together they carried the mother to the girls' room and sat her down on the sofa. Then Fahmy asked her anxiously and fearfully, "Tell me what's the matter, Mother. I want to know everything."

She leaned her head back and did not say anything while she tried to catch her breath. Meanwhile Khadija, Aisha, Umm Hanafi, and Kamal were weeping so loudly that they got on Fahmy's nerves. He scolded them till they stopped. Then he caught hold of Kamal to ask, "How did the accident come about? What did the people there do to the driver? Did they take you to the police station?" Without any hesitation Kamal answered his questions in full, giving most of the details.

The mother followed the conversation, despite her feeble condition. When the boy finished, she summoned all the strength she had and said, "I'm fine, Fahmy. Don't alarm yourself. They wanted me to go to the police station, but I refused. Then I came along as far as the end of the Goldsmiths Bazaar, where my strength suddenly gave out. Don't be upset. I'll get my strength back with a little rest."

In addition to his alarm over the accident Yasin was extremely upset, since he was responsible for suggesting what they would later term the ill-omened excursion. He said they should get a doctor. Without waiting to hear what anyone else thought of his idea, he left the room to carry it out. The mother shuddered at the mention of the doctor just as she had earlier at the reference to the police station. She asked Fahmy to catch his brother and dissuade him from going. She asserted that she would recover without any need for a doctor, but her son refused to give in to her request. He explained to her the need for one.

Meanwhile the two girls assisted each other in removing the wrap. Umm Hanafi brought a glass of water. Then they all crowded around her, anxiously examining her pale face and asking over and over how she felt. So far as she was able, she pretended to be calm. When the pain got bad, the most she said was: "There's a slight pain in my right shoulder." Then she added, "But there's no need for a doctor." The truth was that she did not like the idea of sending for a doctor. She had never had a doctor before, not merely because her health had been good but also because she had always succeeded in treating whatever ailed her with her own special medicine. She did not believe in modern medicine and associated it with major catastrophes and serious events. Furthermore, she felt that summoning a doctor would have the effect of highlighting a matter she wanted to hush up and conceal before her husband returned. She did her best to explain her fears to her children, but at that delicate moment they were only concerned about her well-being.

Yasin was not gone more than a quarter of an hour, since the doctor's clinic was in Bayt al-Qadi Square. He returned ahead of the doctor, whom he took to his mother the moment he arrived. They emptied the room of everyone except Yasin and Fahmy. The doctor asked the mother where she hurt and she pointed to her right shoulder. Her throat was dry with fear, but she swallowed and said, "I feel pain here."

Guided by what she said and what Yasin had told him before in general terms, he set about examining her. The examination seemed to take a long time, both to the young men waiting inside and to the women with throbbing hearts who were listening from the other side of the door. The doctor turned from his patient to Yasin and said, "There's a fracture of the right collarbone. That's all there is to it."

The word "fracture" caused dismay both inside and outside the room. They were all astonished that he had said, "That's all there is to it." It sounded as though there was something about a fracture that made it bearable. All the same, they found the phrase and the tone in which it was delivered reassuring. Torn between fear and hope, Fahmy asked, "Is that serious?"

"Not at all. I'll move the bone back where it belongs and fix it there, but she'll have to sleep a few nights sitting up with her back supported by a pillow. It'll be hard for her to sleep on her back or side. The fracture will set within two or three weeks at the most. There's no cause for alarm at all. . . . Now let me get to work."

They all breathed a sigh of relief after having been worried sick, especially those outside the door. Khadija murmured, "May the blessing of our master al-Husayn rest with her. The only reason she went out was to visit him."

Kamal asked in astonishment, as though her words had reminded him of something important he had forgotten for too long, "How could this accident happen after she was blessed with a visit to our master al-Husayn?"

Umm Hanafi replied with great simplicity, "Who knows what might have befallen her, we take refuge in God, had she not been blessed by visiting her master and ours?"

Aisha had not recovered from the shock. All the talk was getting on her nerves. She cried out fervently, "Oh, my Lord, when will everything be over, as though it had never happened?"

With sorrow and regret Khadija spoke again: "What was she doing in al-Ghuriya? If she had returned home directly, immediately after the visit, nothing would have happened to her."

Kamal's heart pounded with fear and alarm. In his eyes his offense appeared an abominable crime. Even so, he tried to evade their suspicions. In a disapproving tone he said, "She wanted to walk along the road and I tried in vain to talk her out of it."

Khadija gave him an accusing look. She started to reply, but she stopped out of sympathy and concern for his pale face. She told herself, "We've got enough troubles for the time being."

The door opened and the doctor left the room. He told the two young men, who followed him, "I'll have to see her every day until the fracture sets, but as I told you, there's absolutely no cause for alarm."

They all rushed into the room. They saw their mother sitting on the bed with her back supported by a pillow folded behind her. The only difference was a bulge in her dress over her right shoulder that betrayed the existence of a bandage beneath it. They rushed over to her and called out, "Praise to God."

When the doctor had been treating her fracture, the pain had been intense. She had moaned continually. Had it not been for her natural reserve, she would have screamed aloud. The pain was gone now, or so it appeared. She felt relatively comfortable and peaceful. The diminution of her sharp pain, though, allowed her mind to resume its energetic activity and she was able to think about the situation from different points of view. She was soon consumed by fear. With her eyes wandering back and forth between them she asked, "What can I say to your father when he returns?"

This question, like a protruding boulder blocking the safe passage of a ship, mockingly challenged the wisps of reassurance they had grasped. It did not take their minds by surprise. It had perhaps insinuated itself into the crowd of painful emotions their hearts had harbored since they were first confronted by the news, but it had been lost sight of in the confusion. Consideration of it had been postponed for a time. Now it had returned to occupy the place of honor in their souls. They found no alternative to confronting it. They considered it to be more threatening to them and their mother than the fracture from which she would soon recover. When her question was greeted by silence, the mother felt isolated, like a guilty person whose comrades desert him when an accusation is lodged against him. She complained softly, "He'll certainly learn about the accident. Moreover, he'll discover I went outside, because that's what led up to it."

Although Umm Hanafi was no less worried than the family members and understood the seriousness of the situation just as well as the others, she still wanted to say something reassuring to lighten the atmosphere. She also felt it her duty as a longtime and devoted servant of the family not to keep quiet when calamity struck. She was afraid they might think she did not care. Even though she was well aware that her words were remote from reality, she observed, "When my master learns what happened to you, he'll have to overlook your mistake and praise God for your safe recovery."

Her comment was received with the neglect it deserved from people who could see the reality of the situation quite clearly. All the same, Kamal believed it. As though completing Umm Hanafi's statement, Kamal said enthusiastically, "Especially if we tell him we only went out to visit our master al-Husayn."

The woman looked back and forth from Yasin to Fahmy with her half-closed eyes, and asked, "What can I say to him?"

Yasin, who was overwhelmed by the weight of his responsibility, said, "What demon led me astray so that I advised you to go out? A word slipped from my tongue. I wish it never had. But the fates wanted to cast us into this painful predicament. Even so, I assure you that we'll think of something to tell him. In any case, you shouldn't trouble your mind about what might happen. Leave the matter to God. The pains and fears you've endured today are enough for you now."

Yasin spoke with intensity and affection. He was pouring out his indignation against himself and his affection for their mother. He was commiserating with her situation. Although his words did not help or hinder anything, they provided some relief for his oppressive feeling of anguish. At the same time he was probably expressing what was going through the minds of those standing there with him. He spared them from having to express it themselves.

He had learned from experience that sometimes the best way to defend one's actions is to attack them. A confession of guilt would promote goodwill as much as an attempt to defend himself would have aroused anger. What he had most to fear was that Khadija would seize this golden opportunity to attack him openly about his responsibility for the consequences of his advice. She could use it to assail him. He had anticipated her plan and pulled the rug out from under her.

He was right about his hunch, for Khadija was just about to demand that he, as the person with primary responsibility for what had happened, should find them some solution. After he had made his little speech, she was ashamed to attack him, especially since she did not usually assail him in anger but only when they were bickering. Thus Yasin's situation was slightly improved, but the overall situation remained bad. Nothing improved it, until Khadija volunteered, "Why don't we claim she fell on the stairs?"

Her mother looked at her with a face that yearned for salvation by any means. She looked at Fahmy and Yasin too. There was a glimmer of hope showing in her eyes. All the same, Fahmy asked anxiously, "What about the doctor? He'll be checking on her day after day. Father will certainly bump into him."

Yasin refused to close the door through which a breath of hope had slipped to hint he might be rescued from his pains and fears. He said, "We can reach an agreement with the doctor about what Father should be told."

They looked back and forth at each other, trying to decide whether to accept or reject this idea. Then the gloomy atmosphere became festive, and a mutual feeling of salvation was evident in their faces. It was like a blue streak appearing unexpectedly in the middle of dark clouds. By an amazing miracle, the blue streak spread in just a few minutes until it covered the entire celestial dome and the sun came out.

Yasin said, "We've been saved, praise God."

After Khadija recovered her normal vivacity in the new climate, she told Yasin, "No, you've been saved. You're the one who thought it all up."

Yasin laughed until his huge body shook. He replied, "Yes, I've been saved from the scorpion sting of your tongue. I've been expecting it would reach out and bite me."

"But it's my tongue that saved you. For the sake of the rose, the thorns get watered."

In their happiness at being saved they had almost forgotten that their mother was confined to bed with a broken collarbone, but she herself had almost forgotten it too.

29

She opened her eyes and found Khadija and Aisha sitting on the bed by her feet. They were gazing at her with expressions wavering between hope and fear. She sighed and turned toward the window. She saw bright daylight streaming through the gaps in the shutters. She murmured in disbelief, "I slept a long time."

Then Aisha said, "Just a few hours. It was dawn before you closed your eyelids. What a night! I'll never forget it, no matter how long I live."

The mother was visited once again by memories of the past night dominated by sleeplessness and pain. Her eyes expressed her sorrow for herself and the two girls who had sat up with her all night, sharing her pain and insomnia. She moved her lips as she inaudibly sought God's protection. Then she whispered, almost in embarrassment, "I've really worn you out. . . ."

In a playful tone Khadija answered, "Wearing ourselves out for you is relaxing, but you had better not scare us again." Then she continued in a voice that showed emotion was getting the better of her: "How could that dreadful pain pick on you? . . . I'd think you were sound asleep and in good shape and lie down to get some sleep myself, only to wake up hearing you moan. You kept going 'Oh . . . oh' till dawn."

Aisha's face shone with optimism as she said, "In any case, here's good news. This morning I told Fahmy how you were doing when he asked about your health. He told me the pain troubling you was a sign the broken bone was starting to mend."

Fahmy's name brought Amina back from the depths of her thoughts. She asked, "Did they all get off safely?"

Khadija replied, "Of course. They wanted to speak to you and reassure themselves about you, but I wouldn't let anyone wake you after we'd gotten white hair waiting for you to doze off."

Their mother sighed with resignation, "Praise to God in any case. May our Lord make everything turn out for the best. . . . What time is it now?"

Khadija said, "It's an hour till the noon call to prayer."

The lateness of the hour prompted her to lower her eyes thoughtfully. When she raised them again, her anxiety was reflected in her look. She murmured, "He may be on his way home now. . . ."

They understood what she meant. Although they could feel fear creeping through their hearts, Aisha said confidently, "He's most welcome. There's no reason to be anxious. We've agreed on what has to bc said, and that ends the matter."

All the same, his impending arrival spread anxiety through Amina's feeble soul. She asked, "Do you think it will be possible to conceal what happened?"

In a voice that became noticeably sharper as her anxiety increased, Khadija answered, "Why not? We'll tell him what we agreed on, and the matter will pass peacefully."

Their mother wished that Yasin and Fahmy could have stayed by her side at that hour to give her courage. Khadija had said, "We'll tell him what we agreed on, and the matter will pass peacefully," but could what had happened remained a closed secret forever? Would the truth not find some opening through which it could reach the man? She feared lying just as much as she feared the truth. She did not know what destiny lay in wait for her. She looked affectionately at one girl and then the other. She had opened her mouth to speak when Umm Hanafi rushed in. She whispered, as though afraid someone outside the room might hear, "My master has come, my lady."

Their hearts beat wildly. The girls got off the bed in a single bound. They stood facing their mother. They all exchanged glances silently. Then the mother mumbled, "Don't you two say anything. I'm afraid of what might happen to you if you deceive him. Leave the talking to me, may God provide assistance."

A tense silence reigned like that of children in the dark who hear footsteps they think are those of jinn prowling around outside. Then they could hear al-Sayyid Ahmad's footsteps coming up the stairs. As they drew nearer, the mother struggled to break the nightmare silence. She mumbled, "Should we let him climb up to his room and not find anyone?"

She turned to Umm Hanafi and said, "Tell him I'm here, sick. Don't say anything more."

She swallowed to wet her dry throat. The two girls shot out of the room, each trying to escape first. They left her alone. Finding herself cut off from the entire world, she resigned herself to her destiny. Frequently this resignation on her part, since she was deprived of any weapon, seemed a passive kind of courage. She collected her thoughts in order to remember what she was supposed to say, although her doubt that she was doing the right thing never left her. It hid at the bottom of her emotions and announced its presence whenever she was anxious and tense or her confidence dwindled.

She heard the tip of his stick striking the floor of the sitting room. She mumbled, "Your mercy, Lord, and assistance."

Her eyes watched the doorway until he blocked it with his tall and broad body. She saw him come in and approach her. He gave her a searching look with his wide eyes. When he reached the center of the room he stopped and asked in a voice she imagined was more tender than usual, "What's the matter with you?"

Lowering her eyes, she said, "Praise to God for your safe return, sir. I'm well so long as you are."

"But Umm Hanafi told me you're sick. . . ."

With her left hand she pointed to her right shoulder and said, "My shoulder has been injured, sir. May God not expose you to any evil."

Examining her shoulder with concern and anxiety, the man asked, "What injured it?"

It was destined to happen. The crucial moment had arrived. She had only to speak, to utter the saving lie. Then the crisis would be safely concluded. She would receive even more than her share of sympathy. She raised her eyes in preparation for it. Then her eyes met his, or, more precisely, were consumed by his. Her heart beat faster, pounding mercilessly. At that moment all the ideas she had collected in her mind evaporated. The determination she had accumulated in her will was dispersed. Her eyes blinked from dismay and consternation. Then she gazed at him with a bewildered expression and said nothing.

Al-Sayyid Ahmad was amazed to see her confusion. He was quick to ask her, "What happened, Amina?"

She did not know what to say. She did not seem to have anything to say, but she was now certain she would not be able to lie. The opportunity had escaped without her knowing how. If she renewed the attempt, the words would come out in a disjointed and damning way. She was like a person who after having walked over a tightrope in a hypnotic trance is asked to repeat the trick in a conscious state. As the seconds passed she felt increasingly nervous and defeated. She was on the brink of despair.

"Why don't you speak?" His tone seemed to suggest he was growing impatient and would soon start shouting angrily. By God, she certainly needed some assistance. What demon had tempted her to go on that ill-omened excursion?

"Strange. Don't you want to speak?"

The silence then was more than she could bear. Driven by despair and defeat, she murmured in a shaking voice, "I have committed a grave error, sir. . . . I was struck by an automobile."

His eyes widened with astonishment. A look of alarm coupled with disbelief could be seen in them. It seemed he had begun to doubt her sanity. The woman could no longer bear to hesitate. She resolved to give a complete confession, no matter what the consequences. She was like a person who risks his life in a dangerous surgical operation to get relief from a painful disease he can no longer endure. Her feeling of the seriousness of her offense and the danger of her confession doubled. Tears welled up in her eyes. In a voice she did not attempt to keep free from sobs, either because she could not help it or because she wanted to make a desperate appeal to his sympathy, she said, "I thought I heard our master al-Husayn calling me to visit him. So I obeyed the call. . . . I went to visit his shrine. . . . On the way home an automobile ran into me. . . . It's God's decree, sir. I got up without anyone needing to help me." She spoke this last sentence very distinctly. Then she continued: "At first I didn't feel any pain. So I thought I was fine. I walked on until I reached the house. Here the pain started. They brought me a doctor, who examined my shoulder. He decided it was broken. He promised to return every day until the fracture is healed. I have committed a grave error, sir. I have been punished for it as I deserve. . . . God is forgiving and compassionate."

Al-Sayyid Ahmad listened to her without commenting or moving. He did not turn his eyes away from her. His face revealed nothing of his internal agitation. Meanwhile she bowed her head humbly like a defendant waiting for the verdict to be pronounced. The silence was prolonged and intense. The oppressive atmosphere was shot through with intimations of fearful threats. She was nervous about it and did not know what decree was being worked up or what fate would be allotted her.

Then she heard his strangely calm voice ask, "What did the doctor say? . . . How serious is the fracture?"

She turned her head toward him in bewilderment. She had been ready for anything except this gracious response. If the situation had not been so terrifying, she would have asked him to repeat it so she could be sure she had heard him correctly. She was overcome by emotion. Two large tears sprang from her eyes. She pressed her lips tightly together to keep from being choked up by weeping. Then she mumbled contritely and humbly, “The doctor said there’s absolutely no reason to worry. May God spare you any evil, sir.”

The man stood there for a time, struggling with his desire to ask more questions. He got control of himself and then turned to leave the room, saying, “Stay in bed till God heals you.”

30

Khadija and Aisha rushed into the room after their father left. They stopped in front of their mother and looked at her inquisitively. Their expression revealed their concern and anxiety. When they noticed that their mother's eyes were red from crying they were disturbed. Although her heart was fearful and pessimistic, Khadija asked, "Good news, God willing?"

Blinking her eyes nervously, the mother limited herself to replying tersely, "I confessed the truth to him."

"The truth!"

With resignation she said, "I wasn't able to do anything but confess. There was no way the affair could have been kept from him forever. I did the best thing."

Khadija thumped her chest with her hand and cried out, "What an unlucky day for us!"

Aisha was struck dumb. She stared at her mother's face without uttering a word. The mother smiled with a mixture of pride and embarrassment. Her pale face blushed when she remembered the affection he had showered on her when she had been expecting nothing but his overwhelming anger that would blow her and her future away. Yes, she felt both pride and embarrassment when she started to talk about their father's sympathy for her in her time of need and how he had forgotten his anger because of the affection and pity that had seized hold of him.

Then Amina murmured in a soft voice that was barely audible, "He was merciful to me, may God prolong his life. He listened silently to my story. Then he asked me what the doctor had said about the seriousness of the fracture and left. He directed me to stay in bed till God would take me by the hand."

The two girls exchanged astonished and incredulous glances. Then their fear quickly left them. They both sighed deeply with relief, and their faces became bright with joy. Khadija shouted, "Don't you see? It's the blessing of al-Husayn."

Her prediction having come true, Aisha commented proudly,

"Everything has its limits, even Papa's anger. There was no way he could be angry with her once he saw her in this state. Now we know how much she means to him." Then she teased her mother, "What a lucky mother you are! Congratulations to you for the honor and affection shown you."

The blush returned to the mother's face and she stammered modestly, "May God prolong his life...." She sighed and continued, "Praise to God for this salvation."

She remembered something and turned to Khadija. She told her with concern, "You've got to go to him. He'll certainly need your help."

The girl was nervous and uncomfortable in her father's presence. She felt she had fallen into a trap. She replied angrily, "Why can't Aisha go?"

Her mother said critically, "You're better able to serve him. Don't waste time, young lady. He may be needing you this very moment."

Khadija knew it would be pointless to protest, since it always was when her mother asked her to undertake a task for which she thought Khadija better suited than her sister. All the same, she was determined to voice her objection as she always did at such times, driven by her fiery temper as well as her aggressive nature that made her tongue its most willing and incisive weapon. She wanted to force her mother to say once more that she was more proficient at this or that than Aisha. That would be an admission from her mother, a warning to her sister, and a consolation for her.

The fact was that if one of these important tasks had been awarded to Aisha instead of her, she would have been even more furious and would have intervened. In her heart she still felt that performing these duties was one of her rights. They set her apart as a woman worthy of her status as second-in-command to her mother in the household. Yet she refused to acknowledge openly that she was exercising one of her rights when she undertook the task. It was, rather, a heavy burden that she accepted only under duress. Thus anyone summoning her to do something would feel uncomfortable about it. If she objected, she would be able to protest with an anger that would provide her some relief. She could make whatever commentary she wished about the situation. Finally, she would be reckoned to be doing the person a favor meriting his thanks.

Therefore as she left the room, she said, "In every crisis you call on Khadija, as though there was no one else at hand. What would you do if I weren't here?"

The moment she left, her pride abandoned her. Its place was taken by terror and agitation. How could she present herself to him? How would she go about serving him? How would he treat her if she stuttered or was slow or made a mistake?

Al-Sayyid Ahmad had removed his street clothes by himself and put on his house shirt. When she stood at the door to ask what he needed, he ordered her to make a cup of coffee. She hastened to fetch it. Then she presented it to him, walking softly with her eyes lowered, feeling shy and afraid. She retreated to the sitting room just outside his door to wait there for any signal from him. Her sense of terror never left her. She wondered how she would be able to continue serving him through all the hours he spent at home, day after day, until the three weeks were over. The matter seemed nerve-racking to her. She perceived for the first time the importance of the niche her mother filled in the household. She prayed for her speedy recovery out of both love for her mother and pity for herself.

Unluckily for her, al-Sayyid Ahmad was of a mind to rest up after the fatigue of his journey and did not go to the store as she hoped. Accordingly, she was obliged to remain in the sitting room like a prisoner. Aisha came up to the top floor and crept silently into the room where her sister was sitting. She came to parade herself before Khadija. She winked at her to ridicule her situation. Then she returned to her mother, leaving her sister boiling with rage. The thing that infuriated Khadija most was for someone to tease her, even though she happily teased everyone else. Khadija regained her freedom, and then just provisionally, only when her father fell asleep. Then she flew to her mother and began to tell her about all the real and imaginary services she had rendered her father. She described to her the signs of affection and appreciation for her services that she had noticed in his eyes. She did not forget to turn on Aisha and rain abuse and reprimands on her for her childish conduct.

She went back to her father when he woke up and served him lunch. After the man finished eating, he sat reading over some papers for a long time. Then he summoned her and asked her to send Yasin and Fahmy to him the moment they got home.

The mother was upset about his request. She was afraid that the man's soul had some concealed anger trapped inside and that he now wished to find a target for his anger—namely, the two young men.

When Yasin and Fahmy came home and learned what had happened and that their father had ordered them to appear before him, their minds entertained the same thought. They went to his room with fearful forebodings, but the man surprised them by greeting them more calmly than usual. He asked them about the accident, the circumstances surrounding it, and the doctor's report. They recounted at length what they knew while he listened with interest. Finally he asked, "Were you at home when she went out?"

Although they had expected this question from the outset, when it came after this unexpected and unusual calm, it alarmed them. They feared it was a prelude to change from the harmony they had enjoyed with relief, thinking they were safe. They were unable to speak and chose to remain silent. All the same, al-Sayyid Ahmad did not insist on his question. He seemed to attach little importance to hearing the answer he had guessed in advance. Perhaps he wanted to point out their error, without caring whether they confessed. After that he did nothing but show them the door, allowing them to depart. As they were walking out, they heard him say to himself, "Since God has not provided me with any sons, let Him grant me patience."

Although the incident appeared to have shaken al-Sayyid Ahmad enough that he was altering his conduct to an extent that amazed everyone, it could not dissuade him from enjoying his traditional nightly outing. When evening came he dressed and left his room, diffusing a fragrance of perfume. On his way out he passed by his wife's room to inquire about her. She prayed for him at length, gratefully and thankfully. She did not see anything rude in his going out when she was confined to bed. She may have felt that for him to stop to see her and ask after her was more recognition than she had expected. Indeed, if he refrained from pouring out his anger on her. was that not a boon she had not even dreamt of?

Before their father had left his room, the brothers had asked, "Do you suppose he'll forsake his evening's entertainment tonight?"

The mother had replied, "Why should he stay home when he's learned there's nothing to be worried about?" Privately she might have wished he would complete his kind treatment of her by renouncing his night out, as was appropriate for a husband whose wife had suffered what she had. Since she knew his temperament well, though, she fabricated an excuse for him in advance, so that if he did rush off to his party, as she expected, she could put a pleasant face on her situation. She would justify his departure with the excuse she had already invented and not let it seem to be caused by his indifference.

All the same, Khadija had asked, "How can he bear to be at a party when he sees you in this condition?"

Yasin had answered, "There's nothing wrong with his doing that once he's satisfied himself that she's all right. Men and women don't react to sorrow the same way. There's no contradiction between a man going out to a party and feeling sad. It may actually be his way of consoling himself so he'll be able to carry on with his difficult life." Yasin was not defending his father so much as his own desire to step out that was beginning to stir deep inside him.

His cunning did not work on Khadija. She asked him, "Could you stand spending the evening in your coffee shop?"

Although he cursed her secretly, he quickly replied, "Of course not. But I'm one thing and Papa's something else."

When al-Sayyid Ahmad left the room, Amina felt again the relief that follows a rescue from genuine danger. Her face lit up with a smile. She observed, "Perhaps he thought I'd already been punished enough for my offense. So he forgave me. May God forgive him and all of us."

Yasin struck his hands together and objected, "There are men as jealous as he is, some of them friends of his, who see no harm in permitting their women to go out when it's necessary or appropriate. What can he be thinking of to keep you imprisoned in the house all the time?"

Khadija glanced at him scornfully and asked, "Why didn't you deliver this appeal for us when you were with him?"

The young man began laughing so hard his belly shook. He replied, "Before I can do that I need a nose like yours to defend myself with."

Her days in bed passed without a recurrence of the pain that had devastated her the first night, although the slightest movement would make her shoulder and torso hurt. She convalesced quickly because of her sturdy constitution and superabundant vitality. She had a natural dislike of being still and sitting around and that made obedience to the doctor's orders a difficult ordeal. The torment it caused her overshadowed the pains of the fracture at their worst. Perhaps she would have violated the doctor's commands and gotten up prematurely to look after things if her children had not watched her so relentlessly.

Yet her confinement did not prevent her from supervising household affairs from her bed. She would review everything assigned to the girls with a tiresome precision, especially the details of tasks she was afraid they might neglect or forget. She would ask persistently, "Did you dust the tops of the curtains? . . . The shutters? . . . Did you burn incense in the bathroom for your father? . . . Have you watered the hyacinth beans and jasmine?"

Khadija got annoyed by this once and told her, "Listen, if you took care of the house one carat, I'm taking care of it twenty-four."

In addition to all this, her compulsory abandonment of her important position brought with it some ambivalent feelings that troubled her a great deal. She asked herself whether it was true that the house and its inhabitants had not lost anything, in terms of either order or comfort, by her relinquishing her post. Which of the two alternatives would be preferable: for everything to remain just the way it ought to be, thanks to her two girls who had been nurtured by her hands, or that there should be sufficient disturbance of the household's equilibrium to remind everyone of the void she had left behind her? What if it was al-Sayyid Ahmad himself who sensed this void? Would that be a reason for him to appreciate her importance or a reason to become angry at her offense that had caused all this? The woman wavered for a long time between her abashed fondness for herself and her open affection for her daughters. It became clear that any shortcoming in the management of the house disturbed her immensely. On the other hand, if it had retained its perfection as though nothing had happened, she would not have been totally at ease.

In fact, no one did fill her place. Despite the earnest and energetic activity of the two girls, the house showed evidence of being too large for them. The mother was not happy about that, but she kept her feelings to herself. She defended Khadija and Aisha sincerely and vehemently. Even so, she suffered from alarm and pain and could not endure her seclusion patiently.

31

At dawn on the promised day, the day for which she had waited so long, she hopped out of bed with a youthful nimbleness derived from her joy. She felt like a king reclaiming his throne after being exiled. She went down to the oven room to resume her routine that had been interrupted for three weeks. She called Umm Hanafi. The woman woke up and could not believe her ears. She rose to greet her mistress, embracing her and praying for her. Then they set about the morning's work with an indescribable happiness.

When the first rays of the rising sun could be seen, she went upstairs. The children greeted her with congratulations and kisses. Then she went over to where Kamal was sleeping and woke him. The moment the boy opened his eyes he was overcome by astonishment and joy. He clung to her neck, but she was quick to free herself gently from his arms. She asked him, "Aren't you afraid my shoulder will get hurt again?"

He smothered her with kisses. Then he laughed and asked mischievously, "Darling, when can we go out together again?"

She replied in a tone that had a ring of friendly criticism, "When God has guided you enough so you don't lead me against my will to a street where I almost perish."

He understood she was referring to his stubbornness that had been the immediate cause of what befell her. He laughed until he could laugh no more. He laughed like a sinner who has been reprieved after having his offense hang over his head for three weeks. Yes, he had been terribly afraid that the investigation his brothers were conducting would reveal the secret culprit. The suspicions entertained by Khadija at one time and Yasin at another had come close to uncovering him in his redoubt. He had been spared only because his mother had defended him firmly and had resolved to bear responsibility for the accident all by herself. When the investigation had been transferred to his father, Kamal's fears had reached their climax. He had expected from one moment to the next to be summoned before his father. In addition to this fear, he had been tormented during the past three weeks by seeing his beloved mother confined to bed, suffering bitterly, unable either to lie down or to stand up. Now the accident was past history. Gone with it was its bad taste. The investigation was terminated. Once again his mother had come to wake him in the morning. She would put him to bed at night. Everything had returned to normal. Peace had unfurled its banners. He had a right to laugh his heart out and congratulate his conscience on its reprieve.

The mother left the boys' room to go to the top floor. When she approached the door of al-Sayyid Ahmad's room she could hear him saying in his prayers, "Glory to my Lord, the Magnificent." Her heart pounded and she stood hesitating, a step away from the door. She found herself wondering whether to go in to wish him good morning or prepare the breakfast tray first. She was less interested in the actual question than in fleeing from the fear and shame rampant in her soul, or perhaps she was interested in both. At times a person may create an imaginary problem to escape from an actual problem he finds difficult to resolve.

She went to the dining room and set to work with redoubled care. Even so, her anxiety increased. The period of delay she had granted herself was worthless. She did not find the relief she had hoped for. The ordeal of waiting was more painful than the situation she had shrunk from confronting. She was amazed that she had been scared to enter her own room, as though she were preparing to enter it for the first time. All the more so because al-Sayyid Ahmad had continued to visit her, day after day, during her convalescence. The fact was that her recovery had removed the protection afforded her by ill health. She sensed that she would be meeting him without anything to hide behind for the first time since her error had been disclosed.

When the boys arrived for breakfast one after the other, she felt a little less desolate. Their father soon entered the room in his flowing gown. His face revealed no emotion on seeing her. He asked calmly as he headed for his place at the table, "You've come?" Then, taking his seat, he told his sons, "Sit down."

They began to consume their breakfast while she stood in her customary place. Her fear had peaked when he came in, but she started to catch her breath after that. The first encounter after her recovery had taken place and passed peacefully. She sensed that she would find no problem in being alone with him shortly in his room.

The breakfast ended, al-Sayyid Ahmad returned to his room. She joined him a few minutes later carrying a tray with coffee. She placed it on the low table and stepped aside to wait until he had finished.

Then she would help him get dressed. Her husband drank the coffee in profound silence, not the silence that comes naturally either as a rest, when people are tired, or as a cloak for someone with nothing to say. It was a deliberate silence. She had not given up her hope, however faint, that he was fond enough of her to grant her a kind word or at least discuss the subjects he usually did at this hour of the morning. His deliberate silence unsettled her. She began asking herself again whether he still harbored some anger. Anxiety was pricking her heart once more. Yet the heavy silence did not last long.

The man was thinking with such speed and concentration that he had no taste for anything else. It was not the kind of thought that arises on the spur of the moment. It was a type of stubborn, long-lasting thought that had stayed with him throughout the past days. Finally, without raising his head from his empty coffee cup, he asked, "Have you recovered?"

Amina replied in a subdued voice, "Yes, sir, praise God."

The man resumed speaking and said bitterly, "I'm amazed, and never cease to be amazed, that you did what you did."

Her heart pounded violently, and she bowed her head dejectedly. She could not bear his anger when defending a mistake someone else had made. What could she do now that she was the guilty person? . . . Fear froze her tongue, although he was waiting for an answer.

He continued his comments by asking her disapprovingly, "Have I been mistaken about you all these years and not known it?"

At that she held out her hands in alarm and pain. She whispered in troubled gasps, "I take refuge with God, sir. My error was really a big one, but I don't deserve talk like this."

Nevertheless, the man continued to talk with his terrifying calm, compared to which screaming would have been easy to bear. He said, "How could you have committed such a grave error? . . . Was it because I left town for a single day?"

In a trembling voice, its tones swayed by the convulsions of her body, she replied, "I have committed an error, sir. It is up to you to forgive me. My soul yearned to visit our master al-Husayn. I thought that for such a blessed pilgrimage it was possible for me to go out just once."

He shook his head fiercely as though saying, "There's no point trying to argue." Then he raised his eyes to give her an angry, sullen look. In a voice that made it clear he would tolerate no discussion, he said, "I just have one thing to say: Leave my house immediately."

His command fell on her head like a fatal blow. She was

dumbfounded and did not utter a word. She could not move. During the worst moments of her ordeal, when she was waiting for him to return from his trip to Port Said, she had entertained many kinds of fears: that he might pour out his anger on her and deafen her with his shouts and curses. She had not even ruled out physical violence, but the idea of being evicted had never troubled her. She had lived with him for twenty-five years and could not imagine that anything could separate them or pluck her from this house of which she had become an inseparable part.

With this final statement, al-Sayyid Ahmad freed himself from the burden of a thought that had dominated his brain during the past three weeks. His mental struggle had begun the moment the woman tearfully confessed her offense when confined to her bed. At the first instant he had not believed his ears. As he started to recover from the shock, he had become aware of the loathsome truth that was an affront to his pride and dignity but had postponed his wrath when he saw her condition. In fact, it would be correct to say that he was unable to reflect then on the challenge to his pride and dignity because of his deep anxiety for this woman, verging on fear and alarm. He had grown used to her and admired her good qualities. He was even fond enough of her to forget her error and ask God to keep her safe. Confronted by this imminent threat to her, his tyranny had shrunk back. The abundant tenderness lying dormant within his soul had been awakened. He had gone back to his room that day sad and dispirited, although his face had remained expressionless.

When he saw her make rapid and steady progress toward recovery, his composure returned. Consequently he began to review the whole incident, along with its cause and results, with a new eye, or, more accurately, the old one he was accustomed to using at home. It was unfortunate, unfortunate for his wife, that he reviewed the matter when he was calm and all alone. He convinced himself that if he forgave her and yielded to the appeal of affection, which he longed to do, then his prestige, honor, personal standards, and set of values would all be compromised. He would lose control of his family, and the bonds holding it together would dissolve. He could not lead them unless he did so with firmness and rigor. In short, if he forgave her, he would no longer be Ahmad Abd al-Jawad but some other person he could never agree to become.

Yes, it was unfortunate that he reviewed the situation when he was calm and all alone. If he had been able to give vent to his anger when she confessed, his rage would have been satisfied. The accident would have passed without trailing behind it any serious consequences. The problem was that he had not been able to get angry at the suitable moment and his vanity would not let him announce his anger after she had recovered, when he had been calm for three weeks. That kind of anger would have been more like a premeditated reprimand. When his anger flared up, normally it was because of a combination of premeditation and natural emotion. Since the latter element had not found an outlet at the appropriate time, premeditation, which had been provided with plenty of quiet time to review its options, was left to discover an effective method of expressing itself in a form corresponding to the seriousness of the offense. Thus the danger that threatened her life for a time, which protected her from his anger by stirring up his affection, turned into a cause of far-reaching punishment, because the scheming side of his anger had been given so much time to plan and think.

He rose with a frown and turned his back on her. He reached for his garments on the sofa and said, "I'll put my clothes on myself."

She had stayed put, oblivious to everything. His voice roused her. She quickly grasped from his words and stance that he was ordering her to leave. She headed for the door, making no sound as she walked.

Before she got through it she heard him say, "I don't want to find you here when I come back this noon."

32

Her strength gave out in the sitting room, and she threw herself down on the edge of the sofa. His harsh, decisive words were bouncing around inside her. The man was not joking. When had he ever told a joke? Much as she wanted to flee, she could not leave immediately. If she left before him that would be contrary to the normal routine and arouse the boys' suspicions. She did not want them to begin their day and go off to their jobs digesting the news of her being thrown out of the house. There was another sentiment at work as well, possibly embarrassment, that kept her from wishing to see them when she was in the humiliating status of a discarded wife. She decided to stay where she was until he had left. Better still, she would take refuge in the dining room so he would not see her on his way out. With a broken heart she slipped into that room and, gravely and despondently, sat down on a pallet.

What did he really mean? Was he evicting her temporarily or forever? She did not believe he intended to divorce her. He was more noble and generous than that. Yes, he was irascible and tyrannical, but only extreme pessimism could hide from her his gallantry, chivalry, and mercy. Could she forget how sympathetic he had been when she was confined to bed? He had visited her day after day to inquire about her health. A man like that would not lightly destroy a house, break a heart, or wrest a mother from her children.

She began pondering these ideas as though trying to restore some composure to her shaken soul. She persisted at this task, but her persistence only revealed the fact that composure refused to settle in her soul. Similarly, the weaker some invalids feel, the more they boast of their strength. She did not know what to do with her life or what meaning life would have if her hopes were dashed and the worst did happen.

She heard his stick tapping on the floor of the sitting room as he made his exit. She lost her train of thought and listened intently to the succession of taps, until he had departed. At that moment she felt the enormous pain of her situation and was furious at the iron will that had made no allowance for her weakness.

She rose feebly and left the room to go down to the first floor. At the head of the stairs she could make out the voices of the boys as they descended one after the other. She stretched her head out over the railing and caught sight of Fahmy and Kamal. They were trailing after Yasin on their way to the door that led to the courtyard. Affection rushed through her heart and overwhelmed it. She was amazed at herself. How could she let them go without saying goodbye? She would not be able to see them again for days or even weeks. Perhaps for the remainder of her life, she would see them only infrequently, as though they were strangers. She stood where she was on the stairs, without budging, while affection surged through her heart. Although her heart was filled with emotion, she could not accept the painful thought that this gloomy fate was her destiny. She had a limitless belief in God, who had protected her in the past when she was alone with the jinn. Her trust in her husband also continued undimmed. No evil had yet afflicted her that was serious enough to deprive her quiet life of its confident trust. For all these reasons, she was inclined to consider her ordeal a harsh trial through which she would pass unscathed.

She found Khadija and Aisha embroiled in a quarrel as usual, but they abandoned it when they noticed her sorrow and the dead look of her eyes. They feared, perhaps, that she had left her bed before fully recovering her health. Khadija asked anxiously, "What's the matter, Mother?"

"By God, I don't know what to say. I'm going."

Although the last phrase emerged in a terse and impromptu fashion, it acquired a gloomy meaning from her despairing look and plaintive tone. Both girls were frightened by it and cried out together, "Where?"

She had been apprehensive beforehand about the effect her words would have on them and even on herself. Now she said brokenly, "To my mother."

They rushed to her in alarm and said at the same time, "What are you saying? . . . Don't say that again. . . . What happened?"

She found some consolation in her daughters' dismay, but—as often happens in such circumstances—that only caused her sorrows to burst forth even more. Struggling with her tears, she said in a trembling voice, "He hasn't forgotten anything and hasn't forgiven anything." She said this with an anguish that revealed the depth of her sorrow. She continued: "He was angry with me and postponed doing something about it till I recovered. Then he told me, 'Leave my house immediately.' He also said, 'I don't want to find you here when I come back this noon.'" Then she remarked in a voice that betrayed both disappointment and melancholy censure, "Hear and obey . . . hear and obey."

Khadija, in a state of nervous agitation, yelled at her, "I don't believe it. I don't believe it. Say something else. . . . What's happened to the world?"

Aisha shouted in a broken voice, "This will never do! Does our happiness mean so little to him?"

Khadija asked again, angrily and sharply, "What's he got in mind? . . . What does he plan to do, Mother?"

"I don't know. That's exactly what he said, with no additions or deletions."

At first this was all she would say, perhaps because she wished to increase their sympathy and gather some consolation from their dismay. Then her pity for them and her desire to reassure herself got the better of her and she went on: "I suspect that all he plans to do is separate me from you for a few days to punish me for my misadventure."

"Wasn't what happened to you enough for him?"

The mother sighed sadly and murmured, "The matter's in God's hands. . . . Now I must go."

Khadija blocked her way. She said in a voice choked by sobs, "We won't let you go. Don't leave your home. I don't think he'll persist in his anger if he returns and finds you with us."

Aisha implored her, "Wait till Fahmy and Yasin get back. Father will think twice about tearing you away from all of us."

In rebuttal, their mother admonished them: "It's never wise to challenge his anger. A man like him becomes softer when people obey him and fiercer if people rebel."

They tried to protest once more, but she silenced them with a motion of her hand and observed, "There's no point in talking. I've got to go. I'll gather my clothes and set off. Don't be alarmed. We won't be separated long. We'll be reunited again, God willing."

The woman went to her room on the second floor with the two girls at her heels. They were crying like babies. She started to remove her clothes from the armoire, but Khadija seized her hand and asked her passionately, "What are you doing?"

The mother felt that her tears were about to get the best of her. She refrained from speaking for fear her voice would give her away or she would start weeping. She was determined not to cry when her daughters could see her. She gestured with her hand as if to say, "Circumstances require me to get my clothes together."

Khadija said sharply, "You're only going to take one change of clothing with you . . . just one."

A sigh escaped from her. At that moment she wished the whole affair was a frightening dream. Then she said, "I'm afraid he'll be furious if he sees my clothing in the usual place."

"We'll keep it in our room."

Aisha collected her mother's clothes, except for a single outfit, as her sister had suggested. Their mother yielded to them with deep relief. It seemed to her that so long as her clothes remained in the house she retained her right to return there. She got out a bag and stuffed in it the clothing she was permitted to take. She sat down on the sofa to put on her stockings and shoes. Her daughters stood facing her. They looked at her with sad, bewildered eyes. Her heart melted at the sight and, pretending to be calm, she said, "Everything will return to normal. Be brave, so you don't make him angry at you. I entrust the house and family to you with full confidence in your abilities. Khadija, I'm certain you'll find Aisha helpful to you in every way. Do what we used to do together just as though I were with you. Each of you is a young woman fully prepared to found and nurture a home."

She rose to get a cloth to wrap around herself. Then she lowered a white veil over her face with deliberate slowness to delay the painful, frightening final moment as long as she could. They all stood facing each other, not knowing what would come next. Her voice refused to say goodbye. Neither of the girls had the courage to fling herself into her mother's arms as she wished. Seconds ticked by, made heavy by suffering and anxiety. Finally, the woman, who had steeled herself, feared her resolve would desert her. She moved a step closer and bent toward them to kiss them, one after the other. She whispered, "Never lose heart. Our Lord is with all of us."

At that they clung to her. They were sobbing too hard to speak.

The mother left the house, her eyes filled with tears, and the street seemed to dissolve as she looked at it through them.

33

As she knocked on the door of the old house she was thinking with painful embarrassment about the alarm and distress her arrival as a chastised wife would cause. The door was located on a dead-end alley that branched off from al-Khurunfush Street. At the end of the alley there was a little mosque of a Sufi religious order where prayers had been said for a long period before the building was finally abandoned because of its age. The crumbling ruins were left to remind her, each time she visited her mother, of her childhood, when she would wait by the door for her father to finish his prayers and come to her. She would poke her head inside while people were praying. She found it diverting to watch the men bow and prostrate themselves on the floor. At times she would observe members of various mystical Sufi orders who met in the alley next to the mosque. They would light some lamps, spread mats on the ground, and attempt to establish contact with God by chanting His name while swaying back and forth.

When the door was opened, the head of a black servant in her fifties peeked out. The moment she saw who it was, her face shone and she called out to welcome the visitor. She stepped aside to make room for her, and Amina entered. The servant waited there as though expecting a second person. Amina understood what her stance implied. She whispered in a vexed tone, "Close the door, Sadiqa."

"Didn't al-Sayyid Ahmad come with you?"

She shook her head and pretended to ignore the servant's astonishment. She crossed the courtyard, with the oven room in the center and a well in the left corner, and went to the narrow stairway to climb to the first and final floor. Then she passed through the vestibule into her mother's room. When she entered, she saw her mother seated cross-legged on a sofa at the front of the small chamber. She was grasping with both hands a long string of prayer beads that dangled down to her lap, and her eyes were directed inquisitively at the door. She had no doubt heard someone knock and footsteps approach. When Amina drew near, her mother asked, "Who is it?"

As she spoke, her lips parted in a gentle smile of happiness and welcome as though she had guessed the identity of the visitor. Amina answered her, in a voice made soft by her depression and sorrow, "It's me, Mother."

The elderly woman stretched her legs out. Her feet searched the floor for her slippers. When they were located, she shoved her feet in. She stood up and spread out her arms eagerly. Amina threw her bag on the edge of the sofa and wrapped herself in her mother's arms. She kissed her mother on the forehead and both cheeks, while the other woman planted a kiss wherever her lips landed, on her daughter's head, cheek, and neck. When they finished embracing, the old lady patted her on the back affectionately and stayed where she was, facing the door. The smile on her lips announced a welcome for someone else as she made the assumption Sadiqa had before. Once again, Amina understood what was implied by her posture. With vexed resignation she said, "I came by myself, Mother...."

Her mother turned her head toward her curiously and muttered, "By yourself?" Then, affecting a smile to ward off the anxiety that afflicted her, she added, "Glory to God, who never changes."

She retreated to the sofa and sat down. With a voice that revealed her anxiety this time, she asked, "How are you?... Why didn't he come with you as usual?"

Amina sat down beside her. Like a pupil confessing how atrocious his answers were on an examination, she said, "He's angry at me, Mother...."

The mother blinked glumly. Then she muttered in a sad voice, "I take refuge in God from Satan, who deserves to be pelted with stones. My heart never deceives me. I was upset when you told me, 'I came by myself, Mother.' What do you suppose made him angry at a gracious angel like yourself whom no man before him was lucky enough to possess? ... Tell me, daughter."

With a sigh, Amina said, "I went to visit the shrine of our master al-Husayn during his trip to Port Said."

Her mother reflected sadly and dejectedly. Then she asked, "How did he learn about the visit?"

From the very beginning, Amina, out of compassion for the old lady and to make her own responsibility seem lighter, had been careful not to refer to the automobile accident. Thus she gave her an answer she had worked up in advance: "Perhaps someone saw me and told on me...."

The elderly woman said sharply, "There's not a human being who would know you except the people in the house with you. Isn't there someone you suspect? . . . That woman Umm Hanafi? Or his son by the other woman?"

Amina quickly intervened to say confidently, "Possibly a neighbor woman saw me and told her husband, without meaning any harm, and the man brought it to al-Sayyid Ahmad's attention, without understanding the dangerous consequences. Suspect anyone you like, but not a member of my household."

The old lady shook her head skeptically and observed, "Your whole life you've been too trusting. God alone can decipher and overcome the schemes of crafty people. But your husband? . . . An intelligent man going on fifty . . . can he find no other way to express his anger than by throwing out the companion of a lifetime and separating her from the children? . . . O Lord, glory to You. Most people get wiser as they get older, while we grow older and become foolhardy. Is it a sin for a virtuous woman to visit our master al-Husayn? Don't his friends, who are just as jealous and manly as he is, allow their wives to leave the house for various errands? . . . Your father himself, who was a religious scholar and knew the Book of God by heart, permitted me to go to neighbors' homes and watch the procession of pilgrims setting out for Mecca."

There was a long period of despondent silence until the old woman turned toward her daughter with a perplexed, critical smile. She asked, "What tempted you to disobey him after that long life of blind obedience? . . . This is what puzzles me the most. . . . No matter how fiery his temper, he's your husband. The safest thing to do is to be careful to obey him, for your own peace of mind and for the happiness of your children. Isn't that so, daughter? . . . I'm amazed because I've never found you needed anybody's advice before. . . ."

A smile appeared at the corners of Amina's mouth, suggesting a slight relaxation of her anxiety and embarrassment. She mumbled, "The devil made me do it."

"God's curse on him. Did the cursed one cause your feet to slip after twenty-five years of peace and harmony? . . . Well, he was the one who got our father Adam and our mother Eve expelled from paradise. . . . It makes me very sad, daughter, but it's just a summer cloud that will disperse. Everything will return to normal." She continued as though addressing herself: "What harm would it have done him to be more forbearing? But he's a man, and men will always have enough defects to blot out the sun." Then, pretending to be happy and welcoming, she told her daughter, "Take off your things and make yourself comfortable. Don't be alarmed. What harm will it do you to spend a short holiday with your mother in the room where you were born?"

Amina's eyes glanced inattentively at the old bed with its tarnished posts and at the shabby carpet, threadbare and frayed at the edges, even though the design of roses had retained its reds and greens. Her breast was too affected by separation from her loved ones to be receptive to a flood of distant memories. Her mother's invitation did not arouse the kind of nostalgia in her heart that memories of this room, of which she was so fond, ordinarily did. All she could do was sigh and confess, "The only thing bothering me is that I'm anxious about my children, Mother."

"They're in God's care. You won't be away from them long, if God the Compassionate and Merciful permits."

Amina rose to remove her wrap while Sadiqa, sad and mournful because of what she had heard, retreated from her post by the entrance to the room, where she had remained as they talked. Amina sat down again next to her mother. They discussed the matter inside and out, backward and forward.

The juxtaposition of the two women appeared to illustrate the interplay of the amazing laws of heredity and the inflexible law of time. The two women might have been a single person with her image reflected forward to the future or back into the past. In either case, the difference between the original and its reflection revealed the terrible struggle raging between the laws of heredity, attempting to keep things the same, and the law of time, pushing for change and a finale. The struggle usually results in a string of defeats for heredity, which plays at best a modest role within the framework of time. It was the law of time that had transformed Amina's elderly mother into a gaunt body with a withered face and blind eyes. There had also been internal changes hidden from the senses. All of the splendor of life that she retained was what is known as "the charm of old age"—that is, a calm manner, a somber new dignity, and a head adorned with white. Although she was descended from generations of people who had lived to a ripe old age and not given up without a fight, her protest against time, once she reached seventy-five, was limited to rising in the morning in exactly the same way she had for the past fifty years and groping her way to the bathroom without any assistance from the maid. There she would perform her ablutions before returning to her room to pray. The rest of the day she passed with her prayer beads, praising God and meditating in total privacy. The servant was usually busy with the housework, but when she was free to sit with her mistress, the old lady enjoyed conversing with her.

The lady's enthusiasm for work and zest for life had definitely not abandoned her. For example, she supervised every detail of the household budget, the cleaning and arranging. She took the servant to task if she spent too long on a job or was late returning from an errand. Not infrequently she made her swear on a copy of the Qur'an to assure herself of the veracity of the maid's accounts of scrubbing the bathroom, washing the pots and pans, and dusting the windows. Her meticulousness verged on paranoia. Her insistence on this may have been a continuation of a custom that became embedded in her when she was young or a flaw introduced by old age.

Her perseverance in staying on in her house in almost total isolation after the death of her spouse and her insistence on remaining there even after she lost her sight could also be attributed to this extremism of her character. She had turned a deaf ear to the repeated invitations of al-Sayyid Ahmad to move to his house, where she could be cared for by her daughter and grandchildren. In this way, she exposed herself to the accusation of being senile. Al-Sayyid Ahmad finally stopped inviting her. The truth was that she did not want to leave her house, because she was so attached to it and because she wished to avoid the unintentional neglect she might find in the new one. Her presence there might also impose new burdens on the shoulders of her daughter, who already had many weighty responsibilities. Nor was she eager to squeeze herself into a home headed by a man known to his family for his ferocity and anger. She might inadvertently fall victim to his comments and thus threaten her daughter's happiness. Finally, the sense of honor and pride she harbored deep inside herself caused her to prefer living in the house she owned, dependent only upon God and the pension left her by her late husband.

There were other reasons for her insistence on remaining in her house that could not be attributed to her sensitivity or common sense, like her fear that if she moved out of the house she would find herself forced to choose between two options. She would either have to allow strangers to live there, even though the house was what she treasured most dearly, after her daughter and grandchildren, or leave it deserted and let the jinn appropriate it as their playground, after it had been the home of a religious scholar who knew the Qur'an by heart—her husband. For her to move into al-Sayyid Ahmad's house would also create awkward problems that in her opinion had no easy solution. At that time she had brooded about it. Should she accept his hospitality and give nothing in return—and she certainly would not be comfortable with that—or surrender her pension to him in return for staying in his house? Giving him her pension would upset her instinctive need to own things, which, along with old age, became one of the primary elements of her general paranoia.

At times when he urged her to move to his house she even imagined that he had greedy designs on her pension and the house she would vacate. She chose to refuse him with blind obstinacy. When al-Sayyid Ahmad bowed to her will, she told him with relief, "Don't be offended by my stubbornness, son. May our Lord honor you for the affection you have shown me. You see, don't you, that I'm just not able to move out of my house? It's good of you to humor an old woman with her many shortcomings. All the same, I ask you to swear to God that you'll allow Amina and the children to visit me from time to time, now that it's difficult for me to leave the house."

Thus she had remained in her house as she wished, enjoying her mastery and freedom as well as many of the customs of her cherished past. Some of these, like her excessive concern with her house and her money, were hardly compatible with the serenity and tolerance of wise maturity. Therefore, they appeared to be accidental infirmities of old age. There was another practice she had retained that could adorn youth and lend majesty to maturity. It was worship, which continued to be the central interest of her life and the source of her hopes and happiness. She had absorbed religion as a young girl from her father, who was a religious scholar. It had become deeply ingrained in her through her marriage to another religious scholar, who was no less pious and God-fearing than her father. She had continued to worship with love and sincerity, although in her earnestness she did not discriminate between true religion and pure superstition. She was known to the women of the neighborhood as "the blessed shaykha."

Sadiqa, the maid, was the only person who knew both her good and bad sides. After a tiff had flared up between them, Sadiqa might say, "My lady, wouldn't worship be a better use of your time than quarreling and squabbling over trivial things?"

Her mistress would answer sharply, "Vile woman, you're not advising me to pray out of love for it. All you want is to be left free to mess around, neglect your duties, roll in filth, and loot and plunder. God commands us to be clean and honest. Keeping close track of you is both a form of worship and a reward."

Since religion played such an important role in her life, she had held her father and then her husband in even higher esteem than that required by their relationship. She had often envied them the honor they had of housing the words of God and His prophet in their breasts. She may have remembered this as she consoled and encouraged Amina, "By expelling you from your house, al-Sayyid Ahmad merely intended to show his anger at your failure to obey his command. He will not do more than discipline you. Yes, evil cannot befall a woman who had a father and grandfather like yours."

Amina was cheered by the reference to her father and grandfather. She was like a person lost in the dark who hears the voice of the watchman calling out. Her heart believed what her mother had said, not only because she was eager to be reassured but because she believed in the sanctity of those two departed scholars. She was a replica of her mother in body, faith, and most traits of character. At that moment, memories of her father swarmed into her mind. When she was a girl, he had filled her heart with love and faith. She prayed to God to rescue her from her predicament out of respect for his holiness. The old lady returned to her consoling remarks. With a tender smile on her dry lips she said, "God in His compassion is always looking out for you. Remember the epidemic, may God never repeat it. God spared you and took your sisters. You weren't harmed at all."

A smile triumphed over Amina's gloom and appeared on her lips. She searched back through a twilight region of the past almost obliterated by forgetfulness. Out of a jumble of memories she could discern clearly an image that awakened echoes within her from that terrible era. She was a little girl skipping outside closed doors behind which her sisters were stretched out on beds of sickness and death. She was by the window watching the endless stream of coffins go by as people fled from them. Another time she was listening to the masses of people who, in their terror and despair, sought out a religious leader like her father. They were lamenting and praying fervently to the Lord of the heavens. Despite the serious threat to her and the loss of all her sisters, she had escaped safe and unharmed from the clutches of the epidemic. The only thing disturbing her serenity had been the lemon juice and onion she had been forced to consume once or twice a day.

Her mother started speaking again, in a tender and affectionate voice that revealed she was abandoning herself to her dreams. Memory seemed to have taken her back to a bygone age. She was recalling the life and memories of that time, which were dear and precious because of their association with her youth. With the pains forgotten, they were cleansed of any blemish. She remarked, "It was your good fortune that not only were you saved from the epidemic but you were treasured as the only child left in the family. You were all the family possessed in this world, its hope, consolation, and happiness. You flourished in a nursery formed by our hearts."

After these words, Amina no longer saw the room the way she had before. Now everything had the freshness of youth breathed back into it: the walls, carpet, bed, her mother, and Amina herself. Her father had returned to life and taken his customary place. Once again she listened to his whispered expressions of love and affection. She was dreaming of the stories of the prophets and their miracles, recalling the extraordinary exploits of good people against the infidels, from the Prophet's companions down to the struggle of the nineteenth-century Egyptian patriot Urabi Pasha against the English. Her past life was resurrected along with its magical dreams and promising hopes for happiness.

Then the old lady said, as though drawing a conclusion from the premises she had previously laid out, "Hasn't God preserved and protected you?"

Although the comment was meant to console her, it made her remember her present condition. She awoke from the dream of her happy past to return to her current melancholy. A person who has forgotten his sorrows can be forced to confront them once more when someone with the best intentions favors him with a word of comfort. Amina sat idly and grimly beside her mother. The only time she had felt like this had been during her recent confinement in bed. She disliked it and was uncomfortable. Her continuing conversation with her mother only occupied half her attention. The other half was given over to restless anxiety.

At noon, when Sadiqa brought in a tray with lunch, the old lady told her, mainly to distract her daughter, "A new watchman has come to discover your thefts."

Just then Amina was not interested in whether the maid stole or acted honestly. The servant did not respond to her mistress, out of respect for the guest and because she had grown so accustomed to both the bitter and sweet sides of her mistress that she would have missed one without the other.

As the day wore on, Amina thought even more desperately about her household. Al-Sayyid Ahmad would be returning home for his lunch and siesta. Then after he went back to his store the boys would be arriving, one after the other. Her imagination derived extraordinary power from her pain and homesickness. She could see the house and its inhabitants as though they were present. She saw al-Sayyid Ahmad removing his cloak and caftan without any assistance from her. She was afraid he might have gotten used to that during her long stay in bed. She attempted to read the thoughts and intentions hidden behind his forehead. Did he sense the void she had created by leaving? How did he react when he found no trace of her in the house? Hadn't he made some reference to her for one reason or another? Here were the boys returning home, rushing to the sitting room after waiting impatiently for the coffee hour. They found her place empty. They were asking about her. They were answered by their sisters' gloomy and tearful looks. How would Fahmy take the news? Would Kamal understand the significance of her absence? This question made her heart throb painfully. Were they deliberating for a long time? What were they waiting for? Perhaps they were already on their way, racing toward her. . . . They must be on their way. Or had he ordered them not to visit her? They must be in al-Khurunfush already. . . . A few minutes would tell.

"Were you talking to me, Amina?"

This question from the old lady interrupted Amina's train of thought. With a mixture of astonishment and embarrassment she came to her senses. She inferred that some words from her internal dialogue had inadvertently slipped out and been picked up by her mother's sharp ear. She found herself obliged to answer, "I was asking, Mother, if the boys won't come visit me."

"I think they've arrived." The elderly woman was listening intently and leaning her head forward.

Amina listened silently. She heard the door knocker telegraphing quick, consecutive beats like a voice urgently calling out for help. She recognized Kamal's touch in these nervous raps. She knew who it was just as well as when she heard him knock on the door of the oven room at home. She quickly dashed to the head of the stairs and called to Sadiqa to open the door. She looked down over the railing. She saw the boy leaping up the steps with Fahmy and Yasin following him. Kamal clung to her and prevented the others from embracing her for a while.

When they entered their grandmother's room they were all talking at the same time, heedless of the others' comments because their souls were so agitated and their minds so confused. Then they saw their grandmother, standing with her arms spread out and her face beaming in a smile of welcome filled with love, and they stopped talking so they could kiss her, one after the other.

The room was relatively quiet except for the soft noise of their kisses. At last Yasin cried out in a sad voice of protest, "We no longer have a home. We will never have a home until you return to us."

Like a fugitive seeking asylum, Kamal climbed into his mother's lap. For the first time he stated his decision that he had kept secret at home and on the way: "I'm staying here with Mother. . . . I'm not going back with you."

Fahmy had been gazing at her silently for a long time the way he did when he wanted to tell her something with a look. This silent glance was the best expression for her of what both their hearts were feeling. He was her darling and his love for her was exceeded only by hers for him. When he talked to her, he rarely spoke openly of his feelings, but his thoughts, words, and deeds all revealed them. He had seen a look of pain and embarrassment in her eyes that upset him terribly. He said sadly and painfully, "We're the ones who suggested you should go out. We encouraged you to do it. But here you're the only one getting punished."

His mother smiled in confusion and said, "I'm not a child, Fahmy. I shouldn't have done it. . . ."

Yasin was touched by this exchange. His distress increased because he was so upset at being the proponent of the ill-omened suggestion. He hesitated for a long time between repeating his apology for the suggestion within earshot of their grandmother, who would criticize him or harbor a grudge against him, and keeping silent, even though he wanted to get some relief by expressing his anguish. He overcame his hesitation and chose to repeat Fahmy's comment in different words. He said, "Yes, we're the guilty ones, and you're the one who got accused." Then with special emphasis, as though reacting to his father's stubbornness and rigidity, he continued: "But you will return. The clouds overshadowing all of us shall be dispersed."

Kamal took hold of his mother's chin and turned her face toward him. He showered her with a stream of questions about the meaning of her departure from the house, how long she would stay at his grandmother's house, what would happen if she returned with them, and so on. None of her answers was able to calm his mind. Not even his determination to stay with his mother was able to reassure him, for he was the first one to doubt that he would be able to carry through on it.

After each of them had finished expressing his feelings, the course of the conversation changed. They began to discuss the situation in a new way, for as Fahmy said, "There's no point talking about what has happened. We need to think about what will happen."

Yasin replied, "A man like our father is not willing to let an incident like Mother's excursion pass unnoticed. He will inevitably express his anger in a way that's hard to forget. But he will never exceed the limits of what he has already done."

This opinion seemed plausible and everyone was relieved by it. Fahmy expressed both his satisfaction and his hopes when he said, "The proof you're right is that he hasn't done anything else. Someone like him doesn't postpone something once he's resolved to do it."

They talked a lot about their father's heart. They agreed that he had a good heart, even though he was severe and easily enraged. They thought it highly unlikely that he would do something to injure his reputation or harm anyone.

At that point the grandmother said, just to tease them, since she knew what an impossible request it was, "If you were men, you would search for some way to touch your father's heart and make him stop being so stubborn."

Yasin and Fahmy exchanged sarcastic glances about this pretense of manliness that would melt at the first mention of their father. The mother for her part was afraid that the discussion between the two young men and the grandmother would lead to some reference to the automobile accident. She motioned to them, pointing to her shoulder and then her mother, to tell them she had kept it a secret from her. As though springing to the defense of the virility of the two youths, she told her mother, "I don't want either of them to expose himself to the man's anger. Leave him alone until he's ready to forgive."

Then Kamal asked, "When is he going to forgive you?"

The mother gestured upward with her index finger and murmured, "Forgiveness comes from God."

As usual in a situation like this, the conversation went full circle. Everything that had been said before was repeated in the same words or different ones. Rosy thoughts continued to predominate. The conversation went on, without bringing up anything new, until night fell and the time came to leave. Their hearts were overwhelmed by the pervasive gloom of departure, and they were too busy thinking about it to have anything to say. A silence reigned, like that before a storm, broken only by words intended to soften its impact or to make it seem it was not yet time to say goodbye. Out of compassion for the other side, no one was willing to take responsibility for saying goodbye.

At this time the old lady guessed what was troubling the people around her. She blinked her sightless eyes and ran her fingers through her prayer beads quickly and devoutly. Minutes passed which, despite their brevity, were unbearably oppressive, like the moments when a dreamer expects, in his nightmare, to fall from a great height. Then she heard Yasin's voice say, "I think it's time for us to go. We'll return soon to fetch you, God willing."

The old lady listened intently to see whether her daughter's voice trembled when she answered, but she did not hear anyone speak. All she heard was the movement of people rising and then the sound of kisses and a hum of farewells. Kamal protested against being forcibly removed and started crying. Now it was her turn to say goodbye to them in an atmosphere fraught with sorrow and foot-dragging. Finally the footsteps went off, leaving her alone and apprehensive.

Amina's light steps returned. The old lady listened anxiously. Finally she cried out to her, "Are you crying? . . . What a dunce you are! . . . Can't you bear to pass a couple of nights with your mother?"

34

Of all of them, Khadija and Aisha appeared to be the most distressed by the absence of their mother. In addition to their sorrow, which was shared by their brothers, the two of them had to bear the burdens of looking after the house and serving their father. The household chores did not weigh nearly so heavily on them as serving their father, for that required taking a thousand things into account. Aisha tended to flee from anything having to do with her father. Her excuse was that Khadija had assisted him when their mother was confined to bed. Khadija found herself obliged to return to those terrifying and delicate situations she endured if she was near her father or doing some task for him. The very first hour after her mother's departure, Khadija said, "This situation had better not last long. Life in this house without her is unbearable suffering."

Aisha concurred in what her sister said, but the only way she could respond was by bursting into tears. Khadija waited to explain what she had in mind until her brothers returned from her grandmother's house, but before she could, they began to tell her about their mother in her place of exile. Khadija found their comments strange and objectionable, as though they were telling her about strangers she had never been permitted to meet.

She was overcome by emotion and said sharply, "If we're all content to keep silent and wait, days and weeks may go by while she's separated from her house and consumed by grief. Yes, talking to Papa is an arduous task, but it's no more oppressive than keeping quiet, which wouldn't be right. We must find some way. . . . We must talk."

Although the expression "we must talk" concluding her remarks embraced everyone present, it was naturally understood to refer to one or two individuals, each of whom felt uncomfortable for obvious reasons. Even so, Khadija continued: "The task of speaking to him about matters that came up was no easier for Mother than it would be for us. She never hesitated to speak to him as a favor to one of us. It's only fair for us to make the same sacrifice for her sake."

Yasin and Fahmy exchanged a glance that revealed they felt they were choking. That sensation was rapidly overwhelming them. Yet neither of them dared to open his mouth for fear his words would lead to his selection as the sacrificial lamb. Like a mouse succumbing to a cat, each waited for the outcome of the discussion. Khadija left the general plane to get specific and turned toward Yasin. She said, "You're our oldest brother. In addition to that, you're an employee —in other words, you're really a man. You're the one best suited for this mission."

Yasin breathed in deeply and then exhaled. He was playing with his fingers in obvious anxiety. He stammered, "Our father has a fiery temper and does not accept corrections for his opinions. I, for my part, am no longer a boy. I have become a man and an employee, as you pointed out. What I fear most is that he'll get angry and I'll lose control of myself and become angry too."

Despite their shattered nerves and sad spirits, they had to smile. Aisha almost laughed and hid her face in her hands. It was possibly their tension itself that helped them smile so they could get some temporary relief from it and their pain. At times people who are extremely sad become lighthearted for the most trivial reasons, merely to obtain the relief furnished by the exactly opposite condition. In other words, the family considered what Yasin had said a joke deserving sarcastic laughter. He himself realized better than anyone else how totally incapable he was of even thinking about getting angry or contending with his father. He was the first to recognize that he had only said that to keep from having to confront his father and out of fear of his wrath. When he saw they were making fun of him, all he could do was smile along with them and shrug his shoulders as though to say, "Leave me alone."

Fahmy was the only one careful not to smile too much. He was afraid he might get tapped even before his smile had faded. His fears were confirmed when Khadija turned away from Yasin with scornful despair and told Fahmy with affectionate entreaty, "Fahmy . . . you're our man!"

He raised his eyebrows in confusion and gave her a look that seemed to say, "You know very well what the consequences will be." He did in fact possess qualities none of the rest of the family had. He was a law student and the most intellectual and influential of the children. He could control himself well in awkward situations and had demonstrated his courage and manliness. To appear before his father, however, was enough to cause all his strengths of character to vanish, leaving blind obedience his only recourse. He seemed not to know what to say. Khadija nodded her head to tell him to speak. In dismay he observed, "Do you think he's going to accept my request? No. He'll rebuff me and say, 'Don't interfere in what doesn't concern you.' That's if he doesn't get angry and say even worse things to me."

Yasin was comforted by this wise statement, which he found could also serve as a defense for himself. As though completing his brother's thought, he commented, "Our meddling might lead to our being examined again about our position on the day she went out. We'll be exposing ourselves to charges we won't know how to rebut."

The girl turned on him, enraged and furious. She said bitterly and sarcastically, "We won't expect any help from you. You've done enough harm already."

Fahmy had derived some new energy from the instinct of self-preservation. He said, "Let's think about this matter in the broadest possible terms. I think he won't accept a request from me or Yasin, since he considers us accomplices against him in this error. The case will be lost if one of us tries to defend her. But if either of you girls spoke to him, perhaps you would succeed in appealing to his sympathies. Even in the worst case you would only meet with a calm rejection free of any violence. Why doesn't one of you speak to him? . . . You, for example, Khadija?"

The girl had fallen into the trap. Her heart sank and she glared at Yasin, not Fahmy. She said, "I thought this was a job more suitable for men."

Fahmy continued his nonviolent offensive, saying, "The reverse is true, if we focus on the success of the endeavor. Let's not forget that all your lives you two have been exposed to his anger only on rare occasions that don't count. He's as used to being gentle with you as he is to being brutal to us."

Khadija bowed her head thoughtfully. She did not try to hide her anxiety. She seemed to fear that if she was silent too long the attack against her would intensify and she would be drafted into the dangerous mission. She raised her head to say, "If you're right, then it would be better for Aisha to talk to him than me."

"Me! . . . Why?" Aisha spoke with the alarm of a person who finds herself on the firing line after calmly assuming for a long time the position of a spectator with no special involvement in the case. Since she was young and still something of a pampered child, she was not entrusted with anything important, let alone the most perilous assignment any of them could have. Even Khadija could think of no clear justification for her suggestion, but she insisted on it with an obstinacy overflowing with bitter irony. She replied to her sister, "We need your golden hair and blue eyes for our project to succeed."

"What do my hair and eyes have to do with a confrontation with Father?"

At that moment Khadija was not so interested in being convincing as she was desperate to find a way to escape, even if she had to distract their minds with matters that were almost humorous to prepare for her retreat and escape by the safest possible route. A person in trouble who lacks an adequate line of defense will resort to humor in order to allow himself to escape in happy clamor rather than let himself be subjected to scorn and condescending laughter. Khadija said, "I know they have a magical effect on everyone who comes in contact with you . . . Yasin, Fahmy . . . even Kamal. Why shouldn't they have the same effect on Father?"

Aisha blushed and said in panic, "How could I speak to him about something like this when my mind becomes a complete blank the moment his eyes light on me?"

Then, after everyone in succession had evaded this dangerous task and no one felt directly threatened, they all found that their salvation had not spared them from feeling guilty. In fact, it was possibly the main reason they felt that way. In a crisis a person will concentrate his thoughts on saving himself. Once he is safe, his conscience will start to give him trouble. Similarly, when a member of the body is ill, the body drains vital energies from other areas to try to heal it. When the diseased member recovers, these energies must be redistributed equally to other, neglected parts of the body. Khadija seemed to be trying to assuage her feeling of guilt when she said, "Since none of us is able to speak to Papa, let's ask Maryam's mother to help us."

The moment she mentioned the name Maryam she noticed Fahmy's involuntary reaction. Their eyes met for an instant. The young man was uncomfortable with her suggestion. He turned his face away, pretending to be uninterested. No one had mentioned this name in his presence since his idea of getting engaged to her had been renounced. Everyone had either respected his feelings or felt that Maryam had acquired a new significance after Fahmy had admitted his love for her. She had entered the corps of sacrosanct topics that house rules did not permit to be discussed openly in the presence of the person involved. Even so, Maryam herself had continued to visit the family, pretending she did not know what had taken place in secret.

Yasin did not miss the awkward exchange between Fahmy and Khadija. He wanted to blunt the probable outcome by shifting their attention in a new direction. Putting his hand on Kamal's shoulder, he said in a half-sarcastic and half-provocative way, "Here's the right man for us. He's the only one who can beg his father to give him back his mother."

No one took his words seriously, particularly not Kamal. All the same, the next day when the boy was walking across Bayt al-Qadi Square on his way home from school, after spending most of the day thinking about his banished mother, he suddenly remembered what Yasin had said. He stopped going toward Qirmiz Alley and headed back to al-Nahhasin Street. His sad heart was pounding with distress and pain. He proceeded to al-Nahhasin with slow steps. He had not made up his mind about what he would do. He was led forward by the torment he was suffering from the loss of his mother. He was held back by the fear that overcame him when he merely thought about his father, not to mention talking to him or begging him for something. He could not picture himself standing in front of his father to discuss this affair. He was well aware of the fears that would probably overwhelm him if he did. He had not made up his mind about anything, but nonetheless, as though he longed to relieve his tortured heart even if only indirectly, he kept walking ahead slowly until his eyes fell on the door of the shop. He was like a mother kite circling overhead but lacking the courage to attack the predator seizing her chicks. He approached within a few meters of the store and stopped. He paused there for a long time without advancing or retreating. He had not been able to decide what to do. Suddenly a man emerged from the store laughing uproariously. There was Kamal's father, following the man to the threshold to say goodbye. He too was engulfed in laughter. Kamal was stunned. He stood nailed to the spot, taking in his father's relaxed, laughing face with indescribable incredulity and astonishment. He could not believe his eyes. He imagined that a new person had taken over his father's body or that this laughing man, much as he resembled Kamal's father, was a different individual whom he was seeing for the first time. The man laughed. He laughed uproariously. His face beamed with happiness like the sun radiating light.

When al-Sayyid Ahmad turned to go back into the store, his eyes fell on the boy who was looking at him in bewilderment. The father was astonished to see him standing there like that. Al-Sayyid Ahmad's features quickly regained their serious and sedate expression. Scrutinizing his son's face, he asked him, "What brings you?"

At once, despite the boy's bewilderment, his soul was permeated by the instinct of self-defense. He went up to his father and stretched out his small hand. He leaned over and kissed his father's hand politely and deferentially, without uttering a word. Al-Sayyid Ahmad asked, "Do you want something?"

Kamal swallowed but did not find anything to say. Choosing to remain on the safe side, he remarked that he wanted nothing and was simply on his way home.

His father was impatient and noticed the boy's anxious expression. He told him roughly, "Don't stand there like a statue. Tell me what you want."

The roughness of his father's voice penetrated Kamal's heart and he trembled. He was tongue-tied. His words were stuck to the roof of his mouth. Al-Sayyid Ahmad became even more impatient and shouted at him sharply, "Speak. . . . Have you forgotten how?"

The boy summoned all his strength for one purpose and that was to end his silence at any cost and save himself from his father's anger. He opened his mouth to say anything that would come out: "I was on my way home from school. . . ."

"What made you stand here like an idiot?"

"I saw . . . I saw your honor, so I wanted to kiss your hand."

A skeptical look appeared in the gentleman's eyes. Dryly and sarcastically he remarked, "Is that all there is to it? . . . Did you miss me so much? Couldn't you have waited till tomorrow morning to kiss my hand, if that's what you wanted? . . . Listen . . . you better not have done something wrong at school. . . . I'll find out all about it."

Kamal replied quickly and uneasily, "I haven't done anything. I swear by our Lord."

His patience exhausted, the man said, "Then go. . . . You've wasted my time for nothing. . . . Get lost!"

Kamal started off. He was so shaken he was barely able to see where he was putting his feet. Al-Sayyid Ahmad moved to go back into his store. The moment his father's eyes turned away, the boy revived. Afraid the man would leave and the opportunity be lost, without pausing to consider what he was doing Kamal shouted, "Bring back Mama, God help you." Then he sped away as fast as the wind.

35

Al-Sayyid Ahmad was having his afternoon coffee in his room when Khadija entered and said in a voice that was so deferential it was barely audible, "Our neighbor Umm Maryam wishes to see you, sir."

Her father asked in amazement, "The wife of Mr. Muhammad Ridwan? What does she want?"

"I don't know, Papa."

Attempting to curb his amazement, he ordered her to show the woman in. Although it did not happen often, this would not be the first time one of the respectable ladies from the neighborhood came to call on him, either for some matter relating to his business or because he was trying to reconcile her and a husband who was one of his friends. All the same, he thought it unlikely that this lady was coming to see him for one of these reasons. While he was wondering about this, he happened to think of Maryam and his discussion with his spouse concerning a possible engagement; but how could there be any connection between that secret, which would not have gone beyond the limits of his family circle, and this visit? Then he thought of Mr. Muhammad Ridwan and the possibility that the visit had some link to him. Yet he had never been anything more than a neighbor. Their relationship had never been elevated to the rank of friendship. In former times they had visited each other only when it was necessary. Once the other man became paralyzed, he had called on him a few times, but after that he had knocked on his door only during the religious festivals.

In any case, Maryam's mother, Umm Maryam, was no stranger to him. He remembered she had been in his store once to buy some items. On that occasion she had introduced herself to him to assure herself favorable treatment. He had been as generous with her as he thought appropriate for a good neighbor. Another time he had met her at the door of his house when his departure coincided with her arrival. Although accompanied by her daughter, she had astonished him then with her daring, for she had greeted him openly, saying, "Good afternoon, your honor, sir."

His dealings with his friends had taught him that some of them were lenient where he was strict. He was extreme in his insistence on retaining traditional standards for his family. These other men saw nothing wrong with their wives going out to visit or shop. They were not disturbed by an innocent greeting like Umm Maryam's. Despite his ultraconservative, Hanbali bias in religion, he was not one to attack his friends over what they found appropriate for them and their women. Indeed, he saw nothing wrong with the fact that some of the more distinguished ones took their wives and daughters along when they went in a carriage for outings in the countryside or to frequent wholesome places of entertainment. All he would do was repeat the saying "You've got your religion and I've got mine." In other words, he was not inclined to impose his views blindly on other people. Although he could distinguish what really was good from what was bad, he was not willing to embrace every "good" thing. In that respect he was influenced by his sternly traditional nature, so much so that he considered his wife's visit to the shrine of al-Husayn a crime deserving the gravest punishment he had meted out during his second marriage. For these reasons, he had felt an astonishment mixed with panic when Umm Maryam had greeted him, but he had not thought any the worse of her.

He heard someone clearing her throat outside his door. He perceived that the visitor was warning him she was about to enter. When she did come in, she was swathed in her wrap and her face was concealed behind a black veil. Large black eyes enhanced by kohl could be seen on either side of the golden cylinder connecting her veil to her scarf. She brought her ample and corpulent body with its swaying hips close to him. He rose to greet her. Putting out his hand, he said, "Welcome. You honor our house and family."

She held her hand out to him after wrapping it in a corner of her cloth, so she would not nullify his state of ritual cleanliness. She replied, "Sir, your honor, may our Lord hold you in high esteem."

He invited her to have a seat. Then he sat down and asked her for the sake of politeness, "How is al-Sayyid Muhammad?"

As though the question had reminded her of her sorrows, she sighed audibly and responded, "Praise to God who is the only one we praise for adversity. May our Lord be gracious to all of us."

Al-Sayyid Ahmad shook his head as though he were grieved and murmured, "May our Lord take him by the hand and grant him patience and good health."

The exchange of pleasantries was followed by a short silence while the lady began to prepare for the serious conversation that had brought her. She resembled a musician preparing to sing after the instrumental prelude has ended. Al-Sayyid Ahmad lowered his eyes decorously while retaining a smile on his lips to announce his welcome for the expected conversation. She said, "Al-Sayyid Ahmad, you're such a chivalrous person that you're proverbial throughout the whole district. A person who comes to you and appeals to your chivalry is not disappointed."

Although he was wondering to himself, "What's behind all this," he murmured modestly, "I ask God's forgiveness."

"The fact is that I came just now to visit my sister Umm Fahmy. How appalled I was to learn that she's not here in her house and that you're angry with her."

The woman fell silent to gauge the effect of her words and to hear what he might think of them. For his part, al-Sayyid Ahmad took refuge in silence, as though he could not think of anything to say. Although he felt uncomfortable that this topic had been raised, the smile of welcome remained plastered on his lips.

"Is there a lady finer than Umm Fahmy? She is a wise and modest lady, a neighbor for twenty years or more. During that time we have never heard anything but the nicest things about her. What could she possibly have done that would merit the anger of a just man like you?"

Al-Sayyid Ahmad persisted in his silence and ignored her question. Some ideas occurred to him that increased his discomfort. Had the woman merely come to the house by accident or had she been invited to carry out some schemer's plan? . . . Khadija? Aisha? Amina herself? The children would never tire of defending their mother. Could he forget how Kamal had dared to scream in his face and ask him to bring back his mother? That incident had led to a beating so fiery that smoke had poured from the boy's ears.

"What a fine lady she is. She doesn't deserve such punishment. . . . And what a noble gentleman you are. Violence does not become you. It's the work of cursed Satan, may God humiliate him, but your excellence will prevail to spoil his scheme."

At that point, he felt he could no longer remain silent, not even out of politeness to his guest. He muttered with deliberate brevity, "May our Lord remedy the situation."

Encouraged by her success in getting him to talk, Umm Maryam said zealously, "How it hurts me for our fine neighbor to leave her home after a long life of seclusion and honor."

"The streams will return to their banks, but there is a right time for everything."

"You are like a brother to me. Indeed, you're dearer than a brother. I won't add a single word."

A new element had entered the affair and did not escape his attentive mind. He registered it the way an observatory might record a distant earthquake, regardless of how faint it seemed. He imagined that when she said, "You are like a brother to me," her voice had been tender and sweet. When she said, "Indeed, you're dearer than a brother," her voice had revealed a warm affection that lent a pleasant fragrance to the embarrassed atmosphere. He was amazed and wondered about it. Perplexed, he could no longer bear to keep his eyes lowered. He raised them hesitantly. He stole a look at her face. Contrary to his expectations, he found her looking at him with her large black eyes. He was flustered and lowered his again quickly. He was partly surprised and partly embarrassed. To cover up his emotions, he continued the conversation: "Thank you for considering me your brother. . . ."

He wondered whether she had been looking at him that way throughout their conversation or whether he had merely raised his eyes at a moment when she happened to glance at him. What could be said about her not lowering her eyes when their eyes met? He immediately scoffed at these ideas, telling himself that his infatuation with women and experience with them made him especially prone to think ill of them. No doubt the truth was as far removed as possible from what he imagined. She might be one of those women whose nature gushes with affection, so that people who do not know them think they are flirting when they are not. In order to confirm his opinion, since confirmation was needed, he looked up again. How appalled he was to see her still looking at him. He was a little more courageous this time and fixed his eyes on her for a moment. She kept gazing at him submissively but boldly. In total confusion he lowered his eyes. At that time he heard her soft voice say, "After this request I'll see whether I'm truly favored by you."

Favored? If the word had not been spoken in this atmosphere filled with emotion and charged with doubt and confusion, it would have passed without leaving any trace. But now . . . ? With considerable embarrassment he looked at her again. He discerned some hints in her eyes that tantalized his suspicions. Had his feeling been right? Was this possible at the very moment she was interceding for his wife? For a man as experienced with women as he was, that would be no surprise . . . a playful wife with a paralyzed husband. His consciousness was permeated by surges of delight that filled him with warmth and pride. When had this sentiment begun? Was it an old one that had simply been waiting for an opportunity? Had she not visited him at the store once without doing anything to excite his suspicions? Even so, the store was not a place where a woman like her would feel comfortable revealing a secret passion, as the performer Zubayda had, with no prior preparation for the announcement. Was it a sentiment born of the moment that had arisen along with the golden opportunity when she found herself alone with him? If that was true, then she was merely another Zubayda disguised in a lady's clothing.

Although he knew a lot about passionate women, it was not surprising that he had overlooked her. He was zealous to respect the honor of his neighbors in the most exemplary way. If she was flirting with him, how should he respond? Should he say, "You're more in favor with me than you can imagine"? It would be a pretty phrase, but she might see it as a welcoming response to her invitation. He certainly did not want that. He was completely opposed to it and not merely because he was still enthralled with Zubayda. He would not agree to a situation deviating from his principles, which called for total respect for the reputations of honorable people in general and of friends and neighbors in particular. In spite all his amorous and sensual excesses, there was not a single blot on his page to embarrass him with a friend, neighbor, or virtuous person. It had always been his custom to fear God as much when he was amusing himself as when he was being serious. He had only allowed himself things he considered licit or within the bounds of minor offenses. This did not imply that he had been endowed with supernatural willpower shielding him from passion. What he did was revel in every passion allowed him and turn his eyes away from respectable women. Throughout his entire life he had never deliberately looked at the face of a woman from his district. He was known to have rejected a promising affair out of concern for the feelings of an acquaintance. A messenger had come one day to invite him to meet the sister of that man, a middle-aged widow, on a night he would name. Al-Sayyid Ahmad had received the invitation silently and shown the messenger out with his customary politeness. Then he had avoided the street where her house was for years afterward.

Umm Maryam was possibly the first person to test his principles face to face. Although he found her attractive, he refused to answer the temptations of passion. The voice of wisdom and sobriety won out, protecting his much-discussed reputation from a world of reproaches. His good reputation seemed to mean more to him than seizing a proffered pleasure. He consoled himself with the opportunities that arose from time to time for romances with no unpleasant consequences.

This will to respect his obligations and act honorably with friends remained with him even in the realms of amusement and desire. He had never been accused of making a pass at the mistress of a companion or of looking lustfully at the sweetheart of a friend. He chose friendship over passion. He would say, "The affection of a friend endures. A girlfriend's passion is fleeting." For this reason, he was content to select his lovers from unattached women or to wait until a woman had ended her previous relationship. Then he would seize his opportunity. At times he would even ask permission from her former companion before beginning to court her. Thus he was able to conduct his amorous adventures with a delight free of regret and a serenity unblemished by ill will. In other words, he had successfully balanced the animal within him that was voracious for pleasure with the man in him that looked up to higher principles. He had succeeded in harmoniously joining these two sides of his personality in a compatible whole. Neither side dominated the other, and each was able to pursue its own special interests easily and comfortably. Just as he had reconciled the opposing forces of sensuality and ethics, he was also able to merge piety and debauchery successfully into a unity free of any hint of either sin or repression.

Yet his good faith was not inspired merely by loyalty to a code of ethics. It was based most of all on his innate desire to continue to be loved and enjoy a fine reputation. The success of his amorous forays made it easier for him to avoid love marred by betrayal or depravity. Moreover, he had never known a true form of love that could have pushed him into succumbing either to emotion, without regard to principles, or to a fierce emotional and moral crisis, in which he could not keep from being burned.

Umm Maryam represented nothing more to him than a delicious kind of food, which, if it threatened his digestion, he could easily turn down in favor of some of the other tasty but wholesome dishes that covered the table. Therefore, he answered her tenderly, "Your mediation is accepted, God willing. You will hear something that will please you shortly."

The woman said as she rose, "May our Lord be generous to you, sir, your honor."

She stretched out her soft hand. He took it, but lowered his eyes. He imagined that she squeezed his hand a little when they were saying goodbye. He began to wonder whether this was the way she usually shook hands or if she had deliberately squeezed it. He tried to remember what her handshake had been like when she arrived, but he could not. He spent most of the time before he returned to the store thinking about the woman, what she had said, her tenderness, and her handshake.

36

"Our aunt, the widow of the late Mr. Shawkat, wishes to see you."

Al-Sayyid Ahmad threw Khadija a fiery look and shouted at her, "Why?"

His angry voice and irritated looks proclaimed that he meant more than this "why" implied and that he would have liked to tell her, "I've barely gotten rid of the intermediary who came yesterday when you bring me a new one today. Who told you these tricks would work on me? How can you and your brothers dare to try to put something over on me?"

Khadija's face became pale. In a trembling voice she replied, "I don't know, by God."

He nodded his head as though to say, "Yes, you do know, and I know too. Your cunning will achieve nothing but the most disastrous consequences for you." Resentfully he declared, "Let her come in. I won't be able to drink my coffee with a calm mind after this. My room has turned into a court with judges and witnesses. That's the kind of rest I find at home. God's curse on all of you!"

Before he could finish speaking, Khadija had vanished like a mouse that has heard the floor creak. Al-Sayyid Ahmad glowered angrily for a few moments. Then he remembered the sight of Khadija retreating so fearfully that her foot stumbled in its wooden clog and her head almost collided with the door. He smiled sympathetically. His impulsive fury was wiped away and left him feeling affectionate. What children they were! They refused to forget their mother even for a single minute.

He directed his eyes toward the door and readied a beaming face to greet the visitor, as though he had not just seconds earlier fumed with anger at the thought of her visit. When he got angry at home for the most trifling reason or for none at all, he was not bluffing, but this visitor, as the widow of the late Mr. Shawkat, had a special status and outranked all the women who called at the house from time to time. Her husband had been a special friend and the two families had been linked by a bond of affection since the days of their grandparents. The departed gentleman had been like a father to him. His widow continued to be a mother to him and, consequently, to his entire family. It was she who had arranged his engagement to Amina. She had helped bring his children into the world. In addition to all of these considerations, the Shawkat family were people it was a privilege to know. Not only were they of Turkish origin, but they had a high social standing and owned real estate in Cairo between al-Hamzawi and al-Surayn. If al-Sayyid Ahmad was in the middle ranks of the middle class, they were indisputably members of its top echelon. Perhaps it was the woman's maternal feelings toward him and his filial feelings for her that made him indignant and uncomfortable about her anticipated intercession.

She was a person who would mince no words when she spoke to him. She would not weary of appealing to his emotions. Moreover, he knew her to be scathingly frank. Her excuses for it were her age and her status. Yes, she was not one to . . .

He stopped brooding when he heard her footsteps. He rose to greet her: "Welcome. It's as though the Prophet himself were visiting us."

The elderly lady approached him. She was hobbling along, leaning on her parasol. She looked up at him with a face that was fair and full of wrinkles. Her transparent white veil did little to conceal her features. She responded to his greeting with a smile that revealed her gold teeth. She shook his hand and sat down beside him casually. She said, "A person who lives a long time sees a lot. Even you, pride of mankind . . . and even in this house . . . things are happening that are unpleasant to discuss. . . . By the God of al-Husayn, you've grown senile. Your dotage has arrived unexpectedly."

She rattled on, giving her tongue free rein to say whatever it pleased without allowing al-Sayyid Ahmad an opportunity to interrupt or comment. She told him how she had come to visit and had discovered his wife was absent. "I thought at first that she was out visiting someone. So I pounded my chest in astonishment. I exclaimed, 'What's become of the world?' . . . How could her husband have permitted her to leave the house? Does he think so little of the decrees of God, of human law, and of the edicts of the Ottoman Empire?" She had quickly learned the whole truth. "I regained my senses and said, 'Praise to God, the world's just fine. This truly is al-Sayyid Ahmad. This is the least one could expect from him.' "

Then she abandoned her mocking tone and began to scold him for his harshness. She was outspoken in her laments for his wife, whom she considered the last woman to deserve punishment. Whenever he attempted to interrupt she would yell at him, "Hush. Not a word. Save your sweet talk that you make so flowery. It won't fool me. I want you to do the right thing, not say something eloquent." She told him frankly that he was excessively conservative in his treatment of his family. It was abnormal. It would be a good thing if he would act in a kindlier, more indulgent way.

Al-Sayyid Ahmad listened to her for a long time. When she allowed him to speak, only after she was exhausted from talking, he explained his point of view to her. Her passionate defense of his wife and his respect for her did not prevent him from asserting to her that his treatment of his family was based on principles he would not abandon. He did promise at the end, as he had promised Umm Maryam earlier, that everything would turn out for the best. He thought the time had come for the meeting to conclude.

Before he knew what was happening she said, "The absence of Mrs. Amina was an unpleasant surprise to me, since I needed to see her for an extremely important reason. Because of my health it's not an easy matter for me to go out. Now I don't know whether it would be better for me to tell you what I was going to tell her or to wait till she returns."

Al-Sayyid Ahmad replied with a smile, "We are all ready to serve you."

"I would have liked her to be the first to hear, even though you leave her no voice in the matter. Since this opportunity has escaped me, I'll console myself by preparing a happy reason for her return."

The gentleman was baffled by her statement. He wondered as he stared at her, "What's behind all this?"

Stabbing the carpet with the point of her parasol, she said, "I won't keep you in suspense. I have chosen Aisha to be my son Khalil's wife."

He was astounded. He was taken by surprise and by something totally unexpected. He felt uneasy and even alarmed for reasons that were hardly secret. He perceived immediately that he would have to drop his long-standing resolve that the younger daughter should not marry before the elder. He could not ignore this precious request announced by a person who was well acquainted with his resolution. She had obviously rejected it in advance and would refuse to be ruled by his judgment.

"Why are you silent as though you hadn't heard me?"

Al-Sayyid Ahmad smiled in confusion and embarrassment. Then, in order to say something pleasant while pondering the issue in all its aspects, he replied, "This is an enormous honor for us."

The lady shot him a look that seemed to say, "Don't use your honeyed phrases on me." She said combatively, "I don't need to be made fun of with empty words. Nothing will satisfy me but total acceptance. Khalil entrusted me with the task of finding a wife for him. I told him, 'I've the best bride you could hope for.' He was pleased by my choice. He had no reservations about becoming your son-in-law. . . . Has the time come that you meet a request like this, from me, with silence and evasion? My God, my God."

How long would he be tormented by this difficult problem, which he could not resolve without inflicting a rude shock on one of his daughters? He looked at her as though trying to beg her sympathy for his situation. He mumbled, "The matter's not the way you imagine. Your request is my command, but . . ."

"A pox on 'but.' Don't tell me you've decided not to let the younger marry until the elder has. Who are you to decree this or that? Leave God's work to God. He's the most compassionate one of all. If you want, I can give you tens of examples of younger sisters who married before the older ones without their marriages keeping their sisters from excellent matches. Khadija is an extraordinary young woman. She will not go wanting for a fine husband as soon as God wills it. How long will you stand in the way of Aisha's destiny? Doesn't she too deserve your affection and compassion?"

He asked himself, "If Khadija's such an extraordinary young woman, why don't you choose her?" He thought about putting her on the spot the way she had him, but he was afraid she would toss him an answer that would insult, however innocently, Khadija and thus him as well. In a voice that was very serious and earnest he said, "It's just that I feel sorry for Khadija."

She replied sharply as though she was the one making the concession, "Every day things like this happen without upsetting anyone. God dislikes it if His servant is stubborn and proud. Accept my request and trust in God. Don't reject my hand. I haven't made this offer to anyone before you."

The gentleman cloaked his feelings with a smile and said, "This is an enormous honor, as I told you a moment ago. . . . If you would just be patient with me for a short time while I pull myself together and straighten things out, you will find that my opinion corresponds to your wishes, God willing."

She said, in the tone of a person wishing to terminate a conversation, "I won't waste any more of your time than I have. The longer this give-and-take is drawn out, the more I think you're not really accepting my request. A woman like me wants you to say yes at once and not beat around the bush when she asks for something. I'll only add one word to what I've said: Khalil is as much your child as mine and the same holds true for Aisha."

She rose and al-Sayyid Ahmad stood up to say goodbye to her. He was expecting only a word of farewell, but she insisted on reiterating everything she had said. She seemed to fear he might miss some nuance and so repeated it all in detail. Before he knew what was happening, or she did either, she was harking back to corroborate some of her ideas and substantiate others. One idea led to another and she rambled on without interference until she had repeated most of what she had earlier said about the engagement. Nor did she care to conclude her remarks before paying her respects to the subject of the banished mother with a word, or two, or three. Then once more she was overpowered by the association of ideas and carried on until the man had trouble controlling his nerves. He almost laughed when she finally told him, "I won't waste any more of your time than I already have."

He escorted her to the door, apprehensive at each step that she might stop walking and take another shot at conversation. When he could at last sit down again, he was breathing heavily. He was distressed and dejected. He had a sensitive heart, more sensitive than most people would have suspected. In fact, it was too sensitive. How could anyone believe that who had only seen him grinning, bellowing, or laughing sarcastically? . . . Sorrow was going to scorch his flesh and blood in a way that could spoil his whole life, making it seem ugly to him. How happy it would make him to spare no expense to delight both his daughters, the one in whose beautiful face he could detect a resemblance to his mother's and the other girl who had only received a faint glimmer of good looks. Each of them was a vital part of him.

The husband whom the widow of the late Mr. Shawkat was offering was a catch in every sense of the word. He was a young man of twenty-five with a monthly income of not less than thirty pounds. It was true that, like many members of the elite, he had no occupation and little education, the latter not extending beyond knowledge of reading and writing. All the same, he had many of his father's good qualities. He was pleasant, generous, and polite.

What should he do? He had to make up his mind. He did not

usually hesitate or ask for advice. It was not acceptable, even for a brief moment, for him to appear indecisive to his family, as though he did not know what he thought. Could he not consult with his closest friends? He was not ashamed to do that when something serious came up. In fact, their evenings usually began with a discussion of worries and problems before wine transported them to a world where worries and problems were unknown. He realized that he was very opinionated and would not deviate from what he believed. He was the kind of person who requests advice to shore up his opinion, not to undermine it. Even so, that would provide consolation and relief.

When the man was exasperated with thinking he cried out, "Who would believe that the unbearable state I'm in results from a blessing God has bestowed upon me?"

37

Amina had no occupation during her exile other than sitting beside her mother and discussing at length anything that came to mind. They had talks about the distant and not so distant past and the present, ranging from precious memories to the current drama. Had it not been for the painful separation and the specter of divorce, she would have been content with her new life. It was like a restful holiday after the burden of her duties or a voyage to a world of memories.

When days passed with nothing happening to frighten her and when she heard about the mediation by Umm Maryam and Widow Shawkat, she felt less apprehensive and more relaxed. Moreover, the evening visits of the boys continued without interruption and breathed new hope into her breast. She got to spend almost as much time with them in the new house as in the old one. In both instances, she was separated from them until they were free to come to the evening reunion. Even so, she longed for them like an emigrant in a distant land parted by fate from her loved ones. She yearned for them, feeling deprived because she could not breathe the same air, share their memories, and supervise their workaday and leisure activities. Every inch a person's body travels on the road of separation seems like miles to the heart.

When the old lady found her silent or sensed that her daughter's thoughts were wandering, she would tell her, "Patience, Amina. I feel sorry for you. A mother away from her children is a stranger. She's a stranger even if she's staying in the house where she was born."

Yes, she was a stranger. The house might just as well not have been the only home she had known as a child. Her mother was no longer that mother she could not bear to leave for even a moment. So long as the house was her place of exile where she waited regretfully for a word of pardon from heaven, it could not be her home.

After a long interval her pardon did arrive. The boys brought it one evening. When they came, their eyes flashed like lightning. Her heart pounded so hard it shook her whole chest. She was apprehensive about giving this sign a grander interpretation than it deserved, but Kamal ran toward her and put his arms around her neck. Then, beside himself with joy, he yelled to her, "Put on your wrap and come with us."

Yasin roared with laughter and said, "It's all over."

Then he and Fahmy together said, "Father summoned us and told us, 'Go get your mother.' "

She lowered her eyes to hide her overwhelming joy. She could not conceal the emotions rocking her soul. Her face seemed an extremely accurate mirror, registering everything that was inside her, no matter how small. She wanted so much to receive the happy news with a composure befitting her maternal role, but she was transported by joy. The features of her face laughingly expressed her childish delight. At the same time she felt ashamed, although she did not know why. She remained motionless for so long that Kamal's patience was exhausted. He pulled her by the hand, putting his entire weight into it until she yielded and rose. She stood for a little while in a strange confusion. Before she realized what she was doing she turned and asked, "Should I go, Mother?"

This question sounded peculiar and slipped out with an inflection of confusion and embarrassment. Fahmy and Yasin smiled. Only Kamal was astonished and almost alarmed. He affirmed to her once more the news of the pardon they brought.

The grandmother had sensed everything her daughter was feeling and surmised what was going on inside her. Her heart was touched. Taking care not to appear surprised by the question, not even registering so much as a faint smile, she replied seriously, "Go to your house, and may the peace of God go with you."

Amina went to put on her wrap and bundle up her clothes, with Kamal following at her heels. The grandmother asked the young men in a critical tone softened by a tender smile, "Wouldn't it have been more appropriate for your father to come himself?"

Fahmy answered apologetically, "Grandmother, you know very well what my father's like."

Yasin laughed and observed, "Let's thank God for what's happened."

The grandmother muttered something they could not understand. Then she sighed and said, as though replying to her own muttering, "In any case, al-Sayyid Ahmad's not a man like the others."

They left the house with their grandmother's prayers and blessings ringing in their ears. For the first time in their lives they walked along the street together. They found it an extraordinary event. Fahmy and Yasin exchanged smiling glances. Kamal remembered the day he had gone along, as he was now, holding his mother's hand tight and leading her from alley to alley. Then there had ensued the pains and fears that were even worse than a nightmare. He marveled about it for some time but soon was able to overlook the sorrows of the past in favor of the joy of the present. He found himself wanting to jest. He laughingly suggested to his mother, "Come on, let's sneak off to our master al-Husayn."

Yasin laughed and commented allusively, "May God be pleased with him. He's a martyr and loves martyrs."

They could see the protruding wooden balcony of their house and two shapes moving behind the spindles of its latticework. The mother's heart fluttered with affection and longing at the sight of her daughters. Just inside the door she found Umm Hanafi waiting to welcome her and smother her mistress's hands with kisses. In the courtyard she met Khadija and Aisha, who clung to her like little girls.

They climbed the stairs in a tumultuous parade with exhilarating and frenzied happiness. They came to a halt in her room. Each one tried to help her remove her wrap, that symbol of the loathsome separation, as they roared with laughter. When she sat down among them she was breathless from the impact of her emotions. Kamal wanted to tell her how happy he was. The best way he found to put it was: "Today's dearer to me even than the procession with the holy shrine on the camel when the pilgrims leave for Mecca."

For the first time in a long while all the regulars were present at the coffee hour. They resumed their evening chat in an atmosphere of delight. Its splendor was doubled by the days of separation and dejection preceding it, just as the pleasure of a warm day is greater if it follows a frigid week. The joy of the reunion notwithstanding, the mother did not forget to ask the girls about the household affairs, progressing from the oven room all the way up to the hyacinth beans and jasmine. She also asked a lot about their father. She was delighted to learn that he had not allowed anyone to assist him with removing or putting on his clothes. Whatever rest she might have afforded him by her absence, a change had crept into the system of his life, which had without doubt imposed a burden on him that would disappear now that she was back. Her return, and that alone, would guarantee him the kind of life he was accustomed to and comfortable with.

One thing that did not occur to Amina was that some of the hearts happy at her return discovered in this return itself a reason for brooding about their sorrow and pain. Yet this is what happened. These hearts, distracted from their sorrows by their mother's, began to think again about their own worries now they were reassured about their mother's well-being. In the same way, when we have acute but temporary intestinal pain we forget our chronic eye inflammation, but once the intestinal distress is relieved, the pain in the eyes returns.

Fahmy was telling himself, "It appears that every sorrow has an end. My mother's affliction is over. But it seems my sorrow will never end." Aisha resumed her own reflections, to which no one else was privy. Her dreams and memories visited her, although compared with her brother she was considerably calmer and readier to forget.

Amina could not read their thoughts, and nothing disturbed her serenity. When she retired to her room that night it was clear she would not be able to sleep, her mind was so overflowing with happiness. She only dozed off a few times before she got out of bed at midnight. She went to the balcony as usual to gaze through the latticework screens at the wakeful street until the carriage bringing her husband home swayed into sight.

Her heart beat violently, and she blushed with shame and confusion. She might well have been meeting her husband for the first time. Had she not reflected about this moment for a long time . . . the awaited moment of reunion and how she would approach him? How would he treat her after this long separation? What could she say to him, or him to her? If only she could pretend to be asleep. But she had no talent at all for acting and could not bear for him to find her lying down when he came in. Yes, she would not be able to neglect her duty to go to the stairway with a lamp to light the way for him. Over and above all these considerations, after winning the right to return and overcoming his anger at her, she felt good. She forgave everything that had happened and assumed full responsibility for the offense, to the point of thinking that, although her husband had not taken the trouble to go to her mother's house to reach a settlement with her, he deserved to be treated in a conciliatory fashion.

She took the lamp and went to the staircase. She held her arm out over the railing and stood there with a throbbing heart, listening to the sound of his approaching footsteps, until he made his way up to her. She greeted him with her head bowed, so she did not see his face when they met. She did not know if any change had taken place in his appearance since she last saw him. She heard him say in a normal voice that bore no trace of the painful recent past, "Good evening."

She mumbled, "Good evening, sir."

He went to his room. She trailed after him holding up the lamp. He began to remove his clothes silently. She went to assist him. She set to work, privately heaving sighs of relief. She remembered the ill-fated morning of the separation when he had risen to don his clothes and told her harshly, "I'll put my clothes on myself." The memory, though, lacked any of the feelings of pain and sorrow that had overwhelmed her at the time. As she carried out this service for him, which he had not allowed anyone else to perform, she felt she was reclaiming the dearest thing she possessed in all the world.

He took his place on the sofa and she sat cross-legged on the pallet at his feet, without either of them uttering a word. She expected him to put the painful past to rest with some word of advice or admonition. She had prepared herself for that in a thousand different ways. All he did was ask her, "How's your mother?"

Sighing with relief, she answered, "Fine, sir. She sends you her greetings and prayers."

Another period of silence passed before he remarked with apparent disinterest, "The widow of the late Mr. Shawkat disclosed to me her wish to choose Aisha as Khalil's wife."

Amina looked up at him in an astonishment that eloquently revealed the impact of the surprise on her. He shrugged his shoulders as though it was nothing. Fearing she might express an opinion that happened to agree with his decision, which he had kept secret from everyone, and would then suspect he had taken her advice, he quickly added, "I've thought about the matter for a long time and have decided to accept. I don't want to interfere with my daughter's fortune any more than I have already. The matter is in God's hands, both now and later."

38

Aisha received the good news with the joy of a girl who since early childhood had cherished the dream of getting married. She could scarcely believe her ears when she was told about it. Had her father actually agreed? Had marriage become an imminent reality and not a dream or a cruel joke? No more than three months had passed since the disappointment she had suffered. Although the impact on her of that experience had been harsh and intense, with the passing days it had become lighter and weaker, turning into a pale memory, which when aroused would excite only a gentle sorrow of no particular significance.

Everything in the house yielded blindly to a higher will with a limitless authority almost like that of religion. Within these walls even love itself had to creep into their hearts timidly, hesitantly, and diffidently. It did not enjoy its normal influence or dominance. The only dominant force here was that higher will. Therefore, when her father had said no, his verdict had become lodged in the depths of her soul. The girl had firmly believed that everything was really over, since there was no way to escape or to ask for a review. She had no hope that anything would help. It was as though this "no" were one of the processes of nature, like the alternation of night and day. No objection to it would be of any significance, since only obedience was allowed. This belief of hers, whether conscious or not, worked to terminate everything, and terminated it was.

Aisha wondered privately whether her current good fortune did not embrace an incomprehensible contradiction. Less than three months after one rejection, permission had been granted for her to marry. Thus she would not be part of the destiny of the young man for whom her heart had yearned. She kept this thought to herself, and no one learned about it, not even her mother. To announce her happiness with a suitor, even one of whom she had only the vaguest concept, would be a wanton affront to modesty. It would have been inconceivable for her to express a desire for some specific man. In spite all this and despite the fact that she knew nothing about the new bridegroom except what her mother had mentioned in a general discussion of his family, Aisha was happy beyond words with the good news. Her eager emotions had found a pole toward which to gravitate. Her love seemed to be more a disposition than an attachment to any particular man. Even if one man was disqualified and another took his place, she was satisfied and everything was fine. She might prefer one man over another but not enough to destroy her taste for life or to push her into rebellion and revolt.

Now that she was in good spirits and her heart fluttered with delight, she felt, as she usually did in such circumstances, pure affection and sympathy for her sister. She wished that Khadija had married first. By way of apology and encouragement she told her, "I wish you'd been the first to marry . . . but it's fate and destiny. It will all come soon."

Khadija did not enjoy affectionate words of comfort when defeated. She received Aisha's statement with unconcealed annoyance. Their mother had already apologized to her delicately: "We all wanted your turn to come first. We acted on this assumption more than once, but perhaps it is our stubbornness about something beyond our control that has thwarted your luck until now. Let's allow things to proceed as God wills. Something good comes out of every delay."

Khadija found that Yasin and Fahmy were also full of affection for her, whether they expressed it in words or revealed it by being nice to her, at least for the moment, instead of resorting to the stinging humor customary between them, especially between her and Yasin. The only thing matching Khadija's sorrow at her bad luck was her nervousness about the affection smothering her, but not because of an innate aversion to sympathy. She was like a patient with influenza whose health would be harmed by exposure to the fresh air that would normally invigorate him when well. She discounted this affection as a trifling substitute for lost hope and may well have been suspicious of their motives for showering it on her. Was her mother not always the intermediary between the matchmakers and her father? How could Khadija know whether her mother's mediation had been confined to carrying out the duties of the mistress of the house and had not been influenced by a covert desire for Aisha to get married? Was it not Fahmy who brought the message from the officer at the Gamaliya police station? Could he not have acted deftly behind the scenes to change the officer's mind?

Was it not true that Yasin . . . but why should she blame Yasin when a brother even more closely related to her than Yasin had let her down? What kind of affection was this? No, one should ask what kind of hypocrisy and what kind of a lie. Therefore she was impatient with all the sympathy. It reminded her of their ill treatment, not their beneficence. She was filled with resentment and anger but concealed that deep inside her so as not to appear displeased by her sister's happiness. She did not care to expose herself, as her suspicious nature made her think she might, to the abuse of anyone wishing to revile her. In any case, there was no alternative to suppression of her emotions, because in this family that was an ingrained custom and a moral imperative established by threat of paternal terror. Between her hatred and resentment on one side and concealment and pretended delight on the other, her life was a continual torment and an uninterrupted effort.

What about her father? What had made him alter his former opinion? How could she seem so unimportant to him now, after he had cherished her? Had he lost patience waiting for her to get married and decided to sacrifice her, leaving her to her fate? She could not get over her amazement at the way they were abandoning her as though she did not exist. In her rebellious mood, she forgot how they had stood up for her previously. Now all she remembered was their betrayal.

Her anger for everyone in general was nothing compared with the feelings of jealousy and resentment against Aisha that she had packed into her breast. She hated her happiness. Most of all she hated Aisha's attempt to hide her happiness. She hated her beauty, which to Khadija's eyes appeared to be an instrument of torture and oppression. In much the same way, a man stalking prey finds the glistening full moon oppressive. She hated life too. It held nothing for her but despair. The progression of days only added to her sorrows as the presents of the bridegroom were brought to the house along with little tokens of his affection. While the house was filled with an atmosphere of unadulterated delight and happiness, she found herself in a forlorn isolation that was as fertile a breeding ground for sorrows as a stagnant pond is for insects.

Then al-Sayyid Ahmad began to outfit the bride. Talk about the trousseau dominated the family's evening reunions. The bride was shown various styles of furniture and clothing. She would praise one and shun another, comparing one color with a second with such concern that everyone forgot the elder sister and her need for consolation and flattery. Khadija was even forced, since she was pretending to be delighted about everything, to join energetically and enthusiastically in their interminable discussions. This complex emotional situation might have appeared to a stranger to portend only evil, but there was a sudden change when attention was directed to making the wedding gown. Then all eyes were fixed on Khadija with great interest and hope. She had dreaded this task as an inescapable duty she hated to accept but was unable to decline, for fear of revealing her concealed emotions. But her resentment faded away and modesty brought her rebellion under control once their attention was focused on her.

Her mother urged her to do a good job for her sister. Aisha's eyes were filled with embarrassment and entreaty when she gazed at Khadija. Fahmy told Aisha in her hearing, "You won't be a real bride until Khadija makes your wedding gown."

Yasin agreed: "You're right . . . that's a fact."

Khadija's latent good nature came to the surface like a green plant emerging from a seed hidden beneath the mud once sweet water has been provided. She did not suspect the motives of this interest in her the way she had previously. She knew this was genuine and directed at her unquestionable skill. It constituted a general admission of her importance and significance. Although happiness was not hers to enjoy, it would not be fully realized until she contributed to it. She set about this new project with a heart totally cleansed of her hostile emotions. Although members of this family, like most other people, were subject to feelings of anger, they never were so afflicted that their hearts were hostile in a consistent or deep-rooted fashion. Some of them had a capacity for anger like that of alcohol for combustion, but their anger would be quickly extinguished. Then their souls would be tranquil and their hearts full of forgiveness. Similarly in Cairo, during the winter, the sky can be gloomy with clouds and it even drizzles, but in an hour or less the clouds will have scattered to reveal a pure blue sky and a laughing sun.

Khadija had not forgotten her sorrows, but her generosity had purified them of malice and resentment. With each passing day she was less inclined to find fault with Aisha or some family member and more apt to blame her luck. Ultimately she made it the target of her resentment and grumbling. Her luck had been too stingy to make her beautiful. It had delayed her marriage until she was over twenty and clouded her future with fears and anxiety.

Finally, like her mother, Khadija surrendered to the fates. Her fiery side, inherited from her father, and the complex of characteristics arising from her interaction with the environment were both unable to deal with her fortune. She found peace of mind by relying on her tranquil side, which she had inherited from her mother. So she yielded to her destiny. She resembled a commander who, unable to achieve his objective, chooses a naturally fortified location for his remaining forces to make a stand or asks for a truce or peace.

Khadija would express her grief when she performed her prayers or was alone with God the Compassionate. Since childhood she had imitated her mother's piety and observance of religious duties with a persistence that showed an awakened spirituality. Aisha, on the other hand, worshipped in isolated bouts of religious enthusiasm but could not bear to keep it up for long. Khadija was often amazed when she compared her fortune with that of her sister. Why did she achieve such poor results with her religious devotion while Aisha was richly rewarded for being slack.

"I perform my prayers regularly, but she can't do it for more than two days in a row. I fast during the whole month of Ramadan, while she fasts for a day or two and then just pretends. She slips secretly into the pantry and fills her belly with nuts and dried fruit. When the cannon is fired in the evening to mark the end of the daily fast, she rushes to the table ahead of those who have been fasting."

Khadija would not even concede wholeheartedly that her sister was more beautiful. Of course, she did not announce her opinion to anyone and frequently chose to attack herself in order to prevent others from being tempted to do so. But she would look at herself in the mirror for long periods and tell herself, "No doubt Aisha is beautiful, but she's skinny. Being plump is half of beauty. I'm plump. The fullness of my face almost compensates for the size of my nose. All I need is for my luck to improve." She had lost her self-confidence during the recent crisis. Although in the past she had frequently repeated to herself similar observations about beauty, plumpness, and luck, now she made them to ward off her unnerving feeling of being unsure of herself. In the same way, we resort at times to logic to reassure ourselves about matters, like health or illness, happiness or misery, and love or hate, that bear no relationship whatsoever to logic.

In spite of her many chores as mother of the bride, Amina did not forget Khadija. Her happiness for the bride reminded her of her sorrow for her other daughter, just as the relief provided by an anesthetic drug reminds us of the pain that will return eventually. Aisha's wedding reawakened her old fears about Khadija. Searching for reassurance without being too particular about the source, she sent Umm Hanafi with one of Khadija's handkerchiefs to Shaykh Ra'uf at al-Bab al-Akhdar for him to read her fortune. The woman returned with good news. She related that the shaykh had told her, "You'll be bringing me a kilo of sugar soon when my prediction comes true." Although this was not the first augury of glad tidings for Khadija the servant had brought, Amina hoped for the best. She welcomed the news as a sedative to calm the anxiety that had been hounding her.

39

"Isn't it time yet, bitch? I've melted away, Muslims. I've dissolved like a bar of soap. Nothing's left but the suds. She knows this and doesn't care to open the window. Go ahead, play the coquette, you bitch. Didn't we agree on a date? But you're right to hold back . . . one of your breasts could destroy Malta. The second would drive Hindenburg out of his mind. You've got a treasure. May our Lord be gracious to me. May our Lord be gracious to me and to every poor rogue like me who can't sleep for thinking about swelling breasts, plump buttocks, and eyes enhanced by kohl. Eyes come last, because many a blind woman with a fleshy rump and full breasts is a thousand times better than a skinny, flat-chested woman with eyes decorated with kohl. You're the performer's daughter and a neighbor of al-Tarbi'a Alley. The performer has taught you to flirt, and the alley has supplied you with its secret beauty potions. If your breasts have grown full and round, it's because so many lovers have fondled them. We agreed on this date. I'm not dreaming. Open the window. Open up, bitch. Open up. You're the most beautiful creature ever to arouse my passion. Holding your lip between mine . . . sucking on your nipple. . . . I'll wait until dawn. You'll find me very docile. If you want me to be the rear end of a donkey cart that you rock back and forth on, I'll do it. If you want me to be the ass pulling the cart, I'll do that. What a mishap, Yasin! Your life is destroyed, you son of Ahmad Abd al-Jawad. How the Australians gloat at your fate. Woe to me, expelled from the Ezbekiya entertainment district, a prisoner in al-Gamaliya. It's all the fault of the war. Kaiser Wilhelm launched it in Europe and I have become its victim here in al-Nahhasin. Open the window, delight of your mother. Open up, my delight. . . ."

This was the way Yasin had begun talking to himself as he sat on a bench in the coffee shop of al-Sayyid Ali. His eyes were gazing at the house of the performer Zubayda through the small window overlooking al-Ghuriya. The more anxious he became, the more he sank into his dreams and musings, which soothed his anxiety but aroused his desires, just as some sedatives deal with insomnia but tire the heart. He had progressed a step forward in his courtship of the lute player Zanuba. He had advanced from the preparatory stage—frequenting the coffee shop of al-Sayyid Ali in the evening, watching for her, walking behind her donkey cart, smiling, twisting his mustache, and raising his eyebrows playfully—to the stage of negotiating and getting down to business.

He had taken this step in al-Tarbi'a Alley, which was long and narrow with a canvas roof. There were small stores clustered on either side like the cells of a beehive. He was certainly not unfamiliar with al-Tarbi'a, a bazaar frequented by women of all classes. They thronged there to purchase something that was light to carry and had much to offer. They were shopping for various types of perfume useful in promoting delight and beauty. He headed for this market whenever he had no other special destination. It was a favorite haunt of his Friday mornings. Going from one end to the other, he would walk along slowly, both because of the congestion and because he wanted it that way. He pretended to examine the shops as though wanting to select something. Actually, he was scrutinizing the faces, visible when veils were momentarily lifted, and the outlines of bodies, discernible where the ladies' wraps were drawn tight. He saw some features in their entirety and others only in part. He took in the charming fragrances here and there as well as the voices that slipped out from time to time or their whispering laughter. He usually kept within the bounds of good manners because of the preponderance of respectable women there. He was content to observe, compare, and criticize. From what he saw he gathered extraordinary pictures with which to decorate his mental museum. Nothing made him so happy as to come upon a clearer complexion than he had ever seen before, an unusual glance from an eye, a breast that was astonishingly round, or buttocks unique in size or build. When he reviewed them later, he would say, "The winner in today's competition for full breasts was the lady standing in front of so-and-so's shop," or "Today's the day of the rump surpassing size five," or "What a full bag, what a bag . . . today's the day for splendid bags."

It was characteristic of him to devote all his attention to a woman's body and neglect her personality. He also tended to concentrate on individual parts of the body and ignore the way they fit together. These investigations allowed him to keep his hopes alive, refreshing them with possible opportunities he could set aside for today or tomorrow. He seemed a man with no goal in the world that took precedence over women. On rare occasions he succeeded in making a good catch on these sexual excursions.

Late one afternoon he was sitting beneath the small window in al-Sayyid Ali's coffee shop when he saw the lute player leave the house alone. He rose at once to follow her. She turned into al-Tarbi'a Alley, and he turned too. When she stopped at a store, he stood beside her. She had to wait while the proprietor of this perfume shop tended to some other customers. So Yasin waited. She did not turn toward him. From her attempt to pretend he was not there, he inferred she was aware of his presence. She must also have guessed from the outset that he was following her. He whispered into her ear, "Good evening."

She continued to look straight ahead of her, but he noticed her mouth move slightly in a smile of greeting or at least of recognition for all the time he had spent following her, evening after evening. He sighed with relief and victory, confident now that he would pluck this fruit he had patiently pursued. Lust surged inside him, the way a ravenously hungry man's mouth waters when his nose smells meat being broiled for him.

He thought the best thing would be to pretend they had come together. So he paid for her purchases of henna and tonic with the good humor of a man who believes he will acquire an enjoyable and entertaining right by rendering this small service. He did not mind when she seemed inclined to purchase several more things once she was sure he was paying. As they returned, he told her, with the haste of a person who fears the end of the road is in sight, "Beautiful and lovely lady, I have spent my whole life following after you, as you have seen. Can't a lover aspire to be rewarded with at least a meeting?"

She cast him a mischievous glance and asked sarcastically, "At least a meeting?"

He was almost consumed by laughter, body and soul, the way he usually was when intoxicated by joy, but he quickly shut his mouth tight to keep from causing a commotion that would attract attention. He answered her with a whisper, "A rendezvous and everything that goes with it."

She observed critically, "Each of you asks for a rendezvous, as though there were nothing to it, but it's an important matter that does not take place for some people until after a proposal, negotiation, recitation of the opening prayer of the Qur'an, a dowry, a trousseau, and the arrival of a religious official to write the contract. Isn't that so, sir . . . you, the gentleman who's as tall and broad as a camel?"

He blushed in confusion and said, "No matter how harsh your rebuke, coming from your lips it's like honey. Hasn't passion always been like this, beautiful lady, since God created the earth and the people on it?"

She raised her eyebrows until they were level with the top of the cylinder connecting her veil to her scarf and resembled the spreading wings of a bee. "My camel, how would I know about passion?" she asked. "I'm just a musician. Do you suppose passion has things that go with it too?"

Trying not to laugh, he replied, "They're the same things that go along with a rendezvous."

"No more and no less?"

"No more and no less."

"Not one more than another?"

"Not more of one thing than another."

"Perhaps that's what they call illicit sex."

"One and the same thing."

A laugh escaped from her. She said, "You've got a deal . . . wait in the coffee shop of al-Sayyid Ali, where you've spent all these evenings. When I open the window, come to the house."

He waited evening after evening after evening. One evening she went in the cart with the troupe. Another evening she went in a carriage with the chanteuse. Still another evening there was no sign of life in the house. Here he was waiting. His head was worn out from looking up at her window for so long. It was past midnight, the shops were closed, the road was deserted, and al-Ghuriya was enveloped in darkness. He found, as he often did, that the darkness and emptiness of the street acted as a strange stimulus for the desire latent in his body. He became more and more agitated.

Yet everything has an end, even waiting that seems endless. He made out a rattling noise coming from the direction of the window, which was lost in the darkness. This breathed a spirit of new hope into his senses just as the drone of an airplane inspires a person lost at the North Pole with hope that people are arriving to search for him in the snow. Light could be seen coming from the opening of the window. Then the musician's silhouette was visible at the center of the opening.

He got up at once and left the coffee shop to cross the street to the performer's house. He pushed against the door without knocking. It swung open as though it had been left unlatched on purpose. He made his way inside, where it was too dark for him to find the staircase. He stayed put in order not to bump into something or trip. A question that made him a little nervous leapt into his head. Did the performer know that Zanuba had invited him? Did she allow the girl to meet her lovers in this house? But he dismissed the thought disdainfully. No obstacle was going to make him abandon this adventure. In any case, there was no need to worry about the consequences of a lover's being caught in a house that depended for its very existence on lovers.

He cut short these reflections when he saw a pale light coming from upstairs. Then he noticed it slowly advancing down the walls. He could make out that he was an arm's length from the bottom step of the staircase. It was not long before he saw Zanuba approaching with a lamp in her hand. He went to her, drunk with desire. He pressed her forearm affectionately with gratitude and lust. She laughed softly. Despite the softness of her laugh, it showed she was not trying to be cautious. She asked mischievously, "Did you have to wait long?"

He touched the hair at his temples and complained, "My hair turned gray while I waited, may God forgive you." Then he whispered, "Is the lady here?"

She jestingly imitated his whisper: "Yes . . . she's alone with a fantastic man."

"Won't she be angry if she learns I've come at this hour?"

She turned around, shrugging her shoulders in disdain. She started up the stairs saying, "Is there a more appropriate hour for a lover like you to come?"

"So she won't see anything wrong with our meeting in her house?"

With a dancing motion of her head, she replied, "Perhaps she would think it very wrong if we didn't meet."

"Long live the lady!"

She resumed speaking, proudly this time, "I'm not just her lute player. I'm her sister's daughter. She's not stingy with me. . . . You can enter in peace."

When they reached the foyer upstairs they could hear some delightful singing accompanied by lute and tambourine. Yasin listened a little and then asked, "Are they alone or is it a party?"

She whispered in his ear, "Alone and a party both. The sultana's lover is a good-humored man who loves music. He wouldn't bear for even an hour of his soiree to pass without lute, tambourine, wine, laughter . . . and you know what else."

She turned to open a door and entered, setting the lamp on a table bracketed to the wall. She stood in front of the mirror to examine her reflection carefully. Yasin forgot about Zubayda and her musical lover. He riveted his greedy eyes on Zanuba's desirable body, which he was seeing for the first time stripped of the wrap. He fixed his eyes on her with force and concentration and moved them deliberately and delightedly from top to bottom and from bottom to top. Before he could act on any of the tens of wishes racing through his breast, Zanuba remarked, as though continuing the same conversation, "He's a man with no equal in his graciousness or sensitivity to music. As for his generosity, we could talk about that from today till tomorrow . . . that's what lovers should be like . . . otherwise . . ."

He did not miss the implications of her reference to the generosity of the performer's lover. He had accepted from the start that his new romance would cost him dearly, but her reference to it seemed in poor taste and offended him. Motivated by an instinct of self-defense, he found himself forced to say, "Perhaps he's a rich man."

Responding to his maneuver, she said, "Wealth is one thing, generosity is another. Many a wealthy man is stingy."

He inquired, not because he wanted to know but merely to avoid silence, which he was afraid would seem to express disapproval, "Who do you suppose this generous man is?"

Turning the knob to raise the wick on the lamp, she answered, "He's from our district. You must have heard of him . . . al-Sayyid Ahmad Abd al-Jawad."

"Who!"

She turned toward him in astonishment to see what had frightened him. She found him in a rigid pose with his eyes bulging out. She asked him disapprovingly, "What's the matter with you?"

The name she had spoken had come upon him like a hammer falling violently on top of his head. The question had escaped from him unintentionally in a scream of alarm. For some moments he was bewildered and oblivious to his surroundings. When he saw Zanuba's face again and its expression of astonishment and disapproval, he was afraid he would give himself away. He exerted his willpower to defend himself. To conceal his alarm, he resorted to some playacting. He clapped his hands together, as though he could not believe what had been said about the man, because he thought he was so respectable. He muttered incredulously, "Al-Sayyid Ahmad Abd al-Jawad! . . . With a store in al-Nahhasin?"

She gave him a bitterly critical look for alarming her for no reason. She asked him scornfully, "Yes, him. . . . So what made you cry out for help like a virgin being deflowered?"

He laughed in a perfunctory way. Praising God secretly that he had not told her his full name the day they met, he replied with mock astonishment, "Who would believe this of such a pious, respectable man?"

She looked at him with skepticism before asking him sarcastically, "Is this what really alarmed you? . . . Nothing but that? Did you think he was a sinless saint? . . . What's wrong with his doing this? Can a man attain perfection without having an affair?"

He said apologetically, "You're right . . . there's nothing in this world worth being astonished at." He laughed nervously and continued: "Imagine this dignified gentleman flirting with the sultana, drinking wine, and swaying to the music. . . ."

In her same sarcastic tone she said, as though to continue his statement, "And playing the tambourine better than a professional like Ayusha and telling one gem of a joke after another until everyone with him is dying of laughter. It's not surprising, given all of this, that in his store he's seen to be a fine example of sobriety and earnestness. You should be serious about serious things and playful when you play. There's an hour for your Lord and an hour for your heart."

He plays the tambourine better than a professional like Ayusha. . . . He tells jokes that make his companions die from laughter. . . . Who could this man be? His father? . . . Al-Sayyid Ahmad Abd al-Jawad? That stern, tyrannical, terrifying, God-fearing, reserved man who kills everyone around him with fright?

How could he believe what his ears had heard? How, how? . . . There must be some confusion between two men with similar names. There could be no relationship between his father and this tambourine-playing lover. But Zanuba had agreed he owned a store in al-Nahhasin. There was only one store in al-Nahhasin that bore this name and it was his father's. Lord, was what he had heard true or was he raving? He wanted dearly to learn the truth for himself, to see it with his own eyes. That desire gained control of him. This investigation appeared to him the most important thing in life. He was unable to combat the desire. He smiled to the girl and shook his head sagely as though to say, "What days we live in. Each more amazing than the last." Then he asked her, as if motivated by nothing but curiosity, "Isn't there some way I could see him without being seen?"

She objected, "You're strange! What need is there to spy?"

He entreated her: "It's a sight worth seeing. Don't deprive me of it."

She laughed contemptuously and commented, "You've got the brains of a child in the body of a camel. Isn't that so, my camel? But death to anyone who disappoints one of your requests. . . . Hide in the foyer while I take them a dish of fruit. I'll leave the door open till I come back."

She left the room and he trailed after her with a pounding heart. He hid in a dark corner of the hall while the lute player continued on her way to the kitchen. She soon returned with a dish of grapes. She went to the door from which the singing came and knocked. She waited a moment and then went in, leaving the door open. There he saw a divan at the end of the room. Zubayda sat in the middle of it cradling a lute. She accompanied herself as she sang, "O Muslims, O People of God."

Sitting next to her was his father, not someone else. When he saw him, his heart pounded harder. His father had removed his cloak and rolled up his sleeves. He was shaking the tambourine and gazing at the performer with a face brimming with joy and happiness. The door was open only so long as Zanuba was in the room, one or two minutes, but during that time he witnessed an amazing sight: a secret life, a long story with many ramifications. He awoke like a person emerging from a long, deep sleep to the convulsions of a violent earthquake. In those two minutes he saw a whole life summed up by one image, like a brief scene in a dream that brings together diverse events that would take years in the real world. He saw his father the way he truly was—his father, not some other man, but not as he was accustomed to seeing him. Never before had he seen him without his cloak, at a relaxed, spontaneous party. He had never seen him with his black hair sticking up as though he had been running around bareheaded. He had never seen his naked leg as it appeared at the edge of the divan, sticking out from his gown, which had been pulled up. He had never seen, by God, the tambourine in his hands as he shook it with a dancing rhythm gracefully interspersed with taps on the skin. Perhaps most amazing of all, he had never before seen his face smile. It was glistening with such affection and goodwill that Yasin was stunned, just as Kamal had been when he saw their father laughing in front of his store, the day he went to see him driven by his desire to get his mother released.

Yasin saw all of this in two minutes. Once Zanuba had closed the door and gone to her room he remained where he was, listening to the singing and the jingling of the tambourine with a spinning head. It was the same sound he had heard when he entered the building, but how differently it affected his soul, what new images and ideas it brought to his mind now. . . . When a child who has not started school yet hears a school bell ring, he smiles, but once he is a pupil it sounds like a warning of the many hardships ahead.

Zanuba rapped on the door of her room to summon him. He awoke from his daze and went to her. He was trying to gain control of himself so he would not appear disturbed or stunned when she saw him. He entered with a broad smile on his face.

"Did you see something to make you forget yourself?"

He replied in a contented and relieved tone, "It was a rare sight, and the singing was excellent."

"Would you like us to do what they're doing?"

"On our first night? . . . Certainly not. . . . I wouldn't want to mix anything else with you, not even singing."

At first he had been forcing himself to talk so he would appear to her, and to himself, to be calm and natural. He got caught up in what he was saying and no longer needed to pretend. He found he had returned to normal faster than he would have imagined. Similarly, a person who pretends to cry at a funeral may end up weeping profusely. Even so, Yasin was suddenly struck with astonishment and told himself, "What an amazing situation! It would never have occurred to me. Here I am with Zanuba and my father's in a nearby room with Zubayda. Both of us in the same house!" He soon shrugged his shoulders and continued to himself: "But why should I bother to be amazed at something that seems incredible when it's an actuality I've observed myself? There it is, so it's silly to wonder with astonishment whether I can believe it. I'll believe it and stop marveling at it. What's wrong with that?"

He felt not only relief but happiness beyond measure. He needed no encouragement to continue his sex life, but like most men indulging in forbidden pleasure, he was interested in the company of a like-minded person. How incredible to have found this person in his father, the traditional role model, who had terrified him for so long, whether consciously or not, because he assumed they held contradictory views. He set aside everything but his joy, which seemed the most precious thing he had achieved in life. He felt new love and admiration for his father, unlike the old types he had previously known, which had a thick coating of awe and fear. This new emotion sprang from the depths of his soul and was intertwined with the roots of his being. It seemed identical to his love and admiration for himself. His father was no longer a man who was distant, hard to reach, a closed door. He was near at hand, a bit of his own soul and heart. Father and son were a single spirit. The man in there shaking the tambourine was not al-Sayyid Ahmad Abd al-Jawad but Yasin himself, the way he would be in the future and the way he should be. Nothing separated them except secondary considerations of age and experience.

"Good health to you, Father," he thought to himself. "Today I've discovered you. Today's your birthday in my soul. What a day and what a father you are. . . . Until tonight I've been an orphan. Drink and play the tambourine even better than Ayusha. I'm proud of you. Do you sing too, I wonder?"

"Doesn't al-Sayyid Ahmad Abd al-Jawad sing sometimes?"

"Are you still thinking about him? Why can't people leave each other alone? . . . Yes, he sings, my camel. . . . When he's drunk, he joins in singing the choruses."

"How's his voice?"

"As full and beautiful as his neck."

"All the singing voices in our family go back to this source," he mused. "Everyone sings. It's a family with deep roots in music. I wish I could hear you, even just once. The only memory I have of your voice is of yelling and scolding. The only refrain of yours we all know is 'Boy! Ox! Son of a bitch!' I'd like to hear you sing 'Affection's rare with good-looking people' or 'I'm in love, my beauty.' What are you like when you're drunk, Father? What are you like when you get rowdy? I must know so I can follow your example and live according to your traditions. How are you when you're in love? How do you embrace?"

He remembered Zanuba. He saw her in front of the mirror smoothing her hair with her fingers. The armhole of her dress revealed smooth, clear skin sloping down to a breast like a round loaf of unbaked bread. Intoxicating desire swept through his body, and he fell on her like a bull elephant crushing a gazelle.

40

Three automobiles proffered by friends of al-Sayyid Ahmad stopped in front of his house to wait for the bride and her party, whom they were to convey to the Shawkat residence in Sugar Street, or al-Sukkariya. It was late in the afternoon. The rays of the summer sun had withdrawn from the street and were resting on the houses opposite the bride's home. There was no hint of a wedding there, except for the roses decorating the lead vehicle. These caught the eyes of the nearby shop owners and of many of the passersby.

The engagement had been arranged previously. The presents had arrived. The trousseau had been sent. The marriage contract had been signed. At no time during all of this had there been any ululations of joy from the house, any decorations on the door, or any other of the customary signs of a wedding to reveal what was going on inside. Families were usually proud to make a display on such occasions, using weddings as an excuse to express their concealed longing for delight with song, dance, and shrieks of joy.

Everything had been concluded in calm silence. No one knew about the marriage except for relatives and friends and a select group of neighbors. Al-Sayyid Ahmad had refused to budge from his sense of decorum or to allow any member of his family to escape from it even for an hour. Consequently, accompanied by the women of her family, the bride left the house in silence despite the protestations of Umm Hanafi. Aisha dashed for the automobile at breakneck speed, as though she feared that the eyes of the onlookers might scorch her wedding gown or her white silk tiara and veil, which were decorated with different varieties of jasmine. Khadija and Maryam followed her, together with some other girls. The mother and women relatives and neighbors found their places in the other automobiles. Meanwhile Kamal took his seat beside the driver of the bride's car.

The mother wanted the procession to pass by al-Husayn so she could have a fresh look at his shrine, which her desire to see had cost her so dearly once before. She wished to ask al-Husayn's blessing on her beautiful bride. The automobiles went along the streets she had taken that day with Kamal. Afterward they turned into al-Ghuriya at the corner where she had almost met her death. Finally they dropped their passengers at Mutawalli Gate in front of the entrance to Sugar Street, which was too narrow for cars to enter. They all dismounted and entered the alley, where wedding decorations could be seen. The boys of the district rushed toward them while screams and trills resounded from the Shawkat residence, the first house on the right as they entered the alley. The windows of the house were crowded with the heads of people peering down and trilling with joy. The bridegroom, Khalil Shawkat, stood at the entrance with his brother Ibrahim Shawkat as well as Yasin and Fahmy. Khalil smilingly approached the bride and offered her his arm. She did not know what to do and would not have moved if Maryam had not taken her arm and put it around his. Then he escorted her inside. They passed by the crowded courtyard as roses and sweets were showered at the bride's feet and those of the bridal party until the women disappeared behind the door of the women's quarters.

Although the marriage contract for Aisha and Khalil had been signed a month or more earlier, the sight of their arms being intertwined and of them walking side by side affected Yasin and Fahmy, and especially the latter, with an astonishment mixed with embarrassment and a feeling almost of disapproval. The family code did not seem to make any exception for wedding ceremonies conducted in full accord with Islamic law. This reaction was even more pronounced in Kamal, who pulled on his mother's hand in alarm and pointed to the bridal couple preceding everyone else up the stairs. He seemed to be appealing to her to prevent an outrageous evil

The two young men wanted to steal a look at their father's face to see what effect that rare sight had on him. They quickly looked all around but found no trace of him. He was not at the entrance or in the adjacent courtyard, where benches and chairs were arranged in rows with a platform up in front for the singers. The fact was that al-Sayyid Ahmad had shut himself up with some of his best friends in a reception room opening on the courtyard and had not left it since he had set foot in the house. He was determined to stay there until the evening was concluded. He wanted to keep some distance between himself and the "masses" clamoring around outside. Nothing made him so uncomfortable as to be with his family at a wedding party. He did not want to impose his supervision on them at a time set aside for delight and did not care to observe at close hand their relaxed response to a festive occasion. What he hated most of all was for any of them to see him lapse from the stern dignity to which they were accustomed. If the matter had been left to him, the wedding would have been carried out in complete silence. The widow of the late Mr. Shawkat had met his suggestion with totally inflexible opposition. She had refused for the bride to be welcomed to her home with anything less than a gala evening party. For the entertainment she had hired the female vocalist Jalila and the male vocalist Sabir.

Kamal was so ecstatic with the freedom and enjoyment he was allowed that he could have been the bridegroom. He was one of the few individuals permitted to move freely back and forth between the women's section inside and the men's area in the courtyard by the stage. He stayed for a long time with his mother, gazing at the women's ornaments and jewelry and listening to their jokes and conversations, which were dominated by the topic of marriage. He also heard the performer Jalila there. She sat at the front of the hall, resembling in both her huge size and her ornamentation the ceremonial camel litter sent with the pilgrims to Mecca. She proceeded to sing some popular songs, while openly drinking wine.

The jovial atmosphere was strange and attractive to Kamal, and he felt very comfortable. The most important thing of all to him was Aisha, who was dressed up more magnificently than he had ever dreamed possible. His mother encouraged him to stay with her so she could keep an eye on him. After a time she changed her mind and was forced, for reasons she had not anticipated, to urge him in a whisper to go find his brothers. One reason was his intense interest in Aisha, now with her dress and the next time with her ornaments. Amina was afraid he would spoil her outfit. Then, too, he let some childishly frank observations slip out concerning some of the ladies present. For example, one time he pointed to a woman from the bridegroom's family and called out to his mother, "Look at the nose of that lady, Mother. Isn't it bigger than Khadija's?"

When Jalila was singing he had surprised everyone by joining with the troupe in the chorus: "Beautiful dove . . . where can I find her?" The performer had invited him to sit with the members of her ensemble. In this way and in others he had attracted a lot of attention, and the women had begun teasing him. His mother was not comfortable with the commotion he was causing. Apprehensive that he might upset some people and worried that he might be admired more than was safe for him, she reluctantly chose to have him leave the room to join the men's party.

He wandered among the rows of chairs and then stood between

Fahmy and Yasin until Sabir had finished singing "You beauty, why are you already in love?" Then Kamal started roving around again. When he passed by the reception room, his curiosity prompted him to have a look inside. He poked his head in and before he knew it his eyes met his father's. Kamal felt nailed to the spot and unable to turn his eyes away. One of his father's friends, al-Sayyid Muhammad Iffat, saw him and called him. To avoid angering his father, he found himself forced to obey this summons. He approached the man fearfully and reluctantly and stood before him, straight as a ramrod with his arms at his sides, as though a soldier at attention. The man shook his hand and said, "God's will be done ... what year in school are you, Uncle?"

"Third year, fourth section. . . ."

"Splendid ... splendid. . . . Did you hear Sabir sing?"

Although the boy was answering Muhammad Iffat, he had been careful from the beginning to answer in a way that would please his father. He did not know how to reply to the last question or at least he hesitated. The man took pity on him and quickly asked, "Don't you like singing?"

The boy said emphatically, "Certainly not."

It was clear that some of the men present planned to make a joke about this response, the last they would have expected from a person related to Ahmad Abd al-Jawad, but their host cautioned them against it with his eyes, and they kept quiet.

Then Mr. Muhammad Iffat asked Kamal, "Isn't there something you like to listen to?"

Looking at his father, Kamal said, "The Holy Qur'an."

Expressions of approval were heard and the boy was allowed to depart. Thus he did not get to hear what was said about him behind his back. Al-Sayyid al-Far laughed out loud and commented, "If that's true, the boy's a bastard."

Al-Sayyid Ahmad Abd al-Jawad laughed and, pointing to where Kamal had been standing, said, "Have you seen anyone craftier than that son of a bitch, pretending to be pious in front of me? ... One time when I got home, I heard him singing 'O bird, you up in the tree.' "

Al-Sayyid Ali observed, "Oh, you should have seen him standing between his two brothers and listening to Sabir with his lips moving as he sang along, keeping time perfectly, even better than Ahmad Abd al-Jawad himself."

Then Muhammad Iffat addressed an inquiry to al-Sayyid Ahmad: "The important thing is to tell us whether you liked his voice when he sang 'O bird, you up in the tree.' "

Al-Sayyid Ahmad laughed. Pointing at himself, he said, "He's this lion's cub."

Al-Far cried out, "God have mercy on the lioness who gave birth to you."

Kamal escaped from the reception room to the alley. He seemed to be awakening from a nightmare. He stood amid the crowd of boys on the street. He soon recovered his spirits and walked along, proud of his new clothes, delighted with his freedom that allowed him to go anywhere he wanted, except for the frightening reception room. There was no one to restrict or supervise him. What a historic night for him! Only one thing troubled his serenity whenever he thought of it. That was Aisha's moving to this house, which they had begun referring to as her home. This move had been accomplished in spite of him, without anyone being able to convince him that it was right or beneficial. He had asked repeatedly how his father could allow it, since he would not allow even the shadow of one of his women to be seen through the crack of a window. The only answer he received was loud laughter. He had asked his mother critically how she could do something so extreme as giving Aisha away. She had told him he would grow up one day and take a girl like her from her father's house, and that she would be escorted to his house with cries of joy.

Kamal had asked Aisha if she was really happy about leaving them. She had said no, but the trousseau had been carried to the stranger's house. Aisha, whose place on the cup was Kamal's favorite, had followed her trousseau. Although it was true that the present festivities were helping him forget things he had thought he would be unable to forget even for a moment, sorrow veiled his cheerful heart like a small cloud passing in front of the moon on a clear night.

It was interesting that his pleasure in the singing that night surpassed his other pleasures, like playing with the boys, observing the women and the men having a good time, or even eating the "palace" bread pudding and the fancy gelatin dessert at supper. All the men and women who noticed him were astonished at the serious interest he took in listening to Jalila and Sabir. It seemed unusual for a child his age, but no one in his family who knew his background in music as Aisha's student was surprised. He had a fine voice, which was considered second in the family only to Aisha's, although their father's voice, which they had only heard screaming, was the best of all. Kamal listened for a long time to both Jalila and Sabir. He found to his surprise that he preferred the singing of the male vocalist and the music of his troupe. They made a greater impact on his heart. Some lines from their songs stuck in his memory, like "Why are you in love? . . . Because that's the way it is." After the night of the wedding, he frequently repeated these lines in the hyacinth bean and jasmine bower on the roof of their home.

Amina and Khadija also enjoyed some of the same delights and freedom as Kamal. Like him, neither of them had ever witnessed an evening so filled with fellowship, music, and merriment. Amina was especially delighted by the attention and flattery she received as mother of the bride, since she had never before been afforded either. Even Khadija's grief disappeared in the festive lights just as the gloom of night gives way to morning's radiance. She forgot her sorrows under the influence of soft laughter, sweet tunes, and pleasant conversation. It was all the easier for her to forget, because she had a new sorrow, an innocent one that arose from her feeling of regret over Aisha's imminent departure. This feeling engendered sincere love and affection. Her former sorrows were obscured by this new one, just as feelings of animosity may be obliterated by generosity. Similarly, a person who both loves and hates someone may find that the sorrow of parting obscures the hatred, leaving only the love. Moreover, Khadija felt a new confidence in herself from appearing with makeup and fine clothes that attracted the attention of some of the women, who praised her enthusiastically. Their praise filled her with hope and dreams and provided her some happy moments.

Yasin and Fahmy sat side by side, alternately chatting and listening to the music. Khalil Shawkat, the bridegroom, joined them from time to time, whenever he had a break from the duties of his enjoyable but taxing evening. In spite of the atmosphere of celebration and delight, Yasin was rather anxious. There was a lingering, vacant look in his eyes. He would ask himself occasionally whether it would be all right for him to quench his thirst, if only with a glass or two of wine. For that reason, he leaned toward their friend Khalil Shawkat and whispered, "Rescue me before the whole evening is lost."

The young man reassured him with a wink of his eye and said, "I've set aside a table in a private room for friends like you."

Yasin was cheered by that, and his interest in conversation, jokes, and music revived. He did not intend to get drunk, for in a place like this, overflowing with family and acquaintances, even a little wine had to be considered a great victory. Although his father was secluded in the reception room, he was not far away. Yasin's penetration of his father's secrets did not shake the man's traditional authority over him. Al-Sayyid Ahmad continued to occupy his heavily fortified stronghold of awe and reverence, and Yasin had not stirred from his own position of obedience and veneration. He had not even thought of revealing his father's secret, which he had discovered surreptitiously, to anyone, not even to Fahmy. For all these reasons, Yasin was at first satisfied with a glass or two with which to cajole his unruly appetite. It would help prepare him to enjoy the merriment, conversations, music, and other pleasures that lost their savor for him without wine.

Unlike Yasin, Fahmy did not find and doubted he ever would find anything to quench his thirst. His grief had been aroused unexpectedly by the arrival of the bride. He had gone with the bridegroom and Yasin to welcome her with a carefree heart. Then he had seen Maryam walking directly behind the bride. Her mouth was resplendent with a smile of greeting for everyone. Distracted by the trills of joy and the roses, she did not notice him. Her silk veil was so sheer that the clear complexion of her face was visible. He had followed her with his eyes, his heart pounding, until she disappeared behind the door to the women's quarters. He returned to his seat as shaken as a skiff suddenly caught in a violent storm. Before he saw her, he had been calm, apparently distracted enough by conversation to have forgotten everything. In fact, long periods would pass when he was in this oblivious, forgetful state, while his heart became a reservoir for his suffering. The moment a thought occurred to him, a memory stirred, someone mentioned her name, or anything similar happened, his heart would throb with pain and exude one grief after another. It was like a decayed tooth with an inflamed gum. For a time the toothache may die down until the tooth presses against a morsel of food or touches a solid object. Then the pain erupts. Thus Fahmy's love would beat against his ribs from the inside as though craving a breath of air, shouting at the top of its lungs that it was still a prisoner. No amount of consolation or forgetfulness had set it free.

He often hoped she would remain invisible to other suitors until he could get established as a free man, acting and deciding his own fate. As days, weeks, and months passed without a suitor asking for her hand, it seemed his wish had been granted, but he did not enjoy any real peace of mind. He was prey to anxiety and fear, which took turns, time and again, ruffling his serenity, spoiling his dreams, and conjuring up for him many different types of pain and jealousy, which although imaginary were no less ferocious and cruel than if his fears had been realized. Even this desire itself and the delay in the occurrence of the misfortune became incentives for more anxiety and fear and consequently for pain and jealousy. Whenever his torment was severe, he wished the calamity would take place so he could receive his share of grief all in one blow. Perhaps afterward, through his despair, he could attain the tranquillity and repose he had not been able to achieve through his pipe dreams.

He could not yield to his emotions at a musical soiree where he was surrounded by the looks of friends and relatives. Yet the impact the sight of Maryam had made on him as she walked behind his sister could not pass without provoking some noticeable reaction. Since Fahmy was not able to brood about his sorrows or reveal his hidden emotions, he softened their impact by going to the other extreme. He talked, laughed, and pretended to be blissfully happy, but whenever he had even a moment to himself, he felt deep inside the alienation of his heart from everything around him. With the passing of time he realized that the sight of Maryam walking in the bridal court had aroused his love the way a sudden racket decisively arouses an anxious person with a tendency toward insomnia. For that evening at least, Fahmy would be unable to enjoy any peace of mind. Nothing happening around him would be able to remove from his mind her image or the smile with which she responded to the warm welcome composed of trills of joy and roses. It was a pure, sweet smile, suggestive of a carefree heart aspiring to calm and happiness. It was a smile that seemed too pretty ever to be replaced by a grimace of pain. The sight of her ripped into his heart, disclosing to him that only he was suffering. He alone bore his troubles. But had he not been laughing boisterously just now and moving his head to the music as though he was happy and glad? Was it not possible that someone looking at him might be deceived and think the same thing of him that he did of her? He derived some consolation from that thought but was no more convinced than a typhoid patient who asks himself, "Isn't it likely that I'll recover the way so-and-so did?"

Fahmy remembered her message Kamal had brought him some months before: "Tell him that she won't know what to do if a suitor asks to marry her during this long period of waiting." He asked himself, as he had tens of times before, whether any emotion lay behind those words? Indeed, no man, no matter how obstinate, could blame her for a single one of them. Nor could he overlook the good sense and wisdom they contained. Yet, for this very reason, he felt powerless against them and hated them. Good sense and wisdom are seldom happy with the impetuousness of emotion, which characteristically knows no limits.

Fahmy returned to the present, to the musical evening, and his raging love. It was not merely the sight of her that had rocked him so violently. Perhaps seeing her for the first time in a new place had done it. She had been here in the courtyard of the Shawkat residence, far removed from his house. He had never seen her in any other area before. For her to remain put in the old location established her in the mechanical daily routine, whereas her sudden appearance in a new place re-created her before his eyes and gave her a new existence in his consciousness, which in turn reawakened her original, latent presence in his mind. Both old and new visions of her had joined together to create this violent jolt. Moreover, her former existence linked to his house was separated from him by a wall of despair created by the stern rules of his family. Here, far removed from that house, her new existence was attended by a feeling of freedom and liberation as well as a spirit of parade and vivacity unknown to him. Her new existence was in the context of a wedding and thoughts of love and union. All of these circumstances helped to free her from her confinement atop a pedestal. Now his heart could see her as a possible goal. She seemed to be telling him, "Look where I am now. Just one more step and you'll find me in your arms." This hope soon collided with the thorny reality, helping create his violent jolt. Perhaps the sight of her in this new location also worked to establish her even more firmly in his soul, embed her in his life, and fix her in his memories. Images penetrate more deeply into us when they are associated with the different places we know from our experiences. Previously Maryam was associated with the roof of his house, the arbor of hyacinth beans and jasmine, Kamal, listening to his English lesson, the coffee hour, and talking to his mother in the study, and the message Kamal brought back from her. Henceforth she would be associated with Sugar Street, the courtyard of the Shawkat residence, the evening's musical entertainment, the singing of Sabir, Aisha's wedding procession, and everything else that was crowding in through his senses. Such a transformation could not occur without adding to the violent shock that had stunned him.

During one of Sabir's intermissions, the voice of the female vocalist happened to carry through the windows overlooking the courtyard so the men could hear her. She was singing "My lover's departed." Fahmy set about listening eagerly and with enormous interest. He concentrated all of his attention on absorbing the music, not because he particularly liked Jalila's voice, but because he thought Maryam would be listening to her at that moment. The lyrics would be speaking to both of them at the same time. Jalila united the two of them in a single experience of listening and possibly of feeling. She had created an occasion for their spirits to meet. All of these considerations made him revere her voice and love her song. He wished to share this one sensation with Maryam. He tried for a long time to get through to her soul by retreating deep into himself. He sought to contact the vibrations of her reactions by following his own. Notwithstanding the distance and the thick walls separating them, he wished to live for a few moments inside her essence. To accomplish this, he attempted to determine from the lyrics the effect they would have on his beloved's soul. What would her response be to "My lover's departed" or "It's a long time since he sent me a letter"? Had she been lost in a sea of memories? Had not at least one of those waves slipped away to reveal his face? Had not her heart felt a stabbing pain or a piercing grief? Or was she in such a daze throughout that she saw nothing in the song but enjoyable music?

Fahmy imagined her listening attentively to the music, free of her veil, parading her vitality, or her mouth parted in a smile like the one he had glimpsed when she arrived, which had upset him since he had inferred from it that she had forgotten him. She might be talking to one of his sisters as she frequently enjoyed doing. He envied his sisters that privilege, which would daze him to the point of panic, whereas they regarded it as an ordinary conversation like any they conducted with girls in the neighborhood. Indeed, he had frequently been amazed by his sisters' attitude toward her, not because they took an interest in her, for they did love her, but because they loved her exactly the same way they did the other girls in the neighborhood, as though she was just some girl. How could they greet her without getting flustered and do it in an ordinary manner, the way he greeted any passing girl or his fellow law students? How could they talk about her and say, "Maryam said this" or "Maryam did that" and pronounce the name like any other one, Umm Hanafi, for example? Hers was a name he had only pronounced once or twice in someone else's presence. Then he had been amazed by its impact on him. When he was alone, he would only repeat her name as though it were one of the venerable names of Muslim saints engraved in his imagination along with the ornamentation provided by legends. These were names he would not pronounce without immediately adding one of the appropriate religious formulas: "May God be pleased with him" or "Peace on him." How could he explain that not merely the name but even Maryam herself lacked any magic or sanctity for his sisters?

When Jalila finished singing, there were shouts of appreciation and applause. Fahmy concentrated on that with even greater interest than he had given the song, since Maryam's voice and hands were participating. He wished it was possible for him to make out her voice among all the others and to isolate her clapping from all the rest, but that was no easier than distinguishing the sound of one wave from the roar of all those beating against the shore. So he responded lovingly to the cries of applause and the clapping without distinction, as a mother prays for blessings and peace collectively when she hears the voices of pupils from a school her son attends.

Although their reasons differed, no one so resembled Fahmy in his inner isolation as his father, who did not leave the chamber where he was surrounded by some of his very best friends. Some companions had not been able to endure the sober atmosphere in there when music was resounding outside. They had broken away from his circle to scatter among the listeners where they could enjoy the music and have a good time. The only people left with al-Sayyid Ahmad were those who loved his company even more than having a good time. They all observed an unaccustomed solemnity as though performing a duty or attending a funeral. These old friends had understood in advance it would be like this when he had invited them to the wedding. They knew from experience that there were two sides to his character. One was reserved for his friends and the other was for his family. There was a paradoxical contradiction between this somber behavior with which they were celebrating a wedding and their boisterous nightly reunions when they had nothing to celebrate. They did not hesitate to joke about their dignified conduct, but in a calm and delicate manner. When Mr. Iffat's voice was raised in laughter once, Mr. al-Far put his finger to his lips as though warning him to lower his voice. He whispered in his ear to caution and scold him: "We're at a wedding, man."

Another time, when they had been silent for a while, Mr. Ali looked around at their faces and, raising his hand to his head, congratulated them: "May God thank you for your effort."

At that, al-Sayyid Ahmad asked them to join their other friends outside and have fun, but Mr. Iffat told him in a critical tone of voice,

"Should we leave you alone on a night like this? Do you know who your friends are until you're in need?"

Al-Sayyid Ahmad could not keep from laughing. He commented, "It will only take a few more wedding nights before God forgives all of us."

A wedding had other ramifications beyond mandatory solemnity at a party devoted to merrymaking and music. There were implications for him in particular as a father with an unusual temperament. He had ambivalent feelings about his daughter's marriage. He was not comfortable about it, even though reason and religion did not support his position. It was not that he did not wish for his two daughters to marry. Like all other fathers, he wished to protect his daughters, but would have preferred that marriage was not the only way to provide this protection. He may even have wished that God had created girls in a manner that made marriage unnecessary or that he had never had any daughters. Since his wishes had not been and could not be fulfilled, he was forced to hope his daughters would marry, like a man who longs for an honorable or painless death, since he knows life cannot last forever.

Al-Sayyid Ahmad had often expressed his reluctance in many different ways, both conscious and unconscious. He would tell some of his loyal friends, "You ask me about fathering females? It's an evil against which we are defenseless, but let us thank God. In any case, it's a duty. This is not to say that I don't love my daughters. In fact, I love them as much as I do Yasin, Fahmy, and Kamal, each equally. But how can my mind be at rest when I know that I will carry them to a stranger one day. However attractive he may seem on the outside, only God knows what's inside him. What can a weak girl do when she's faced by a strange man far from the supervision of her father? What will her fate be if her husband divorces her one day, after her father has died? She must take refuge in her brother's house to endure a life of neglect. I'm not afraid for any of my sons. No matter what happens to one of them, he's a man and is able to confront life. But a girl . . . my God, preserve us."

He might say with apparent candor, "A girl is really a problem. . . . Don't you see that we spare no effort to discipline, train, preserve, and care for her? But don't you also see that after all of this we ourselves hand her over to a stranger and let him do as he wishes with her? Praise to God who alone is praised for adversity."

Al-Sayyid Ahmad's anxious and ambivalent feelings found expression in the critical attitude he adopted toward Khalil Shawkat, the bridegroom. It was a harsh, faultfinding attitude that kept searching to discover some defect to satisfy its obstinacy. Khalil seemed not to count as a member of the Shawkat family, which had been bound to his own family by ties of affection and friendship for more than a generation. He seemed not to be the young man whose manliness, good looks, and honor were attested to by everyone who knew him. Al-Sayyid Ahmad was not able to deny the boy's good qualities but hesitated for a long time over his full face and the calm, heavy look of his eyes that seemed indicative of laziness. He was pleased to infer from these signs that he was sluggish. The gentleman told himself, "He's nothing but a bull, living only to eat and sleep." His recognition of the young man's good qualities followed by his search for any defect was an emotional dialectic reflecting al-Sayyid Ahmad's latent emotions. He both desired the girl to get married and detested the idea of marriage. His acknowledgment of Khalil's qualities had made it possible for the marriage to take place. His search for Khalil's defects helped relieve his hostilities toward the marriage. He was like an opium addict, enslaved by its pleasures and terrified by its danger, searching for it by any means, while cursing it. For the moment, al-Sayyid Ahmad ignored his ambivalent feelings. He was surrounded by his best friends and consoled himself alternately with conversing and listening to the distant music. He allowed contentment and joy a place in his heart and prayed that his daughter would be happy and lead a tranquil life. Even his critical attitude toward Khalil Shawkat was reduced to a scornful feeling free of any rancor.

When the guests were invited to the dinner tables, Fahmy and Yasin were separated for the first time. Khalil Shawkat conducted the latter to a special table where wine was in ample supply. Conscious of the possible consequences, Yasin was cautious at first. He announced that two glasses were enough for him. He resisted with courage (or was it cowardice?) the freely flowing wine, until he reached the first stage of intoxication. Then his memories of the pleasures of drunkenness were stirred, and his willpower weakened. He wanted to get more intoxicated without exceeding the limits of safety. He had a third glass and fled from the table, although he took the precaution of hiding a half-filled bottle in a secret place so he could retrieve it if there was a pressing need. He kept one eye on paradise, while the other was peering down at hell. The young men returned to their seats with vibrant new spirits that imparted to the atmosphere a delight freed from restrictions.

In the women's quarters, intoxication had gained firm control over the performer Jalila. She started looking around at the faces of the women in the audience, asking, "Which of you is the wife of al-Sayyid Ahmad Abd al-Jawad?"

Her question attracted their attention and aroused everyone's interest. Amina was too shy to utter a word. She began to stare at the entertainer's face with anxiety and disapproval. When the performer repeated the question, Widow Shawkat pointed to Amina and volunteered, "There she is. Why do you ask?"

The performer examined her with piercing eyes. Then she let out a resounding laugh and said with satisfaction, "A beauty, by the truth of God's house. Al-Sayyid Ahmad's taste is unbeatable."

Amina was so embarrassed she was like a tongue-tied virgin. Embarrassment was not her only emotion. She asked herself with anxiety and alarm what the implications were of the entertainer's question about al-Sayyid Ahmad Abd al-Jawad's wife and of her praise for his taste. She had spoken in a tone that only a person who knew him well would adopt. Aisha and Khadija felt the same way. Khadija glanced back and forth from some of her friends to the performer, as though asking them what they thought of this tipsy woman. Jalila paid no attention to the panic her words had provoked. She turned her eyes to the bride and examined her as she had the mother previously. Then she wriggled her eyebrows and declared admiringly, "As beautiful as the moon, by the Messenger of God! You're really your father's daughter. Anyone seeing those eyes would immediately remember his." She laughed boisterously before continuing: "I see you are all wondering how this woman knows al-Sayyid Ahmad.... I knew him before his wife herself did. He was a neighbor and childhood playmate. Our fathers were friends. Do you think a performer doesn't have a father? My father was head of a Qur'anic primary school and a blessed man. What do you think about that, you beauty?"

She directed this question to Amina, whose fear, natural indulgence, and good humor prompted her to answer, as she struggled with her embarrassed confusion, "May God have mercy on him. We're all children of Eve and Adam."

Narrowing her eyes, Jalila began to rock her head left and right. Her memories and expressions of piety seemed to have made a great impact on her, or perhaps her drunken head enjoyed this routine. She began speaking again: "He was a man with a jealous sense of honor. But I grew up with a natural tendency to be playful, as though I had been suckled on coquetry in the cradle. When I laughed on the top floor of our house, the hearts of men in the street would be troubled. The moment he heard my voice, he would rain blows upon me and call me the worst names. But what point was there in trying to discipline a girl who was so gifted in the arts of love, music, and flirtation? His attempts were in vain. My father went to paradise and its delights while I was fated to adopt the epithets he hurled at me as my banner in life. That's the way the world is. . . . May our Lord nourish you with the good things in life and spare you the evil. . . . May God never deprive us of men, whether through marriage or affairs."

Laughter rang out from all sides of the room. It drowned the shocked exclamations of some women here and there. The reaction was perhaps primarily caused by the apparent contradiction between the final, licentious prayer and the expressions preceding it which at least outwardly seemed serious and regretful. The woman had cloaked her expressions with a serious and dignified veil, before finally revealing her joke. Even Amina, uneasy though she was, could not keep from smiling, although she bowed her head so no one would see. At a party like this, women were able to entertain the drunken jokes of the performers and respond to their humor, although the limits of decency were occasionally surpassed. They seemed to enjoy a break from their normal primness.

The intoxicated entertainer continued her discourse: "My father, may God make paradise his final abode, had good intentions. For example, he brought me a fine man like himself one day and wanted to marry him to me." She roared with laughter. "What kind of marriage would that have been, my dear? What was left for a husband after what had already happened? I told myself, 'Jalila, you'll be disgraced. You've fallen into a tar pit.' "

She paused for a time to whet their appetite or to enjoy the attention focused on her, which was even greater than when she was singing. Then she went on: "But God was gracious. I was saved a few days before the anticipated disaster. I ran off with the late Hassuna al-Baghl, a drug dealer. He had a brother who played the lute for the entertainer Nayzak. He taught me how to play it. Since he liked my voice he also taught me how to sing. He coached me until I got into Nayzak's troupe. When she died, I took her place. I've been singing for ages and have had a hundred lovers, plus. . . ."

She frowned as she tried to remember how many more than a

hundred there had been. Then she turned to ask her tambourine player, "How many, Fino?"

The musician quickly responded, "Plus five—like the five fingers of the Prophet's granddaughter Fatima held up to ward off the evil of infidels."

Laughter resounded once more. Some of the women most fascinated by the performer's account attempted to silence the laughing ladies so she would resume speaking, but she rose suddenly and headed for the door. She paid no attention to the women asking her where she was going. Although they received no answer, no one pressed her, because she was notorious for her outbursts, which she made no effort whatsoever to resist.

Jalila descended the staircase to the door of the women's quarters and stepped into the courtyard. When her sudden appearance attracted the attention of nearby eyes, she paused to allow everyone to see her. She wanted to enjoy the interest that the sight of her would arouse in them and use it to challenge Sabir, who had worked his audience to a peak of enthusiasm. Her wish was granted. The contagion of turning to look at her spread as quickly as a yawn from one man to the next. Her name was repeated by every tongue. Although Sabir was carried away by his own singing, he too noticed the sudden rift between him and his audience. He turned to see what was attracting everyone's attention and his eyes came to rest on the chanteuse, who was gazing at him from afar with her head tilted back in a mixture of intoxication and pride. Sabir was compelled to stop singing and motioned to his musicians to cease playing. He raised his hands to his head to greet her. He knew about her outbursts and, unlike most people, also knew how kindhearted she was. Taking into consideration the dangers of antagonizing her, he displayed unreserved affection for her. His ruse succeeded, and the woman's face shone with delight. She called out to him, "Continue singing, Sabir. That's what I've come to hear."

The guests applauded and jubilantly returned to Sabir. Then Ibrahim Shawkat, the bridegroom's elder brother, approached her and asked politely what she needed. His question reminded her of the real reason she had come. She asked him in a voice that carried to many of the men present and most importantly to Yasin and Fahmy, "Why don't I see al-Sayyid Ahmad Abd al-Jawad? Where has the man hidden himself?"

Ibrahim Shawkat took her arm and smilingly escorted her to the reception room. Meanwhile Fahmy and Yasin exchanged an astonished and incredulous glance. Their eyes followed Ibrahim and the entertainer until they disappeared behind the door.

Al-Sayyid Ahmad was no less astonished than his sons to see her strutting toward him. He stared questioningly at her in alarm, while his companions exchanged smiling, knowing looks.

Jalila looked everyone over quickly and said, "A fine evening to you, gentlemen."

She focused her eyes on al-Sayyid Ahmad. She could not keep herself from laughing heartily. Then she asked sarcastically, "Has my visit frightened you, al-Sayyid Ahmad?"

He gestured to caution her about the people outside. He replied seriously, "Restrain yourself, Jalila. What has motivated you to visit me here under the eyes of all the people?"

Although her sarcastic smile never left her, she replied apologetically, "I would have hated to miss congratulating you on the marriage of your daughter."

Al-Sayyid Ahmad responded uneasily, "Thank you, lady, but didn't you think about the suspicions your visit might arouse in the minds of those who saw you?"

Jalila clapped her hands together and said almost as a reprimand, "Is this the best welcome you have for me?" Then she addressed his companions: "Gentlemen, you're my witnesses. Observe how this man, who used to be unhappy if he couldn't stick the tip of his mustache in my belly button, can't bear the sight of me."

Al-Sayyid Ahmad gestured to her as if to say, "Don't make the mud any wetter." He entreated her, "God knows I'm not unhappy to see you. The only problem is, you see, the awkward situation. . . ."

At this point, Mr. Ali tried to remind her of something she should not forget: "You lived together as lovers and parted friends. There's nothing to be revenged. But the women of his family are upstairs and his sons are outside."

Continuing to try to infuriate al-Sayyid Ahmad, Jalila asked, "Why do you pretend to be pious around your family when you're a pool of depravity?"

He threw her a look of protest and said, "Jalila! . . . There's no might or power except with God."

"Jalila or Zubayda, you saint?"

"I rely on God and the blessings of his deputy the Prophet. . . ."

She wriggled her eyebrows at him as she had in honor of Aisha before him, but this time it was sarcastic and not a sign of admiration.

In a calm voice as serious as a judge's in pronouncing a verdict, she said, "It's all the same to me whether you're Zubayda's lover or some other woman's, but by the head of my mother it troubles me to see you roll in the dirt after being up to your ears in cream here." She pointed to herself.

Mr. Muhammad Iffat, who was the closest to her, rose at that point. He was afraid her intoxication would lead her to do something with unfortunate consequences. He took her hand and gently pulled her toward the door as he whispered in her ear, "I adjure you by al-Husayn to return to your audience, who are waiting impatiently for you."

After some resistance, she obeyed him, but as she slowly moved off, she turned toward al-Sayyid Ahmad to say, "Don't forget to give my greetings to the filthy bitch, and I'll give you some sisterly advice. Wash yourself off with alcohol after you've been with her, otherwise her sweat will affect your blood."

Al-Sayyid Ahmad saw her off with a furious look. He was cursing his luck which had decreed for him to be disgraced before the eyes of many, including his family, who knew him as a shining example of earnestness and dignity. Well, there was still hope that not everyone in his family had heard about the incident, but it was only a feeble one. There was also a chance that in their innocence they would not really understand if they did hear about it, although that possibility was hardly guaranteed, and for more than one reason.

Even assuming the worst, there was no reason for him to be alarmed. Their subservience to him and his domination over them both assured that no convulsion would shake them, not even this scandal. Moreover, he had never assumed it was out of the question that one of his sons, or even the whole family, might discover the truth about him, but he had not been overly worried about that, because of his confidence in his power and because in rearing them he had not relied on either setting an example or persuasion. There was no need to fear that they would swerve off the high road if they discovered he had. He thought it unlikely they would learn anything about him before they came of age, when he would not care much whether they did uncover his secret. Yet none of this could lighten his regret at what had happened, although the event had also pleased and flattered his pride in his sexual appeal. For a woman like Jalila to seek him out to greet him, tease him, or even to make fun of his new sweetheart was a real event that would have a great impact on the circles where he passed his nights. It was an occurrence with far-reaching significance for a man like him who enjoyed nothing so much as love, music, and companionship. But how much purer his happiness would have been if the beautiful event had taken place at a distance from this family atmosphere.

Yasin and Fahmy had not turned their eyes away from the door to the reception room from the moment Jalila disappeared through it till she emerged again, escorted by Mr. Muhammad Iffat. Fahmy was so astonished his head spun like Yasin's when he had heard Zanuba reply, "He's from our district. You must have heard of him . . . al-Sayyid Ahmad Abd al-Jawad. . . ." Now Yasin was overcome by a voracious curiosity. With a happiness that awakened in his heart a frenzy of the same admiration and feeling of affinity for his father that he had felt in Zanuba's room, he realized that Jalila was another adventure in his father's life, which Yasin had begun to picture as a golden chain of romantic escapades. The man surpassed everything he had imagined about him. Fahmy was still hoping and praying he would eventually learn that the entertainer had merely wanted to meet his father for some reason or other connected with her contract to perform at Aisha's wedding.

Then Khalil Shawkat came and laughingly told them that Jalila had been "teasing" their father and had "treated him affectionately, like a good friend."

With that, Yasin could no longer bear to keep his secret. The intoxication of the wine encouraged him to reveal his information. He waited until Khalil left. Then he leaned close to his brother's ear and, trying not to laugh, told him, "I've kept some things from you that I was uneasy about disclosing at the time. Now that you've seen what you have and heard what you have, I'll tell you." He started narrating to his brother what he had heard and seen in the home of the performer Zubayda.

As Yasin told the story with all its details, Fahmy kept interrupting him in bewilderment with, "Don't say that," or "Have you lost your senses?" and "How do you expect me to believe you?" Because of Fahmy's strong faith and idealism, he was not prepared to understand, let alone digest, his father's secret life, which was revealed to him for the first time, especially since his father was one of the pillars of Fahmy's creed and one of the buttresses of his idealism. There may have been some similarity between his feelings when he was first experiencing these revelations and those of a child, if imagination is to be trusted, when he leaves the stability of the womb for the chaos of the world. He could not have been more incredulous or

panic-stricken if he had been told that the mosque of Qala'un had been turned upside down, with its minaret below the building and the tomb on top, or that the Egyptian nationalist leader Muhammad Farid had betrayed the cause of his mentor and predecessor Mustafa Kamil and sold himself to the English.

"My father goes to Zubayda's house to drink, sing, and play the tambourine. . . . My father allows Jalila to tease him and be affectionate with him. . . . My father gets drunk and commits adultery. How could all this be true? Then he wouldn't be the father he knew at home, a man of exemplary piety and resolve. Which was correct? I can almost hear him now reciting, 'God is most great. . . . God is most great.' So how is he at reciting songs? A life of deception and hypocrisy? . . . But he's sincere. Sincere when he raises his head in prayer. Sincere when he's angry. Is my father depraved or is licentiousness a virtue?"

"Astonished? . . . I was too when Zanuba mentioned his name, but I quickly got over it and I asked her what's wrong with it? . . . A sin? Men are all like this or ought to be."

"This statement is entirely appropriate for Yasin. Yasin's one thing and my father's something else. Yasin! . . . What about Yasin? How can I repeat this now, when my father, my father himself doesn't differ at all from Yasin except in having sunk lower. . . . But no, it's not depravity. . . . There must be something I don't know. . . . My father hasn't done anything wrong. . . . He can't do anything wrong. He's above suspicion. In any case, he doesn't merit contempt."

"Still bewildered?"

"I can't imagine that anything you've said could have happened."

"Why? . . . Laugh and enjoy the world. He sings. So what's wrong about singing? He gets drunk, and believe me, drinking is even better than eating. He has affairs and so did the Muslim caliphs. Read about it in the ancient poems contained in Abu Tammam's anthology *Diwan al-Hamasa* or see its marginal glosses. Our father isn't doing anything sinful. Shout with me, 'Long live al-Sayyid Ahmad Abd al-Jawad! Long live our father!' I'll leave you for a moment while I visit the bottle I hid under a chair for just such an occasion."

On the return of the entertainer to her troupe, the news of her meeting with al-Sayyid Ahmad Abd al-Jawad spread through the women's quarters. It passed from mouth to mouth until it reached the mother as well as Khadija and Aisha. Although his family was hearing something like this about him for the first time, many of the ladies whose husbands were friends of al-Sayyid Ahmad were hardly surprised by the news and smilingly winked as if to say they knew more than was being said. But none of them let herself be tempted to plunge into the topic. To bring it up publicly in front of his daughters would not have seemed appropriate to them. Courtesy dictated remaining silent about it in the presence of Amina and her two daughters. Widow Shawkat did jokingly tell Amina, "Watch out, Madam Amina. It seems Jalila's eye has strayed to al-Sayyid Ahmad."

Amina smiled and pretended not to be concerned but blushed with shame and confusion. For the first time she had tangible evidence for the doubts she had entertained long ago. Although she had trained herself to be patient and submissive about what happened to her, her collision with this tangible evidence had cut her to the quick. She felt a torment she had never experienced before. Her pride had also taken a beating.

A woman who wished to add a flattering comment appropriate for the mother of the bride said, "Anyone with a face as beautiful as Mrs. Amina's doesn't have to worry about her husband's eyes straying to another woman."

Amina was deeply moved by the praise, and her vivacious smile returned. In any case, it provided her some consolation for the silent pain she was suffering. Yet when Jalila began a new song, filling their ears with her voice, Amina suddenly became angry and felt for a few seconds she was about to lose control of herself. She quickly suppressed her anger with all the force of a woman who did not acknowledge that she had a right to get angry. Meanwile Khadija and Aisha received the news with astonishment and exchanged an anxious glance. Their eyes were asking what it was all about. Their astonishment was not coupled with panic like Fahmy's nor with pain like their mother's. Perhaps they understood that for a woman like Jalila to leave her troupe and take the trouble of going down to where their father was sitting to greet him and talk to him was something to be proud of. Khadija felt a natural desire to look at her mother's face. She stole a glance at her. Although Mrs. Amina was smiling, her daughter grasped right away the pain and uneasiness she was enduring, which were robbing her of her peace of mind. Khadija felt upset and became angry at the entertainer, Widow Shawkat, and the gathering as a whole.

When it was time for the wedding procession, everyone forgot his personal concerns. No matter how many weeks and months passed, the picture of Aisha in her wedding gown would not leave their minds.

Al-Ghuriya was dark and quiet when the family left the bride's new home to return to al-Nahhasin. Al-Sayyid Ahmad walked alone in front followed a few meters back by Fahmy and Yasin. The latter was exhausting himself by trying to act sober and walk straight, for fear his giddiness would reveal he had drunk too much. At the rear came Amina, Khadija, Kamal, and Umm Hanafi. Kamal had joined the caravan against his will. If his father had not been there to lead them, Kamal would have found some way to free himself from his mother's hand and run back to where they had left Aisha. He was looking behind him at Bab al-Mutawalli from one step to the next to bid farewell sadly and regretfully to the last trace of the wedding, that shining lamp a worker on a ladder was removing from its hook over the entrance to Sugar Street. Kamal was heartbroken to see that his family had relinquished the person he loved best after his mother. He looked up at his mother and whispered, "When will Aisha come back to us?"

She whispered, "Don't say that again. Pray for her to be happy. She'll visit us frequently and we'll call on her a lot."

He whispered to her resentfully, "You've tricked me!"

She motioned toward al-Sayyid Ahmad up in front, who had almost been swallowed up by the darkness. She pursed her lips to whisper, "Hush."

But Kamal was preoccupied with recalling images of things he had happened to see during the wedding. He thought them extraordinarily odd, and they made him uneasy. He pulled his mother's hand his way to separate her from Khadija and Umm Hanafi. Then, pointing back, he whispered to her, "Do you know what's going on there?"

"What do you mean?"

"I peeked through a hole in the door."

The mother felt distressed and alarmed, because she could guess which door he meant, but refusing to trust her intuition, she asked, "What door?"

"The door of the bride's room!"

The woman said with alarm, "It's disgraceful for a person to look through holes in doors."

He immediately whispered back, "What I saw was even more disgraceful."

"Be quiet."

"I saw Aisha and Mr. Khalil sitting on the chaise longue . . . and he was . . ."

She hit him hard on his shoulder to make him stop. She whispered in his ear, "Don't say shameful things. If your father heard you, he'd kill you."

He persisted and told her, as though revealing something to her she could not possibly have imagined, "He was holding her chin in his hand and kissing her."

She hit him again, harder than she ever had before. He realized that he had certainly done something wrong without knowing it. He fell silent and was afraid. When they were crossing the courtyard of their house, straggling behind the others except for Umm Hanafi, who had waited behind to bolt the door, lock it, and latch it, Kamal's anxiety and curiosity overcame his silence and fear. He asked pleadingly, "Why was he kissing her, Mother?"

She told him firmly, "If you start that again, I'll tell your father."

41

Yasin was quite intoxicated when he retired to the bedroom. Since Kamal had fallen sound asleep the moment his head touched the pillow, Yasin was alone with Fahmy. Free at last from parental supervision, he felt in the mood for a noisy row as a release from the nervous strain he had been under all evening, especially on the way home when he had struggled to control himself and act right. Since the room was too cramped for rowdiness, he felt like relieving his tensions by talking. He looked at Fahmy, who was getting undressed, and said sarcastically, "Compared with our brilliant father, we're failures. He's truly some man."

Although this statement revived Fahmy's pain and anxiety, he was content to answer with a bitter smile, "You've been blessed too. What an excellent son!"

"Are you sad our father's one of the great skirt chasers?"

"I wish there had been no change in the ideal picture I've had in my soul."

Rubbing his hands merrily, Yasin said, "The real picture is even more splendid and delightful. He's more than a father. He's the ultimate. Oh, if you had only seen him grasping the tambourine, with a glass shining in front of him. Bravo . . . bravo, al-Sayyid Ahmad!"

Fahmy asked uneasily, "What about his prudence and piety?"

Yasin frowned in order to concentrate on the question, but he found it easier to merge opposites than to reconcile them. Motivated by nothing but admiration, he replied, "There's absolutely no problem there at all. Your cowardly intellect's just creating the problem from nothing. My father's prudent, a Muslim, and loves women. It's as simple and clear as one plus one equals two. Perhaps I'm the one who most resembles him, because I'm a Muslim believer and love women, although I'm not too prudent. You yourself are a believer, prudent, and love women, but you base your acts on faith and prudence while shying away from the third alternative: women." He laughed. "It's the third that lasts."

Yasin's final statement was only remotely linked to his admiration for his father that had started him rattling on and was only superficially in defense of him. It was really an expression of a burning feeling Yasin's intoxication had aroused. Once the guardians he respected were out of the way, he experienced a raging lust incited by an imagination charged with alcohol. His body felt a mad craving for love, and his willpower was unable to bridle it or coax it away. But where could he find what he wanted? Did he have enough time? . . . Zanuba? . . . What was keeping him from her? It wasn't far. It wouldn't take long to make love with her. Then he could come home and sleep deeply and calmly. He was delighted by these visions and seemed not to have a brain to make him think twice. He was in a rush to bring them to pass with no further delay. He quickly told his brother, "It's hot. I'm going up to the roof to enjoy the moist night air."

He left the room for the outer hall and groped his way down the steps in total darkness, being extremely careful not to make a sound. How could he get in touch with Zanuba at this hour of the night? Should he knock on the door? Who would open it? What could he say when the person asked him what he wanted? What if no one woke up to answer the door? What if the night watchman, with his knack for arriving at the wrong time, should catch him? These thoughts floated on the surface of his brain like bubbles and then were carried off by the swift current of the wine. They did not seem obstacles with consequences to be taken seriously. They were little jokes to make him smile during this lonely adventure. His imagination flew past them to Zanuba's room overlooking the intersection of al-Ghuriya and al-Sanadiqiya streets.

He pictured her in a diaphanous white nightgown that curved obediently around her breasts and buttocks, with the bottom pulled up to reveal rosy legs with gold bangles. He went wild and would have leapt down the steps had it not been so dark. In the courtyard it was brighter because of the faint light from the stars. After the total darkness of the stairway it appeared almost light. When he had taken two steps toward the outer door at the end of the courtyard, he noticed a feeble glow, which came from a lamp sitting on a meat block in front of the oven room. He looked at it in surprise until he spotted nearby a body flung down on the ground, illuminated by its light. He recognized Umm Hanafi, who had evidently chosen to sleep out in the open to escape the stifling atmosphere of the oven room. He started to continue on his way, but something made him stop. He turned his head once more toward the sleeping woman no more than a few meters away, whom he could see with unexpected clarity from where he stood. He saw her stretched out on her back. Her right leg was bent, creating a pyramid in the air with the edge of her dress, which clung to her knee. At the same time, the bare skin of a section of her left thigh near the knee was revealed. The opening that was formed where her dress stretched between her raised knee and the other leg, extended on the ground, was drowned in darkness.

Although Yasin's feeling of being pressed for time and in a rush to get what he wanted had not diminished, he kept looking at the supine body, apparently unable to tear his eyes away. He was unwittingly drawn into observing it with an interest evident in the alertness of his bloodshot eyes and the way his full lips spread open. As he examined the fleshy form, which occupied as much space as a plump female water buffalo, the alertness of his eyes turned into unnerving desire. They came to rest on the dark opening between the raised leg and the extended one. There was a change of course for the current raging through his veins, and its momentum directed him toward the oven room. He seemed to have discovered for the first time the woman with whom he had rubbed shoulders for years.

Umm Hanafi had not been favored with a single attribute of beauty. Her gloomy face made her look older than her forty years. Even her treasure of flesh and fat, because it lacked proportion or harmony, seemed a bloated swelling. Perhaps also because she was hidden away in the oven room so much of the time and because he had lived with her since he was a boy, he had never paid any attention to her.

Yasin was in such turmoil that he was unable to reason clearly. He was blinded by lust. What kind of lust was it? A lust kindled by a woman simply because she was a woman, not because of any of her qualities or associations. It was a lust that loved beauty but would not turn away from ugliness. In these crises, everything was equivalent. He was like a dog that eagerly devours whatever scraps it finds.

At this juncture, Yasin's first choice for an escapade—Zanuba—seemed surrounded by obstacles with unknown consequences. He no longer considered going to her at this hour of the night, knocking on the door, thinking of something to say when the door was opened, and avoiding the night watchman to be laughing matters. They were real impediments and enough to cause him to shy away from her.

With his mouth hanging open, he advanced gently and cautiously. He was oblivious to everything except the mountain of flesh spread at his feet. To his greedy eyes this body appeared to be preparing itself to receive him. He hesitated before her legs. Then, almost unconscious of what he was doing, little by little he leaned down over her, driven by urgent internal and external stimuli. Before he knew it, he was sprawled out on top of her. He had perhaps not intended to go this far all at once. Perhaps he had intended to indulge in some of the foreplay that ought to precede the final violent motions, but the body on top of which he was sprawled began to heave with terror, and a resounding scream escaped, before his hand could stifle it. The pervasive silence was shattered and his brain was dealt a blow that brought him back to his senses. He put his hand over her mouth as he whispered anxiously and fearfully in her ear, "It's me. Yasin. It's Yasin, Umm Hanafi. Don't be afraid."

He kept repeating these words until he was certain she understood who he was. Then he removed his hand, but the woman, who had never stopped resisting, was finally able to push him off. She sat up straight, panting from her exertion and emotion, and asked him in a voice that was loud enough to alarm him, "What do you want, Mr. Yasin?"

Whispering, he entreated her, "Don't raise your voice like that. I told you not to be afraid. There's absolutely nothing to be afraid of."

Although she lowered her voice a little, she asked sternly, "What brings you?"

He began to caress her hand affectionately and sighed with anxious relief, since he saw in the lowering of her voice an encouraging sign. He asked, "Why are you angry? I didn't mean to hurt you." Then he said amiably, "Come into the oven room."

In a troubled but decisive manner, she replied, "Certainly not, sir. Go to your room. Go. God's curse on Satan. . . ."

Umm Hanafi was not able to weigh her words carefully. They escaped from her in reaction to the situation. Perhaps they did not express her wishes so much as her surprise at a proposition that had not been preceded by any hint but had pounced on her while she slept like a predatory kite swooping down on a chicken. She rejected the young man and scolded him without taking time to think whether she wanted to.

He took her words the wrong way and was filled with resentment. Ideas raged through his head. "What's to be done with this bitch? I can't retreat after revealing my intentions and going far enough to cause a scandal. I must get what I want even if I have to resort to force."

He thought quickly about the best way to overcome any resistance she might display, but before he could reach a decision he heard an unexpected sound, perhaps footsteps, coming from the door of the stairway. He jumped to his feet, totally overcome by panic. He swallowed his lust the way a thief swallows a stolen diamond when caught unawares in his hideout. He turned toward the door anxiously and saw his father crossing the threshold, holding his arm out with a lamp. Yasin stayed nailed to the spot, pale with fear, resigned, stunned, and desperate. He realized at once that Umm Hanafi's scream had not been in vain. The rear window of his father's room had served as an observatory. But what use was hindsight? He had fallen into a snare set by divine decree and destiny.

Trembling with rage, al-Sayyid Ahmad began to examine Yasin's face grimly and silently, dragging out the silence. Without taking his pitiless eyes off Yasin, he pointed with his hand to the door, ordering him inside. Although at that moment disappearing would have been dearer to Yasin than even life itself, he was paralyzed by fear and confusion. The father was outraged, and his scowl showed he was about to explode. His eyes seemed to shoot off sparks as they reflected the light of the lamp, which trembled as the hand holding it shook. He rebuked him loudly, "Go upstairs, you criminal. You son of a bitch."

Yasin became even more paralyzed. Then al-Sayyid Ahmad fell upon him. He grabbed Yasin's right arm roughly and yanked him toward the door. Yasin yielded to this extraordinary force and almost fell on his face. Regaining his balance, he turned around in terror. He fled for his life, leaping up the stairs, heedless of the darkness.

42

Besides his father and Umm Hanafi, two other people knew about Yasin's scandal, Mrs. Amina and Fahmy. They had heard Umm Hanafi's scream and watched from their windows what transpired between the young man and his father. They were able to guess what had happened without too much thought.

Al-Sayyid Ahmad mentioned his son's blunder to his wife and asked her in some detail about Umm Hanafi's morals. Amina defended her servant's character and integrity, reminding him that had it not been for the woman's scream, no one would have been the wiser. The man spent an hour cursing and swearing. He cursed Yasin and cursed himself for fathering children who would destroy his peace of mind with their evil passions. His anger boiled over, and he damned his house and all the people in it.

Amina remained silent, as she did later, when she pretended to know nothing about it. Fahmy also feigned ignorance of the subject. He pretended to be sound asleep when his brother returned to the room, out of breath after forfeiting the battle. Fahmy never gave any indication that he knew about it. He respected his older brother and would have hated for him to realize he was aware of the shameful depravity to which Yasin had stooped. Fahmy's respect for Yasin was not shattered by this discovery of his reckless antics, by his own superiority to Yasin in education and culture, or even by Yasin's nonchalance about whether his brothers respected him. Yasin would joke with them and let them tease him as though they were his equals. Fahmy still respected him. Perhaps his desire to continue respecting him could be attributed to Fahmy's own manners, seriousness, and sense of dignity, which made him seem older than he was.

Khadija did not fail to observe the morning after the incident that Yasin was not eating with his father. She asked incredulously why. He claimed he had suffered indigestion at the wedding. The girl, by nature acutely suspicious, felt there must be some reason other than indigestion. She asked her mother about it, but did not receive a convincing answer.

When Kamal returned from the dining room, he also asked. He

was not motivated by curiosity or regret but by the hope of good news of a prolonged period during which the field would be empty of a dangerous competitor for food like Yasin.

The matter might have been forgotten had Yasin not left the house in the evening without participating in the customary coffee hour. Although he apologized to Fahmy and their mother and claimed he was tied up with an appointment, Khadija said bluntly, "There's something going on. I'm no fool. . . . I'll cut my arm off if Yasin hasn't changed."

The mother was forced to announce that al-Sayyid Ahmad was angry at Yasin for some unknown reason, and the coffee hour was devoted to their conjectures about the cause. Amina and Fahmy guessed along with the others, in order to conceal the truth.

Yasin avoided eating with his father until he was summoned one morning to meet him before breakfast. The invitation did not come as a surprise and yet it alarmed him. He had expected it from day to day. He was certain his father would not feel there had been an adequate response to his offense. His father would return to the subject by one avenue or another. Yasin expected to be treated in a manner inappropriate for a gainfully employed person like himself. At times he thought of leaving the house temporarily or for good. For his father, especially the father he had learned about in Zubayda's house, to make such a catastrophe out of his blunder was not nice. It was also not right for Yasin to expose himself to treatment incompatible with his manly status. The best thing would be for him to leave, but where to? He would have to live alone. That was not out of the question. He considered the matter from every angle, estimated his expenses, and asked himself how much would be left over for his entertainment in al-Sayyid Ali's coffee shop, in Costaki's bar, and with Zanuba. At this point his enthusiasm flagged. Then it was extinguished like the flame of a lamp when a strong gust of wind hits it.

Although he knew he was not being totally honest, he told himself, "If I obey Satan and leave home, I'll create a bad precedent that would be wrong for our family. No matter what my father says or does, he's my father. It's absurd to think his discipline would be unjust." Then he continued with the candor he affected when in a playful mood: "Have some humility, Yasin Bey. Spare us the talk about honor, by the life of your mother. Which do you love more: your honor or Costaki's cognac and Zanuba's navel?"

Thus Yasin abandoned the thought of leaving home and kept on waiting for the anticipated summons. When it arrived, he pulled himself together and set off, reluctantly and apprehensively. He entered the room, walking softly, his head bowed. He stopped at some distance from his father and did not dare offer him a word of greeting. Yasin waited while al-Sayyid Ahmad gave him a long look. Then the father shook his head in amazement and said, "God's will be done! So tall and broad . . . a mustache and a wide neck. If someone saw you on the street he'd comment admiringly, 'What a fine son for some lucky man.' If only he'd come to the house to see you in your true colors."

The young man became even more distressed and embarrassed but said nothing. Al-Sayyid Ahmad continued to examine him angrily. Then in a stern and commanding voice he told him tersely, "I've decided you're going to get married."

Yasin was so astonished he could scarcely believe his ears. Curses and rebukes were all he had been expecting. It had never occurred to him that he would hear an important decision altering the whole course of his life. He could not keep himself from raising his eyes to look at his father's face. When they met his father's piercing blue ones, he looked down, blushed, and kept silent.

Al-Sayyid Ahmad realized that his son had been expecting rough treatment and was caught off guard by these blissful tidings. The father was enraged at the circumstances that dictated this mild-mannered approach, fearing it would shake Yasin's faith in his reputation for tyranny. He vented his anger in his voice as he said with a frown, "I don't have much time. I want to hear your answer."

Since the man had decided Yasin was to marry, there was only one possible answer, and there was nothing to prevent him from hearing the answer he wanted. In this case, Yasin's obedience to his father was also obedience to his own desire. Yes, no sooner had his father announced the decision than Yasin's imagination shot off, depicting his beautiful bride. He would have a woman entirely to himself, to be at his beck and call. The image delighted him so much, his voice almost gave him away when he answered, "The decision's up to you, Papa."

"Do you want to marry or not? . . . Speak."

With the caution of a person wanting to get married but financially unprepared, the young man replied, "Since this is your wish, I agree with all my heart."

Al-Sayyid Ahmad softened the roughness of his voice when he said, "I'll request for you the daughter of my friend Mr. Muhammad

Iffat, a textile merchant in al-Hamzawi. She's a treasure who's too good for an ox like you."

Yasin smiled delicately and, trying to ingratiate himself with his father, said, "With your help I'll try to be a good husband for her."

His father glared at him as if attempting to pierce through his flattery and said, "No one hearing you would imagine what you're capable of doing, you hypocrite. . . . Get out of my sight."

Yasin started to leave, but his father stopped him with a gesture of his hand. Al-Sayyid Ahmad added, as though he had just happened to think of the question, "I suppose you've saved up enough for the dowry?"

Yasin did not have an answer. He became more upset. His father was enraged and remarked incredulously, "Even after you got a job you continued to live at my expense the way you did when you were a student. What have you done with your salary?"

All Yasin did was move his lips without uttering a word. His father shook his head in annoyance. He remembered speaking to him a year and a half before. When Yasin got his government position, al-Sayyid Ahmad had told him, "If I were to ask you to take care of your own expenses like an adult, I would not be deviating from the norm between fathers and sons, but I will not ask you for a single penny, so you can have an opportunity to put aside a sum of money to have at your disposal when you need it." In this way he had shown his confidence in his son.

He could not imagine that one of his sons, after the stern discipline and training he had meted out, would have an inclination for any of the passions that squander money. He could not imagine that his little boy would turn into a philandering drunkard. The wine and women al-Sayyid Ahmad considered a harmless form of recreation for himself, fully compatible with manly virtue, became an unforgivable crime when they defiled one of his sons. The young man's blunder in the courtyard, which al-Sayyid Ahmad had discovered, reassured him to the same extent that it angered him. It would have been impossible, in his opinion, for Umm Hanafi to tempt the young man if he had not been struggling to maintain an intolerable level of chastity and rectitude.

He could not imagine that his son had wasted his money on wine and women, but he did remember noticing Yasin was fond of elegance, choosing expensive suits, neckties, and shirts. He had been uncomfortable about that and had warned him against throwing away his money. His warning had been mild, because he did not think elegance a crime and because it was an interest he shared with his son. He saw no harm in his sons imitating him in this manner. It made him feel kindly and well disposed toward them. What had been the result of that lenience? It was clear to him now that Yasin had squandered his money on unimportant luxuries. The man snorted with rage and told his son bitterly, "Get out of my sight."

Yasin departed from the room, leaving his father angry at him for squandering his money, not, as he had anticipated, for his moral lapse. Being a spendthrift had never troubled Yasin before. He had let it happen without any thought or planning. He would spend whatever he had in his pocket until it was gone. He was immersed in the present, turning a blind eye to the future, as though it did not exist. Yasin left the room upset, cowering from his father's scolding, but he felt a deep relief since he realized that this scolding meant he would not be thrown out of the house and also that his father would bear the expenses of his wedding. He was like a child who, having pestered his father for a coin, gets it and is shoved outside. Then the happiness of the boy's triumph makes him forget the strength of the push.

Al-Sayyid Ahmad was still angry and began to repeat, "What an animal he is. He's got a big, strong body, but no brain." He was angry that Yasin had squandered his money, as though he himself never had. He saw nothing wrong with extravagance, any more than he did with his other passions, so long as it did not bankrupt him, make him forget his obligations, or harm his character. But what guarantee did he have that Yasin would be as resolute? Al-Sayyid Ahmad did not forbid his son what he allowed himself merely out of egoism and authoritarianism, but because he was concerned about him. Of course, this concern of his revealed how confident he was of himself and how little he trusted his son, and neither sentiment was entirely free of conceit. As usual, his anger abated as quickly as it had flared up. His peace of mind returned, and his features relaxed. Matters began to appear to him in a new, agreeable, tolerable light.

"You want to be like your father, ox? . . . Then don't adopt one side and neglect the others. Be Ahmad Abd al-Jawad completely if you can, otherwise know your limits. Did you really think I was angry at your extravagance because I wanted you to get married at your own expense? Far from it. . . . I simply hoped to find you had been careful with your money so I could marry you off at my expense and leave you with a surplus. This is the hope you disappointed. Did you suppose I wouldn't have thought about choosing a wife for you until I caught you philandering? What a wretched excuse for sex that was, wretched, like your taste and your mother's. No, you mule, I've been thinking about your married bliss since you became a government employee. How could it be otherwise, since you were the first to make a father of me? You're my partner in the torment to which your damned mother has exposed us. So don't I have the right to give you, in particular, a festive wedding? I'm going to have to wait a long time to marry off the other ox, your brother, who's a prisoner of love. Who knows who'll be alive then?"

The following moment he recalled something directly related to his present situation. He remembered how he had told Mr. Muhammad Iffat about Yasin's "crime" and how he had scolded him and yanked him by the arm in a way that almost made him fall on his face. That revelation had been apropos of his request for the hand of the man's daughter for his son. The fact was that the two men had already agreed on the marriage before he brought it up with Yasin.

Muhammad Iffat had asked him, "Don't you think it would be appropriate to change the way you treat your son, as he grows more mature, especially now that he has a job and has become a responsible adult?" He had laughed before continuing: "It's clear you're a father who doesn't ease up until his sons openly rebel."

Al-Sayyid Ahmad had answered his friend: "It's out of the question that the relationship between me and my sons should change with time." He had felt a boundless confidence and pride in this answer but later had acknowledged that his treatment actually had changed, although he had tried to keep anyone from detecting his hidden intention to change. He had added: "The truth is that I'm no longer willing to lift my hand against Yasin or even Fahmy. I only yanked Yasin like that because I was so angry. I didn't mean to get carried away." Then, reverting to a time in the distant past, he had continued: "My father, God's mercy on him, raised me so strictly that my severity with my sons seems lenient, but he quickly changed the way he treated me once he asked me to help him in the store. Then after I married Yasin's mother, his treatment changed into a father's friendship. My self-esteem became so great that I opposed his final marriage, because he was much older than the bride. All he did was to say, 'Do you oppose me, ox? . . . What's it got to do with you? I'm better able than you to satisfy any woman.' I couldn't keep from laughing, and I apologetically set about conciliating him."

While al-Sayyid Ahmad was recalling all of this, a saying came to his mind: "When your son grows up, make him your brother." Perhaps more than ever before he felt how complicated it is to be a father.

That same week, their mother announced Yasin's engagement at the coffee hour. Fahmy had learned about it from Yasin himself. Khadija instinctively recognized that there was some relationship between the engagement and her father's anger at Yasin. She suspected his anger had arisen from Yasin's desire to get married, going on the analogy of what had happened between her father and Fahmy. She stated her opinion bluntly, but in the form of a question.

Glancing at their mother with shame and embarrassment, Yasin laughed and said, "The truth is that there's a very strong link between the anger and the engagement."

In order to make a sarcastic joke, Khadija pretended to be skeptical. She said, "Papa can be excused for getting angry, because you won't do him much credit with a close friend like al-Sayyid Muhammad Iffat."

Yasin countered her sarcasm: "Father's position will become even more difficult when the aforementioned personage learns the bridegroom has a sister like you."

Then Kamal asked, "Will you leave us, Yasin, the way Aisha did?"

His mother replied with a smile, "Of course not. A new sister, the bride, will join our household."

Kamal was relieved at this answer, which he had not been expecting. He was relieved because his storyteller was staying to entertain him with stories, anecdotes, and conviviality. But then he asked why Aisha had not stayed with them too.

His mother replied that it was customary for the bride to move to the bridegroom's house and not vice versa. Kamal wondered who had established this custom. He dearly wished it had been the other way round, even if he had had to sacrifice Yasin and his droll stories. He was not able to state this desire openly, and so he expressed it with a look directed at his mother.

Fahmy was the only one saddened by the news. Although he was happy for Yasin, marriage had become a subject that awakened his emotions and stirred up his sorrows, just as talk of victory stirs up the sorrows of a mother who has lost her son in a triumphal battle.

43

The carriage set off to take the mother, Khadija and Kamal to Sugar Street. Was Aisha's wedding the harbinger of a new era of freedom? Would they finally be able to see the world from time to time and breathe its fresh air? Amina had not let herself get her hopes up or become too optimistic. The man who had forbidden her to visit her mother, except on rare occasions, was equally capable of preventing her from calling on her daughter. She could not forget that many days had passed since her daughter's wedding. Al-Sayyid Ahmad, Yasin, Fahmy, and even Umm Hanafi had visited Aisha, but he had not given her permission to go, and her courage had not been up to asking. She was wary about reminding him that she had a daughter on Sugar Street whom she needed to see. She remained silent, but the image of her little girl never left her mind. When the pain of waiting grew too great to bear, she summoned all her willpower to ask him, "Is my master planning to visit Aisha soon, God willing, so we can be sure she's all right?"

Suspecting that her question was motivated by a hidden desire, al-Sayyid Ahmad got angry at her, but not because he had decided to prevent her visit. It was typical of him in such cases to wish to grant permission as a gift, without a prior request. He did not want her to think her request had had any influence on him. He assumed she was trying to remind him with this sly question. At an earlier time he had thought about this question apprehensively and had been annoyed to realize that such a visit was unavoidable. So he shouted at her furiously, "Aisha's in her husband's house and doesn't need any of us. Besides, I've visited her, and her brothers have too. Why are you anxious about her?"

In her despair and defeat, her heart sank and her throat felt dry. Al-Sayyid Ahmad had decided to punish her for what he considered her unforgivable cunning by remaining silent, as though the subject was closed. He ignored her for a long time, although he glanced stealthily at her sorrowful expression. When it was time for him to leave for work, he said tersely and gruffly, "Go visit her tomorrow."

Her face, which was incapable of hiding any emotion, immediately became radiant with joy. She looked as happy as a child. It did not take long for his anger to return. He shouted at her, "You'll never see her after that, unless her husband allows her to visit us."

She made no reply to this remark but did not forget a promise she had made to Khadija when they discussed bringing up the topic with him. Hesitantly and apprehensively she asked, "Will my master allow me to take Khadija?"

He shook his head as though to say, "God's will be done.... God's will be done." Then he replied sharply, "Of course, of course! Since I've agreed to let my daughter get married, my family's got to join the demimonde parading through the streets. Take her! May our Lord take all of you away."

Her joy was even more complete than she had thought possible. She paid no attention to the final curse, which she often heard when he was angry or pretending to be angry. She knew it came from his lips and not his heart, which felt quite the opposite way. He was like a mother cat which appears to be devouring her kittens when she is actually carrying them.

The wish was granted, and the vehicle started on its way to Sugar Street. Kamal seemed happiest of all, for three reasons. He was going to visit Aisha, he was on an excursion with his mother and sister, and he was riding in a carriage. As though he could not keep his joy a secret and wished to announce it to everyone or attract attention to himself sitting in the carriage between his mother and sister, he suddenly stood up and cried out, "Amm Hasanayn, look!" when the vehicle approached the barbershop. The man looked at him. Discovering that Kamal was not alone, he quickly lowered his eyes and smiled. The mother was terribly embarrassed and upset. She grabbed Kamal by the edge of his jacket, so he would not repeat his performance as they passed the other shops, and scolded him for the crazy thing he had done.

The house on Sugar Street appeared to be ancient, a relic. It looked quite different without its decorative wedding lights. The very age and mass of the building and the expensive furnishings all suggested power and prestige. The Shawkats were an old family, although not much was left of their former glory, except their name, especially since the family fortune had been divided up over the years by inheritance. The fact that they shunned modern education had not helped either. The bride had taken up residence on the second floor. Because of her age, Widow Shawkat had difficulty climbing the stairs and moved down to the first floor with her elder son, Ibrahim. The third floor remained vacant. They did not try to use it and refused to rent it out.

When the family entered Aisha's apartment, Kamal wanted to rush off on his own, the way he would at home, in order to scout around until he found his sister all by himself. He looked forward to the pleasure of the surprise and pictured it to himself as he climbed up the stairs, but his mother would not let him escape from her grip, no matter how hard he tried. Before he knew what was happening, the servant had led them to the parlor and left them there alone. Kamal felt they were being treated like strangers or company. He was dejected and depressed and began to repeat with alarm, "Where's Aisha? . . . Why are we waiting here?"

The only answer he received was "hush" and a warning that he would not be allowed to visit again if he raised his voice. His pain quickly left him once Aisha came running in, her face beaming with a smile of such brilliance it outshone her magnificent clothes and dazzling finery. Kamal ran to her and put his arms around her neck. He clung to her all the time she was exchanging greetings with her mother and sister.

Aisha appeared to be ecstatic about herself, her new life, and her family's visit. She told them about the visits from her father, Yasin, and Fahmy and how her desire to see the rest of the family had conquered her fear of her father. She had been daring enough to ask permission for them to call on her.

She said, "I don't know how my tongue obeyed me and let me speak. Perhaps it was his new image that encouraged me. He seemed to be charming, mild-mannered, and smiling. Yes, by God, he was smiling. Even so, I hesitated for a long time. I was afraid he would suddenly revert back to form and scold me. Finally I put my faith in God and spoke."

Her mother asked her how he had replied. Aisha answered, "He said, in as few words as possible, 'God willing.' Then he continued quickly in a serious tone that sounded like a warning: 'But don't think this is a game. There's a limit to everything.' My heart pounded and I proceeded to invoke blessings on him for a long time to try to humor and placate him."

Then she skipped back a little to describe how she had felt when she was told, "The head of your family is in the parlor."

She said, "I raced to the bathroom and washed my face to get off every trace of powder. Mr. Khalil asked me why I was doing that, but I told him, 'Believe me, I can't even meet him in this summer dress, because my arms show.' I didn't go till I wrapped myself in my cashmere shawl."

Then she said, "When Mother . . ." She laughed. "I mean my new mother. When she heard about it, because Mr. Khalil told her what happened, she said, 'I know al-Sayyid Ahmad extremely well. He's like that and worse.' Then she turned to me and said, 'Shushu, you should realize that you're no longer part of the Abd al-Jawad family. Now you're one of the Shawkats. So pay no attention to anyone else.' "

Aisha's splendid appearance and her conversation awakened their love and admiration. Kamal gazed at her as he had the night of the wedding and asked contentiously, "Why didn't you look like this when you were at our house?"

She laughed and immediately answered him, "Back then, I wasn't a Shawkat."

Even Khadija looked at her affectionately. The girl's marriage had eliminated all the reasons for the name-calling that used to break out between them when they were cooped up together. Moreover, only a small trace was left of the resentment Khadija had felt when permission was granted for the younger sister to marry first, since she blamed her misfortune on luck, not her sister. Her heart held nothing but love and longing for her. She missed her frequently, particularly when she needed a companion to confide in.

Then Aisha talked about her new home with the enclosed balcony overlooking Mutawalli Gate, the minarets that shot up into the sky nearby, and the steady flow of traffic. Everything around her reminded her of the old house and the streets and buildings surrounding it. There was no difference except for the names and some secondary features. "And, come to think of it, you don't have anything comparable to the huge gate where you live."

Then, with a trace of disappointment, she admitted, "Although Mr. Khalil told me the procession of pilgrims setting off for Mecca does not pass by our balcony. . . ."

She continued: "Directly under the balcony there's a spot where three men sit all day long until night comes: a crippled beggar, a vendor of red leather shoes, and a fortune-teller who makes his predictions by reading patterns in sand. They are my new neighbors. The geomancer is the most successful. Don't ask me about the droves of women and men who squat in front of him to find out what their fortune will be. . . . How I wish my balcony were a little lower so I could hear what he tells them. The most entertaining sight of all is the Suarès omnibus coming from al-Darb al-Ahmar when it meets a wagon of stones on its way from al-Ghuriya. The entrance of the gate is too narrow for both of them, and each of the drivers gets it into his head to challenge the other and force him to retreat and make way. At first the language is relatively polite, but then it becomes sharp and rude. Their throats bellow out curses and insults. Meanwhile the donkey carts and the handcarts arrive on the scene till the road is choked with them and no one has any idea how to get things back to normal. I stand there at the peephole trying not to laugh as I watch the faces and the sights."

The courtyard of Aisha's new home was quite similar to theirs, with an oven room and a pantry. Her mother-in-law ruled the courtyard with the help of the maid Suwaydan. "I don't have any work to do. If I even mention the kitchen, a tray of food is brought to me."

At that, Khadija could not keep from laughing. She commented, "You've finally got what you always wanted."

Kamal did not find much of interest in this discussion, but its general tone left him with the impression that Aisha was settling here permanently. He was alarmed and asked her, "Aren't you coming back to us?"

The room was filled by a voice answering, "She won't return to you, Mr. Kamal." It was Khalil Shawkat, who entered the room laughing. He strutted in, his medium-sized body arrayed in a white silk house shirt. He had a full, oval face with white skin. His eyes bulged out slightly, and his lips were full. His large head was topped by a narrow brow and thick black hair parted at the crown. The color and styling of his hair resembled that of al-Sayyid Ahmad. There was a good-humored, languid look in his eyes, possibly the result of his life of rest, relaxation, and fun. He bent over his mother-in-law's hand to kiss it, but she quickly withdrew it in embarrassment and discomfort, stammering her thanks. He greeted Khadija and Kamal and sat down—as Kamal put it later—as though he were one of them. The boy seized the opportunity presented by the bridegroom's conversation with the others to scrutinize his face for a long time. It was a stranger's face that had suddenly appeared in their lives, where it occupied a prominent position that entitled the man to be one of their closest relatives—in fact, Aisha's husband. Whenever Kamal thought of this new relationship, he remembered the loss of Aisha, just as surely as the thought of white brings to mind the color black. He looked at Khalil's face for a long time and repeated to himself Khalil's confident words: "She won't return to you, Mr. Kamal." Kamal disapproved of Khalil. He found him repulsive and resented him. These sentiments had almost gained control of Kamal when the man rose suddenly, returning shortly with a silver tray with different kinds of sweets. He gave Kamal a fine selection of the very best varieties. Khalil smiled pleasantly at Kamal, even though two of his teeth overlapped each other.

Then Widow Shawkat appeared, leaning on the arm of a man they assumed to be Khalil's older brother, since he looked so much like him. Their assumption was confirmed when the widow introduced him: "My son Ibrahim . . . don't you know him yet?" She noticed how upset Amina and Khadija were when greeting him and said with a smile, "We've been like a single family for a long time, but some of us are only now seeing each other for the first time . . . never mind!"

Amina understood that the woman was encouraging her and trying to make it easy for her. She smiled but felt anxious. She wondered whether her husband would consent to have her meet this man when she was not wearing a veil, even if he was as much a new member of the family as Khalil. Should she tell her husband about the encounter or avoid mentioning it in the interests of peace?

Ibrahim and Khalil could have been twins except for the difference in age, for their other differences seemed slight indeed. In fact, but for Ibrahim's short hair and twisted mustache, there would have been nothing to distinguish him from Khalil, even though Ibrahim was in his forties. His youthfulness and general appearance seemed not to have been affected by the passing years. Amina remembered what her husband had told her once about the late Mr. Shawkat, that he "looked twenty years or more younger than he really was." He had also said that he, "despite his good nature and nobility, was like an animal in never allowing thought to ruffle his serenity." How strange that Ibrahim looked thirty, even though he had married when young and had had two children by his wife, who had subsequently died along with their children. He had emerged unscathed and unharmed from this grim experience, returning to his mother to live the indolent, calm life of leisure of all the Shawkats.

Khadija amused herself, whenever no one was watching her, by stealing glances at the brothers who resembled each other in amazing ways. Each had a full, oval face and wide protruding eyes. They were both portly and languid. These traits stirred Khadija's sense of irony, and she laughed about them to herself. She began to store up images in her memory that she could make use of at the coffee hour. Because of her propensity for sarcasm, she was prone to mischief and comedy. She searched carefully for a descriptive and critical epithet she could apply to them, like the ones she gave to her other victims, on a par with their mother's nickname, "the machine gun," inspired by the way her spit flew when she talked.

Glancing furtively at Ibrahim, Khadija was terrified to find his wide eyes looking at her. Peering out from beneath his thick eyebrows, they were examining her face with interest. She lowered her eyes in shame and confusion. She asked herself with alarm what he might infer from her look. Then she found herself thinking nervously about her appearance and the impression it would make on him. Would he ridicule her nose the way she had his corpulence and lassitude? She became engrossed in these anxious thoughts.

Even though he had been reunited with Aisha, Kamal was bored. They were being treated like guests. None of his wishes had been realized, except for the sweets he had been given. He sidled up to the bride and gestured to her that he wished to be alone with her. She rose and, taking his hand, left the room. She thought he would be satisfied to sit with her in the central living room, but he pulled her into the bedroom and slammed the door behind them. His face beamed and his eyes shone. He looked at her for a long time and then studied the room from corner to corner. He sniffed the new furniture fragrance which blended with a sweet aroma possibly left from the activities of the wedding perfumers. Then he looked at the comfortable bed and the pair of rose-colored cushions lying side by side at the point where the bedspread covered the pillows. He asked her, "What are they?"

She replied, "Two small pillows."

He asked, "Do you sleep on them?"

She said with a smile, "No, they're just for decoration."

He pointed at the bed and asked, "Where do you sleep?"

Still smiling, she answered, "Inside it."

As though he wanted to make certain whether her husband slept with her, he asked, "What about Mr. Khalil?"

Giving his cheek a gentle pinch, she said, "Outside."

Then he turned toward the chaise longue in amazement and went over to sit on it. He invited her to sit beside him and she did. He was soon lost in his memories. He had to lower his eyes to hide their uneasy look. His disquieting suspicions had been aroused by the intensity of his mother's attack on him after the wedding when he was confiding to her what he had seen through a hole in the door. He was tempted to tell Aisha his secret and ask her about it. This temptation contained an element of cruelty. Embarrassment and doubt prevented him from asking. He suppressed his desire, in spite of himself. He raised his clear eyes to look at her and smiled.

She smiled back and leaned toward him to kiss him. Then she rose. Her face was covered by a sweet smile when she said, "I've got to fill your pockets with chocolates."

44

The boys massed near the door of the house and along the sidewalk by the historic cistern building were all yelling back and forth to each other. Among the screams of joy, Kamal's voice could be heard proclaiming, "I see the bride's car." He repeated that three times. Yasin, splendidly attired in his best clothes, left the group of men waiting at the entrance to the courtyard to stand in front of the door, facing toward al-Nahhasin. He caught sight of the bridal procession, which was advancing slowly, as though on parade.

At that hour so full of both happiness and dread, Yasin appeared steady and resolute, despite the eyes staring at him from inside the house and out, from above and below. He was charged with manliness and virility, and one factor that helped steady him was his sensation of being the focus of attention. He wrestled courageously with his internal discomfort so people would not think him unmanly. He may also have known that his father was out of sight, having withdrawn to a spot behind the group at the entrance composed of the male members of the families of the bride and bridegroom. Thus Yasin was in full control of himself when he saw the automobile decorated with roses that was bringing him his bride. The girl had been his wife for more than a month now, although he had not set eyes on her yet. Yasin's resolve was also strengthened by the hope forged by his dreams, which were thirsty for happiness and would not be satisfied with anything transitory.

The first automobile in the long line came to a halt in front of the house. Yasin prepared for the auspicious arrival. He hoped once more that he could see through the silk veil well enough to get a first look at the face of his bride. The door of the car was opened and out stepped a black maid in her forties. She was powerfully built and had gleaming skin and large eyes. He surmised on the basis of her confident and proud gestures that she was the servant selected to continue serving the bride in her new home. She moved aside to plant herself like a sentry and smile with pearly-white teeth before addressing Yasin in a resounding voice: "Come take your bride."

Yasin approached the door of the automobile and leaned partway inside. He saw the bride in her white garments sitting by two young ladies. He was greeted by the fragrance of a captivating perfume. Dazzled, he lost himself in the beautiful atmosphere. Although his eyes had not adjusted from the light outside and could scarcely discern anything, he held out his arm. The bride's shyness restrained her, and she made no movement. The girl to her right intervened to take the bride's hand and place it on his arm. She whispered merrily to her, "Take heart, Zaynab."

They entered the house side by side, but because of her modesty she held a large fan of ostrich feathers between them to hide her head and neck. Passing between two rows of male guests, they crossed the courtyard. They were followed by the women from her family, who let out their trilling shrieks of joy, paying no attention to the presence nearby of al-Sayyid Ahmad. Thus joyful cries rang out in this silent house for the first time, and the tyrannical master was present to hear them. If the members of his household were astonished, it was an astonishment mixed with delight and even a trace of innocent and merry malice, which revived their spirits after his stern and weighty decree that there would be no shouts of joy, no singing, and no entertainment. The wedding night of his eldest son was to be just like any other night.

Amina, Khadija, and Aisha exchanged smiling but quizzical looks. They crowded up against the peephole in the window grille overlooking the courtyard to observe al-Sayyid Ahmad's reaction. They saw him talking and laughing with Mr. Muhammad Iffat. Amina murmured, "All he can do tonight is laugh, no matter what he notices that he doesn't like."

Umm Hanafi seized this golden opportunity to slip her barrel-like figure in among the ladies doing the trilling. She let loose with a powerful, ringing cry that drowned out all the others. With it, she sought to make up for all the opportunities for merriment and delight during the engagements of Aisha and Yasin that had been lost because of the dread house rules. She came upstairs to be with the ladies and trilled until they were dying from laughter. She told them, "Give a trill of joy even if it's the only time in your life. . . . He won't know tonight who's doing it."

After escorting his bride to the door of the women's quarters, Yasin returned and came upon Fahmy, who had an apprehensive and uneasy smile on his lips, possibly because of this forbidden but splendid racket. He was peeking furtively at his father. Then he looked back at his brother and laughed briefly in a halfhearted way. Yasin reacted indignantly and asked, "What's wrong with enlivening a wedding night with gaiety and cries of joy? How would it have harmed him to hire a female vocalist or a male singer?"

The family had wanted to have a singer, but they had found no way to express this wish, although Yasin had encouraged Mr. Muhammad Iffat to intervene with his father. Al-Sayyid Ahmad had declined. He had refused to allow any music at the wedding. The joys of the evening would be confined to a sumptuous dinner.

Yasin continued sorrowfully: "I won't have anyone to provide music for a real bridal procession tonight. I'll never have another chance. I'll enter the bridal chamber without any send-off, songs, or tambourines. I might as well be a dancer trying to wiggle his torso without a percussion accompaniment."

A naughty, cheerful smile could be seen in his eyes when he added, "There's no doubt that the only place our father can tolerate women entertainers is in their own homes."

Kamal remained for a time on the top floor, which had been prepared to receive the women guests. Then, in search of Yasin, he went down to the first floor, where the male guests were being entertained. He found his brother in the courtyard inspecting the mobile kitchen the caterer had set up. Kamal approached him happily, proud of having carried out the mission his brother had entrusted to him. He told him, "I did just what you said. I followed the bride to her room and examined her after she removed the veil from her face."

Yasin took him aside and asked with a smile, "So? . . . How's she built?"

"Her build's like Khadija's."

Yasin laughed. "Nothing wrong with that. . . . Did you like her as much as Aisha?"

"Of course not. . . . Aisha's much prettier."

"A pox on your house. Do you mean to say she looks like Khadija?"

"Of course not. She's prettier than Khadija."

"A lot prettier?" Yasin shook his head thoughtfully and ordered the lad impatiently, "Tell me what you liked about her."

"Her nose is small, like Mama's. . . . Her eyes are like Mama's too."

"And then?"

"She has a fair complexion. Her hair is black. She has a beautiful fragrance."

"Praise God. May our Lord be gracious to you." Yasin imagined that the boy was struggling with a desire to say something more. He said to him somewhat anxiously, "Tell everything. Don't be afraid."

"I saw her take out a handkerchief and blow her nose." Kamal twisted up his lips in disgust, as though he thought it terrible that a bride at the height of her charms should do such a thing.

Yasin could not keep himself from laughing. He said, "Up to this point, everything's great. May our Lord make everything that follows good too." He cast a despairing look at the courtyard, which was empty except for the caterer and his assistants and a few children. He thought there should have been some decorations and a tent where musicians could perform for the guests. Who had decreed it should be this way? His father . . . the man who devoted his energies to buffoonery, rowdiness, and music. What a strange man he was to sanction forbidden forms of entertainment for himself while denying his family legitimate enjoyments. Yasin began to imagine his father the way he had seen him in Zubayda's room, with his glass of wine and the lute. Before he knew it, a strange thought jumped into his mind. Although it was extremely clear to him now, it had never occurred to him before. He saw a similarity between his father's character and that of his own mother. Both of them were sensual and pleasure-seeking. They recklessly ignored conventions. Perhaps if his mother had been a man she would have been just as enamored of wine and music as his father. The relationship between them had ended quickly, because a man like him could not stand a woman like her, and vice versa. In fact, married life would have been impossible for his father, if he had not happened upon his current wife. Yasin laughed, but his dismay at this strange idea robbed his laughter of any delight. "I know now who I am. I'm nothing but the son of these two sensual people. It wouldn't have been possible for me to turn out any other way."

The next moment he asked himself whether he had been mistaken when he neglected to invite his mother to the wedding. He wondered about it, even though he remained convinced he had done the right thing. His father had probably been trying to ease his conscience when he offered a few nights before the wedding: "I think you ought to inform your mother. If you want to, you can invite her to the wedding party." Yasin assumed he had spoken with his tongue, not his heart. He could not imagine that his father would want him to go to the residence inhabited by that miserable man his mother had married after all her many other spouses. He would not want Yasin to try to ingratiate himself with her, inviting her to his wedding while that man watched. Neither the wedding nor any other happiness he could attain in this world would make him reestablish the link that had been severed between him and that woman . . . that scandal . . . that disgraceful memory.

At the time he had merely replied to his father, "If I truly had a mother she would be the first person I would invite to my wedding."

Yasin suddenly noticed that the children in the courtyard were staring at him and whispering to each other. He singled out some of the little girls and asked them in a jovial but loud voice, "Are you already dreaming of marriage, girls?"

He headed for the door of the women's quarters and remembered Khadija's mocking words from the day before: "Don't let embarrassment get the better of you tomorrow when you're with the guests. Otherwise, they'll realize the bitter truth that it's your father who's paying your wedding costs, your dowry, and all the expenses of the party. Keep circulating and don't stop. Move from room to room among your guests. Laugh with this one and talk to that one. Go upstairs and come back down. Inspect the kitchen. Yell and shout. Perhaps you'll make people think you're really the man of the evening and its master."

Yasin laughed as he went on his way. He intended to follow her sarcastic advice. He strutted among the guests with his tall and massive body. He was exceptionally elegant, attractive, good-looking, and in the prime of his youth. He went back and forth and up and down, even if there was no need for it. All this activity dispelled any doubts he might have had. His soul became immersed in the charms of the evening.

When Yasin thought about his bride, a bestial tremor passed through his body. Then he remembered the last night, a month before, that he had spent with the lute player Zanuba. He had informed her of his impending marriage and told her he was saying goodbye to her.

She had screamed in a sham rage, "You son of a bitch! . . . You kept the news secret until you got what you wanted. The boat you're leaving on is better than the one coming here. You deserve to be beaten a thousand times with a slipper, you bastard." Zanuba no longer meant anything to him, nor did any other woman. He had lowered the curtain on that side of his life forever. He might return to drinking, because he thought his desire for that would not die, but as for women, he could not imagine his eyes straying when he had a beauty at his disposal. His bride was a renewable resource and a spring of water for the wild thirst that had troubled his existence so frequently.

Yasin went on to imagine what life had in store for him that night and the following ones, for the next month and the next year, for the rest of his life. His face was radiant with delight at his good fortune. Fahmy noticed that with an eye filled with curiosity, calm happiness, and not a little regret.

Kamal, who had been into everything, suddenly appeared. With joy at the good news visible in his face, he informed Yasin, "The caterer told me that there's more dessert than will be needed for the guests. There'll be lots left over."

45

With the addition of Zaynab, the coffee hour acquired a new face, one glowing with youth and the joy of being married. The three rooms adjoining the parents' bedroom on the top floor had been outfitted with the bride's furniture. Otherwise, Yasin's marriage brought little change to the general organization of the house in terms of either domestic politics or household management. The residents remained subservient in every sense of the word to the authority and will of al-Sayyid Ahmad. Housekeeping remained a subsidiary department under the direction of the mother, just as it had been before the marriage. The real change was emotional and mental, and it was easily observable. It would have been hard for Zaynab to occupy the position of wife of the eldest son, or for her and her husband to unite together with the other members of the family in a single household, unless there had been a significant development of the family's emotions and sentiments.

The mother regarded Zaynab with a mixture of hope and caution. What sort of person was this girl who was destined to live with her for a long time, possibly for the rest of her life? What was she hiding behind her tender smile? On the whole, she welcomed the girl the way a landlord greets a new tenant, warily hoping for the best.

Khadija, notwithstanding the flattering comments she and Zaynab exchanged, began to focus on Zaynab her penetrating eyes, which were naturally inclined toward sarcasm and suspicion. She probed for defects and shortcomings with an eagerness inspired by her resentment and hidden annoyance against Zaynab for joining the household and marrying her brother. When Zaynab stayed in her chambers the first few days after the marriage, Khadija asked her mother in the oven room, "Do you suppose the oven room isn't good enough for her?"

Although her mother found some relief for her own anxious thoughts in Khadija's attack on Zaynab, she defended the girl and replied, "Be patient. She's still a bride starting out on a new life."

In a tone revealing her disapproval, Khadija asked, "Who decreed that we should be servants for brides?"

Her mother asked, as though putting the question to herself, "Would you prefer her to have her own kitchen?"

Khadija cried out in protest, "If the money were her father's and not my father's, that would be all right. But I think she ought to work with us."

A week after the wedding when Zaynab decided to assume some of the tasks in the oven room, Khadija's heart did not welcome this step toward cooperation. She began to observe the bride's work with critical attention to detail and told her mother, "She hasn't come to assist you but to exercise what she may claim is her right." Khadija would remark sarcastically, "We hear so frequently about the Iffat family and how elite they are. They don't eat what other people do. . . . Have you found anything extraordinary about her cooking?"

One day Zaynab suggested that she would make a "Circassian" chicken dish with hazelnut sauce, since it was a favorite at her father's table. That was the first time this Circassian dish was served in al-Sayyid Ahmad's home, where it garnered everyone's admiration, and most especially Yasin's. Their mother felt a twinge of jealousy. Khadija became frantic and made fun of it: "They said, 'Circassian,' and we said, 'The longer a teacher lives, the more he learns,' but what did we see? Rice and sauce strategically arranged and a taste that's neither here nor there. It's like a bride who's shown to the bridegroom in her wedding procession, splendidly attired, with glittering jewels, but when she takes off her gown, she's just an ordinary girl predictably composed of flesh, bones, and blood."

Scarcely two weeks after the wedding Khadija said in the hearing of her mother, Fahmy, and Kamal that although the bride had a fair complexion and a moderate share of good looks, she was just as dull as her Circassian chicken. She said that even though she was then mastering the dish with her customary proficiency.

Some comments escaped from Zaynab—innocently, since the time for malice had not yet arrived—that stirred up their thoughts and cast a shadow of doubt over her. Whenever an opportunity arose she bragged about her Turkish origin, although she did so politely and graciously. She also enjoyed telling them what she had seen when she rode in her father's carriage and accompanied him to the gardens or other places of innocent recreation. All this talk startled and alarmed the mother. She was amazed by that kind of life, which she was hearing about for the first time. She had not thought such things possible and privately disapproved of this strange freedom more than words could tell. Zaynab's pride in her Turkish origin, no matter how polite and innocent, displeased Amina a great deal, because despite her humble and unobtrusive character, she was very proud of her father and her husband. She felt that because of them she had attained the highest possible rank, but she suppressed her reactions. Zaynab always received her full attention and a polite smile.

If the mother's desire to keep the peace had not been so strong, Khadija would have exploded angrily with unfortunate results. She revealed her resentment in more covert ways that were not a threat to the peace. For example, since she could not openly state her opinion about the carriage rides, she exaggerated the way she showed her astonishment. Gazing at the face of the speaker, she would cry out, "Oh, my goodness!" She might strike her breast and exclaim, "The men passing by saw you walking in the park?" Again, she might say, "My Lord, I would never have thought that possible," or other similar things. Her words did not express any disapproval, but her dramatic or melodramatic tone implied more than one meaning, like the scolding tone assumed by a father who is reciting from the Qur'an and saying his prayers when he notices that his son nearby has acted improperly or impolitely, for that is easier than breaking off his prayers and scolding his child openly.

To relieve her rage, as soon as Khadija was alone with Yasin she told him, "Goodness gracious, what a promenader your wife is."

He laughingly answered, "That is the Turkish fashion. It's hard for you to understand."

The word "Turkish" reminded her of Zaynab's boasts of her ancestry, which Khadija found hard to bear. She commented, "By the way, the lady of the house brags a lot about her Turkish ancestry. Why? Because the grandfather of the grandfather of the grandfather of the grandfather of her grandfather was Turkish? Watch out, brother. Turkish women end up going crazy."

Countering her sarcasm, he replied, "I prefer insanity to a person who has a nose that would drive anyone with good taste crazy."

The battle brewing between Khadija and Zaynab was evident to members of the family with any ability to predict the future. Fahmy warned Khadija to watch her tongue lest the other girl learn of her rude remarks. He also secretly cautioned Kamal, who kept flitting back and forth between them and the bride like a butterfly carrying pollen from flower to flower. But Fahmy could not have foreseen, no more than anyone else in the family, that fate was at work to separate the two girls.

Widow Shawkat and Aisha paid the house a visit crowned with an ending none of them could have imagined. In the presence of Khadija, the old lady addressed the mother: "Mrs. Amina, I have come to visit you today in order to ask for Khadija's hand for my son Ibrahim."

It was a joy that came with no warning, although they had awaited it for an unbearably long time. The woman's words were beautiful poetry to the mother's ears. Amina could not remember any previous statement ever bringing such a balm of comfort and peace to her breast. She was almost giddy with happiness when she replied in a trembling voice, "Khadija's no more mine than yours. She's your daughter. She will certainly find twice as much happiness in your custody as she has in her father's home."

This happy conversation went on for some time, but Khadija's attention drifted away. She was in a kind of daze. She lowered her eyes from modesty and confusion. The mocking spirit that so often gleamed in her eyes abandoned her. She became uncommonly meek and yielded to the current of her thoughts. The proposal had come as a surprise, and what a surprise. Troublesome when absent, it was incredible now that it had taken place. But her happiness was almost submerged by a wave of consternation. "To ask for Khadija's hand for my son Ibrahim. . . ." What had come over him? Despite his languor, which had aroused her ridicule, he had a handsome face. He was a prince among men. So what had come over him?

"It's fortunate that the two sisters will be united in one home."

The voice of Widow Shawkat confirmed the reality and vouched for it. There was no doubt about it, then. Ibrahim had as much money and status as Khalil. The fates had reserved a fine destiny for her. How unhappy she had been when Aisha married first. She had not known that Aisha's marriage was destined to open the doors of good fortune for her.

"How lovely it is that the sister-in-law will also be a sister. This will remove one of the basic causes for headaches in a family." She laughed and continued: "That leaves only her mother-in-law and I think she'll be easy to deal with."

"Since her sister-in-law is her sister, then her mother-in law will be a mother for her."

The two mothers continued to compliment each other. Khadija loved the old lady who brought her these glad tidings as much as she had hated her when she came to ask for Aisha's hand. Maryam must be told the news today. She could not bear to put it off. She did not know the reason for this insistent desire. Perhaps it was Maryam's comment about Aisha's engagement: "How would it have hurt them to wait until you got engaged?" At the time Khadija had been suspicious of the question's apparent innocence.

When the Shawkat family had left, Yasin wanted to tease and provoke Khadija. He remarked, "As soon as I saw Ibrahim Shawkat I told myself, 'This ox of a man, who looks incapable of distinguishing between black and white, will probably choose a wife like Khadija someday.' "

Khadija smiled briefly but said nothing. Yasin cried out in astonishment, "Have you finally learned manners and modesty?" Even as he teased her, his face revealed his pleasure and delight for her.

Nothing spoiled their good cheer until Kamal asked anxiously, "Is Khadija going to leave us too?"

To console him and herself, his mother replied, "Sugar Street's not far away."

Kamal could not express what he felt with complete freedom until he was alone with his mother that night. He sat on the sofa facing her and asked in a voice of protest and reproach, "What's happened to your mind, Mother? . . . Are you going to give up Khadija the way you abandoned Aisha?"

She explained to him that she was not abandoning either of the girls but was pleased by what would make them happy. As though pointing out something she had overlooked before and was about to overlook again, he warned, "She'll leave us too. Perhaps you think she'll return, the way you did with Aisha. But she won't return. If she visits you, it'll be as a guest. The moment she's drunk her coffee, she'll tell you goodbye. I say quite frankly that she'll never return."

Then, cautioning and preaching at the same time, he continued: "You'll find yourself alone with no companion. Who will help you sweep and dust? . . . Who will assist you in the oven room? Who will keep us company in the evening? . . . Who will make us laugh? You won't find anyone except Umm Hanafi, who will see the way clear to steal all our food."

She explained to him that happiness has a price. He protested, "Who told you marriage brings happiness? I can tell you that there's absolutely no happiness in marriage. How can anyone be happy when separated from his mother?"

He added fervently, "And she doesn't want to get married any more than Aisha did before her. She told me that one night in her bed."

His mother argued that a girl needs to get married. Then he could not keep himself from saying, "Who says a girl's got to go to the home of strangers? What will she do if that other man makes her sit in a chaise longue and takes her chin in his hand too and . . . ?"

She scolded him and ordered him not to talk about things that did not concern him. Then he struck his hands together and warned her, "You can do what you want . . . but you'll see."

That evening Amina was kept awake by her happiness as though by brilliant moonlight. She stayed awake until after midnight when her husband returned and she told him the good news. Despite his strange ideas about the marriage of a daughter, he received the news with such delight that it cleared the hangover from his head. But he frowned suddenly and asked, "Has Ibrahim been allowed to see her?"

The woman asked herself why his delight, which was so rare, could not have lasted longer than half a minute. She mumbled anxiously, "His mother . . ."

He interrupted her angrily, "Has Ibrahim been allowed to see her?"

For the first time that evening her happiness deserted her, and she said, "Once when we were in Aisha's apartment he entered the room as a member of the family. I did not see anything wrong with that."

He observed furiously, "But I didn't know about it."

Everything pointed to an evil outcome. Would he deal the girl's future a fatal blow? She could not keep the tears from welling up in her eyes. Ignoring his sullen anger, she said, before she knew what she was doing, "Master, Khadija's life is in your custody. It's hardly likely that fortune will smile at her a second time."

He threw her a harsh look and began to snarl, growl, mutter, and grumble as though his anger had reduced him to communicating with the sounds his first ancestors had used. But he said nothing more. He had perhaps intended from the start to agree but had refused to yield until he had expressed his anger, like a politician who attacks an opponent, even though supporting the same goal, in order to defend his principles.

46

During his honeymoon Yasin devoted all his energy to his new life as a married man. Since his wedding coincided with his summer holiday, he did not have to depart for work during the day. At night he did not go out in search of entertainment and left the house only for a pressing necessity like buying a bottle of cognac. Otherwise, he found no employment, meaning, or identity outside the conjugal framework. He poured himself into marriage with all the energy, enthusiasm, and optimism of a man who imagined he was carrying out the initial steps of a huge program for carnal enjoyment that would last day after day, month after month, and year after year.

During the final ten days of the month, he realized he had been a little too optimistic in at least one respect. A flaw he did not completely understand had appeared in his life. He was extremely perplexed and for the first time ever suffered from that illness native to the human soul known as boredom. He had not experienced it before when he was with Zanuba or even with the woman who sold doum palm fruit, because they had not been his property the way Zaynab was. She was securely settled in his own home. This secure, peaceful form of ownership inspired a kind of apathy. Marriage's external appearance was beguiling, tempting enough to die for, but inside it was so staid and sedate that a person might become indifferent or disgusted. It was like a trick chocolate presented on April Fools' Day with garlic stuffed inside the sweet coating. What a calamity it was that the intoxication of body and soul should be lost in a self-conscious, mechanical, planned, repetitive, and cold habit that destroyed the emotion and novelty of married love. In the same manner a tranquil, spiritual vision may be transformed into a verbal prayer inattentively repeated by rote.

The young man began to wonder what had happened to his rebellious nature and what had calmed his demons. Why was he satiated? How had that happened? Where had the temptation gone? Where was the old Yasin and where was Zaynab? Where were the dreams? Was marriage itself at fault or was he? What if months went by followed by more months? Yasin had not lost all desire for his wife, but it was no longer the desire of a fasting person for a tasty delicacy. He was appalled to find his desire becalmed when he had expected it to flourish. His perplexity was increased by the fact that the girl showed no comparable reaction. As a matter of fact, her vivacity and desire had increased. When he would think that sleep had become a necessity after such a long period of activity, before he knew it her leg would be flung over his as if of its own accord. So he told himself, "How amazing . . . she's the one who's realizing my dreams for our marriage."

In addition to all this, although he had enjoyed it at first, now when he embraced her he was embarrassed, because it ultimately made him lose himself in memories to which he thought he had said farewell forever. Zanuba and his other women rose from the depths to dominate his mind the way objects thrown into the sea float to the surface when a storm is over. He had entered the nest of matrimony with no leftover desires and a heart full of good intentions, but after comparing, contrasting, and pondering his alternatives, he became convinced that a bride was not the magic key to the world of women. He did not know how he could really be faithful to the good wishes with which he had strewn the path of matrimony. It seemed that at least one aspect of his naïve dreams would be difficult to achieve—namely, his assumption that in the arms of his wife he would have no need for anything else in the world and would be able to remain in her shelter his whole life. That had merely been a dream inspired by his innocent lust. He would find it increasingly difficult to cut himself off from his former world and habits, and what need was there for that? He had to search for some method or other to escape frequently from himself, his thoughts, and his failure. Similarly, when even an excellent singer spends too much time on the instrumental preludes to his vocal improvisations, the listener feels a desire for the main part of the piece to begin.

Liberation from his prison would also give him a chance to meet with some of his married friends. Perhaps they had reassuring answers to the perplexing questions that troubled him, even if not a panacea for every malady. From this moment on, how could he believe a panacea existed? The best thing would be for him to stop trying to make long-range plans that would soon come to naught and mock his vision. He should satisfy himself with proceeding in life a step at a time so that he could see where he was ending up. He would begin by acting on a suggestion that she, his wife, had made for them to go out together.

To the family's amazement, Yasin and his wife left the house without informing anyone of their destination, even though they had both been chatting with them that evening. Because of the lateness of the hour and because they were residents of the home of al-Sayyid Ahmad, their excursion seemed a strange event and aroused various suspicions. Khadija did not hesitate to summon Nur, the bride's servant, to ask her what she knew about her mistress's outing. With great simplicity, the maid answered in her ringing voice, "Lady, they went to Kishkish Bey."

Khadija and her mother both exclaimed at the same time, "Kishkish Bey!"

They were not unfamiliar with that name, which had taken the world by storm. Everyone and his brother were singing the songs about this vaudeville character created by al-Rihani, but all the same he seemed as distant as a legendary hero or the zeppelin, that Satan of the skies. For Yasin to take his wife to see him was an extremely different matter. They might as well have been hauled into court. The mother cast her eyes back and forth between Khadija and Fahmy and asked with apparent fear, "When will they return?"

With an inane smile decorating his lips, Fahmy replied, "After midnight, perhaps a little before dawn."

Their mother excused the servant and waited until her footsteps could no longer be heard. Then she blurted out emotionally, "What's come over Yasin? He sat here with us in full control of his senses. . . . Has he stopped worrying about what his father will think?"

Khadija said resentfully, "Yasin's too smart to plan a trip like this. It's not sense that he lacks, but he's too meek. That doesn't suit a man. I'll cut off my arm if she isn't the one who goaded him into it."

Motivated by a desire to lighten the tense atmosphere, although he instinctively shunned his brother's recklessness, Fahmy said, "Yasin's always liked the theater."

His defense of Yasin increased Khadija's anger. She burst out: "It's not Yasin and his likes or dislikes that concern us. He can love places of amusement all he wants or continue to stay out until dawn whenever he wants, but to take his cloistered wife with him is an idea that could not have originated with him. Perhaps it came up because it was obvious he wouldn't be able to resist, especially now that he's so docile, like a house cat in her arms. So far as I can tell, she would not think twice about this. Haven't you heard her describe her excursions with her father? If she had not inspired him to do it, he wouldn't have taken her with him to Kishkish Bey. What a scandal! . . . In these dark days when grown men hide at home like mice in their holes for fear of the Australians."

The incident had stirred everyone so deeply that, whether they supported it, opposed it, or were neutral, they kept commenting on it. Only Kamal followed the heated discussion with alert silence. He could not grasp the secret that had turned Kishkish Bey into a reprehensible crime meriting all this discussion and distress. Was not Kishkish the model for the little doll sold in the markets with a body that jumped around playfully, a laughing face with a thick beard, a loose gown, and a conical turban? Was he not the figure to whom those jolly songs were ascribed? He had memorized some of them to sing with his friend Fuad, who was the son of Jamil al-Hamzawi, the assistant to Kamal's father. Why were they attacking this pleasant character who was linked in Kamal's imagination with fun and mirth? Perhaps the reason for their distress was the fact that Yasin took his wife with him, not anything about Kishkish Bey himself. If that were so, he agreed with their alarm at Yasin's daring, especially since he could not forget the excursion he had made with his mother to see al-Husayn and the ensuing events. Yes, it would have been better for Yasin to go alone or to take Kamal, if he wanted a companion, particularly since Kamal was on his summer holiday and had done very well on the school examination. Before he knew it, he was moved to voice his thoughts: "Wouldn't it have been better for him to take me?"

His question broke into their conversation like a Western theme incorporated into a purely Eastern piece of music. Khadija commented, "From now on we'll know to excuse you for your lack of sense."

A laugh escaped from Fahmy. He observed, "The son of the goose is a good swimmer."

The proverb did not sound right to him once he said it, and the surprised stares from his mother and Khadija confirmed that it had not been well received. He realized his unintentional slip and, feeling upset and embarrassed, corrected himself: "The brother of the goose is a good swimmer. . . . That's what I meant to say."

Taken as a whole, their conversation betrayed Khadija's prejudice against Zaynab and the mother's fear of the consequences, although Amina did not divulge everything she felt. That evening she had learned things about herself she had not known before. She had frequently felt disappointed or uneasy with Zaynab but never to the point of hating or disliking her. She had blamed the problem on the girl's pride, whether or not it was justified. Today she was appalled to find Zaynab violating common decency and tradition. In Amina's opinion, Zaynab was arrogating to herself masculine prerogatives. She took exception to this conduct, precisely because she was a woman who had spent her life shut up inside her house, a woman who had paid with her health and well-being for an innocent visit to al-Husayn, the glory of the Prophet's family—not to Kishkish Bey. Her silent criticism was mixed with a feeling of bitterness and rage which she seemed to be rationalizing when she observed to herself, "Either that woman is punished too or life has no meaning."

Thus in one month of living with this new woman, Amina's pure, devout soul was soiled by rancor and resentment after a lifetime of earnestness, discipline, and fatigue during which her heart had known nothing but obedience, forgiveness, and serenity. When she retired to her room, she did not know whether she wished that God would conceal Yasin's crime, as she had stated in front of her children, or whether she hoped that he or, more appropriately, his wife would receive the scolding and punishment she merited. That night nothing in the world seemed to matter to her except preserving the family's traditions from being tampered with and defending them from the attack launched against them. Her moral fervor was keen enough to be cruel. She buried her normal, tender emotions deep inside herself in the name of sincerity, virtue, and religion, as an excuse for ignoring her troubled conscience. A dream may similarly reveal suppressed drives in the name of freedom or some other lofty principle.

Amina was in this determined state of mind when her husband returned, but the sight of him sent shivers of fright up her spine. She could nct bring herself to speak. She listened to what he had to say and answered his questions absentmindedly. Her heart was pounding and she did not know how to express the thought raging through her mind. As the minutes passed and bedtime approached, a nervous desire to talk troubled her. She wished with all her heart that the reality would reveal itself. If Yasin and his wife returned before the father fell asleep, then al-Sayyid Ahmad would learn firsthand about Yasin's reprehensible deed. The frivolous bride would be confronted by his opinion of her conduct, without the mother having to interfere. That would no doubt grieve her but also relieve her mind.

Anxiously and apprehensively, she listened for a long time for someone to knock on the door. She waited minute after minute until her husband yawned and told her in a relaxed voice, "Put out the lamp."

With defeat at hand, she found her voice. In a soft but troubled tone, she said as though thinking about it to herself, "It's late, and Yasin and his wife aren't home yet."

Al-Sayyid Ahmad stared at her and asked in amazement, "His wife? . . . Where did they go?"

The woman swallowed. She was afflicted by fear not only of her husband but of herself as well. She found herself forced to answer, "I heard the maid say they went to Kishkish Bey."

"Kishkish!"

His voice sounded loud and petulant. Sparks seemed to fly from his eyes inflamed by alcohol. He proceeded to ask her question after question, storming and snarling, until he felt wide awake again. He refused to go to bed until the two reprobates returned. He waited, seething with fury. His anger cast a shadow of terror over her. She was as terrified as if she had been the guilty person. She was consumed by regret for what she had said, regret that descended on her immediately after she had revealed her secret. She almost seemed to have spoken in order to regret it. She would have given anything then, no matter how costly, to be able to correct her error. She was merciless and accused herself of being responsible for the evil that would occur. If she really wanted to reform them rather than get revenge, should she not have covered up for them and waited till the next day to point out their error to them? She had intentionally yielded to malice. She had wanted something bad to happen. She had prepared for the young man and his bride a calamity they had never dreamed of and had brought down on herself remorse that was savagely eating away at her tormented heart. Although she was ashamed to mention His name, she prayed to God to be merciful to all of them. Each minute that passed made her feel worse.

She was roused by her husband's voice saying with bitter sarcasm, "Mr. Kishkish has arrived."

She listened carefully and looked out the open window to the courtyard. She heard grating as the main door was closed. Al-Sayyid Ahmad rose and left the room. She got up mechanically but remained frozen where she stood from cowardice and shame. Her heart pounded wildly until she heard his loud voice tell the newcomers, "Follow me to my room." She was terribly frightened and slipped away to escape.

Al-Sayyid Ahmad returned to his seat, followed by Yasin and Zaynab. Ignoring Yasin, he gave the girl a penetrating look and said firmly, but not coarsely or rudely, "Listen to me carefully, my little girl. Your father is like a brother to me, or even closer and dearer. You are my daughter just as much as Khadija and Aisha. I would never want to trouble your peace of mind, but there are matters that I cannot be silent about without committing what I consider an unforgivable crime. One of these is for a girl like you to stay out of her house until this hour of the night. Do not imagine that the presence of your husband excuses such perverse behavior, for a husband who demeans his honor to this degree is unfit to steady the person whom he has unfortunately been the first to shove. Since I am certain you are innocent or, rather, that your only offense was complying with his wishes, my hope is that you will assist me in reforming him by refusing to submit to his enticements again."

The girl was speechless and overwhelmed by astonishment. Although she had enjoyed a measure of freedom in her father's care, she could not work up the courage to argue with this man, not to mention oppose him. After living for a month in his home, her character had been infected with the virus of submission to his will, which terrified everyone in the house. Her conscience protested that her father himself had allowed her to accompany him to the cinema more than once. It was not right for this man to forbid her something that her husband allowed. She was satisfied that she had not done anything wrong or disgraceful. Her conscience told her this and more, but she was unable to speak a single word when faced by his eyes, which demanded obedience and respect, and his large nose, which when his head was tilted back looked like a revolver aimed at her. Her internal dialogue was concealed behind a façade of polite agreement, just as sound waves seem to hide inside the wireless receiver once it is turned off.

Before she knew what was happening, she heard him ask her, as though continuing his conversation, "Do you have any objection to what I have said?"

She shook her head in the negative and the word "no" was traced on her lips although she did not say it. So he told her, "We've agreed, then. You may retire to your room in peace."

She left the room with a pale face, and al-Sayyid Ahmad turned toward Yasin, who was looking at the ground. Shaking his head with great sorrow, he said, "The matter is extremely serious, but what can I do? You're no longer a child. If you were, I'd break your head. But, alas, you're a man and an employee and a husband too, even if you don't abstain from frivolous entertainments on account of your marriage. So what can I do with you? Is this the result of the education I've given you?" Then he continued even more sorrowfully: "What came over you? . . . Where's your manhood? . . . Where's your sense of honor? By God, I can scarcely believe what I've heard."

Yasin did not raise his head and did not speak. His father assumed that his silence showed he was afraid and felt he had been in error. He did not imagine that his son might be drunk. Yasin's apparent contrition was no consolation to him. The offense seemed too outrageous to be left without some decisive remedy, even though the former one, the stick, was out of the question. He would have to be firm or the family structure would be destroyed.

He said, "Don't you know that I forbid my wife to leave the house even if only to visit al-Husayn? How could you have given in to the temptation to take your wife to a bawdy show and stayed there with her until after midnight? You fool, you're propelling yourself and your wife into the abyss. What demon has hold of you?"

Yasin thought it best to seek refuge in silence, for fear his voice or his garrulousness would reveal his intoxication. This strategy seemed especially necessary since his mind, scoffing at his serious situation, insisted on stealing out of the room and shooting off to the far horizons, which to his drunken head appeared to be dancing at times and swaying at others. No matter how much his father's voice terrorized him, it could not silence the tunes the comedians had sung at the theater. They leapt to his mind, in spite of himself, like ghosts appearing to a frightened person at night, and whispered:

I'll sell my clothes for a kiss
From your creamy cheek, you Turkish delight;
You, there, sweet as a tart,
You're a pudding too or even smoother.

The song would be banished by his fear, only to bounce back.

His father became upset by his silence and shouted angrily, "Speak! Tell me what you think. I'm determined that this incident will not slide by."

Afraid that silence would prove harmful, Yasin abandoned it fearfully and uneasily. Making a valiant effort to gain control of himself, he said, "Her father treated her somewhat leniently." Then he added hastily, "But I'll admit I made a mistake."

Overlooking the last phrase, al-Sayyid Ahmad screamed angrily at him, "She's no longer in her father's house. She must respect the rules of the family to which she now belongs. You're her husband and master. It's up to you to make her see things the way you want. Tell me: Who's responsible for her going with you: you or her?"

Despite his intoxication, Yasin was aware of the trap laid for him, but fear forced him to equivocate. He mumbled, "When she learned of my intention to go out, she begged me to let her go too."

Al-Sayyid Ahmad beat his hands together and said, "What kind of man are you? . . . The proper reply to her would have been a blow. Only men can ruin women, and not every man is capable of being a guardian for them." (Qur'an 4:34.)

Then, furious at his son, he said, "You take her to a place where women dance half naked?"

In his imagination Yasin saw once more the scenes his father's appearance at the head of the stairs had spoiled. The tunes rang through his head again: "I'll sell my clothes . . ."

Before Yasin knew what was happening the man was threatening him: "This house has rules which you know. Reconcile yourself to respecting them if you wish to remain here."

47

Aisha took charge of beautifying Khadija for her wedding and accomplished the task with unparalleled zeal and extraordinary skill, as though she felt the adornment of Khadija was in every way the most rewarding accomplishment of her life. Khadija really looked like a bride and prepared herself to move to the bridegroom's house. In keeping with her custom of downplaying the value of services other people performed for her, she claimed that the credit should go to her plumpness more than to anything else. Moreover, her beauty was no longer the focus of her concern, since a man who had happened to see her himself had asked for her hand.

Despite all the manifestations of happiness surrounding her, they were not able to obliterate her pulsing homesickness at the prospect of the impending separation. It was exactly what one would expect of a girl whose heart pounded with love for nothing so much as for her family and house—from her parents, whom she adored, to the chickens, hyacinth beans, and jasmine. Not even marriage itself, for which she had longed and yearned so impatiently, was able to diminish the bitterness of parting. Before anyone had asked for her hand she had seemed oblivious to her love and respect for the house. Any minor vexation would suffice to mask her authentic feelings, for love is like health. It is taken lightly when present and cherished when it departs. With her mind put at ease about her future, her heart refused to make the change from one life to another without intense anguish that seemed an attempt to atone for some offense or a stingy reluctance to part with something of value.

Kamal gazed at her silently. He no longer asked, "Will you return?" He had learned that a girl who marries does not return. He murmured to his sisters, "I'll visit both of you frequently in the afternoon when school lets out."

Although they indicated they would welcome his visits, Kamal was no longer beguiled by false hopes. He had visited Aisha often without ever finding the old Aisha. In her place he found another woman, all decked out, who received him with such exaggerated affection that he felt like a stranger. Even if he was alone with her for a moment, her husband would soon join them. Khalil did not leave the house and amused himself with various pastimes like smoking his cigarettes or water pipe or strumming his lute. Khadija would be no better than Aisha. The only companion he would have left in the house would be Zaynab, and she was not as affectionate to him as she should be, unless his mother was watching. Then she seemed to try to ingratiate herself with Mrs. Amina by being nice to him. Whenever the mother left, Zaynab would ignore him, as though he were invisible.

Although Zaynab did not feel she would be losing a dear friend with the departure of Khadija, she disapproved of the quiet and serious atmosphere enveloping the wedding day. She used that as a pretext for expressing some of the resentment and rage she harbored against the domineering spirit of al-Sayyid Ahmad. She observed sarcastically, "I've never seen a house like yours where what's licit is forbidden. . . . What's the wisdom of that?" Since Zaynab did not feel like saying goodbye to Khadija without a polite word, she praised her abilities highly and said she was a good homemaker who would be a credit to her husband.

Aisha agreed with that and added, "The only thing wrong with her is her tongue. Haven't you experienced it, Zaynab?"

Zaynab could not help laughing. She replied, "Praise God, I haven't, but I've heard it used against other people."

Everyone laughed, and Khadija was the first. Then they saw suddenly that the mother was trying to listen to something. She said, "Hush." They all stopped laughing immediately. They could hear people shouting outside.

Khadija said at once in alarm, "Al-Sayyid Ridwan has died."

Maryam and her mother had excused themselves from the wedding because of the acute condition of Mr. Muhammad Ridwan. It was not strange, then, that Khadija should infer from the clamor that he had died. The mother rushed out of the room. After a few minutes she returned to say with great sorrow, "Shaykh Muhammad Ridwan has indeed passed away. . . . What an awkward situation."

Zaynab said, "Our excuse is as obvious as the sun. It's no longer in our power to postpone the wedding or to keep the bridegroom from celebrating his special night in his house, which, praise God, is far away. What more can they expect from you than this profound silence?"

Khadija, though, was lost in other thoughts that cast fear in her heart. She saw an evil portent in this sad news. She murmured as though to herself, "O Gracious Lord. . . ."

Her mother read her thoughts and became upset too, but she refused to yield to this uninvited emotion or to allow her daughter to do so. Pretending to play down the importance of the coincidence, she commented, "We should not second-guess God's decree. Life and death are in His hands. Looking for evil omens is the work of Satan."

Yasin and Fahmy joined the assembled women in the bride's room once they had finished dressing. They told the mother that al-Sayyid Ahmad had gone to represent the family, in view of the pressure of time. He would bear the necessary condolences to the family of al-Sayyid Ridwan.

Yasin looked at Khadija and said with a laugh, "Al-Sayyid Ridwan refused to remain in this world once you decided to move out of our neighborhood."

She responded with a pale smile that gave no indication of her feelings. He began to examine her carefully and nod his head in approval. He sighed and remarked, "Whoever said, 'Dress up a reed and you can make it look like a bride,' was right."

She frowned to indicate she was not prepared to banter with him. She brushed him off: "Be quiet. I don't think it's a good omen that al-Sayyid Ridwan has died on my wedding day."

He laughed and said, "I don't know which of you is more to blame." He laughed some more and continued: "Don't worry about the man's death. What I'm afraid does not augur well is your tongue. My advice for you, which I never tire of repeating, is to soak your tongue in sweet syrup till it's fit for you to converse with the bridegroom."

At that, Fahmy said in a conciliatory way, "Putting aside the question of al-Sayyid Ridwan, your wedding day coincides with a blessing for which the world has been waiting a long time. Don't you know that the armistice has been announced?"

Yasin cried out, "I almost forgot about that. Your wedding isn't today's only miracle. Something happened for the first time in years. The fighting stopped and Kaiser Wilhelm surrendered."

Their mother asked, "Will the high prices and the Australians go away?"

Yasin laughed and replied, "Naturally . . . of course. The high prices, the Australians, and Miss Khadija's tongue."

Fahmy looked thoughtful. He remarked as if to himself, "The Germans were defeated. . . . Who would have imagined that? There's no longer any hope that Khedive Abbas or the nationalist leader Muhammad Farid will return. All hopes of restoring the Muslim caliphate have been lost. The star of the English continues in the ascendant while ours sets. We're in His hands."

Yasin said, "The two who got something from the war are the English and Sultan Fuad. Without it, the former could never have dreamed of getting rid of the Germans and the latter could never have dreamed of ascending the throne of Egypt." He was quiet for a moment and then continued merrily: "And there's a third party whose luck was equal to theirs. She's the bride who never dreamed of finding a husband."

Khadija cast him a threatening glance and remarked, "You insist on provoking me to say something vicious about you before I leave the house."

He backed down, saying, "I'd better ask for an armistice. I'm no mightier than Kaiser Wilhelm or Hindenburg." Yasin looked at Fahmy, who seemed more pensive than was appropriate for such a happy occasion. Yasin advised him, "Put politics behind you and prepare for music, delicious food, and drinks. . . ."

Although many thoughts were running through Khadija's mind and dream upon dream filled her heart, an insistent memory from just that morning almost obliterated all her other concerns because of its intense impact on her. Her father had invited her to a private meeting in honor of the day that was the beginning of a new life for her. He had received her with a graciousness and compassion that were a healing balm for the shame and terror that afflicted her, making it difficult for her to walk without stumbling. He had told her, with a tenderness that made a strange, unprecedented impression on her, "May our Lord guide your steps and grant you success and peace of mind. I cannot give you any better advice than to imitate your mother in every respect, both great and small."

He had given her his hand, which she kissed. Then she had left the room, so moved and touched she could scarcely see what was in front of her. She kept repeating to herself, "How gracious, tender, and compassionate he is. . . ."

With a heart filled with happiness she remembered his words: "Imitate your mother in every respect, both great and small."

Her mother had listened to her with a blushing face and flickering eyelids when Khadija asked, "Doesn't this mean he thinks you're the best model for the best kind of wife?" She had laughed and continued: "What a lucky woman you are! Who could have believed all this?

It's like a happy dream. Where was all this beautiful affection stored away?" She had invoked God's blessing for him until her eyes flowed with tears.

Then Umm Hanafi came to inform them that the automobiles had arrived.

48

The coffee hour lost Khadija just as it had previously lost Aisha, but Khadija left a void that remained unfilled. She seemed to have taken with her the session's spirit, plundered its vitality, and deprived it of the qualities of fun, mirth, and squabbling that were so important to it. As Yasin observed to himself, "In our conversations she was like the salt in food. Salt by itself doesn't taste good, but what taste is there to food without it?" Out of consideration for his wife, he did not make his opinion public. Although his hopes for marriage were so disappointed that he no longer sought a remedy at home, he at least worried about hurting her feelings, if only to keep her from growing suspicious of his spending night after night "at the coffee shop," as he claimed.

Yasin preferred mirth to seriousness so much that there was little of the serious about his character. Now he had lost the companion who inspired his jokes and taunted him in return. Thus all he could do was content himself with the few remnants of his traditional observance of the coffee hour. He sat on the sofa with his legs folded under him, sipped some coffee, and looked at the sofa opposite, where the mother, his wife, and Kamal were absorbed in meaningless chatter. For perhaps the hundredth time he was amazed at Zaynab's earnestness. He remembered that Khadija had accused her of being dull and was inclined to accept that opinion. He would open *al-Hamasa*, Abu Tammam's collection of ancient poems, or *The Maiden of Karbala*, a novel by Jurji Zaydan, and read to himself or relate to Kamal some of what he had read.

When he looked to his right, he found that Fahmy wanted desperately to talk. What would it be about? The nationalist leaders Muhammad Farid and Mustafa Kamil? Yasin had no idea, but it was clear that Fahmy was going to speak. Indeed, today, ever since returning from the Law School, he had looked like a sky threatening to rain. Should he stir him up? No, there was no need for that. Fahmy was acknowledging his glance with intense interest and staring at Yasin as though he was about to address him. He asked, "Don't you have any news?"

Fahmy asked him what news he had! "I've got too much news to count," he thought. "Marriage is just a big deception. After a few months as tasty as olive oil, your bride turns into a dose of castor oil. Don't feel sad that you didn't get to marry Maryam, you callow politician. Do you want some other news? I've got a lot, but it definitely wouldn't interest you. Even if I wanted to, I'm not courageous enough to reveal it in my wife's presence."

To his surprise, Yasin found he was reciting to himself a verse from the medieval poet al-Sharif al-Radi:

I have passionate messages I won't mention,
But if we weren't being watched,
I would have shared them with your mouth.

Yasin asked Fahmy in turn, "What news do you mean?"

Fahmy replied excitedly, "Amazing news is spreading among the students. Today it was all we talked about. A delegation or "wafd" composed of the nationalist leaders Sa'd Zaghlul Pasha, Abd al-Aziz Fahmy Bey, and Ali Sha'rawi Pasha went to the British Residency in Cairo yesterday and met with the High Commissioner, requesting that the British protectorate over Egypt be lifted and independence declared."

Yasin raised his eyebrows to show his interest. A look of astonished doubt appeared in his eyes. The name of Sa'd Zaghlul was not new to him, but there was little he could attach to it except some obscure memories connected with incidents he had forgotten long ago. They had made no appreciable impact on him emotionally, for he paid slight attention to public affairs. He was hearing about the other men for the first time. But the strangeness of their names was nothing compared with their strange action, if what Fahmy had said was true. How could anyone think of requesting independence for Egypt from the English immediately after their victory over the Germans and the Ottoman Empire? He asked his brother, "What do you know about them?"

With the resentment of a person who wished these men were members of the National Party, Fahmy replied, "Sa'd Zaghlul is Vice President of the Legislative Assembly and Abd al-Aziz Fahmy and Ali Sha'rawi are members of it. The truth is, I don't know anything else about the last two. As for Sa'd, I don't see anything wrong with him, based on what many of my fellow students who are nationalists tell me. They disagree about him a lot. Some of them think he has sold out totally to the English. Others acknowledge his outstanding qualities that make him worthy of being ranked with the men of the National Party. In any case, the step he took with his two colleagues was a magnificent act, and he's said to have been the instigator. He may be the only one left who could have done something like that, since the prominent members of the National Party have been banished, including their leader, Muhammad Farid."

Yasin tried to appear serious so his brother would not think he was making fun of his enthusiasm. As though wondering aloud, he repeated the words: "Requesting that the British protectorate over Egypt be lifted and independence declared. . . ."

"We also heard that they requested permission to travel to London to lobby for Egyptian independence. For that reason they met with Sir Reginald Wingate, the British High Commissioner for Egypt."

Yasin could no longer conceal his anxiety. His features revealed it, and he asked in a slightly louder voice, "Independence! . . . Do you really mean it? . . . What do you mean?"

Fahmy replied nervously, "I mean the expulsion of the English from Egypt: what Mustafa Kamil called an 'evacuation' when he advocated it."

What a hope! Yasin was not naturally inclined to seek out conversations about politics, but he would accept Fahmy's invitation in order to avoid upsetting his brother and to amuse himself with this novel form of entertainment. His interest in politics was aroused occasionally, but never to the point of enthusiasm. He may have shared his brother's hopes in a calm, passive way, but he had never demonstrated much interest in public affairs at any time in his life. His only goal was enjoyment of the good things in life and its pleasures. For this reason, he found it difficult to take Fahmy's statements seriously. He questioned his brother again: "Does this fall within the realm of possibility?"

Fahmy replied with a combination of enthusiasm and censure: "So long as there's life there's hope, brother."

This sentence, like the others before it, prompted Yasin's sarcasm, but pretending to be in earnest, he asked his brother, "How can we expel them?"

Fahmy thought for a moment and then said with a frown, "That's why Sa'd and his colleagues asked permission to journey to London."

The mother had been following their conversation with interest. She was concentrating her full attention on it to try to understand as much as she possibly could. She always did whenever the conversation turned to public affairs remote from domestic chatter. These matters intrigued her, and she claimed to be able to understand them. She did not hesitate to participate in such a discussion, if the opportunity arose, and was oblivious to the scorn mixed with affection that her opinions often provoked. Nothing could daunt her or prevent her from taking an interest in these significant matters, which she appeared to follow for the same reasons she felt compelled to comment on Kamal's lessons in religious studies or to debate what he related to her about geography and history in the light of her religious and folkloric information. Because of her serious attention, she had acquired some knowledge of Mustafa Kamil, Muhammad Farid, and "Our Exiled Effendi," the Khedive Abbas II. Her love for those men was doubled by their devotion to the cause of the Muslim caliphate, making them seem in her eyes, which were those of a person who judged men by their religious stature, almost like the saints of whom she was so fond. Thus when Fahmy mentioned that Sa'd and his colleagues were asking permission to travel to London, she suddenly asked, "Where in God's world is this London?"

Kamal answered her immediately in the singsong voice pupils use to recite their lessons: "London is the capital of Great Britain. Paris is the capital of France. The Cape's capital is the Cape. . . ." Then he leaned over to whisper in her ear, "London is in the land of the English."

His mother was overcome by astonishment and asked Fahmy, "They're going to the land of the English to ask them to get out of Egypt? This is in very bad taste. How could you visit me in my house if you're wanting to throw me out of yours?"

Her interruption annoyed the young man. He gave her a look that was smiling and critical at the same time, but she thought she would be able to convince him. So she added, "How can they ask them to leave our lands after they have been here all this long period. When we were born and you as well, they were already in our country. Is it humane for us to oppose them after this time we've spent living together as neighbors and to tell them bluntly, and in their country at that, to get out?"

Fahmy smiled in despair. Yasin guffawed, but Zaynab said seriously, "Where do they get the nerve to tell them that in their own country? Suppose the English kill them there. Who would know what happened to them? Haven't their soldiers made walking in streets of Cairo far from home hazardous and uncertain? So what will happen to someone who storms into their country?"

Yasin wished he could encourage the two women to keep saying these naïve things in order to satisfy his thirst for fun, but he noticed Fahmy's annoyance and was apprehensive about making him angry. He turned toward his brother to continue their interrupted conversation: "They both have a point, although they might have expressed it more clearly. Tell me, brother, what can Sa'd do against a nation that now considers itself the unrivaled mistress of the world?"

The mother nodded her head in agreement, as though he had been addressing her. She stated: "The revolutionary leader Urabi Pasha was one of the greatest men and one of the most courageous. Sa'd and the others are nothing compared with him. He was in the cavalry, a fighting man. What did he get from the English, boys? They imprisoned him and then exiled him to a land on the other side of the world."

Fahmy could not keep himself from entreating her crossly, "Mother! . . . Won't you let us talk?"

She smiled in embarrassment, for she was anxious not to anger him. She changed her zealous tone, as though announcing by this change of tone a total shift of her opinion, and said gently and apologetically, "Sir, everyone who tries hard deserves some reward. So let them go there in God's safekeeping. Perhaps they'll win the sympathy of the great queen. . . ."

Without thinking about what he was doing, the young man asked her, "Which queen do you mean?"

"Queen Victoria, my son. Isn't that her name? . . . I often heard my father talk about her. She's the one who ordered Urabi banished, although according to what was said she admired his courage."

Yasin commented sarcastically, "If she banished the cavalry knight Urabi, she's even more liable to banish that old man Sa'd."

The mother said, "All the same, she's a woman and no doubt still bears in her chest a sensitive heart. If they speak to her the right way and know how to win her affection, she'll be sympathetic to their views."

Yasin was delighted by their mother's logic and the way she spoke about the historic queen as though she were talking about Maryam's mother or some other neighbor. He no longer felt like conversing with Fahmy. To encourage her to say more he asked, "Tell us what they should say to her?"

The woman, who was delighted by this request recognizing her political acumen, sat up straight. As was appropriate for a "conference," she began to think with an intensity apparent in the way her eyebrows were bunched together, but Fahmy did not give her time to think through the subject to the end. Tersely and indignantly he told her, "Queen Victoria died a long time ago. Don't wear yourself out pointlessly."

Yasin noticed then from the cracks between the shutters that it was starting to get dark outside. He realized it was time to excuse himself from the coffee hour to go off in search of entertainment. Since he was certain that Fahmy's thirst for conversation had not yet been quenched, he sought to apologize for his departure by putting his weight behind the news that had captured Fahmy's interest. Rising, he said, "They are men who doubtless know the danger of their undertaking. Perhaps they've worked out a winning strategy. Let's pray they succeed." He left the group after gesturing to Zaynab to follow and get his clothes ready.

Fahmy watched him depart with a look that was slightly hostile. He was angry that he had not found a partner to share the excitement of his ardent soul. Talk of national liberation excited great dreams in him. In that magical universe he could visualize a new world, a new nation, a new home, a new people. Everyone would be astir with vitality and enthusiasm. The moment his mind returned to this stifling atmosphere of lassitude, ignorance, and indifference, he felt a blazing fire of distress and pain that desired release from its confinement in order to shoot up to the sky. At that moment he wished with all his heart that the night would pass in the twinkling of an eye so he could be surrounded once more by a group of his fellow students. Then he would be able to quench his thirst for enthusiasm and freedom and ascend with their blazing zeal to that great world of dreams and glory.

Yasin had asked what Sa'd could do face to face with a country that now was justly considered the mistress of the world. Fahmy did not know exactly what Sa'd would do or what he could do himself, but he felt with all the power of his being that there was work to be done. Possibly there was no example in the real world, but he sensed it existed in his heart and blood. It had to manifest itself in the light of life and reality. Otherwise, life and reality would be in vain. Life would be a meaningless game and a bad joke.

49

The street in front of al-Sayyid Ahmad's store did not look any different, for it was crowded with pedestrians, vehicles, and customers of the shops crammed along either side. Overhead there was a decorative, misty quality to the light. It was a pleasant November day and the sun was obscured by thin clouds. There were pure white billows resembling pools of light over the Qala'un and Barquq minarets. Nothing in the sky or on the ground seemed to differ from what al-Sayyid Ahmad saw every day, but the man's soul, those of the people connected to him, and perhaps those of everyone else too, had been exposed to a powerful wave of excitement almost making them lose control of themselves. Al-Sayyid Ahmad went so far as to say he had never experienced times like these when people were so united by a single piece of news, their hearts all beating with the same emotion.

Fahmy, usually silent in his father's presence, had initiated a conversation to tell him in great detail what he had learned about Sa'd's meeting with the High Commissioner. That same evening at al-Sayyid Ahmad's musical soiree, some of his friends had confirmed the truth of the information.

In his shop, customers who did not know each other had, on more than one occasion, plunged into a discussion of this meeting. That very morning, to his surprise, Shaykh Mutawalli Abd al-Samad had burst into the store after a long absence. He had not been satisfied to recite some verses from the Qur'an and receive the customary gift of sugar and soap but had insisted on recounting news of the visit as though making the first announcement.

When al-Sayyid Ahmad had asked him playfully what he thought the outcome of the visit would be, the shaykh had replied, "It's impossible! . . . It's impossible that the English will leave Egypt. Do you think they're crazy enough to leave the country without a fight? . . . There certainly would be fighting, and we would lose. So there's no way to expel them. Perhaps our men could succeed in getting the Australians sent away. Then order could be restored. Things would revert to the way they used to be. There'd be peace."

In these days of news and overflowing feelings al-Sayyid Ahmad was intensely receptive to infectious nationalist political aspirations. He was in such an expectant and attentive mood that he read with passionate enthusiasm the newspapers, which for the most part seemed as if they had been published in some other country where there was no passion or awakening. He greeted his friends with an inquisitive look that yearned to discover anything new they had learned.

It was in this fashion that he greeted Mr. Muhammad Iffat when he hurried into the store. The penetrating look and energetic motions of the man indicated that he was not just a casual visitor stopping by the store to drink some coffee or tell an amusing anecdote. The proprietor found that his friend's appearance matched his own anxious feelings, which were full of nationalist aspirations. While his friend was still making his way through the customers being served by Jamil al-Hamzawi, al-Sayyid Ahmad welcomed him: "It's a damp morning. What do you know, you lion?"

Mr. Muhammad Iffat sat down next to the desk. He smiled proudly, as though the proprietor's question, "What do you know?"—the same question he repeated whenever he met one of his friends—was a recognition of Mr. Iffat's importance during these especially significant days, because of his ties of kinship to some influential Egyptian personalities. Mr. Iffat was also a link between the original group of merchants and those distinguished civil servants and attorneys who had joined them later. Of all these men, al-Sayyid Ahmad held the most cherished spot in his friend's affection because of his personality and disposition. Although the value of Mr. Iffat's connections had never been lost on his old friends who looked up to the civil servants and people with titles, it had increased now that fresh information was more important than water or food.

Mr. Iffat spread out a sheet of paper he had been holding in his right hand. Then he said, "Here's a new step. I'm no longer simply reporting news. I've become a messenger to bring you and other noble people this joyous authorization petition. . . ." Murmuring, "Read it," he offered the paper to him with a smile.

Al-Sayyid Ahmad took it and read aloud: "We, the signatories of this document, authorize Messrs. Sa'd Zaghlul Pasha, Ali Sha'rawi Pasha, Abd al-Aziz Fahmy Bey, Muhammad Ali Alluba Bey, Abd al-Latif al-Makabbati, Muhammad Mahmud Pasha, and Ahmad Lutfi al-Sayyid Bey, and those persons they choose to include in their number, to strive by all legal and peaceful means available to them to achieve the total independence of Egypt."

The proprietor's face was radiant when he read the names of the Egyptian delegation, for he had heard them mentioned when nationalism was discussed. He asked, "What does this paper mean?"

The man replied enthusiastically, "Don't you see these signatures? Put yours below them and get Jamil al-Hamzawi to sign too. This is one of the authorization petitions the delegation has had printed up for citizens to sign. They'll use them to show that they represent the Egyptian nation."

Al-Sayyid Ahmad took a pen and signed with a delighted gleam in his blue eyes. He smiled in a sensitive way that revealed his happiness and pride at having Sa'd and his colleagues represent him. Although those men had not been famous long, they had been welcomed into everyone's heart, arousing deep, suppressed desires. Their encouraging impact was like that of a new cure on a patient with an old malady that has resisted treatment, even though he is trying the medicine for the first time. The proprietor summoned al-Hamzawi, who also signed. Then he turned to his friend and remarked with intense interest, "It seems the matter is serious."

The man pounded on the edge of the desk with his fist and said, "Extremely serious. It's all progressing with forceful determination. Do you know what motivated the printing of these petitions? It's said that 'the man,' the British High Commissioner, asked in what capacity Sa'd and his colleagues had spoken with him on the morning of November the thirteenth. So the delegation has had to rely on these petitions to prove that they speak in the name of the nation."

The proprietor commented emotionally, "If only Muhammad Farid were here with us too."

"Some of the men of the National Party have joined the delegation: Muhammad Ali Alluba Bey and Abd al-Latif al-Makkabati. . . ." He shrugged his shoulders as though to shake away the past and then said, "We all remember Sa'd from the enormous row he stirred up when he was appointed Minister of Education and then Minister of Justice. I still remember that the nationalist newspaper *al-Liwa'* welcomed him when he was nominated to the cabinet, although I can't forget its attacks on him afterward. I won't deny that I was influenced by his critics because of my devotion to the late Mustafa Kamil, but Sa'd has always shown that he merits admiration. His most recent move entitles him to the highest regard."

"You're right. It's a blessed undertaking. Let's pray to God it meets with success." Then he asked with concern, "Do you think they'll be allowed to make the trip? . . . What do you think they'll do if they go there?"

Mr. Muhammad Iffat rolled up the petition. Then as he rose he said, "Tomorrow's not far off. . . ."

On their way to the door, the proprietor's playful spirit got the better of him and he whispered into his friend's ear, "I'm so happy about this petition that I could be a drunkard lifting his eighth glass between Zubayda's thighs."

Muhammad Iffat waggled his head enthusiastically, as though intoxicated by the picture his imagination had conjured up at the mention of a glass of wine and Zubayda. He murmured, "Oh, what we'll soon be hearing. . . ."

Then he left the store and his smiling friend called after him, "And what we'll see after that. . . ."

Al-Sayyid Ahmad returned to his desk. His face showed the happy impact of the jest, even though his patriotic enthusiasm had not subsided in his heart. He was like this in all concerns of life, so long as they had no connection to his home. He could be totally serious when that was called for but would not hesitate to lighten the atmosphere with humor and mirth whenever he felt like it, motivated by an irresistible urge. He had an unusual ability to reconcile seriousness and mirth, without either one suppressing or spoiling the other. His jesting was not a luxury of marginal importance to his life but was as much a necessity as seriousness. He had never been able to achieve total seriousness or to concentrate his energies on it. Consequently, he had been content to limit his patriotism to an emotional and psychic participation, not taking any action that might have altered the life he enjoyed so much that he would not have exchanged it for any other. For this reason he had never thought of joining one of the committees of the National Party, even though he was deeply attached to its principles. He had never even taken the trouble to go to one of their rallies. Would that not have been a waste of his precious time? The nation did not need his time, and he was eager to have every minute of it to spend on his family, on his business, and especially on his amusements with his friends and chums. Thus his time was reserved for his own life, and the nation was welcome to a share of his heart and emotions. It was easier to part with money than time. He was not stingy about contributing to the cause. He did not feel he was neglecting his duty in any way.

On the contrary, he was known among his comrades for his patriotism, both because none had a heart as liberal with its emotions as his and because even those with liberal hearts were not as generous with their financial contributions. His patriotism set him apart so that he was known for it. It was added to the rest of the fine qualities on which he secretly prided himself. He could not imagine that the nationalist cause could ask any more of him after he had given so generously. Although his heart was filled with romance, music, and humor, he still found room for patriotism. Even if his nationalist fervor was confined to his heart, it was strong and deep, preoccupying and engrossing his soul.

His patriotism had not come to him accidentally. It had matured with him since childhood, when he had heard the previous generation recount tales of the heroism of the Egyptian revolutionary Urabi. It had been enflamed by articles and speeches printed in the nationalist newspaper *al-Liwa'*. And what a unique sight it had been, arousing both laughter and concern, the day he was seen crying like a baby over the death of Mustafa Kamil. His companions were touched because none of them had been indisposed at all by their sorrow. At their party that evening they had roared with laughter when they recalled the improbable sight of the "Lord of Laughter" sobbing with tears.

Today, after years of the war, now waning, after the death of the youthful leader of the National Party and the banishment of his successor, after all hope for the return of "Our Effendi" Khedive Abbas II had been lost, after the defeat of Turkey and the victory of the English, after all of this or in spite of all of this, there came amazing news, the facts of which seemed like legends: presenting to the Englishman, the High Commissioner, demands for independence, signing nationalist petitions, and wondering about the next step. Hearts were shaking off the dust to separate out what was vital to them. Souls were radiant with their hopes. What was behind all of this? His pacific soul, accustomed to passivity, wondered about this turn of events to no avail. He could hardly wait for nightfall so he could rush to his musical gathering, where political talk had become the appetizer before the drinks and music. It fit in with the other attractions that made him long for his evening's entertainment, like Zubayda, his love for his comrades, the drinking and the music. In that enticing atmosphere, it appeared pleasantly refreshing and induced emotions like enthusiasm and love without asking more of the heart than it could bear.

Al-Sayyid Ahmad was thinking about all of this when Jamil al-Hamzawi came over to him and asked, "Have you heard about the new name that's being given to the home of Sa'd Pasha? . . . They're calling it 'the House of the Nation.' " He leaned toward his employer to tell him how this news had reached him.

50

While the nation was preoccupied by its demand for freedom, Yasin was likewise resolutely and determinedly striving to take charge of his own destiny. He was struggling for the right to go on his nightly outings, which he had virtuously given up for several weeks following his marriage. An excuse he frequently repeated to himself was that he could not have imagined while intoxicated by the dream of marriage that he would ever return to the life of idling his time away at the coffee shop and Costaki's bar. He had sincerely believed he had set that aside for good, since he harbored only the best of intentions for his married life. When the hopeless and total disappointment of marriage overwhelmed him, his nerves were agitated by enduring the boredom or "the emptiness of life," as he put it. With all the strength of his pampered and sensitive soul, he sought escape through relaxation, entertainment, and distraction at the coffee shop and the bar. This was no longer the temporary life of amusement he had thought it to be when he treasured the hope of getting married. It was all that life had left for him to enjoy after marriage had become a bitter disappointment. He was like a person whose hopes forced him away from his native land but whose failure brought him back repentant.

Zaynab had once experienced his warm affection and greedy flattery. She had even been so cherished by him that he had taken her to the theater to see Kishkish Bey in defiance of the bulwark of stern conventions his father had constructed around the family. Now this same Zaynab had to endure his staying out until midnight evening after evening and coming home staggering drunk. It was a blow she found painful to bear.

She could not keep herself from expressing her sorrows to him. He had known instinctively that a sudden transformation in his married life could not be accomplished peacefully. From the beginning he had expected some form of resistance, whether criticism or a quarrel. He had taken precautions to secure his position with the same forcefulness his father had employed on intercepting him the night he returned from Kishkish Bey, when he had told Yasin, "Only men can ruin women, and not every man is capable of being a guardian for them."

As soon as she voiced her complaints, he told her, "There's no reason to be sad, darling. Since antiquity, houses have been for women and the outside world for men. Men are all like this. A sincere husband is as faithful to his wife when he's away from her as when he's with her. Moreover, the refreshment and delight I derive from my outings will make our life together thoroughly enjoyable."

When she mentioned his drinking and protested that she was afraid for his health, he laughed and observed in a tone that blended tenderness with resolve, "All men drink. Getting drunk is good for my health." Then he laughed some more and suggested, "Ask my father or yours."

Even so, she tried to drag out the discussion, guided by false hopes. He was resolute, drawing courage from his boredom, which made it easier than before to feel indifferent about angering her. He proceeded to emphasize that men have an absolute right to do anything they want and women a duty to obey and abide by the rules. "Look at my father's wife. Have you ever seen her object to his conduct? . . . In spite of that, they are a happy couple and a stable family. There will be no need to talk about this subject again."

Perhaps if he had left it up to his feelings, he would not have spoken to her so diplomatically, for his disappointment with marriage made him feel something like a desire for revenge. At other times, he felt a kind of intermittent loathing for her, although neither of these sentiments kept him from wanting her. He was considerate of her feelings out of fear or respect for his father, who was very fond of Mr. Muhammad Iffat. Nothing disturbed him so much as his fear that she might complain about him to her father, who would then complain to al-Sayyid Ahmad. He had even decided that if something like that happened he would take a separate house, no matter what the consequences.

His fears were not realized. Despite her grief, the girl proved that she was "reasonable," as though she were the same type of woman as his father's wife. She evaluated her position carefully and resigned herself to the situation. She had to fall back on her husband's oft-repeated assertions of his fidelity and of the innocence of his nightly excursions. She was content to air her pain and sorrow within the narrow family circle at the coffee hour, where she received no real support. How could she in a household that viewed submission to men as a religion and a creed? Mrs. Amina disapproved of her complaints and was annoyed at her strange craving to monopolize her husband. The mother was unable to imagine women being any different from her or men from her husband. She saw nothing strange in the enjoyment Yasin derived from his freedom. What seemed strange to her was his wife's complaint.

Only Fahmy appreciated her sorrows. He took it on himself to repeat them to Yasin, although he was certain from the start that he was defending a lost cause. He may have been encouraged to bring up the topic because they met frequently at the coffee shop of Ahmad Abduh in Khan al-Khalili. That coffee shop was situated belowground like a cave hewn from a mountain. Residences of this ancient district formed its roof. Its narrow rooms faced each other around a courtyard with an abandoned fountain, cut off from the outside world. Its lamps were lit both day and night, and it had a calm, dreamy, cool atmosphere.

Yasin had chosen this coffee shop because it was close to Costaki's bar and because he had been forced to abandon al-Sayyid Ali's coffee shop in al-Ghuriya after breaking up with Zanuba. The antique look of this new haunt also appealed to his poetic inclinations. Fahmy had not learned the route to coffeehouses as the result of any setback to his career as a diligent student. He came in response to the troubled times, which called on the students and everyone else to meet and consult. He and some comrades had chosen Abduh's coffeehouse for the antique characteristics that made it a refuge from prying eyes. They sat there evening after evening to talk, scheme, predict, and await forthcoming events.

The two brothers met frequently in one of the small rooms, if only for a short time before Fahmy's colleagues arrived or Yasin moved on to Costaki's bar. On one of these occasions, Fahmy alluded to Zaynab's distress. He expressed his astonishment at his brother's conduct, which was not compatible with the married life of a young couple. Yasin laughed as though he felt he had every right to mock his brother's naïveté in offering advice about something of which he was totally ignorant. He did not wish to justify his conduct directly, preferring to say whatever came to mind. He told the young man, "You wanted to marry Maryam. No doubt you were deeply saddened when Father prevented that desire from being fulfilled. I tell you, and I really know what I'm talking about, that if you had known then what marriage conceals beneath the surface you would have praised God for your failure."

Fahmy was astonished and even alarmed. He had not expected to be assaulted so abruptly by phrases combining the words "Maryam," "marriage," and "desire," which had played unforgettable roles on the stage of his heart. He may have exaggerated his astonishment to conceal the emotional impact of these memories. Perhaps that was the reason he was unable to say a word.

Gesturing to express his weariness and boredom, Yasin continued: "I never imagined that marriage would be so dreary. In fact, it's nothing more than a false dream. It's a cruel and evil swindler."

These words seemed difficult for Fahmy to stomach and aroused his suspicion. That was only to be expected from a young man whose emotional life was centered on a single goal which could be pictured only in the form of a wife and under the rubric "marriage." Fahmy was disturbed to have his irresponsible brother attack this revered category with such bitter sarcasm. He muttered in evident astonishment, "But your wife's perfect . . . a perfect lady."

Yasin cried out sarcastically, "A perfect lady! That she is. Isn't she the daughter of a respected gentleman? And her stepmother's from a distinguished family. Beautiful? . . . Refined? . . . Yes, but some unknown demon in charge of married life turns these qualities into trivial characteristics of little interest through the sickening boredom of marriage. These noble but meaningless qualities are like the noble and happy expressions we rain down on a poor person when we offer him our condolences for his poverty."

Fahmy replied simply and truthfully, "I don't understand a word you've said."

"Wait till you learn for yourself."

"Why have people kept on getting married, then, since the beginning of creation?"

"Because warnings and caution are as futile for marriage as for death." Yasin continued as though to himself: "My imagination really tricked me. It lifted me up to worlds of delight superior even to those of my dreams. I kept asking myself: Is it actually true that I'll share a house with a beautiful maiden forever? What a dream! . . . But I assure you that there's no disaster more oppressive than being united with a beautiful woman under one roof forever."

With the bewilderment of a person so buffeted by youthful passions that he found it difficult to imagine boredom, Fahmy murmured, "Perhaps you've discovered something else concealed inside a flawless exterior?"

Laughing bitterly, Yasin replied, "I'm not complaining about anything except the flawless exterior. . . . My complaint is actually based on the beauty itself. . . . It's beauty that's made me so bored I'm sick. It's like a new word that dazzles you the first time. Then you keep repeating it and using it until it's no different for you than words like 'dog,' 'worm,' 'lesson,' and other commonplace expressions. It loses its novelty and appeal. You may even forget its meaning, so that it becomes a strange, meaningless word you can't use. Perhaps someone else will come across it in your essay and be amazed at your brilliance, while you're amazed at their ignorance. Don't wonder about the disaster of being bored by beauty. It's a boredom that appears inexcusable and consequently totally condemnable. It's difficult to try to avoid groundless despair. Don't be surprised at what I'm saying. I excuse you because you're looking at the situation from a distance. Beauty is like a mirage that can only be seen from afar."

In spite of his brother's bitter tone, Fahmy doubted it was justified, since from the beginning he had been inclined to blame his brother and not human nature for Yasin's deviant behavior. Was it not possible that his complaint could be attributed to his shameless behavior before he got married? Fahmy held firm to this assumption because he refused to allow his fondest dreams to be destroyed. Yasin was not as interested in what his brother thought as in getting some things off his own chest. Smiling sweetly for the first time, he continued: "I've come to understand my father's position perfectly. I know what turned him into that boisterous man who's always chasing after romance. How could he have put up with a single dish for a quarter century when I'm dying of boredom after five months?"

Fahmy was upset that his father had been dragged into the conversation. He protested: "Even if we suppose that your complaint arises from some misery that's an integral part of human nature, the solution you so cheerfully announce . . ." he was about to say, "is far removed from being harmonious or natural," but to seem more logical he switched to: "is far removed from religion."

Yasin was content to limit his observance of religion to belief and paid no serious attention to its commandments or prohibitions. He responded, "Religion supports my view, as shown by its permission to marry four wives, not to mention the concubines with whom the palaces of the caliphs and wealthy men were packed. Religion acknowledges that even beauty itself, once familiarity and experience make it seem trite, can be boring, sickening, and deadly."

Fahmy observed with a smile, "We had a grandfather who spent the evening with one wife and the morning with another. Perhaps you're his heir."

Yasin murmured with a sigh, "Perhaps."

At that time, Yasin had not yet realized any of his rebellious dreams. Although he had returned to the coffeehouse and the bar, he had hesitated before taking the final step of slipping back to Zanuba or some other woman. What had made him reflect and hesitate . . . some feeling of responsibility toward married life? Perhaps he had not freed himself from respect for the religious view that distinguished between an unmarried fornicator and a married adulterer and punished the latter far more severely? Perhaps until he recovered from the disappointment of the greatest hope he had ever nurtured he would be alienated from worldly pleasures? None of these reasons would have been a serious obstacle capable of restraining him, had he not found an unavoidable and irresistible temptation in the example provided by his father's life.

Yasin associated the reasonableness of his wife with that of his stepmother. His imagination busied itself sketching out a plan for her future with him based on Mrs. Amina's life with his father. Yes, he deeply wished that Zaynab would settle down in the life for which she was destined the way his father's wife had. Then he would embark on a series of daring escapades like his father's. He would come home at the end of the night to a calm house and a compliant wife. In that manner and that alone, marriage appeared bearable. Indeed, it would be desirable, with qualities he would otherwise miss out on.

"What more does any woman want than a home of her own and sexual gratification? Nothing! Women are just another kind of domestic animal, and must be treated like one. Yes, other pets are not allowed to intrude into our private lives. They stay home until we're free to play with them. For me, being a husband who is faithful to his marriage would be death. One sight, one sound, one taste incessantly repeated and repeated until there's no difference between motion and inertia. Sound and silence become twins. . . . No, certainly not, that's not why I got married. . . . If she's said to have a fair complexion, then does that mean I have no desires for a brown-skinned woman or a black? If she's said to be pleasingly plump, what consolation will I have for skinny women or huge ones? If she's refined, from a noble and distinguished family, should I neglect the good qualities of girls whose fathers push carts around in the streets? . . . Forward . . . forward."

51

Al-Sayyid Ahmad was bent over his ledgers when he heard a pair of high-heeled shoes tapping across the threshold of the store. He naturally raised his eyes with interest and saw a woman whose hefty body was enveloped in a wrap. A white forehead and eyes decorated with kohl could be seen above her veil. He smiled to welcome a person for whom he had been waiting a long time, for he had immediately recognized Maryam's mother, or the widow of the late Mr. Ridwan, as she had recently become known. Jamil al-Hamzawi was busy with some customers, and so the proprietor invited her to sit near his desk. The woman strutted toward him. As she sat down on the small chair her flesh flowed over the sides. She wished him a good morning.

Although her greeting and his welcome followed the customary pattern repeated whenever a woman customer worth honoring came into the store, the atmosphere in the corner near the desk was charged with electricity that was anything but innocent. Among its manifestations were the modest lowering of her eyelids, visible on either side of the bridge connecting her veil to her scarf, and the glance of his eyes, which were lying in wait above his huge nose. The electricity was hidden and silent but needed only a touch to make it shine, glow, and burst into flame.

He seemed to have been expecting this visit, which was an answer to whispered hopes and suppressed dreams. The death of Mr. Muhammad Ridwan had made him anticipate it, arousing his desires the way the death of winter excites youthful hopes in creatures. With his neighbor's passing, al-Sayyid Ahmad's chivalrous scruples had vanished. He reminded himself that the deceased man had merely been a neighbor, never a friend, and that he was now dead. Today he could recognize the woman's beauty, which he had previously tried to ignore to help preserve his honor. He could express this recognition and allow it a measure of enjoyment and life.

His affection for Zubayda was starting to go bad, like a fruit at the end of its season. In contrast to the last time, now the woman found him an uninhibited male and uncommitted lover. The unwelcome idea that this might be an innocent visit crossed his mind, only to be banished on the evidence of the tender and exquisitely provocative hints she had let drop at their last encounter. The fact that she was making an unnecessary call on him proved that his doubts were unfounded. An old hand at this game, he finally decided to try his luck. Smiling, he told her tenderly, "What a fine idea!"

Somewhat uneasily she replied, "May God honor you. I was just returning home when I passed by the store and it occurred to me to do my shopping for the month myself."

He considered her excuse but refused to believe it. That it had seemed a good idea to do her shopping for the month was not convincing. There had to be some other motive, especially since she would know instinctively that a second visit after the overtures of the past one would be apt to excite his suspicions and inevitably appear provocative. Her haste to apologize also increased his confidence. He commented, "It's an excellent opportunity for me to greet and serve you."

She thanked him briefly, but he did not give her his full attention. He was busy thinking about what to say next. Perhaps he ought to mention her late husband and ask God's mercy on him, but he abstained for fear it would destroy the mood. Then he wondered whether he should go on the offensive or encourage her advances? Either method had its pleasures, but he could not forget that for her to come alone to see him was a giant step on her part that deserved a warm reception from him. He added to his previous greeting: "Indeed it's an excellent opportunity to see you."

Her eyelids and eyebrows moved in a way that revealed modesty or discomfort, or both at once, but most of all that she understood the hidden meanings behind his flattery. Yet he viewed her embarrassment more as a reaction to her own feelings, which had moved her to visit him, than to his statement. He felt certain his hunch was correct and proceeded to repeat his words tenderly: "Yes, an excellent opportunity to see you."

At that, she replied in a tone with a bite of concealed criticism, "I doubt that you consider seeing me an 'excellent opportunity.'"

Her criticism pleased and delighted him, but he protested, "Whoever said that some forms of doubt are sinful was right."

She shook her head to tell him that such talk proved nothing. Then she said, "It's not merely a doubt. I'm certain of it. You're a man who doesn't lack understanding. Even if you suspect otherwise, I'm that way too. . . . So it wouldn't be right for either of us to try to deceive the other."

He felt scornful and bitter that a woman would say such things only two months after the death of her husband but thought up an excuse for her, something he would not have considered doing in other circumstances, and told himself, "Her patience during his long illness has to be considered on her behalf." Spurning this uninvited feeling, he told her with feigned regret, "You're angry with me? . . . That's an evil fate I don't deserve."

She said somewhat impetuously, perhaps because the restrictions of time and place did not allow much playful repartee, "I told myself when I was on the way here, 'You shouldn't go.' So now I have only myself to blame."

"Why so angry, lady? I ask myself what crime I've committed."

She asked provocatively, "What would you do if you greeted someone and he didn't return your greeting?"

He realized immediately that she was referring to her display of affection on her previous visit, which he had met with silence, but he pretended not to understand the reference. Imitating her allusive style, he said, "Perhaps he wasn't able to hear the greeting for one reason or another."

"His hearing's excellent and so are his other senses."

His mouth opened in an uncontrollable and self-satisfied smile. Like a sinner starting to confess, he said, "Perhaps he was too bashful or pious to return the greeting."

With a candor that pleased and stirred him, she replied, "As for bashfulness, he's not at all bashful, and how could a serious person accept the remainder of the excuse?"

A laugh escaped from him, but he cut it short and glanced at Jamil al-Hamzawi, who seemed engrossed in the business of assisting some customers. Then al-Sayyid Ahmad said, "I would prefer not to rehash the complications troubling me at the time. All the same, I shan't despair so long as regret, repentance, and forgiveness remain."

She asked skeptically, "Who says there's regret?"

In an ardent tone that he had perfected over the years, he replied, "With God as my witness, I have been consumed by regret."

"And repentance?"

Boring deep into her with a flaming look, he said, "The greeting is returned ten times over."

She asked flirtatiously, "How do you know there's forgiveness?"

He answered suavely, "Isn't forgiveness one of the qualities of noble people?" Then he continued with delirious intoxication: "Forgiveness is frequently the secret word granting entry into paradise." Gazing at the sweet smile he detected in her eyes, he concluded, "The paradise I refer to is located at the intersection of Palace Walk and al-Nahhasin. Fortunately, the door opens onto a side alley far from prying eyes and there's no watchman."

It crossed his mind that her late husband, who had been the watchman guarding the terrestrial paradise he was attempting to enter, was now an occupant of the heavenly paradise. His mind was troubled by fear that the woman might have realized the same ironic truth, but he found she was daydreaming. He sighed and secretly asked God's forgiveness.

Jamil al-Hamzawi had finished taking care of his customers and approached to attend to her requests. Al-Sayyid Ahmad had an opportunity to mull things over. He began to remember how his son Fahmy had once wanted to get engaged to Maryam, this woman's daughter, and how God had inspired him to turn Fahmy down. At that time he had believed he was merely acting according to his principles. It had not occurred to him that he was sparing his son the most terrible tragedy that can befall a husband. What course would a girl follow but her mother's? . . . And what a mother! A thoroughly dangerous woman. . . . Although she was a precious jewel to skirt chasers like him, on the domestic front she would be a bloody disaster. What had she been up to during the long years when her husband was as good as dead? All the evidence pointed in one direction. Perhaps many of the neighbors knew. Indeed, if anyone in his home had been skilled at observing these affairs, he would have known all about it, and his wife, who even now believed in her, would not have remained a friend. He felt once more a desire, which had first seized him after her doubt-provoking visit, to separate this wanton woman from his pure family. He had found no way then to fulfill it without arousing suspicion. Because of his anticipated liaison with her, he saw that it was time to act on this desire. He would suggest that she gradually terminate her friendship with his wife, and thus, without any damage to her reputation, he would achieve his goal by making use of a legitimate excuse. The closer this woman got to his heart, the farther she was removed from his respect.

When al-Hamzawi finished getting what she needed, she rose and held out her hand to al-Sayyid Ahmad. He accepted it with a smile and said softly, "Until we meet again."

As she started to leave, she murmured, "We'll be waiting for you."

She left behind her a man who was overjoyed and intoxicated by pride at his conquest, but she had also created a problem for him that would occupy a prominent place among his daily concerns. He would have to think about the safest way to withdraw from Zubayda's house, as seriously as he pondered what the military authority was doing, what the English were up to, and what Sa'd was planning. Yes, as usual, this new happiness carried a tail of thought behind it. If he had not craved for people to love him—and it was this love that brought him his happiest moments—it would have been easy for him to leave the entertainer. His love had become threadbare, its bloom had faded, and satiation had plunged it into a brackish swamp, but he was always apprehensive about leaving behind an angry heart or a spiteful soul. Whenever he got bored with a relationship he would hope for his lover to initiate the separation so that he would be the one left, not the one departing. How he wished that his relationship with Zubayda could end like those previous ones when a temporary unpleasantness had been washed away by choice farewell presents. Then this former liaison would evolve into a solid friendship.

He suspected that Zubayda was as satiated as he was. Would she accept his apologies graciously? Could he hope that his presents would adequately compensate for his leaving her, which he was determined to do? Would she prove to be as bighearted and generous as her colleague Jalila, for example? He would have to think about these questions at length to prepare the most satisfying excuses for himself. He sighed deeply, as though complaining that love should be so transitory. If it were lasting, it would spare the heart troublesome passions. Then his imagination wandered off to nightfall. He could see himself creeping along in the darkness, groping his way to the appointed house where the woman was waiting with a lamp in her hand.

52

"England proclaimed the Protectorate of its own accord without asking or receiving permission from the Egyptian nation. It is an invalid protectorate with no legal standing. In fact, it was one of those things necessitated by the war and should end now that the war has ended."

Fahmy dictated these words, one at a time, deliberately and in a clear voice, while his mother, Yasin, and Zaynab followed this new dictation exercise Kamal was tackling. He concentrated his attention on the words without understanding anything he wrote down, whether he got it right or not. It was not unusual for Fahmy to give his younger brother a lesson in dictation or some other subject during the coffee hour, but the topic seemed different, even to the mother and Zaynab.

Yasin looked at his brother with a smile and remarked, "I see these ideas have gained control of you. Has God not inspired you with any dictation for this poor boy except this nationalist address that could get a person thrown into prison?"

Fahmy quickly corrected his brother: "It's an address Sa'd gave in front of the occupation forces in the Legislative and Economic Assembly."

Yasin asked with interest and astonishment, "How did they reply?"

Fahmy said passionately, "Their answer hasn't come yet. Everyone's anxiously and apprehensively wondering what it will be. The speech was an outburst of anger in the face of a lion not known for restraint or justice." He sighed with bitter exasperation and continued: "This angry outburst was inevitable after the Wafd Delegation was prevented from making their journey and Rushdi resigned as Prime Minister. Sultan Ahmad Fuad disappointed our hopes when he accepted the Prime Minister's resignation."

Fahmy hurried to his room, returning with a piece of paper, which he unfolded. He presented it to his brother and said, "The speech isn't all I've got. Read this handbill, which has been distributed secretly. It contains the letter from the Wafd Delegation to the Sultan."

Yasin took the handbill and began to read:

"Your Majesty,

"The undersigned, members of the Egyptian Wafd Delegation, are honored to represent the Nation by presenting these concerns to Your Majesty:

"Since the belligerents agreed to make the principles of freedom and justice the basis for the peace treaties and announced that peoples whose status had been altered by the war would be consulted about self-government, we have taken upon ourselves an effort to liberate our country and to defend its case at the Peace Conference. Since the traditionally dominant power has disappeared from the arena and since our country, with the dissolution of Turkish sovereignty over it, has become free of every claim against it, and since the Protectorate, which the English proclaimed unilaterally without any agreement from the Egyptian nation, is invalid and merely one of the necessities of war, which ends with the end of the war, based on these circumstances and the fact that Egypt has suffered as much as could be expected of her while serving in the ranks of those claiming to protect the freedom of small nations, there is nothing to prevent the Peace Conference from acknowledging our political freedom pursuant to the principles it has adopted as its foundation.

"We submitted our request to travel to your Prime Minister, His Excellency Husayn Rushdi Pasha. He promised to assist us, confident that we expressed the views of the Nation as a whole. When we were not permitted to travel and were confined within the borders of our country by a tyrannical force with no legal authority, we were prevented from defending the cause of this distressed nation. When His Excellency the Prime Minister was unable to bear the responsibility for retaining his post while the will of the people was obstructed, he resigned along with his colleague His Excellency Adli Yeken Pasha. Their resignations were welcomed by the people, who honored these men and acknowledged the sincerity of their nationalism.

"People believed that these two men in their noble stand in defense of liberty had a powerful ally in Your Majesty. Therefore no one in Egypt expected that the final solution to the question of the journey of the Wafd Delegation would have been acceptance of the resignation of the two ministers, which will further the purposes of those desiring to humiliate us and strengthen the obstacle placed in the path of the delivery of the Nation's plea at the Conference. It also makes it appear that we consent to the perpetuation of foreign rule over us.

"We know that Your Majesty may have been forced for dynastic considerations to accept the throne of your illustrious father when it became vacant on the death of your late brother Sultan Hasan, but the Nation, for its part, believed that when you accepted this throne during a temporary, invalid protectorate for those dynastic considerations, you would not be deterred from working for the independence of your country. Resolution of the problem by accepting the resignation of the two ministers who demonstrated their respect for the will of the Nation is impossible to reconcile with the love for the good of your country to which you are naturally disposed or with your respect for the wishes of your subjects. Therefore, people have been amazed that your advisers have not sided with the Nation at this critical time. That is what is requested of you, O wisest of the descendants of our great liberator Muhammad Ali, so that you will be the mainstay in the achievement of the Nation's independence, no matter what the cost to you. Your zeal is too lofty to be limited by the circumstances. How did it escape the attention of your advisers that Rushdi Pasha's resignation guarantees that no patriotic Egyptian will agree to replace him? How did it escape them that a cabinet dedicated to programs contrary to the wishes of the people is destined to fail?

"Pardon, Your Majesty, if our intervention in this affair seems inappropriate. In other circumstances perhaps it would be, but the matter has now gone beyond consideration of any concern other than the good of the Nation, of which you are the faithful servant. Our Sovereign holds the highest position in the country and therefore holds the greatest responsibility for it. The greatest hopes are placed in him. We will not be misrepresenting our advice to him if we implore him to take into account the views of his Nation before reaching a final decision regarding the current crisis. We affirm to His Majesty that there is no one among his subjects, from one end of the country to the other, who does not seek independence. Obstruction of the Nation's request is a weighty responsibility which Your Majesty's advisers did not consider with the necessary care. Therefore, our duty to serve our country and our loyalty to Our Sovereign have compelled us to bring to the attention of His Majesty the feelings of his Nation, which hopes fervently for independence now and greatly fears what the agents of the colonial party may do to it. The Nation has a right, which it seeks to exercise, for its sovereign to be angry when it is angry and for him to side with it. This is the goal the Nation has chosen.... And God is capable of granting that...."

Yasin raised his head from the handbill. There was an astonished look in his eyes and his heart pounded with a new excitement. He shook his head and exclaimed, "What a letter! . . . I doubt I would be able to send anything like that to the headmaster of my school without being severely punished."

Fahmy shrugged his shoulders disdainfully and said, "The matter has now gone beyond consideration of any concern other than the good of the Nation." He repeated the words from memory, just as they appeared in the handbill.

Yasin could not keep himself from laughing. He observed, "You've memorized the handbill . . . but that doesn't surprise me. You seem to have been waiting all your life for a movement like this in order to throw your whole heart into it. Although I may share your feelings and hopes, I'm not happy about your holding on to this handbill, especially after the cabinet has resigned and martial law has been proclaimed."

Fahmy said proudly, "I'm not just keeping it. I'm distributing it as much as I can."

Yasin's eyes widened in astonishment. He started to speak, but the mother spoke first. She said with alarm, "I can scarcely believe my ears. How can you expose yourself to danger when you're such an intelligent person?"

Fahmy did not know how to answer her. He felt the awkwardness of the situation his recklessness had created. Nothing could be more difficult for him than discussing this matter with her. He was closer to the heavens than he was to convincing her that he had a duty to expose himself to danger for the sake of the nation. In her eyes, the nation was not worth the clippings from his fingernail. The expulsion of the English from Egypt seemed easier to him than persuading her of the necessity of expelling them or inducing her to hate them. Whenever the subject came up in a conversation she would remark quite simply, "Why do you despise them, son? . . . Aren't they people like us with sons and mothers?"

Fahmy would reply sharply, "But they're occupying our country."

She would sense the bitter anger in his voice and fall silent. There would be a veiled look of concern in her eyes that would have said if it could have spoken, "Don't be like that."

Once when he was exasperated by her reasoning, he had told her, "A people ruled by foreigners has no life."

She had replied in astonishment, "But we're still alive, even though they've been ruling us for a long time. I bore all of you under their rule. Son, they don't kill us and they don't interfere with the mosques. The community of Muhammad is still thriving."

The young man had said in despair, "If our master, Muhammad, were alive, he would not consent to being ruled by the English."

She had responded sagaciously, "That's true, but what are we compared to the Prophet, peace and blessings on him? . . . God sent His angels to assist him."

He had cried out furiously, "Sa'd Zaghlul will do what the angels used to."

She had raised her arms as though trying to fend off an irresistible calamity and shouted, "Ask your Lord's forgiveness. O God, Your mercy and forgiveness!"

That was what she was like. How could he answer her now that she had realized the danger threatening him because he was distributing the handbill? All he could do was resort to lying. Pretending to dismiss the matter lightly, he said, "I was just joking. There's nothing for you to be alarmed about."

The woman spoke again entreatingly, "This is what I believe, son. How I would hate for my hopes in the person with the best sense of all to be disappointed. . . . And what business of ours are these affairs? If the pashas think the English should be expelled from Egypt, let them expel the English themselves."

Throughout the conversation, Kamal had been trying to remember something important. When the conversation reached this point, he shouted, "Our Arabic language teacher told us yesterday that nations gain their independence through the decisive actions of their sons."

The mother cried out in annoyance, "Perhaps he meant big pupils. Didn't you tell me once that some of the other pupils already have mustaches?"

Kamal asked innocently, "Isn't my brother Fahmy a big pupil?"

His mother replied with unaccustomed sharpness, "Certainly not! Your brother's not an adult. I'm amazed at that teacher. How could he have succumbed to the temptation of discussing something with you that wasn't part of the lesson? If he really wants to be a nationalist, he should address such talk to his sons at home, not to other people's children."

This conversation would have grown progressively more heated had not a chance remark intervened to change its direction. Zaynab wanted to gain her mother-in-law's approval by supporting her. She attacked the teacher and called him "a despicable mosque student to whom the government gave a responsible position despite the changing times."

The moment the mother heard this insult aimed at students in

Islamic universities like al-Azhar, she was distracted from her former concerns. She refused to let the remark slip by unchallenged, even though it had been said to support her. She turned to Zaynab and said calmly, "Daughter, you are disparaging the best thing about him. The religious shaykhs carry on the work of God's messengers. The man is to be blamed for exceeding the boundaries of his noble calling. He should have contented himself with being a student at a mosque and a religious scholar."

Yasin was not blind to the secret behind his stepmother's change of direction. He quickly intervened to erase the bad impression left by his wife's innocent remark.

53

"Look at the street. Look at the people. After all this, who could say that the catastrophe hasn't taken place?"

Al-Sayyid Ahmad did not need to look. Everyone was asking about the event and trembling. His friends plunged into heated discussions in which grief, sorrow, and anger played equal parts. The news was repeated by everyone, friends and customers alike. They all agreed that Sa'd Zaghlul and his closest associates had been arrested and transported to an unknown location, either in Cairo or outside it.

Mr. Muhammad Iffat, his face flushed with anger, said, "Don't question the accuracy of the rumor. Bad news has a stench that stops up the nose. Wasn't this to be expected after the Wafd's letter to the Sultan? . . . And after Sa'd's rejection of the British threats with that stupendous letter to the British cabinet?"

Al-Sayyid Ahmad said despondently, "They arrest the great pashas. . . . What a terrifying event! What do you suppose they'll do with them?"

"Only God knows. The country is stifling under the shadow of martial law."

Mr. Ibrahim al-Far, the copper merchant, rushed in. He cried out breathlessly, "Have you heard the latest news? . . . Malta!" He struck his hands together and proceeded: "Exile to Malta. None of them is left here with us. They've exiled Sa'd and his colleagues to the island of Malta."

They all exclaimed at the same time, "Exiled them!" The word "exile" stirred up sad old memories that had stayed with them since childhood concerning the revolutionary leader Urabi Pasha and what had happened to him. They could not help feeling anxious, wondering if the same fate lay in store for Sa'd Zaghlul and his colleagues. Would they really be exiled from their nation forever? Would these great hopes be nipped in the bud and die?

Al-Sayyid Ahmad felt a kind of grief he had never experienced before. It was a heavy, dull sorrow that spread through his chest like nausea. Under its weight he felt rigid, dead, choked. They began to exchange eloquently somber and gloomy looks that screamed out their feelings soundlessly, inciting each other without a single shout. There was a bitter taste in all their mouths.

On the heels of al-Far came another friend and then a second and a third to repeat the same news, hoping the other men would be able to calm their inflamed souls. All they found was silent sorrow, dejected gloom, and suppressed rage.

"Will today's hopes be for naught like those of yesterday?"

No one answered. The questioner kept looking from face to face, but to no avail. There was no answer to comfort a soul's turmoil, even though they refused to admit publicly the fear that was killing them. Sa'd had been exiled.... That was true, but would Sa'd return, and if so, after what length of time? How would Sa'd return? What power could bring him back? If Sa'd did not return, what would become of these vast hopes? From their new hope a profound and fervent life had sprung that was too overwhelming to abandon to despair. Yet they did not know how their souls could justify reviving it again.

"But isn't there any way that the information might be a false rumor?"

No one paid any attention to that suggestion. Even the person making it was not surprised to be ignored. He had only offered his remark in an attempt to find some escape, however imaginary, from the stifling despair.

"The English have imprisoned him.... Who is there to stand up to the English?"

"He was a man unlike other men. He inspired our lives for a dazzling moment and vanished."

"Like a dream.... He'll be forgotten. Nothing more will be left of him than is left from a dream by midmorning."

Someone exclaimed in a voice hoarse with pain, "God exists!"

They all shouted together, "Yes ... and He's the most merciful of all who are compassionate." The mention of God's name was like a magnet attracting and assembling around it their roving thoughts which had been scattered by despair.

That evening, for the first time in a quarter century or more, the assembled friends seemed averse to fun and music. They were overwhelmed by gloom. All their comments concerned the exiled leader. Sorrow had subjugated them. Even if one of them was torn between his sorrow and a desire to drink, sorrow would win out over drinking, because of his respect for the feelings of the group and his sense that it was inappropriate under those circumstances. When the conversation had dragged on until they had exhausted all aspects, they took refuge in silence. A covert anxiety afflicted them that revealed the itching addiction to alcohol active within them. They seemed to be waiting for a sign from someone daring enough to lead their forces.

Mr. Muhammad Iffat said suddenly, "It's time for us to return to our homes."

He did not mean what he said. He merely wanted to warn them that they were allowing the time to pass and would soon be forced to go home. Their long familiarity with each other had taught them to understand each other's hints.

Abd al-Rahim, the flour merchant, was encouraged by the hidden content of this warning to say, "Are we to part without a glass of wine to lighten today's suffering?"

His statement cheered them up the way a surgeon's does when he leaves the operating room to tell the family of a sick patient, "Praise God . . . the operation was a success."

Yet a man whose sorrow was struggling with his desire to drink pretended to protest, while concealing the relief gladdening his heart: "Should we drink on a day like this?"

Al-Sayyid Ahmad cast him a knowing look. Then he said ironically, "Let them drink by themselves and we'll go outside, you . . . son of a bitch."

They laughed for the first time, and bottles of wine were brought in. Apparently wanting to apologize for this behavior, al-Sayyid Ahmad said, "A little fun won't alter what's in a man's heart."

They applauded his words. Throughout the evening they had hesitated a long time before answering the call of their physical yearnings. Stirred by the sight of the wine bottles, al-Sayyid Ahmad soon observed, "Sa'd's rebellion was intended to cheer the Egyptians, not to torment them. So don't let your sorrow for him make you feel embarrassed about drinking."

His own grief did not prevent him from joking, although it was not an enjoyable or carefree evening. Al-Sayyid Ahmad described it later as "a sick night which had to be treated with doses of wine."

The family began their coffee hour with unprecedented gloom. Fahmy launched into a long revolutionary speech with tears in his eyes. Yasin listened sorrowfully and sadly. The mother wanted to dispel the despair and lighten their affliction but was afraid she would only make things worse. Then the infectious sorrow soon passed into her heart. She felt sorry for the old man they had taken away from his house and wife to a distant place of exile.

Yasin commented, "It's a sad affair. All our men: the Khedive Abbas II, the nationalists Muhammad Farid and Sa'd Zaghlul . . . all have been driven far from the nation."

Fahmy exclaimed passionately, "What rogues the English are! . . . We address them in the same terms they used to gain sympathy during their ordeal and they answer with military threats, exile, and banishment."

The mother could not bear to see her son so upset. She forgot about the leader's tragedy and said gently and soothingly, "Don't take it so hard, son. May our Lord be gracious to us."

This gentle tone only made him more upset. Without turning to look at her he shouted, "If we don't confront terrorism with the anger it deserves, may the nation never live again. It's unthinkable for the nation to be at peace when its leader who has sacrificed himself for it suffers the torments of captivity."

Yasin commented thoughtfully, "It's fortunate that Hamad Basil Pasha was one of those exiled. He's the chieftain of a ferocious tribe. I doubt that his men will keep quiet about his banishment."

Fahmy replied sharply, "What about the others? . . . Aren't there men behind them too? . . . The case doesn't just concern one tribe, it concerns the whole nation."

The conversation continued without interruption and grew even more bitter and violent. The two women kept still out of anxiety and fear. Zaynab could not understand the reasons for this emotional outburst. It seemed meaningless to her. So what if Sa'd and his men had been exiled? Clearly, if they had lived the way God's children should, no one would have thought of banishing them. But they were not content to live like that. They wanted things it was dangerous to desire. There was no necessity for what had occurred. Regardless of what had happened to them, why was Fahmy so insanely angry, as though Sa'd were his father or his brother? Indeed, what was making Yasin, a man who never retired to bed sober, so sad? Were men like him and the others really saddened by Sa'd's banishment? Did her life need anything else to upset it so that Fahmy had to spoil the serenity of this brief gathering with his tantrum? She thought about this as she observed her husband from time to time with vexed amazement. Her expression seemed to say, "If you're really sincere about your sorrow, then don't go out this evening, just this one evening, to the bar."

She did not utter a word. She was too wise to cast her icy reflections into that fiery stream. Her mother-in-law resembled her in this. Her courage rapidly evaporated when confronted by anger, no matter how trivial. For that reason, she retreated into silence and kept her intense discomfort to herself as she apprehensively followed the raging, unruly conversation. She was better able than Yasin's wife to fathom the reasons for these storms. She remembered Urabi with her mind, and her heart still felt sad about "Our Effendi," the Khedive Abbas II. Yes, the word "exile" was a meaningful concept to her. Indeed, the way she understood the term it lacked the hope that could tantalize a person like Fahmy. In her mind, like those of her husband and his friends, it was not associated with any possibility of return. If it meant something else, where was "Our Effendi"? Who deserved to return to his nation more than he did? Would Fahmy's sorrow last as long as Sa'd's banishment? What was so unlucky about these days that coming and going brought news to shake their security and destroy their peace of mind? How she wished peace would return to its abode and that this gathering would be pleasant again, the way it had been all their lives. She wished Fahmy's face would smile and that the conversation would be amiable. How she wished it....

"Malta! Here's Malta!" Kamal yelled suddenly, raising his head from a map of the Mediterranean Sea. He had set his finger on the outline of the island and now looked at his brother with triumph and delight, as though he had found Sa'd Zaghlul himself. All he saw of Fahmy was a scowling, gloomy face. There was no response to his cry of discovery. His brother paid no attention to him at all. The boy subsided and looked back down at the drawing of the island in confusion and embarrassment. He gazed at it for a long time while he measured with his eyes the distance between Malta and Alexandria and then between Malta and Cairo. He tried to imagine what the real Malta looked like. He pictured the men they had been talking about who had been transported there. Since he had heard Fahmy say the English had taken Sa'd away at spearpoint, he could only visualize him being carried on the points of spears. The great leader was not in pain or screaming, as one would expect in such a situation, but "steadfast as a mountain," as his brother had also described him at another stage of the conversation. How Kamal wished he could ask his brother about the essence of that wonderfully magical man who rested as steadfast as a mountain on the points of spears. In view of the outpouring of anger that had destroyed the peace of the entire gathering, Kamal postponed any action on his desire until a more suitable opportunity.

Fahmy finally grew uncomfortable at dominating the session, after he had ascertained that the emotions he felt were too great to be relieved by a conversation with Yasin in this setting, where the latter, even if sympathetic, still played the part of a spectator. Fahmy's soul urged him to join his comrades at the coffee shop of Ahmad Abduh, where he would find hearts as responsive as his own and souls that vied with his to express the perceptions and ideas raging inside. There he would hear an echo of the anger crackling in his heart. He would be able to formulate his daring and unruly impulses in a splendid atmosphere of yearning for total freedom. Fahmy leaned toward Yasin and whispered, "To Ahmad Abduh's coffee shop."

Yasin sighed deeply, because he had begun to wonder with great discomfort about some graceful way of slipping out of the coffee hour to go off in search of entertainment without adding any more fuel to Fahmy's flaming anger. Yasin's grief had not been fabricated, at least not entirely. The momentous news shook his heart, but left to his own devices he would have forgotten it without much effort. In view of the strain on his nerves of trying to keep up with Fahmy, to flatter him and show respect for his unprecedented anger, Yasin left the room saying to himself, "I've done enough for the nationalist movement today. Now it's my body's turn."

54

Fahmy opened his eyes when he heard the sound of dough being pounded in the oven room. The shutters were closed, and the room was almost dark except for the pale light coming through the openings between the slats. He could hear Kamal's regular breathing and turned his head toward his brother's nearby bed. Memories of his life, fresh this morning, swarmed through his mind. He was waking up from a deep sleep resulting from his total exhaustion of mind and body. He had not known whether he would wake up in this bed or never wake up again. He had not known, nor had anyone else, for death was roaming the streets of Cairo and dancing along its arcades.

How amazing! Here was his mother making bread as always. Here was Kamal, sound asleep, rolling around as he dreamt. Yasin's footsteps overhead indicated that he had wrenched himself out of bed. His father was probably taking a cold shower. Here was the morning light, both splendid and shy. Its first rays were gently seeking entry. Everything was proceeding as usual, as though nothing had happened, as though Egypt had not been turned upside down, as though bullets were not searching for chests and heads, as though innocent blood was not enriching the earth and walls. The young man closed his eyes with a sigh. He smiled at the swelling current of his emotions that carried zeal, sorrow, and belief in successive waves.

During the last four days he had lived a life of far greater scope than he ever had known before. His only comparable experience had been in shadowy daydreams. It was a pure, lofty life, ready to sacrifice itself in good conscience for the sake of something glorious, a goal worthier and more exalted than life itself. It did not care whether it risked death, which it greeted resolutely and attacked scornfully. If it escaped from death's clutches once, it returned to attack again, shunning any consideration of possible consequences. This life always had its eyes fixed undeviatingly on a magnificent light and was driven by an irresistible force. It submitted its fate to God, whom it felt encompassing it like the air.

Life considered as a means to something else was despicable. It was less significant than an atom. Life considered as an end in itself was so exalted it was equal to the heavens and the earth. Life and death were brothers. They were like one hand in the service of one hope. Life strengthened this hope with exertion, and death strengthened it with sacrifice. If the awesome upheaval had not occurred, Fahmy would have perished from grief and distress. He could not have stood for life to have continued on in its calm, deliberate way, treading beneath it the destinies and hopes of men. The upheaval had been necessary to relieve the pressure in the nation's breast and in his own. It was like an earthquake providing relief to the pressures that accumulate inside the earth.

When the struggle began, it found him ready. He threw himself into the midst of it. When and how had that happened? He was riding a streetcar to Giza on his way to the Law School when he found himself in a band of students who were waving their fists and protesting: "Sa'd, who expressed what was in our hearts, has been banished. If Sa'd does not return to continue his efforts, we should be sent into exile with him."

The other passengers, their fellow citizens, joined in their discussion and threats. Even the conductor neglected his work and stopped to listen and talk with them. What a moment! . . . After a dark night of grief and despair, Fahmy's hope shone anew. He was certain that this blazing fire would not grow cold.

When they reached the courtyard of the school, it was swarming with clamorous students creating a great uproar. Their hearts raced ahead of them as they rushed to their colleagues. They sensed that something was brewing. Someone immediately began calling for a strike. . . . That was new and unheard of then. While they were shouting for a strike with their law books under their arms, the head of the Law School, Mr. Walton, came to greet them with unusual graciousness and advised them to enter their classrooms. In response, a young man climbed up the stairway leading to the secretary's office and began to address them with extraordinary zeal. All the dean could do was withdraw.

Fahmy listened to the speech with rapt attention. His eyes were fixed on the speaker, and his heart was beating rapidly. He would have liked to climb up there too and pour out the contents of his raging heart, but he did not have a background in public speaking. He was content for someone else to repeat the outbursts of his own heart. He listened to the speaker attentively and enthusiastically until the first pause. Then Fahmy shouted along with all his comrades at the same time, "Independence!"

He listened to the continuation of the speech with an interest enlivened by the shouting. When the speaker reached a second stopping point, Fahmy cried out with everyone else, "Down with the Protectorate!" Then, his body rigid with emotion and his teeth clenched to hold back the tears inspired by the agitation of his soul, he kept on listening until the speaker reached his third stopping place. With all the others, he shouted, "Long live Sa'd!" That was a new chant. Everything seemed new that day, but this was a ravishing chant. Deep inside him, his heart reverberated to it and kept repeating it with its successive beats, as though echoing his tongue. But the cry on his tongue was actually echoing his heart.

He remembered now that his heart had repeated this chant silently all through the night prior to the uprising. He had spent that night in grief and distress. His stifled emotions, love, enthusiasm, aspirations, idealism, and dreams had been scattered in disarray until the voice of Sa'd had rung out. They had been drawn to him like a pigeon floating in the sky drawn back by its master's whistle.

Before they knew what was happening, Mr. Amos, the assistant British judicial counsel in the Ministry of Justice, was making his way through their midst. They greeted him with a single chant: "Down with the Protectorate!" He was gruff with them and not even civil, advising them to return to their lessons and leave politics to their fathers.

At that point one of them protested: "Our fathers have been imprisoned. We won't study law in a land where the law is trampled underfoot."

The cry from the depths of their hearts resounded like a peal of thunder, and the man quickly withdrew. For a second time, Fahmy wished he were the speaker. How many ideas were swarming through his mind, but other students proclaimed them first. His enthusiasm became even more intense. He was consoled by the fact that what he expected to happen would more than compensate for anything he had missed.

Matters progressed rapidly. Someone called for them to leave the school. They went off in a demonstration, heading for the School of Engineering, where the students joined them at once, and then on to Agriculture, where the students rushed out chanting as though they had been expecting them. They went to Medicine and Commerce. As soon as they reached al-Sayyida Zaynab Square they merged with a mass demonstration of citizens. Shouts were raised for Egypt, independence, and Sa'd. With every step they took, they gained more enthusiasm, confidence, and faith, because of the impulsive participation and spontaneous response of their fellow citizens. They encountered people whose souls were primed, reeling with anger that found expression in their demonstration.

Fahmy's astonishment that the demonstration had occurred almost overpowered his feelings about the demonstration itself. He wondered, "How did all this happen?" Only a few hours had passed since morning, when he had been despondent and dejected. Now here he was a little before noon taking part in a turbulent demonstration where he discovered in every other heart an echo of his own, repeating his chant and imploring him not to hesitate but to persevere to the end. How joyful he was and how enthusiastic. . . . His spirit soared off into the heavens with boundless hope. It regretted the despair that had overcome it and was ashamed of the suspicions it had entertained about innocent people.

In al-Sayyida Zaynab Square he witnessed another of the novel scenes of that amazing day. He was one of those who saw groups of mounted policemen commanded by an English officer advancing on them, trailing plumes of dust behind the horses. The earth shook with their hoofbeats. He could well remember how he had stared at them in dismay. He had never before found himself exposed to such unexpected danger.

He looked around him at faces that glowed with enthusiasm and anger. He sighed nervously, but kept on waving his fist and chanting. The mounted policemen surrounded them. Of the formidable ocean in which he was surging he could only observe a limited area and even there everyone else was craning his head to see. Then they heard that the police had arrested many students, those who had confronted them defiantly or had been at the head of the demonstration. For the third time that day he had an unfulfilled wish. He wished he were one of those arrested, but he could not have extricated himself from the band he was in without extraordinary effort.

That day had been relatively peaceful compared with the next. Monday morning began with a general strike and a demonstration in which all the schools participated, carrying their banners, together with untold throngs of citizens. Egypt had come back to life. It was a new country. Its citizens rushed to crowd into the streets to prepare for battle with an anger that had been concealed for a long time. Fahmy threw himself into the swarms of people with intoxicating happiness and enthusiasm, like a displaced person rediscovering his family after a long separation.

The demonstration, which was thronged by onlookers, passed by the homes of influential politicians, voicing its protests in various terms, until it reached Ministries Street. Then a violent disturbance passed through the swarms of people and someone shouted, "The English!" Bullets immediately started flying and drowned out the sound of the protesters. The first fatalities occurred. Some people continued on with insane zeal, while others seemed nailed to the ground. Many separated off and sought shelter in homes and coffeehouses. Fahmy was in this last category. He slipped into a doorway, his heart beating wildly in alarm. He stopped thinking about anything except his life. He stayed there for he knew not how long until silence prevailed everywhere. Then he stuck out his head, followed by his feet, and set off for home, incredulous that he had survived. He was in a kind of daze when he reached his house. In his sorrowful solitude he wished that he had been one of the departed or at least one of those who had held their ground. In a blaze of harsh self-criticism, Fahmy promised his stern conscience to act more thoughtfully the next time. Fortunately the arena for thoughtful action was vast and near at hand.

Tuesday and Wednesday were like Sunday and Monday. They were comparable in both their joys and sorrows. There were demonstrations and chants, bullets and victims. Fahmy threw himself totally into all of this. Driven by his enthusiasm, he reached far-flung horizons of lofty sentiment. He was troubled that he was still alive and regretted his escape. His zeal and hopes were doubled by the spread of the spirit of anger and revolution. It was not long before the tramway workers, the drivers and street sweepers went on strike. The capital appeared sad, angry, desolate. There was good news that attorneys and civil servants were about to strike. The heart of the nation was throbbing. It was alive and in rebellion. The blood would not have been shed in vain. The exiled leaders would not be forgotten. A self-conscious awakening had rocked the Nile Valley.

The young man rolled over in bed. He turned his mind away from the deluge of memories and began to follow the beats of the dough once more. He looked around the room, slowly becoming visible as the sun rose outside the closed shutters. His mother was making bread! She would continue to knead the dough morning after morning. God forbid that anything should distract her from concentrating her attention on preparing the meals, washing the clothes, or cleaning the furnishings. Great activities would not interfere with minor ones. Society would always be flexible enough to embrace exalted and trivial matters and to welcome both equally. But not so fast. . . . Was a mother not part of life? She had given birth to him, and sons fueled the revolution. She fed him, and nourishment fueled the sons. In fact, nothing about life was trivial. But would not some day come when a great event would rock all the Egyptians, leaving none of the differences of opinion that had been present at the coffee hour five days ago? How remote that day seemed. . . . Then a smile came to his lips when this question leapt into his mind: What would his father do if he learned about his continual struggle, day after day? What would his tyrannical, despotic father do about it and his tender, affectionate mother? He smiled anxiously, because he knew he would be exposed to problems no less significant than if the military authority itself should learn his secret.

He pulled back the covers and sat up in bed murmuring, "It's all the same whether I live or die. Faith is stronger than death, and death is nobler than ignominy. Let's enjoy the hope, compared to which life seems unimportant. Welcome to this new morning of freedom. May God carry out whatever He has decreed."

55

No one could claim any longer that the revolution had not changed at least some aspect of his life. Even Kamal's freedom to go to school and return by himself, which he had enjoyed for a long time, was affected by a development he found obnoxiously burdensome, although he could not prevent it. His mother had ordered Umm Hanafi to follow him on his way to and from school. She was not to let him out of her sight and to bring him home if they ran into a demonstration. He would not have a chance to loiter or obey any frivolous impulses.

The news of the demonstrations and disturbances made the mother's head spin. Her heart trembled at the savage attacks on the students. She spent gloomy days filled with alarm and panic, wishing she could keep her two sons at home until matters returned to normal. She was unable to achieve her goal, especially after Fahmy promised he would definitely not participate in any strike. Her confidence in his good sense had not been shaken. Her husband rejected the idea of keeping Kamal home from school, because he knew the school would prevent the younger pupils from participating in the strike. Reluctantly the mother agreed that the brothers could go to school, but she had stipulated Umm Hanafi's supervision for Kamal, telling him, "If I were able to go out, I would follow you myself."

Kamal had objected as forcefully as he could, because he realized intuitively that this supervisor, who would keep nothing about him secret from his mother, would put a decisive end to all the mischief and tricks he enjoyed in the street. That would destroy this brief, happy time of his day as he went from one of his prisons to the other: home and school. He was also intensely annoyed at walking down the street accompanied by this woman whose excessive weight and faltering step would certainly attract attention. He was forced to submit to her supervision, since his father had ordered him to accept her. The most he could do to comfort himself was to scold her whenever she got too close to him, since he had decreed that she should stay several meters behind him.

In this manner they made their way to Khalil Agha School on

Thursday morning, the fifth day of the demonstrations in Cairo. When they reached the door of the school, Umm Hanafi approached the gatekeeper and, acting according to her daily instructions received at home, asked him, "Are the pupils in the school?"

The man answered her indifferently, "Some have gone in and others have left. The headmaster is not interfering with anyone."

This answer was a bad surprise for Kamal. He was prepared to hear the response he had come to expect since Monday—namely: "The pupils are on strike." Then they would return home where he would spend the whole day in freedom. That made him love the revolution from afar. His soul urged him to flee to escape the consequences of this new reply. He told the gatekeeper, "I'm one of those who leave."

He walked away from the school with the woman behind him. When she asked him why he had not gone in with the others who were staying, he implored her repeatedly, for the first time in his life, to deceive his mother by telling her that the pupils were on strike. To strengthen his entreaty and gain her affection, he prayed for her to have a long and happy life when they were passing by the mosque of al-Husayn. Umm Hanafi was unable to keep the truth, as she had heard it, from his mother, who chided him for being lazy and ordered the woman to take him back to school. They left the house again and Kamal treated her to a fierce tongue-lashing and accused her of treachery and betrayal.

In school, he found only boys his age, the youngsters. The others, the overwhelming majority, were on strike. About a third of the pupils were present in his class, which contained a higher percentage of younger students than any other. The teacher ordered them to review the previous lessons. Meanwhile he busied himself correcting their exercises and ignored them as though they actually were on strike. Kamal opened a book. He pretended to read but paid no attention to the book. He did not like staying at school with nothing to do, when he could have been with the strikers or at home enjoying the vacation that these amazing days had unexpectedly granted him. He found school oppressive in a way he had not before.

His imagination flew away to the strikers outside with astonishment and curiosity. He often wondered which view of them was accurate. Were they "daredevils" as his mother claimed, with no feeling for themselves or their families, unnecessarily putting their lives in jeopardy? Or were they "heroes" as Fahmy described them, sacrificing their lives to struggle against God's enemy and their own?

He was often inclined to agree with his mother because of his resentment toward the older pupils at his school who were among the strikers. They had made the worst possible impression on him and the other young pupils like him with the rough treatment and contempt they meted out in the school courtyard, where they challenged the younger boys with their enormous bodies and insolent mustaches.

Yet he could not totally accept this view, because Fahmy's opinion always carried a lot of weight with him and was hard to ignore. Kamal could not deny them the heroism Fahmy ascribed to them. He even wished he could observe their bloody battles from a safe place. Something extremely serious was no doubt underway, otherwise why were the Egyptians striking and banding together to clash with the soldiers? . . . And what soldiers? The English! The English . . . when a mention of that name had once sufficed to clear the streets. What had happened to the world and to people? This amazing struggle was so overwhelming that its basic elements were engraved in the boy's soul without his having made any conscious effort to remember them. The terms "Sa'd Zaghlul," "the English," "the students," "the martyrs," "handbills," and "demonstrations" became active forces inspiring him at the deepest levels, even if he was only a perplexed bystander when it came to understanding what they stood for. His bewilderment was doubled by the fact that the members of his family reacted differently to the events and at times in contrary ways. While Fahmy was outraged and attacked the English with lethal hatred, yearning for Sa'd so much it brought tears to his eyes, Yasin discussed the news with calm concern and quiet sorrow that did not prevent him from continuing his normal routine of chatting, laughing, and reciting poetry and stories followed by an evening on the town that lasted until midnight. Kamal's mother kept praying that God would bring peace and make life secure again by cleansing the hearts of both the Egyptians and the English. Zaynab, his brother's wife, was the most disconcerting of them all. She was frightened by the course of events, and the only person she could find to vent her anger on was Sa'd Zaghlul himself, whom she accused of having caused all the evil. "If he had lived the way God's children should, meekly and peacefully, no one would have harmed him in any manner and this conflagration would not have broken out."

Thus the boy's enthusiasm was set on fire by the thought of the struggle itself, and his sorrow overflowed at the thought of death in the abstract, without his having any clear understanding of what was going on around him, locally or nationally. He would have had a fine opportunity to observe a demonstration at close range or to participate in one, if only in the school courtyard, the day the pupils of Khalil Agha School had been called to strike for the first time, had not the headmaster, to Kamal's distress, immediately shut the younger pupils up in their classrooms. He had lost that opportunity and found himself kept indoors, although he could listen to the loud chanting with a mixture of astonishment and secret delight, inspired perhaps by the chaos affecting everything and mercilessly wreaking havoc with the tedious daily routine. He had missed the chance then to participate in a demonstration, just as he had lost the opportunity today to enjoy a holiday at home. He would remain confined to this boring assembly, looking at a book with eyes that saw nothing, cautiously and fearfully exchanging pinches with a friend across a book bag until the end of the long day came.

Then, suddenly, something attracted his attention. It might have been an unfamiliar voice at some distance or a ringing in his ears. He looked around him to determine what he had heard. He found that the pupils' heads were raised and that they were looking at each other. Then everyone stared at the windows overlooking the street. It was a reality, not something imaginary, that had attracted their attention. Different voices were blended together into an enormous, incomprehensible sound. Because of the distance, it seemed like the roaring of waves far away. As it grew closer it could be termed a din, or even an advancing din. There was a commotion in the classroom. Pupils started whispering. Then a voice called out: "A demonstration!"

Kamal's heart pounded. His eyes took on a gleam of joy mixed with dismay. The din came closer and closer until the chanting could be heard clearly, thundering and raging in all directions, surrounding the school. His ears were bombarded by the words that had filled his mind during the past days: "Sa'd," "independence," "protectorate." . . .

The chanting came even nearer and got louder, until it filled the school courtyard itself. The pupils were dumbfounded. They were sure this deluge would flood them, but they welcomed it with a childish delight that shunned any consideration of the consequences, because of their zealous yearning for anarchy and liberation. Next they heard footsteps coming toward them and noisy shouting. The door swung wide open from the impact of a violent shove. Bands of students from the University and al-Azhar poured into the room like water rushing through an opening in a dam. They were shouting, "Strike! Strike! . . . No one can stay here."

In a matter of moments, Kamal found himself swept away by a tumultuous wave pushing him forward so forcefully that resistance was impossible. He was extremely upset. He moved along slowly like a coffee bean revolving in the mouth of the grinder. He did not know where to look. All he knew of the world were bodies crammed together, not to mention the clamor assaulting his ears, until he discerned from the appearance of the sky overhead that they had reached the street. He was being squeezed ever more tightly till he could scarcely breathe. He was so frightened he screamed a loud, continuous, piercing wail. Before he knew what was happening, a hand had grabbed his arm and yanked him forcibly, making a way for him through the crowd until it pushed him up on the sidewalk and against a wall. He started panting and searching around him for a safe place. He discovered that the metal security door of Hamdan's pastry shop had been pulled down until it was close to the ground. He rushed over and got on his knees to crawl under it. When he stood up inside he saw Uncle Hamdan, who knew him quite well, two women, and a few young pupils. He rested his back against the side of the counter with the trays on it while his chest rose and fell repeatedly. He heard Uncle Hamdan say, "Students from al-Azhar and the University, workers, citizens . . . all the roads leading to al-Husayn are jammed with people. Before today I wouldn't have thought the earth could support so many people."

One of the women said in astonishment, "How can they keep on demonstrating after they've been fired on?"

The other woman commented sadly, "May our Lord provide guidance . . . they're all good boys, alas."

Uncle Hamdan said, "We've never seen anything like this before. May our Lord protect them."

The chanting burst out from the demonstrators' throats, convulsing the atmosphere, at times so near it resounded in the shop and at other times at a distance in a great, incomprehensible hullabaloo like the roaring of the wind. It continued without interruption, its slow but steady motion revealed by the differing degrees of intensity and loudness between the waves of people as they approached and drew away.

Whenever he thought it had ended, another wave came along. It seemed it would never end. Kamal concentrated his whole being in his ears to listen attentively, although he felt uneasy and anxious. As time passed without anything terrible happening, he was able to catch his breath and regain his composure. Then he was finally able to consider the situation as transitory. It would soon be over. He wondered whether he should tell his mother what had happened to him once he got home: "A demonstration without beginning or end burst into our classrooms, and before I knew it, I was surrounded by the raging current, which swept me out into the street. I shouted along with everyone else, 'Long live Sa'd! Down with the Protectorate! Long live independence!' I was carried from street to street until the English attacked us and opened fire."

She would be so alarmed she would weep, hardly able to believe he was still alive. She would recite many verses from the Qur'an as she shuddered.

"A bullet went by my head. I can still hear its drone ringing in my ear. People were bumping into each other like madmen. I would have perished with the others if a man had not pulled me into a store."

His daydreams were cut short by loud, sporadic screams and footsteps rushing past in confusion. His heart pounded, and he looked at the faces surrounding him. He saw that they were staring at the door with an expression suggesting they expected to be hit on the head. Uncle Hamdan went to the door and leaned down to peer out the gap at the bottom. Jumping back, he quickly lowered the door until it was flush with the ground. He stammered in confusion, "The English!"

Many people were shouting outside, "The English! . . . The English!"

Others called out, "Stand firm . . . stand firm."

Someone else yelled, "We die, but the nation lives."

Then for the first time in his short life the boy heard shots fired nearby. He recognized them instinctively and shook all over. When the women let out a scream of terror, he burst into tears.

Uncle Hamdan was saying in a shaky voice, "We proclaim that God is one . . . one."

Kamal felt afraid, and a deathly chill crept throughout his body from his feet to his head. The shots kept on coming. Their ears were assailed by a clatter of wheels and a neighing of horses. Voices and movement were heard in extraordinarily rapid succession and then they were joined by roars, screams, and moans. To those crouching behind the door, a fleeting moment of combat seemed an eternity spent in the presence of death. Then a frightening silence prevailed, like a swoon following an onslaught of pain.

Kamal asked in a hoarse and trembling voice, "Have they gone?"

Uncle Hamdan put his finger to his lips and murmured, "Hush." Then he recited the Throne Verse from the Qur'an (2:255) about the omnipotence of God.

Kamal recited another verse about God, to himself since he no longer felt able to speak. "Say: He is God, one, only one." (Qur'an, 112:1). Perhaps this verse would drive away the English as effectively as it drove away the jinn in the dark.

The door was not opened until the noon prayer, when the boy ran out into the deserted street and dashed off like the wind. Passing by the steps leading down to Ahmad Abduh's coffee shop, he noticed a person coming up whom he recognized as his brother Fahmy. He rushed to him like a drowning man grabbing at a life preserver. As Kamal grasped his arm, the young man turned in alarm. When he recognized his little brother he shouted at him, "Kamal? . . . Where were you during the strike?"

The boy noticed that his brother's voice was so hoarse it was hard for him to speak. He replied, "I was in Uncle Hamdan's shop. I heard the shots and everything."

Fahmy told him quickly and hastily, "Go home and don't tell anyone you met me. . . . Do you hear?"

The boy asked him in bewilderment, "Aren't you coming home with me?"

He replied in the same tone, "Of course not . . . not now. . . . I'll return at my usual time. Don't forget, you didn't run into me at all."

He pushed him away, leaving him no opportunity for discussion. The boy galloped off until he reached Khan Ja'far Alley. There he saw a man standing in the middle of the road. He was pointing to the ground and addressing several others. Looking in the direction he was pointing, Kamal saw red splotches in the dust. He heard the man say, as though delivering a funeral oration, "This innocent blood screams out to us to continue the struggle. It was God's will that blood should be shed in the sacred precincts of al-Husayn, the Prince of Martyrs, to link our present trials to our past. God is on our side."

Kamal was terrified. He turned his eyes away from the bloody ground and ran off like a madman.

56

In the early morning darkness, Amina was groping her way to the door of the room cautiously and deliberately to avoid waking her husband when she heard a strange commotion coming from the street that sounded like the droning of bees. At this, her usual time to arise, she normally heard only the clatter of garbage carts, a cough from someone heading for work early, and the shouts of a man who liked to break the pervasive silence after he returned from the dawn prayer by crying out from time to time, "Proclaim Him one." She had never heard this strange commotion before. She was at a loss to explain it and curious to learn its source. She walked softly to the window in the sitting room that overlooked the street. She raised the cover of the peephole and poked her head out. She found it was dark with a glimmer of light at the horizon, but that was not enough for her to be able to see what was happening below her. The commotion grew louder and more mysterious at the same time. She could hear human voices of unknown origin. As her eyes became slightly more accustomed to the darkness, she looked around. Below the historic cistern building on Palace Walk and near it at the intersection of al-Nahhasin with Qirmiz Alley she could make out indistinct human figures, as well as things shaped like small pyramids and other objects like short trees. She stepped back anxiously and went downstairs to the room Fahmy shared with Kamal. Then she hesitated. Should she wake him up to solve this puzzle for her or postpone it until he woke by himself? She could not bring herself to disturb Fahmy and decided to wait until the normal time for him to awaken at sunrise, which was not far off.

She performed her prayers and then went back to the window, driven by her curiosity. She peered out. Rays from the rising sun were beginning to adorn the gown of night. The light of morning was streaming off the peaks of the minarets and the domes. She was able to see the road much more clearly. Her eyes examined the shapes that had alarmed her when it was dark. She could see what they really were. A moan of terror escaped her, and she stepped back to rush to Fahmy's room. She woke him without any hesitation.

The young man shuddered and sat up in bed. He asked in alarm, "What's wrong, Mother?"

Trying to catch her breath, she replied, "The English are filling the street below our house."

The young man jumped out of bed to run to the window. Looking down, he saw a small encampment on Palace Walk under the cistern building at a vantage point for the streets that branched off there. It consisted of a number of tents, three trucks, and several groups of soldiers. Adjacent to the tents, rifles had been stacked up in groups of four. In each bunch the muzzles leaned in against each other and the butts were separated, forming a pyramid. The sentries stood like statues in front of the tents. The other soldiers were scattered about, speaking to each other in a foreign language and laughing. The young man looked toward al-Nahhasin and saw a second encampment at the intersection of al-Nahhasin with the Goldsmiths Bazaar. There was a third encampment in the other direction at the corner of Palace Walk and al-Khurunfush.

His first impulse was to think that these soldiers had come to arrest him, but he soon decided that was silly. He attributed the idea to his rude awakening, from which he had not quite recovered, and to his sense of being followed that had not left him since the revolution had broken out. Then the truth gradually became clear to him. The district that had frustrated the occupying forces with its continual demonstrations had been occupied by troops. He went on looking through the blind, examining the soldiers, tents, and wagons while his heart pounded with terror, sorrow, and anger. When he turned away from the window he was pale and muttered to his mother, "It's the English, just as you said. They've come to intimidate people and to stop the demonstrations at their source."

He began to pace the room back and forth, while he commented to himself resentfully, "Incredible . . . preposterous."

Then he heard his mother say, "I'll wake your father to tell him about it." The woman made that statement as though it were the only alternative left. She implied that al-Sayyid Ahmad, who solved all the problems of her life, was equally capable of finding a solution for this one and of guiding them to safety.

Her son told her sadly, "Leave him alone until he wakes up at the normal time."

Terrified, the woman asked, "What are we going to do, son, with them stationed outside the entrance of our house?"

Fahmy shook his head anxiously and repeated her question: "What are we going to do?" Then in a more confident tone he continued: "There's no reason to be afraid. They're only trying to frighten the demonstrators."

Swallowing because her mouth felt dry, she remarked, "I'm afraid they'll attack peaceful citizens in their homes."

He thought for a little while about what she had said. Then he murmured, "Of course not . . . If their goal had been to attack the houses, they wouldn't have waited there quietly this long." He was not totally sure about his statement but thought it was the best thing to say.

His mother came back with yet another question: "How long will they stay here with us?"

He replied with a blank stare, "Who knows? . . . They've pitched tents, so they're not leaving soon."

He noticed that she was addressing questions to him as though he were a military commander. He looked at her affectionately and did not let her see the ironic smile that had formed on his pale lips. He thought for a moment about teasing her, but the situation was distressing enough to deter him. He became serious once more. Similarly, when Yasin recounted one of their father's exploits to him, the very nature of the anecdote would make him want to laugh, but the anxiety that afflicted him whenever he learned something about the hidden side of his father's character would restrain him.

They heard footsteps hurrying toward them. Then Yasin, followed immediately by Zaynab, stormed into the room. His eyes looked swollen and his hair was disheveled. He shouted, "Have you seen the English?"

Zaynab cried out, "I'm the one who heard them. So I looked out the window and saw them. Then I woke up Mr. Yasin."

Yasin continued: "I knocked on Father's door until he woke up, so I could tell him. When he saw them himself he ordered that no one should leave the house and that the bolt on the door should not be opened. But what are they doing? . . . What can we do? . . . Isn't there a government in this country to protect us?"

Fahmy told him, "I don't think they'll interfere with anyone except the demonstrators."

"But how long are we going to remain captives in our houses? . . . These houses are full of women and children. How can they set up encampments here?"

Fahmy muttered uneasily, "Nothing's happening to us that isn't happening to everyone else. Let's be patient and wait."

Zaynab protested nervously, "All we hear or see anymore is something frightening or sad. God damn the bastards."

At that point, Kamal opened his eyes. He looked with astonishment at all the people unexpectedly assembled in his room. He sat up in bed and looked inquisitively at his mother, who went to him and patted his large head with her cold hand. Then in a whisper she recited the opening prayer of the Qur'an, while her thoughts wandered off.

The boy asked, "Why are you all here?"

His mother wanted to break the news to him in the nicest way, and so she said gently, "You won't be going to school today."

He asked with delight, "Because of the demonstrations?"

Fahmy replied a bit sharply, "The English are blocking the road."

Kamal felt he had discovered the secret that had brought them all together. He looked at their faces with dismay. Then he ran to the window and looked for a long time through the blind. When he returned, he remarked uneasily, "The rifles are in groups of four." He looked at Fahmy as though pleading for help. He stammered fearfully, "Will they kill us?"

"They won't kill anyone. They've come to pursue the demonstrators."

There was a short period of silence. Then the boy commented, as though to himself, "What handsome faces they have!"

Fahmy asked him sarcastically, "Do you really like their looks?"

Kamal replied innocently, "A lot. I imagined they'd look like devils."

Fahmy said bitterly, "Who knows? . . . perhaps if you saw some devils you'd think they were handsome."

The bolt on the door was not pulled back that day. None of the windows overlooking the street was opened, not even to freshen the air or let in sunlight. For the first time ever, al-Sayyid Ahmad conducted a conversation at the breakfast table. He said, in a voice that implied he knew what he was talking about, that the English were going to take strong measures to stop the demonstrations and that it was for this reason they had occupied the areas where most of the demonstrations had taken place. He said he had decided they would stay home all day until matters became clearer.

Al-Sayyid Ahmad was able to speak with confidence and preserve his customary awesome appearance. Thus he prevented anyone from discerning the anxiety that had afflicted him since he had hopped out of bed in response to Yasin's knocks.

It was also the first time that Fahmy had dared question one of his father's ideas. He remarked politely, "But, Father, the school may think I'm one of the strikers if I stay home."

Al-Sayyid Ahmad naturally knew nothing of his son's participation in the demonstrations. He replied, "Necessity has its own laws. Your brother as a civil servant is in more jeopardy than you are, but you both have a clear excuse."

Fahmy was not courageous enough to ask his father a second time. He was afraid of angering him and found his father's order forbidding him to leave the house an excuse that eased his conscience for not going into the streets occupied by soldiers thirsty for the blood of students.

The breakfast group broke up. Al-Sayyid Ahmad retired to his room. The mother and Zaynab were soon busy with their daily chores. Since it was a sunny day with warm spring breezes, one of the last of March, the three brothers went up on the roof, where they sat under the arbor of hyacinth beans and jasmine. Kamal got interested in the chickens and settled down by their coop. He scattered grain for them and then chased them, delighted with their squawking. He picked up the eggs he found.

His brothers began to discuss the thrilling news that was spreading by word of mouth. A revolution was raging in all areas of the Nile Valley from the extreme north to the extreme south. Fahmy recounted what he knew about the railroads and telegraph and telephone lines being cut, the outbreak of demonstrations in different provinces, the battles between the English and the revolutionaries, the massacres, the martyrs, the nationalist funerals with processions with tens of coffins at a time, and the capital city with its students, workers, and attorneys on strike, where transportation was limited to carts. He remarked heatedly, "Is this really a revolution? Let them kill as many as their savagery dictates. Death only invigorates us."

Yasin, shaking his head in wonder, observed, "I wouldn't have thought our people had this kind of fighting spirit."

Fahmy seemed to have forgotten how close he had been to despair shortly before the outbreak of the revolution, when it took him by surprise with its convulsions and dazzled him with its light. He now asserted, "The nation's filled with a spirit of eternal struggle flaming throughout its body stretched from Aswan to the Mediterranean Sea. The English only stirred it up. It's blazing away now and will never die out."

There was a smile on Yasin's lips when he observed, "Even the women have organized a demonstration."

Fahmy then recited verses from the poem by the Egyptian author Hafiz Ibrahim about the ladies' demonstration:

Beautiful women marched in protest.
I went to observe their rally.
I found them proudly
Brandishing the blackness of their garments.
They looked like stars,
Gleaming in a pitch-black night.
They took to the streets;
Sa'd's home was their target.

Yasin was touched. He laughed and said, "I'm the one who should have memorized that."

Fahmy happened to think of something and asked sadly, "Do you suppose news of our revolution has reached Sa'd in exile? Has the grand old man learned that his sacrifice has not been in vain? Or do you think he's overcome by despair in his exile?"

57

They stayed on the roof until shortly before noon. The two older brothers entertained themselves by observing the small British encampment. They saw that some of the soldiers had set up a field kitchen and were preparing food. Soldiers were scattered between the intersections of Qirmiz Alley and al-Nahhasin with Palace Walk in an area otherwise deserted. From time to time many would fall into line at a signal from a bugle. Then they would get their rifles and climb into one of the vehicles, which would carry them off toward Bayt al-Qadi. This suggested that demonstrations were underway in nearby neighborhoods. Fahmy watched them line up with a pounding heart and flaming imagination.

When the two older brothers finally went downstairs to the study they left Kamal alone on the roof to amuse himself as he saw fit. Fahmy got his books to review what he had missed during the past days. Yasin selected Abu Tammam's medieval collection of Arabic poetry, called *al-Hamasa*, and Jurji Zaydan's historical romance *The Maiden of Karbala* and went out to the sitting room. He was counting on these books to help pass the time, which accumulated as plentifully behind the walls of his prison as water behind a dam. Although novels, including detective stories, had the greatest hold over his affections, he was also fond of poetry. He did not like to exert himself too much when he learned a poem. He was content to understand the parts that were easy to grasp and to enjoy the music of the difficult sections. He rarely referred to the margin of the page packed with glosses. He might memorize a verse and recite it, even though he understood very little of its meaning. He might ascribe a meaning to it that bore almost no relationship to the real one or not even try to attribute a meaning to it. Nevertheless, certain images and expressions settled in his mind. He considered them a treasure to brag about and exploit determinedly when appropriate and even more often when not. If he had a letter to write, he prepared for the assignment as though he were a novelist and crammed it full of any resounding expressions he could recall, inserting whatever remnants of the poetic heritage of the Arabs God allowed him to remember. Yasin was known among his acquaintances as eloquent, not because he really was but because the other men fell short of his attempts and were stunned by his unusual accumulation of knowledge.

Until that time, he had never experienced such a long period of enforced idleness, deprived of all forms of activity and amusement for hour after hour. If he had possessed the patience for reading, that might have helped, but he was only accustomed to read when he was with other people and then only during the short periods preceding his departure for his evening's entertainment. Even on those occasions, he saw nothing wrong with interrupting his reading to join in the coffee hour conversations or to read a little and then summon Kamal to narrate to him what he had read. He enjoyed the boy's passionate response to storytelling, typical of children of that age. Consequently, neither the poetry nor the novel was able to brighten his solitude on such a day. He read some verses and then a few chapters of *The Maiden of Karbala*. He choked on his boredom, drop after drop, while he cursed the English from the depths of his heart. He passed the time until lunch in a bad mood, feeling vexed and disgruntled.

The mother served them soup and roast chicken with rice, but there were no vegetables because of the blockade around the house. She ended the meal with cheese, olives, and whey, substituting molasses for the sweet. The only person with a decent appetite was Kamal. Al-Sayyid Ahmad and the two older brothers were not much inclined to eat, since they had spent the day without any work or activity. This nourishment did assist them to escape from their boredom by helping to put them to sleep, especially the father and Yasin, who were able to fall asleep whenever and however they wanted.

Yasin got up from his nap shortly before sunset and went downstairs to attend the coffee hour. The session was short, since the mother was not able to leave al-Sayyid Ahmad alone for long. She had to withdraw to return to his room. Yasin, Zaynab, Fahmy, and Kamal remained behind to chat with each other listlessly. Then Fahmy excused himself to go to the study. He asked Kamal to join him, leaving the couple alone.

Yasin wondered to himself, "What can I do from now till midnight?" The question had troubled him for a long time, but today he felt depressed and humiliated, forcibly and tyrannically separated from the flow of time which was plunging ahead outside the house with its many pleasures. He was like a branch that turns into firewood when cut from the tree.

Had it not been for the military blockade, he would have been in his beloved seat at the coffeehouse of Ahmad Abduh, sipping green tea and chatting with his acquaintances among its patrons. He would have been enjoying himself in its historic atmosphere. He was captivated by its antiquity, and his imagination was stirred by its subterranean chambers buried in the debris of history. Ahmad Abduh's coffeehouse was the one he loved best. He would not forsake it, unless scorched by some desire, for as they say: "Desire's a fire." It was desire that had attracted him in the past to the Egyptian Club, which was close to the woman who sold doum palm fruit. Desire had also been responsible for tempting him to move to al-Sayyid Ali's coffeehouse in al-Ghuriya, situated across the street from the home of the lute player Zanuba. He would exchange coffeehouses according to the object of his desire. He would even exchange the patrons who had offered him their friendship. Beyond satisfying the desire itself, the coffeehouse and his friends there were meaningless. Where were the Egyptian Club and those friends? They had gone out of his life. If he ran into one of them, Yasin might pretend not to know him and avoid him. It was now the turn of Ahmad Abduh's coffeehouse and its regulars. God only knew what coffeehouses and friends the future had in store for him.

In any case, he did not spend too much of his evening at Ahmad Abduh's. He would soon slip over to Costaki's grocery store, or, more exactly, to his secret bar to get a bottle of red wine, or "the usual," as he liked to call it. Where was "the usual" on this gloomy night? At the memory of Costaki's bar, a shudder of desire passed through his body. Then a look of great weariness showed in his eyes. He seemed as fidgety as a prisoner. Staying home appeared to him to be prolonged suffering. The sharpness of the pain intensified when he entertained the images of bliss and memories of intoxication associated with the bar and the bottle. These dreams tormented him and doubled his anguish. They encouraged his ardent longing for wine's music of the mind and the games it played with his head. Those made him warm and happy, overflowing with delight and joy. Before that evening he had never realized how incapable he was of patiently abstaining from alcohol for even a single day. He was not sad to discover how weak he was and how addicted. He did not blame himself for the overindulgence that had ended up making him miserable for such a trivial reason. He was as far as one could be from blaming himself or being annoyed. The only cause for his pain that he could remember was the blockade the English had set up around his house. He was consumed by thirst when the intoxicating watering hole was near at hand.

He glanced at Zaynab. He found her examining his face with a look that seemed to say resentfully, "Why are you so inattentive? Why are you so glum? Doesn't my presence cheer you up at all?" Yasin felt her resentment in the fleeting moment their eyes met, but he did not respond to her sorrowful criticism. To the contrary, it annoyed and riled him. Yes, he disliked nothing so much as being forced to spend a whole evening with her, deprived of desire, pleasure, and the intoxication on which he relied to endure married life.

He began to look at her stealthily and wonder in amazement, "Isn't she the same woman? . . . Isn't she the one who captured my heart on our wedding night? . . . Isn't she the one who drove me wild with passion for nights and weeks on end? . . . Why doesn't she stir me at all? What's come over her? Why am I so restless, disgruntled, and bored, finding nothing in her beauty or culture to tempt me to postpone getting drunk?"

As usual, he was inclined to find her deficient in areas where women like Zanuba excelled. They were clever at providing him special services, but Zaynab was the first woman who had attempted to live with him in a permanent relationship. He had not spent much time with the lute player or the doum fruit vendor. His attachment to them had not been great enough to prevent him from moving on when he felt like it. Many years later he would recall these anxious moments and his reflections on them. Then he would realize things from his own experience and from life in general that had not occurred to him at the time.

He was awakened from his thoughts by her question: "I guess you're not happy about staying home?"

He was not in a condition to deal with criticism. Her sarcastic question affected him like a careless blow to a sore. He shot back with painful candor: "Of course not."

Although she had tried to avoid quarreling with him from the beginning, his tone hurt her badly. She replied sharply, "There's no harm in that. Isn't it amazing how you can't bear to miss your carousing for even one night?"

He said angrily, "Mention one thing that would make staying home bearable."

She became enraged and said in a voice that showed she was on the verge of tears, "I'll leave. Perhaps then you'll like it better."

She turned her back on him to flee. He followed her with a stony glare. "How stupid she is! She doesn't know that only divine decree keeps her in my house."

Although the quarrel had relieved a little of his anger, he would have preferred for it not to have happened, if only because it served to increase his depressing boredom. If he had wanted to, he could have appeased her, but the listlessness of his mind had overwhelmed all his feelings.

In a few minutes, a relative calm took possession of him. The cruel words he had thrown at her echoed in his ears. He acknowledged that they were harsh and uncalled for. He felt almost regretful, not because he had suddenly discovered some dregs of affection for her in the corners of his heart, but because of his desire to treat her politely, perhaps out of respect for her father or fear of his. He had not exceeded these bounds, even during the nerveracking period of adjustment when with decisive firmness he had undertaken to make her accept his policies. He had apologized when he got too angry.

Anger was nothing out of the ordinary for this family. The only time they attempted to control their tempers was when the father was present, monopolizing for himself all rights to anger. Their anger was like a bolt of lightning, quick to flare up and quick to die down. They would be left with various forms of regret and sorrow. Yasin was like this, but he was also obstinate. His regret did not motivate him to seek a reconciliation with his wife. He told himself, "She's the one who made me angry. . . . Couldn't she have spoken to me in a gentler tone?" He wanted her to be consistently patient, forbearing, and forgiving, so that he could shoot off in pursuit of his passions, confident about the home front.

After she got angry and withdrew, he felt even more uncomfortable with his imprisonment. He left the room to go to the roof. He found the air pleasant there. The night was tranquil. It was dark everywhere but more profoundly so under the arbor of hyacinth beans and jasmine. On the other side of the roof, the dome of the sky was visible, studded with stars like pearls. He began to pace back and forth on the roof between the wall adjoining Maryam's house and the end of the hyacinth bean garden with its view of the Qala'un mosque. He gave himself over to contemplation of various mental images.

As he was walking slowly by the entrance to the arbor a rustling sound or perhaps a whisper caught his ear. He could hear someone breathing. Surprised, he stared into the darkness and called out, "Who's there?"

A voice he easily recognized replied in ringing tones, "Nur, master."

He remembered immediately that Nur, his wife's maid, retired at night to a wooden hut containing a few sticks of furniture, next to the chicken coop. He looked across the roof until he made out her figure standing a few feet away, like a condensed and solidified piece of night. He saw the whites of her eyes, as pure white as circles drawn in chalk on a jet-black form. He kept on pacing and said nothing more, but her features were automatically traced on his imagination. She was black, in her forties, and solidly built. She had thick limbs and a full chest. Her rear was plump. She had a gleaming face, sparkling eyes, and full lips. There was something powerful, coarse, and unusual about her, or he had thought of her that way since she had appeared in his house.

Suddenly and unexpectedly, an inclination to assault her exploded within his breast like fireworks going off without any warning. This was a forceful, dominating lust. The whole point of his life seemed to be concentrated in it. It got control of him just as it had the night of Aisha's wedding, when he had seen Umm Hanafi in the courtyard as he was reaching the threshold. His languid being was permeated by a bubbling new life. Restless desire spread through his veins, electrifying him. His ennui and boredom were replaced by an insane, raging, hot interest. All of this happened in the twinkling of an eye. His gait, thought, and imagination all became energetic. Unconsciously he stopped pacing the entire width of the roof. He cut back on the distance by a third and then half. Whenever he passed her, his body was troubled by tempestuous desire.... A black maid?... A servant? So what? It would not be the first time for him. Women like Zanuba definitely were not the only ones he craved. Just one beautiful feature was enough for him, like the kohl-enhanced eyes of the doum fruit vendor in al-Watawit, which had compensated for the stench of her armpits and the mud caked on her legs. Even ugliness, so long as there was a woman attached to it, was excused by his blind lust, as it had been with Umm Hanafi or with the one-eyed geomancer with whom he had enjoyed some private moments behind al-Nasr Gate.

Nur at any rate had a solid, firm body. Touching it would no doubt inspire him to be virile and active. The very fact that she was a black maid would lend interest to the tryst and novelty to the experience. He would be able to verify the rumor about girls of her heritage, who were said to be hot and passionate.

The circumstances seemed propitious. It was dark and secure on the roof. His desire intensified. His nervous energy was bounding. His heart raced. He cast a piercing glance in her direction and changed course slightly so that he would just happen to rub against her one way or another when he passed her. He would postpone making an open declaration of his intentions until he had a chance to sound out the situation cautiously, for fear that she might be a fool like Umm Hanafi and cause the house to echo with a new scandal.

Staring at her, he advanced with deliberate steps. He wanted to have all the lust raging inside him conveyed to her by the message in his eyes, in spite of the encompassing darkness. When he got close to her, his heartbeats became irregular. He came up beside her and his elbow touched the upper part of her body. He kept on walking, as though it had been an accident. A tremor passed through his body when he collided with her. He was not sure what he had touched, for he was wandering in a trance world. All he could remember as his mind cleared a bit at the edge of the roof was that he had felt something tender and appealing and she had stepped back nonchalantly. His suspicion that she was not worried about him was corroborated by her reaction.

He turned around, determined to attack again. He went back toward her with his arm folded so his elbow would touch one of her breasts. His senses did not mislead him this time. He did not move his elbow away, as one would have expected from a person who had simply lost his way. He left it there to brush gently past the other breast, no longer trying to avoid awakening her suspicions. He walked on, telling himself, "She'll no doubt understand what I'm after. Perhaps she has understood and wanted to step aside but was slow to do it. Perhaps she was taken by surprise and startled. At any rate, she didn't push me away with her hand and she remained still. She won't start screaming suddenly like that other bitch. Let's try a third time."

On this occasion his pace was quick and impatient. He slowed down when he reached her. Then he stretched his elbow out to her breasts that swelled like a full pair of little waterskins. He moved his arm in a hesitant, doubtful manner. He started to walk on, driven by a desire to flee, but found her so yielding or dull that the remnants of his conscious mind were drowned in an insane flood. He stopped.

With a voice that emerged from a fog of lust, trembling and fading away, he asked, "Is that you, Nur?"

The maid, who was backing away from him, replied, "Yes, master."

To prevent her from escaping, he pursued her until her back was against the wall and he was almost touching her. He wanted to say anything he could think of to declare his inner turmoil, like a boxer waving his fist in the air while watching for an opportunity to deal a final blow. Breathing on her forehead, he asked, "Why didn't you go into your room?"

Blockaded by him, she stammered, "I was enjoying the fresh air a little."

His greedy appetite overcame his hesitation. He put his hand on her waist. Then he pulled her gently toward his breast. She put up some resistance and kept him from achieving his goal. Putting his cheek next to hers, he whispered in her ear, "Come to the room."

She muttered uneasily, "Shame on you, master."

Her voice rang out in the silence in a way that disturbed him. She had not raised her voice intentionally, but it did not appear easy for her to whisper or her whisper had a resonance to it, even if less pronounced than that of her normal voice. His panic quickly deserted him, both because his lust was fully ignited and because her tone lacked the protest that her words suggested. He took her by the hand as he murmured, "Come along, sweetheart."

She did not attempt to free her hand, either because she was pleased or because she was obedient. He was lavishing kisses on her cheek and neck, swaying from the intense emotional impact, in a delirium of happiness. He began to say, "What's kept you from me all these months?"

She answered him in her normal tone of voice, lacking any ring of protest, "Shame on you, master."

Smiling, he commented, "Your objections are very attractive. Make some more."

She did resist a little when they reached the entrance to the room and said, "Shame on you, master. . . ." Then, as though to caution him, she added, "The room's full of bedbugs."

He pushed her inside, whispering with his mouth at the nape of her neck, "I'd lie among scorpions for your sake, Nur."

She was a servant in every sense of the word. She stood submissively in front of him in the dark while he placed his lips on hers and kissed her in a fiery, passionate manner. She was still and submissive, as though watching a scene in which she had no part. He told her emotionally, "Kiss me!" He put his lips to hers again and kissed her. Then she kissed him.

He wanted her to sit down. She repeated her phrase, "Shame on you, master," which was becoming comic through monotonous repetition.

He sat her down himself and she complied without any resistance. He began to enjoy the juxtaposition of her protests and her obedience. He sought to elicit more. Her verbal resistance continued, combined with her active obedience. He forgot the time.

He imagined that the darkness around him was moving or that there were strange creatures prancing about in it. Perhaps the exertion was beginning to tell on him after he had stayed at it such a long time—if he had been there long. He certainly did not know how much time he had spent with her. Perhaps the raging currents crashing against each other in his head had impinged on his vision, causing him to see imaginary lights. But not so fast . . . the walls of the room were undulating. A faint light flowed over them into which the pitch-black darkness dissolved so thoroughly that the room's secrets were disclosed. He raised his head to stare. He saw a faint light slipping through the cracks in the wooden wall, intruding on his privacy.

Then his wife's voice was raised to call the maid: "Are you asleep, Nur? Nur. . . . Have you seen Mr. Yasin?"

His heart trembled in alarm. He leapt up and quickly and regretfully grabbed his clothes to put them on. With roving eyes he searched the room on the chance that he might find a hiding place among its cast-off furnishings. One look was enough to make him despair of concealing himself. Meanwhile the sound of approaching slippers assaulted his ears. The maid could not keep herself from saying in a tearful voice, "It's all your fault, master. What am I going to do now?"

He hit her hard on the shoulder to make her stop. He stared at the door with terror and despair. Without thinking about what he was doing, he retreated to the corner farthest from the entrance and pressed against the wall. He froze there and waited. The calls were repeated, but no one answered. Then the door was pushed open. Zaynab's arm appeared, holding a lamp in front of her. She was crying, "Nur . . . Nur."

The maid was forced to murmur in a sad, weak voice, "Yes, madam."

She chided her in an angry voice, "How quick you are to fall asleep, old lady. . . . Have you seen Mr. Yasin? My father-in-law sent for him. I looked for him downstairs and in the courtyard. Now I haven't been able to find him on the roof. Have you seen him?"

As soon as she finished speaking, her head poked inside the room. She looked down at the compromised maid in astonishment. Then, instinctively, she turned to her right and her eyes fell upon her husband, whose enormous body was plastered against the wall, looking flabby and weak from shame and disgrace. Their eyes met for an instant before he looked down. Another instant of lethal silence passed. Then a scream like a howl escaped from the girl. She retreated. Beating her breast with her left hand, she cried out, "You scandalous black slut . . . You! You!"

She began to tremble and the lamp in her hand trembled along with her. The light reflected on the wall opposite the door shook. Then she turned and fled. Her wail rent the silence.

Swallowing, Yasin told himself, "I'm ruined. What's done is done." He remained standing where he was, oblivious to everything around him. When he came to his senses, he left the room for the roof, without thinking about going any farther. He did not know what to do. How widely known would the scandal become? Would it be confined to his own apartment or travel to the other one? He began to scold himself for being too stunned and weak to catch up with her in order to contain the scandal in the smallest possible circle. He wondered with intense discomfort how he would deal with this scandal. Would he be resolute? Perhaps he could be if the news did not get through to his father.

He heard movement coming from the direction of the ill-omened room. He turned and saw the figure of the maid leaving it with a large bundle in her hand. She hastened to the door of the stairway and departed. He shrugged his shoulders disdainfully. When he touched his chest he realized he had forgotten to put on his undershirt and quickly returned to the room.

58

Someone knocked on the door early in the morning. It was the shaykh, or supervisor, of the district. He met with al-Sayyid Ahmad and told him that the authorities had instructed him to inform the residents of the occupied areas that the English would not interfere with anyone except the demonstrators. It was incumbent upon al-Sayyid Ahmad to open his store, on the pupil to go to school, and on the civil servant to go to his place of employment. The shaykh cautioned him against keeping pupils home lest they be suspected of striking. He directed his host's attention to the orders strictly forbidding demonstrations and strikes.

In that manner the house resumed the activities with which it normally greeted the morning. The men breathed a sigh of relief after the captivity of the previous day. People felt refreshed, attaining a certain degree of composure and tranquillity.

After the visit from the shaykh of the district, Yasin told himself, "Conditions outside the house have begun to improve, but inside it's nothing but mire and muck."

Most members of the family had passed a hideous night dominated by the scandal. The misfortune had torn the family apart. Zaynab's patience, which had kept her sorrows and grievances confined to her breast, could not stand up to the shocking vision in her maid's room. Her reserve exploded and threw flames in every direction. She deliberately intended for her wail to reach the ears of al-Sayyid Ahmad.

He rushed to her, wondering what was the matter. The scandal was revealed. She told him everything, emboldened by her insane passion. Without it, her courage would not have been up to confronting him with her story, since she still dreaded him more than anyone else. In this manner, she got revenge for her wounded honor and for the patience she had shown, voluntarily at times and resentfully on many other occasions.

"A maid! A servant! Old enough to be his mother! In my house! So what do you suppose he does elsewhere?"

She was not weeping from jealousy, or perhaps her jealousy was temporarily hidden behind a thick veil of disgust and anger, like fire concealed by clouds of smoke. It seemed she would prefer death to staying under the same roof with him, even for a single day, after what had happened. In fact, she abandoned her bed to spend the night in the parlor. She was awake most of it, delirious as though she had a high fever. The short time she slept, her slumber was deep but troubled like an invalid's. When she awoke, she was determined to leave the house. This decision was virtually the only thing that provided any relief from her pains. What could even her father-in-law do? He could not undo the reprehensible act after it had occurred. No matter how tyrannical he was, he could not punish her husband as much as he deserved and heal her wounded heart. The most he could do would be to reprimand and pour out his wrath upon his son. The debauched sinner would listen with head bowed but then continue with his nasty style of life. How preposterous!

Al-Sayyid Ahmad had implored her to leave the matter to him. He had advised her at length to overlook her husband's slip and rely on the patience of virtuous women like herself. But she could not bear to be patient or forgiving any longer. A black servant over forty! No! This time she would leave him without any hesitation. She would tell her father all her sorrows and remain in his custody until Yasin came to his senses. If he then came to her repentant, having reformed his behavior, she might return. Otherwise, this whole life, with its good and bad aspects, could go to the devil.

Yasin was wrong to think she was too reasonable and sensible to reveal her worries to other people. The truth was that from the beginning she had been so apprehensive she had shared her concerns with her mother, who had demonstrated how sensible she was by making sure the complaint did not reach Zaynab's father. She had counseled her daughter to be patient, telling her that men, like her father for example, spent their evenings out and drank. Zaynab should be satisfied if her household was well provided for and if her husband returned to her, no matter how late or how drunk. The girl had heeded her mother's advice grudgingly and had attempted to the best of her abilities to adorn herself with patience. She had spared no effort to content herself with the reality and trim her vast dreams down, to be satisfied with what she actually had, especially since she was pregnant and looking forward to the proud status of motherhood. With her grievances buried deep inside her, she was content to surrender, consoling herself at different times with her mother's example and that of the mistress of her new home.

There was room enough for doubt. Her heart was troubled occasionally about what her husband might be doing at his drinking parties. She confided her fears to her mother. Indeed, she did not conceal from her the man's diminished interest. Her sensible mother explained to her that this decrease in passion was definitely not caused by what she had in mind. It was "something natural," common to all men. She would become convinced of that herself as she became more experienced in life. Even if her suspicions were correct, what did she think she was going to do about it? Should she leave her home just because her husband had sex with other women? Of course not . . . a thousand times no! If a woman renounced her position for a reason like this, households would soon run short of honest women. A man might set his sights on one woman or another, but he would always return home, so long as his wife was worthy of being his last resort and enduring refuge. Patient women would be the winners. She proceeded to remind her daughter of women who had been divorced for no fault of their own and of women whose husbands had more than one wife. Was her husband's fickleness, even if a reality, not a lighter matter than the conduct of those other types of men? Moreover, Yasin was a young man of only twenty-two. It was inevitable that he would become more reasonable in time and return to his home, occupying himself with his children to the exclusion of the rest of the world. The moral of all this advice was that she had to be patient, even if her suspicions were true. What if they were not? What then? The mother had repeated this and other, similar advice until the girl's defiance was tamed. She had come to believe in patience and had resigned herself to it, but with one fatal blow the incident on the roof had completely destroyed the entire structure of patient resignation.

Al-Sayyid Ahmad did not comprehend this distressing fact. He thought the girl had resolved to follow his advice. Even so, his anger was too great to be easily assuaged. The maid had done the right thing when she fled, but Yasin had not left the roof, where he was anticipating with alarm the storm that awaited him. When he heard his father's voice calling him, it sounded like whips cracking. His heart pounded, but he did not answer or obey. Feeling desperate, he stayed put. Before Yasin knew what was happening, the man stormed up to the roof. He stood there snarling for some moments while he searched the area. When he made out his son's shape, he headed toward him, coming to a stop nearby. He folded his arms across his chest and glared at Yasin severely and haughtily. He remained silent for a long time to increase his son's torment and terror. He seemed to want his silence to express his feelings, which words could not convey. He may also have wished it to symbolize the violent kick and punch he would have used to discipline his son had he not been a man and a husband like himself.

When he could not stand to be silent any longer, shaking with anger and rage, he rained down insults and rebukes on Yasin: "You defy me within my hearing and sight. . . . You and your disgrace can go to hell. . . . You've defiled my house, you scoundrel. There's no way this house can ever be pure again so long as you're in it. You had an excuse before you got married, alas. What excuse do you have now? . . . If my words were addressed to an animal, it would behave itself, but they're directed to a stone. . . . A household that includes you is likely to be cursed." He relieved his flaming breast of words like hot lead.

Yasin stood before him still, silent, with his head bowed, as though he were about to melt away into the darkness. When the father had screamed as much as he could, he turned his back on him and left the place, cursing him and his father and mother. In his rage, he thought that Yasin's slip was a crime deserving the ultimate punishment. In his fury, he neglected to remember that his own past was a long and repeated series of slips like Yasin's. He had persisted with this conduct even halfway through his fifth decade, when his children were growing up and some were married. His rage did not really make him forget, but he allowed himself liberties he did not permit any of his family. He had a right to do what he wanted, but they were expected to adhere to the limits he imposed on them.

His anger was possibly greater at the elements present in Yasin's offense of challenge to his will, disdain for his existence, and distortion of the image he wanted to have of his children than at the offense itself. But as usual his anger did not last long. Its flames soon died down and its blaze abated. He slowly became calm, although his façade, and just his façade, remained despondent and distressed. He was now able to see Yasin's "crime" from more than one angle. He could contemplate it with a clear head. Its darker side faded to reveal its various comic aspects, which entertained his enforced solitude. The first thing that occurred to him was to look for an excuse for the guilty party. It was not from any love of lenience, for he hated to be lenient at home. He wanted to use this excuse as an explanation for Yasin's apparent violation of his will. He seemed to be telling himself, "My son did not disobey me. . . . Far from it! His excuse is such and such."

Should his youth be considered an excuse, since it was a time of recklessness and rashness? Certainly not . . . Youth might be an excuse for the offense, but it was no excuse for defying his will. Otherwise Fahmy and even Kamal would be allowed any extremes in ignoring his instructions. The excuse should be sought, then, in his status as a man. It was his manhood that gave him a right to free himself from his father's will, if only to a limited extent, and spared al-Sayyid Ahmad from bearing responsibility for his son's deeds. The father seemed to be telling himself, "He did not disobey me. Far from it! He's just reached an age when it's not an offense to deviate from my will." Needless to say, he would not admit this truth to Yasin and would never have forgiven his son if Yasin had dared to make this demand. Indeed, he would not admit it to himself unless there was a rebellious act requiring some justification. To reassure himself, he did not forget even under such circumstances to remind himself that he had been unusually hard on his son when he was growing up. Few fathers were so strict. Yasin had submitted totally to this discipline in a way that few sons would have.

He turned his mind thoughtfully to Zaynab, but he felt no sympathy for her. He had tried to comfort her out of respect for her father, who was his dear friend, but he felt the girl was not really worthy of her father. It was not appropriate for a good wife to implicate her husband in a scandal as she had, no matter what the circumstances. How she had wailed! How she had screamed! What would he have done if Amina had surprised him one day in a comparable situation? But what was she compared with Amina? More over, how shamelessly she had recounted to him everything she had seen. . . . Pshaw! Pshaw! If this girl had not been Muhammad Iffat's daughter, Yasin would have been within his rights to discipline her for what she had done. He himself would not have been happy to allow this incident to pass without a scolding to punish her. Yasin had made a mistake, but she had made an even greater one.

Then his thoughts quickly returned to Yasin. With inner joy he thought about the temperament they both shared. They had no doubt inherited it from the grandfather. It might well be blazing in Fahmy's chest behind a veil of culture and morality. In fact, did he not remember how he had come home unexpectedly one day and heard Kamal singing "O bird, you up in the tree"? He had waited outside the door, not merely to pretend he had arrived after the song was completed but also to follow the voice, savoring its timbre and probing its length of breath. When the boy had finished the tune, he had banged the door and coughed when he entered. He had concealed inside his breast his delight, which no one had detected. He was pleased to see himself flourishing once more in the lives of his sons—at least during calm and serene times. But not so fast. . . . Yasin's disposition was peculiar to him and not something they shared. They did not have a single temperament, if the precise meaning of the word was to be respected. Yasin was a blind animal. . . . He had assaulted Umm Hanafi once and had been caught again with Nur. He thought nothing of wallowing in the mud. He himself was not like that!

Yes, he could understand how vexing it had been for Yasin to be forced to spend the night in something like a prison. He understood, because he had endured it too, feeling depressed and sad, as though he had lost a loved one. Suppose he had been strolling around the roof garden like the boy and had come upon a maid—assuming she was to his liking—would he have embarked on this adventure? Certainly not . . . absolutely not! But what obstacle would have restrained him? Perhaps the location? The family! Perhaps his maturity. . . . Oh, he became irritated when this last possibility came to mind. He imagined that he envied Yasin both his youthful appetite and the folly of his slip. . . . No, however that might be, they had two different temperaments.

Al-Sayyid Ahmad was not infatuated with women per se, with no conditions or stipulations. His lust was always distinguished by a taste for luxury. It was propelled by a refined sense of selection. It was concerned about social qualifications, which it lumped together with the customary physical ones. He was infatuated with feminine beauty in all its flesh, coquetry, and elegance. Jalila, Zubayda, Maryam's mother, and tens more like them had all possessed at least some of these characteristics. In addition to that, it was not like him to be comfortable or content without a delightful setting and a congenial gathering, along with the wine, pleasant conversation, and music that went with such occasions. He did not need to spend much time with a new lover before she would realize what he desired and prepare the kind of setting his soul yearned for, with a fragrant atmosphere redolent of roses, incense, and musk.

Just as he loved beauty in the abstract, he loved it in its glittering social framework. He liked to be noticed and to have a widespread reputation. Therefore he enjoyed sharing his love and lovers with his special friends, except on those rare occasions when circumstances required him to be discreet and secretive, as with Maryam's mother.

This social use of his love did not require him to sacrifice beauty, for in his circle beauty and reputation went hand in hand, like an object and its shadow. Beauty was most often the magic wand that opened the door to reputation and noteworthy status. He had been the lover of some of the most famous entertainers of his time. Not one of them had disappointed his yearning for beauty or his craving for loveliness.

For these reasons he thought scornfully of Yasin's conquests. He repeated disapprovingly, "Umm Hanafi! . . . Nur! . . . What a beast he is!" He himself was innocent of such abnormal lusts, although he did not need to wonder too long about their source. He had not forgotten the woman who had given birth to Yasin. She had passed on to him her character with its passion for the sordid. He was responsible for the strength of Yasin's lust, but she had to answer for the nature of this lust and its base inclinations.

The next morning he thought seriously about the issue again. He almost summoned the couple to try to reconcile them with each other and with him, but he deferred it to a more appropriate time than morning.

When Fahmy asked Yasin why he stayed away from the breakfast table, he answered tersely, "It's just some trivial thing. I'll tell you about it later."

Fahmy remained in the dark about the secret reason his father was angry with Yasin until he learned that the maid Nur had disappeared. He was then able to guess everything. The morning started off in an unusual way for the family, because Yasin left the house early and Zaynab stayed in her room. Then the other men of the family left the house. They were agitated and careful not to look at the soldiers. Behind the peephole of the window, the mother prayed for God to protect them from any harm.

Amina did not want to become involved in the "incident" on the roof. She went down to the oven room and waited from one moment to the next for Zaynab to join her as usual. She would not admit that Zaynab had a right to be angry about her honor. She considered it a form of coquetry of which she disapproved. She began to ask herself, "How can she claim rights for herself that no other woman has ever claimed?"

It was clear that Yasin had done something wrong. He had defiled a pure house. But he had wronged his father and stepmother, not Zaynab. . . . "I'm an angel compared with that girl. . . ."

As the waiting became protracted, she could no longer pretend to ignore the girl. She convinced herself that it was her duty to go console her. She went up to her apartment and called her. She entered the room and found no trace of her. She went from room to room, calling her until she had searched the whole house. Then she struck her hands together and exclaimed, "O Lord . . . has Zaynab seen fit to leave her home?"

59

Amina found no relief from her anxiety all day long. The possibility that the soldiers would stop one of her men going or coming never left her head. Fahmy was the first to return. On seeing him, she felt slightly less anxious, but when she noticed he was frowning she asked, "What's the matter, son?"

He complained, "I hate these soldiers."

The woman told him apprehensively, "Don't let them see it. If you love me, don't do it."

Even without her entreaty he would not have. He was not bold enough to challenge them with even a look as he walked along at their mercy. He kept his eyes from turning to gaze at any of them. On his way home he had asked himself sarcastically what they would do with him if they knew he was returning from a demonstration during which a violent confrontation had taken place and that early in the morning he had distributed tens of handbills inciting people to resist the soldiers.

He sat down to pass in review the events of the day. He recalled a few of them as they had actually happened but most as he wished they had been. It was his notion to work during the day and dream in the evening. In both cases, he was motivated by the most sublime and most hideous emotions: patriotism and a desire to kill and devastate. His dreams would intoxicate him for some time and then he would rouse himself, sad that they were impossible to carry out and depressed because they seemed silly. The fabric of these dreams was woven from the battles he would lead like Joan of Arc. Having seized the enemy's weapons, he would attack, achieving the defeat of the English, and then deliver his immortal speech in Cairo's Opera Square. The English would be forced to announce the independence of Egypt. Sa'd would return triumphant from exile. Fahmy would meet the leader, who would address the nation. Maryam would be present at the historic inauguration. Yes, his dreams were always crowned by the image of Maryam, even though, like the moon hidden behind storm clouds, she had been tucked away all this time in a remote corner of his heart that was beset by distractions.

Before he knew what was happening, his mother, tightening the kerchief around her head, told him uneasily, "Zaynab's angry and has left for her father's home."

Oh . . . he had almost forgotten what had happened to his brother and family that morning. His speculations when he learned that the maid, Nur, had disappeared were now confirmed. He avoided his mother's eyes in embarrassment. He did not want her to discern what was passing through his mind, especially since he was sure she knew the truth of the matter. He thought it likely that she realized he knew about it too or at least suspected he did. He did not know what to say, since in his conversations with her he was not accustomed to pretending things he did not feel. He hated nothing so much as having wiles replace candor in their relationship. He limited himself to muttering, "May our Lord remedy the situation."

Amina said nothing more, as though the disappearance of Zaynab was a trivial event to be dismissed with a declarative statement and a pious wish.

Fahmy had to hide a smile, which almost betrayed that he knew more than he was saying. He realized that his mother was suffering too. She was uneasy because she had no natural talent for acting. She was not good at lying. Even if she was forced to prevaricate at times, her temperament, which was too straightforward to allow the veils of deception to cling, would give her away.

Their confusion did not last long, for in a few minutes they saw Yasin heading toward them. From the way he looked up at them, they imagined he did not realize what problems lay in store for him in the house, although even they did not know the extent of the trouble. Fahmy was not surprised, for he knew that Yasin paid little attention to problems other people found oppressive.

Yasin was overwhelmed by the breathtaking sensation of having emerged triumphant from an adventure that had caused him to forget most of his problems, if only temporarily. He had been on his way to the house when a soldier, apparently popping up from nowhere, had blocked his way. Yasin had trembled all over, expecting unprecedented evil or at least a distressing insult that would be observed by the shop owners and passersby. He had not hesitated to defend himself, addressing the soldier gently and ingratiatingly, as though asking permission to pass: "Please, sir."

The soldier had asked for a match and smiled. Yes, he had smiled. Yasin had been so astonished to see him smile that he had encountered difficulty understanding what he wanted until the soldier repeated his request. He had never imagined that an English soldier would smile that way. Even if English soldiers smiled like other human beings, he would not have thought one would smile at him so politely. He had been transported by delight and remained frozen for a few moments, neither offering an answer nor making a motion. Then with all the energy he could muster, he had tackled this simple assignment for the mighty, smiling soldier. Since he did not smoke and did not carry any matches, he had gone at once to al-Hajj Darwish, who sold beans, and purchased a box of matches. Then he had rushed back to the soldier, holding it out to him. The soldier had taken it and said, in English, "Thank you."

Yasin had not yet recovered from the impact of that magical smile. Now here was "thank you." It was like a glass of beer a person drinks to refresh himself when he has had enough whiskey. It filled Yasin with gratitude and pride. His pudgy face blushed and beamed as though the words "thank you" were a high decoration with which he had been publicly invested. It practically guaranteed that he would be able to go and come as he pleased in perfect safety. As soon as the soldier gave the first sign of moving away, Yasin told him in a friendly manner that came straight from his heart, "Good luck, sir."

Yasin proceeded to the house almost reeling with joy. What good luck he had had.... An Englishman—not an Australian or an Indian—had smiled at him and thanked him.... An Englishman—in other words, the kind of man he imagined to embody all the perfections of the human race. Yasin probably detested the English as all Egyptians did, but deep inside he respected and venerated them so much that he frequently imagined they were made from a different stuff than the rest of mankind. This man had smiled at him and thanked him.... Yasin had answered him correctly, imitating English pronunciation so far as his mouth would allow. He had succeeded splendidly and had merited the man's thanks.

How could he believe the brutal acts attributed to them? Why had they exiled Sa'd Zaghlul if they were so gracious? His enthusiasm faded the moment his eyes fell on Mrs. Amina and Fahmy. From their expressions he could grasp that something was wrong. His worries, from which he had been temporarily severed, wound round him like a rope. He realized that he was confronted once more by the problem from which he had fled early that morning. Pointing upstairs, he asked, "Why isn't she sitting with you? Is she still angry?"

Amina exchanged a glance with Fahmy. Then she muttered nervously, "She's gone to her father."

He raised his eyebrows in astonishment or alarm. Then he asked her, "Why did you let her go?"

Amina replied with a sigh, "She slipped out without anyone noticing."

He felt he ought to say something to defend his honor in front of his brother and stepmother. He declared scornfully, "Whatever she wants."

Fahmy decided to resist his urge to keep silent. He wanted his brother to think he knew nothing about his secret and also wished to dispel any suspicion that he had heard it from his mother. He asked simply, "What caused this misfortune?"

Yasin gave him a searching look. He waved his large hand and grimaced as if to say, "Nothing's caused any misfortune." Then he observed, "Girls today no longer have the ability to get along with people." Looking at Mrs. Amina, he asked, "Where are the ladies of yesteryear?"

Amina bowed her head, apparently from embarrassment but actually to hide a smile that got the better of her when her mind tried to reconcile the image of Yasin now—contemplative, hortatory, and victimized—with the Yasin of the previous evening when he had been caught on the roof. All the same, Yasin's discomfort was far greater than the circumstances allowed him to admit. Despite the oppressive disappointment he had sustained in his married life, he had never thought for a moment of terminating it. He found in marriage a secure haven and refuge, not to mention the promise of imminent fatherhood, which he welcomed enthusiastically. He had always hoped to have his marriage waiting for him when he returned from his various sorties like an explorer returning to his homeland at the end of the year. He was not oblivious to the new conflict between him and his father as well as Mr. Iffat that would result from his wife's departure. All of this would be further clouded by the scandal. Its odor would be diffused until it stopped up everyone's nostrils. . . . The bitch! He had been fully determined to bring her around gradually to confessing that her error was more serious than his. Indeed, he may even have been so convinced that he felt it would certainly happen. He had sworn to make her apologize and to discipline her, but she had departed. She had turned his plans upside down and left him in an extremely awkward crisis. The bitch!

He was wrenched from his stream of thoughts by a scream that rent the silence enveloping the house. He turned toward Fahmy and his stepmother. He found they were trying hard to listen, looking concerned and anxious. The screaming continued, and they easily ascertained that it came from a woman. Their eyes showed that they were wondering what direction it came from and what the cause was. Was it announcing a death or a fight or calling for help? Amina began to ask God's protection against all evils.

Then Fahmy said, "It's near . . . perhaps on our street." He rose suddenly, furrowing his brow, and asked, "Could it be that the English have attacked a woman who walked past them?"

He rushed to the balcony with the others trailing behind. The screaming stopped, leaving no indication of the direction from which it had come. The three of them looked through the peephole in the latticework to search the street. Their eyes came to rest on a woman who attracted attention by the strange way she was standing in the center of the street and by the circle of passersby and storekeepers gathered around her. They recognized her immediately and cried out together, "Umm Hanafi! . . ."

Amina had sent the servant to get Kamal from school. She asked, "Why don't I see Kamal with her? What's making her stand there like a statue?"

"Kamal. . . . My Lord . . . where's Kamal?"

Relying on her intuition, the mother said, "She's the one who screamed. I recognize her voice now. . . . Where's Kamal? Save me. . . ."

Neither Fahmy nor Yasin uttered a word. They were busy searching the roadway in general and the English camp in particular for Kamal. They saw people looking toward the soldiers, most notably Umm Hanafi. They were certain that it was Umm Hanafi who had screamed and thus gathered the people around her. They felt instinctively that she was calling for help because some danger was threatening Kamal. Their fears centered on the English. But what was the danger? Where was Kamal? What had happened to the boy?

The mother kept appealing for help. They did not know how to comfort her and probably needed some reassuring themselves. . . . Where was Kamal? Some of the soldiers were sitting down, others stood or walked along minding their own business. Each was preoccupied with his own activities, as though nothing had happened, as though there was no crowd of people gathered in the street.

Suddenly Yasin punched Fahmy's shoulder and yelled, "Don't you see those soldiers standing in a circle under the cistern building on our street? Kamal's standing in the middle. . . . Look."

The mother could not keep herself from screaming, "The soldiers have Kamal. . . . There he is, O my Lord . . . Lord . . . save me."

Four giant soldiers had linked arms to form a circle. Fahmy's eyes had searched in that direction more than once without discovering Kamal. This time he noticed the boy in the center of the circle, visible through an opening between the legs of a soldier who was standing with his back to them. The family imagined the soldiers were going to kick him back and forth like a ball until they did him in.

Fahmy's fear for his brother made him forget his own safety. He turned around and said excitedly, "I'm going to him, no matter what."

Yasin's hand grabbed his shoulder. Yasin told Fahmy decisively, "Stop." Then with a calm, cheerful voice he told the mother, "Don't be afraid. If they had wanted to harm him, they would not have hesitated. . . . Look. He seems to be involved in a long conversation. And what about this red thing in his hand? I wager it's a piece of chocolate. . . . Calm yourself. They're just having some fun with him." He sighed and continued: "He's frightened us for no reason at all."

Yasin regained his composure. He still remembered his happy adventure with the soldier. He did not think it too unlikely that some of the man's fellow soldiers were as gracious and gentle as he was. Then he thought he would shore up and corroborate what he had said for the sake of the mother's agonized heart. He pointed to Umm Hanafi, who had not moved, and observed, "Don't you see that Umm Hanafi kept screaming until she realized there was no need for it? The people around her are beginning to move away. They seem reassured."

The mother murmured in a shaky voice, "My heart won't be reassured until he comes to me."

They focused their attention on the boy or what they could see of him from time to time. The soldiers unlinked their arms and relaxed their legs as though they were confident that Kamal would not run away. Now Kamal could be seen in his entirety. He was smiling, and they could tell from the movement of his lips and from the gestures of his hands, which he used to get a point across, that he was talking. The fact that he and the soldiers seemed to understand each other indicated that they could use the Cairo dialect of Arabic to some extent. But what was he telling them and what were they saying to him? None of them could guess that, but they calmed down. Even the mother in her anxious astonishment was finally able to watch silently, without any wail or call for help, the strange scene unfolding before her eyes.

Yasin laughed and said, "It's clear we were far too pessimistic when we assumed that the occupation of our district by these soldiers would create endless problems for us."

Although Fahmy appeared to be grateful that the soldiers were treating Kamal correctly, he did not appreciate Yasin's remark. Without turning his eyes away from the boy, he commented, "The way they treat men and women may differ from their treatment of children. Don't get too optimistic."

Yasin almost burst out with an account of his happy adventure, but he stopped himself in time for fear of enraging his brother. To be polite and ingratiating he said, "May our Lord free us safely from them."

Amina asked impatiently, "Isn't it time for them to let him go, with our thanks?"

It appeared that the circle of men around Kamal were expecting something else to happen. One of the four had gone off to a nearby tent to fetch a wooden chair, which he placed in front of Kamal. The boy immediately jumped on the chair. He stood there erect, with his arms hanging down straight at his sides, as though reviewing a formation of soldiers from an elite guard. His fez had slipped down over the back of his head, probably without his noticing it, to reveal his large, protruding forehead. What was he doing? Why was he standing like that? They did not have long to wonder, for his clear voice soon rang out with this song:

I want to go home,
Darling.
They've taken my boy,
Darling.

He sang it all the way through in his pleasing voice while the soldiers watched, their mouths open and smiling. They clapped their hands in appreciation at the end of each phrase. One of them was touched when he understood part of the meaning of the song and began to shout, "I'm going home. . . . I'm going home."

Kamal was encouraged by the enthusiastic response of his audience. He sang his very best, taking special care with his vibrato and projection. He finished the song to applause and praise, in which his family at the peephole participated, after singing along with him in their hearts, filled with joy and apprehension. Yes, the family participated in praising him after sharing vicariously in the singing, which they had followed anxiously, praying that he would excel and not make any mistakes. They might almost have been singing through him. It was as though their honor, both individually and as a family, was riding on his success.

Amina forgot her fears in the midst of these other feelings. Even Fahmy thought of nothing but the song and his hopes for its success. When the song was concluded successfully they all sighed deeply and wished Kamal would hurry home before anything happened to spoil the impact.

It seemed clear that the party was about to break up, for Kamal jumped down from the chair. He shook hands with each of the soldiers and raised his hand in salute. Then he shot off toward the house. The family rushed from the balcony to the sitting room to be ready to greet him. He arrived flushed and out of breath, with perspiration on his brow, his eyes and features contented, his limbs moving jerkily and aimlessly from his joyful feeling of victory. His young heart was filled to overflowing with happiness, which he could not help but proclaim in every possible way, calling the others to share in it. It was like a swelling deluge the riverbanks cannot retain that floods the fields and valleys. One look would have been enough to show him the impact of his adventure on their faces, but he was blinded by his joy and shouted, "I've got news you won't believe. You couldn't imagine it. . . ."

Yasin laughed loudly and sarcastically, "What news, my darling?"

This phrase lifted the veil from his eyes, like a light suddenly glowing in the darkness, so he could see the eloquent expressions of their faces. His knowledge that they had witnessed his adventure compensated for missing the opportunity to astonish them with his amazing account. He burst into laughter, slapping his knees with his hands. Then, struggling with his giggles, he asked, "Did you really see me?"

At that the voice of Umm Hanafi was heard complaining, "It would have been better if they had seen how I suffered. . . . What's all this joy about after I was almost undone? . . . One more incident like that and it'll be time for God to have mercy on me." She had not removed her black wrap and looked like a sack of coal full to bursting. Her face appeared pale and sickly. There was a strange look of resignation in her eyes.

Amina asked her, "What happened? . . . Why did you scream? God was kind to us and we didn't see anything alarming."

Umm Hanafi leaned her back against the door and commenced: "I'll never forget what happened, lady. We were on our way home when a devil of a soldier jumped in front of us and motioned to Mr. Kamal to go with him. Frightened, he ran toward Qirmiz Alley, but another soldier cut him off there. He turned into Palace Walk. He was screaming and my heart plunged from fear. I started to call for help at the top of my lungs. My eyes did not leave him for a minute while he ran from one soldier to another until they surrounded him. I was so afraid I almost died, and I couldn't see straight. I could not see much of anything. Before I knew it, people had gathered around me, but I kept on screaming until Uncle Hasanayn, the barber, told me, 'May God spare him from being harmed by those bastards. Proclaim the oneness of God. They're being nice to him.' Oh, lady, our master al-Husayn was with us and protected us from evil. . . ."

Kamal objected, "I never screamed."

Umm Hanafi beat her hand against her breast and said, "Your screaming was so loud it hurt my ears and drove me crazy."

In a low voice, as though apologizing, he said, "I thought they were going to kill me, but one of them began to whistle and patted my shoulder. Then he gave me a piece of chocolate." Kamal patted his pocket before continuing: "I stopped feeling afraid."

Amina's happiness left her. Perhaps it had been a hasty, spurious joy. The fact she should not lose sight of was that Kamal had been terrified for some minutes. She would need to pray to God for a long time to spare Kamal any evil effects. She did not think of fright merely as a transitory sensation. Certainly not. . . . It was an abnormal state with a mysterious, invisible halo around it. The jinn sought refuge there like bats in darkness. A frightened person, particularly someone young, would be harmed. There would be bad consequences. In her opinion, fear required special care and precautions, whether recitation of verses from the Qur'an, incense, or amulets. She remarked sadly, "They frightened you! May God destroy them. . . ."

Yasin, reading her thoughts, joked, "Chocolate is a useful charm against fright." Then he addressed Kamal: "Did you talk to them in Arabic?"

Kamal embraced the question, because once more it opened for him the doors to imagination and adventure, rescuing him from the vexations of reality. With his face beaming again, he replied, "They spoke to me in a strange kind of Arabic. . . . I wish you had heard it yourself." He went on to imitate the way they talked until everyone was laughing. Even his mother smiled.

Yasin, who envied his brother, asked him, "What did they say to you?"

"Lots of things! . . . 'What's your name?' 'Where's your house?' 'Do you like the English?' "

Fahmy asked sarcastically, "How did you reply to that wonderful question?"

Kamal looked at him and hesitated, but Yasin answered for him: "Of course he said he loves them. . . . What would you have wanted him to say?"

Kamal spoke up again to add fervently, "But I also told them to bring back Sa'd Pasha."

Fahmy could not restrain himself from laughing out loud. He asked Kamal, "Really! . . . What did they say to that?"

Feeling better now that his brother had laughed, Kamal replied, "One of them tweaked my ear and said in English, 'Sa'd Pasha, no.' "

Yasin had another question: "What else did they say?"

Kamal replied innocently, "They asked me if there weren't any girls in our house?"

For the first time since Kamal had arrived they looked at each other grimly. Fahmy asked him with concern, "What did you tell them?"

"I told them my sisters Aisha and Khadija got married, but they didn't understand what I was saying. So I said there's no one at home except 'Nina.' They asked what that meant and I told them 'Mama.' "

Fahmy gave Yasin a look that said, "Do you see how appropriate my suspicions were?" Then he remarked sarcastically, "They didn't give him the chocolate simply for the love of God."

Yasin smiled feebly and muttered, "There's nothing to be worried about." He was not willing to allow this subject to cloud their reunion. So he asked Kamal, "Why did they invite you to sing?"

Kamal laughed. He said, "During the conversation one of them began to sing in a low voice. Then I asked them if they wanted to hear me."

Yasin laughed loudly. He remarked, "What a daring boy you are. . . . Weren't you afraid when you were surrounded by their legs?"

"Not at all," Kamal boasted. Then he said with feeling, "How handsome they are! I've never seen anyone more handsome before. Blue eyes . . . golden hair . . . gleaming white skin. They look like Aisha!"

He suddenly ran off to the study, where he raised his head to see the picture of Sa'd Zaghlul on the wall next to those of the Khedive Abbas II, Mustafa Kamil, and Muhammad Farid. When he returned he said, "They're a lot better-looking than Sa'd Pasha."

Fahmy shook his head sadly and remarked, "What a traitor you are. . . . They bought you with a piece of chocolate. You're not so young you can be excused for saying that. Pupils in your school are dying as martyrs every day. May God grant you failure."

Umm Hanafi had brought in the brazier, coffeepot, cups, and the container with the coffee. Amina began to prepare the coffee for the time-honored session. Everything had returned to normal except that Yasin had begun to think once more of his angry wife. Kamal went off by himself and took the chocolate out of his pocket. He began to remove its gleaming red wrapper. Fahmy's attempt to make him feel bad seemed to have been in vain, for in his heart there was nothing but contentment and love.

60

Yasin's marital problems became more complex. They were more momentous than anyone had expected. Before al-Sayyid Ahmad knew what was happening, Muhammad Iffat appeared in the store the day after Zaynab had fled. Even before he freed his hand from al-Sayyid Ahmad's handshake of greeting, he said, "Al Sayyid Ahmad, I've come to you with a request. Zaynab must be divorced today. Before tomorrow, if possible."

Al-Sayyid Ahmad was staggered. Yes, he had been totally disgusted by Yasin's behavior, but he had never thought it would inspire an honorable man like Mr. Muhammad Iffat to request a divorce. He had certainly not imagined that these "errors" would require a divorce. Indeed, it had never occurred to him that a request for divorce would come from the wife. It seemed to him that the world had been turned upside down. He refused to believe the man was in earnest. In the gracious tone that had so often captivated the hearts of his friends, he said, "I wish the brothers were here to observe you hurling this harsh language at me. . . . Listen to me. In the name of our friendship I forbid you to mention the word 'divorce.' "

He examined his friend's face to gauge the impact of his words on him but found Muhammad Iffat frowning glumly in a determined way that boded ill. He began to sense the seriousness of the situation and to feel pessimistic. He invited his visitor to have a seat. Mr. Iffat sat down but looked even glummer. Al-Sayyid Ahmad knew him to be a stubborn, intractable man. When he got angry, affection and kindness were useless. All ties of kinship and friendship were ripped apart by the cutting edge of his wrath.

Al-Sayyid Ahmad said, "Declare the oneness of God . . . and let's talk calmly."

Muhammad Iffat replied, in a tone he seemed to have borrowed from the angry fire of his cheeks, "Our friendship is not in question, so let's leave it out of this. Your son Yasin is not fit to live with. I ascertained this after learning everything. How patient the poor girl has been. . . . She kept her worries to herself for a long time. She hid everything from me. Then she revealed it all after her heart was broken. . . . He stays out all night and returns at dawn so drunk he can't walk straight. He has scorned her and rejected her. What has been the result of all her patience? She catches him in her house with her servant." He spat on the ground before continuing: "A black maid! . . . My daughter wasn't made for this. Absolutely not, by the Lord of Heaven. You know better than anyone else how I feel about her. No . . . by the Lord of Heaven. I would not be Muhammad Iffat if I kept quiet about this."

It was the same old story but with a new element that stunned and shocked him: Mr. Iffat's statement that Yasin "returns at dawn so drunk he can't walk straight." Had he learned his way to the bar as well? When? How? . . . Oh, he did not have time to think about it or to be upset. He needed to control his emotions. The hour required calmness and control. He had to take charge of the situation to ward off any irreparable damage. He observed in a sad voice, "What distresses you distresses me twice as much. Unfortunately, none of the disgraceful actions you have mentioned ever reached me or came to my attention, by God, except the last incident. I have disciplined him more severely for that than any other father would have thought permissible. What can I do? I have subjected him to stern discipline since he was a boy. Beyond our wills, there are the devils and the world of the flesh, which mock our determination and spoil our best intentions."

Avoiding al-Sayyid Ahmad's eyes by looking at the desk, Muhammad Iffat replied, "I have not come to blame you or to criticize you. You are a model father who can be imitated but never equaled. But that does not alter the distressing fact that Yasin has not turned out the way you wished. In his current condition he is not fit for married life."

Al-Sayyid Ahmad protested, "Not so fast, Mr. Muhammad."

The other man corrected himself while remaining resolute: "In any case, he is not a fit husband for my daughter. He will find some woman who accepts him with his faults, but not her. My daughter was not made for this. You know better than anyone how I feel about her."

The proprietor moved his head close to his friend's and said in a low voice and with a hint of a smile, "Yasin's not unusual as husbands go. Lots of them get drunk and boisterous and do things they shouldn't."

Muhammad Iffat frowned to make it clear he would not allow the situation to be turned into a joke. He answered sternly, "If you're referring to our group or to me in particular, it is true that I get drunk, become rowdy, and take lovers, but I refrain from wallowing in the mud. We all do. A black maid. . . . Is my daughter destined to share a husband with her in a polygamous marriage? By the Lord of Heaven, no. She will not be Yasin's wife and he will not be Zaynab's husband."

Al-Sayyid Ahmad perceived that Muhammad Iffat, perhaps like his daughter, might be ready to forgive many things, but not Yasin's attempt to have both the girl and her black maid. He knew Muhammad Iffat was of Turkish descent and stubborn as a mule. He happened to recall the words of his friend Ibrahim al-Far the day he told him he was asking for Zaynab's hand for his son Yasin. The man had observed, "She's a fine girl from a good family. Muhammad is our brother and friend. His daughter is our daughter. But have you thought carefully about the girl's status with her father? Have you considered the fact that Muhammad Iffat does not allow the tiniest speck of dust to settle on her?" Although that was true, al-Sayyid Ahmad had found it difficult to judge matters by any standards but his own and had always boasted that Muhammad Iffat, despite his atrocious temper, had never gotten angry with him even once throughout their long friendship.

He said, "Take it easy. Don't you see we're all made of the same stuff, even if the details differ? A black maid and a female vocalist—aren't they both women?"

Muhammad Iffat flew into a rage. He pounded on the edge of the desk with his fist. He burst out: "You don't mean what you're saying. A servant's a servant and a lady's a lady. Why don't you take servants for mistresses then? Yasin's not like you. I'm sorry my daughter's pregnant by him. I hate for my grandchild to have such filth in his veins."

The last sentence stung al-Sayyid Ahmad and he was enraged, but he was able to suppress his anger by using the forbearance he lavished on his acquaintances and friends, the strength of which was matched only by that of his irascibility with his family. He replied calmly, "I would like to suggest that we postpone this conversation to some other time."

Muhammad Iffat said angrily, "I want my request carried out immediately."

Al-Sayyid Ahmad was extremely vexed. There was nothing unsavory about divorce as a solution, but he was apprehensive about his lifelong friendship, and it was hard for him to admit defeat. Was he not the man whose mediation people requested to settle disputes and mend quarrels between friends and spouses? How could he accept defeat and divorce when he was defending his own son? What good were his forbearance, diplomacy, and finesse?

"I attempted to strengthen our friendship through this marriage tie between our families. How can I accept a weakening?"

His visitor answered disapprovingly, "Our friendship is not in doubt. . . . We're not children, but my honor is not going to be sullied."

Al-Sayyid Ahmad asked gently, "What will people say about a marriage that doesn't even last a year?"

Muhammad Iffat replied haughtily, "No intelligent person will blame my daughter."

Oh . . . once again, a new insult, but he met it with the same forbearance. His annoyance at failing to achieve a reconciliation seemed to have eclipsed that aroused by the angry man's words. He was not nearly so concerned about the blast directed against him as about justifying his own lack of success. He began to console himself with the thought that the divorce was in his hands alone. If he wanted to, he could grant it. If he did not, he could prevent it. Muhammad Iffat knew that perfectly well. It was for this reason he had come to ask for it in the name of their friendship, which was the only mediator he had to fall back on. If al-Sayyid Ahmad said no, that would settle the matter. The girl would return to his son, voluntarily or involuntarily. Their lengthy friendship would be in the past tense. If he said yes, the divorce would take place, but the friendship would be preserved and he would have the credit for doing his friend a favor. In the future, it would not be difficult to bring all these considerations into play to reunite what had been severed. Although the divorce was a defeat, it was a temporary one, which clearly demonstrated his goodwill and nobility. In time it might turn into a victory. Once he was even partially reassured about his position, he felt a desire to criticize his friend for taking him for granted. He warned him, "The divorce will not take place without my consent. . . . Do you disagree? . . . I will not reject your request, if you are still determined to proceed with it, out of respect for you and the friendship you slighted when you spoke to me. . . ."

Muhammad Iffat sighed, either from relief at achieving the desired result or in protest against his friend's criticism, or both. Then with a voice free of the sharp edge of anger for the first time, he said resolutely, "I told you a thousand times that our friendship was not in jeopardy. You haven't wronged me in any way. To the contrary, you have honored me by granting my request, although you didn't want to."

Al-Sayyid Ahmad echoed his words sadly, "Yes . . . I didn't want to."

The moment his visitor passed from sight, al-Sayyid Ahmad's resentment flared up. His suppressed rage exploded, encompassing himself, Muhammad Iffat, and Yasin, especially Yasin. He asked himself whether the friendship would really remain secure and not be muddied by events to come. Oh . . . he would have spared no expense to protect himself from a rude jolt like this. . . . But it was all because of Turkish obstinacy. No . . . the devil, no . . . Yasin . . . Yasin, not anyone else.

He told his son angrily and scornfully, "You have spoiled the purity of a friendship no number of days would have been able to harm, even if they had conspired to that goal."

After repeating to Yasin what Muhammad Iffat had said, he concluded: "You have disappointed my hopes in you so much that only God and His blessings can ever repay me. I raised and disciplined you. I watched over you. . . . Then all my efforts lead to what? . . . An alcoholic wretch who talks himself into raping the most humble servant in his family's home. There is no power or might save with God. I never imagined that my discipline would produce a son like you. Everything is in God's hands, the past and the future. What can I do with you? If you were a juvenile, I'd smash your head in, but time will certainly take care of that. You'll receive your just deserts. Decent families will wash their hands of you and let you go for a song."

He may have been sorry for his son, but his anger got the upper hand. Then all he could feel was contempt. Although Yasin was virile, handsome, and large, he no longer brought delight to his father's eyes. He wallowed in the mud, as Muhammad Iffat (may God destroy him) had observed. Yasin had been too weak to tame an unruly woman. How callow he was. His recklessness had soon been rewarded by a degrading disaster from which he had been unable to save himself. How contemptible he was! Let him get drunk, carouse, and take lovers, on condition that he remain the unchallenged master of his family. But his shameful defeat made him seem totally contemptible to his father. As Muhammad Iffat (may God destroy him) had also observed: Yasin was not like him.

"I do what I want and still I'm al-Sayyid Ahmad. That's all there is to it. What a fine idea it was for me to try to rear my sons to be outstanding examples of rectitude and purity, since it would be difficult for them to balance my lifestyle with my honor and rectitude. But, alas, my effort was in vain with this son by Haniya."

"Did you agree, Father?" Yasin's voice reverberated like a death rattle.

"Yes," he answered gruffly, "to preserve a long-lasting friendship and because it was the best solution, at least for now."

Yasin's hand began to contract into a fist and then unfold, in a mechanical, nervous gesture. The blood drained from his face until he looked extremely pale. He felt more humiliated by this than by anything else in his life except his mother's conduct. His father-in-law was asking for a divorce! In other words, Zaynab was requesting one or at least consenting to one.... Which of them was the man and which the woman? There was nothing strange about a man casting out a pair of shoes, but shoes were not supposed to throw away their owner. How could his father agree to this unprecedented humiliation for him? He glared at his father harshly but also in a way that reflected the cries for help surging in his breast. In a voice he desperately strove to keep free of any hint of protest or objection, as though trying to remind his father there might be a more appropriate solution, he remarked, "A husband has legal means of forcing a wife to return and obey him if she's rebellious...."

Al-Sayyid Ahmad sensed what his son was going through and was touched. Therefore he shared some of his own thoughts with him. He told him, "I know that, but I've decided we should be generous. Muhammad Iffat has an inflexible, Turkish mentality but a heart of gold. This is not the last word. It's not the end. I'm not forgetting your welfare, even though you don't deserve it. Let me proceed as I wish."

"As you wish," Yasin thought. "Who has ever gone against your wishes? You marry me and divorce me. You give me life and take it away. I don't really exist. Khadija, Aisha, Fahmy, Yasin... all the same thing. We're nothing. You're everything. No.... There's a limit. I'm no longer a child. I'm just as much a man as you are. I'm the one who is going to decide my destiny. I'm the man who will grant the divorce or have her legally confined to my house until she's ready to obey me. Muhammad Iffat, Zaynab, and your friendship with her father can all lick the dust from my shoes."

"What's the matter? Don't you have anything to say?"

Without hesitation, Yasin answered, "Whatever you want, Father."

"What a life! What a household! What a father!" Yasin reflected. "Scoldings, discipline, and advice. . . . Scold yourself. Discipline yourself. Give yourself some advice. Have you forgotten Zubayda? Jalila? The music and the wine? After all that, you appear before us wearing the turban of the most authoritative Muslim legal scholar, the Shaykh al-Islam, and carrying the sword of the Caliph, the Commander of all Muslims. . . . I'm not a child anymore. Look after yourself and leave me and my affairs alone. 'Marry.' Whatever you say, sir. 'Divorce.' Whatever you say, sir. . . . Curses on your father."

61

The intensity of the demonstrations decreased in the Husayn district after the British soldiers occupied it, and al-Sayyid Ahmad was able to resume a favorite custom he had temporarily been forced to curtail, that of attending the Friday prayer service at al-Husayn Mosque, accompanied by his sons. It was a practice he had scrupulously observed for a long period. He had invited his sons to join him, when they were old enough, in order to direct their hearts toward religion early in life. He hoped it would be a blessing to him, his sons, and the entire family. Amina was the only one with reservations about this caravan that set out at the end of each week, consisting of her three men, as big as camels, resplendent and virile. She watched them through the balcony peephole and imagined that everyone was staring enviously at them. In her alarm, she prayed to God to spare them the dangers of the evil eye. One day she felt compelled to confide her fears to her husband, who seemed swayed by her warning momentarily but did not yield. He told her, "The blessing of the religious duty we fulfill by attending the Friday prayer service is sufficient protection against any evil."

Since childhood, Fahmy had cheerfully obeyed the summons to attend the Friday service with a heart eager to perform his religious duties. He was motivated not only by his father but by sincere religious sentiment, enlightened by views drawn from the teachings of the influential Egyptian theologian Muhammad Abduh and his disciples. He was the only one in the family to adopt a skeptical attitude toward incantations, charms, amulets, and the amazing deeds performed by saints. His mild temperament kept him from making his doubts public or announcing his disdain for such things. He accepted without protest the amulets from Shaykh Mutawalli Abd al-Samad that his father brought him from time to time.

Yasin complied with his father's request to attend prayers with him because he had no alternative. Left to his own devices he might never have thought of squeezing his huge body in among the masses of worshippers, not from any religious doubt but from laziness and a lack of interest. On Fridays, Yasin suffered from a special distress all morning. When it was time to go to the mosque he grumpily put on his suit. He followed behind his father like a prisoner, but gradually as he approached the mosque his grouchiness decreased. By the time he entered the sanctuary he felt at peace with the world and performed the prayer, asking God to forgive him and pardon his sins. He would not ask for repentance, since he secretly feared his prayer might be granted and he would be turned into an ascetic with no taste for the pleasures of life he loved and without which he thought life would be meaningless. He knew beyond the shadow of a doubt that repentance was a necessity and that he could not be pardoned without it. He just hoped it would come at an appropriate time so he could have full enjoyment of both this world and the next. Therefore, despite his laziness and grumbling, in the end he praised the circumstances that forced him to perform a religious duty as important as the Friday prayer. In the final reckoning, it might erase some of his bad deeds and lighten the burden of his sins, especially since it was virtually the only religious duty he did perform.

Kamal had just recently been invited to join them, when he became ten. He obeyed the summons proudly, cockily, and happily. He sensed that the invitation implied recognition of him as a person and almost put him on a par with Fahmy, Yasin, and even his father. He was particularly pleased to follow in his father's footsteps without having to dread some punishment from him. He stood beside him as an equal in the mosque, where everyone copied the motions of the same imam or prayer leader. At home when he prayed, he was totally absorbed in the experience to a degree he could not attain at the Friday prayer service. There he was nervous about performing his prayers surrounded by so many people and apprehensive that he might slip up in some manner his father would detect. When he was in the mosque, the intensity of his devotion to al-Husayn, whom he loved more than himself, also interfered with giving the kind of total attention to God that a person should when praying.

Thus they appeared on al-Nahhasin Street walking briskly toward Bayt al-Qadi, al-Sayyid Ahmad in front with Yasin, Fahmy, and Kamal following in a line behind him. They found places in the mosque and sat listening to the sermon in total silence, their heads craned to see the pulpit. Although the father listened attentively, he was also praying silently. His heart reached out to Yasin in particular, since he thought the young man deserved compassion after his false steps. He prayed to God at length to reform Yasin, straighten him out, and compensate him for everything he had lost. The sermon directed his attention to his own sins, sweeping aside all other considerations. He found himself directly confronted by them. They were given such terrifying vividness by the penetrating and resonant voice of the preacher that al-Sayyid Ahmad imagined he was singling him out and screaming into his ears at the top of his voice. He would not have been surprised to hear the preacher address him by name: "Ahmad, restrain yourself from evil. Cleanse yourself of fornication and wine. Repent and return to God your Lord."

He was troubled by anxiety and doubt just as he had been the day Shaykh Mutawalli Abd al-Samad had argued with him. He usually was not affected this way by the sermon, for he would become distracted, praying for pardon, forgiveness, and mercy. Like his son Yasin, he did not pray for repentance, or if he did it was only with his tongue and not his heart. If his tongue said, "O God, repentance," his heart limited its request to pardon, forgiveness, and mercy. They seemed to be a pair of musical instruments playing together in a single orchestra but rendering different tunes. He could not imagine viewing life in any other fashion than the way it actually appeared to him. Whenever anxiety and doubt threatened to gain control of him, he would rise to defend himself against them, putting his defense in the form of a prayer or a plea for forgiveness. He would say, "O God, You know my heart, my faith, and my love. God, increase my dedication to the performance of my religious duties and my ability to do good deeds. O God, a good deed outweighs ten others. God, You are forgiving and merciful." With such a prayer he would gradually recover his peace of mind.

Yasin did not have this ability to reconcile his piety and his practice or did not feel in need of it. He never thought about it. He wandered through life just as he wanted, believing in God in exactly the same way he believed in his own existence. He would surrender himself to the flow of life, not opposing or resisting it. When the preacher's words reached his ears, he prayed mechanically for mercy and forgiveness with complete peace of mind, for he felt no real danger. God was too merciful to cause a Muslim like himself to burn in hell for transitory lapses that harmed no one. And there was always repentance. . . . It would come one day and erase everything that had preceded it.

Biting on his lip to suppress his laughter, he looked stealthily at his father and wondered what the man might be thinking while he listened with such evident interest to the sermon. "Is he tormented by every Friday service or do you suppose he's a hypocrite and doesn't admit the truth? . . . No, neither one. . . ." He was like Yasin and believed in the vastness of God's mercy. If matters were as grave as the preacher's description implied, then his father would have chosen one of the two conflicting paths. He stole another glance at al-Sayyid Ahmad. He thought he looked like a noble and handsome stallion among the seated worshippers gazing at the pulpit. The admiration and love he felt for him were pure. There was no trace of resentment left in his soul, although on the day of the divorce he had been so angry that he had revealed his anguish to Fahmy: "Your father has destroyed my household and made me a laughingstock for people." Now he had forgotten his resentment along with the divorce, the scandal, and everything else.

The preacher himself was no better than his father. In fact, he was quite certainly more debauched. One of his friends at Ahmad Abduh's coffee shop had told him, "He believes in two things: God in heaven and adolescent boys on earth. He's such a sensitive type that when he's in al-Husayn, his eye twitches if a lad moans in the Citadel." Yasin felt no rancor toward him because of that. On the contrary, the preacher and his father seemed like a trench at the front lines that the enemy would have to storm across first before reaching him.

Then the call to prayer was given. The men rose all at once and positioned themselves in closely packed lines, which filled the courtyard of the great mosque. They brought the building to life with their bodies and souls. The congestion was so intense that Kamal was reminded of the annual procession along al-Nahhasin, or Coppersmiths Street, of the pilgrims leaving for Mecca. Intermingled in the long, parallel lines were men with all different styles of clothing—suits, cloaks, or floor-length shirts—but they all became a single organism, moving in unison, facing in a single direction for prayer. Their whispered recitations reverberated in an all-encompassing hum until the benediction came.

At that moment, the orderly discipline was abandoned. Freedom drew a deep breath, and everyone rose to go wherever he wished. Some went to visit the sepulcher, some headed for the doors to leave, and others stayed behind to chat or to wait until the crowd thinned out. The streams of traffic in different directions frequently got mixed up with each other. The happy moment Kamal had promised himself was at hand, that of visiting the sepulcher, kissing the walls, and reciting the opening prayer of the Qur'an for himself and on behalf of his mother, as he had promised her. He began to move along slowly, following in his father's footsteps.

Before anyone knew what was happening, a young theology student from al-Azhar University suddenly burst out of the crowd to block their way so violently that people started looking. He spread his arms out to thrust people aside. He stepped back to glare at Yasin, frowning as sparks of anger flew from his sullen face. Al-Sayyid Ahmad was startled by him and began to look back and forth between him and Yasin, who seemed even more startled and began in turn to look questioningly from the theology student to his father. People noticed what was happening and focused their attention to watch with curious astonishment.

Al-Sayyid Ahmad could not restrain himself any longer. He asked the young man indignantly, "What's the matter, brother? Why are you looking at us that way?"

The seminarian pointed at Yasin and cried out in a voice like thunder, "Spy!"

The word ripped into the family like a bullet, making their heads spin. Their eyes were fixed on the man, and their bodies became rigid. Meanwhile the accusation was on everyone's lips, repeated with alarm and resentment. People began to gather around them, warily linking their arms together to form a circle from which they could not escape. Al-Sayyid Ahmad must have been the first to come to his senses, although he understood nothing of what was happening around him. He sensed the danger of remaining silent and of retreating into himself. He shouted angrily at the young man, "What are you saying, Mr. Shaykh? What spy do you mean?"

The seminarian paid no attention to the father. He pointed once more at Yasin and yelled, "Beware, people. This fellow's a traitor, one of the spies for the English who has slipped in among you to collect information he turns over to his criminal masters."

Al-Sayyid Ahmad was furious. He took a step toward the young man and, losing control of himself, shouted, "What you're saying doesn't make any sense. Either you're a troublemaker or you're crazy. This young man is my son. He's no traitor or spy. We're all nationalists. This district knows us as well as we know ourselves."

Their adversary shrugged his shoulders disdainfully and shouted oratorically, "A despicable English spy. I have seen him repeatedly with my own eyes conversing privately with the English at Palace Walk. I have witnesses to that. He won't dare deny it. I challenge him. . . . Down with the traitor."

An angry rumble resounded throughout the mosque. Voices were raised here and there, crying, "Down with the spy." Others called out, "Teach the traitor a lesson."

It was clear from the threatening looks in the eyes of those near them that people were just waiting for some initial gesture or sign before pouncing on them. The only thing holding back the tide may have been the impressive sight of al-Sayyid Ahmad, who was standing beside his son as though offering to absorb the harm threatening him, as well as the tears of Kamal, who was wailing. Yasin was standing between his father and Fahmy, barely conscious from alarm and fear. He began to say in a trembling voice no one could hear, "I'm not a spy. . . . I'm not a spy . . . with God as my witness for what I say."

The crowd's anger was becoming a frenzy. People were converging on the circle of prisoners. They were shoving against each other with their shoulders and threatening to harm the spy.

Then a voice cried out from the center of the mob: "Not so fast, gentlemen. . . . This is Yasin Effendi, the secretary of the school on Coppersmiths Street."

Voices roared back, "Coppersmiths or ironmongers, it doesn't matter. Let's teach him a lesson."

Another man was making his way between the bodies with difficulty but also with invincible determination. As soon as he reached the front, he raised his hands and screamed, "Listen! Listen!" When it was a little quieter he pointed at al-Sayyid Ahmad and said, "This is Mr. Ahmad Abd al-Jawad from a well-known family on al-Nahhasin. There's no way his household could harbor a spy. Be patient until the truth is discovered."

The theology student yelled angrily, "I'm not concerned with whether he's Mr. Ahmad or Mr. Muhammad. This young man is a spy, no matter who his father is. I've seen him joking with the executioners who are filling the tombs to overflowing with your sons."

At once countless people were shouting, "Let's beat him with our shoes."

A violent wave surged through the people packed together there. Eager zealots moved in from every direction waving their shoes and boots. Yasin felt desperate and defeated. He glanced all around him and wherever he looked all he saw was the face of someone looking for a fight, bubbling over with anger and hatred. Al-Sayyid Ahmad and Fahmy pressed close to Yasin in an instinctive gesture as though trying to protect him from harm or at least to share it with him. The two of them felt as choked by desperation and defeat as Yasin. Meanwhile Kamal's sobs had turned into a scream that almost drowned out the voices of the mob.

The seminarian was the first to attack. He threw himself on Yasin and grabbed his shirt. Then he pulled hard to drag him out of the refuge he had created for himself between his father and his brother so the blows would not miss him. Yasin grasped the man's wrist to fight him off and al-Sayyid Ahmad intervened. For the first time in his life, Fahmy saw his father in an alarming situation. He was so outraged that he was oblivious to the danger engulfing them. Fahmy shoved the theology student in the chest hard enough to force him back. He shouted at the man threateningly, "Don't you dare come a step closer."

The seminarian lost his temper and screamed, "Get all of them!"

At that moment a powerful voice commanded, "Wait, Mr. Shaykh. . . . Everyone, wait."

Eyes were turned toward the voice. It was a young effendi who emerged from the crowd heading for the circle with the prisoners. He was followed by three others his age, dressed like him in modern clothing. They marched forward in a confident and resolute manner until they stood between the young shaykh and his victim and the victim's family. Many people whispered to ask each other, "Police . . . police?"

The questioning ceased when the theology student held out his hand to the commander of the group, and the two shook hands warmly. The leader asked the seminarian resolutely, "Where's this spy?"

The young shaykh pointed with scorn and loathing at Yasin. The leader turned to scrutinize him coldly. Before he could say a word, Fahmy took a step forward to attract his attention. When the man noticed him, his eyes quickly grew wide in amazement and disbelief. He muttered, "You . . ."

Fahmy smiled wanly and said somewhat sarcastically, "This spy is my brother."

The leader turned to the seminarian to ask, "Are you certain of what you're saying?"

Fahmy answered first: "He may be correct in saying he saw him talk to the English, but he really misinterpreted what was happening. The English are camped in front of our house and confront us whenever we go in or out. At times we're forced to talk to them, against our wills. That's all there is to it."

The theology student started to speak, but the young leader silenced him with a gesture. Putting his hand on Fahmy's shoulder, he addressed the crowd: "This young man is one of our friends among the freedom fighters. We both work on the same committee, so I'll take his word for it. . . . Let them pass."

No one said a thing. The young shaykh from al-Azhar withdrew without any hesitation and the crowd began to disperse. The young patriot shook hands with Fahmy and then went off, followed by his companions. Fahmy patted Kamal on the head until he stopped crying.

Silence reigned while everyone nursed his psychic wounds. Al-Sayyid Ahmad realized that some of his acquaintances had gathered around him. They began to offer him their condolences and apologies for the grave mistake committed by the theology student and those in the crowd whom he had misled. They assured him that they had spared no effort to defend him. He thanked them, although he did not know when they had arrived or how they had defended him. He renounced the visit to al-Husayn's sepulcher, because he was so overwhelmed by emotion. He headed for the door, frowning, his lips pressed tight together. His sons followed him in total silence.

62

Al-Sayyid Ahmad got his breath back in the street, relieved to be away from the people who had participated in the incident, even if only by watching. He hated everything to do with the misadventure and hurled insults at it. He saw scarcely anything of the street along which he was walking. He exchanged greetings twice with acquaintances in a cursory, formal manner he never used. He concentrated on himself and his wounded soul, which was boiling with anger.

"I would rather die than be humiliated like that: the prisoner of a mob of rabble," he reflected. "This ill-fed, louse-infested theology student claiming to be a patriot attacked me shamelessly. He showed no respect for my age or dignity. I wasn't made to be treated like this. I'm not a person who can be humiliated this way. And when I'm with my sons.... Don't be surprised.... Your sons are the source of the problem. This ox, born of misery, will never stop causing trouble for you. He has acted scandalously in my home and alienated me from my dearest friend, crowning the year with a divorce. Was that enough? ... No, Haniya's son feels compelled to chat publicly with the English and let me pay the price of being attacked by riffraff. Take your friends the soldiers to your mother so her museum of lovers can be rounded out with Englishmen and Australians.

"It seems you'll be causing trouble for me as long as I live." This sentence slipped out bitterly, but he resisted the temptation to upbraid his son.

Despite his anger, he could see the state Yasin was in and felt sorry for him. He observed that his son was dazed, pale and ill, and he could not force himself to attack. The trouble Yasin had gotten himself into sufficed for now. He was not the only one giving him trouble. There was the hero. "But let's postpone his case till we recover from the headaches caused by the ox ... an ox at home and in the tavern, a bull with Umm Hanafi and Nur. But in the battle at the mosque, he was totally useless, a spineless wonder." What bastards his sons were.... If God would only dispense with children, descendants, and families.... "Oh ... why are my feet leading me home? Why don't I get a bite to eat away from the poisoned atmosphere of the house? Amina, for her part, will wail when she hears the news. I don't need to feel any more disgusted. I'll get some kabob at al-Dahan's. . . . I'll surely find a friend there to whom I can recount my disaster and tell my troubles. . . . But no, I have other problems that cannot wait that long. The hero . . . a new calamity we must remedy. On to the disastrous dinner. Wail, lament, and cry, woman, and curses on your father too."

Fahmy had only just finished changing clothes when he was summoned to talk to his father. Despite his depleted energy and his distress, Yasin could not keep himself from muttering, "Now it's your turn."

Pretending not to understand the point of his brother's remark, Fahmy asked, "What do you mean?"

Yasin laughed, finally able to, and said, "The traitors have had a turn, and now the freedom fighters will have theirs."

Fahmy wished dearly that the terms his friend had used to describe him in the mosque had been forgotten in all the commotion of the disturbance and the family's dazed reaction, but they had not been. Now Yasin was repeating them. Without any doubt, his father was summoning him to discuss them. Fahmy sighed deeply and departed.

He found his father sitting on the sofa with his legs tucked under him. He was fiddling with his prayer beads, and the look in his eyes was sad and thoughtful. Fahmy greeted him with great courtesy and stopped, submissively and obediently, about two meters away from the sofa. The man nodded his head slightly to return the greeting but the gesture did more to reveal how upset he was than to greet his son. It seemed to imply: "I'm returning your greeting reluctantly and only for the sake of politeness, but this spurious courtesy of yours no longer deceives me."

Al-Sayyid Ahmad directed a frowning glare at his son, which radiated anxiety and thus resembled a lamp used to search for a person concealed in the darkness. He told the boy resolutely, "I've summoned you, to learn everything. I want to know everything. What did he mean when he said you were on the same committee? Don't hesitate to tell me everything with complete candor."

Although Fahmy had grown accustomed during the past few weeks to confronting various dangers and had even gotten used to having bullets whiz past, it was his prerevolutionary heart that surfaced once his father began interrogating him. He was terrified and felt reduced to nothing. He concentrated his attention on skirting this wrath and trying to escape. He told his father gently and politely,

"The matter's quite simple, Papa. My friend probably exaggerated to extricate us from our dilemma."

Al-Sayyid Ahmad's patience was exhausted. He said, " 'The matter's quite simple . . .' Great. . . . But which matter is it? Don't hide anything from me."

With lightning speed, Fahmy considered the subject from different perspectives to select something he could say without fear of the consequences. He responded, "He called it a 'committee' when it's nothing more than a group of friends who talk about patriotic topics whenever they get together."

His father cried out furiously and resentfully, "Is this how you earned the title of 'freedom fighter'?"

The man's voice betrayed intense disapproval, as though he was hurt that his son was trying to put something over on him. The wrinkles of his frowning face looked threatening. Fahmy rushed to defend himself by making a significant admission, in order to convince his father that in every other respect he had been obedient to his commands, just as an accused man may voluntarily confess to a lesser offense in an attempt to plea for mercy. He said rather modestly, "It happens sometimes that we distribute appeals on behalf of nationalism."

Al-Sayyid Ahmad asked in alarm, "Handbills? . . . Do you mean handbills?"

Fahmy shook his head no. He was afraid to admit this, since the word was linked in the official pronouncements to the harshest penalties. When he had found a suitable formula to make his confession seem less dangerous, he said, "They're nothing but appeals that urge people to love their country."

His father allowed the prayer beads to fall to his lap. He clapped his hands together. Unable to control his alarm, he exclaimed, "You're distributing handbills! . . . You!"

Al-Sayyid Ahmad could not see straight, he was so alarmed and angry: distributing handbills . . . a friend of the freedom fighters. "We both work on the same committee!" Had the flood reached his roost? He had often been impressed by Fahmy's manners, piety, and intelligence. He would have lavished praise on his son except that he thought praise corrupted, whereas gruffness was educational and corrective. How had all of this peeled away to reveal a boy who distributed handbills, a freedom fighter? "We both work on the same committee . . ."

He had nothing against the freedom fighters, quite the contrary.

He always followed news about them with enthusiasm and prayed for their success at the conclusion of his normal prayers. News about the strike, acts of sabotage, and the battles had filled him with hope and admiration, but it was a totally different matter for any of these deeds to be performed by a son of his. His children were meant to be a breed apart, outside the framework of history. He alone would set their course for them, not the revolution, the times, or the rest of humanity. The revolution and everything it accomplished were no doubt beneficial, so long as they remained far removed from his household. Once the revolution knocked on his door, threatened his peace and security and the lives of his children, its flavor, complexion, and import were transformed into folly, madness, unruliness, and vulgarity. The revolution should rage on outside. He would participate in it with all his heart and donate to it as generously as he could. . . . He had done that. But the house was his and his alone. Any member of his household who talked himself into participating in the revolution was in rebellion against him, not against the English. Al-Sayyid Ahmad implored God's mercy for the martyrs both night and day and was amazed by the courage their families displayed, according to what people said, but he would not allow one of his sons to join the martyrs nor would he embrace the courage their families had displayed. How could Fahmy have seen fit to take this insane step? How had he, the best of his boys, chosen to expose himself to certain destruction?

The man was more alarmed than he had ever been before, even more than during the melee at the mosque. In a stern and threatening voice as though he were one of the English police inspectors, he asked Fahmy, "Don't you know the penalty for persons caught distributing handbills?"

Despite the seriousness of the situation, which required Fahmy to concentrate his attention on it, the question aroused a recent memory that shook his soul. He remembered being asked this same question, identical in words and import, by the president of the supreme student executive committee—together with many other questions—when he had been chosen a member of the committee. He also remembered that he had replied with determination and enthusiasm, "We are all ready to sacrifice ourselves for our country." He compared the different conditions under which the same question had been addressed to him and felt the irony of it.

Fahmy answered his father in a gentle and self-deprecating tone:

"I only distribute among my friends. I don't have anything to do with general distribution. . . . That way there's no risk or danger."

Al-Sayyid Ahmad, concealing his fears for his son behind the virulence of his anger, shouted harshly, "God does not protect those who expose themselves to danger needlessly. He, may He be glorified, has commanded us not to put our lives in jeopardy." The man would have liked to cite the verse of the Qur'an that dealt with this but had only memorized those short suras of the Qur'an he recited when he prayed. He was afraid that if he tried to quote it he might overlook a word or get it wrong and thus commit an unforgivable sin. He was content to cite the meaning and repeat it in order to make his point.

Before he knew what was happening, he heard Fahmy reply in his refined way, "But God also urges Believers to struggle, Papa."

Afterward Fahmy asked himself in amazement how he had found the courage to confront his father with this statement, which betrayed the fact he had been trying to conceal: that he was sticking to his ideas. Perhaps he thought the Qur'an would protect him if he took refuge behind one of its phrases. He was confident that his father would refrain from attacking him under such circumstances.

Al-Sayyid Ahmad was shocked by both his son's audacity and his argument. He did not give way to anger, though, which might have silenced Fahmy but not his argument. He would ignore the audacity for a moment while he pounded away at Fahmy's argument with a comparable one from the Qur'an, so that the erring child could be provided with correct guidance. Afterward he could settle the other account with him in any manner he wished. God inspired him to say, "That's struggle 'for the sake of God.' " (Qur'an, 9:20.)

Fahmy took his father's answer to show a willingness to debate with him. Once more he found the courage to speak: "We're struggling for God's sake too. Every honorable struggle advances God's cause."

Al-Sayyid Ahmad privately agreed with this statement, but his agreement itself and the feeling of insecurity it occasioned when he was debating with his son made him fall back on anger. Actually he was motivated not just by anger but by wounded pride and his concern that the youth would go too far in his rebellion and get himself killed. He abandoned the debate and asked disapprovingly, "Do you think I called you here to argue with me?"

Fahmy realized the threat his father's words contained. His dreams evaporated and he became tongue-tied. His father continued sharply: "The only struggle for the sake of God is when I intend to advance God's cause in a specifically religious struggle. There's no argument about that. Now I want to know whether my command is going to be obeyed?"

The young man quickly replied, "Most certainly, Papa."

"Then break every link between you and the revolution. . . . Even if your role was limited to distributing handbills to your best friends."

No power in existence could come between him and his patriotic duty. He absolutely would not retreat even one step. The time for that had passed, never to return. This passionate, dazzling life, springing from the depths of his heart and illuminating every area of his soul, could not die away. How preposterous to think he would kill it himself. All this was no doubt true, but could he not find some way to please his father and escape his wrath? He could not defy him or openly declare that he disagreed with the command. He could rebel against the English and defy their bullets almost every day, but the English were a frightening and hated enemy, while his father was his father, a frightening and beloved man. Fahmy worshipped him as much as he feared him. It was hard to disobey him. There was also another feeling Fahmy could not ignore. His rebellion against the English was inspired by noble idealism. His disobedience against his father was associated only with disgrace and misery. What reason was there for this quandary? Why not promise to obey and then do whatever he wanted?

Lying was not considered contemptible or shameful in this household. Living in their father's shadow, none of them would have been able to enjoy any peace without the protection of a lie. They openly admitted this to themselves. In fact, they would all agree to it in a crisis. Had his mother intended to admit what she had done the day she slipped off to visit al-Husayn when her husband was out of town? Would Yasin have been able to drink, Fahmy to love Maryam, and Kamal to get up to all sorts of mischief when walking between Khan Ja'far and al-Khurunfush without the protection provided by lying? None of them had scruples about it. If they had been totally truthful with their father, life would have lost its savor. For all these reasons, Fahmy said calmly, "Your command is obeyed, Papa."

This declaration was followed by silence as each of them rested with relief. Fahmy imagined that his interrogation had been safely concluded. Al-Sayyid Ahmad imagined that he had rescued his son from the pit of hell. While Fahmy was waiting for permission to leave, his father suddenly rose and went to the armoire, which he opened. He thrust his hand inside as the young man watched with uncomprehending eyes. The father returned to the sofa with the Qur'an. He looked at Fahmy for some time. Then he held the Book out to him and said, "Swear it on this Book."

Fahmy jerked back involuntarily as though fleeing from the tongue of flame that had suddenly shot out at him. Then he remained nailed to the spot as he stared at his father's face in desperate, alarmed confusion. Al-Sayyid Ahmad kept his hand stretched out holding the Book and looked at his son with incredulous disapproval. His face became flushed, as though on fire, and there was a frightening gleam to his eyes. He asked in astonishment, as though he could not believe his eyes: "Don't you want to swear?"

Fahmy was tongue-tied. He could not utter a word or make a gesture. His father asked in a calm voice, with a shaky quaver suggestive of the raging anger behind it, "Were you lying to me?"

No change came over Fahmy, although he lowered his eyes to escape his father's. Al-Sayyid Ahmad placed the Book on the sofa. Then he exploded and shouted in such a resounding voice that Fahmy felt he was being slapped on the cheek: "You're lying to me, you son of a bitch. . . . I don't let anyone pull the wool over my eyes. What do you think I am and what do you think of yourself? You're a vile insect, vermin, a son of a bitch whose exterior appearance has deceived people for a long time. I'm not turning into an old lady any time soon. Do you hear? Don't mistake me for some old woman. You sons of bitches are driving me crazy. You've turned me into a laughingstock for people. I'm going to hand you over to the police myself. Do you understand? By myself, you son of a bitch. The only word that counts here is mine. Mine, mine, mine. . . ." He picked up the Book again and continued: "Swear. . . . I command you to swear."

Fahmy appeared to be in a trance. His eyes were fixed on some unusual motifs in the Persian carpet but saw nothing. He stared at the motifs for so long they became imprinted on his mind, only to fragment into chaos and emptiness. With each passing second he plunged deeper into silence and despair. He had no alternative to this desperate, passive resistance.

Al-Sayyid Ahmad rose with the Book in his hand and took one step toward him. Then he roared, "Did you think you were a man? Did you think you could do what you like? If I wanted, I'd beat you till your skull caved in."

Fahmy could not keep himself from crying then, but not from fear of the threat, for in his condition he was oblivious to any harm that might befall him. His tears expressed his sense of defeat and helped relieve the struggle raging within him. He started to bite on his lips to suppress his tears. He felt ashamed at being so weak. When he was finally able to speak, he launched into a rambling plea, because he was deeply moved and wished to conceal his embarrassment: "Forgive me, Papa. I'll obey every command of yours more than willingly, but I can't do this. I can't. We work like a single hand. I can't accept shrinking back and abandoning my brothers, and I don't think you would like me to. There's no way that life would be bearable if I did. There's no danger in what we're doing. Others have more exalted tasks like participating in the demonstrations in which many of them have been martyred. I'm no better than those who have been killed. There are funeral processions for tens of martyrs at a time with no lamentation except for the nation. Even the families of the victims shout slogans instead of weeping. What is my life worth? . . . What is the life of any man worth? Don't be angry, Papa. Think about what I'm saying. . . . I assure you that there's no danger in our little, nonviolent job."

Fahmy was so overcome by emotion that he could no longer bear to face his father. He fled from the room, almost colliding with Yasin and Kamal, who were listening behind the door, their dismay visible on their faces.

63

Yasin was heading for Ahmad Abduh's coffee shop when he ran into one of his mother's relatives in Bayt al-Qadi. The man approached him solicitously, shook his hand, and told him, "I was on my way to your house to see you."

Yasin guessed that this statement presaged some news about his mother, who had already caused him so much trouble. He felt uncomfortable and asked listlessly, "Good news, God willing?"

The man answered with unusual concern, "Your mother's ill, actually very ill. She's been sick for a month or more, but I only learned of it this week. At first they thought it was nerves and didn't worry about it, until it became entrenched. When the doctors examined her, it was diagnosed as a serious case of malaria."

Yasin was astonished by this totally unexpected news. He had anticipated word of a divorce, a marriage, a row, or something along those lines. He had not considered illness. He scarcely knew what he felt, since his emotions were so conflicting. He asked, "How is she now?"

The man replied with a premeditated candor not lost on Yasin, "Her condition's grave. . . . In spite of the prolonged treatment there has not been the least hint of progress. To tell the truth, her condition has continued to deteriorate. She has sent me to tell you frankly that she feels her end is near and that she wants to see you at once." He added in a tone that implied Yasin should carefully consider what he was saying, "You must go to her without any delay. This is my advice to you and my plea. God is forgiving and compassionate."

Perhaps there was a certain amount of exaggeration in the man's words, intended to induce him to go, but they could not be a total fabrication. So he would go, if only from a sense of duty.

Here he was, once again traversing the curve in the road leading to al-Gamaliya, between Bayt al-Mal and Watawit Alley. On his right was al-Tih Street, where the woman who sold doum palm fruit had her place in shimmering memories of darkness. In front of him lay the road of sorrows. He would shortly see the store of the fruit merchant, lower his eyes, and slink past like a fugitive thief. Whenever he thought he would never return here, misfortune brought him back. No power short of death could have brought him to her this time.... Death! "Has her time really come?" he wondered. "My heart's pounding ... with pain? Sorrow? All I know is that I'm afraid. Once she's gone, I'll never return to this place again.... All the old memories will succumb to forgetfulness. What's left of my property will be returned to me, but I'm afraid ... I'm angry at these vicious thoughts. O God, preserve us.

"Even if I gain a more comfortable life and greater peace of mind, my heart will never escape from its pains. On her death I will bid farewell to a mother, with a son's heart ... a mother and a son, isn't that the way it is? I'm a person who has suffered a lot, not a beast or a stone. Death is new to me. I've never witnessed it before. I wish the end could come without it. We all die ... really? I've got to resist my fears. Nowadays we hear about people dying all the time, on Ministries Street, in the schools, and at the mosque of al-Azhar. There are victims of the violence in the city of Asyut daily. Even the poor milkman, al-Fuli, lost his son yesterday. What can the families of the martyrs do? Should they spend the rest of their lives weeping? They weep and then forget. That's death. Ugh ... it seems to me there's no way out of trouble now. At home there's Fahmy and his stubbornness. In front of me there's my mother. How hateful life is. What if it's all a trick and I find her in the best of health? She'll pay dearly.... She'll certainly have to pay a high price for it. I'm not a toy or an object to be ridiculed. She won't find her son until she dies. Do you suppose there's any money left for me? When I go in the house, will I find that man there? I won't know how to treat him. Our eyes will meet for a dreadful moment. Woe to him! Should I ignore him or throw him out? That's a solution. There are violent alternatives the man won't have considered. The funeral will certainly bring us together. What a joke! Imagine her coffin with her first and final husbands following behind it, while her son walks between them with tears in his eyes. By that time there definitely will be tears in my eyes. Isn't that so? I won't be able to evict him from the funeral. Scandal will accompany me to the very end. Then she'll be buried. Yes, she'll be buried, and everything will end. But I'm afraid, hurt, and saddened. May God and His angels pray for me.... Here's the sinister store.... There's the man. He won't recognize me. Far from it.... I'm disguised by age. 'Uncle ... my mother says ...' "

The servant opened the door for him, the same servant who had received him the year before. At first she did not recognize him and looked up curiously, but the questioning look quickly left her face to be replaced by a flash of recognition that seemed to say, "Oh . . . you're the one she's waiting for." Then she made way and pointed to a room on the right as he entered. She said, "Step this way, sir. . . . No one else is there."

Her final phrase attracted his attention immediately, since it addressed one of his major concerns. He realized that his mother had removed this obstacle. He headed for her room, cleared his throat, and entered. His eyes met his mother's as she looked up from her bed, to his left. Her eyes, known for their clarity, were clouded, so that her gaze seemed faint, as though coming from far away. Despite the feebleness of her eyes and their apparent disinterest, occasioned by their fading strength, she fixed them on him with a look of recognition. The delicate smile of her lips betrayed her feelings of victory, relief, and gratitude. Since she was wrapped in a blanket up to her chin, only her face was visible, a face that was far more changed than her eyes. Once full and round, it now looked withered and elongated, pale instead of rosy. Her delicate skin revealed the outlines of her jaw and protruding cheekbones, giving the pitiable appearance of a face wasting away. He stopped in stunned disbelief, incredulous that any power in existence would dare play such a cruel joke. His heart was seized by alarm, as though he were staring at death itself. He was stripped of his manhood and seemed to have become a child again, searching everywhere for his father. Irresistible emotion drew him to the bed. He bent over her, murmuring in sorrowful tones, "Never mind. . . . How are you?"

He felt genuinely sympathetic. In the warmth of this emotion his chronic pains disappeared. Similarly, in rare cases the symptoms of a hopeless medical condition, like paralysis, may disappear because of a sudden, overwhelming onslaught of terror. He seemed to be rediscovering the mother of his childhood whom he had loved, before pain had hidden her from his heart. Gazing at her faded face, he clung to this rejuvenated feeling which had also rejuvenated him, taking him back years before the pain, just as an exhausted invalid clings to a moment of lucidity he fears intuitively may be almost his last. Yasin clung to this sentiment with all the intensity of a man fully conscious of the strength of the forces threatening him. The very way he clung to this emotion revealed that those pains still existed deep inside him. He was aware of the sorrow awaiting him if he carelessly allowed this pure emotion to become spoiled by letting it mix with other feelings.

The woman extracted from the covers a gaunt, emaciated hand with dry skin washed with faded black and blue as though it had been mummified for thousands of years. Immensely touched, he took it in his own hands. At that moment he heard her weak, husky voice say, "As you can see, I've turned into a phantom."

He murmured, "May our Lord bring His mercy to bear on you and make you all well again."

Her head, which was covered with a white scarf, nodded prayerfully as if to say, "May our Lord hear you." She gestured to him to sit down. When he sat on the bed, she started talking with renewed strength derived from his presence: "At first I felt strange shivers. I thought it was something that would go away, that it was caused by nerves. People advised me to make a pilgrimage to the shrines and to burn incense. So I went to the mosques of al-Husayn and his sister al-Sayyida Zaynab and burned various different types of incense—Indian, Sudanese, and Arab—but my condition only got worse. Sometimes I was overcome by a constant shaking that wouldn't leave me until I was almost dead. At times my body would feel as cold as ice. On other occasions, fire would go through my body until I screamed, it was so hot. Finally we decided, I and Mi . . ." She stopped herself from mentioning the man's name, realizing at the last moment the error she was about to commit. "Finally I sent for the doctor, but his treatment did not make me any better and may even have set me back some. Now there's no hope."

Gently squeezing her hand, Yasin said, "Don't despair of God's mercy. His compassion is universal."

Her pale lips smiled and she said, "It pleases me to hear that. It pleases me to hear it from you more than from anyone else. You're dearer to me than the world and all its inhabitants. You're right. God's mercy is universal. I've had bad luck for so long. I don't deny that I've slipped up and made mistakes. Only God is infallible."

He noticed, uneasily, that her conversation was verging on confession. He was upset and alarmed that things he could not bear would be repeated in his hearing, even if only with reflective regret. He became tense and jumpy. He implored her, "Don't tire yourself out with talking."

She raised her eyes with a smile and answered, "Your visit has given me back my spirit. I want to tell you that never in my life did I want to harm anyone. Like everyone else, I was seeking peace of mind, but my luck tripped me up. I didn't harm anyone, but many people have harmed me."

Yasin felt that his prayer for the hour to pass peacefully would not be answered and that his pure emotion would suffer a crisis that would spoil it. In the same tone of entreaty he said, "Forget these people, both the good and the bad ones. Your health is more important now than anything else."

She patted his hand, as if asking for his affection and tenderness. She whispered, "There are things I should have done. I haven't done all that I should have for God. I wish I could live longer to make up for some of the things I've neglected. But my heart has always been full of faith, with God as my witness."

As though defending both her and himself, he remarked, "The heart's everything. It's more important to God than fasting and prayer."

She pressed his hand gratefully. Then she changed the direction of the conversation. She told him welcomingly, "You've finally returned to me. I didn't dare ask you to come till the illness brought me to the state you see. I felt I was saying goodbye to life, and I couldn't bear to leave it without seeing you. When I sent for you I was more afraid of your refusal than of death itself. But you've had mercy on your mother and come to bid her farewell. So accept my thanks and my prayers, which I hope God will heed."

He was deeply touched but did not know how to express his feelings. Either because of his shyness or lack of practice, loving words felt awkward and clumsy in his mouth whenever he tried to address them to this woman, whom he had grown accustomed to spurning and treating roughly. He discovered he could most effectively and sensitively express himself with his hand. He gently pressed hers and mumbled, "May our Lord make your destiny a safe one."

She kept referring back to the idea expressed in her previous statement, repeating the same words or finding other ways to put it. She paced her conversation by swallowing with noticeable difficulty or by falling silent for short periods while she caught her breath. For this reason, he repeatedly implored her to refrain from talking, but she would smile to cut him off and then continue her conversation. She stopped as her face showed she had just thought of something significant. She asked, "Have you gotten married?"

He raised his eyebrows in embarrassment and blushed, but she misinterpreted his reaction and hastened to apologize: "I'm not upset. . . . Of course, I would have liked to see your wife and children, but it's enough for me to know you're happy."

He could not keep himself from responding tersely, "I'm not married anymore. I got divorced about a month ago."

For the first time he noticed an interested look in her eyes. If they had still been able to sparkle they would have, but a dreamy light emanated from them as though coming through a thick curtain. She murmured, "You're divorced, son. . . . How sorry I am."

He quickly replied, "Don't be sorry. I'm not sorry or sad." He smiled and continued: "She left. Good riddance."

But she asked sadly, "Who chose her for you . . . him or her?"

In a manner that suggested he wished to close the door on this subject, he answered, "God chose her. Everything's fated and destined."

"I know that, but who chose her for you? Was it your stepmother?"

"Oh no. My father chose her. There was nothing wrong with his choice. She was from a good family. It was just a question of fate and destiny, as I said."

"Fate, destiny, and your father's choice," she observed coldly. "That's what it was!"

After a short pause she asked, "Pregnant?"

"Yes. . . ."

She sighed and commented: "May God make your father's life difficult."

He deliberately allowed her remark to go unchallenged, as though it were a sore that might not itch anymore if he did not scratch it. They were both silent. The woman closed her eyes from fatigue but soon opened them and smiled at him. She asked him in a tender voice, with no edge of emotion to it, "Do you think you can forget the past?"

He lowered his eyes and shuddered, feeling an almost irresistible urge to flee. He implored her, "Don't go back over the past. Let it depart, never to return."

Perhaps his heart did not mean it, but his tongue had found the right thing to say. The statement may even have accurately expressed his feeling at the moment, when he was totally absorbed by the current situation. His phrase, "Let it depart, never to return," may have sounded odd to his ears and heart, leaving anxiety in its wake, but he refused to ponder it. He fled from that subject and clung to his sincere emotion, which he had been determined not to relinquish from the beginning.

His mother asked again, "Do you love your mother the way you did in the happy days?"

Patting her hand, he replied, "I love her and pray for her safety."

He soon found himself richly repaid for his anxiety and inner struggle by the look of peace and deep contentment that spread over her withered face. He felt her hand squeeze his, as though to tell him of the gratitude she felt. They exchanged a long, dreamy, calm, smiling look that radiated an ambiance of reassurance, affection, and sorrow throughout the room. She no longer seemed to want to talk or perhaps it was too much effort for her. Her eyelids slowly drooped until they closed. He looked at her questioningly but did not move. Then her lips opened a little and a delicate, recurrent snoring could be heard.

He sat up straight and scrutinized her face. Then he closed his eyes for a bit while he conjured up the image of her other face with which she had looked at him the year before. He felt depressed, and the fear that had dogged him on his way over returned. Would he ever be permitted to see this face again? With what emotions would he encounter her if he returned? He did not know. He did not want to try to picture what lay in the world of the unknown, the future. He wanted his mind to stop and to follow events, not to try to anticipate them. He was afflicted by fear and anxiety. It was strange . . . he had wanted to flee when he was listening to her talk, so much that he had thought he would be relieved if she fell asleep, but now that he was alone he felt afraid. He did not know why. He wished she would wake up from her nap and start talking again. How long should he wait? . . . Suppose she stayed sound asleep until morning? He could not spend that much time at the mercy of fear and anxiety. He had to set a limit to his pains. . . . The next day or the day after that congratulations or condolences would be in order. Congratulations or condolences? . . . Which would he prefer? The uncertainty had to end. "Whether it's congratulations," he thought, "or condolences, I mustn't anticipate events. The most that can be said is that if we are fated to part now, we've parted friends. It will be a good ending to a bad life. But if God prolongs her life . . ."

While his mind wandered, his glance roamed about, until his eyes fell on the mirror of the wardrobe that stood opposite him. He could see reflected in it the bed with his mother's body stretched out under the blanket and he saw himself, almost blocking from view the upper half of his mother except for her hand, which she had removed from the covers when she welcomed him. He gazed at it affectionately and placed it under the covers, which he arranged carefully around her neck. Then he looked back at the mirror. It occurred to him that this mirror might reflect the image of an empty bed by the next day. Her life, in fact anyone's life, was no more permanent than these visions in the mirror. He felt even more afraid and whispered to himself, "I've got to limit my pains. . . . I've got to go." Leaving the mirror, his eyes moved around until they fell upon a table with a water pipe on it. The flexible tube was wound around the neck of the pipe like a snake. He looked at it with astonishment and disbelief, at once replaced by a raging feeling of disgust and anger. That man! . . . No doubt he was the owner of this pipe. He imagined the man sitting cross-legged on the sofa between the bed and the table, slumped over the pipe, inhaling and exhaling with pleasure as Yasin's mother fanned its coals for him. Oh . . . where was he? Somewhere in the house or outside? . . . Had the man seen him from some concealed spot? He could not bear to stay any longer with the water pipe. He cast a final look at his mother and found her fast asleep. He gently got up and went to the door. Seeing the servant in the outer hall, he told her, "Your mistress has fallen asleep. I'll return tomorrow morning."

At the door of the apartment he turned to say once more, "Tomorrow morning." He seemed to want to warn the man about the time so he could keep out of sight.

He headed straight for Costaki's bar. He drank as usual, but it did not cheer him up. He was unable to dispel the fear and anxiety from his heart. Although dreams of his mother's fortune and the comfort it would provide him did not leave his mind, he was unable to erase from his memory the image of sickness and ideas of annihilation.

When he got home at midnight he found his stepmother waiting for him on the first floor. He looked at her in surprise. Then with his heart pounding he asked, "My mother?"

Amina hid her face and said in a soft voice, "A messenger from Palace of Desire Alley came an hour before you returned. Have a long life, son."

64

Kamal's association with the British developed into a mutual friendship. Citing Yasin's misadventure in the mosque of al-Husayn, the family attempted to persuade the boy to sever his relations with these friends, but he protested that he was young, too young to be accused of spying. To keep them from stopping him, he went directly to the encampment when he got back from school, leaving his book bag with Umm Hanafi. There was no way to prevent him except by force, which they did not think appropriate, especially since he was having such a good time in the camp, directly under their eyes, and was welcomed and treated generously wherever he went. Even Fahmy showed forbearance and amused himself by watching Kamal move among the soldiers like a "monkey playing in the jungle."

"Tell al-Sayyid Ahmad," Umm Hanafi suggested once when complaining that the soldiers were fresh with her because of the accursed friendship and that some of them had mimicked the way she walked. For that reason, they deserved "to have their heads cut off." No one took her suggestion seriously, not merely out of consideration for the boy but to spare themselves too, fearing an investigation would reveal that they had concealed this friendship for a long time. They let the boy and his concerns alone. They may also have hoped that the reciprocal good feelings between the boy and the soldiers would protect the rest of them from interference or injury they might otherwise expect from the soldiers when members of the family came and went.

The happiest times of Kamal's day were those inside the encampment. Not all the soldiers were his friends in the ordinary sense of the word, but they all knew him. He would shake hands with his special friends, pressing their hands warmly, but limit himself to a salute for the others. When his arrival coincided with the sentry duty of one of his friends, the boy ran up to him cheerfully and happily, putting out his hand, only to be shocked to find that the soldier remained curiously and disturbingly rigid, as though snubbing Kamal or as though he had turned into a statue. The boy only realized this was not the case when the others burst out laughing.

It was not unusual for the alarm siren to sound suddenly when he was with his friends. They would rush to their tents, returning shortly in their uniforms and helmets and carrying their rifles. A truck would be brought out from behind the cistern building. The soldiers would quickly jump into it, until it was packed full. He would realize from the scene in front of him that a demonstration had broken out somewhere and that the soldiers were going to break it up. Fighting would certainly flare up between them and the demonstrators. The only thing that concerned him at these times was to keep sight of his friends until he saw them packed into the truck. He would gaze at them, as though bidding them farewell. When they headed off for al-Nahhasin, he would spread out his hands to pray for their safety and to recite the opening sura of the Qur'an.

He only spent half an hour each afternoon at the camp. That was the longest he could absent himself from home when he got back from school. During that half hour, all his senses were on the alert every minute. He prowled around the tents and trucks, which he inspected piece by piece. Standing in front of the pyramids of rifles, he examined them in detail, especially the barrel muzzles where death lurked. He was not permitted to get too close to them and suffered terribly because he wanted to play with them or at least touch them.

If his visit coincided with teatime, he went with his friends to the field kitchen set up at the entrance to Qirmiz Alley and took his place at the end of the "tea queue," as they called it. Then he would return behind them with a cup of tea and milk and a piece of chocolate. They would sit on the wall of the fountain to drink their tea. The soldiers all sang while he listened with interest, waiting for his turn to perform.

The life of the camp made a deep impression on him, giving an all-encompassing vividness to his flights of imagination and dreams that were engraved in his heart alongside Amina's legends and accounts of the world of mysteries and Yasin's stories and their magical universe, to which Kamal added the phantoms and visions of his daydreams about the lives of ants, sparrows, and chickens, which occupied his mind when he was on the roof surrounded by sprigs of jasmine, hyacinth beans, and pots of flowers. From this inspiration, he created a military encampment, completely equipped and staffed, next to the wall separating their roof from Maryam's. He erected tents of handkerchiefs and pencils. The weapons were twigs, the vehicles wooden clogs, and the soldiers date pits. Near the army camp he had demonstrators, represented by pebbles. He usually began the performance by distributing the pits in groups, some in the tents or by the entrances, others around the rifles. To one side there were four pits surrounding a pebble that stood for himself.

First he imitated the English style of singing. Then it was time for the pebble to sing "Visit me once each year" or "O Darling." He would move over to the pebbles and arrange them in rows as he shouted, "Long live the Nation. . . . Down with the Protectorate. . . . Long live Sa'd." Returning to the camp and giving a warning whistle, he organized the pits in columns, putting a date at the head of each one. He moved a clog as he huffed to imitate the truck's drone. After putting pits on the clog he shoved it toward the pebbles. The battle would break out, and many victims would fall on both sides. He did not allow his personal feelings to influence the course of the battle, at least not at the beginning or even midway through it. His single dominant desire was to make the battle authentic and thrilling. Both sides would struggle, pushing and pulling to try to maintain an equal number of casualties. The outcome would remain in doubt as the advantage passed back and forth, but eventually the battle would have to end. Then Kamal would find himself in an awkward position. Which side should win? His four friends, headed by Julian, were on one side, but on the other side were the Egyptian demonstrators with whom Fahmy was deeply involved emotionally. In the final moment the victory would be accorded to the demonstrators. The truck would withdraw with the few remaining soldiers, including his four friends. One time the battle ended with an honorable armistice, which warriors from both sides celebrated in song at a table set with teacups and different types of sweets.

Julian was his favorite, distinguished from the others by his good looks, gentle temperament, and greater skill in speaking Arabic. He was the one who had issued Kamal a standing invitation to tea. He was also the soldier most touched by Kamal's singing. Almost every day he would ask to hear "O Darling." He would follow the words with interest. Then he would murmur with heartfelt homesickness, "I'm going home to my country. . . . I'm going home."

Kamal appreciated the man's sensitivity and it made him like the soldier all the more. He felt comfortable enough to tell him once quite seriously that the way to escape from his distress was to "return Sa'd Pasha and go back to your country."

Julian did not receive this suggestion with the good humor Kamal had anticipated. To the contrary, he asked the boy, as he had before in comparable circumstances, not to mention Sa'd Pasha. In English he said, "Sa'd Pasha . . . no!" Thus failed the "first Egyptian negotiator," as Yasin dubbed Kamal.

The boy was surprised one day to have one of his friends present him with a caricature he had drawn of him. Kamal looked at it in astonishment and alarm, observing to himself, "My picture? . . . This isn't my picture." Deep inside, he felt it did look like him and no one else. He looked up at the men standing around him and found they were laughing. He realized it was a joke and that he should accept it with pleasure. He laughed along with them to hide his embarrassment.

When Fahmy looked at it, he studied the portrait of Kamal with amazement. Then he said, "O Lord, this picture omits none of your defects and exaggerates them . . . the small, skinny body, the long, scrawny neck, the large nose, the huge head, and the tiny eyes." Laughing, he continued: "The only thing your 'friend' seems to admire is your neat, elegant suit, and that's no fault of yours. All the credit belongs to Mother, who takes such superb care of everything in the house."

With a gloating look, Fahmy told his little brother, "It's clear what the secret of their fondness for you is. . . . They like to laugh at your appearance and foppishness. To put it plainly, you're nothing but a comic puppet to them. What have you gained from your treachery?"

Fahmy's rebuke had no impact on the boy, because he understood how hostile Fahmy was to the English. He thought his brother was plotting to separate him from them.

One day he arrived at the encampment as usual and saw Julian at the far wall of the cistern building looking with interest at the alley where the residence of the late Mr. Muhammad Ridwan was situated. Kamal went toward him and noticed that Julian was waving his hand with a gesture the boy did not understand. Kamal stopped, obeying an instinctive feeling he could not explain. His curiosity tempted him to detour around the tents erected in front of the cistern. He crept up behind Julian and looked in the same direction. There he saw a small window in a wing of the Ridwan family residence which blocked off the short alley. Maryam's smiling and responsive face could be plainly seen there. Stunned, Kamal stood looking back and forth between the soldier and the girl, almost refusing to believe his eyes.

How could Maryam have dared to appear at the window? How could she show herself to Julian in this shameless way? He was waving and she was smiling. . . . Yes, the smile was still evident on her lips. . . . Her eyes were so busy looking at the soldier that she was not aware of Kamal's presence. He accidentally moved and attracted Julian's attention. The soldier burst into laughter when he saw the boy standing behind him and made some remarks that sounded like gibberish to Kamal. Maryam, clearly terrified, retreated at breakneck speed. Kamal stared in a daze at the soldier. The way Maryam had fled only increased his suspicions, although the whole affair seemed extremely mysterious to him.

Julian asked him affectionately, "Do you know her?"

Kamal nodded his head in the affirmative and said nothing. Julian went off for a few minutes, returning with a large parcel, which he presented to Kamal, telling him as he pointed toward Maryam's house, "Take it to her."

Kamal jumped back with alarm. He shook his head from side to side stubbornly. That incident lingered in his mind, and although he sensed from the beginning that it was serious, he did not realize just how serious it was until he told the story at the evening coffee hour. Amina sat up straight, drawing away from him, with the coffee cup still in her hand, not bringing it to her lips or putting it back on the tray. Fahmy and Yasin raced over from their sofa to the one shared by the mother and Kamal and began to stare at him with unexpected interest, astonishment, and alarm.

Swallowing, Amina said, "Did you really see that? . . . Didn't your eyes deceive you?"

Fahmy grumbled, "Maryam? . . . Maryam! . . . Do you know for certain who it was?"

Yasin asked, "Was he gesturing to her and was she smiling back at him? . . . Did you really see her smile?"

Replacing her cup on the tray and leaning her head on her hand, Amina said in a threatening voice, "Kamal! Lying about a matter like this is a crime God will not forgive. Think carefully, son. . . . Didn't you exaggerate something?"

Kamal swore his weightiest oaths. Fahmy commented with bitter despair, "He's not lying. No sensible person would accuse him of lying about this. Don't you see that a person his age wouldn't be able to invent such a story?"

The mother asked in a sad voice, "But how is it possible for me to believe him?"

As though to himself, Fahmy observed, "Yes, how is it possible to believe him? . . ." Then in a serious voice he added, "But it happened . . . happened . . . happened."

The word sank into him like a dagger. When he repeated it, he seemed to be deliberately stabbing himself. It was true that events had distracted him from Maryam and that her memory appeared only at the edges of his daydreams, but this blow to her reputation struck deep into his heart. He was dazed, dazed, dazed, not knowing whether he had forgotten her or not, whether he loved or hated her, was angry out of a sense of honor or jealousy. . . . He was a dry leaf caught up in a howling storm.

"How can I believe him? . . . My trust in Maryam has been like mine for Khadija or Aisha for such a long time. Her mother is a virtuous woman. Her father, may God let him rest in peace, was a fine man . . . neighbors for a lifetime, excellent neighbors. . . ."

Yasin, who had seemed lost in thought all the while, replied in a tone not innocent of sarcasm, "Why are you surprised? . . . Since ancient times, God has created evil people from the loins of pious ones."

Amina, as though refusing to believe that she had been taken in for such a long time, protested, "With God as my witness, I've never observed anything discreditable about her."

Yasin agreed cautiously: "Nor has any of us, not even Khadija, the supreme faultfinder. People far more clever than either of us have been deceived about her."

Fahmy cried out in anguish, "How can I penetrate the world of mysteries? It's a matter that defies the imagination." He was boiling with anger at Yasin. Then it seemed to him that everyone was hateful: the English and the Egyptians in equal measure . . . men and women, but especially women. He was choking. He longed to disappear and be alone to inhale a breath of relief, but he stayed where he was, as though tied down with heavy ropes.

Yasin directed a question to Kamal: "When did she see you?"

"When Julian turned toward me."

"And then she fled from the window?"

"Yes."

"Did she notice that you saw her?"

"Our eyes met for a moment."

Yasin said sarcastically, "The poor dear! . . . No doubt she's imagining our gathering now and our distressing conversation."

"An Englishman!" Pounding his hands together, Fahmy shouted, "The daughter of al-Sayyid Muhammad Ridwan. . . ."

Shaking her head in amazement and sighing, Amina mumbled something to herself.

Yasin observed thoughtfully, "For a girl to flirt with an Englishman is no easy matter. This degree of corruption could not have appeared in a single leap."

"What do you mean?" asked Fahmy.

"I mean that her corruption must have proceeded a step at a time."

Amina implored them, "I ask you to swear by God to give up this conversation."

As though he had not heard her entreaty, Yasin kept on with his observations: "Maryam's the daughter of a lady whose art in adorning herself has been witnessed by the women of our family. . . ."

Amina cried out in a voice filled with censure and rebuke, "Yasin!"

Backing down, Yasin said, "I want to say that we as a family live according to such strict standards that we know little of what goes on around us. No matter how hard we try to guess, we imagine that other people live the way we do. We've associated with Maryam for years without knowing what she's really like, until the truth about her was discovered by the last person one would have expected to uncover the facts." He laughed and patted Kamal on the head.

Amina once again implored them fervently, "I beg you to change the topic of this conversation."

Yasin smiled and said nothing. Silence reigned. Fahmy could not bear to stay with them any longer. He responded to the inner voice that was anxiously calling for help and encouraging him to flee far from other eyes and ears, so that he could be all alone and repeat the conversation to himself from start to finish, word by word, phrase by phrase, sentence by sentence, in order to understand and fathom it. Then he could see where he stood.

65

It was after midnight when al-Sayyid Ahmad Abd al-Jawad left the home of Maryam's mother, Umm Maryam, concealing himself in the darkness of the cul-de-sac. The whole district appeared to be sound asleep, enveloped in the gloom. It had been that way every night since the English had set up camp there. No one chatted in a coffee-house, no vendor roamed about, no shop stayed open late, and no passerby stole along. The only traces of life or light were those coming from the camp. None of the soldiers had ever interfered with him as he came and went, but he felt anxious and apprehensive whenever he approached the camp, especially when returning home late at night exhausted but relaxed and in a daze that made it difficult for him even to attempt to walk safely and steadily.

He went down to al-Nahhasin Street before turning to head back toward his house, glancing stealthily at the sentry until he reached the most dangerous section of the street, where it was illuminated by light from the camp. There he was always seized by the feeling that he was an easy mark for any predator. He quickened his steps to reach the dark area near the entrance to his house but had hardly advanced a step when his ears rang as a rude, gruff voice yelled after him in gibberish. He realized from the violent tone and concision of the words, even though he could not understand them, that an order not subject to debate was being tossed at him. He stopped walking and turned, terrified, toward the voice.

He saw another soldier, not the sentry, heading toward him, armed to the teeth. What new development had brought on this treatment? Was the man intoxicated? Perhaps he had been overcome by a sudden urge to attack someone? Or was he out to plunder and loot? With a pounding heart and a dry throat, al-Sayyid Ahmad watched the soldier approach. The lingering effects of his intoxication fled.

This soldier stopped a few feet away from him and in a commanding voice addressed a few brisk words to him. Al-Sayyid Ahmad naturally did not understand a single one. The soldier pointed toward Palace Walk with his free hand. Al-Sayyid Ahmad looked desperately and ingratiatingly at him, suffering bitterly from his inability to communicate or to convince the man that he was innocent of his accusations. He wished he could at least discover what the man wanted. It occurred to him that the soldier had gestured down Palace Walk to tell him to move away, thinking he did not live in this neighborhood. He pointed in turn to his house, so the man would understand that he was a resident returning home. The soldier ignored his gesture and snarled at him, pointing persistently in the other direction. He motioned with his head, as though urging al-Sayyid Ahmad to go in that direction. Apparently growing impatient, he seized him by the shoulder, forcibly turned him around, and shoved him in the back. Al-Sayyid Ahmad found himself moving toward Palace Walk with the other man behind him. He surrendered to his fate, but his joints felt like rubber. On his way to an unknown destination, he passed the military camp and the cistern building. After that, the last trace of light from the camp vanished.

He waded into the waves of gloomy darkness and profound silence, seeing nothing but phantom houses and hearing only the heavy footsteps that followed him with mechanical precision, as though counting out the minutes or perhaps seconds left for him to live. Yes, he expected at each moment to be dealt a blow that would finish him off. He walked along, waiting for it, his eyes staring into the darkness, his mouth pursed from worry, his Adam's apple jerking up and down as he tried to swallow to relieve his dry, burning throat. He was startled by a gleam of light that made him look down. He almost screamed from dismay, like a child, as his heart plummeted. He saw a circle of light going back and forth and realized that it was caused by rays of light from a battery-powered lantern that his warder had turned on to see where he was going. He got his breath back after his sudden alarm subsided, but this relief was short-lived. He was once more seized by fear, fear of the death to which he was being led. Once more he expected to die from moment to moment. He was like a drowning man flailing about in the water who thinks he sees a crocodile preparing to attack. When it becomes clear that the beast is just some plants floating in the water, he enjoys a momentary relief at being spared this danger, before choking again under the pressure of the real danger presented by the ocean.

Where was the man leading him? If he could only talk that gibberish, he would ask. It seemed he would be forced to go all the way to the cemetery at Bab al-Nasr. There was no trace of any man or beast. Where was the night watchman? He was alone at the mercy of a merciless person. When had he ever suffered like this? Could he remember? In a nightmare . . . yes, it was a nightmare he had had several times when he was sick. Even in a nightmare the gloom is occasionally brightened by a flash of hope, considerately letting the sleeper feel that his dream is not real and he will be saved from it sooner or later. It was farfetched to assume that destiny would grant him any comparable hope. He was awake, not asleep. This soldier, armed to the teeth, was a reality, not a phantom. The street witnessing his humiliation and captivity was frighteningly tangible, not imaginary. His suffering was real, there was no doubt about that. The least sign of resistance from him would probably result in the loss of his head. There was no doubt of that.

Umm Maryam had told him when she said goodbye to him, "Until tomorrow." Tomorrow? Would that day ever come?

"Ask the heavy feet rocking the earth behind your back. . . . Ask the rifle with its sharp-pointed bayonet."

She had also teased him: "The fragrance of wine coming from your lips is about to intoxicate me." Now both the wine and his mind had flown off. The time for passion was gone, although only a few minutes before it had been all that mattered in life. Now suffering was his whole life. . . . Only a few short minutes separated the two conditions. A few minutes?

When he reached the corner of al-Khurunfush, his eyes were attracted by rays of light flashing in the darkness. He looked along the street and saw a lantern carried by another soldier driving before him an uncertain number of figures. He wondered whether the soldiers had been given orders to capture all the men they came across at night. Where were they leading them? What punishment would be meted out? He wondered about these things for a long time with astonishment and alarm, although the sight of these new victims provided some consolation and relief for his heart. At least he was not the only one, as he had thought. He had found some mates to share his affliction. They would keep him from feeling so lonely and would share his fate. He was a short distance ahead of them.

He began to listen to their footsteps with the relief a person lost in a desert feels on hearing human voices carried to him by the wind. His dearest wish was for them to catch up with him so that he could join their group, regardless of whether he knew them or not. Let their hearts beat in unison as they marched briskly to an unknown destination. These men were innocent. He was innocent. So why had they been captured? What special reason could there be for taking him captive? He was not one of the revolutionaries and was not involved in politics. He was not even young. Were the English privy to the secrets in men's hearts or capable of scrutinizing their emotions? Were they going to arrest members of the general public after arresting all the leaders? If only he knew English so he could ask his captor. . . . Where was Fahmy to interpret for him?

He was stung by painful homesickness. Where were Fahmy, Yasin, Kamal, Khadija, Aisha, and their mother? Could his family imagine his disgraceful state? Their only image of him was one of venerable and exalted power. Would they be able to imagine that a soldier had shoved him in the back almost hard enough to make him fall on the ground and herded him along like livestock? When he remembered his family, he felt such painful homesickness that tears almost came to his eyes.

On the way, he passed shadowy houses and stores whose owners he knew and coffeehouses he had frequented, especially when he was younger. It made him sad to walk past them as a prisoner with no one coming to his aid or even offering their condolences for his situation. He really felt that the most distressing form of humiliation was that suffered in his own district.

He looked up to the heavens to transmit his thoughts to God, who could see into his heart. He sent his prayers to Him without saying anything with his tongue, not even under his breath. He was ashamed to mention God's name when his body had not been cleansed of the vapors of wine and the sweat of lovemaking. His fear increased, because his polluted state might interfere with his salvation. He might meet a fate that suited his debauchery. Pessimism and dejection gained control of his emotions. He was on the verge of despair when, approaching the lemon market, he heard unintelligible sounds, instead of the silence broken only by footsteps. Staring into the darkness, he listened intently, alternating between fear and hope. He could hear a clamor but did not know if it came from men or beasts. Before long he could tell it was shouting. He could not keep from exclaiming to himself, "Human voices!"

As the road turned, he saw lights moving. At first he thought they were more lanterns, but it became clear that they were flaming torches. By their light he saw one side of Bab al-Futuh. There were British soldiers standing under this ancient city gate. Then he caught a glimpse of Egyptian policemen. The sight of them quickened his pulse.

"Now I'll know what they want with me," he thought. "It's only a few more steps. Why are the English soldiers and the Egyptian policemen crowded together at the gate? Why are they rounding up citizens from all areas of the district? I'll know everything shortly. Everything? I'll seek God's protection and submit my destiny to Him. I'll remember this dreadful hour for the remainder of my life, if there is a remainder. . . . Bullets, the gallows, not to mention the brutal injustice the English inflicted on the villagers at Dinshawai. . . . Am I going to join the roster of martyrs? Will I become an item of news about the revolution to be passed on by Muhammad Iffat, Ali Abd al-Rahim, and Ibrahim al-Far the way we've been discussing such things at our evening sessions? Can you imagine one of our parties with your place empty? God's mercy on you. . . . 'He's gone and done for.' How they'll weep for you. They'll remember you for a long time. Then you'll be forgotten. How upset I am. Submit your fate to your Creator. O God, encompass us, don't oppose us."

As he approached the British soldiers they looked at him in a stern, cold, threatening manner. He had a sinking feeling along with intense pain in his chest. Was it time for him to stop? He dragged his feet and hesitated uncertainly.

"Enter," an Egyptian policeman shouted to him, pointing to the area inside the great portal. Al-Sayyid Ahmad looked inside questioningly but also ingratiatingly and pitifully. He passed between the English soldiers, barely able to see what was in front of him, he was so scared. He wished he could hide his head in his arms in response to his instinctive fear. What he saw under the gateway explained, without any need for questions, why he was wanted. He saw that a deep pit like a trench had been dug there to obstruct the road. He likewise saw a swarm of citizens working nonstop to fill the hole under the supervision of the police. They were carrying baskets of dirt, which they emptied into the trench. Everyone was working zealously and quickly while their eyes glanced stealthily and fearfully at the English soldiers stationed at the entrance to the gate.

A policeman came up to him and threw him a basket, telling him in a gruff voice that sounded threatening, "Do what the others are doing." Then he added in a whisper, "Be quick so you don't get hurt."

This final sentence was the first humane expression he had encountered during his terrifying journey, and it felt like air in the throat of a man close to asphyxiation. Al-Sayyid Ahmad bent over the basket to pick it up by the handle and asked the policeman in a whisper, "Will I be set free when the work's completed?"

The policeman whispered, "God willing."

He sighed profoundly and felt like crying. It seemed he had been born anew. With his left hand he lifted the bottom of his cloak and tucked it into the belt of his caftan so it would not impede his work. He took the basket to the sidewalk where dirt was piled. Putting the basket at his feet he filled his hands with dirt and emptied them into the basket. When it was full, he carried it to the hole and threw the dirt in before returning to the sidewalk. He kept on with this, surrounded by groups of men, both old and young, some in modern dress and others wearing traditional turbans. They all worked with a high degree of energy stemming from their desire to live.

He was refilling his basket when an elbow nudged him. He turned to see who it was and recognized a friend named Ghunaym Hamidu, the owner of an olive-oil-pressing firm in al-Gamaliya and a guest at some of al-Sayyid Ahmad's parties. They were delighted to see each other and soon were whispering together.

"So you got caught too!"

"Before you. I arrived a little before midnight. I saw you getting your basket, so as I went back and forth with my basket I began to follow a path that would gradually bring me over to you."

"Welcome . . . welcome. Aren't any more of our friends here?"

"You're the only one I've found."

"The policeman told me they'll let us go when we finish the work."

"I was told that too. May our Lord hear us."

"They've ruined my knees, may God destroy their homes."

"So far as I can tell, I don't even have knees anymore."

They exchanged a quick smile. "How did this pit get here?"

"I was told that a bunch of the boys from al-Husayn dug it at the beginning of the night to prevent the trucks from coming through here. They also say a truck fell in."

"If that's true, then you can say goodbye to us."

The second time they worked beside each other at the dirt pile they were somewhat more resigned to their situation. Their spirits had revived and they could not keep themselves from smiling as they filled their baskets with dirt like construction workers.

Ghunaym whispered, "May God and His blessings repay us for these sons of bitches."

Al-Sayyid Ahmad smiled and whispered back, "I hope they're going to pay us the normal wage."

"Where did they catch you?"

"In front of my house."

"It figures."

"What about you?"

"I had taken some dope, but I got over it fast. The English are stronger than cocaine."

"They're even more effective than throwing up."

By the light of the torches the men went back and forth quickly between the sidewalk with the dirt and the ditch. They stirred up the dust until it spread throughout the vaulted area of the gate, filling the air. They had trouble breathing. Sweat poured from their brows and plastered their faces with mud. They were coughing from inhaling the dust. They looked like ghosts brought to light when the hole gaped open.

In any case, he was no longer alone. There was this friend and the other men from his district. Even the Egyptian policemen were with them in their hearts. The fact that they had been stripped of their weapons was evidence of that. They no longer had swords in metal scabbards dangling from their belts.

"Be patient," he advised himself. "Be patient. Perhaps this suffering will pass. Did you think you'd work until morning or even almost till noon? Buck up. You won't always be carrying dirt and exploited to fill the hole. . . . The hole refuses to fill up. . . . There's nothing to be gained from complaining. To whom would you complain? Your body's powerful and strong and can take it, despite being impaired by the evening's inebriation. What time is it? It wouldn't be prudent to check now. If this had not happened to me, I'd be stretched out in bed enjoying a sound sleep. I would be able to wash my head and face and get a refreshing drink flavored with orange blossoms from the water jug. Congratulations to us for this participation in the hell of the revolution. Why not? The country is in revolt every day. Every hour there are casualties and martyrs. Reading the papers and passing on news is one thing, but carrying dirt at gunpoint is something else. Congratulations to all of you asleep in your beds. O God, preserve us. . . . I'm not meant for this . . . not meant for this. God vanquish those who doubt Your power. We are weak. . . . I'm not meant for this.

"Does Fahmy realize the dangers threatening him? He's reviewing his lessons now, unaware of what is happening to his father. He said no to me for the first time in his life. He said it with tears in his eyes, but it means the same thing. I didn't tell his mother and I won't. Should I reveal my lack of power to her? Should I seek help from her weakness after my power has failed? Certainly not. . . . Let her remain ignorant of the whole affair. He says he's not exposing himself to any danger. Really? God, hear my prayer. If it had not been for that, I wouldn't have been so easy on him. God preserve him. God preserve all of us from the evil of these days. What time is it now? Once it's morning, we'll be safe. They won't kill us in front of the people."

"I spat on the ground to clear the dust from my throat," his friend remarked, "and one of the policemen shot me a look that made my hair stand on end."

"Don't spit. Do like me. I've swallowed enough dirt to fill this hole."

"Perhaps Zubayda cursed you?"

"Perhaps."

"Wasn't filling her hole better than filling this one?"

"It was even more strenuous!"

They smiled quickly at each other. Then Ghunaym said with a sigh, "God help me, my back's broken."

"Me too. Our only consolation is that we're sharing some of the pains of the freedom fighters."

"What do you think? Should I throw my basket in the soldiers' faces and cry out at the top of my lungs, 'Long live Sa'd'?"

"Has the dope started working again?"

"What a loss! . . . It was a piece the size of the pupil of your eye. I stirred it in my tea three times. Afterward I went to al-Tambakshiya to listen to Shaykh Ali Mahmud recite poetry in the home of al-Hamzawi. On my way back, shortly before midnight, I was telling myself, 'Your old lady's waiting for you now. There's nothing to be gained from disappointing her.' Then that monkey popped up and drove me along in front of him."

"May our Lord compensate you."

"Amen."

Soldiers brought in more men, some from al-Husayn and others from al-Nahhasin, who were quickly incorporated into the work force. Al-Sayyid Ahmad looked around. The place was almost packed full of people. They spread out around the trench in every direction, going between the sidewalk and the hole without taking a break, their panting faces illuminated by light from the torches. They looked thoroughly exhausted, humiliated, and afraid. There was blessed safety in numbers. "They won't slaughter this swarm of people," he reflected. "They wouldn't take the innocent along with the guilty. Where do you suppose the guilty ones are? Where are those brave young men? Do they know their brothers have fallen in the hole they dug? May God destroy them. Did they think that digging a hole would bring Sa'd back or drive the English out of Egypt? I'll certainly abandon my nightlife if God grants me a new lease on life. Abandon my nightlife? It's no longer safe to go out at night. Will life retain any savor? Life loses its savor in the shadow of the revolution. Revolution . . . in other words, a soldier takes you captive, you carry dirt in your hands, Fahmy says no to you. No! When will the world return to normal? A headache? . . . Yes, a headache and I want to throw up too. A few minutes to rest. I don't want anything more than that. Maryam's mother, Bahija, is sound asleep. Amina's waiting for me like Ghunaym's "old lady." There's no way you could imagine what's happened to your father. O Lord, the dust's filling my nose and eyes. O Master Husayn. . . . Fill, fill . . . isn't all this enough dirt for you? O grandson of the Messenger of God, Husayn. . . . The Battle of the Trench, that's what the revered preacher called it. The Prophet Muhammad, God's peace and blessings on him, fought a Battle of the Trench and worked alongside the other men, digging the dirt out with his own hands. His enemies were pagans back then. Why are the pagans winning today? It's a corrupt age. . . . The times are corrupt. I'm corrupt. Will they remain camped in front of my house until the revolution's over?"

"Did you hear the cock?"

Al-Sayyid Ahmad listened intently and mumbled, "The cock's crowing! Is it dawn?"

"Yes, but the hole won't be filled up until morning. . . . The important thing is that I need to relieve myself, badly."

Al-Sayyid Ahmad's mind thought about the lower part of his body. He realized that he needed to go too. Part of his pain was no doubt related to his swollen bladder. Thinking about it seemed to make it much worse, and the pressure of his bladder was intense. "Me too," he said.

"What can we do?"

"There's no solution at hand."

"Look over there at that monkey pissing in front of Ali al-Zajjaj's store. . . ."

"Oh. . . ."

"Getting a little urine out of my body's more important to me now than getting the English out of Egypt."

"Get the English out of all of Egypt? Let them get out of al-Nahhasin to begin with."

"O Lord. . . . Look. The soldiers are still bringing people in."

Al-Sayyid Ahmad saw a new batch making their way toward the trench.

66

When al-Sayyid Ahmad awoke it was almost time for the afternoon prayer. News of his mishap had spread among his family and friends. Many of them stopped by the house to congratulate him on his deliverance. Despite the seriousness of the topic, he told them the whole story in a style graced by comic touches and flourishes that inspired their comments.

Amina was the first to hear the story, which he recounted while still psychologically shattered and physically weak, scarcely able to believe he had escaped alive. She heard the terrifying aspects uncensored. Once he fell asleep, she wept profusely and began to pray to God to watch over her family with His care and mercy. She prayed so long she felt she was losing her voice.

Al-Sayyid Ahmad, on finding himself surrounded by friends, especially close ones like Ibrahim al-Far, Ali Abd al-Rahim, and Muhammad Iffat, recovered his spirits and had difficulty ignoring the humorous aspects of the incident, which finally won out over everything else. His rendition turned the episode into a comedy. He might have been telling them about one of his escapades.

While the top floor was crowded with male visitors, the family gathered on the lower floor, except for the mother, who was busy with Umm Hanafi preparing coffee and cold drinks. Once again the sitting room witnessed a reunion of Yasin, Fahmy, Kamal, Khadija, and Aisha for the traditional coffee hour. Khalil and Ibrahim Shawkat had been with them all day long but had gone to the father's room shortly after he had awakened, leaving the brothers and sisters alone. Their sorrow over what had happened to their father vanished as they became reassured. Their hearts were filled with affection, and they jumped at the chance to chat and joke with each other the way they had in the past. They had felt anxious until they had seen their father with their own eyes. They had gone to him, one after the other, kissed his hand, and prayed he would have a long and peaceful life. Then they had left his room with military order and discipline.

Although the father had merely held his hand out to Yasin, Fahmy, and Kamal without saying a word, he had smiled at Khadija and

Aisha, asking them tenderly how they were doing and if they were in good health. They had been treated to this tenderness only after they got married. Kamal had noticed it with delighted astonishment, as though he were the recipient. In fact, Kamal was the happiest of anyone whenever his sisters visited. On those occasions he enjoyed a profound happiness tarnished only by anticipation of the visit's end. The warning would come when one of the men, Ibrahim or Khalil, stretched or yawned. Then he would say, "It's time for us to leave." The phrase was a command to be obeyed, not rejected.

Neither of Kamal's sisters was gracious enough, even once, to tell her husband, for example, "You go. I'll join you tomorrow."

In time, Kamal became accustomed to the strange bond linking his sisters to their husbands and accepted its authority. He contented himself with their short visits every now and then and rejoiced without longing for more. Yet he could not keep himself from asking wishfully sometimes, "Why don't you return and live here the way you used to?"

His mother would quickly reply, "May God spare them the evil of your good wishes."

The most amazing thing he had noticed about their married life was the bizarre change that had befallen their bellies and the attendant symptoms, which seemed as frightening as a disease and as exotic as legends. He had learned some new concepts, like pregnancy and cravings, and associated ones like vomiting, malaise, and the consumption of pellets of dry clay. . . . So what was the matter with Aisha's belly? When would it stop growing? It looked like an inflated waterskin. Khadija's belly too appeared to be undergoing the same transformation. If Aisha with her ivory complexion and golden hair craved mud, what would Khadija crave? As it turned out, Khadija confounded his fears and craved pickles.

Kamal had countless questions but was unable to elicit a satisfactory answer for any of them. His mother told him that Aisha's belly, as well as Khadija's, would produce a tiny baby, who would be the apple of his eye. But where was this baby living? How was it living? Did it hear and see? What did it hear and see? How did it come into existence? Where did it come from? For these significant questions he received answers that deserved to be added to the lore about saints and jinn, amulets and spells, and other such matters he had gleaned from his mother's personal encyclopedia. Therefore he asked Aisha with concern, "When will the baby come out?"

She laughed and replied, "Be patient. It won't be long."

Yasin asked, "Aren't you in your ninth month?"

She answered, "Yes, although my mother-in-law insists I'm in my eighth."

Khadija observed sharply, "It's just that our mother-in-law always wants to have a different opinion. That's all there is to it."

Since everyone knew of the frequent disputes that flared up between Khadija and her mother-in-law, they looked at each other and laughed.

Aisha said, "I want you to move to our house and stay with us until the English evacuate your street."

Khadija said enthusiastically, "Yes. Why not? The house is large. You'll be comfortable and have plenty of space. Papa and Mama can stay with Aisha because she's on the middle floor, and the rest of you can stay with me."

Kamal was overjoyed by the suggestion and to prod them asked, "Who will tell Papa?"

Fahmy shrugged his shoulders and said, "You both know perfectly well that Papa will not agree."

"But he likes to go out at night, and he'll be exposed to interference from the soldiers," Khadija protested. "What criminals they are! To lead him off in the dark and make him carry dirt. . . . My head spins whenever I think about it."

Aisha said, "I waited for my turn to kiss his hand so I could examine him from head to toe, to reassure myself. My heart was pounding and my eyes were blinking away tears. . . . God's curse on those dogs, the bastards."

Yasin smiled. Winking at Kamal, he cautioned Aisha, "Don't insult the English. They have a friend among us."

Fahmy observed sarcastically, "Perhaps it would amuse Papa to know that the soldier who captured him last night was just one of Kamal's buddies."

Smiling at Kamal, Aisha asked, "Do you still love them after what they've done?"

Blushing from embarrassment and confusion, Kamal stammered, "If they had known he was my father, they wouldn't have harmed him."

Yasin could not keep himself from laughing so loudly he had to put a hand over his mouth. He looked up at the ceiling warily, as though afraid the sound of his laughter might reach the upper story. Then he said mockingly, "What you ought to say is: If they had realized that Kamal was Egyptian they would not have tormented Egypt and the Egyptians. They just don't know any better."

Khadija said fiercely, "You should leave this talk to someone else.... Are you denying that you have befriended them too?" She addressed Kamal in as biting a tone: "Will you be brave enough to perform the Friday prayer at the mosque of our master al-Husayn now that people know about your friendship with them?"

Yasin understood her allusion and replied with mock regret, "It's permissible for you to give me a hard time now that you're married and have acquired some basic human rights...."

"Didn't I have this particular right before?"

"God's mercy on those bygone years ... but it's marriage that returns the spirit to wretched girls. Bow down in thanks to the saints ... and to Umm Hanafi's incantations and prescriptions."

Trying not to laugh, Khadija retorted, "You've gained the right to attack people, whether or not what you say is true, after inheriting from your late mother and becoming a man of property."

With childish glee Aisha said, as though she knew nothing about it, "My brother's a man of property.... How lovely to hear that.... Are you really rich, Mr. Yasin?"

Khadija said, "Let me enumerate his properties for you. Listen, lady: the store in al-Hamzawi, a residence in al-Ghuriya, the house in Palace of Desire Alley ..."

Shaking his head and lowering his eyes, Yasin recited, "And from the evil of the envious person when he envies ..." (Qur'an, 113:5)

Khadija continued her comments without paying any attention to his interruption: "And valuables like jewelry and coins worth even more than the real estate."

Yasin cried out with genuine sorrow, "That all disappeared, by your life. Stolen. That son of a bitch stole them. Father asked him if she had left jewelry or money, but the thief said, 'Search for yourselves. God knows I paid her expenses during her illness from my own money.' What a man! His 'own money' ... that son of a washerwoman."

Aisha said sympathetically, "The poor dear ... sick, confined to bed, at the mercy of a man who wanted her money ... without a friend or a loved one. She left the world without anyone to grieve for her."

Yasin asked, "Without anyone to grieve for her?"

Khadija pointed through the half-open door at Yasin's clothes hanging on a rack. She protested ironically, "And this black bow tie? . . . Isn't that a sign of mourning?"

Yasin said seriously, "I really did mourn for her, may our Lord be merciful to her and forgive her sins. Didn't we become reconciled at our last meeting? May God be merciful to her and forgive her and the rest of us."

Khadija lowered her head a little and raised her eyebrows to gaze at him, as though looking over the top of a pair of spectacles. She said, "Ahem, ahem . . . listen to our revered preacher." She cast him a skeptical look and continued: "But I suspect that your sorrow was not too deep?"

He looked at her furiously and replied, "Praise to God, I did not fall short in my duties to her. I received people and had the Qur'an recited for three nights. Every Friday I visit the cemetery with fragrant herbs and fruit. Do you want me to strike my face, wail, and spread dirt on my head? Men grieve differently from women."

She shook her head as though to say, "You have assisted me. May God assist you." Then with a sigh she remarked, "Oh, the grief of men! . . . But tell me, by my life, didn't the shop, apartment, and house alleviate some of the torment of your grief?"

He grumbled, "The person was right who said, 'An ugly tongue bespeaks an ugly face.' "

"Who said that?"

Smiling, he replied, "Your mother-in-law!"

Aisha laughed. Fahmy laughed too and asked Khadija, "Haven't relations between you improved?"

Aisha answered for her, "Relations between the English and the Egyptians will improve before theirs do."

Khadija for the first time spoke resentfully: "She's a strong-willed woman. May our Lord hold it against her. By God, I'm innocent and falsely accused."

"We all believe you," Yasin commented sarcastically. "There's no need for an oath. We'll testify to that before God on Judgment Day."

Fahmy asked Aisha, "How are you doing with her?"

Glancing apprehensively at Khadija, she replied, "As well as could be hoped."

Khadija shouted, "Fie on your sister Aisha. She knows when to lead and when to bow her head. Fie. . . ."

Pretending to be serious, Yasin said, "At any rate, may God be merciful to your mother-in-law and my sincere congratulations to you."

Khadija observed sarcastically, "God willing, the real congratulations will soon be for you when you're escorted to your second bride. Isn't that so?"

He could not help but laugh. "May God hear your prayer," he said.

Aisha asked with interest, "Really?"

He thought a little. Then he said somewhat seriously, "The Believer does not put his hand back in the lair to be bitten a second time, but who knows what the morrow will bring? Perhaps second, third, and fourth brides."

Khadija exclaimed, "That's what I expect. May God be compassionate to your grandfather."

They all laughed, even Kamal. Then Aisha said sadly, "Poor Zaynab! She was such a fine girl."

"She was . . . and also stupid, with a father as unbearable as my own. If she had been content to live with me the way I wanted, I would never have renounced her."

"Don't admit that. Protect your honor. Don't give Khadija a chance to gloat over your misfortune."

He said scornfully, "She got what she deserves. Let her father brew her up and drink her down."

Aisha muttered, "But she's pregnant, poor dear. Are you pleased that your child will grow up in someone else's custody until returned to you as a boy?"

Oh, she had drawn blood. His child would grow up in the mother's custody the way Yasin had before him. Perhaps he would suffer misery like Yasin's or even worse. He might grow up hating his mother or father. In any case, it was miserable. Frowning, he said, "Let his fate be like his father's. There's nothing that can be done about it."

They were quiet for a time until Kamal asked Khadija, "And you, sister, when will your baby come out?"

Laughing and feeling her belly, she answered, "He's still in his first stage."

Studying her face, he told her innocently, "You've really gotten thin, sister, and your face has become ugly."

They all laughed, covering their mouths with their hands. They laughed so much that Kamal felt embarrassed and confused. Khadija was unable to take offense at Kamal and was inclined to flow with the current. Laughing, she agreed: "I confess that during this time of special cravings I have lost all the flesh that Umm Hanafi worked hard for so many years to create. I've grown thin, my nose sticks out, and my eyes are sunken. I imagine my husband's looking everywhere in vain for the bride he married."

They laughed again. Yasin commented, "The truth is that your husband has been wronged. Despite his obvious stupidity, he's good-looking. Glory to God who united a stallion and a jenny."

Khadija pretended to ignore him. Pointing toward Aisha, she told Fahmy, "Both her husband and mine are slow. They hardly leave the house by night or day. They have no interests or jobs. Her husband squanders his time smoking or playing the lute like those beggars who go to people's houses at the festivals. My husband is always lying around smoking or chattering so much it makes me dizzy."

"Aristocrats don't work," Aisha said apologetically.

Khadija sneered. "I beg your pardon. . . . It's right for you to defend that life. The truth is that God never united two such identical people as when he united the two of you. When it comes to laziness, mildness, and indolence you're the same person. Mr. Fahmy, by the Prophet, her husband spends the whole day smoking and playing music while she adorns herself and flits back and forth in front of the mirror."

Yasin inquired, "Why not, so long as what she sees in the mirror is pretty?" Before Khadija could open her mouth, he quickly asked, "Tell me, sister, what will you do if your child looks like you?"

She was fed up with his attacks and answered him seriously, "With God's permission he will resemble his father, grandfather, grandmother, or aunt. . . . If . . ." She laughed. "If he insists on resembling his mother, then he'll deserve to be banished even more than Sa'd Pasha."

With the tone of a man of experience, Kamal told her, "The English don't care about beauty, sister. They like my head and nose a lot."

Khadija struck her breast with her hand and cried out, "They claim to be your friends when all the time they're making fun of you. . . . May our Lord send another zeppelin after them."

Aisha cast a tender look at Fahmy and said, "How your prayer would please some people."

Fahmy smiled and muttered, "How can I be happy when they have gullible friends in our house?"

"What a pity your influence has failed with the boy."

"Some people aren't helped by good influences."

Kamal protested, "Didn't I ask Julian to bring back Sa'd Pasha?"

Khadija laughed and said, "Next time have him swear by that head of yours he likes so much."

More than once Fahmy had felt they were trying to draw him into the conversation and distract him every chance they got, although that did nothing to dissipate his feeling of alienation, which for a long time had come between him and his family whenever he was with them. He would feel alienated or alone no matter how crowded the coffee hour was. He would withdraw into his heart, grief, and zeal when surrounded by giddy, laughing people. When they could, they even made a joke out of Sa'd's banishment.

He glanced stealthily at each of them in succession and found they were all happy. Aisha was flourishing, although a little tired because of the pregnancy. She was happy about everything, even her fatigue. Khadija was bouncy and quick to laugh. Yasin's health was outstanding, and he looked blissful. Who among them cared what was happening nowadays? Who among them was concerned whether Sa'd was in Egypt or in exile and whether the English left or stayed? He felt like a stranger or at least estranged from these people. Although this feeling was usually blunted by his magnanimous spirit, now he felt angry and resentful, perhaps because of what he had been going through over the past few days. He had frequently expected to hear that Maryam was getting married. He had been concerned and troubled about that, even though he had already resigned himself to it in despair. As time passed he had almost accepted the idea. Even his love had retreated from center stage in his emotions while he was distracted by weighty concerns. But the incident with Julian had been like an earthquake. What was the meaning of her flirtation with an Englishman she could not hope to marry? Would anyone but a shameless woman do such a thing? Was Maryam a shameless woman? What had happened to the object of his dreams?

The first chance he had had to be alone with Kamal he had asked his little brother to tell the story again, insisting on all the details. How had he observed what took place? Where was the soldier standing? Where was Kamal standing? Was he certain that it was Maryam herself who was in the little window? Was she really looking at the soldier? Did he see her smile at the man? Where . . . ? Was . . . ? Did . . . ? Clenching his teeth as though trying to crush the distress that was tormenting him, Fahmy had asked, "Did she act scared and leave when she saw you?"

Afterward Fahmy had visualized the whole episode, gesture by gesture and scene by scene. He imagined her smile at length until he could almost see her lips parting, the way he had seen them the day of Aisha's wedding when the girl was following along after the bride in the courtyard of the Shawkat family residence.

"It seems Mama won't join us today," Aisha said sadly.

Khadija commented, "The house is full of visitors."

Yasin laughingly remarked, "I'm afraid the soldiers will become suspicious of the number of people coming here and think a political rally is being held in our home."

Khadija said proudly, "Papa's friends are so numerous they could hide the sun."

Aisha observed, "I saw Mr. Muhammad Iffat himself at the head of the procession."

Khadija confirmed her sister's statement: "He's been his best friend since before we saw the light of day."

Shaking his head, Yasin said, "Papa accused me falsely of destroying their friendship."

"Doesn't divorce separate even the dearest friends?"

Yasin smilingly replied, "Not your father's friends!"

Aisha boasted, "Who would ever want to oppose Papa? By God, there's no one in the whole world who's equal to him." Then with a sigh she continued: "Whenever I think of what happened to him last night, my hair turns gray."

Khadija had finally had enough of Fahmy's despondency. She decided to attack it directly, after indirect methods had failed. She turned toward him and asked, "Brother, do you see how gracious our Lord was the day you were denied your wish with regard to . . . Maryam?"

Fahmy looked at her with astonished embarrassment. All eyes were immediately focused on him with concern, even Kamal's. Profound silence reigned, revealing the existence of a stifled sentiment that had been ignored or concealed until Khadija expressed it so boldly. They looked at the young man as though awaiting his reply, almost as though he was the one who had asked the question.

Yasin thought he had better end the silence before it got any worse and caused more pain. Pretending to be happy, he commented, "The reason is that your brother's a saint, and God loves His saints."

Fahmy, suffering from anguish and embarrassment, said tersely, "This is an old issue that's been forgotten."

To shield him, Aisha said, "Mr. Fahmy wasn't the only one to be deceived by her. We were all taken in."

Khadija defended herself as best she could against this alleged oversight: "Well, I was never convinced for a moment—even when I believed she was innocent—that she was worthy of you."

Pretending to dismiss the whole affair, Fahmy said, "This is an old issue that's been forgotten. An Englishman, an Egyptian, it's all the same thing. Let's skip all this."

Yasin found himself thinking once again about the "issue" of Maryam. . . . Maryam? He had never looked at her in the past if she came into view except in a cursory fashion. Fahmy's attachment to her had increased Yasin's desire to ignore her, until her scandal had been broadcast in the family. That had aroused his interest, and he had wondered for a long time what sort of girl she was. He would have liked to study her carefully and observe the girl who had aroused the desire of an Englishman sent to fight, not flirt. Yasin's anger at her was only a conversational device. He was actually enraptured by the presence nearby of a daring "fallen woman," separated from him by a single wall. His broad, sturdy chest was pervaded by a bestial intoxication bringing out the hunting instinct in him, but he held back in honor of Fahmy's sorrow, for he loved his brother. He limited himself to a passive, emotional delight, although no one in the whole district so stirred his interest as Maryam.

"It's time to leave," Khadija remarked as she rose. She had heard the voices of Ibrahim and Khalil, who were coming in from the hall. Everyone stood up. Some stretched while others adjusted their clothing. Only Kamal remained seated. He looked at the door of the sitting room mournfully, his heart pounding.

67

Al-Sayyid Ahmad sat at his desk bent over his ledgers, immersing himself in his daily tasks, which helped him forget, if only temporarily, his personal worries as well as the bloody public ones that were in the news all the time. He had grown to love the store as much as his evenings of fellowship and music, because in both situations he successfully freed himself from the hell of thinking. Although the store's atmosphere was full of haggling, selling, buying, making money, and similar concerns of ordinary, daily life, it restored his confidence that everything could return to normal, to the original condition of peace and stability. Peace? Where had it gone and when would it be ready to return? Even in his store there were distressing, whispered conversations about bloody events. Customers were no longer content just to bargain and buy. Their tongues kept belaboring the news and bewailing events. Over the bags of rice and coffee beans he had heard about the battle of Bulaq, the massacres at Asyut, the funeral processions with tens of coffins, and the young man who had wrested a machine gun away from the enemy, intending to bring it back into al-Azhar Mosque, only to be killed before he could get there as swarms of bullets sank into his body. News like this, tinged crimson with blood, assaulted his ears from time to time in the very place where he had taken refuge, seeking to forget.

How miserable it was to live constantly in the shadow of death. Why did not the revolution achieve its objectives quickly before he or any of his family was harmed? . . . He was not stingy with money and did not begrudge it his emotional involvement, but sacrificing a life was another matter. What kind of punishment was God inflicting on His flock? Life had become cheap and blood was flowing. . . . The revolution was no longer a thrilling spectacle. It threatened his security whenever he came or went and menaced the life of his rebellious son. His enthusiasm for it, but not for its goal, had dwindled. He still dreamt of independence and the return of Sa'd, but without a revolution, bloodshed, or terror. He chanted slogans with the demonstrators and was zealous with the zealots, but his mind was attached to life and struggled to resist this current, like a tree trunk in a flood, its branches torn off by storms. Nothing, no matter how great, would weaken his love for life. Let him keep his love for life to the end of his days. If only Fahmy felt that way too, so that he would not sacrifice his life; Fahmy, the disobedient son who had thrown himself into the stream without a life preserver.

"Is al-Sayyid Ahmad here?"

He heard the voice and sensed that someone was hurtling into the shop like a human projectile. He looked up from his desk and saw Shaykh Mutawalli Abd al-Samad in the middle of the room blinking his inflamed eyes, futilely trying to peer toward the desk. Al-Sayyid Ahmad's spirits rose. With a smile he shouted at the visitor, "Make yourself at home, Shaykh Mutawalli. We are blessed by your presence."

The shaykh appeared reassured. He advanced, his torso swaying backward and forward as though he were riding on a camel. Al-Sayyid Ahmad leaned over his desk, putting out his hand to take his visitor's and press it firmly, saying gently, "The chair's to your right. Please sit down." Shaykh Mutawalli leaned his stick against the desk and took his seat. Putting some of the weight of his shoulders on his hands, which were placed on his knees, he said, "May God preserve you and sustain you."

The proprietor responded wholeheartedly, "How fine your prayer is and how much I've needed it." Turning toward Jamil al-Hamzawi, who was weighing rice for a customer, he advised him, "Don't forget to prepare the parcel for our master the shaykh."

Jamil al-Hamzawi responded, "Who could forget our master the shaykh?"

The shaykh spread out his hands and raised his head, moving his lips in a quiet prayer of which only an intermittent whisper could be heard. Then he returned to his former pose and was silent for a moment. By way of invocation he said, "I begin with a prayer for the Prophet, our guiding light."

Al-Sayyid Ahmad said fervently, "The finest of all blessings and peace on him."

"I ask a double portion of mercy for your father of blessed memory."

"May God have great mercy on him."

"Then I ask God to delight your eyes with your family and offspring for generations to come."

"Amen."

Sighing he continued: "I ask Him to return to us 'Our Effendi' the Khedive Abbas II, Muhammad Farid, and Sa'd Zaghlul."

"May God hear your prayer."

"And devastate the English for their past and present sins."

"Glory to the Omnipotent Avenger."

At that point, the shaykh cleared his throat and wiped his face with his palm before saying, "I saw you in a dream waving your hands. As soon as I opened my eyes I resolved to visit you."

The proprietor smiled somewhat sadly and replied, "That's not surprising, because I'm in desperate need of your blessings, may God multiply them."

The shaykh leaned his face toward al-Sayyid Ahmad affectionately and asked, "Is what I heard about the incident at Bab al-Futuh correct?"

Al-Sayyid Ahmad smiled and answered him: "Yes . . . I wonder who told you."

"I was passing by the oil-pressing establishment of Ghunaym Hamidu when he stopped me and said, 'Haven't you heard what the English did to me and your dear friend al-Sayyid Ahmad?' In alarm I asked him to explain. So he told me, wonder of wonders."

Al-Sayyid Ahmad recounted the whole story with every detail. He never tired of repeating it, even though he had told it tens of times over the past few days.

As the shaykh listened, he recited the Throne Verse about God under his breath (Qur'an, 2:255). "Were you frightened, my son?" he asked. "Describe your fear to me. Tell me about it. There is no power or might save from God. Were you convinced you would be saved? Have you forgotten that fright doesn't just go away? You prayed for a long time and asked God for salvation. That's excellent, but you'll need an amulet."

"Why not! . . . It will bring us added blessings, Shaykh Mutawalli. And the children and their mother—weren't they frightened too?"

"Of course . . . their hearts are weak, inexperienced with brutality or terror. . . . An amulet. . . . An amulet's the remedy."

"You are goodness and blessing, Shaykh Mutawalli. God rescued me from a grave evil, but there's another evil still threatening me that keeps me awake nights."

Once again the shaykh's face leaned toward al-Sayyid Ahmad affectionately. He asked, "May God forgive you. What's troubling you, son?"

The proprietor looked at him despondently and muttered angrily, "My son Fahmy."

The shaykh raised his white eyebrows inquisitively or in alarm and commented hopefully, "He's safe, with the permission of God the Merciful. . . ."

Al-Sayyid Ahmad shook his head sorrowfully and said, "He disobeyed me for the first time. The matter's in God's hands."

The shaykh spread his arms out in front of him as though to ward off affliction and shouted, "I take refuge in God. Fahmy's my boy. I'm certain he's dutiful by nature."

Al-Sayyid Ahmad said with annoyance, "His honor insists on doing just what the other boys are doing at this bloody time."

The shaykh was astonished and incredulous. He protested, "You're a resolute father. There's no doubt about that. I would never have imagined that one of your sons would dare oppose you in anything."

These words cut him to the quick and drew blood. He felt upset and inclined to downplay his son's rebellion in order to defend himself, both to the shaykh and to himself, against the accusation of weakness. He said, "Of course he did not dare do so directly, but I asked him to swear on a copy of the Qur'an that he would not participate in any revolutionary activity. He wept instead of having the courage to say no. What can I do? I can't lock him up in the house. I can't keep him under surveillance at school. I'm afraid that the current of events at this time will be too strong for a boy like him to resist. What should I do? Threaten to beat him? Beat him? But what good is a threat when he doesn't mind risking death?"

The shaykh stroked his face and asked anxiously, "Has he thrown himself into the demonstrations?"

Shaking his broad shoulders, the proprietor answered, "Of course not. But he distributes handbills. When I pressured him, he claimed he only distributed them to his best friends."

"Why is he interested in such activities? . . . He's the mild-mannered son of a mild-mannered father. These activities are for a different type of man. Doesn't he know that the English are brutes with rough hearts unaffected by mercy who feed on the blood of the poor Egyptians from dawn to dusk? Talk to him amicably. Preach to him. Show him the difference between light and darkness. Tell him that you're his father, that you love him and are afraid for him. For my part, I'll make several amulets of a special type and remember him in my prayers, especially the Dawn Prayer. It's God who is our help from first to last."

The proprietor said mournfully, "Every hour there's more news of fatalities. That should be warning enough for anyone with half a mind. What's happened to his intellect? The son of al-Fuli, the milkman, was lost in an instant. Fahmy attended the funeral with me and offered his condolences to the boy's poor father. The lad was distributing bowls of curdled milk when he ran into a demonstration. He was tempted by fate to join it, without giving the matter any thought. Then in not much more than an hour he was slain in front of al-Azhar Mosque. There's no might or power save with God. We are from God and return to God. When he was late getting back, his father became anxious and went to his customers to ask after him. Some of them said he had brought the milk and departed and others said he had not passed by them as usual. When he reached Hamrush, who sells sweet shredded pasta bars, he found the boy's tray and the remaining bowls that hadn't been distributed. Hamrush told the father that the boy had left them with him while he participated in a demonstration that afternoon. The poor man went crazy and proceeded at once to the Gamaliya police station. They sent him to the Qasr al-Ayni Hospital, where he found his son in the autopsy room. Fahmy heard the story with all the details, just the way al-Fuli related it to us when we were at his house to offer him our condolences. Fahmy learned how the boy had been lost and might just as well have never existed. He witnessed the father's excruciating grief and heard the wails of the family. The poor lad perished, but Sa'd didn't return and the English didn't leave. If Fahmy were a stone, he would have understood something. Still, he's the best of my children, for which I praise and thank God."

In a sad voice, Shaykh Mutawalli said, "I knew that poor boy. He was the oldest of al-Fuli's children, isn't that so? His grandfather was a donkey driver, and I used to hire his donkey to go to Sidi Abu al-Sa'ud. Al-Fuli has four children, but he was fondest of the one who died."

For the first time Jamil al-Hamzawi entered into their conversation: "In these crazy times, people can't think straight, not even the youngsters. Yesterday my son Fuad told his mother he wanted to take part in a demonstration."

Al-Sayyid Ahmad said anxiously, "The young ones participate in demonstrations and the big ones are struck down in them. Your son Fuad's a friend of my son Kamal, and they both go to the same school. Hasn't he, haven't they both been tempted to join in a demonstration? . . . Huh? Nothing seems amazing anymore."

Al-Hamzawi regretted having let that slip out and observed, "It hasn't gone this far, al-Sayyid Ahmad, sir. I disciplined him mercilessly for his innocent wish. Mr. Kamal never goes out unless he's accompanied by Umm Hanafi, may God preserve and watch over him."

They were silent. The only thing that could be heard in the store was the rustling of the paper in which al-Hamzawi was wrapping the present for Shaykh Mutawalli Abd al-Samad. Then the shaykh sighed and commented, "Fahmy's a bright boy. He mustn't let the English threaten his dear soul. The English! . . . May God make it up to me. Haven't you heard what they did in the villages of al-Aziziya and Badrashin? . . ."

The proprietor was so perturbed he did not really wish to inquire what had happened. He expected it would be the same sort of thing he kept hearing about. He merely raised his eyebrows to seem interested.

The shaykh commenced: "The day before yesterday I was visiting the esteemed and noble Shaddad Bey Abd al-Hamid in his mansion in al-Abbasiya. He invited me to have lunch and supper, so I presented him with some amulets for him and the members of his household. There I learned what happened at al-Aziziya and Badrashin."

The shaykh was silent for a bit. Al-Sayyid Ahmad asked, "The well-known cotton merchant?"

"Shaddad Bey Abd al-Hamid is the greatest of all the cotton merchants. Perhaps you knew his son Abd al-Hamid Bey Shaddad? He was closely linked with Mr. Muhammad Iffat once."

Al-Sayyid Ahmad spoke slowly to give himself time to think: "I remember I saw him at one of Mr. Muhammad Iffat's parties before the outbreak of the war. Then I heard he had been exiled following the fall of 'Our Effendi' Abbas II. What news is there of him?"

Shaykh Mutawalli replied quickly in passing, as though putting his words in parentheses so he could return directly to his original topic, "He's still in exile. He lives in France with his wife and children. Shaddad Bey is intensely worried he will die before he sees his son again in this world." He fell silent. Then he began to shake his head right and left, reciting in a musical voice as though chanting the opening of a poem in praise of the Prophet, "Two or three hours after midnight when the people were sleeping, a few hundred British soldiers armed to the teeth surrounded the two towns."

Al-Sayyid Ahmad's attention was rudely awakened. "They surrounded the villages when the people were sleeping? Weren't the besiegers similar to the soldiers camped in front of the house? They began by attacking me. What's the next step they plan?"

The shaykh slapped his knee as though trying to set the rhythm for his recitation as he continued: "In each village they burst into the home of the magistrate, ordering him to surrender his weapons. Then they penetrated the women's quarters, where they plundered the jewelry and insulted the women. They dragged them outside by their hair, while the women wailed and called for help, but there was no one to help them. Have sympathy, God, for Your weak servants."

"The homes of the two magistrates! Isn't the magistrate a government official? I'm no magistrate, nor is my house the home of one. I'm just a man like any other. What might they do to people like us? Imagine Amina being dragged by her hair. Is it fated that someday I'll wish I were insane? . . . Insane!"

Shaking his head, the shaykh continued with his account: "They forced the magistrates to show them where the village elders and the leading citizens lived. Then they stormed those houses, breaking down the doors and plundering everything of value. They attacked the women in a most criminal fashion, after killing those who tried to defend themselves. They beat the men violently. Then they moved out of the towns, leaving nothing precious untouched and no honor undefiled."

"Let them take anything precious with them straight to hell," al-Sayyid Ahmad brooded. "But 'no honor undefiled' . . . where was God's mercy? Where was His vengeance? . . . The flood and Noah . . . the nationalist leader Mustafa Kamil. . . . Imagine! How could a woman remain under one roof with her husband after that? And what fault had she committed? How could he countenance it?"

The shaykh struck his knee three times before resuming his account. His voice had begun to tremble and he lamented, "They set fire to the villages, pouring gasoline over the poles and thatch forming the roofs of the houses. The towns awoke in dreadful terror. Residents fled from their homes, screaming and wailing as though they had gone mad. The tongues of flame reached everywhere until both villages were engulfed."

Al-Sayyid Ahmad cried out involuntarily, "O Lord of heaven and earth!"

The shaykh proceeded: "The soldiers formed a ring around the burning villages to wait for the wretched inhabitants, who rushed off in every direction followed by their livestock and dogs and cats, looking for some way to escape. When they reached the soldiers, the latter fell upon the men, beating and kicking them. Then they detained the women to strip them of their jewelry and divest them of their honor. Any woman who resisted was killed. Any husband, father, or brother who lifted a hand to protect them was gunned down."

Shaykh Mutawalli turned to look at the stunned proprietor. He struck his hands together and shouted, "And they led the survivors to a nearby camp, where they forced them to sign a document containing their confessions to crimes they had not committed and their admission that what the English had done to them was an appropriate punishment. Al-Sayyid Ahmad, this is what happened to al-Aziziya and Badrashin. This is an example of the kind of punishment imposed on us, mercilessly and heartlessly. O God, bear witness, bear witness."

A despondent, oppressive silence reigned while each of the men wrestled with his own thoughts and images. Then Jamil al-Hamzawi moaned, "Our Lord exists."

"Yes!" shouted al-Sayyid Ahmad, applauding his statement. Gesturing in all four directions, he said, "Everywhere!"

Shaykh Mutawalli advised the proprietor, "Tell Fahmy that Shaykh Mutawalli counsels him to stay away from danger. Tell him, 'Surrender to God your Lord. He alone is capable of devastating the English as He has devastated those who disobeyed Him in the past.'"

The shaykh leaned over to grasp his stick. Al-Sayyid Ahmad gestured to Jamil al-Hamzawi, who brought the present. He put it in the shaykh's hand and helped him rise. The shaykh shook hands with both men and recited as he left, " 'The [God-fearing] Byzantines have been defeated in a nearby land, but after their defeat, they will be victorious' [Qur'an, 30:2–3], and not the friends of the pagans. The words of God Almighty are true."

68

At dawn, when darkness was slowly giving birth to light, a servant from Sugar Street knocked on the door of al-Sayyid Ahmad's house and informed Amina that Aisha's labor had begun. Amina, who had been in the oven room, turned her work over to Umm Hanafi and rushed to the stairway.

For perhaps the first time in the long history of her employment in the house, Umm Hanafi appeared to be indignant. Was it not obligatory for her to be present when Aisha gave birth? She had every right to be there, just the same as Amina. Aisha had first opened her eyes in Umm Hanafi's lap. Every child in the family had two mothers: Amina and Umm Hanafi. How could she be separated from her daughter at such a terrifying time?

"Do you remember what it was like when you had your child?" she asked herself. "The apartment in al-Tambakshiya. . . ." The master had been out as usual. She had been alone, although it was after midnight. Umm Hasaniya had been both a friend and a midwife. "Where is Umm Hasaniya now? Is she alive today?" Then her son Hanafi had arrived amid moans of pain. He had departed amid moans of pain too, when he was still in the cradle. If he had lived, he would be twenty. "My little mistress will be suffering, while I'm stuck here preparing food."

Amina's heart was filled with the same apprehensive joy she had felt when she first prepared to give birth. Here was Aisha getting ready to deliver her first child and commence life as a mother, as she herself had begun with Khadija. Thus the life that had sprung from her would continue on endlessly. She went to her husband to announce the good news to him in a quiet, courteous way. She tried her best to appear shy and polite, so her ardent desire to rush off to her daughter would not show. Al-Sayyid Ahmad received the news calmly and then ordered her to go without delay. She got dressed quickly, appreciative of the wonders motherhood could work at times for a weak woman like herself.

The brothers learned the news when they woke up, shortly after the mother's departure. They smiled and exchanged questioning glances.

"Aisha's a mother!"

"Isn't that strange?"

"What's strange about it? Mother was younger than Aisha when Khadija was born."

"Has Mother gone to deliver the baby with her own hands?" Kamal's question was answered by two smiles.

"This is a warning for me," Yasin observed. "The bitch will have her baby soon. . . ."

"Who do you mean?"

"Zaynab."

"Oh, if Papa ever heard you . . ."

"Aisha's a mother and I'm a father."

"And I'm an uncle twice over," Fahmy remarked. "You will be too, Mr. Kamal."

"I'm going to have to stay out of school today to go to Aisha's."

"That's great. Just ask Papa's permission at breakfast, if you're able."

"Oh! We need more births to keep up with the dent the English are making in our population."

"If I stay home from school, that won't be a problem. Three-fourths of the students have been on strike for more than a month."

"Tell Papa that. He'll surely be convinced by your argument. Then he'll hit you in the face with a plate of beans."

"Oh! A new baby. . . . In an hour or two Papa will become a grandfather and Mama a grandmother. We'll all be uncles. This is a significant event. How many children are being born at this moment, do you suppose? And how many people are dying right now? We need to let Grandmother know."

"I can go to al-Khurunfush and tell her, if I stay home from school. . . ."

"We've explained that your school is none of our business. Tell Papa. He'll welcome your idea."

"Oh! Perhaps Aisha's suffering now. The poor darling. . . . Golden hair and blue eyes won't make the labor pains any lighter."

"May our Lord bring her through it safely. Then we'll drink the traditional broth and light some candles."

"A boy or a girl?"

"Which do you prefer?"

"A boy, of course."

"Perhaps she'll begin with a girl, like her mother."

"Why not start with a boy, like her father?"

"Ah . . . by the time school lets out, the baby will already have arrived. Then I won't get a chance to watch him come out."

"You want to see him being born?"

"Of course."

"You'd better postpone this desire until it's your own child."

Kamal was the most deeply affected by the news. It preoccupied his mind, heart, and imagination. Had he not felt that the school disciplinarian was keeping track of him and watching his every move to report in detail to his father, he would have been unable to resist the temptation to go to Sugar Street. He remained in school, but only in body. His spirit was hovering over Sugar Street, inquiring about the new arrival he had been awaiting for months, in hopes of learning its secret.

He had once seen a cat give birth when he was not quite six. She had attracted his attention with her piercing meows. He had rushed to her, finding her on the roof under the arbor of hyacinth beans, writhing in pain with her eyes bulging out. When he saw her body part with an inflamed bit of meat, he had backed away in disgust, screaming as loudly as he could. This memory haunted his mind, and he felt the same old disgust. It was a pesky, distressing memory, encompassing him like a fog, but he refused to let himself be frightened. He could not imagine any connection between the cat and Aisha, except the slight relationship between an animal and a human being, whom he believed to be as far apart as earth from heaven. But what was going on in Sugar Street, then? What strange things were happening to Aisha? These were vexing questions that appeared to have no easy answers. The moment he got out of school that afternoon he dashed off at full speed to Sugar Street.

He was panting when he entered the courtyard of the Shawkat residence. He went to the door of the women's quarters but chanced to peer into the reception room. To his chagrin, he found himself looking straight into his father's eyes. The man was sitting down, grasping with both hands the top of the walking stick held between his legs. Kamal froze, staring as though hypnotized, not blinking or moving. He felt he must have unwittingly done something wrong. He waited for the punishment to fall on him, as the chill of fear spread through his limbs. Then al-Sayyid Ahmad started talking to the person sitting beside him and turned in that direction. Kamal averted his eyes and swallowed. He caught a glimpse of Ibrahim Shawkat, Yasin, and Fahmy in the pavilion before he fled. He leapt up the stairs till he reached Aisha's floor. The door was partway open and he went in. There he found Khalil Shawkat, Aisha's husband, standing in the sitting room. He noticed that the bedroom door was closed. He could hear voices conversing inside. He recognized those of his mother and Widow Shawkat, but there was a third he did not know. He said hello to Khalil and, looking up at him with smiling eyes, asked, "Has Aisha had her baby yet?"

The man put a finger to his lips to caution him and said, "Hush."

Kamal realized that he and his question were not welcome, although Khalil usually greeted him warmly. Kamal was embarrassed and felt uneasy for no particular reason. He wanted to go over to the closed door but was stopped by Khalil's voice yelling at him peremptorily, "No."

Kamal turned toward him questioningly. The man told him quickly and urgently, "Be a good boy and go downstairs and play."

The boy was crushed. Disheartened, he retreated with heavy feet. It hurt him to be rewarded so shabbily for the torment of waiting he had endured all day. Just as he was about to leave, a strange sound coming from the closed room made his ears ring. It began high, shrill, and piercing and then became husky and disjointed, even raucous, before ending as a long, harsh rattle. It died away just long enough for the person to breathe. Afterward there was a deep moan of complaint. At first Kamal did not recognize the voice, but despite its shrillness, huskiness, and rattling, there was something distinctive about its tortured sound that revealed the person's identity. It was the voice of his sister Aisha, without any doubt, or of Aisha exhausted and fading away. When the deep, complaining moan was repeated, he knew he was right. He trembled all over. He imagined her writhing in pain. That reminded him of the cat. He glanced toward Khalil and found him contracting and relaxing his fists as he murmured, "O Gracious Lord."

Kamal imagined that Aisha's body was contracting and relaxing like her husband's hands. He lost control of himself and raced off, unable to say anything because of his sobs. When he reached the door of the women's quarters he heard footsteps behind him. He looked up and saw the servant Suwaydan hurrying down. She passed without paying any attention to him. Stopping at the door, she called her master Ibrahim. When the man hastened to her, she told him, "Praise to God, master." She added nothing further and did not wait to hear his reply. She turned on her heels and rushed back up the steps without any delay.

Ibrahim went to the reception chamber with a beaming face. Kamal stayed where he was, alone, not knowing what to do. In less than a minute Ibrahim returned, followed by al-Sayyid Ahmad, Yasin, and Fahmy in that order. The boy stepped aside to let them pass and then trailed after them with a pounding heart.

Khalil received them at the door of the apartment. Kamal heard his father say, "Praise to God for good health."

Khalil muttered despondently, "Praise to God in any case."

With concern, al-Sayyid Ahmad asked him, "What's the matter?"

In a low voice Khalil said, "I'm going to call the doctor."

Al-Sayyid Ahmad asked anxiously, "For the baby?"

He replied as he shook his head no, "Aisha! . . . She's not in good shape. I'll get the doctor at once."

He departed, leaving behind him undisguised dejection and anxiety. Ibrahim Shawkat invited them into the parlor. They went there silently. Widow Shawkat arrived soon and greeted them. She smiled to reassure them. When she sat down she said, "The poor dear suffered so long that her strength gave out. It's just a temporary condition and will soon pass. I'm sure of what I say, but my son seems to be unusually fearful today. In any case, there's no harm in having the doctor come." Then she commented in a low voice to herself, "The real doctor is our Lord. He's the true physician."

Though surrounded by his sons, al-Sayyid Ahmad was unable to maintain his customary composure. With evident anxiety he asked, "What's the matter with her? . . . Can't I see her?"

The woman smiled and said, "You'll see her shortly, when she's feeling better. It's my crazy son's fault that he alarmed you unnecessarily."

Within his broad, powerful chest that seemed so resolute, dignified, and awe-inspiring was a grievously tormented heart. Inside those grave, despondent eyes was a frozen tear. "What's happened to my little girl? The doctor! Why is the old lady keeping me from seeing her? A tender smile or an affectionate word from me, from me in particular, would certainly lessen her pains. Marriage, husband, pain. . . . She never tasted the bitterness of pain in my house. The beautiful, darling little girl . . . mercy, God. Life's lost its flavor. The taste is destroyed by the least harm threatening them. Fahmy . . . I see he's dejected and in pain. . . . Has he understood the meaning of pain? How could he know what a mother's heart feels? The old lady's calm and confident of what she says. Her son upset us for no reason at all. O God, hear our prayer. You know the state I'm in. You'll save her the way You saved me from the English. My heart can't take this torment. God is merciful. He's capable of saving my children from every evil. Otherwise, life would have no taste. What enjoyment would I get from gaiety, music, and entertainment if there was a sharp thorn planted in my side? My heart prays for their deliverance, because it's a father's heart. It can't enjoy amusements unless it's free from worry. Will I go to the party tonight with a heart at ease? When I laugh, I like it to resound from the depths of my sincere heart. An anxious heart is like a string that's out of tune. Fahmy's enough for me to worry about. He pesters me like a toothache. How hateful pain is! A world without pain . . . nothing is too much for God. A world without pain, even if only for a brief time . . . a world in which my eye's delighted by my children. Then I would laugh, sing, and play. Most Merciful of the merciful. . . . Have mercy on Aisha, O God."

Khalil returned with the doctor after an absence of three-quarters of an hour. They entered the door at once, closing it behind them. When al-Sayyid Ahmad learned they had arrived, he rose and went to the door of the parlor. He stood at the threshold for a little while, looking at the closed door. Then he went back to his place and sat down.

Widow Shawkat said, "We'll see how right I am once the doctor speaks to us."

Al-Sayyid Ahmad raised his head heavenward and murmured, "Pardon comes from Him."

He would soon know the truth and escape from the fog of doubt, regardless of the outcome. His heart pounded rapidly. Let him be patient. It would not be long. His faith in God was deep, profound, and not easily shaken. He should surrender the affair to Him. No matter how long the doctor stayed inside, he would eventually come out. Then he would ask what it was all about. A doctor? . . . He had not thought about that before. . . . A doctor at a delivery, face to face with her womb. Was not that so? But he was a doctor. . . . What could be done? "The important thing is for our Lord to take her by the hand. We ask him for deliverance."

In addition to being worried, al-Sayyid Ahmad felt embarrassed and annoyed. The examination lasted about twenty minutes. Then the door opened. He rose and went at once to the sitting room, followed by the boys. They gathered around the doctor, who knew al-

Sayyid Ahmad. Shaking his hand, he said with a smile, "She's in good health." He continued more seriously: "They brought me for the mother, but I found the one really in need of my care was the baby girl."

Al-Sayyid Ahmad sighed with relief, feeling better for the first time in about an hour. With a gracious smile brightening his face, he asked, "Can I be sure of what you say, then?"

Pretending to be astonished, the doctor said, "Yes, but aren't you concerned about your granddaughter?"

Smiling, he replied, "I'm not familiar yet with the duties of a grandfather."

Khalil asked, "Isn't there any hope she'll live?"

Knitting his brows, the doctor answered, "Lives are in God's hands. I found that her heart's weak. It's likely she'll die before morning. If she makes it safely through the night, she'll be out of immediate danger, but I think she won't live long. In my judgment, she won't live past her twenties. But who knows? Only God controls our lives."

When the doctor had gone off about his business, Khalil turned toward his mother with a sad smile. He told her, "I was intending to name her Na'ima, after you."

The woman gestured with her hand to scold him and observed, "The doctor himself said, 'Lives are in God's hands.' Are you going to have less faith than the doctor? Name her Na'ima. You must name her Na'ima in my honor. God willing, her life will be as long as her grandmother's."

Al-Sayyid Ahmad was thinking to himself, "The fool called a doctor to look at his wife for no reason, no reason at all. What an idiot he is!" Unable to contain his fury, although he disguised it in a gentle tone, he said, "It's true that fear makes men do foolish things, but shouldn't you have thought a little before rushing off to bring an outsider to take such a searching look at your wife?"

Khalil did not respond. He glanced at the people around him and remarked earnestly, "Aisha must not know what the doctor said."

69

"What's happening in the street?" al-Sayyid Ahmad wondered as he rose hastily from his desk. He went to the door, followed by Jamil al-Hamzawi and some of their customers. Al-Nahhasin was not a quiet street, quite the contrary. Its strident noise did not abate from one dawn until shortly before the next. There were the loud cries of vendors, haggling of shoppers, pleas of crazed beggars, and wisecracks of passersby. People conversed as though delivering a public oration. Even the most personal discussions ricocheted everywhere, flying up to the minarets. To this general commotion the Suarès omnibus added its clanking and the donkey carts their clatter. In no sense was it a quiet street, but a sudden clamor had arisen, at first heard in the distance like the roar of waves, then growing stronger and more raucous until it sounded like a howling wind. It enveloped the whole district, near and far. Even on this noisy street it was out of the ordinary and exceptional.

Al-Sayyid Ahmad thought a demonstration had broken out, as anyone who had experienced those days would have, but cries of joy were audible in the uproar. Wondering what it was, he went to the door where he bumped into the shaykh, or supervisor, of the district, who had rushed up. He was crying out with a jubilant face, "Have you heard the news?"

Even before he heard any more, the proprietor's eyes began to glow optimistically. "No," he said. "What's it all about?"

The man replied enthusiastically, "Sa'd Pasha has been freed."

Al-Sayyid Ahmad could not restrain himself from yelling, "Really?"

The shaykh affirmed, "Allenby broadcast a bulletin with this good news just now."

The next moment the two men were hugging each other. Al-Sayyid Ahmad was deeply moved. His eyes filled with tears. Laughing to disguise his emotions, he said, "He's known for broadcasting threats, not good news. What's made him change, that old son of a gun?"

The shaykh of the district replied, "Glory to the one who never changes." He shook hands with the proprietor and then left the store shouting, "God is most great. *Allahu akbar*. Victory to the Muslims."

Al-Sayyid Ahmad stood at the door of the shop, looking up and down the street with a heart that had recaptured the delight and innocence of childhood. The effect of the news about Sa'd was evident everywhere. The entries of the shops were jammed with their owners and customers, who were congratulating each other. The windows of the houses were crowded with children, and ululating trills of joy could be heard from the women at the peepholes of the window grilles. Impromptu demonstrations took place between al-Nahhasin, the Goldsmiths Bazaar, and Bayt al-Qadi, with people yelling their hearts out for Sa'd, Sa'd, Sa'd, and then Sa'd. The muezzins went up to the balconies of their minarets to give thanks, pray, and shout. There were tens of donkey carts with hundreds of women, fully covered in wraps, dancing and singing patriotic songs. All he could see were people, or, more precisely, people shouting. The earth had disappeared and the walls were concealed by them. Shouts for Sa'd were heard everywhere. The air seemed to have turned into a tremendous phonograph record, spinning incessantly on a turntable, repeating his name. News bounced along the mass of heads that the English were striking their camps, which had been set up at the street corners, in preparation for redeployment of the soldiers to al-Abbasiya. The enthusiasm increased and delirium reached a fever pitch. Al-Sayyid Ahmad had never seen such a sight before. He looked every which way with sparkling eyes and a bounding heart. Under his breath, he sang along with the women dancers, "O Husayn . . . a burden has been lifted."

Then Jamil al-Hamzawi put his head close to the proprietor's ear to say, "The shops are distributing cold drinks and putting up flags."

Al-Sayyid Ahmad told him enthusiastically, "Do what the others are doing and more. Put your whole heart into it." Then with a trembling voice he added, "Hang Sa'd's picture under the calligraphy of 'In the Name of God.' "

Jamil al-Hamzawi looked reluctant and cautioned him, "In that place it can be seen from outside. Wouldn't it be better for us to bide our time until things return to normal?"

The proprietor replied scornfully, "The era of fear and bloodshed has passed, never to return. Don't you see that demonstrations are going on under the eyes of the English, who aren't making any attempt to interfere with them? Hang up the picture and trust in God."

"The days of fear and bloodshed have vanished. Isn't that so? Sa'd is free and at liberty. He's probably on his way now to Europe. Only a step or a word stands between us and independence. These are demonstrations with trills of joy, not bullets. Those of us who are still alive are happy people, having passed safely through the fires. God's mercy on the martyrs. . . . Fahmy? He's escaped from a much greater danger than he ever imagined. He's escaped, praise and thanks to God. Yes, Fahmy has escaped. What are you waiting for? Pray to God your Lord."

When the family gathered that evening, their hoarse voices revealed that they had spent the day shouting. It was a happy evening. Joy was evident in their eyes, lips, gestures, and words. Even Amina's heart imbibed some of the overflowing happiness. She realized that Sa'd's release brought good news of a return to peace and joy.

"From the balcony I saw something no one has ever seen before," she commented. "Has Judgment Day come with the scales to weigh our sins? Were those women crazy? The echo of their singing still rings in my ears: 'O Husayn . . . a burden has been lifted.' "

Laughingly messing up Kamal's hair, Yasin said, "It was a word of farewell to speed the departing English on their way, just as you see off an unwelcome guest by breaking a jug after him."

Kamal looked at his brother without saying anything. Then Amina had another question: "Is God finally pleased with us?"

Yasin replied, "No doubt about it." Then he asked Fahmy, "What do you think?"

Fahmy, who seemed as happy as a child, said, "The English wouldn't have freed Sa'd if they weren't agreeing to our demands. He'll travel to Europe and then return with independence. This is what everyone says. No matter what else happens, April 7, 1919, will remain the date marking the success of the revolution."

Yasin exclaimed, "What a day! Government employees participated openly in the demonstrations. I didn't think I was capable of walking that distance or yelling for so long."

Fahmy laughed. He said, "I wish I could have seen you shouting zealously. Yasin takes part in a demonstration. He gets excited and yells. What a rare spectacle!"

It truly was an amazing day. Yasin had been swept along by its swelling current and carried by its strong waves like a tiny, weightless leaf, fluttering everywhere. He could scarcely believe that he had been able to regain control of himself and had retreated to a quiet observation tower where, through its glass, he had calmly watched what was happening, without any emotional involvement. In the light of Fahmy's observation, he began to recall the state he had been in while he was in the demonstration. He remarked with astonishment, "A man forgets himself in the strangest way when he's with so many people. He almost seems to become a new person."

Fahmy asked him with interest, "Did you really feel enthusiastic?"

"I shouted for Sa'd so much my throat became sore. I had tears in my eyes once or twice."

"How did you get into the demonstration?"

"We heard the news that Sa'd had been released when we were at school. I was really ecstatic. Were you expecting that? Then the teachers suggested joining the large demonstration outside. I didn't feel like it and thought I'd slip off home but was forced to walk with them until I could get an opportunity to escape. Then I found myself in a swirling sea of people. There was an electric atmosphere of enthusiasm. Before I knew it, I forgot myself and merged with the stream. I was as zealous and optimistic as a person can be. Please believe me."

Fahmy shook his head and murmured, "Amazing. . . ."

Yasin laughed out loud and asked, "Did you think I had lost my sense of patriotism? The thing is, I don't like noise and violence. I don't have any problem reconciling love of country and love of peace."

"What if that reconciliation is shattered?"

Yasin smiled and answered without any hesitation, "I put love of peace first. I come first. . . . Is it impossible for my country to be happy unless it consumes my life? God's deliverance! I'm not taking any chances with my life, but I'll love my country so long as I'm alive."

"That's very wise," Amina commented. Then, looking at Fahmy, she asked, "Does my master think otherwise?"

Fahmy replied calmly, "Of course not. It's very wise, as you said. . . ."

Kamal was not happy to be left out of the conversation, especially since he was convinced that he had played a vital role that day. He volunteered, "We went on strike too, but the headmaster told us we were still children and would be trampled underfoot if we left school. He gave us permission to demonstrate in the school courtyard. So we assembled there and chanted for a long time, 'Long live Sa'd.' " He repeated the chant in a loud voice. "After that we didn't go back to the classes, because the teachers had left the school to join the demonstrators outside."

Yasin threw the boy a sarcastic look and remarked, "But your friends have gone. . . ."

"To hell," Kamal said, in spite of himself. The comment did not express his true feelings at all, but he felt that circumstances required it and, faced with Yasin's sarcasm, he wished to mask his defeat. In his heart he felt bewildered and slandered. He could not forget how, on his return from school, he had stood in the deserted campsite, casting his eyes in every direction in painful silence as tears welled up in his eyes. It would be a long time before he forgot tea on the sidewalk by the cistern, the admiration his singing had garnered, his affectionate treatment by the soldiers and especially by Julian, and the friendship that linked him to those outstanding gentlemen whom he believed to be superior to the rest of mankind.

Amina said, "Sa'd Pasha's a lucky man. The whole world is chanting his name. Not even 'Our Effendi' Abbas II was treated like that. Sa'd's no doubt a Believer, because God grants real victories only to Believers. Sa'd's been victorious over the English, who even defeated the zeppelin. What greater victory can you ask for? The man was born auspiciously on the Night of Destiny in Ramadan, which commemorates the Qur'an's descent."

"Do you love him?" Fahmy asked with a smile.

"I love him, since you do."

Fahmy spread his hands out and raised his eyebrows disapprovingly. "That doesn't mean anything," he said.

She sighed somewhat uneasily and explained, "Whenever I got some sad news, tearing my heart to pieces with sorrow, I would ask myself, 'Do you suppose this would have happened if Sa'd had not started his rebellion?' But a man loved by everyone must also be loved by God." Sighing audibly, she continued: "I grieve for those who have perished. How many mothers are weeping sorely now? How many a mother finds that today's joy only adds another sorrow to her regrets?"

Fahmy winked at Yasin and told her, "A really patriotic mother would trill with joy at her son's martyrdom."

She put her fingers in her ears and shouted, "May God be my witness to what the young master has said. . . . A mother trills with joy when her son is martyred? Where? On this earth? Not here or even underground where the devils reside."

Fahmy laughed loudly. He thought for a while. Then with twinkling eyes he said, "Mama . . . I'm going to tell you a terrible secret that can be revealed now. I participated in the demonstrations and met death face to face."

She looked at him gravely and incredulously. With a bewildered smile she said, "You? . . . Impossible. You're part of my flesh and blood. Your heart comes from mine. You're not like the others. . . ."

Smiling at her, he declared, "I swear to you by God Almighty that it's true."

Her smile disappeared and her eyes grew wide with consternation. She looked back and forth between him and Yasin, who was also staring inquisitively at Fahmy. After swallowing, she mumbled, "O Lord! . . . How can I believe my ears?" Shaking her head in helpless agony, she exclaimed, "You!"

He had expected her to be upset, but not to the extent that she clearly was. After all, his confession came after the danger had passed. Before she could say anything more, he told her, "That's ancient history. It's over and done with. There's no reason to be alarmed now."

She responded with nervous insistence, "Hush! You don't love your mother. May God forgive you."

Fahmy laughed disconcertedly. With a mischievous smile, Kamal told his mother, "Do you remember the day I was fired on in the pastry shop? I saw him in the deserted street on my way home. He warned me not to tell anyone I had seen him." Then he turned to Fahmy and asked with avid interest, "Tell us, Mr. Fahmy, what you experienced in the demonstrations. How did the battles start? What happened when people fell dead? Were you armed?"

Yasin interrupted the conversation to tell the mother, "It's ancient history, dead and buried. It would be better to thank God he's safe than get alarmed."

She asked him harshly, "Did you know about it?"

He quickly replied, "No, by my mother's grave." For fear that might not be adequate, he added, "And by my religion, faith, and Lord."

He rose to go to her. He put a hand on her shoulder and told her tenderly, "Did you relax when you should have been alarmed only to be alarmed now that you can relax? Declare that God is one. The danger has passed and peace has returned. Here's Fahmy in front of you. . . ." He laughed. "By tomorrow we'll be able to walk the length and breadth of Cairo by day or night without fear or anxiety."

Fahmy said earnestly, "Mama, please don't spoil our good spirits with pointless sorrow."

She sighed and opened her mouth to speak, but no words came out, even though her lips moved. She smiled wanly to announce her compliance with his request. Then she bowed her head to hide her eyes filled with tears.

70

By the time Fahmy fell asleep that night he had made up his mind to get back into his father's good graces no matter what it cost him. The next morning he decided to act on his resolve without delay. Although he had never harbored any angry or defiant feelings toward his father during his rebellion, a guilty conscience was a heavy burden for his sensitive heart, which was imbued with dutiful obedience. He had not defied his father verbally but had acted against his will and had done so repeatedly. Moreover, he had refused to swear an oath the day his father had asked him to, announcing with his tears that he would stick to his principles despite his father's wishes. To his unbearable regret, all these acts had put him in the position, regardless of his good intentions, of being wickedly disobedient. He had not attempted to make peace with his father earlier from fear of scraping the scab off the wound without being able to bandage it. He had assumed his father would ask him to take the oath again as penance for what he had done and that he would be forced once more to refuse, thus reviving his rebellion when he wanted to apologize for it.

The situation today was different. His heart was intoxicated with joy and victory, and the whole nation was drunk on the wine of delight and triumph. He could not stand for a barrier of suspicion to separate him from his father a moment longer. They would be reconciled and he would receive the pardon he craved. Then there would be true happiness, unblemished by any defect.

He entered his father's room a quarter of an hour before breakfast and found his father folding up the prayer rug as he mumbled a prayerful entreaty. The man no doubt noticed him but pretended not to and went to sit on the sofa without turning toward his son. He sat facing Fahmy, who stood at the door, looking ashamed and confounded. Al-Sayyid Ahmad stared at him impassively and disapprovingly as though to ask, "Who is this person standing there and why has he come?"

Fahmy got the better of his consternation and quietly walked toward his father. He leaned over his hand, which he took and kissed with the utmost respect. He was silent for some time. Then in a scarcely audible voice he said, "Good morning, Papa."

His father continued to gaze at him silently, as though he had not heard the greeting, until the boy lowered his eyes in confusion and stammered in a despairing voice, "I'm sorry. . . ." Al-Sayyid Ahmad persisted in his silence.

"I'm really sorry. I haven't had a moment's peace of mind since . . ." He found his words were leading him up to a reference to something he wanted with all his heart to skip over. So he stopped.

Before he knew what was happening, his father asked him harshly and impatiently, "What do you want?"

Fahmy was overjoyed that the man had abandoned his silence and sighed with relief as though he had not noticed the harsh tone. He entreated his father, "I want your approval."

"Get out of my sight."

Feeling the grip of despair loosening a little around his neck, Fahmy said, "When I have your approval."

Becoming sarcastic suddenly, al-Sayyid Ahmad asked, "My approval! . . . Why not? . . . Have you, God forbid, done anything to make me angry?"

Fahmy welcomed his father's sarcasm twice as much as his renunciation of silence. Sarcasm with his father was the first step toward forgiveness. When he was really angry, he would slap, punch, kick, curse, or do all at once. Sarcasm was the first sign of a change of heart.

"Seize the opportunity," Fahmy told himself. "Speak. Speak the way a man preparing to be a lawyer should speak. This is your opportunity. Say, 'Answering the call of the nation should not be considered rebellion against your will, sir. I really didn't do much by way of patriotic deeds . . . distributing handbills to friends. . . . What did that amount to? What am I compared with those who willingly gave their lives? I understood from your words, sir, that you were afraid for my life, not that you really rejected the idea of patriotic duties. I simply did a little of my duty. I'm confident that I actually did not disobey your wishes.' . . . And so forth and so on."

Then Fahmy did say, "God knows it never occurred to me to disobey you."

Al-Sayyid Ahmad responded sharply, "Empty words. You pretend to be obedient now that there's no reason to rebel. Why haven't you asked for my approval before today?"

Fahmy said sadly, "The world was full of blood and grief. I was preoccupied by sorrow."

"Too preoccupied to ask for my approval?"

Fahmy replied ardently, "I was too preoccupied to think about myself." In a low voice he added, "I can't live without your approval."

Al-Sayyid Ahmad frowned, not from anger as he made it appear, but to hide the good impression his son's words had made on him. "This is the way a person should speak," he reflected. "Otherwise, forget it. He's really good at using words. This is eloquence, isn't it? I'll repeat what he said to my friends tonight to see what impact it makes on them. What do you suppose they'll say? The boy takes after his father. . . . That's what they ought to say. People used to tell me that if I had completed my education I would have been one of the most eloquent attorneys. I'm quite an eloquent person even without a higher education and a law practice. Our daily conversation is exactly like the law in revealing one's gift for eloquence. How many attorneys and important civil servants have cowered like sparrows before me at our parties. Not even Fahmy will be able to replace me one day. They'll laugh and say the boy's really a chip off the old block. His refusal to swear that oath still troubles me, but don't I have a right to be proud that he participated in the revolution, even if only remotely? Since God has allowed him to live to see this day, I wish he had done something important in it. From now on, I'll say he waded into the midst of the revolution. Do you think he was content just to distribute handbills as he claimed? The son of a bitch threw himself into the bloody stream of events. 'Al-Sayyid Ahmad, we must acknowledge your son's patriotism and courage. We did not wish to tell you this during the danger, but now that peace has come, there's no harm saying it.' Do you disown your patriotic feelings? Didn't the people collecting donations for the nationalist Wafd Party commend you? By God, if you were young, you would have done much more than your son has. But he defied me! He defied your tongue and obeyed your heart. What can I do now? My heart wishes to forgive him, but I'm afraid he'll think then that it's okay to disobey me."

He finally spoke: "I can never forget that you disobeyed me. Do you think the meaningless oration you have delivered this morning, before I even had breakfast, can influence me?"

Fahmy started to speak, but his mother entered at that moment to announce, "Breakfast is ready, sir."

She was astonished to find Fahmy there. She looked from one to the other and tarried a little in hopes of hearing part of what was being said. But the silence, which she was afraid her arrival had caused, made her leave the room quickly. Al-Sayyid Ahmad rose to go to the dining room, and Fahmy moved out of his way. The boy's intense sorrow was evident to his father, who hesitated a few moments before finally saying in a conciliatory voice, "I hope that in the future you won't insist on being so stupid when you address me."

He walked off, and the young man followed after him with a grateful smile. As they went through the sitting room he heard his father say sarcastically, "I suppose you put yourself at the head of those who liberated Sa'd."

Fahmy left the house happy. He went at once to al-Azhar, where he met with his colleagues on the supreme student committee. They were discussing arrangements for the enormous, peaceful demonstrations the authorities were allowing so that the nation could express its delight. It had been decided that representatives of all segments of the population would participate.

The meeting lasted quite a while. Then the participants separated, each going off about his business. Fahmy rode over to Ramses Square in front of the central railroad station, after learning of his assignment to supervise the groups of students from the secondary schools. Although the tasks he was customarily assigned could be considered rather secondary, compared with those of the others, he undertook them with precision, care, and joy, as though each was the happiest moment of his life. Even so, his industry was accompanied by a slight feeling of discontent, which he did not share with anyone else, originating from his conviction that he was less daring and forward than his other comrades. Yes, he had never hesitated to attend a demonstration the committee supported but he became discouraged when the trucks carrying soldiers appeared, especially once shots were fired and victims started to fall. One time he had sought refuge in a coffee shop, trembling. Another time he had run so far he ended up in the cemetery for theology students. What was he compared with the man who had carried the flag in the Bulaq demonstration, or massacre, as it had come to be called? That fellow had died a martyr, clasping the flag with his hands, standing his ground at the head of the procession, shouting at the top of his lungs for everyone to stand firm. What was Fahmy compared with that martyr's companions who had rushed to raise the flag again only to be shot down around him with their breasts decorated heroically by bullet holes? What was he compared with that martyr who had grabbed the machine gun from the hands of the enemy at al-Azhar? What was he compared with all those men and the others whose heroism and martyrdoms were always in the news? Heroic acts appeared to him to be so dazzling and magnificent that they were breathtaking. He frequently heard an inner voice daring him to imitate the heroes, but his nerves had always let him down at the decisive moment. When the fighting started, he would find himself at the rear, if not hiding or fleeing. Afterward he would regain his determination to double his efforts to struggle tenaciously, but with a tortured conscience, an anxious heart, and a limitless desire for perfection. He would console himself at times by saying, "I'm just an unarmed warrior. Even if stunning deeds of heroism have passed me by, it's enough that I've never hesitated to throw myself into the thick of the fray."

On his way to Ramses Square, he began to observe the streets and vehicles. It appeared that everyone was heading his way: students, workers, civil servants, and ordinary folk, riding or walking. They had a relaxed look about them, appropriate for people going to a peaceful demonstration sanctioned by the authorities. He too felt the way they did. It was not the same as when he had searched for the appointed place with an excited soul and a heart that pounded hard whenever he thought about perishing. That was in a former time. Today he went along, feeling secure, with a smile on his lips. Was the struggle over? Had he emerged from it safely with no losses or gains? No gains? . . . If only he had suffered something like the thousands who had been imprisoned, beaten, or wounded slightly by gunfire. Wasn't it sad that security should be the reward for a person with a heart and enthusiasm like his? He was like a diligent student unable to obtain a diploma.

"Do you deny you're happy that you're safe? Would you have preferred to be a martyr? Certainly not. . . . Would you have liked to be one of those wounded but not killed? Yes. That was in your reach. Why did you recoil from it? There was no way to guarantee that the wound wouldn't be fatal or the imprisonment temporary. You don't regret your current deliverance, but you wish you had been afflicted in some way that wouldn't interfere with this happy ending. If you ever engage in another struggle like this again, you had better have your fortune told. I'm going to a peaceful demonstration with a calm heart and an uneasy conscience."

He reached the square around one o'clock. It was two hours before the demonstration was due to commence. He took his place at the spot assigned to him, the door of the railroad station. There was no one in the square except for supervisory personnel and scattered groups from various religious factions. The weather was mild, but the April sun poured down on those exposed to its scorching rays. He did not have long to wait, for groups began to throng into the square from the different streets leading to it. Each group went to the location where its banner was displayed. Fahmy set to work with pleasure and pride. Although the task was simple, consisting of nothing more than the organization of each of the schools behind its banner, Fahmy was filled with pride and conceit, especially since he was supervising many students who were older than he was. His nineteen years did not seem like much in a mass of students with twisted mustaches going on twenty-two or twenty-four.

He noticed eyes that were looking at him with interest and lips that were whispering about him. He heard his name, accompanied by his title, being repeated by some tongues: "Fahmy Ahmad Abd al-Jawad, representative of the supreme committee." That touched the strings of his heart. He pressed his lips together to keep them from smiling, out of concern for his dignity. Yes, he must look the part of a representative of the supreme committee by being serious and stern, as was only proper for the elite corps of young freedom fighters. He wanted to leave room for the imaginations of those looking at him to guess what deeds of heroism and valor were concealed behind his imposing façade. Let the spectacular deeds he had been unable to carry out in reality be performed in their imaginations. He had no desire to discourage them but was stung by the unvarnished truth. He had distributed handbills and been part of the rear guard. That was all he had been. Today he was entrusted with supervision of the secondary schools and had a leadership role. Did others think he had played a more important part than he did himself? How much respect and affection they were awarding him. . . . They had not had a meeting without taking time to hear his opinion.

"Oratory? There was no need for you to deliver speeches, isn't that so? You can be great without being an orator, but what a pity it will be for you on the day the supreme committee appears before the great leader if, when the orators try to outdo each other, you take refuge in silence. No, I won't remain silent. I'll speak. I'll say exactly what I feel, whether or not I excel at it. When will you stand before Sa'd? When will you see him for the first time and feast your eyes on him? My heart is pounding and my eyes long to weep. It will be a great day. All of Egypt will come out to welcome him. What we're doing today will be like a drop of water in the sea compared with that time. O Lord! The square's full. The streets feeding into it are full: Abbas, Nubar, al-Faggala. There's never been a demonstration like this before. A hundred thousand people, wearing modern fezzes and traditional turbans—students, workers, civil servants, Muslim and Christian religious leaders, the judges . . . who could have imagined this? They don't mind the sun. This is Egypt. Why didn't I invite Papa? Yasin was right. . . . A person forgets himself in a crowd of people. He rises above himself. What are my personal ambitions? Nothing. How my heart is pounding. I'll talk about this for a long time tonight and after that too. Do you suppose Mama will tremble with fear once again? It's a magnificent spectacle, which humbles a person and calms him. I would like to be able to gauge its impact on those devils. Their barracks overlook the square. Their cursed flag is fluttering in the wind. I see heads in the windows there. What are they whispering to each other? The sentry's like a statue, seeing nothing. Your machine guns did not stop the revolution. Do you understand that? Soon you'll be seeing Sa'd return victoriously to this square. You exiled him by force of arms and we are bringing him back without any weapons. You'll see, before you evacuate."

The enormous parade began to move. Successive waves rolled forward, chanting patriotic slogans. Egypt appeared to be one great demonstration . . . united in one person and a single chant. The columns of the different groups stretched out for such a long distance that Fahmy imagined the vanguard would be approaching Abdin Palace before he and his group had budged from their position in front of the railroad station. It was the first demonstration that machine guns had not interrupted. No longer would bullets come from one side and stones from the other.

Fahmy smiled. He saw that the group in front of him was starting to move. He turned on his heels to direct his own personal demonstration. He raised his hands and the lines moved in anticipation and with enthusiasm. Walking backward, he chanted at the top of his lungs. He continued his twin tasks of directing and chanting until the beginning of Nubar Street. Then he turned the chanting over to one of the young men surrounding him, who had been waiting for their chance with anxious, excited voices, as though they had labor pains that would only be relieved by being allowed to lead the chants. He turned around once again to walk facing forward. He craned his neck to look at the procession. He could no longer see the front of it. He looked on either side to see how crowded the sidewalks, windows, balconies, and roofs were with all the spectators who had begun to repeat the chants. The sight of thousands of people concentrated together filled him with such limitless power and assurance it was like armor protecting him, clinging tightly to him so that bullets could not penetrate.

Now the police force was helping to maintain order, after they had been unable to suppress the demonstrations by their attacks. The sight of these men going back and forth on their horses, like guards associated with the demonstration, delegated to assist it, was the most eloquent proof of the victory of the revolution. The chief of police! . . . Was that not Russell Bey? Of course, he recognized him perfectly. There was his deputy trotting along behind him, looking at everything impassively and haughtily as though protesting silently against the peace reigning over the demonstration. What was his name? How could he forget a name that everyone had been repeating during the bloody, dark days? Did it not begin with a *g* or a *j*? "Ja . . . Ju . . . Ji . . ." He could not recall it. "Julian!" Oh, how did that hated name slip into his mind? It fell on him like dirt, putting out the fire of his zeal. "How can we respond to the call of zeal and victory when the heart is dead? My heart dead? It wasn't dead a minute ago. Don't surrender to sorrow. Don't let your heart become separated from the demonstration. Haven't you promised yourself to forget? In fact, you really have forgotten. Maryam . . . who is she? That's ancient history. We live for the future, not the past. Guise, Mr. Guise, I think that's the name of the deputy police chief, may God curse him. Start chanting again to shake off this dusty cloud of regret."

Fahmy's own part of the demonstration slowly approached Ezbekiya Garden. The lofty trees could be seen over the banners that were displayed all along the street. Then Opera Square was visible in the distance looking like an endless mass of heads that all seemed to spring from a single body. He was chanting forcefully and enthusiastically, and the crowd repeated his chants with a sound that filled the air like the rumble of thunder. When they came near the wall of the garden, suddenly there was a sharp, resounding pop. He stopped chanting and in alarm looked around questioningly. It was a familiar sound that had often assaulted his ears during the past month and had frequently echoed in his memory during the quiet nights, although he had never gotten used to it. The moment it rang out he became pale and his heart seemed to stop pumping.

"A bullet?"

"Incredible. Didn't they sanction the demonstration?"

"Did you forget to allow for treachery?"

"But I don't see any soldiers."

"Ezbekiya Garden is an enormous camp, packed full of them."

"Perhaps the explosion was an automobile tire blowing out."

"Perhaps."

Fahmy listened intently to what was going on around him without regaining his peace of mind. It was only a few moments before a second explosion was heard. "Oh. . . . There could no longer be any doubt. It was a bullet like the one before. Where do you suppose it hit? Isn't it a day of peace?"

He felt the uneasiness moving through the ranks of the demonstrators, coming from the front like the heavy wave that a steamboat plowing down the center of a river sends to the shore. Then thousands of people started to retreat and spread out, creating in every direction insane and unruly outbursts of confusion and consternation as they collided with each other. Terrifying shouts of anger and fear rose from the masses. The orderly columns were quickly scattered and the carefully arranged structure of the parade collapsed. Then there was a sharp burst of shots in close succession. People screamed in anger and moaned in pain.

The sea of people surged and swelled, and the waves thrust through every opening, sparing nothing in its way and leaving nothing behind it.

"I'll flee. There's no alternative. If the bullets don't kill you, the arms and feet will." He meant to run or retreat or turn, but he did not do anything. "Why are you standing here when everyone has scattered? You're in an exposed position. Flee."

His arms and legs began a slow, limp, disjointed motion. "How loud the clamor is. But what are they screaming about? Do you remember? How quickly memories are slipping away. What do you want? To chant? What chant? Or just call out? To whom? For what? There's a voice speaking inside you. Do you hear? Do you see? But where? There's nothing. Nothing. Darkness and more darkness. A gentle motion's pushing with the regularity of the ticking of a clock.

The heart is flowing with it. There's a whisper accompanying it. The gate of the garden. Isn't that so? It's moving in a fluid, rippling way and slowly dissolving. The towering tree is dancing gently. The sky ... the sky? High, expansive ... nothing but the calm, smiling sky with peace raining from it."

71

Al-Sayyid Ahmad Abd al-Jawad heard footsteps at the entrance to the store. He glanced up from his desk and saw three young men approaching him. They looked serious and grave. They stopped just in front of his desk and said, "Peace to you and the compassion of God."

Al-Sayyid Ahmad rose and with his customary politeness responded, "And to you peace and the compassion of God and His blessings." He motioned to the chairs and said, "Please sit down."

They graciously declined his invitation. The boy in the center asked, "Sir, are you Mr. Ahmad Abd al-Jawad?"

The proprietor smiled, although there was a questioning look in his eyes, and replied, "Yes, sir."

"What do you suppose they want?" he asked himself. "It's not likely that they came to purchase anything. Their military gait and serious tone wouldn't be appropriate if they were buying something. Moreover, it's after seven o'clock. Don't they see that al-Hamzawi is putting the bags up on the shelves to show that the store is closing? Are they collecting donations? But Sa'd's been released, and the revolution has concluded. I'm not fit for anything now except my evening party. Fellows, you should understand that I haven't bathed my head and face with cologne, combed my hair and mustache, adjusted my cloak and caftan just to meet you. What do you want?"

When he looked at the young man who had addressed him, the face seemed familiar. Had he seen him before? Where? When? He tried to remember. He was certain this was not the first time he had seen him. Then the proprietor's face relaxed and he asked with a smile, "Aren't you the fine young man who came forward to save us just in time the day people attacked us in the mosque of al-Husayn, may God be pleased with him?"

The youth said in a subdued voice, "Yes, sir."

"So I was right," he thought. "Fools say that wine weakens the memory? But why are they looking at me that way? See! These stares don't look like good news. O God, make it good. I take refuge in

God from Satan, who should be pelted with stones. For some reason I feel depressed. They've come about something relating to . . ."

"Fahmy?" he asked. "Have you come looking for him? . . . Perhaps you . . ."

The young man lowered his eyes and said in a trembling voice, "Our mission is hard, sir, but it's a duty. May our Lord grant you endurance."

Al-Sayyid Ahmad suddenly leaned forward, supporting himself on the edge of the desk. He cried out, "Endurance? . . . For what! . . . Fahmy?"

The young man said with obvious sorrow, "We are sad to inform you of the death of our brother freedom fighter Fahmy Ahmad. . . ."

Although there was an unmistakable look of belief and dismay in his eyes, the father rejected the news, shouting, "Fahmy?"

"He fell a martyr in the demonstration today."

The boy on his right said, "A noble patriot and sterling martyr was conveyed to a world of pious souls."

Their words fell on ears deafened by misery. His lips were sealed and his eyes gazed blankly and vacantly. They were all silent for a time. Even Jamil al-Hamzawi was frozen to the spot where he stood beneath the shelves, looking dazed and staring at his employer with sorrowful eyes. Finally the young man murmured, "His loss has deeply saddened us, but we have no choice but to submit to God's decree with the patient endurance of Believers, of whom you, sir, are one."

"They are offering you their condolences," al-Sayyid Ahmad realized. "Doesn't this young man know that I excel in offering condolences in circumstances like these? What meaning do they have for an afflicted heart? None! How could words put out the fire? Not so fast. . . . Didn't your heart feel something was dreadfully wrong even before he spoke? Yes . . . the specter of death appeared before my eyes. Now that death is a reality, as you hear, you refuse to believe it. How can I believe that Fahmy is really dead? How can you believe that Fahmy, who requested your approval just hours ago, when you were short with him—Fahmy, who was full of health, good spirits, hope, and happiness when we left home this morning—is dead? Dead! I'll never see him again at home or anywhere else on the face of the earth? How can I have a home without him? How can I be a father if he's gone? What has become of all the hopes attached to him? The only hope left is patience. . . . Patience? Oh. . . . Do you feel the searing pain? This really is pain. You were mistaken previously when you occasionally claimed to be in pain. No, before today you've never known pain. This is pain. . . ."

"Sir, be strong and turn your concerns over to God."

Al-Sayyid Ahmad looked up at the young man. Then in a sick voice he said, "I thought the time for killing had passed."

The youth answered angrily, "The demonstration today was peaceful. The authorities had given permission for it. Top men from all walks of life participated in it. At first it proceeded safely, until the middle section reached Ezbekiya Garden. Before we knew what was happening, bullets fell upon us from behind the wall, for no reason at all. No one had confronted the soldiers in any manner. We had even forbidden any chants in English to avoid provoking them. The soldiers were suddenly stricken by an insane impulse to kill. They got their rifles and opened fire. Everyone has agreed to send a strong protest to the British Residency. It's even been said that Allenby will announce his regrets for what the soldiers did."

In the same sick tone, the proprietor complained, "But he will not bring the dead back to life."

"Alas, no."

Al-Sayyid Ahmad, racked by distress, said, "He's never participated in any of the violent demonstrations. This was the first demonstration he took part in."

The young men looked knowingly at each other but did not utter a word. Al-Sayyid Ahmad seemed to be growing impatient with the way they were separating him from Fahmy and the rest of the world. He moaned and said, "The matter's in God's hands. Where can I find him now?"

The young man answered, "In the Qasr al-Ayni Hospital." When he saw that the proprietor was in a hurry to leave, he gestured for him to wait. "There will be a funeral procession for him and thirteen of his fellow martyrs at exactly three o'clock tomorrow afternoon."

The father cried out in distress, "Won't you allow me to begin his funeral procession at his home?"

The young man said forcefully, "No, his funeral will be with his brothers in a public ceremony." Then he entreated the man, "Qasr al-Ayni is cordoned off by the police. It would be better to wait. We intend to allow the families of the martyrs to pay their last respects to them in private before the funeral procession. It would not be right for Fahmy to have an ordinary funeral like a person who dies at home." In parting he held his hand out to the bereaved father and said, "Endure patiently. Endurance is from God."

The others shook hands with al-Sayyid Ahmad, repeating their condolences. Then they all departed. He leaned his head on his hand and closed his eyes. He heard the voice of Jamil al-Hamzawi offering his condolences in a sobbing voice, but he seemed distressed by kind words. He could not bear to stay there. He left his seat and moved slowly out of the store, walking with heavy steps. He had to get over his bewilderment. He did not even know how to feel sad. He wanted to be all alone, but where? The house would turn into an inferno in a minute or two. His friends would rally round him, leaving him no opportunity to think. When would he ponder the loss he had undergone? When would he have a chance to get away from everyone? That seemed a long way off, but it would no doubt come. It was the most consolation he could hope for at present. Yes, a time would come when he would be all alone and could devote himself to his sorrow with all his soul. Then he would scrutinize Fahmy's life in light of the past, present, and future, all the stages from childhood to the prime of his youth, the hopes he had aroused and the memories he had left behind, giving free rein to tears so he could totally exhaust them. Truly he had before him ample time that no one would begrudge him. There was no reason to be concerned about that. Consider the memory of the quarrel they had had after the Friday prayer at al-Husayn or that of their conversation that morning, when Fahmy had appealed for his affection and he had reprimanded him—how much of his time would they require as he reflected, remembered, and grieved? How much of his heart would they consume? How many tears would they stir up? How could he be distressed when the future held such consolations for him? He raised his head, which was clouded by thought, and saw the blurred outline of the latticed balconies of his home. He remembered Amina for the first time and his feet almost failed him. What could he say to her? How would she take the news? She was weak and delicate. She wept at the death of a sparrow. "Do you recall how her tears flowed when the son of al-Fuli, the milkman, was killed? What will she do now that Fahmy's been killed.... Fahmy killed? Is this really the end of your son? O dear, unhappy son! ... Amina ... our son was killed. Fahmy was killed.... What? ... Will you forbid them to wail just as you previously forbade them to trill with joy? Will you wail yourself or hire professional mourners? She's probably now at the coffee hour with

Yasin and Kamal, wondering what has kept Fahmy. How cruel! I'll see him at Qasr al-Ayni Hospital, but she won't. I won't allow it. Out of cruelty or compassion? What's the use, anyway?"

He found himself in front of the door and stretched his hand toward the knocker. Then he remembered the key in his pocket. He took it out and opened the door. When he entered, he heard Kamal's voice singing melodiously:

Visit me once each year,
For it's wrong to abandon people forever.

Acknowledgments

I want to thank Mary Ann Carroll
for being the first reader,
Jacqueline Kennedy Onassis
for her sensitive editing,
Riyad N. Delshad for assistance
with some obscure vocabulary and expressions,
and Sarah and Franya Hutchins
for their patience.
Although others have contributed
to this translation, I am happy
to bear responsibility for it.

—William Maynard Hutchins

About the Author

Naguib Mahfouz was born in Cairo in 1911 and began writing when he was seventeen. A student of philosophy and an avid reader, he has been influenced by many Western writers, including Flaubert, Balzac, Zola, Camus, Tolstoy, Dostoevsky, and, above all, Proust. He has more than thirty novels to his credit, ranging from his earliest historical romances to his most recent experimental novels. In 1988, Mr. Mahfouz was awarded the Nobel Prize for Literature. He lives in the Cairo suburb of Agouza with his wife and two daughters.

ern Arabic Writing

ican University in Cairo Press

)ther Place • *No One Sleeps in Alexandria*
llah *The Mountain of Green Tea*
uzeid *The Last Chapter*
Aslan *Nile Sparrows*
swany *Yacoubian Building*
Hala El Badry *A Certain Woman*
Salwa Bakr *The Wiles of Men*
Hoda Barakat *The Tiller of Waters*
Mourid Barghouti *I Saw Ramallah*
Mohamed El-Bisatie *A Last Glass of Tea* • *Houses Behind the Trees*
Clamor of the Lake
Fathy Ghanem *The Man Who Lost His Shadow*
Randa Ghazy *Dreaming of Palestine*
Gamal al-Ghitani *Zayni Barakat*
Tawfiq al-Hakim *The Prison of Life*
Yahya Hakki *The Lamp of Umm Hashim*
Bensalem Himmich *The Polymath*
Taha Hussein *A Man of Letters* • *The Sufferers* • *The Days*
Sonallah Ibrahim *Cairo: From Edge to Edge* • *Zaat* • *The Committee*
Yusuf Idris *City of Love and Ashes*
Denys Johnson-Davies *Under the Naked Sky: Short Stories from the Arab World*
Said al-Kafrawi *The Hill of Gypsies*
Edwar al-Kharrat *Rama and the Dragon*
Naguib Mahfouz *Adrift on the Nile* • *Akhenaten, Dweller in Truth*
Arabian Nights and Days • *Autumn Quail* • *The Beggar*
The Beginning and the End • *The Cairo Trilogy: Palace Walk*
Palace of Desire • *Sugar Street* • *Children of the Alley*
The Day the Leader Was Killed • *The Dreams* • *Echoes of an Autobiography*
The Harafish • *The Journey of Ibn Fattouma* • *Khufu's Wisdom*
Midaq Alley • *Miramar* • *Naguib Mahfouz at Sidi Gaber*
Respected Sir • *Rhadopis of Nubia* • *The Search* • *Thebes at War*
The Thief and the Dogs • *The Time and the Place*
Wedding Song • *Voices from the Other World*
Ahlam Mosteghanemi *Memory in the Flesh* • *Chaos of the Senses*
Buthaina Al Nasiri *Final Night*
Abd al-Hakim Qasim *Rites of Assent*
Somaya Ramadan *Leaves of Narcissus*
Lenin El-Ramly *In Plain Arabic*
Rafik Schami *Damascus Nights*
Miral al-Tahawy *The Tent* • *Blue Aubergine*
Bahaa Taher *Love in Exile*
Fuad al-Takarli *The Long Way Back*
Latifa al-Zayyat *The Open Door*

Modern Arabic Writing

from the American University in Cairo Press

Ibrahim Abdel Meguid *The Other Place • No One Sleeps in Alexandria*
Yahya Taher Abdullah *The Mountain of Green Tea*
Leila Abouzeid *The Last Chapter*
Ibrahim Aslan *Nile Sparrows*
Alaa Al Aswany *Yacoubian Building*
Hala El Badry *A Certain Woman*
Salwa Bakr *The Wiles of Men*
Hoda Barakat *The Tiller of Waters*
Mourid Barghouti *I Saw Ramallah*
Mohamed El-Bisatie *A Last Glass of Tea • Houses Behind the Trees*
Clamor of the Lake
Fathy Ghanem *The Man Who Lost His Shadow*
Randa Ghazy *Dreaming of Palestine*
Gamal al-Ghitani *Zayni Barakat*
Tawfiq al-Hakim *The Prison of Life*
Yahya Hakki *The Lamp of Umm Hashim*
Bensalem Himmich *The Polymath*
Taha Hussein *A Man of Letters • The Sufferers • The Days*
Sonallah Ibrahim *Cairo: From Edge to Edge • Zaat • The Committee*
Yusuf Idris *City of Love and Ashes*
Denys Johnson-Davies *Under the Naked Sky: Short Stories from the Arab World*
Said al-Kafrawi *The Hill of Gypsies*
Edwar al-Kharrat *Rama and the Dragon*
Naguib Mahfouz *Adrift on the Nile • Akhenaten, Dweller in Truth*
Arabian Nights and Days • Autumn Quail • The Beggar
The Beginning and the End • The Cairo Trilogy: Palace Walk
Palace of Desire • Sugar Street • Children of the Alley
The Day the Leader Was Killed • The Dreams • Echoes of an Autobiography
The Harafish • The Journey of Ibn Fattouma • Khufu's Wisdom
Midaq Alley • Miramar • Naguib Mahfouz at Sidi Gaber
Respected Sir • Rhadopis of Nubia • The Search • Thebes at War
The Thief and the Dogs • The Time and the Place
Wedding Song • Voices from the Other World
Ahlam Mosteghanemi *Memory in the Flesh • Chaos of the Senses*
Buthaina Al Nasiri *Final Night*
Abd al-Hakim Qasim *Rites of Assent*
Somaya Ramadan *Leaves of Narcissus*
Lenin El-Ramly *In Plain Arabic*
Rafik Schami *Damascus Nights*
Miral al-Tahawy *The Tent • Blue Aubergine*
Bahaa Taher *Love in Exile*
Fuad al-Takarli *The Long Way Back*
Latifa al-Zayyat *The Open Door*